BAEN BOOKS by CHARLES E. GANNON

THE TERRAN REPUBLIC SERIES

Fire with Fire

Trial by Fire

Raising Caine

Caine's Mutiny

Marque of Caine

Mission Critical (with Griffin Barber, Chris Kennedy & Mike Massa)

Endangered Species

Protected Species

Killer Species, forthcoming

Admiral and Commander (with Chris Kennedy), forthcoming

THE VORTEX OF WORLDS SERIES

This Broken World

Into the Vortex

Toward the Maw, forthcoming

THE RING OF FIRE SERIES (WITH ERIC FLINT)

1635: The Papal Stakes

1636: Commander Cantrell in the West Indies

1636: The Vatican Sanction

1637: No Peace Beyond the Line

1636: Calabar's War (with Robert E. Waters)

JOHN RINGO'S BLACK TIDE RISING SERIES

At the End of the World

At the End of the Journey

THE STARFIRE SERIES (WITH STEVE WHITE)

Extremis

Imperative

Oblivion

PROTECTED SPECIES

PROTECTED SPECIES

CHARLES E. GANNON

BAEN

Protected Species

A Baen Books Original

Baen Publishing Enterprises
P.O. Box 1403
Riverdale, NY 10471
www.baen.com

ISBN: 978-1-9821-9307-2

Cover art by Kurt Miller
Maps by Rhys Davies

First printing, December 2023

Distributed by Simon & Schuster
1230 Avenue of the Americas
New York, NY 10020

Library of Congress Cataloging-in-Publication Data

Names: Gannon, Charles E., author.
Title: Protected species / Charles E. Gannon.
Description: Riverdale, NY : Baen Publishing Enterprises, 2023. | Series: Terran Republic series ; 7
Identifiers: LCCN 2023037783 (print) | LCCN 2023037784 (ebook) | ISBN 9781982193072 (hardcover) | ISBN 9781625799418 (ebook)
Subjects: LCGFT: Science fiction. | Novels.
Classification: LCC PS3607.A556 P76 2023 (print) | LCC PS3607.A556 (ebook) | DDC 813/.6—dc23/eng/20230828
LC record available at https://lccn.loc.gov/2023037783
LC ebook record available at https://lccn.loc.gov/2023037784

Printed in the United States of America
10 9 8 7 6 5 4 3 2 1

DEDICATION

To my family—my wife Andrea and children Alexandra and Pierce—without whom I could not have completed this book.

and

To Joy Freeman, and both her proofreaders and my own, whose swift and prodigious labors made it possible for this book to reach your hands at all.

CONTENTS

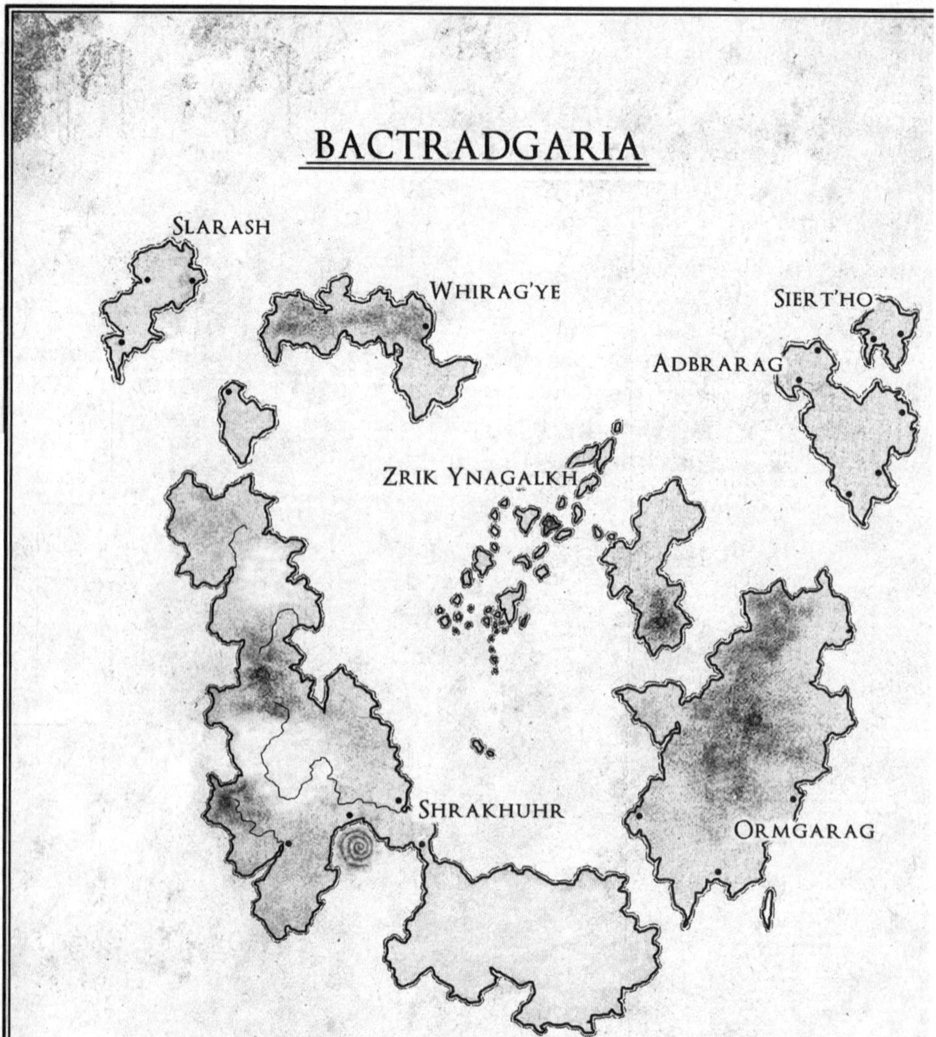
BACTRADGARIA
SLARASH
WHIRAG'YE
SIERT'HO
ADBRARAG
ZRIK YNAGALKH
SHRAKHUHR
ORMGARAG

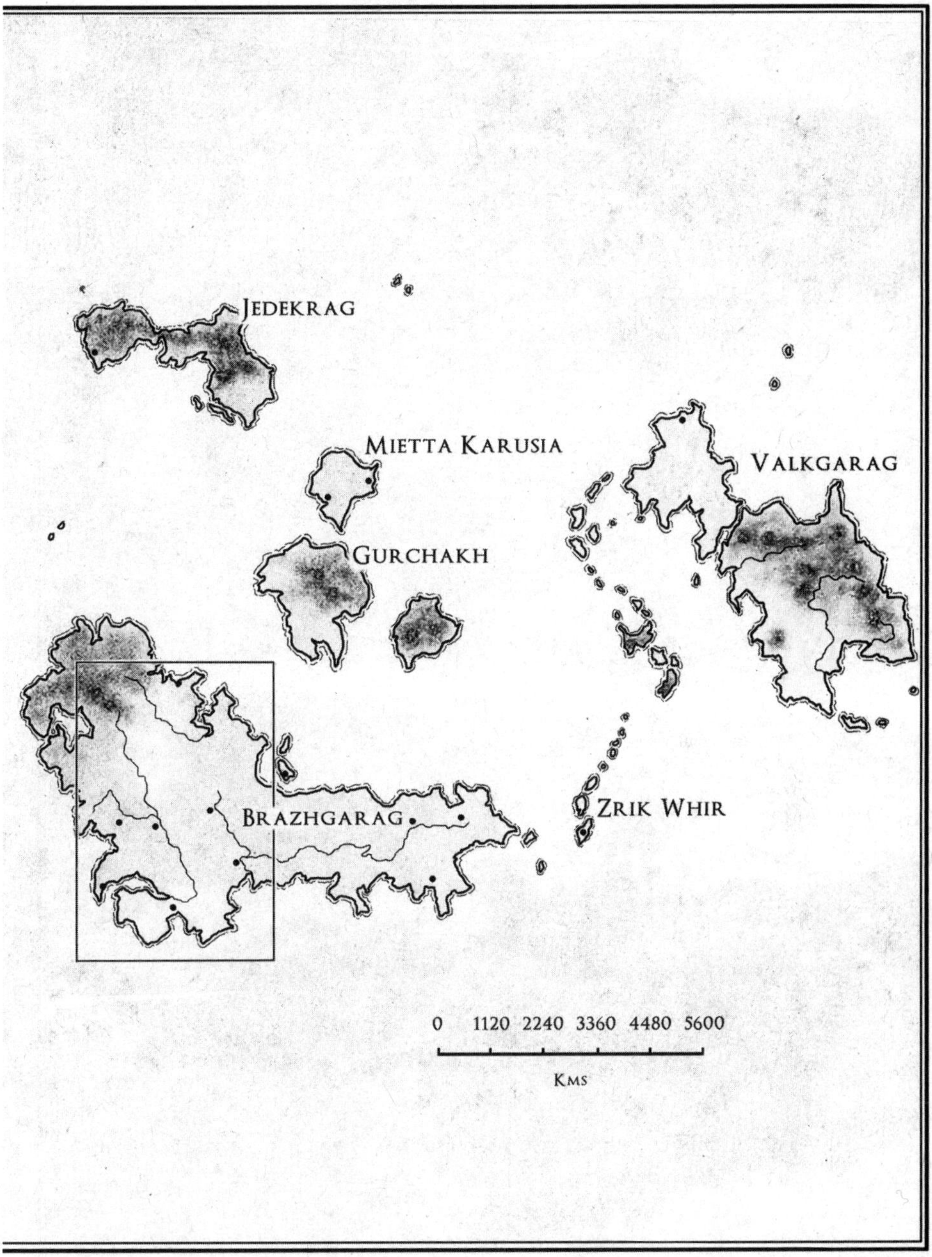

Jedekrag
Mietta Karusia
Valkgarag
Gurchakh
Brazhgarag
Zrik Whir
0 1120 2240 3360 4480 5600
Kms

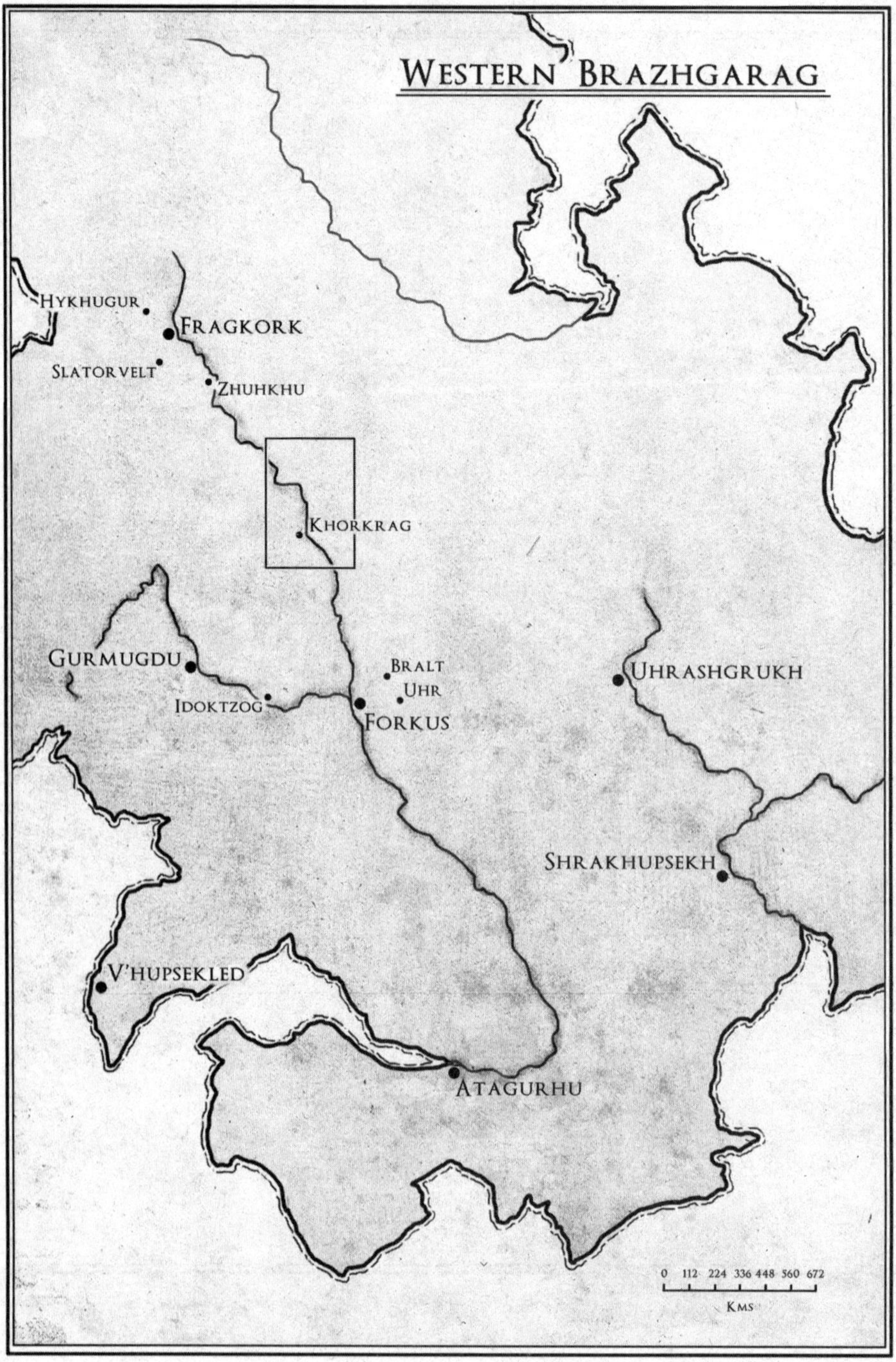
Western Brazhgarag
Hykhugur
Fragkork
Slatorvelt
Zhuhkhu
Khorkrag
Gurmugdu
Idoktzog
Bralt
Uhr
Forkus
Uhrashgrukh
Shrakhupsekh
V'hupsekled
Atagurhu
0 112 224 336 448 560 672
Kms

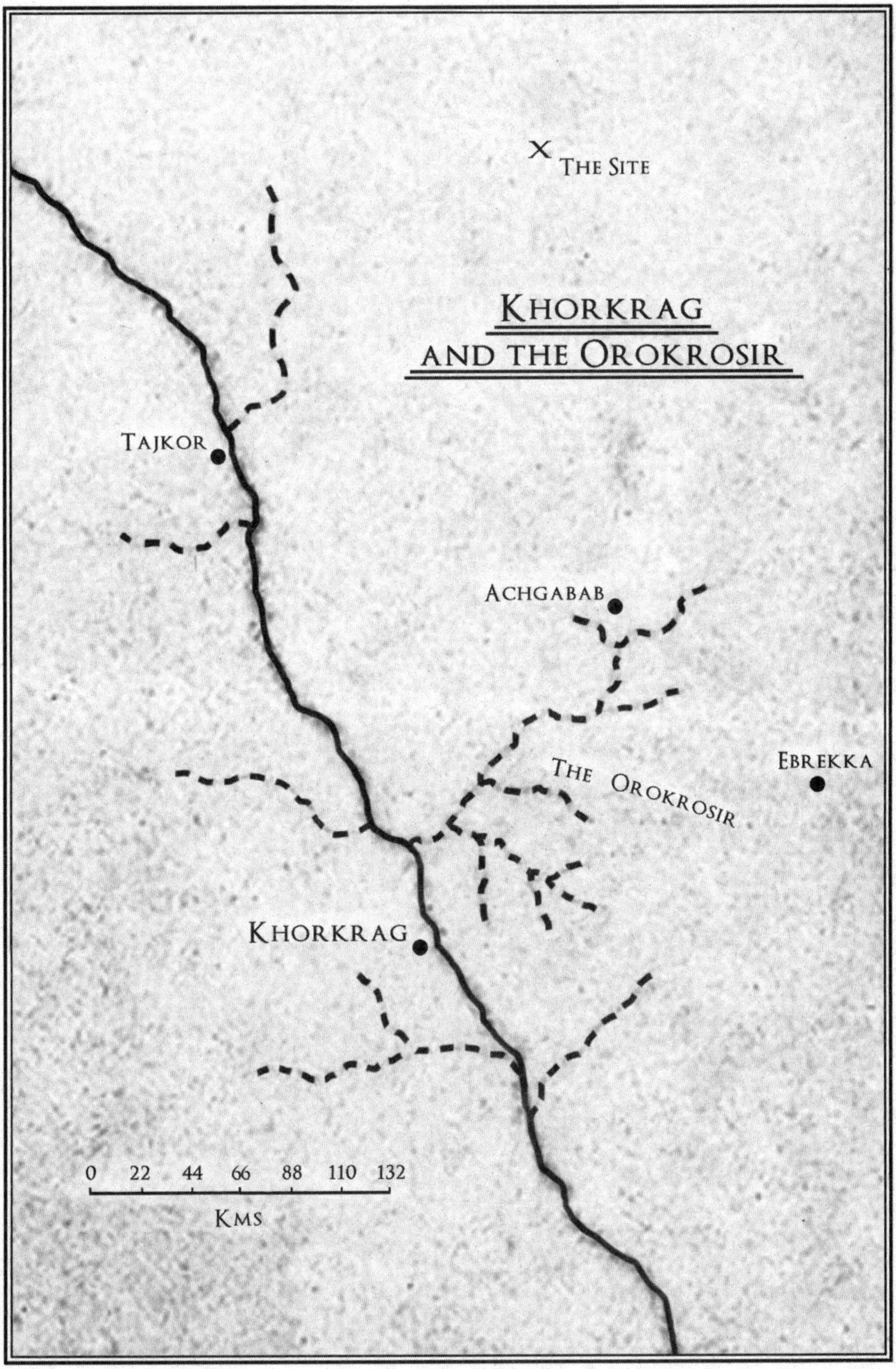

The Site
Khorkrag
and the Orokrosir
Tajkor
Achgabab
The Orokrosir
Ebrekka
Khorkrag
0 22 44 66 88 110 132
Kms

PART ONE

Muster to the Colors

Bactradgaria
May–June 2125

Chapter One

"Commodore Riordan," urged Craig Girten's voice as a hand cautiously shook his upper arm, "you're needed." Caine's dreams became a vapor of fading images through which he struggled up toward—

Fighting. Shouts. Then a scream—all from *inside* the perimeter.

Riordan snapped upright, abdominal muscles spasming. "Girten," he muttered as he reached around for his gear, "report."

"The trogs, sir. They're fighting. Come quick!"

At least we're not under attack. Cinching the straps of the hide cuirass he slept upon, Caine stumbled after the paratrooper who'd last fought in the Battle of the Bulge. "Are they arguing?"

"Bit more than that, sir," Girten said, drawing to the side as he stopped.

Of the four figures on the ground, two were unmoving. Two opposing groups—trog bearers and handlers on one side, scouts and kajhs on the other—were leaning inward, their agitation mounting faster than their numbers. Several started forward.

A figure jumped into the gap: Bey, the only reliable liaison between Caine's Crewe and the locals. The two glowering groups paused, straightened. Some even leaned away from each other. But a few kept pushing forward.

Riordan turned to Girten, ordered, "Crossbow," snatched it out of the surprised sergeant's hands and discharged it into the ground between the rival sides. "Stand down!" Actually, he used the equivalent local phrase, which, transliterated, was "Be still or be meat." It had proven a crude but effective warning on the march north from Forkus.

This time was no exception. The opposed groups became motionless. Then, individuals at the back of each started drifting away.

"Stop! Stay where you are." Riordan glanced at Girten. "Sergeant, bring Dr. Baruch here on the double. Healer Ne'sar, too."

He turned toward Bey. "If you wish to speak to anyone here, bring them to the command post, put them in the custody of the duty officer, and return."

"Yes, Leader Caine."

Riordan managed not to marvel at how, though trogs generally chafed at military discipline, they almost revered its exercise. He pointed at a cluster that was not part of either group. "You three will wait for Dr. Ba—eh, Leader Newton, and carry out his orders. If he asks you to move the wounded, you will do so carefully or answer for your negligence." Caine raised his voice. "The rest of you, back to your furs. Twenty minutes to formation. Dismiss!"

The fight-churned ground was soon empty except for the three trogs who were waving the doctor over toward the two motionless bodies. Newton Baruch did not go to them; a short glance assured him of what Caine could only guess. Their contorted positions amid two wide pools of blood meant they were either dead or soon would be.

Bey's footsteps approached from behind. "I return, Leader Caine. It is my faul—"

Riordan held up a hand; he'd come to know Bey well enough to anticipate what was coming. "You had the *middle* watch, didn't you?"

She nodded. "Yes, but—"

"Then you are without fault; you had to sleep during the last watch. You can't be awake every second of every hour. If you were, you could not lead your people."

"But if I knew them well enough, I would have foreseen this, Leader Caine."

"Bey, it's only been three days since we destroyed the caravan these trogs were accompanying. There is no way you could have come to know them well enough to anticipate their behavior."

Her nod was short, sharp: acceptance without agreement. "I shall hear the accounts of those I sent to the command post. And quickly, that you may make a swift judgment."

Riordan frowned. "The judgment is *yours*. That is why you are their leader, and why we did not make you our vassal."

Bey nodded tightly. "I understand, but just as I do not know the new trogs yet, they do not know me. Until I lead them in battle, many will doubt I am a worthy leader."

"You mean, because you are female."

She nodded. "But even more because I am a truthteller."

Riordan frowned. "Why does that undermine your authority?"

"Because trogs expect that their leaders will employ deceit to overcome foes. I cannot."

Riordan nodded, still frowning as he gestured toward the Crewe's camp circle. "They may not trust you yet, but *we* do. And because you are *exactly* the leader we want—and need—they will come to associate our power and success with you."

"Perhaps, but during these early days, it is best that the judgment comes from you. It will be accepted without question and will not give the new trogs reason to hate or question me." She paused. "Besides, there is another problem. The ones who were behind this fight are cavers."

Riordan had given up trying to conceal his general ignorance of life on Bactradgaria. "I know cavers are considered less civilized, but how does that figure into the fight?"

"They are not merely uncivilized, Leader Caine; they have no regard for other races. At a guess, this fight arose because they were trying to usurp the place of other, more powerful trogs. I will not hide my opinions of them; their kind and my people—the Free Tribes—have been enemies as long as memory or song recalls. So I cannot claim that I would make an objective decision. Cavers killed many of my forebears, and even my own family." Her eyes grew hard. "My mother's older brother fell to them just before she and I were taken away to Forkus."

Caine saw pain behind her stare. "Do you remember him?"

Bey shrugged. "I was very young, so those memories are jumbled, uncertain. But my mother told me much of my uncle."

Riordan wondered how much of that attachment she had transferred to her recently murdered adoptive "uncle." "And do those memories remind you of Zaatkhur?"

She darted a surprised look at him. "Is it written so plainly on my face?"

Riordan shrugged. "Not to the others. But they didn't see you on the bank after giving him to the river or when you faced your sleeping furs alone."

She nodded. "You may not understand many of our ways, but you understand our hearts well enough." She straightened. "You follow your own advice: 'a good leader knows his people.'" She nodded curtly. "I shall bring you what I know within one hour."

"Take two, if it's necessary."

"If the questioning takes that long, I shall send a runner." She gave the abbreviated bow that was the local equivalent of a lazy salute and stalked away, calling for the half-human *prakhwai*—or trogans, as Chief O'Garran had nicknamed them—to gather to her.

"Glad she's on our side," said a new voice from over his shoulder: Bannor Rulaine. "Sorry I'm late to the party, sir."

Riordan waved off the Special Forces colonel's apology and formality. "Like I told Bey, we all have to sleep sometime."

Bannor shrugged. "Orders, sir?"

Riordan nodded, rubbed his eyes, tried to remember the watch rota, decided to just ask the guy who'd set it. "Who's on duty besides Girten?"

"You mean the Crewe, sir?" Riordan nodded at the collective term for all the marooned off-worlders. "Katie Somers, sir."

Riordan stifled a yawn as Craig returned. *Well, that's* one *piece of good news: having someone on patrol who's wearing a Dornaani vacc suit.* "Sergeant Girten, find Somers. I want her running perimeter sweeps from the high ground at the south end of camp. Monoscope is to be set for maximum light amplification and thermal. Motion tracking, too, but low sensitivity."

Craig responded to Riordan's last caveat by swatting an insect on his neck. "Yeah, with all these bugs flying around now, max motion makes everything look jumpy, hazy." He glared at the large fly squashed on his palm. "I guess Bactradgaria has more life as you get closer to the equator."

"Or," Bannor Rulaine countered, "it's not so different from spring back on Earth." He smiled, nodded at the GI from the twentieth century. "On your way, Sergeant."

"Yessir."

Bannor waited until Girten was out of earshot. "Why the

sweeps? Expecting that all the shouting will bring in a breakfast crowd?"

Riordan sighed. "The early monster gets the worm. Or corpse." He glanced at the wet-slate skies to the west. "The carrion from the caravan ambush is probably gone by now, and there's always more hungry mouths—well, maws—than meals out here."

"Do you want me to rouse a few more of the Crewe? Have them standing ready with survival rifles?" Which was a ridiculous misnomer, but it beat reeling off the accurate term: electromagnetic coil guns.

Riordan shook his head. "No, we're going to stick to the 'crisis-only' use criterion. Girten's got a crossbow and so does Katie. That will do."

"I'm not a bad hand with one, either, Caine."

This time, Riordan did chuckle. "Understatement of the century. But I'd rather keep you focused on command issues."

"Why? You going back to sleep?" Bannor grinned at Riordan's baleful stare. "So since we're both up, *you* handle the command issues and let your XO be a grunt again for half an hour. Yeah?"

Caine smiled. "Yeah. Sure."

Bannor didn't move off immediately. He was staring at the two unattended bodies still sprawled in the moist dust; Newton had no intention of losing his three ad hoc orderlies by sending them on a grave detail. "After marching thirty-six days north from Forkus without a scuffle, I didn't see this coming."

Riordan shrugged. "Neither did Bey. None of us could have. So right now, my only concern is whether our people can get another thirty minutes of sleep."

"I doubt any dozed through the noise, Caine."

"No, but I'll bet at least half—the veterans—were snoring again within five minutes. At least I hope so. It's going to be another hard march today."

"Better than waiting in the rain or wading through mud."

Riordan nodded. The day after the caravan ambush, the weather had closed in and hammered them with torrents. The dust-sand of the wastes became so fluid that any attempt to prop up their shelter-halves sent the ground stakes slipping sideways into the gritty porridge. "With any luck, this fight was just an unsettled grudge left over from the caravan," he muttered, jutting a stubbled chin at the bodies.

Bannor frowned. "If not, it could mean more infiltrators. Hell, maybe some of this bunch was supposed to link up with the two traitors that Bey caught marking our trail."

Riordan shrugged. "There's no logical connection between them and the caravan, but I won't rule it out until we learn more about these two." He nodded toward the corpses. "But we've got to settle both issues soon, or it's going to send the wrong message to the rest of the trogs."

"You mean, that we're weak?"

Riordan shook his head. "That and maybe a dozen other things." He sighed. "There are days I wonder if we are ever going to get ahead of the learning curve, here."

"Me, too. Any idea on how you're going to deal with one pair of traitors and another pair of murderers?"

Caine stared at the dove grey smudge of dawn on the eastern horizon. "The traitors? Well, it seems the locals already have their own answer for that. But the right response to this morning's fight depends on finding out why it happened at all."

"Which means, you're going to go talk to Bey again."

Caine shrugged. "Who else?"

Chapter Two

Riordan had walked halfway to the center of camp when he spotted Bey approaching from that direction. Nodding at each other, they angled toward a spot without sleeping circles.

"It is as I thought, Leader Caine," she reported, face set in hard lines. "The two cavers from the caravan were behind the argument. They approached a pair of tinkers to help them prevent the trog scouts from rising in social rank and privileges."

Riordan hoped his question sounded more intelligent and informed than it was. "And how did the cavers hope to achieve that?"

She shrugged. "By rallying the worker trogs to their cause. Between our group and the Legate forces under Sharat, there are over forty such *urldi*, whereas there are only eight scouts.

"The cavers also hoped that the other two dozen porters afflicted with milder *s'rillor*—the pawns—would side with them. But like most city trogs, the workers routinely abused and stole from the pawns: the group just beneath them. So the pawns aligned themselves with the scouts, instead."

Riordan nodded. "How did it start?"

Bey leaned closer, as if someone might hear her. "An urldi rebuffed the tinker's appeal to join the cavers. One of the cavers overheard and threatened the worker. A pawn saw the confrontation and blocked the caver.

"Anger became blows. Or in the case of the caver, stabs; his second thrust killed the pawn. A scout heard the cries and killed the caver, but not before being wounded himself."

"And the injured tinker?"

"He was foolish enough to try breaking up the fight."

Caine shook his head. "But what did the cavers hope to gain by displacing the scouts?"

"Cavers do not require a practical reason to satisfy their cravings for violence and control." Bey's tone was more sardonic than Riordan had ever heard. "Besides, tempers are already high, since there were few females among the caravan trogs."

Riordan nodded. "Leader O'Garran speculated that there would be arguments over who got to sleep in which fur piles... and with whom."

Bey's brow became carefully straight. "Leader O'Garran is an excellent warrior, but his understanding of trog-ways remains... incomplete. The tension he noticed was not over mating. It was over safety, even survival.

"Please try to make your people understand, Leader Caine: among trogs, fur bonds are not just a group's primary relationships, but crucial to individual survival. Even in the cities, one benefits from the warmth of other bodies on the coldest nights. But here in the often frigid wastes, it is a matter of life and death. So too is being able to sleep back-to-back with one whom you trust."

Riordan frowned. "But didn't the caravan trogs already have fur-mates and sleeping piles from before we captured them?"

"That might be the case if the caravan had all come from one source. But he who sent it, Liege Azhdrukh in Fragkork, only provided the commanders and senior x'qai. The rest of its forces were levied from Azhdrukh's vassals and vavasors, including the two humans. So any trogs who have the least stature now will soon be on the outermost layer of the sleeping piles, exposed directly to the cold."

Riordan wondered how trogs, particularly the lowest, endured at all. "Fur bonds don't seem to guarantee safety."

"'Guarantee safety,'" Bey repeated wistfully. "I do not know where you are from, Leader Caine, but here, there is no such thing. Sometimes we are fortunate and keep the same fur-mates for many years. It was thus with Zaatkhur, but that is very, very rare among city trogs."

Riordan nodded. "So this morning's fight had nothing to do with, eh, mating?"

Bey sighed. "Not directly, no, but mating concerns do shape trog groups. That is why I cannot take a new fur-mate; I would be suspected of favoring that person in all ways."

"So the cavers were also exploiting the workers' fears that they'd be unable to find sexual mates?"

Bey nodded. "Cavers never cease striving to be the most feared, the most powerful, among trogs." Her eyes grew hard. "And if they found mates of their own, that would only be the beginning of our troubles."

"How so?"

She glanced at him. "Cavers have very different attitudes toward mating."

Riordan heard hatred in her low tone. "Different in what way?"

Her look said: *Do you really not hear what I mean?* "Leader Caine, cavers compel unwilling urldi to submit to their rutting."

Riordan crossed his arms. "Does this not happen among city trogs?"

She started. "If it did, what little order exists in a gang would be lost."

"So, who prevents such violations?"

"Other urldi."

"You mean, females?"

"No, I mean *urldi*." One of her eyebrows edged up. "Cavers mate as much for power as to satisfy their urges. For many, it does not matter overmuch if they violate males or females."

"So how do the urldi prevent violations?"

"By the certainty that they will exact vengeance. One does not need to be a warrior to wield an unseen knife at night in a fur pile."

Riordan folded his arms. "What about the senior caver, the kajh? Did he become involved in the fight?"

"Not personally." She frowned. "Unfortunately."

"What do you recommend doing with him?"

Bey reflected a moment. "Speak to Sharat. He might add him into his formation."

"And if he won't?"

She shrugged. "Since neither caver is part of any plot that stretches back to Forkus, I suppose there would be little harm in releasing him." Her tone said that she considered doing so more repugnant than cleaning a privy.

"I'll ask Sharat. For now, take the caver's weapons and keep him under guard. Now, what about the wounded tinker?"

"He must be disciplined. Sharply." When Riordan frowned, she leaned in to press her point that much harder. "You have seen how the other tinkers have changed after the fight? How they are now always on the verge of groveling? That is because they know the eyes of the trogans are hard upon them, even harder than when they were the tinkers' taskmasters in the caravan." She held his gaze. "The trogans will be expecting orders from you. Harsh orders."

Riordan thought for a moment. "What if this was purely a trog group, with you in charge of the trogans? What would *you* do?"

She nodded slowly, eyes not seeing him. "First, I would have already assigned one trogan as my assistant and another as my strong hand."

"A lieutenant and an enforcer," Riordan offered, managing to suppress a grin. *No matter where you go, all gangs work the same way.*

She glanced up and nodded, eyes slightly wider. "I would have my lieutenant inform the entire band of the tinker's deeds and his punishment. He would summon the enforcer to mete out the punishment before the rest."

Riordan unfolded his arms. "Then do that."

"But I—"

"Bey, you told me that if the trogs took their oath through you, then both of us had the right to punish them if they broke it. So you'll do just that. And I presume you've already identified the two trogans you'd choose as lieutenant and enforcer, respectively."

When she hesitated, he leaned in. "I trust your judgment, and right now, we need fast action to settle the tinker's disloyalty. As you said, it should be done in a manner that your people understand. Which, in turn, means it should come from the leader we've put in charge of them: you."

Her eyes grew slightly wider. "The traitors from my gang in Forkus took the same oath there, also through me." The cords in her well-muscled neck stood out in high relief as she waited for him to respond. When Riordan did not acknowledge her implicit request, she resorted to stone-eyed frankness: "They killed Zaatkhur."

He sighed. "Punishing a tinker is one thing, but executing two—"

She almost pushed up against him. "You rightly executed eight in Forkus who only *intended* betrayal and murder. These two actually committed both crimes. And by your own words, they are *my* responsibility."

Her appeal became guttural. "Leader Caine, every day they live, there is a chance that some unforeseeable event or accident will free them. They know our numbers, our intended destination, our strengths, and our weaknesses. They would seek those who have placed bounties on humans in the Orokrosir."

Riordan paused long enough to hold her eyes. "Bey, is this justice or revenge?"

"Does it matter if it is both?" she hissed, before calming herself. "We cannot take any chances. They must be disposed of. Quickly."

Riordan looked away. *Well, you were the one who insisted that trogs be allowed to govern their own wherever possible. And these are the consequences.* He turned back to her. "Carry out the executions according to your ways."

Bey nodded deeply. "Thank you, Leader Caine. I will tend to all these matters. Immediately."

Riordan watched her go, tried not to notice the eager quiver in her widening steps.

Chapter Three

Riordan handed the two Terran Republic duty suits to Eku. "Do you think you can repair these?"

Eku's answering smile revealed his utterly perfect teeth: the result of Dornaani genetic screening. "As a factotum for the Custodians, it often fell to me to maintain or examine unfamiliar items. These present no challenges." He frowned at the deep seam cut into one of them. "I do not have a way to fill such furrows, however."

Duncan Solsohn leaned forward. "Can you apply a patch? Maybe cured x'qai hide? We took a suit of it from the caravan. The locals claim it's as sturdy as the Dornaani vacc suits."

"I doubt they would know," Eku muttered. "But Tirolane cautioned us against using any materials derived from x'qai."

Pandora Veriden was suddenly alert and attentive. "He did? Why?"

"I am unsure. He was somewhat oblique. He also used local words to explain. When I submitted them to the translator, it suggested they were linguistically related to the concept of contagion, but not disease."

Riordan nodded. "Both Ta'rel and Bey have said something similar. The lore of both the Mangled and trogs claims that x'qao hide and bone either makes you easier to locate or influence."

"By whom?" Peter Wu asked, suddenly interested.

"That's not clear either. Maybe other x'qai or lieges." Caine shrugged. "The tales are warnings, not explanations."

"So," Chief O'Garran sighed, "is this yet another resource we're going to set aside because the locals swear it's bad hoodoo?"

Dora glowered at him. "I thought you got it through your thick little head that there really *is* mindspeaking here."

"Yeah, maybe... but where does all the mumbo jumbo stop? To listen to the trogs, everything is magical or the will of some spirit. Or god."

"So, are you saying *you* know how Tirolane waved the x'qao caravan leader right off his dustkine?"

Miles O'Garran was bristling with an imminent retort, but Riordan put up his hand. "This is neither the time nor place to continue that discussion. At the caravan, the caver who was wearing that cured x'qao hide kept moving, even after being hit by almost half a dozen arrows. Those fired by longbows barely penetrated; the rest didn't. So clearly, if trogs won't so much as touch armor that effective, I'm going to follow their lead." *Particularly since every time we haven't, we've regretted it.* "Eku will just have to patch the duty suits as best he can. Including Yaargraukh's."

The Hkh'Rkh extended his long neck-head slightly. "That way, I shall be able to remain where I wish: near our enemies." Even sitting, his head was higher than a human's.

Riordan glanced at him. "Just because you're the only one who can wear that duty suit doesn't mean you're always going to be out on the perimeter."

The big exosapient's black-bead eyes protruded slightly from beneath the bony shelf that protected them. "Once again, Commodore, you dash my fondest hopes." His black, wormlike tongue wriggled out of his central nostril for an instant: the Hkh'Rkh equivalent of a small, quick smile.

Eku was oblivious to the banter as he stared at the exosapient's armor. "I may require some assistance carrying that," he murmured.

"I shall be honored to bring it to you when you have completed your work on the two human suits," Yaargraukh assured him with a respectful lowering of his neck.

Eku nodded, yawned, held his broken arm carefully as he stood. "Commodore, with your permission—"

Riordan waved him toward his sleeping fur; although it was not yet sunset, the factotum was pale with fatigue. "Get some rest, Eku. Another long day tomorrow."

Offering a casual version of the Dornaani splay-fingered farewell, Eku walked carefully toward the Crewe's camp circle.

Pandora waited until he was out of earshot before turning wide eyes upon Caine and then Bannor. "Well, neither of you look like you've gone loco, so maybe you have an explanation for why we're not all using the Dornaani vacc suits, now? They've kept us safe, and their sensors have given us the edge in every fight. They're *perfect.*"

Bannor nodded. "Yes, they're perfect. Too perfect to risk every time we get into a scrap. That's why we need different armor. If the suits take too much damage, they won't be able to hold pressure or run the programs driving those sensors."

Craig Girten blew out a long, exasperated sigh. "Yes, sir, but like Dora says, saving the suits won't matter much if we're not around to wear them. It's great to preserve their Wizard of Oz magic, but not at the cost of our lives."

Ayana Tagawa nodded to acknowledge the paratrooper's point even as she disagreed. "We need their 'magic' no less now than when we deorbited."

"Ma'am, I fully agree. Without all their bells and whistles, we probably wouldn't have gotten down in one piece. I know *I* wouldn't have. But now that we're here, well, I care a whole hell of a lot more about staying alive than keeping the suits safe!"

Caine nodded. "We all do, Craig. But here's the catch: we're going to need that magic at least one more time if we're to have any chance of getting home."

"Whaddya mean, sir?"

Newton was nodding. "The commodore means that if no one is coming to rescue us—and how or why would anyone do so?—we will need the suits intact in order to return to space."

"Return to—?" Craig leaned away, looked around the group. "Do any of you still think we can get back to the ship? I mean, what are the odds?"

Ayana glanced at Caine before answering slowly, calmly. "It is pointless to assess odds in the absence of meaningful data. But until we determine it is impossible, our logical first priority is to reclaim the ship. And to do so, we must have working vacc suits."

"And not just for EVA ops," Duncan added emphatically. "Without their sensors and computing power, I'm not sure we could effect rendezvous, then get aboard, and *then* access the ship's systems." He shrugged. "If their advanced functions don't work, we might as well start calling Bactradgaria home sweet home.

Craig shrugged. "I think 'home' means more to you all than it does to me, but I get what you're saying. I guess."

Yaargraukh's neck wobbled slightly. "I do not understand your ambivalence, Sergeant Girten."

"Well, it may be different for your kind, Yaargraukh. Sounds to me like you have traditions that keep things from changing too much. Or at least, too quickly. But me? Everything I grew up seeing and hearing has been gone for almost two centuries." Craig shook his head. "What would I do? Where would I go?

Dora frowned. "Most of the other Lost Soldiers seemed eager to get back to Earth."

"Yeah, well, Lost Soldiers aren't any more alike than other folks, I guess. Besides, most of us who were taken before that war in Vietnam weren't as enthusiastic as those who were grabbed later."

Girten shrugged. "I guess by then, kids were growing up in the middle of science fiction, weren't they? Spaceships landing on the moon, nuclear power, television, computers, and movies that showed a future that is, well, kind of what you have now.

"But none of that was around when I disappeared just before Christmas, 1944. And only twenty years later, they were calling it 'ancient history' and 'old-timey.'" His smile was small and sad. "Like me, I guess."

Katie Somers leaned against him. "Och, ye've a family in us, y'know. And the other Lost Soldiers, too. And once ye're back on Earth, you can bet you'll never want for fame, much less food and a roof."

He glanced sideways at her. "Assuming they don't sweep us Lost Soldiers under the rug. Six feet under, to be exact."

"Aye, but that applies to *all* of us, now, eh, Colonel?"

Bannor nodded. "Unless things change back home, we can't return to Earth either, Craig." He smiled crookedly. "So it's likely you're stuck with us."

The GI's smile was pained but genuine. "Well, I guess I could've done worse."

Dora was frowning. "And you still could."

"You mean, you could all start getting mean and nasty?"

"No. I mean we could all start getting dead."

Duncan flinched. "Huh?"

Veriden tossed her hair. "*Merde*! I cannot tell if you do not see what we must do or you just don' *want* to see."

Caine leaned toward her. "What are we missing, Dora?"

She scratched her hair irritably. "We got to do what the locals do: make ourselves safer however we can."

"That's why we're fixing the duty suits and getting better armor."

"Yeah, but we need more than armor for each of us. We need armor that protects *all* of us."

The Crewe stared, puzzled... except for Miles and Ayana Tagawa. The former nodded as the latter explained, "Dora means we need armor on *other* bodies. *Many* other bodies."

Miles rolled his eyes when half of the Crewe continued to stare blankly. "Other bodies—as in, ones we'll keep between us and the rest of this shithole planet."

Katie Somers was frowning. "I think the term ye're looking for is 'cannon fodder,' Chief." Her voice was tight and hard.

"Yeah, if you like. Might as well call them what they are."

Dora looked around the circle of faces. "Don' you see how it is, here? The leaders stay alive by keeping a layer of protection around them. Jus' like the foam shields that kept us alive during planetfall, yeh? Because it don' matter how good our own armor or guns are; there are too many things waiting to kill us here. *Coño*: it's like this whole damn world is made to do just that. Sooner or later, it will succeed if we don't learn its first lesson of survival: get other bodies to do the dying for you."

"That is a very cold calculus, Ms. Veriden," rumbled Yaargraukh.

"It is," Peter agreed, "and yet, her equation proves out. Even more sweepingly than she means.

"When alone, every creature—human or otherwise—attracts opportunistic attacks. But in a unified and well-led group, none need fear casual tests of their vulnerability. So it is actually the weaker who derive the greatest benefit, even those who are used so poorly here."

Caine pointed at Peter. "Yes, but the groups who don't use the weak so poorly are the only ones that have been able to stand up to the x'qai. Look at the h'achgai, the mangles, even the Free Tribes. It's precisely because they reject the 'cannon fodder' model that they survive and even thrive."

Wu shrugged. "And yet, that is not the case with our single strongest ally: the Legate."

Caine shook his head. "There were no slaves or serfs at Tasvar's fortress. The least of his servitors were not only allowed, but required, to become party to a *mutual* oath in which Tasvar was as bound by his promises to them as they were to the ones they made to him." Riordan thumped his knuckles against the ground. "Our success here depends upon taking that foundation of mutual commitment one step further: to never forsake our own, to reward merit and effort, and for all to live and die by the same rules."

Miles stretched. "Sounds okay, as long as they always remember who's the boss and that their main job is to keep us alive, come what may." He looked around the group. "So how do we start? Grab five trogs as personal security, cycle them through ten-day duty cycles until they're all familiar with the drill? After that, we start pushing them through training—"

Riordan shook his head. "No."

Miles stopped in mid-word. "But . . . I thought you just approved the idea of having meat-shields, sir."

"Firstly, that term dies right here, right now. Second, just because I've agreed to the concept doesn't mean I like it one damn bit." He sighed. "That said, I think what you're proposing is fine, except that we can't be the ones assigning them to, or training them for, protection duty."

O'Garran shrugged. "Okay, then just order Bey to take care of it."

"No. Can't happen."

Others faces in the camp circle were beginning to look as confused as Miles, albeit not as exasperated. "Sir, she's *our* asset. We can simply—"

"No, Chief, that is precisely where you are wrong. She is *not* 'our asset.' That's why I kept her from taking an oath of fealty. And why she received all the trogs' oaths on our behalf. Not just because she's a truthteller, but because she's a local."

Before O'Garran could object again, Bannor broke in. "The commodore is not willing, ethically or legally, to assume direct control over the natives of Bactradgaria."

Miles glanced at the Special Forces colonel as if he'd defected to the enemy; the phrasing was almost straight out of the manual for managing insurgents.

Riordan saw, and understood, the near-glare. "Chief, those

words, and the policy behind them, are coming from *me*. And this doesn't just apply to trogs. It applies to *all* locals. It's why the oaths taken by the two humans we freed—Enoran and Orsost—are temporary: to keep them independent. Same with Tirolane, who's traveling with us as an equal, no strings attached." Seeing the short SEAL's frown, he asked, "So you think they'd be *more* useful as servitors, instead of allies?"

"Well..." O'Garran began hesitantly.

"Look, Chief, there's a practical dimension to this as well. Do you want to spend your time training all those trogs? Do you want to whip them into shape and discipline them? Without any deep understanding of how they think and react?" Riordan shook his head. "We're not the ones with those skills. The *locals* are. Like Bey, who will do that job better, and with less hand-holding, if she's our ally rather than our vassal. It's equally true for the humans. And for Tirolane."

Newton raised an eyebrow. "The way you phrased that, sir: do you suspect that Tirolane is not a human like the others?"

Duncan nodded. "Kinda wondered the same thing, after what he did at the caravan."

Riordan shrugged. "It doesn't matter if Tirolane's human any more than if Bey's a crog or a trog or something else. The same principles apply: they are both locals who can manage situations we don't fully understand and maybe never will. And by keeping them as allies, we're letting them do what they do best. Which frees us up for the tasks that only we have the knowledge and training to perform."

"Yeah," Dora agreed with a frown, "but there's one drawback, Boss. An ally can always walk away. That gives them leverage."

Riordan lifted an eyebrow. "I would think you, of all people, would want them to have leverage, Dora. But from a purely practical standpoint, that leverage works both ways. We, too, can require changes in the terms of an alliance. Both parties have to be satisfied with it; that's how they remain equal and independent.

"Look: this isn't about us carrying the torch of democracy to the locals. We all know how many times that was attempted on Earth and how many times it was a disaster. We're just laying out the basic concepts, which they'll develop as they choose. Or not."

Bannor nodded. "And I'm just as happy not to be a feudal overlord, thank you very much."

Caine nodded. "However you look at it, we want allies, not servitors. And not just because it's ethical; it ensures that the locals retain both control and culpability when it comes to their actions."

Miles' sideways stare was dubious. "Sir, if that shit ever hits the fan, do you really think anyone is going to give a good god-damn about those dainty diplomatic distinctions?"

Riordan smiled. "Only time will tell, Chief. But I started seeing the situation differently the moment Bey told me that the praakht renamed themselves trogs." O'Garran grinned, having originated the term. "I can't shake the feeling that we might be at the birth of a movement: maybe a rebellion, maybe something more sweeping. Something that could build and change very rapidly, once it starts.

"Either way, this is not our world and we don't know its ways. The right and smart paths are one and the same: to avoid becoming part of the local system and to refrain from imposing our own. If we start as friends and allies—no more and no less—we have a good chance of staying that way in the times to come."

Yaargraukh emitted a contemplative phlegm-warble. "It shall be interesting to see when and what kind of benefits we shall derive from the relationships you have set forth, Commodore."

"You'll see one soon, my friend."

"Indeed? Of what kind?"

"The grimmest kind. Bey has taken charge of the execution."

Duncan whistled appreciatively. "At least the blood isn't on our hands this time. When is it happening?"

"Sometime early tomorrow," Riordan answered.

Bannor glanced over at his tone. "I can't tell whether you're more relieved or worried that Bey is carrying out the sentence."

Remembering her look of grim determination, Caine sighed. "I'm not sure either, Colonel."

Chapter Four

By the time Riordan and a few others arrived at the trog sleeping circles the next morning, they saw only one unusual activity. The wounded tinker was already waist-deep in a hole he had evidently been digging for several hours. Flanked by two trogans, Bey was watching the slow process with arms crossed.

"So he's digging the traitors' graves?" Katie asked her.

"Graves?" Bey had to think a moment, then shook her head. "We do not, eh, bury the dead."

"Then why the hole?"

"To keep their remains from attracting predators."

Yaargraukh glanced about. "Where are the traitors?"

Bey jutted her chin toward what they had thought were a pile of hide tarps. "They are there, Leader Yaargraukh."

His eyes protruded slightly. "The sentence has already been carried out?"

She nodded. "At first light."

Katie craned her neck, seeking the covered bodies. "I was expecting it would be, well, public."

Bey shrugged. "That is not the way of the Free Tribes."

O'Garran frowned. "Damn. I'd have thought every gang boss would use public executions as a message to their followers: 'Betray me, and you're next.'"

Bey nodded. "In cities, that is what most do. But those who are confident of their position execute offenders without ceremony; they have no need to remind others of their power." She glanced at Riordan and his companions. "That is why you have commanded respect. You do not shout or threaten. Your word is quiet, but it is law."

The chief crossed his arms. "I'll bet it doesn't hurt that the trogs know we've destroyed every enemy we've faced, too."

Bey nodded. "That is why your quiet ways are mostly seen as confidence, not weakness."

Riordan nodded toward the tinker, who was hissing and groaning; each cycle of the crude shovel pulled at his wounds. "Is he almost done? We need to move within the hour."

"He has little digging left to do. But then the bodies must be shambled so they fit in the hole."

"Shambled?" Yaargraukh echoed uncertainly.

"An old word for butchering," Bannor muttered. "Won't nearby predators smell the remains and dig them up?"

"Almost certainly," Bey answered. "But that will keep them busy until we are long gone."

Riordan nodded. "Send word to me and Sharat when the discipline is complete. We will start out immediately after."

"Yes, Leader Caine," she said, hard eyes on the covered bodies.

As the Crewe walked away, Dora muttered, "Every time I think that this place can't surprise me anymore, I see something that makes it just that much worse." She stalked ahead.

Miles, however, was hanging back. "Commodore, can I have a word?"

Riordan nodded, waved the others on.

"Sir, I've got a few questions of my own for Bey. Didn't want to ask in front of the others. An idea started banging around my brain about the bounties on our heads and how we might use our new recruits to help deal with it."

Riordan raised an eyebrow. "And what is this idea?"

Miles shook his head. "Like I said, sir, at this point, I don't even know if it's possible. But I should have an answer in time for our nightly Fireside Chat. Is that acceptable, sir?"

Riordan nodded, waved Miles back toward Bey and her trogan lieutenants, who looked on impassively as the tinker struggled to drag the first of the traitors' corpses toward the hole in which he stood.

✧ ✧ ✧

"You want to do *what*?" Duncan Solsohn exclaimed, putting down his last strip of dried dustkine.

"Major," Chief O'Garran said patiently, "you said, along with everyone else, that you'd hear me out. It's not as crazy as it sounds."

Dora snorted. "Sure, sure. Taking a bunch of trogs into water-soaked wadis is so *very* sane."

Miles sighed, looked around the circle of faces, half of which were disbelieving, shocked, or both. "Everybody done with the wisecracks, now?"

"Half of us never uttered any, Chief O'Garran," Yaargraukh observed.

"Uh . . . that was just a figure of speech."

"Yes." The Hkh'Rkh's tongue-tip slipped out. "I know."

O'Garran rolled his eyes. "Ha. And ha. Last time I fall for you playing the straight man." He grinned at the exosapient. "So to speak."

Yaargraukh's neck circled slightly. "I believe the idiom is 'now we are even.' Please continue."

Miles nodded. "I'll start by getting all the logical objections out of the way. Yes, it's spring and the wadi country will be wet. But we're in no rush and it will be getting drier every day. Also, we have something the bounty-hunting bastards don't: Ta'rel. In addition to his survival skills, he knows the Orokrosir almost as well as the local mangles. Enough to keep us near good shelter and get us moving toward higher ground when the weather's closing in. Yidreg has also agreed to come along, and he's no slouch when it comes to knowing the terrain. So that also answers the predictable question about getting ambushed: not likely with those two. And we'll have a monoscope with us, so that's 10X magnification versus naked eyes.

"Will we need to carry a lot of supplies? You bet. That's why twenty percent of the team are porters. And before anyone gets anxious that we could run out before we return, Ne'sar has given Ta'rel the locations of hidden caches and bolt-holes maintained by the mangles. So we'll never be more than two days away from resupply, shelter, and a hiding place. And we'll have a tinker along to provide basic field maintenance."

Miles put up a hand as if anticipating objections. "It's true that we can't rule out bumping into groups larger than ours.

But according to both the h'achgai and mangles, those would be spring hunting parties, not bountiers. And if any of those big groups came after us, they'd regret it."

Peter frowned. "Why?"

"Because we'll have nine or ten better marksmen equipped with bigger bows and crossbows. None of the groups we might run into—whether hunter, raider, or bountier—are likely to have more than a few small ones. If that."

Newton crossed his arms. "Even hunting parties have so few bows?"

Duncan's stare was fixed on something impossibly far beyond the twilit horizon. "It's because we're in the ass end of nowhere. Remember Khorkrag? Even from across the river, you could see the signs of it. Almost no metal. Cruder weapons and armor. Buildings that were smaller, half-collapsed. So they're probably no better off when it comes to making bows, fletching arrows, or having chances to use them." He leaned back, eyes returning to the dinner circle as he speared the last morsel on his platter. "Everything's harder because they're as poor as dirt."

O'Garran nodded before turning toward Newton. "By the way, Doc, what they've got up here aren't really hunting parties. Scouts find the dustkine and then the x'qa just run them down. When they're done gorging themselves, the trogs come along to shamble anything that remains."

Ayana sat very straight. "I am satisfied that you will not be in extreme danger, Chief O'Garran. But I have not yet heard what you mean to accomplish with this—this—"

"I call it Operation Swamp Phase, owing to the spring wet *and* our colonel's worthy origins, back when he was still a soldier—I mean, enlisted man."

Bannor waved a dismissive hand at Miles' cryptic references, explained it for those who were still frowning at it. "I started as a Ranger; Swamp Phase is part of our training. And yes, it's as nasty as it sounds. But let's return to Aya—Ms. Tagawa's question: What, beyond some salvaged enemy equipment, is the objective?"

"Crafting better armor, sir." Miles clearly enjoyed the perplexity induced by his response.

"Come again, Chief?"

"Direct result of our convo last night. We need trogs—allies—to be our armor. But it's not like we can, or even want to, increase our numbers very quickly. So I figured we could refine and harden the armor we've already got."

He nodded at Riordan. "I've heard the commodore and the colonel talking about setting up training cycles when we reach Achgabab. But the more I thought about it, the more I felt that skills aren't enough. Might not even be the most important thing."

He jerked his thumb back toward the trog sleeping circles. "We've got to shake these new guys out. The x'qai don't teach trogs to work together; they keep them suspicious of each other. We've got to stop that, reverse it.

"That's not the kind of thing we can achieve at Achgabab. We have to set these guys straight where no one will see or eavesdrop or comment or sympathize or pat their heads. Isolated, just like boot camp—except here, we're playing for keeps, right away." He stopped scanning the faces around him.

Riordan smiled. "Go on, Chief."

"First order of business: we've got to sort out the grudges they've brought with them. Best way to do that is to throw them straight into the shit. That's where you *have* to work together if you want to survive—and dying is what happens when you do anything else.

"How they face those challenges will show us which ones will, or can learn to, pull for each other and the mission. If any of them can't, we'll be in the best place to either fix them or get rid of them: far away from their pals and softhearted human leaders."

Newton's tone and face were dour. "And how do you mean to 'get rid' of those who seem untrustworthy, Chief O'Garran? Executions based on the presumption of crimes they haven't yet committed?"

"Hell, no! Uh, sir. The opposite. *We* won't have to do anything to them: Bactradgaria will. They'll be pushed to the point where only hard work and loyalty will keep them alive. Any trog who manages to do that is a trog we can salvage."

"And for those who can't or won't demonstrate that reliability?"

"They'll keep walking point and pulling the shittiest details until they come around or die resisting. Just that simple. Like I said, Doc: this planet will weed out whoever can't cut it.

"But I doubt we'll have many problems. All but one of the kajhs I've chosen were commanded by Orsost and which he recommended as the most reliable and level-headed of the bunch.

The team's small size will make it easier to train them to think and act like soldiers. When they come back, we'll put them in positions where they'll spread those lessons by example. They'll also see Bey's ability as a leader, which should convince them to accept and support her in that role."

Ayana nodded at the chief's summary, but asked, "What of the kajh that was not picked by Orsost? Why is he being included?"

"Because that's the one who we *know* needs to step up. Or be weeded out."

"Ah," Ayana murmured, frowning. "The caver."

"Yes, ma'am."

"Are you not concerned that, because your team will be small and isolated, the caver might seek opportunities to escape?"

"Maybe, Ms. Tagawa. But from what the mangles tell me, if he tries, he might as well slit his own throat. The wadis are a maze, and he won't be carrying his own rations."

She nodded, but her frown persisted. "I am more concerned with unexpected events, such as if you detect an enemy group too late in the day to engage it, but is still close enough that he flees toward it. He would almost certainly be able to buy his survival by revealing our location, numbers, and plans."

Miles nodded. "No doubt, ma'am. But he's never going to be alone or unwatched. If he tries to give us the slip, we'll put a stop to that with a crossbow bolt between his shoulders."

Peter leaned back. "You mentioned including a tinker. Given their role among the cavers, do you feel it safe to include one?"

O'Garran's smile became a sneer. "Lemme tell you, the tinkers are no fans of the cavers. They may be repairmen, but they get treated more like whipping boys." Miles stretched. "It'll take some time, but I'll get the whole menagerie sorted out and on task."

Katie Somers looked up from beneath beetled brows. "An' am I the only one bothered by the direction we're headed, here?"

"You mean getting recruits? I'm ecstatic."

"No, Chief. I mean your referring to the locals as a 'menagerie.' We hate the x'qai for breeding us as if we were livestock, yeh? But now we're talking about how to 'manage' trogs and crogs and cavers and tinkers to achieve our goals. So tell me: how are we any better?"

Riordan was tempted to lean in, but his gut told him to let the debate run its course—for now.

"Firstly," O'Garran said tensely, "that 'menagerie' happens to include humans, too."

"And that makes it better?" Katie turned to Riordan. "Sir, you can't be deaf to all this!"

Riordan kept his voice very level. "Corporal Somers, I assure you my hearing, and perception, are unimpaired. If what you're really asking is whether I detect echoes of 'manifest destiny' in all this, I do. But I also detect crucial distinctions."

"But—!"

"Lissen," O'Garran said, index finger unfolding at Somers like a switchblade, "you might want to check some of your assumptions, 'lassie.' Like maybe asking how two of my meemaw's great-grandparents felt about Jim Crow laws."

Katie turned very red, eyes narrowed—

"Look," Dora broke in, "if anyone here has the right to be sensitive about all this shit, it's me, yeah? I mean, take your pick of colonizers. Odds are I've got their blood in my veins, flowing right alongside that of the people they raped and sold and killed."

She flung a pausing hand toward the center of the group. "But this isn't about different color or sex or anything like that. It's like Bey says: these are different *species.* Some aren't entirely human, and are so different that they can't breed together safely. So even if the x'qai monsters weren't in charge, genes would still have to be tracked, yeah? Or is it more important for them—or us—to pretend they're all the same than it is to keep mothers from dying in childbirth?"

Riordan suppressed a sigh; time to step in. "Everyone take a step back and a deep breath." He waited a moment for the tension to fade. "Dora makes a crucial point: this situation *is* fundamentally different from any in our own past. So it has to be approached and resolved differently, too.

"But as Katie points out, if we aren't careful, we could find ourselves falling into this hellhole's worst pattern: acting as though some lives are more important or more valuable than others. Because from there, it's a dangerously short step to *believing* that they are."

Miles scratched the back of his head. "But right now, Commodore, isn't that the reality of our situation here?" He put up a hand against Riordan's stare. "Look: I am *all* for using anyone in any role they're best at. I don't give a damn who or what they are. I am also one hundred percent behind destroying the x'qai and what they've created. Christ, they make the worst American and Spanish slave owners look like choirboys. But right now, the only thing we can do is play the hand we've been dealt, no matter how dirty the game."

Dora nodded. "There's one way in which this planet *is* like Earth: you've got to free the slaves before you can change their lives. And we're a long, long way from doing that."

Riordan exhaled slowly before responding. "If anyone believes I lack a full appreciation of the brutal realities of this planet, this is the moment to speak up." He waited until the Crewe started avoiding his eyes. "Firstly, I don't disagree with you. Any of you. The facts of life on Bactradgaria are harder and colder than any we've encountered.

"And that is precisely why we need to keep Katie's warning in mind. Over time, the conditions here could seem so commonplace that we won't realize we're already on the slippery slope of becoming accustomed to them."

Mouths began opening; Riordan held up a hand. "I'm not suggesting any of you would become indifferent to what's around us. But bear this grim possibility in mind: that in fighting to change Bactradgaria, we may have no choice but to adopt some of our enemies' methods. And if we become accustomed to *that*, we're no longer part of the solution; we're part of the problem."

Bannor nodded, murmured, "Remaining alert to those choices, and their costs, is the only way we will keep our souls."

He glanced at O'Garran. "Remaining alert to unexpected outcomes actually brings me to the one possibility your plan doesn't address, Chief."

Miles frowned, concentrating. Then he shook his head. "Sorry, sir: I'm not seeing it."

Rulaine shrugged. "What if it's *too* successful?"

O'Garran's eyebrows rose. "Not sure I understand you, Colonel."

"Chief, your objective is to find enemies, engage them, and return: not merely with some salvaged gear, but with more reliable and seasoned troops. Correct?"

"Correct, sir."

Bannor leaned forward. "Well, let's assume everything goes as planned." Rueful smiles sprung up at the irony of such a notion. "You'll be the terror of the Orokrosir. You'll have defeated raiders and bounty hunters alike. And so, you will achieve what none of them ever have: you'll become a legend. Or at least stand out from the customary spring mayhem in the wadi country, enough to spur rumors, be remembered... and pick up tails.

"I am not speaking of bounty hunters, but smaller, more careful groups. Groups which could follow you back to Achgabab and eventually sell that information to those pursuing us."

The chief's eyes were round. "Uh... hadn't really thought of that, sir."

Riordan chuckled. "That's quite all right, Chief. If our places were reversed, I'd have been so focused on selling the idea that I'd never have worried about *over*selling it."

"You've got that right, sir. So, how do we keep from being *too* successful?"

Rulaine leaned back. "In the simplest terms, this is a hunting trip. I'm all for it. But we've got to set a bag limit. And a time limit."

Miles brightened. "Oh, that's easy, sir."

"I'm not sure it is, Chief. Consider how we acquired the forces you're taking with you: defeating enemy forces. Let's say that pattern continues. If it does, your seek-and-destroy mission requires more than typical operational limits on your maximum number of engagements, days in the field, and salvage burden. You've also got to limit how many new 'recruits' you can add before heading for home."

O'Garran nodded. "I hear that loud and clear, sir. If you and the commodore have a little more time, I'd like to talk about those mission-end benchmarks."

Riordan smiled. "If you hadn't suggested it, I'd have ordered it. Let's go do it where we won't keep everyone awake."

Chapter Five

Miles O'Garran topped the ridge and nodded back toward Riordan. "Yep, this is where we part ways." He pointed at the rocky slopes rising above the eastern horizon. "Achgabab."

Yidreg marched up the shallow incline to join the chief. "You see the highlands in which it is hidden." He turned back toward Caine. "Ulchakh and Hresh both know how to proceed from here. They will bring you to a place where the formation must stop. You will be observed for as much as a day. If Vaagdjul, chief of Achgabab, deems it safe, you will be guided in at night. Otherwise, he will send out an envoy."

Riordan stared at the hazy rock piles. "What then?"

Yidreg shrugged. "It is impossible to say. He will decide how many may proceed to Achgabab: all, some, or none. There may be conditions to be met." The h'achga glanced back over the formation, his eyes lingering on the trogs. "It is almost certain that you will be asked to camp at a slight distance from the community itself. Only the most, er, reliable visitors will be allowed within."

And there's the suspicion that keeps species apart, even hostile. But who can blame any of them, with treachery almost as common as breathing? "I understand," Caine said. "We will comply with whatever requirements Vaagdjul sets forth."

Yidreg nodded. "We know this, or you would not have been brought so close." He turned toward Miles. "O-Garun, we should muster our force. If we start soon, we will reach an isolated stretch of old wadi before nightfall. It is excellent cover and not on any route followed by hunters."

O'Garran nodded, smiled at Riordan. "Gotta rally the troops. I'll report when we're ready, sir."

Riordan nodded, smiled at the chief's oversized duty suit: a loan from Craig Girten which they'd swap back and forth for the duration of the mission. "We could spare another suit, you know."

O'Garran waved off the implicit offer. "I'm all for doing this with minimal tech, sir. The locals have to see that, even without our fancy toys, we're as serious and deadly as a heart attack. Don't want the new trogs to see all our gear in action, either. Not yet, anyway. Until we return, there's always the chance that one could shake loose and reveal what they've seen to potential enemies. Right now, all these new guys know is that we kicked the caravan's ass, and rumors say the same about the hovel we hit in Forkus. Just like you pointed out when we set the equipment limits."

Riordan crossed his arms. "About which you had reservations."

Miles' answering eye roll was theatrical. "Aw, c'mon, sir: are you trying to get me to say you were right? Me? Okay: 'you were right.'"

Riordan shook his head. "No. I just want to make sure you have what you need. And if you still had reservations, I was ready to revisit the limits we put on the gear."

"Sir!" O'Garran gasped. "Did you miss the day in OCS where they teach you that an officer is *never* wrong—even if they are?" The chief's concluding smile was so infectious that Caine felt its twin growing on his own lips. "Seriously, Commodore, over the past four days, I've become a convert. Which was your strategy all along, maybe? Let the wisdom sink into my thick SEAL brain?"

"Thought never crossed my mind."

Miles chortled. "You can really do deadpan when you've a mind to, sir. But at this point, I'm in full agreement: if something, er, goes sideways, we have to minimize the amount of tech that could fall into enemy hands. Hell, I've been thinking of leaving behind the survival rifle and the recharge tissues. But the monoscope and duty suit—particularly its radio—are must-haves if we expect to see the OpFor first and give you daily updates."

Craig Girten trudged up to join them. "Hey, Chief, that suit looks mighty fine on you!"

O'Garran frowned. "Watch it, or this fist will leave a mighty fine imprint on your face."

"Commodore, help! My superior is threatening me!"

Riordan grinned. "As I understand it, that would be a 'point of honor' between noncommissioned officers. Falls outside regulations."

Girten laughed as he tried to shout, "Mother! Help!"

O'Garran shook his head. "Gonna be a long mission fer sure. Work on your jokes, Girten. They stink worse than your—feet." He glanced at Riordan. "That was sanitized for the benefit of your delicate ears, Commodore."

"For which I am much obliged. Now, I don't want to keep you gentlemen from setting forth into the wastes."

Girten, oblivious to the cue that the conversation needed to end, peered over the spine of the ridge. "So that's Achgabab, huh?"

"The vicinity," Riordan amended.

Craig shook his head. "Actually, I'm kind of glad to be heading into wadi country."

"Why?"

"Because he's stoopit?" O'Garran suggested.

"No, because I'm not sure Achgabab is going to be any safer. Maybe a whole lot less so, if we've got enemies following us." He looked sideways at Riordan. "I'm still thinking it might be better not to go there at all, sir."

Girten started at Miles' loud, almost outraged rebuttal. "Not go to Achgabab? We *have* to go there! Have you been paying *any* attention? The h'achgai are the only ones who have their shit gathered!"

"'Have their shit *together*,'" Craig corrected quietly. It was a common expression among the last Lost Soldiers the Ktor had abducted.

"Okay: *together*," Miles corrected. "Look: do you have any idea how hard it is to do what the h'achgai did with that boat they sold down in Forkus? They not only had to haul it overland in pieces to Khorkrag, but when they got there, they had to assemble it. Which was only possible because *everything*—every motherf... uh, mother-lovin' piece of it—fit together so precisely that they could build and then waterproof it in a shit-town a thousand klicks from nowhere. And then they sailed it all those klicks down the crazy river we had to cross before meeting up with Sharat's team.

"I'm telling you, Girten: any group able to do all that is a group we *have to* visit!" O'Garran glanced at Riordan. "Isn't that so, sir?"

Riordan smiled. "Since that's where the rest of us are headed, I expect you already know my answer. Let me know when you're ready to set out, Chief. Carry on."

Miles walked along the lower half of the slope, past the loose groups of his task force.

"Chief," asked Girten, "shouldn't we go down and get them moving?"

"No, Craig, not 'we'; as my second-in-command, *you're* going to do that."

"Second-in-command? Me?"

"You see any other 'Craigs' here, gaping at me?" *Just like Girten to never think of himself in that role: something else we'll get sorted.* "You are going to get them to carry out the loosest, sloppiest pass in review they've never heard of." *Because there's no evidence that anyone on this godforsaken planet ever conceived of military traditions of* any *kind. Which stops today.*

"Order the elements as you'd expect, Sergeant. First cadre and advisors, then line troops, and support bringing up the rear. Don't fuss over it. Give them the boot, but make their own leaders sort out any uncertainties. They might as well get used to our expectations." *And to think of themselves not as a mob, but separate parts of a greater whole.* "Looks like you have a question, Sergeant. Particularly since you're still standing here."

"Yes, si—Chief," Girten corrected, seeing O'Garran's reaction to the possibility that he was about to be called "sir." "H'achgai before the trogs?"

Well, well: a good question, after all! "Yes, right behind command staff."

"Because Yidreg and Arashk will be in the first group."

"Yep. Along with Orsost, our third-in-command."

"So, that means I should put the trogans at the front of the trogs."

O'Garran couldn't help smiling. "If you knew all that, then why are you still here bothering me? You've got it under control, Sergeant. Go make it happen!"

Girten saluted, sprinted back toward the task force, stopped to snap yet another salute at an approaching figure: Bannor Rulaine. Who waved him off and ambled toward Miles.

"Come to see the big parade?" O'Garran asked.

"Wouldn't miss it," Rulaine said with a straight face as he stopped alongside the chief. "Frankly, this may be the most courageous undertaking I've witnessed in my entire career." He smiled. "Utterly insane, but still courageous."

"Uh... thanks, Bannor. You say that like you don't expect to see me again."

Rulaine shrugged. "Half the trogs we're taking to Achgabab think this is the last they'll see of the ones going with you."

"And you trust their military judgment over mine?"

"Cool your jets, there. I'm only saying that the locals consider this mission extremely dangerous and they're glad not to be going on it."

"Yeah, until we come marching back. And then they'll wish they had the bragging rights."

"So you're not worried about the outcome?"

O'Garran shook his head once. "I'm worried enough that I won't take any risks. If we come back with nothing other than our skins, it's a success: we'll have some real soldiers to set a standard for the rest. Besides, there's nothing out in that godforsaken wasteland that's worth losing lives over.

"But hell, we're out there looking for the enemy, so something *will* go wrong. But bad enough that we all buy the farm?" He shook his head. "The only thing I'm worried about is getting spotted by one of those damned kiktzo insects with a hoodoo link back to a x'qao watching through its eyes.

"But if there *are* any of those buzzing around out here, then our mission becomes more important: as a decoy. We may be less than half the size of this column and lack vehicles, but we'll be leaving a trail that airborne bugs are far more likely to see."

Bannor's smile was cramped. "You mean, all the enemy bodies strewn behind you?"

"More like all the survivors running the hell away and raising a lot of dust as they do. Just the thing to keep enemy eyes off *your* formation: the one that really matters." He nodded down the ridgeline; the task force was standing and sorting itself into groups. "Nine of our twenty-two are armed with either bows or crossbows. That gives us at least three times the firepower average of the groups we might face. And half of ours are trained marksmen."

Bannor nodded. "A sharp ambush stands a good chance of breaking the morale of locals, if you spring it at optimum range."

Miles nodded. "That's the plan: inflict enough casualties to get 'em running. Destroying any of these groups isn't worth the effort. It would also require closing to melee range." He shook his head. "Not our sweet spot. Our strengths are firepower and much better command and control. If we get close enough for us to start hacking at each other, both those advantages go to hell."

Bannor nodded in the direction of O'Garran's task force. "And here come the troops. No brass band, though."

Miles suppressed a snicker just in time to present a stern face to the uneven procession that began walking, rather than marching, past. His local cadre—Orsost, Yidreg, Arashk, and Ta'rel—nodded toward him. *But of course Ta'rel is* still *smiling like a kid on a playground!*

Whether by chance or design, the two other h'achga were clustered with the two trogans: the reliable, steady warriors. But when Girten bellowed, "Eyes . . . *left*!" they started, then glanced uncertainly toward the two humans observing them from the slope. The three groups that followed—the kajhs, the scouts, and finally the tinker and porters—benefitted from the first one's mistake; all looked over quickly when Craig snapped the order.

"Thank you, Sergeant Girten," Miles shouted when the porters had passed. "Lead the detachment to the groupment area. Last rations and water. I will bring the XO for final walk-through."

"Aye, aye, Chief!"

"Aye, aye?" *Well, bless Craig's Navy-loving heart!* "That's a Bravo Zulu, Sergeant! Now, stop sucking up!"

Girten grinned over his shoulder as he jogged after the task force. Ta'rel passed him heading back toward the main body of the column.

"Going somewhere?" Miles called after the mangle.

A female voice from behind surprised him. "Miles O-Garun, may I still give this to him?"

He and Bannor turned; Ne'sar was approaching from the opposite direction, a long cloak held out in front of her.

Miles frowned. "Well, er, certainly, Miss—uh, Ne'sar." *Even on Bactradgaria, where war never stops, civilians are the same as everywhere else: no sense of military decorum!*

Ne'sar slipped between the two human commanders. She and Ta'rel stopped a long step apart. She held out the cloak. "You must take this."

He nodded and bent his head. "I will if you insist."

"I do."

"Do you not fear traveling without it?"

"Not so much as I fear for you. I travel in safety."

"Still, there is always danger."

Ne'sar shook the cloak under his nose. "Your danger is far, far greater. And if you refuse, I must presume you think me unable to survive just one more day's travel to Achgabab." She stepped closer. "Take it. Please."

She was so close that Ta'rel was able to lean his forehead against hers. "I hear your words. And I would not dare insult the daughter of Ebrekka's *durus'maan*." They smiled, then she stepped back, turned, and walked toward the main column very briskly.

Ta'rel looked after her for a moment, nodded to the two humans, and trotted back to the groupment area.

Miles and Bannor exchanged small, furtive grins. The chief leaned his head sideways. "You think anyone doesn't know about them . . . except *them*?"

Bannor muttered. "Not possible." He straightened. "I believe it's time to inspect your task force, Chief O'Garran."

Miles snapped a lazy salute, took as long a step forward as his short legs allowed and howled. "On your feet, slugs! XO on deck!"

"Commodore?" The voice inquiring from behind Riordan was O'Garran's.

Caine looked up from Eku's patient instruction on how to clean the solar rechargers, which involved ionizing the sediment before "bumping it" off with a brief opposite charge. He nodded thanks to the factotum, handed off the solar tissue, and stood.

The chief snapped a sharp salute. "Final report, sir. XO has cleared the task force to move out."

Riordan returned the salute casually. "Let's take a stroll, Miles. No rank."

"Fine by me, sir."

They walked in the lee of the ridge for less than three seconds before O'Garran asked, "Sir, we're starting out late, but do you still want a check-in today?"

Riordan grinned over at him. The only enemy "Little Guy" seemed to fear was silence. "Yes, Chief. It is priority one that you observe the same time-coded messaging we used after making planetfall. The only difference is that we won't return-send unless we have a critical update for you."

"Understood, sir. No reason to point out the location of the main formation, sir."

"Miles, relax." Caine raised an eyebrow, knew the words that would jolt the SEAL out of his careful formality. "You have the jitters?"

O'Garran's eyes widened in genuine surprise. "'Jitters'?" He jerked a thumb over his shoulder. "About herding that sorry-ass rump platoon? Hell no, sir. I'm worried about leaving all of *you* on your own." And he clearly meant it.

"Well, we'll manage. And I will emphasize this one last time: if you've got a risky situation developing, break radio silence and report."

O'Garran squinted at the suggestion, then shook his head. "Sir, I know I was a pain in the ass about wanting us to send in the clear back when we arrived dirtside. But that was before we learned that some of the locals 'mindspeak' can preemptively seed traitors into our midst, and were able to shadow us with a force that stayed on our tail across thousands of klicks.

"Bottom line, sir: I don't know what to believe anymore. So I've shifted to the SEAL default. I assume that every enemy I can imagine is out there, that everything that can go wrong will, and that it will do so at the worst possible moment. And that means you won't get any comms in the clear unless I've got something world-shaking to report. Or to send a final signal. And if that's the last you hear from me, just make sure that when the Crewe gets back to Earth, you tell my meemaw that I named a whole goddamned planet!"

Riordan chuckled. "You have my word on it." He glanced at the much smaller man. "Meemaw was a Southern term, wasn't it?"

"'Was' a Southern term? Try 'still is'... er, sir. Well, in some parts, at least."

Caine wondered if O'Garran's sudden, prickly regionalism was part of his contrarian bravado or genuine pride. "So, were your family Reculturists?"

"You mean like Katie and Ms. Tagawa?" "Little Guy" snorted through a few guffaws. "There was no *re*-culturing needed 'cause we never lost it. My folks were from Georgia and Tennessee, originally. But Meemaw's people were from Kentucky: back in the hollers and perched on the knobs, as she used to say. Quiet nights and clean mountain air."

"Sounds appealing."

"Huh. Well, it sure was 'rustic.' But sometimes, that ain't all it's cracked up to be. Particularly when indoor plumbing came way late."

Riordan started. "I know basic services spread unevenly, but I never guessed—"

"Naw, Commodore: it wasn't because my meemaw's clan were poor. Not really." Miles grinned with a softening melancholy. "It was pure orneriness. Good trait sometimes, but bad at others."

"And in the balance?"

O'Garran stopped for a moment, head tilted as if trying to hear something distant. "I'd keep the freedom that came with it, but I wish some of those back-hills folks lived longer. They didn't always hold with doctoring. To this day, they don't much trust what they don't know."

Riordan smiled. "So you're the great adventurer?"

He chortled. "Me? Hardly. I was a brat from the 'burbs. We just *visited* my meemaw back in the hollers. I grew up outside Savannah."

"So, coastal life made you choose the SEALs?"

"You kidding, sir? I was just trying to stick it to all the stuck-up Rangers there. First Battalion of the Seventy-Fifth, y'know." He snickered. "Lazy bastards are probably still in garrison as part of the planetary response force."

"And still you get along with Bannor."

He chuckled softly. "See, now that's about the only thing these days that reminds me you're not military. Only real assholes take those service rivalries to heart. It's just our way of pumping ourselves up."

Riordan shrugged. "I've seen fistfights break out over it."

"See? There you go again. Listen: when you've been crawling around in another guy's puke during live-fires, or cramping so bad during hell week that you can hardly move at the end of the day, I gotta tell you, sir: a fistfight ain't no big deal."

Caine raised an eyebrow. "More than a few have ended up as manslaughter."

"Hey, I did say that there *are* assholes that go too far, didn't I?" Miles sighed. "Every fine tradition generally has some lousy price to pay, somewhere along the line. But if you don't live that life, you won't—can't—understand the hate-love we have for all of that precious bullshit."

Caine smiled. "I told all of you time and time again, I'm not a real soldier."

"Little Guy" stopped and laughed straight in Riordan's face. "And that's another thing you don't understand; you *are* a soldier. Have been since you resurfaced in Indonesia. I know lots of guys wearing combat medals who didn't see a tenth the action you did. But what you'll never be is a *grunt*."

He smiled. "And see, we don't want you to be one. First off, you're as officer as they come. And I don't mean the brownnosers who spend most of their time trying to look high-speed and low-drag. I mean the ones who take the job seriously, which means taking their *troops* seriously. Worrying over them. Fighting the brass on their behalf. Working to save as many as they can. Which usually means killing as many enemies as fast as possible. That's you. And that's who we need."

He shrugged. "That you happen to be way too much of a natural diplomat and way too educated to be doing this at all is just a curse we have to live with." He grinned. "Sir."

O'Garran stopped, gave Riordan a very slow, very careful salute, waited until it had been returned. "Permission to cross the line of departure, sir?"

"Permission granted, Chief O'Garran. And Godspeed."

"Thanks, sir." Little Guy started back toward the groupment with a jaunty step. "High time for me to get back." He half-turned, wearing a big grin. "Unlike officers, I work for a living." His gaze drifted to a spot just beyond Riordan's shoulder. "Oh, and sir? Trouble coming up on your six."

Riordan turned. Bey was striding toward him, halted about a meter away. "Do you have any special instructions, Leader Caine?"

A dozen came to mind, but they weren't orders so much as entreaties to caution. They were the military equivalent of telling a family member to remember to take an umbrella in case it rains. Reminders that no professional needed, but, out of respect for rank, would acknowledge with a nod.

"No instructions," Riordan replied. "Just remember that you are our link to all the trogs. So you have to limit the risks to yourself. We can't afford to lose you." Bey was smiling by the time he finished. Caine raised an eyebrow. “I expected you to resist that advice, rather than find it amusing.”

She shrugged. “It is only amusing because that is what your own companions say about you: that you take too many risks for a commander.” She adjusted her rucksack. “Yet another way in which we are alike, perhaps.”

“Perhaps.”

She nodded and marched after Miles. Riordan watched her go.

It took him several long seconds to realize he was still watching her.

Chapter Six

The sun was in the same part of the sky when, a day later, Ulchakh leaned toward Riordan as they neared the last, sharp turn in a narrow canyon. "This is the place where even your closest companions must wait."

Riordan turned and nodded at the group following him and Bannor: roughly half the Crewe. They halted, turned, and waved a confirmation to the much-diminished balance of the formation waiting at the first checkpoint. Sharat's group had processed through to Achgabab an hour earlier, reducing the total number of bodies by half.

Ulchakh walked around the corner, faced left, and raised his hands. He waited almost a minute, then returned. "We are recognized. We may advance."

Several doglegs later, they entered a wide, bright space where the walls of the box canyon fell away and left a space akin to an immense arena. Off to the western side, Sharat's two rads were parked in a growing margin of shade. Along the northern face, a spring emerged from a slightly sloped stone shelf; it flowed hard against the wall until disappearing into it. On the east, a single switchback trail, carved from the rock, ascended toward the canyon's upper reaches, which were seamed by crevices and pocked by shaded alcoves.

Ulchakh sighed in relief, waved a hand at the tableau, and

proudly announced, "Achgabab." His tone was one of celebration, not announcement.

Riordan waited for the h'achga to lead them toward the walkway, but he showed no intent to do so. "Are we waiting for a delegation?"

"No, Friend Caine. We are giving my people a chance to look at you and Friend Bannor, even as they observe your companions." He smiled. "The openings in the canyon wall connect to tunnels that run quite far. Far enough that a sentinel watching through a shaded slit spotted our column before midday yesterday. There are similar hidden places that watch every approach. Without them, we could not have endured."

"I can see why the x'qai never attacked this place," Bannor muttered as he ran his gaze around the steep sides of the canyon.

"Oh, they tried," Ulchakh said ruefully. "But to overcome such defenses, they would need much greater patience than most of them possess. So they have usually driven trogs in before them. But even so, they ultimately have to turn back."

"Because their casualties were too great?"

"In a manner of speaking. The x'qai cared nothing for the trogs they lost. Well, not until the dead were piled so high that they could not advance further." He shrugged. "None of us delude ourselves by believing Achgabab is impregnable. It has simply never been worth the effort and resources required to take it."

Riordan pointed. "Where does the spring's runoff go?"

"Through the stone to a long chain of similar but smaller canyons. It is good hunting there. And at the end of that winding gorge, it empties into the northeast extents of wadi country: grazing and mating grounds for dustkine."

"How many h'achgai dwell here?" Bannor glanced at Ulchakh. "Assuming you may answer that question."

Ulchakh smiled. "I will answer it as much as I may. A generation ago, we were over six hundreds. Now?" He shrugged. "Who can say?"

Riordan smiled back. It was a near certainty that Ulchakh not only knew, but was consulted on the accuracy of the latest headcount. "It must be upsetting to leave Achgabab. It is a unique place."

"Because of its safety?"

Caine shook his head. "Because of its stability."

Ulchakh squinted into the sun. "So it is. Sometimes a little too stable, I suppose. But that is the trader in me, speaking foolishness." He allowed himself a small grin. "Of course, if there were no such foolish h'achgai, we would have little more than stone and bone. So, just as there are families known for hunting, tracking, and metalcraft, there are others known for trading and the learning of languages."

"Such as yours."

The old trader showed surprising strength as he thumped his chest once, sharply: the first wholly simian gesture Riordan had witnessed from him. "I am First Trader Ulchakh of family Awtsha, the Third Branch of Clan Odrej'j." He smiled again. "Which is to say I am from a long line of similarly foolish h'achgai. As I intimated when we first met, our goods do not move in caravans: such routes are too predictable. And, as you so recently proved, that makes them tempting targets. Rather, we sometimes move our goods by boat, but mostly along ancient portage paths, none of which are used more than one year in every four. That way, they all fade back into the dust and are forgotten. Except by us."

Bannor frowned. "So do your communities work together, like a network of small caravansaries?"

Ulchakh's eyelids half-lowered like heavy shrouds. "Ah, swift insight. Humans are well worth the trouble of dealing with them—if they are safe." He smiled at Caine. "And best of all, if they have our *chogruk*."

His attention was caught by something high on the canyon wall. Caine saw nothing. He glanced at Rulaine, who shook his head.

Ulchakh waved at whatever or whoever they had not detected. "An escort shall arrive presently."

"We can find our way, I think," Bannor muttered, nodding toward the dark, prominent cave mouth that bore into the far wall of the canyon.

"Even so, it is our way. Caine Riordan, come with me."

"Wait! What?" Bannor stepped forward briskly.

Ulchakh raised a hand—toward the canyon walls. "Friend Bannor, do not move so quickly. Especially not toward me." He faced the two of them. "I apologize that I neglected to make this next step clear. A leader who comes to meet our chief stays in Achgabab the prior night."

Caine put up a calming hand toward Bannor. "It's fine, Colonel. It makes sense. I'll be—"

"Ulchakh," Rulaine said sharply. "We have come a long way, endured much. My friends have fought to save, feed, and enrich you."

Ulchakh blinked. "This is true," he said quietly.

"Then I ask one favor in exchange: that it is *I* who shall stay in Achgabab for the night. You have said that both of us will have an audience with your chief. Surely, then, it is not so different if I go with you instead of the commodore." Ulchakh hesitated. "Caine is our leader, yes, but who leads in battle more often, and closer to the enemy? Him or me?"

It was the first time since meeting Ulchakh that Caine saw him become uncomfortable. "Well, eh—"

Riordan nodded at him. "Your answer will not insult me, Friend Ulchakh."

The h'achga trader looked as if someone was twisting his very long arm. "You are a high leader at the front of the battles, Bannor, but—"

"Then if the logic of having a leader remain separated from his forces the night before meeting your chief is rooted in defending against treachery by arms, am I not an even wiser choice than Caine?"

Ulchakh looked away and nodded. "You would have made a passable trader yourself, Bannor Rulaine. Very well: Friend Caine, the escort emerging from the cave shall walk you back to your forces. Friend Bannor, I shall settle you in your lodging, but must then go to confer with Chief Vaagdjul. I shall ask that he speak to you both tomorrow, assuming that he has concluded his business with Sharat, who has urgent need to depart quickly. Tomorrow, he hopes."

Riordan was surprised: the Legate captain had not mentioned it. "Why?"

"You must ask him that yourself."

"And will Ne'sar go with him?"

"Again, that is a question only you may put to him. Now, follow the escort. Friend Bannor, you must follow me. Without any sudden motions, please."

A day later, the sun was once again in the same place as Riordan and Yaargraukh sat waiting for Bannor to emerge. Caine leaned toward his friend and pointed at the whispering spring. "It's always in the shade, from sunup to dusk." He stared up at the blinding white sun, gauged the seasonal angle. "Probably not in winter, though. I'll bet that keeps the ice from accumulating."

After a moment, Yaargraukh emitted a distracted huffing sound: the Hkh'Rkh equivalent of an absentminded "uh-huh."

Riordan raised an eyebrow. "What I can't figure out is why all those h'achgai children are urinating in it, though."

For a whole second, Yaargraukh didn't respond, then started, looked up—and discovered Riordan smiling at him. "Ah. Apologies. I was distracted."

Caine smiled. "Couldn't tell." H'achgai had begun emerging from the various apertures lining the highest wall-following walkway. "You've been quiet ever since we left Forkus."

"Is that true?" Yaargraukh's eyes protruded slightly, then retracted: reflection. "I suppose it is as you say. Why have you not mentioned it until now?"

Riordan shrugged. "In the first place, I know just enough about Hkh'Rkh ways and traditions to be aware of how very much I *don't* know. But the executions at the hovel—that left a mark on us all. Everyone's dealt with it differently." Caine discovered he was staring at his palms; he half-expected to see bloodstains. "I thought your way might involve silence."

Yaargraukh's head-neck raised, straightening. "It involves reflection, certainly, but I suspect my concerns are different than yours." He pony-nodded toward Caine. "I was relieved not to be one of the executioners—"

—Riordan winced—

"—and so, am without the burden of having performed such a deed. I am even more grateful not to carry the greater weight of having to order it. Which your face shows even now."

Yaargraukh shook himself irritably. "And yet, honor mutters, unsettled. Even though I am not human, and law and diplomacy both dictated that I take no part in those affairs, you are my comrades—more true and loyal than many Hkh'Rkh—and I did not bear my share of that night's terrible necessities."

His quadrilaterally arranged hands opened and closed sharply: a reflex of frustration. "But my greater concern is with the strange phenomena we have witnessed since then: the mindspeaking and impossibly swift curatives. They are not to be denied, yet they defy science."

Riordan smiled. "Or so we think."

Yaargraukh fluted phlegm in all three nostrils: aggravation. "That uncertainty troubles me even more. If what we have seen cannot be reconciled with our understanding of physics, it threatens further chaos in what are already distempered times. I hoped that Tirolane might explain some of its workings, but he remains silent."

Caine nodded. "I think he senses our eagerness to learn more and is shying away from it."

The Hkh'Rkh fluted air through his nostrils: exasperation. "Perhaps that is why the only time he spends in *our* camp circle is when he retires to his furs."

Riordan shrugged. "I suspect it's sympathy that keeps him with the humans we liberated from the caravan. He understands their life, and upbringing, in a x'qao stable; we don't."

Yaargraukh pony-nodded. "And the mystery of our origins ensures that they understand us even less. Still, Tirolane's solicitude for Orsost and Enoran should not be so time-consuming that it keeps him a stranger to us. If he means to be our companion, his distance is . . . problematic."

Riordan was about to agree when he spied a distinctly non-h'achgan silhouette—leaner and slightly taller—emerge from one of the dark alcoves at the lowest level of the walkway. "There's Bannor." Another figure followed. "And Sharat, I think."

Yaargraukh stood along with Caine. "Shall I return to our laager, or—?"

"No. Best you hear what Bannor has to say. And Sharat, too."

As the two humans crossed the canyon's wide paddock, h'achgai appeared out of the same shadows. Bearing hide sacks, they headed for the Legate-pennoned rads. A single figure started out from between the vehicles: Ne'sar.

She reached Caine and Yaargraukh just a few moments before Bannor called out, "Ulchakh is waiting for us back in the guest quarters. Or maybe the closer translation is 'quarantine zone.'"

Sharat closed the last few strides with hand outstretched. Caine met it—but was surprised when the Legate captain reached further to clasp his forearm in what old films had popularized as a Roman handshake.

"We leave presently," Sharat announced. "It has been an honor fighting and traveling beside you and your, eh, Crewe." He nodded at Bannor and Yaargraukh. "I hope our paths shall cross again."

"Where are you bound?"

"Atorsír. A h'achgan community a third the size of this one. At most."

Yaargraukh emitted an interested rumble. "Where is it located?"

"South. In a cluster of hills and mesas at the approximate center of the wadi country."

Caine turned toward Ne'sar, nodding. "That sounds close to your home in Ebrekka."

"It is certainly much closer than we are here. And I hope I shall see you there in the future." Her tarsier-eyes widened, as if she'd spoken too casually. "However, we could not allow so large a group."

"So, just a small delegation of us?"

The tufts on her ears bunched into vertical columns. "Ebrekka could welcome almost all of your number. Except the trogs."

Riordan nodded. *You, too? Even mangles won't trust trogs?*

Ne'sar apparently saw his thoughts reflected on his face. "Even those trogs who would never share what they see of our secret ways and places cannot resist torture forever. And the x'qai have a method which breaks the resolve of their most stalwart warriors, merely by threatening to apply it."

Yaargraukh's eyes protruded slightly. "And are humans—and mangles—so courageous that they can endure what trogs cannot?"

Ne'sar's eyes lowered. "My people are immune to the threat of which I speak. The x'qai cannot infest us. However, we are not immune to pain. Which is why we carry lethal herbs."

Caine felt her calm revelations wash over him with a double-chill: that x'qai torture was infestation by lethal parasite, and that mangles carried the local equivalent of suicide pills.

Ne'sar had not paused. "Humans, on the other hand, are not frequently tortured. You are too valuable."

"As sources of information?" Yaargraukh wondered.

Sharat almost spat. "No: as breeding stock."

Ne'sar confirmed his answer with a small nod.

Caine put out his hand. "Ne'sar, thank you for your candor and your friendship. Should we ever be close when you have need to travel or shelter with friends, you have but to ask."

The mangle bowed from the waist. "You do me great honor. I shall remember your invitation and be sure to convey the depth of your solicitude to my father. You will surely be received in

Ebrekka with great honor," she concluded, including Bannor and Yaargraukh in a sweeping glance.

She turned to Sharat. "The h'achgai are loading the last of the supplies. I shall prepare myself for travel." With a nod, she started back to the rads; they were being slowly maneuvered to return the way they had come, the windrad hitched to the one with an engine.

Riordan watched the small convoy readying itself. "Sharat, why did you send most of your people back to stay with us?"

He shrugged. "They had to watch our pawns and deadskins."

"And why did you send *them* back?"

He shook his head. "I didn't; the h'achgai do not permit them to come this far."

"Why?"

Sharat shrugged. "Because those with s'rillor could be manipulated by a distant x'qao if they have been blood-bonded. That's why they're called pawns."

Bannor frowned. "Can't a mindspeaker determine if they're, eh, blood-bonded?"

Sharat shook his head. "Detecting such bonds requires a different Talent."

"So a pawn could be, eh, activated to attack once within Achgabab?"

Sharat shrugged. "Yes, but the h'achgai's deepest fear is that a x'qao liege might be able to tap into its senses."

Bannor's voice was low. "You mean, the way they do with the insects? The kiktzo?"

Sharat nodded. "It's a possibility." He straightened. "While we are on the topic of such powers, Tasvar sent a message for you."

Damn: the strangeness just doesn't stop. "Should this message be shared in a more private place?"

"No. And I imagine you will understand its urgency better than I. It seems that Tasvar sent a convoy out the same night you rescued Eku in Forkus, yes?"

"That is correct."

"I was instructed to inform you that it never reached the town of Uhr, its first intended destination."

Bannor crossed his arms. "Considered in the context of the well-paid traitors that marched north with us, I'd say we've attracted the attention of a liege."

Sharat nodded sympathetically. “Sadly, I agree.” He took a step back. “Beyond Atorsír, my travels bend farther south. More than that I may not say, but it would be a fine thing to share another journey with you.”

“Likewise,” Riordan called after him. When the Legate captain was well out of earshot, Caine looked at Bannor. “Remember how, about three days after rescuing Eku, we wondered if we’d put cross hairs on our backs for the rest of our lives?”

“It was four days,” Bannor murmured, “but yes. Don’t you hate being right, sometimes?”

“I’m getting to hate it *all* the time. Let’s find Ulchakh and talk with Chief Vaagdjul. Who knows? If we’re really lucky, we might manage not to sound like fools.”

Chapter Seven

"I now formally present the two humans who seek audience with you, Chief Vaagdjul: Bannor Rulaine, who is their band's high war captain, and Caine Riordan, who is their leader, chief, and has my *chogruk*." The old trader bowed and took two steps back. As he did, Riordan revised his definition of an "old" h'achga. Compared to Vaagdjul, Ulchakh radiated the vigor of middle years.

The chief waved the two humans forward. As he did, the four guards behind him—orang-humanoids whose size and shapes resembled silverback gorillas—tensed but relaxed almost as quickly. In the half hour that it had taken for Ulchakh and his visitors to work through the formal introductions, the immense bodyguards had gone from a trembling readiness to kill the humans to benign watchfulness.

Vaagdjul's long white sidelocks shook along with his head. "Before presenting yourselves, Ulchakh told me that you formally gifted many fine bronze weapons and breastplates of cured hide to the h'achgai who traveled with you from Forkus."

Riordan nodded. "That is true, Vaagdjul."

"Then why did you not tell me so when you stood forth to present your origins, interests, and kindnesses to the h'achgai? You also did not mention how you saved them from ravenous x'qai on your long march. Are you forbidden to speak of such things, that you do not present the greatest reasons that might dispose, or even oblige, me to give you my ear?"

"We do not have, nor would we accept, prohibitions upon our speech," Caine explained. "However, we do not wish you to feel obligated because we fought alongside your people. All but Yidreg were already known to us and good companions. It would be grasping and faithless for us to seek your favor simply because we helped our friends.

"And in the matter of gifting the weapons and armor, it was not kindness: it was merely sharing the spoils of our fight against the caravan."

Vaagdjul's lipless burble was both distinctly simian and dubious. "Come, now, human: what you conferred upon my people was far beyond the measure of their spoils. I know the value of what they received, how much of a force they were, and the great discrepancy between the two." He narrowed his eyes, leaned forward. "Did you give them these gifts in the hope of enticing them to become your servitors, or to follow you in subsequent endeavors?"

Surprised, Riordan shook his head sharply. "No. We—"

Vaagdjul held up his hand. "Go no further, Caine Riordan. It takes me but a moment to know an honest denial when I see and hear it." He smiled. "And I also know the sound of indignation at having one's motives questioned." He eased himself back. "You will forgive that test, or at least the caution behind it. Your presence here is, in every way, unique in my generation. Perhaps many. Perhaps all that have ever been." He waved a hand as seamed as tree bark. "Please: ask what you wish."

"Thank you, Vaagdjul. Among the many names of my companions, you may recall those of Duncan Solsohn and Katie Somers." The ancient h'achga nodded. "I seek permission for them to meet and offer wares and services to any interested traders—under Ulchakh's auspices, of course."

The chief glanced at Ulchakh, whose slow, measured nod almost concealed his eagerness.

Vaagdjul waved a lazy hand. "Granted. Your next request?"

Bannor raised his chin. "We wish to present Achgabab, in the person of yourself, with a gift."

One of the chief's faint eyebrows rose. "A gift? For what?"

"We live here in safety because of your warriors, your precautions, your wisdom. We wish to show our gratitude. Tangibly."

"You have . . . by acknowledging it and giving your thanks." When Bannor leaned forward as if to press the case, Vaagdjul raised a long, tapering hand. "It is well that you asked once. However, to ask a second time risks insulting your hosts. What else?"

"Our next request is not an appeal for your permission, but your counsel."

The chief looked genuinely perplexed. "My counsel? On what?"

Riordan picked up the topic. "You know of our intention to journey to the place two weeks north of here. The dunes-that-do-not-move."

"The ancient site. Yes. I have been informed. Djubaran, the youth who reported their reappearance upon returning from his *cho'urz*, has journeyed back to inspect them more closely."

"That sounds very dangerous."

"It is, but he was determined. Continue."

"You are also aware that we do not know this region and are not yet skilled in the best ways to travel these lands safely."

Vaagdjul could not keep a sly smile from crinkling the corners of his very broad mouth. "This, too, I have heard."

Riordan smiled back. "We admire the knowledge, skill, and integrity of the h'achgai. We have witnessed it in the words and deeds of Ulchakh, Yidreg, Arash, and even young Hresh. So as we plan for our journey to the site, we conceived that our chances of both success and survival would be much improved if we did not undertake it alone. So we wish your counsel in ensuring that we make fair offers to those of Achgabab who might wish to share in that endeavor... and whatever gain might arise from it."

The old h'achga suddenly looked much older. He folded his hands, sighed, and shook his head. "It is a thoughtful inquiry, and your high opinion of our people honors us. But it is my duty to forbid what you mean to do." He gestured vaguely toward Ulchakh. "He and the others with whom you have traveled; they are free to choose to continue on with you.

"But I cannot allow other warriors or hunters or artisans to join your efforts. That is not the best way for us to help you, even though you have Ulchakh's chogruk. It would threaten the continued existence of Achgabab, and that is a much greater treasure—to you as well as us—than anything you might find at that site."

Bannor shook his head. "But how would helping us threaten Achgabab? It is more likely to gain greater power and wealth."

Vaagdjul nodded. "It might. But you will *surely* take much away. Already, Arashk, one of our best war leaders, is a devoted ally who means to travel with you. Ulchakh tells me that Yidreg is now of a like mind, even though he was to become First Hunter within the year. And you are right about Hresh: his mind is every bit as keen as Yidreg's arrows, but it is now trained upon further journeys with you." A brief pulse of anger became exasperation. "You already have too many of the rising generation's most capable leaders, too much of Achgabab's future.

"I cannot and will not diminish it—us—even more. So do not think to reassure me with promises that you would take our younger or less accomplished warriors or artisans and return them much improved. We have heard such promises before, and the price of believing them has been tears shed over absent bodies, abandoned under duress in the shifting dust, lost forever. So we have learned to abide by our oldest rule: that each family must keep their muster commitments to Achgabab and the Great Tribe of the region.

"Without that force always at hand, we cannot be sure that our communities shall remain places of safety, water, food, trade. As a people, we fight well enough, but war is not the first calling of h'achgai. For those who it is, and who strike blows against the x'qai, we support you. That is why we risk bringing you among us—and so, tempt the wrath of the suzerains.

"But if they believe we not only succored you but went afield with you in numbers, we would become more than overlooked irritants to the lieges. We would be infuriating enemies. And that would be the end of us. We do not have your weapons, your learning, your skills, or your mobility. We range far, yes, but we dwell in one place and measure its value not just by the many ways it ensures our survival, but by the generations that have given their devotion, sweat, and blood to strengthening it."

Riordan inclined his head. "I understand and would do no differently, Chief Vaagdjul."

"And I wish we *could*, Caine Riordan. Truly. It is a chafing thing, to hear the entreaty of an ally with whom we could punish our common foes, and yet have to stay my hand from joining yours." He shifted irritably on his seat.

Bannor nodded. "Then perhaps you will smile upon our last request."

"Why?"

"Because," Caine explained, "it will help my hand strike even harder blows against the x'qai."

The h'achgan chief straightened; the motion and his bright-eyed stare belied his age. "Explain."

Chapter Eight

Arms crossed, Bannor watched two of the six stone-tipped arrows hit the tall hide target. Another one hit and glanced off its tarred-bone frame. The last three sailed past, raising a cloud from the pile of sand behind it.

The senior trogan from the caravan, Kogwhé, howled both imprecations and instructions as he stalked along the firing line. The six trogs toeing it either looked sheepish or stoic. They'd learned that their other reactions—indifference or irritation—would earn them a full half-hour of what the small human Peter Wu called "PT."

Rulaine strolled over to where the calm "trainer of trogs" watched the proceedings. Off to one side, the other three in the class busily repointed arrows damaged during practice. "How's it coming?" he drawled as Kogwhé released the trainees to retrieve their shafts.

Wu glanced at Rulaine, one eyebrow raised. "At this rate, they might be ready next year."

"Really? That soon?"

"You are a font of infinite mirth."

"So I've been told."

Peter sighed. "Your actual question is, 'are we going to get any new archers out of this group?'" He shrugged. "Kogwhé claims four show reasonable promise: three of the scouts and one kajh."

"You sound unconvinced."

"I think he is optimistic. However, I am no archer, and he is."

Bannor leaned back to keep himself in the receding shade of the canyon wall. "And the other training?"

Wu shrugged. "Most show promise at sword drills, fewer at fletching and pointing."

Bannor let him finish before clarifying, "I meant, how is the *Crewe's* training coming along?"

Peter started. "Oh, that. Most everyone has had some wilderness survival preparation, so that's going well. The slowest area is in becoming accustomed to using swords while wearing stiff armor. Only half of us had any prior training in melee weapons. Shields only makc it worse."

Bannor nodded. "I heard you stopped that training."

Wu sighed. "Even if we had a qualified instructor, no one wants to give up the advantage of a free hand for weapons, tools, a light. Even for trogs, shields don't confer most the advantages they did on Earth: no one here fights in formation or mounted."

Bannor shrugged. "Just so long as we can fight with local weapons, survive with local gear, and handle them comfortably, not like costume props." He glanced at the sun. "You're not going to the all-hands meeting, I take it?"

Wu shook his head. "The trogs are more diligent when one of us is present. You'll catch me up on anything important?"

Bannor nodded and left the training paddock, wending his way back to their laager.

Duncan put aside the list he'd scribbled on the coarse parchment that was a Bactradgarian standard, and turned toward Bannor. "So, in exchange for most of the gear from the caravan and half our dried food, we got the weapons and armor we wanted." He grinned. "As well as 'items and services yet to be specified.'"

Seeing Dora's frown, Bannor expanded, "Firstly, that kind of open-ended collateral buys us a lot of goodwill and reciprocal trust. Makes it more of a diplomatic than mercantile agreement. Secondly, we still don't know what we'll need when we set out for the 'dunes-that-do-not-move.' We might require porters, diggers, supplies—and maybe a secure fallback point if things go sideways."

Newton frowned. "Has Chief Vaagdjul decided to allow us to hire some of the locals after all?"

Riordan shook his head. "Short-term laborers don't concern him; they'll add more to the local economy working for us than whatever they'd be doing here."

Solsohn rubbed his neck. "Speaking of organization..."

Bannor smiled. "What's on your mind?"

"Well, just that: organization. Ours."

"What about it?"

"Frankly, sirs, we're a damn mess. We have no unit structure, no T.O.O. Until we organize the new trogs into regular groups under steady leadership, they're going to remain as we found them: a mob. When poor Bey comes back, she's gonna have a hell of a time managing them."

Bannor glanced at Caine. "Which points to yet another challenge." Riordan nodded for him to continue. "No local has prior experience forming up and training regular units, because Bactradgaria doesn't have any: just war bands. And they don't fight battles: just big brawls."

Dora was frowning. "So, are you saying we *don't* need to train them up in units?"

"No: it would give us a huge advantage in any engagement. But Bey can't take that on; both the concept and practice are completely alien to her."

Duncan shrugged. "We could help her. Give her the basics and then provide input if she gets in over her head."

Bannor was about to reply but Ayana leaned forward. "However, if she is seen or suspected not to possess the expertise herself, our help could undermine her stature among the trogs."

Riordan began nodding. "True, but I think we could prevent that. Maybe reverse it."

Wu squinted. "How?"

Bannor was careful to remain expressionless as Caine explained. "We include her in our command circle to advise *us* on local matters. That will boost her standing among the trogs, and they'll have no reason to suspect that we, in turn, are advising *her*."

"Sir," Eku sputtered, "a . . . a trog? In the command group?"

Bannor glanced toward Riordan, who managed not to lose his temper. "Yes, Mr. Eku: a trog in the command group—although heaven help you if you call her anything other than a *crog*, now. She's proven her loyalty and commitment, and her skill was never in question. Pending Miles' review of her performance with the task force, I think it's time to include her in our planning sessions."

He gestured toward the world beyond the canyon walls. "All of us see everything on this planet as outsiders. That's why we keep stubbing our toes against things we don't—can't—foresee.

In large part, that's because asking for Bey's input has been the *last* step in our planning. If we'd had her input from the start, I doubt we'd have stepped so wrong so often. Or left so easy a trail for any enemies that might be following us."

Bannor maintained his silence for a moment; Riordan's arguments all made sense but he wasn't putting them forward with his customary calm objectivity. Careful to keep his tone neutral, the ex-IRIS colonel commented, "Adding a local to our command group: that's a big step, sir."

Riordan nodded. "It is. But I think it's the right time. If not overdue."

Duncan's tone was equally cautious. "Sir, I'm sorry if my remarks brought us to this place—"

"Major, I'm glad you brought us to *exactly* this place. If we mean to be change agents on this world, it's both practical and ethical to have a local sitting in on that process." He rose. "Unless there are other pressing matters, I promised Peter I'd look in on the archers, and I'm overdue." He glanced toward Bannor. "Coming along?"

"Already dropped by, sir."

Caine nodded to the group and started toward the practice range.

Katie's small smile became wider along with the distance between him and the Crewe. "The commodore certainly made quite the case for Bey." She nudged Dora. "Bit like the line from the Scottish play, innit?"

Pandora stared at her. "Huh? What play?"

"C'mon, you heard him, yeh?" Katie said, nudging her. "Makin' that fine, *fine* speech about all the reasons we should have Bey sittin' in."

"What are you talking about?"

Katie rolled her eyes. "Och, it's one of the play's most famous lines! You know: 'Methinks the laddie doth protest too much.'" She glanced at Ayana—who barely managed to hide a small smile of her own.

Rulaine stared as Duncan chortled and Yaargraukh rose to leave. "That's not *Macbeth*," Bannor informed Katie sternly. "It's *Hamlet*."

"Och, an' like I care? Er, sir. But tell me: don't you think he was a bit quick to defend Bey's, well, honor?"

"As I said," Bannor muttered, "the play is *Hamlet*. Dismissed."

As he turned to go, he thought he glimpsed Ayana returning a wink in Katie's direction.

Chapter Nine

From the shadows, Fezhmorbal watched the entrance through which Hwe'tsara, Suzerain Ormalg's liege in Forkus, would appear.

He hadn't long to wait. The greater x'qao stamped into his own court in a manner appropriate to the large, heavy monster that he was. "Where's that stoop counselor of mine?" Hwe'tsara demanded of his lieutenant and seneschal, Kh'shra, a young but promising arurkré.

Not waiting for an answer, he bounded upon the crude dais. His harrows and senior scythes stepped back: not out of fear, but to place themselves beyond the unmindful agitation of their liege's wrath. Hwe'tsara stalked toward his roughhewn throne—and stopped: his tribute bowl was waiting, forgotten, on its seat. It was filled with day-old offerings of dead insects and strips of flesh.

The x'qao stared at the bowl as if it had spat at him. Then, furious, he slapped it away. Shattering at the impact of his rough palm, the receptacle's fragments flew toward the far end of the chamber as a widening cloud. Fangs dripping, he raged, "When I find Fezhmorbal, I shall rend—!"

"I am here, Your Horror. In my accustomed place."

Hwe'tsara started as if impaled. "What—? When—? How dare you enter my stronghold without sending word, without finding me first?"

Fezhmorbal bowed, careful not to react to the x'qao lord's complaints since they were completely contradictory. "Apologies,

Terrible Hwe'tsara. I was not aware the protocols had changed since my last visit." *Which they haven't, of course.*

Fezhmorbal noted that, just behind him, his new adjutant had barely stirred at the x'qao's tantrum. *Promising.* His lieutenant Gasdashrag would likely have gulped audibly at the violent display.

The tall, broadly built x'qao slumped into his throne as if he'd never been on the verge of homicidal hysteria. But the monster's furtive glances told Fezhmorbal that Hwe'tsara felt his failure: that once again he'd lacked the ruthless dispassion that a liege must always maintain in the presence of his lessers. *And so he keeps looking over to see if I shall sneer or put on a superior air. I'm not stupid, you abomination. If I did so, that would be the end of my race's infiltration of your court—and maybe my existence, as well.*

In the awkward silence that followed, the smaller, ubiquitous x'qa—bestial 'qo and lean q'akh—crept forth from their lairs in the shadows of Hwe'tsara's great hall. He stared at them and then Fezhmorbal in mounting irritation. "Well, where have you been, *counselor*?" he snapped. "A dubious title, since you have not been here to share your equally dubious wisdom."

Fezhmorbal inclined his head slightly. "As we discussed, Your Horror, the task of retrieving your goods and punishing the thieves promised to be a long process. Once we ascertained that they fled north along the great river, we knew it meant a long pursuit. I have been securing additional forces and sources of information to aid in the search. Happily, those efforts have produced new information."

"Yes, which you didn't report personally, as you should have. I should skin you alive for having the nerve to send me a written report instead, scrawled in some vague sigils."

"My apologies, Dread Liege. I shall endeavor to ensure that the scribe redrafts it more precisely and plainly."

"And how will that help?"

"I presume the problem is that the report was not legible, Your Horror, inasmuch as it was written in x'qao Deviltongue."

Hwe'tsara's eyes quivered in their sockets. His harrows, all literate, were utterly still, as was his far more clever and capable arurkré lieutenant.

Fezhmorbal managed not to smile. *So: you can't even* read, *though you still cling to the hope that some transformation will yet mark you as an arurkré.* Learning that the x'qao had unwittingly revealed himself to be illiterate would have been gratifying enough, but to witness it was delicious.

Hwe'tsara recovered quickly, however. "A scribe incapable of rendering your report readable to a discerning eye will do no better a second time," he scolded haughtily. "Fortunately, my lieutenant has had much experience deciphering the rude scrawls of several species, and so was able to read it out to me. Kh'shra, synopsize that tiresome document, that the deciqadi themselves may confirm that we have the gist of its crack-brained composition."

Kh'shra nodded promptly and addressed his monotone summation to Fezhmorbal. "Your lieutenant Gasdashrag arrived in Khorkrag, where he learned that Ulchakh, a known trader from Achgabab, had been there just days earlier. Since the thieves' trail included what appeared to be h'achgai tracks, he visited the trade station that his species maintains there. However, your lieutenant surmised that Ulchakh's visit was also to determine if it was safe for the humans to use the ferry to cross into the town.

"Ulchakh's return to the other bank was prompt, no doubt because the mood in Khorkrag was too dangerous for the humans. My liege Hwe'tsara's nearest peer in that place—Inikgolg—placed bounties on them even as the spring rains subsided. Gasdashrag visited him and provided funds to increase the size of those bounties."

Hwe'tsara interrupted, glaring at Fezhmorbal. "You and your lieutenant are very openhanded with my wealth, Counselor."

Fezhmorbal shook his head slowly. "Not so, Your Horror. The funds used by Gasdashrag were mine, not yours." He expanded in response to the x'qao's disbelieving stare. "I would of course be grateful should you deign to defray some of those costs. However, I was resolved to spend that coin without recompense to demonstrate how we deciqadi are more than a match for any group of humans, and are both a safer and superior alternative to those you keep at great expense in your stable."

Hwe'tsara's attempt to appear unsurprised and unimpressed was uneven, at best. He gestured for his lieutenant to continue.

Kh'shra did so in the same dull tone. "After the bounties were increased, the groups that departed Khorkrag to seek humans in the wadi country doubled and were larger. They were also encouraged by rumored sightings of Legate rads."

Hwe'tsara nodded to Kh'shra, who stepped back. "So you see, we have heard your 'news' already, Counselor."

"With trembling respects, Your Horror, you have not."

Hwe'tsara's frown was angry, likely because he had a foreboding that, once again, he had missed some subtlety in Fezhmorbal's earlier words. "Kh'shra's summary was complete, without error."

"That is true, Dread Hwe'tsara. But this is not the new information of which I spoke. Gasdashrag has, in the interim, discovered more. Much more."

Rage and curiosity waged a pitched battle for control of Hwe'tsara's face. When words finally rasped out of his mouth, they were more snarl than speech. "Well, do not keep me waiting, stoop!"

Fezhmorbal offered a long bow, long enough to ensure that his own face did not reveal his satisfied gloating. *So you insult my race with a slur instead of seeking to correct yourself. That is yet another reflex that keeps you weak, x'qao. And yet another reason why, soon enough, you will only retain that throne if we "stoops" are here to keep you in it.* "If it pleases you, Your Horror, I would have my new adjutant present the new information, and so, become known to your court and acquainted with your needs."

Hwe'tsara's eyes narrowed. "Is that him, skulking behind you?"

"That is *she*, Famed Hwe'tsara. And yes, Qudzorpla is indeed a redoubtable warrior." *Which, knowing your prejudices, you will simply accept—and so, not question if she has other, far more important, skills.*

The x'qao lord did not disappoint Fezhmorbal's expectations. "You allow females to become warriors, like the trogs?" He shook his head. "You bloodbag species are all either mad, blind, or both. Yes, yes: the she-stoop may step forward and report. But quickly!"

Qudzorpla—as tall as Fezhmorbal and almost as muscled—advanced and announced, "I am honored to present in the court of the Dread Liege Hwe'tsara!" Who impatiently waved away the honorifics, even though omitting them would likely have resulted in her evisceration. "Gasdashrag has communicated these further significant developments. A caravan from the city of Fragkork, bound to stop in Khorkrag before continuing on to Forkus, is now extremely overdue."

The x'qao seemed puzzled. "Was it sent by Sirvashwekh, Fragkork's Ormalg-sworn liege?"

"No, Your Horror. The caravan was sent at the behest of Liege Azhdrukh, suppliant of Zhyombphal."

"Then, as it does not concern the interests of my suzerain, it is of no concern to me. Why do you even mention it?"

"Gasdashrag has heard rumors that it may have been attacked by agents of the Legate, those whose rads were sighted in the wadi country."

Hwe'tsara sat straight. "And is there speculation why the impertinent bloodbags would strike a caravan at such remove from Forkus?"

"Two conjectures have arisen, Dread Liege. Firstly, the caravan's primary cargo was intended for Liege Suradán of Forkus, also suppliant of—"

"Yes, yes: another suppliant of Zhyombphal—whose domains in Forkus border the Legate's. So you conjecture that the bloodbag Tasvar intercepted the caravan anonymously and at distance so as not to instigate a war with his neighbor here on our streets?"

"It is believed so. However, the more valuable parts of the cargo give rise to the second conjecture."

"And this valuable cargo is—?"

"Humans, Your Horror. Azhdrukh is reportedly liquidating his stable."

Hwe'tsara leaned back, eyes narrowing. "Yes, those two factors might draw the Legate as far north as Khorkrag. But I am still waiting to hear how this bears upon *my* stolen property and destroying the thieves."

Qudzorpla nodded tautly. "As Gasdashrag reported last time, there were already rumors that a Legate force was in the area. That propelled even more bounty-hunting bands into the Orokrosir. However, within two weeks, Khorkrag saw many of these groups begin to return. Or rather, what was left of them. Several smaller ones were apparently destroyed outright, their survivors absorbed by rivals. However, one of the largest and oldest bands was reduced to a handful of survivors. Another great gang—gathered expressly for bountying by a newly arrived shaman, Zhathragz—disappeared without a trace."

Hwe'tsara leaned forward. Even Kh'shra's horned brow rose slightly.

"Gasdashrag had no direct contact with the survivors of the first group. But they reportedly claim to have been ambushed by a well-concealed force. If they are to be believed, the enemy broke them with unusually accurate and rapid fire from larger bows and crossbows."

Hwe'tsara raised a long-taloned hand. "Crossbows? On the Orokrosir?"

"Yes, Your Horror. The ambushers targeted commanders first, hitting the x'qao leader in the first volley and then repeatedly thereafter. He never had enough time to organize a response."

Qudzorpla lifted her wizened chin. "Whether a grim fact or a lie to justify their cowardice, the survivors swore that any who did not flee were slain or soon would be. The attackers did not close until the group had been scattered and its leaders eliminated. That is the limit of the new information."

Hwe'tsara sat back slowly. "Spring hunting and raiding are beneath my notice, but had such ambushes ever occurred before, I would surely have heard."

Qudzorpla nodded. "Gasdashrag reports that the opinion in Khorkrag agrees with Your Horror's assertion: from the lowest trogs to the most powerful lieges, there was surprise and disbelief."

The x'qao liege waved the female deciqad back with one hand, pointed at Fezhmorbal with the other. "I will hear what *you* make of all this, Counselor."

He nodded. "The attackers' tactics, weapons, and audacity have no doubt brought you to our own conclusion: this was the work of humans. The only other species which routinely executes plans with such care and forethought is my own. While it is not impossible that other humans may be responsible, logic suggests that this is the work of forces already known to be in that region: the Legate, the thieves, or perhaps both operating in concert."

Hwe'tsara's clenched fists made a stone-grinding sound. "I want them found and destroyed."

"First we must confirm that the thieves had a hand in these attacks. Otherwise, acting upon these reports will neither recover your property nor avenge you upon those who stole it."

With a visible effort, the x'qao leaned back. "How do you propose to determine the ambushers' identity? By scouring the wadi country?"

Fezhmorbal shook his head. "This enemy is too canny to remain in one place after mounting such attacks. So it is already too late to seek them in the Orokrosir. Rather, we must ponder the question, 'where are they headed?'"

"Achgabab? Ebrekka? Some secret haven?"

"All are possibilities, but I consider a secret haven unlikely.

Independent humans are loath to hide so far away from cities, which augment their greatest advantages. So we must first determine if one or both groups are involved and, if both, whether they acted as one combined force or a number of smaller ones."

"Yes, yes," the x'qao lord muttered pettishly. "But do any of the survivors' reports suggest that the attackers had access to artifacts such as those the thieves stole from *me*?"

At last, a productive question. "No, Your Horror, but it is entirely possible that survivors might have witnessed the effects of such devices yet failed to understand what they were seeing."

Hwe'tsara slammed his hands down on the arms of his basalt throne; the impact of his claws sounded like gunfire. "But if it was the thieves, why mount these attacks at all? Why not stay hidden, if they fear pursuit?"

"That, Dread Liege, is not merely an excellent but pivotal question—because there is no logical reason why a *Legate* force would do so. Even if they traveled from Forkus to intercept the missing caravan, they would surely flee to their nearest stronghold or station afterward. A detour to damage seasonal raiders and hunters from Khorkrag is a risk without strategic gain or purpose.

"However, if the ambushes were carried out by the thieves, there is a plausible, if unusual, reason they might have done so. Particularly if they suspect, or know, that they are already being followed by your forces."

Hwe'tsara shook his square, massive head. "You speak riddles, deciqad. If so small a group knew they were already being pursued, they would flee even faster and farther than the Legate's bloodbags."

"Not if the thieves are both clever and very audacious." Fezhmorbal leaned into his explanation. "Bold thieves often choose to do what pursuers least expect—in this case, preemptive counterattacks on forces friendly to us. In short, they turn the tables by hunting the hunters' allies, hoping to confound us with contradictory actions."

"Let us presume they know we shall ponder questions such as, 'If the attackers are the thieves, why don't they flee? If they wish to hide, why do they attack? And if they have already attained their objective, why do they ambush bounty hunters?' All to puzzle us."

"But to what end?"

"To make themselves inconsistent, and so, unpredictable." Fezhmorbal raised a thin, leathery finger tipped by a long, yellowed nail. "However, they have been utterly consistent in one regard: their demonstrated ability to not only destroy groups sent to seek them, but to do so with absolute impunity."

Hwe'tsara nodded. "Thereby chasing most of the bountiers out of the Orokrosir."

Fezhmorbal matched his patron's nod. "From which, I predict, the attackers promptly withdrew."

The x'qao's fangs rasped like bones grinding bone. "And by the time the mewling trogs creep back out, their trail will be gone."

Fezhmorbal kept his voice level and, he hoped, calming. "However, as I remarked at the outset, their trail matters less than our ability to *project* their destination. And in that regard, the ambushes and the missing caravan may have, quite literally, a significant point in common. A map point, to be precise."

"Explain yourself."

"I refer to Achgabab. Consider, Your Horror. There was word that Azhdrukh's caravan passed Fragkork's southernmost town, Zhukhu, as it journeyed along the great river. This means its path would bring it due west of Achgabab."

"But the Orokrosir and ambushes are due *south* of Achgabab."

"Yes, Dread Liege, but at almost exactly the same distance. And let us not forget that Ulchakh was last reported to be traveling with the thieves and that his final destination was Achgabab."

When Hwe'tsara brooded rather than responded, Kh'shra leaned forward. "My liege mentioned Ebrekka as a possible place to which they might safely retire. You have not addressed that." His master looked up, nodded vigorously.

Fezhmorbal inclined his head. "Two factors make it less likely. Firstly, the last marker left by our two trog agents among the thieves indicate that they traversed the river well north of Khorkrag."

Hwe'tsara stirred. "Which they accomplished how?"

"We do not know. But however they managed that feat, the point where they crossed is on the most direct approach to Achgabab. Ebrekka is almost twice as far and well to the southeast."

"You had a second reason they were unlikely to head there?"

Fezhmorbal shrugged. "As Your Horror knows, although the Mangled are proficient at trade and growing moss, they have little skill at, or in interest in, fashioning implements of war. Besides, while useful, the Mangled are not the best partners for these humans, and vice versa."

Hwe'tsara scowled. "They're too cowardly. Even for humans."

"Yes, but I meant that humans prefer activity—training, hunting, fashioning tools—over hiding. Obversely, h'achgai have the same inclinations as humans and many useful skills to support a warrior band."

"Warrior band? We are speaking of thieves, Counselor!"

Fezhmorbal kept his voice low and agreeable. Which he hated. "They are indeed thieves upon whom you must be avenged. However, their actions and methods are not those of skulkers, but soldiers. And that is consistent with their foray into the Orokrosir. Mere thieves would never conceive of it."

Hwe'tsara tilted forward ominously. "Very well. They mimic 'warriors.' How do you propose to kill them and retrieve my goods? Certainly you do not mean to attack Achgabab itself. The few lieges foolish enough to attempt it were so weakened by the losses that their rivals consumed them."

Fezhmorbal nodded. "Our only reasonable strategy is to watch the approaches to Achgabab, albeit at a distance. That in turn will require additional and more capable forces, including x'qai who are bonded to kiktzo. In that way, I can watch from beyond the reach of our quarry's eyes."

Hwe'tsara sat straighter in his stony throne. "Your phrasing—'*I* can watch'—is figurative, surely."

And now I start breaking you to the yoke of depending upon deciqadi. "With regret, Your Horror, I meant it quite literally. In order to pursue your interests decisively and with adequate strength, I must bring almost all my remaining assets to that region. Without them, we cannot watch for, much less respond to, the thieves' movements across so wide an area. It was to this end that I presented Qudzorpla to your court today." He nodded in her direction; she inclined her head toward the throne. "She shall report all developments to you in my place."

Hwe'tsara's neck stiffened. "You speak of 'pursuing my interests.' My interests are best served by having you here, Counselor."

And so you walk into yet another trap of your own making, fool. "Your Horror is kind to say so, but you have so often been displeased with my efforts that I feel at pains to prove myself worthy of your regard." *And also, while away, I am free to increase my own forces and set my race's plans in motion.* "Additionally, avenging you upon the thieves may not only require more assets but direct guidance. Gasdashrag is quite capable, but this is his first outing as war leader and the mission has become unexpectedly complex."

And now to bait you in even further. "My only misgiving is how long it may take for me to gather more servitors to our banner, particularly x'qai with blood-bonded kiktzo. With every passing day, we lose initiative."

Hwe'tsara frowned, held up his hand. "I am swayed by your logic as well as your determination to redeem yourself in my opinion—"

You are swayed by only one thing: the way my "regret at failing you" flatters and reassures your crumbling ego.

"—and so I will not merely allow you to depart from this court, but shall make you a gift of the servitors you most need. From my own host, I shall provide four x'qiigh with blood-bonded kiktzo. Thus you shall need only to recruit whatever trogs and other bloodbag species you deem necessary."

Fezhmorbal bowed low, dared not smile. *Just the assets I needed. And it will be simplicity itself to discern which of the kiktzo are actually blood-bonded to* you, *Hwe'tsara. What a sad misadventure that they shall also be the first to perish.* "Your generosity humbles us, Great Hwe'tsara."

The x'qao almost preened. "More generous than you know, Counselor. Two of those who I remit to your use also have blood-bonded kiksla, which are skilled at sensing x'qai deep in the sleep of the sands. Be warned: such x'qa are ravenous when they awaken, so you must have much meat on hand. But once their feeding frenzy subsides, and if they are given regular opportunities to hunt and gorge, they may prove receptive to taking service with one who is not a x'qao. That assumes the person is a sufficiently strong leader. Perhaps you shall prove so."

"Your Horror's opinion is most kind." *And needless; I have bent many x'qai to my will with far fewer inducements.*

Hwe'tsara seemed to grasp after a few, final strands of flattery in exchange for a last morsel of sage advice. "Normally, I would also recommend that you gather masterless deadskins from the streets, but they have grown scarce of late."

Fezhmorbal frowned. "I have heard the same, that many have disappeared at night without leaving any spoor of kill or combat."

The x'qao nodded. "Insofar as more typical servitors are concerned, I shall send word if I hear of a broken gang you might absorb. But do not count on it. Indeed, you may count on only one thing: that if you fail to keep me apprised of your progress, I shall be dangerously displeased. Now go, Counselor, before the q'akh grow too enamored of the scent of your stringy flesh."

As Fezhmorbal exited and his waiting praakht and prakhbrai kajhs gathered around him in a tight protective ring, Qudzorpla was counting her steps. "What are you doing?" he asked in their native tongue.

"Ensuring we are sufficiently distant before I speak," she muttered. "Forty-nine, fifty." She turned toward him abruptly. "War Leader Fezhmorbal, do you think Hwe'tsara was testing us by asking about the deadskins? That he suspects we are behind the disappearances?"

Fezhmorbal shook his head. "No. I know this variety of x'qao. Neither pureblood nor arurkré, he lacks both the mental discipline and patience to seek ploys within ploys. He will not suspect that my shared perplexity over the disappearance of deadskins was simply misdirection."

"How do you mean to get them out of Forkus, though?"

The deciqadi war leader's smile was vinegary. "Do you actually believe they are still here?" He jerked his head to the north. "They are waiting with newly recruited praakht, grat'r, and a few x'qnarz at the edge of the wastes. They shall meet my group at the river and parallel us. At night we shall camp together."

Qudzorpla frowned. "You mean to go north by boat?"

"How else? I purchased two h'achgai ships the same way I arranged payment for our spies among the thieves: a bondward, retained through a third party."

Qudzorpla leaned closer, whispered even though they were still speaking deciqadi. "I still do not understand why you ordered me to withhold the additional news we received from Gasdashrag this morning."

Fezhmorbal nodded approvingly. It was a prudent question; Qudzorpla would do well in her role. Assuming she was not devoured first. "Before I answer, remember this: never tell an outright lie to x'qai. Some possess a Talent that detects absolute untruths. Now, I had you withhold Gasdashrag's latest report because too much information at one time only frustrates x'qai. Even though they thirst for it."

"Is it because they cannot hold very much in their minds?"

"No, it is because most of them cannot control their impulses. Every new fact excites them. That excitement accumulates until, in the end, it hardly matters whether the news is good or bad; their agitation builds into rash action, often blind violence. So it is wiser, and safer, to parcel out what we have learned gradually."

"Still, would it not have pleased him to learn that Gasdashrag sent a small expedition of his own to observe the bountiers in the Orokrosir?"

Fezhmorbal shook his head. "Perhaps, but it might have led him to ask if and why Gasdashrag remained in Khorkrag. That question would have put us on the horns of a dilemma. Either we lie and claim he was still there, or reveal that he has already traveled north and found the site of the battle that destroyed Azhdrukh's caravan."

Qudzorpla nodded as they approached their base: a small, but tightly fitted paleolithic pyramid. "Had Hwe'tsara learned the fate of the caravan, he would surely insisted we attack."

Fezhmorbal shook his head. "Not just attack, but attack according to *his* instructions—which would have been the product of his spleen rather than his brain. And given his thirst for vengeance, we would have been unable to dissuade or distract him enough to withhold the even more troubling details Gasdashrag reported."

"Such as?"

"Such as the complete lack of graves where the caravan was struck."

Qudzorpla nodded. "Meaning that no humans died in the attack. Hwe'tsara would have become incensed."

"He would have become *ungovernable*. Particularly if he had pressed us further and we had to report that there were almost no signs of praakht casualties, either. Which suggests most of them were captured and added to the humans' own ranks." Fezhmorbal shrugged. "The thieves did not simply prevail; their victory was entirely one-sided."

Qudzorpla shook her head. "Hwe'tsara could not have borne it. He would have ordered a wild attack just as we've learned that our quarry must be approached with greater caution than we anticipated."

Fezhmorbal nodded as he gave the day's countersign to the two deciqadi guarding the entrance to their small stronghold; too many of Forkus' denizens possessed Talents that could trick the eye, the mind, or both. As they emerged into the small courtyard, he confirmed her projections. "By all appearances, the 'thieves' are growing stronger, bolder, and finding allies. We could refuse Hwe'tsara's orders, of course. He might even elect not to force the issue. But he would remember that as a slight, making it far more difficult to seduce him into dependence upon us."

Qudzorpla squinted into the rapidly setting sun. "So by withholding the most inflammatory facts, you have preserved our freedom of action in dealing with these humans. Masterful, War Leader." She glanced at him. "So, what action *do* you mean to take?"

Fezhmorbal sat, glanced at the empty place beside him on the basalt bench. "I intend to wait and watch."

"Watch?" she repeated. "Not seek, or hunt, or close with them?"

Fezhmorbal bared his teeth in what was not a smile. "Consider the viper, Qudzorpla. It spends much time watching, and almost as much approaching, before it strikes with great suddenness. Does it not?"

"Most certainly."

"Then tell me: is the watching not part of the viper's attack? Perhaps the most important part?"

She frowned deeply. "I have never conceived of it that way."

"That is because you are young and eager to prove yourself."

"And you are wise and patient."

"Possibly. Or, possibly neither."

"Why so?"

Fezhmorbal studied the crisp edge of the late-day shadows that cut the courtyard into hard geometries of light and dark. "Because I find these thieves, these humans, singularly troubling."

Qudzorpla nodded. "They seem less threatening than many Legate war companies, and certainly less so than the harrows to which they have been compared."

Fezhmorbal nodded. "So I tell myself daily. Yes, they seem clever and deadly, but as you say, not more so than other human war bands." But as if speaking it aloud, that truth sparked a sudden understanding of his deeper misgivings. "It is not what they have done that troubles me, but what they have *not* done.

"Their equipment led observers to mistake them for a dozen harrows. Surely, then, they could have made any number of highly advantageous alliances here in Forkus. But instead, immediately after retrieving their comrade from the hovel, they started upcountry.

"Why? And if it was a new safehold they sought, surely the great city of Uhrashgrukh would be the logical choice. It is not much more than a month's travel to the east and offers many opportunities for their kind. But instead they pressed north just as far, toward the obscure oasis at Achgabab."

"It makes no sense," Qudzorpla agreed.

Oh, but it might, Fezhmorbal thought uneasily. *There is another objective that might pull the humans north into the high desert. But I dare not mention it.*

At least, not yet.

Chapter Ten

Caine Riordan did not allow his gaze to drift back toward the doglegged passage that connected Achgabab's box canyon with the outside world. Instead, he watched Katie Somers enter the final reconfiguration protocols that would convert the helmet of the late, unlamented Hsontlosh into a second, albeit makeshift, Dornaani translator.

Somers, who was a natural hand with electronics, sped through the selection screens and called up the module dedicated to Low Praakht: the language most common among trogs. "Finished, sir."

Riordan nodded, tried not to return to the cycle of worry and projection that had risen with the sun. It was the eighty-third day of spring: one more than the return ETA Miles had sent three days ago.

Somers' voice pulled him back into the moment. "Ye're worried too, eh, Commodore?"

Riordan arrested the officer-reflex to reassure the troops. The situation was too obvious and the personal stakes too high for that kind of crap. "Yes, Corporal, I am concerned. Not that I have any reason to expect a problem. We knew that the closer the Chief's section came to the canyons, the more his radio would be screened by the high rock. But I'll be a lot happier when the task force comes around that corner." He glanced back at the entry to the box canyon. Still nothing. Which meant the hidden observers who watched the western approaches hadn't seen anything yet.

"Aye," Katie agreed, "seems everybody is waitin' on somebody. Us waitin' on our lads, the h'achgai for their own warriors—and that mad, brave lad Djubaran on his second walkabout. I just hope—"

Shouts echoed out of the dark cleft opposite the dogleg: the one through which the spring ran to the smaller canyons to the east.

Riordan stood as Miles O'Garran emerged from its shadows, barely stooping. "Well, where's the brass band and the town fathers? Hell of a welcome for homecoming heroes!"

Riordan started toward him at a brisk walk, but discovered he was looking beyond "Little Guy," already watching for Yidreg, and Ta'rel, and Orsost. And Bey—whose face, he realized with a start, was the only one he was actually scanning for.

All of those individuals emerged, single file—but no one else.

"Where's the rest of yer lot?" Katie asked anxiously.

"Couldn't bring 'em in here any more'n the other trogs, and certainly not through the secret passage," the small SEAL replied. "Just after I sent our ETA, we caught sight of a larger group moseying toward the western approaches. So we changed course and decided to come in through the east. Which we'd never have been able to do without our master hunter." He nodded gratefully to Yidreg. The hunter returned the nod, bowed slightly toward Riordan, and angled toward the cliff-side openings from which h'achgai were now streaming, hands held high in welcome and joy.

Miles jutted his chin after Yidreg, who was already pressing through the welcoming crowd. "He's gotta get instructions from Vaagdjul on how to handle the rest of us. Probably blindfolds, but that's up to the chief. They're waiting a few small canyons back."

Ta'rel and Bey approached Riordan. "Leader Caine," Bey almost shouted, "we have been successful!"

Riordan grinned. "And hello to you, too, Bey."

A moment of perplexity creased her forehead before it was smoothed by a broad smile. "It is good to be back."

As Riordan suddenly became aware of how dusty they were, Miles started toward the spring. "I could use some of that cool, clean water right about now," he muttered. He glanced around the paddock. "Where's everyone else, sir?"

"Being trained or training others, mostly. Why?"

O'Garran kept his voice low. "After-action report, sir. Some odd activity out on the Orokrosir."

✧ ✧ ✧

It took an hour to get the Crewe gathered at the main encampment. As they started to sit in a circle, Bey stepped back. She was in the middle of a departing nod when Riordan put up a hand. "Join us, please."

She stopped, might have been about to stare, but managed to effect an air of nonchalant aplomb as she sat next to him.

Miles raised an eyebrow, but either had no reservations at including her or hid it extremely well. "Short version, sir?"

"How long would the full after-action report take?"

"Conservative estimate? Until just after dawn."

Eyes rolled. Yes, Chief Miles O'Garran had returned with his irony and facetiousness intact.

Riordan couldn't help smiling. "A shortened AAR will be fine, Chief."

"Okay, then—and Bey, you chime in if I forget something, okay?"

"'Chime in'?"

"Uh, tell everyone what I forgot to mention."

She nodded.

"So bottom line first: it was a success."

Bey exercised her right to interrupt immediately. "Leader O'Garran is incorrect. It was a *great* success... thanks to him."

"Now, Bey," Miles sighed, "here's the first rule of chiming in: don't lie or exaggerate."

"But—!"

"That's a joke, Bey."

"Oh. Still, I stand by my correction."

Bannor smirked at O'Garran. "So: details?"

"Sir, yes, sir, Colonel! Not counting minor slashes and scrapes, only two casualties: one KIA and one MIA, who was probably wounded." Miles held up his hand against the questions that were opening half of the Crewe's mouths. "Specifics will follow. The task force is still rough around the edges, but they learned to follow complex orders and work together. And to top it all off, we picked up thirteen new recruits."

"What?" asked several voices, Caine's being one of them. "How?" asked Bannor and Dora.

"I'm getting there. We also came back with more supplies and gear than we started out, particularly spare kits and weapons. Had to abandon a lot, actually. I never got a chance to run a tally of what we kept."

Duncan rolled his eyes. "Damn it, Miles, I'm the guy obsesses over that stuff—and even *I'm* getting impatient. What actually *happened* out there? Are you waiting for a drum roll?"

The SEAL shrugged. "After splitting off from you, we headed south for about a week. No enemy contact, no handy game. So we had to start hunting. First day we sent out scouts, we ran into one of those armadillo humanoids that everyone says aren't actually x'qai."

"She was an illithrakz," Bey interjected.

"She?" Duncan wondered. "I thought x'qai were sexless?"

Newton huffed. "As the chief reminded just us, illithrakz are not x'qai."

Miles nodded. "Almost as tough as them, though. Despite the monoscope—which was the single most valuable piece of gear we had—we didn't spot her in advance. She was probably behind a ridgeline, and without a Dornaani helmet to process the 'scopes' thermal returns, we didn't detect any glow over the lip.

"Anyhow, she takes Orsost by surprise as he goes around a boulder, trog in tow. Her claws opened up his armor like it was cardboard, but just barely reached his skin. But the force of the blow threw him back on his butt."

"He was a goner but for the trog with him: Falkurg, one of the kajh from the caravan. He stood toe to toe with her. Paid with his life. But as soon as he fell, Sergeant Girten here"—O'Garran shook Craig's shoulder fondly—"put her down with a crossbow quarrel."

Girten shook his head. "The chief is leaving out one little detail: *he* was the first to fire. Hit the illith-whatever in the leg. That's when she saw the rest of us and turned tail. She'd just started limping away when I got in my lucky shot."

Bey crossed her arms. "There was no luck involved, Leader Caine. Your Crewe are skilled warriors, which the rest of the task force noted repeatedly." She smiled at O'Garran. "I am done amending your account, Chief. For now."

Miles smiled. "Wouldn't be a real after-action report if it wasn't derailed every few minutes. So, as I was saying, we'd started looking for dustkine as well as bounty hunters. Between Ta'rel's knowledge of the wadi country and the monoscope, we saw targets half a day or more before they could see us and where they were headed long before they'd get there. That's how we took the first dustkine.

"A few days later, we spotted a big band of bountiers. And by big, I mean two-and-a-half times our size. But we tracked them, saw that they had crap organization, and were headed toward a point where we could ambush them from high ground. Still wouldn't have taken the chance if Ta'rel and Yidreg hadn't known the slope was so rough and steep; if things went sideways, we could run like hell and get hidden before they reached the crest."

Craig laughed. "Wow, talk about worrying about the wrong thing!"

"So things *did* go, er, sideways?" Eku asked.

O'Garran scoffed. "Yeah—for them. We started by taking out the x'qao leader, then his lieutenants—and the whole damn gang just melted away. Well, those that could."

Wu frowned. "So what was the problem?"

"We weren't ready to take that many prisoners scattered across so wide an area. And three of those prisoners—well, recruits now—are *really* big. Two are a pair of trogres—or as the trogs say, *prakhbrai*—who are some kind of celebrities."

"They are twin sons of a famous warrior among their kind," Bey explained.

"Yeah, and you're going to just love the other heavyweight," Miles added, beaming at Yaargraukh. "It's a grat'r that makes your current one look like a midget."

"I presume," the Hkh'Rkh asked in a dry tone, "that you are once again speaking figuratively, Chief O'Garran.

Little Guy waved off the droll inquiry. "Yeah, yeah. He's also sharper than the one from the hovel."

Caine leaned forward. "And you took no casualties?"

Miles frowned. "Only one: the caver kajh. And all I can say for sure is that he went missing, mostly because managing our victory became a total clusterfu—madhouse. The survivors still outnumbered us almost two to one. Bunches were running off in every direction, wounded were crawling away, and about half a dozen stood their ground huddled together. That's where most of our recruits came from.

"But Bey sent a few two-man teams to dog the ones rabbiting for the horizon, partly to make sure they wouldn't regroup and double back, partly to see if we could grab them or at least their gear. At some point, the caver surprised an enemy trog who'd been hiding, got his arm wounded in that fight, then ran after another." O'Garran shrugged. "At least that's what our kajh sweepers saw from a distance. The caver got way out ahead of them chasing the second guy."

Bey frowned. "That assumes he was *chasing* the 'second guy,' rather than deserting."

The chief shrugged. "We'll never know. The weather came in quick from the south: low clouds moving so fast they weren't on the horizon when the ambush began. Rain and mist reduced visibility to damn near zero and we lost sight of the caver."

Bannor leaned toward Bey. "Why do you think the caver would risk striking out on his own?"

Bey's eyes were hard. "As I said from the outset, cavers are not to be trusted. Up until that point, he was cooperative—but no more than that. I suspect he was waiting for just such an opportunity." She looked around the group. "I have not said it so directly before, but I plead with you: do not bring cavers into our force. They will never bend to your ways. To them, loyalty, kindness, and fair dealing are all signs of weakness. I have never known one of them to behave or believe otherwise."

Riordan nodded and looked around the grim-eyed Crewe. "Bey, we will give your advice serious consideration." He turned back to O'Garran. "And after that?"

Little Guy waved at the wastes. "Wandered around for four or five days before spotting another group behind us. Smaller, just as disorganized, but they'd apparently found our tracks. So we danced around each other for a day or two before we decided to play dumb and let them 'find' our camp. They probed us—and that was the end of them. But their leader . . . well, I'll let Bey explain that bit of strangeness."

Bey's chin rose. "The battle was very brief. They were not well equipped. Only their leader had a bronze weapon, and a worn one, at that. Our first two volleys inflicted many casualties and those who could broke and ran. The leader was among the wounded."

"Or so we thought," Craig put in mysteriously.

Bey nodded. "We discerned that the one we believed to be the leader was not. A larger but less well-equipped trog had been the one giving orders."

"And we learned it just in time," O'Garran added, "thanks to her."

Ayana's eyes had not left Bey's face. "What does the chief mean by that?"

Bey shrugged. "The trog was clever. He let the other appear to lead, but he was more powerful. He is a shaman."

"'Is'?" Duncan repeated, sitting straighter.

Bey nodded. "He is one of the prisoners."

"And he could have made real trouble for us if she hadn't known what to look for," Craig added. "But she saw signs—tattoos and, uh, witch-doctor stuff—that marked him for what he was . . . er, is."

Caine nodded slowly. "I am surprised you brought him here. And even more surprised that Yidreg allowed it."

Bey nodded. "Normally, I would not have done so. But the circumstances of this shaman—Zhathragz—were unusual. He was one of the few survivors of a band that clashed with cavers, well to the west. Alone, he fled to Khorkrag and arrived just as an increased bounty was announced: two hundred fifty *gruhs* per human, one hundred for any being traveling with them.

"Gruhs?" Eku asked.

"A day's worth of food," Duncan answered. "Pretty much the only standard of value around here."

Katie was frowning. "That sounds like a verra high bounty."

Bey nodded. "I have never heard of a higher one. Which is why Zhathragz hit upon the idea of gathering a group around him and joining the bountiers fanning out into the Orokrosir. His Gifts made it a fairly simple task."

Dora frowned. "Gifts? Are they like Talents?"

Bey nodded. "He possesses several that make it easier for him to convince others to believe or obey him, and others that find game, water, or approaching predators. I am not learned in the ways of shamans, other than to be certain he has not revealed all the miracles he might summon."

Dora's eyes were wide. "And still you let him travel with you?"

"I felt it safe, in large part because he is not a city trog; he is from a Wild Tribe and born of a mother captured from a Free Tribe. But also, because Ta'rel, who grew up alongside mangle shamans, was unbothered. He pointed out that if Zhathragz had greater Gifts, he would surely have used them to attract more followers."

Baruch was shaking his head. "I cannot believe that we are having such conversations: about the dangers presented by the powers of a shaman."

"You've seen such powers yourself," Peter pointed out.

His friend glowered. "I do not deny they exist. But to discuss them in the same breath as tactics, missions, outcomes…" He shook his head. "I do not know when, if ever, I will become accustomed to it." He glanced at Bey. "So, you trust this witch doctor?"

Bey shrugged. "He is determined not to return to Khorkrag, which often preys upon us tribals, whether Free or Wild. It was he who did not merely suggest, but petitioned, that we attach what was left of his band to our task force."

Bannor glanced at Miles. "And are you also convinced his appeal was made in good faith?"

The chief leaned back on his elbows. "I'll tell you, sir, I've seen a lot of scared locals in my time. Trog or human, they send most of the same signals. This guy Zhathragz doesn't act like a gang leader; he reminds me of a civilian caught in a war zone. Just wants to travel with folks who are relatively sane and would rather not kill for a living. Besides that, he doesn't strike me as a liar, is pretty sharp, and was an easy fit for the task force. Kinda reminds me of Bey," he finished, grinning at her.

She raised one eyebrow. "As is often the case with Leader O'Garran, I cannot tell if he is taunting or praising me, but it is of no matter: Zhathragz has been a promising companion." She looked around the group. "I understand your hesitation at accepting so many new members into your force. I perceive that, where you are from, such things take place gradually and require more tests of loyalty.

"But that is not the case here. Trogs and other beings readily join new groups because attempting to survive alone is extremely dangerous." She shrugged. "It is also true that bonds made swiftly also dissolve more easily. But Zhathragz and his band seem at least as trustworthy as the trogs from the caravan. I say that knowing I shall be responsible for their conduct."

Bannor nodded. "While we're on the topic of your responsibilities, Bey, we'd like you to resume training our recruits. Both old and new."

Bey frowned before nodding slowly. "I would speak plainly, Leader Bannor."

"We wouldn't have you speak any other way."

"Then here is my answer. I believe such training is wise, since I foresee that we will more frequently need to rely upon our skills than our numbers."

Caine smiled. "Our thinking exactly. But I notice that you haven't said 'yes.'"

The smile Bey returned was one of regret. "That is because if I accepted this role, it would lessen my effectiveness as the leader of trogs. Among us, even in the Free Tribes, leaders refrain from teaching. There are many reasons for this, but trogs will only see that as a teacher, I am not at a remove from them—and so, am not a leader."

Riordan nodded: not a surprise. "So if this is a matter of status, would it help if one of us was a student in every group you trained?"

Bey tilted her head, considering. "I think it would, yes." Her concluding nod was firm. "I shall set about it immediately, if I am no longer needed here."

She was on her feet before Riordan stopped her. "Bey, one last thing. We would like you to return here this time tomorrow."

"To report my progress?"

"That—but another matter, also."

One of her eyebrows rose. She inclined her head and departed with strides full of purpose.

Miles glanced at Bannor then at Caine. "That request for Bey to become our master instructor didn't come out of the blue, Commodore. Am I wrong, or do you need to read me in on a new command policy?"

Riordan nodded. "Chief O'Garran, how would you feel about adding Bey to the command group?"

The SEAL emitted a bark of laughter. "Hell, I'd feel *relieved*! That way I don't have to push for it myself!" Several surprised stares fixed on him. "Look, there will be awkward moments, but we've got to have her perspective in our planning sessions. I saw it again and again when we were in the field.

"Don't get me wrong; Yidreg was fine. He knew the land, the basic tactics, was very competent. But Bey?" O'Garran snorted. "She's sharp as a tack and totally gung ho for the mission, even though she's not sure where it might lead."

Duncan nodded. "I'm in, too. Just so long as we remember to refer to 'Shangri-la' whenever we have to talk about reaching orbit, space, or the ship. And 'ronin' if we're talking about the Crewe." O'Garran made a sour expression at Solsohn's second reminder. "What? You don't like that code name?"

Miles couldn't maintain the scowl; the laugh hiding behind it broke through. "The only thing I don't like about 'ronin' is that Ayana and the commodore came up with it." He glared at them. "Damn it, making up catchy nicknames is *my* turf!"

Riordan smiled. "I think we'll be fine; as it is, we only discuss those topics during our Fireside Chats."

Bannor nodded. "Which we'll keep as our Crewe-only tradition."

"Damn," Craig yawned, "just hearing the words 'Fireside Chat' almost puts me to sleep."

"Which you should do." Riordan rose. "You and the chief are off the clock. Same goes for Ta'rel and Orsost. But the rest of us—"

"Yeah, yeah, Boss," Dora griped, rising. "With you it's always 'back to work!'" She smiled at him, shouted "Slavedriver!" and led the others back toward the day's labors.

Chapter Eleven

Rising from the same seat she had occupied the day before, Bey slowly, intentionally, met the eyes of everyone in the circle. Riordan couldn't tell whether she was stunned, overwhelmed with emotion, or simply being deeply respectful. "I accept this honor, to sit among you in all councils. It is hard to imagine that only seventy days ago, I was newly your captive and we were fleeing north from—"

Arashk sprinted around the nearest bend in the pass that wound snakelike to Achgabab.

"Come quickly!" he panted. "All of you! Djubaran has returned. With news! Much news! Quickly! What are you *waiting* for?"

As Caine led the command group into Achgabab's great hall, two immense guards—as large as those who had flanked Chief Vaagdjul—crossed their blades in front of Bey.

Riordan turned on his heel and confronted the barrier from the other side. "Let me pass. I am leaving."

The guards stared at him. "But our chief has requested you."

"We were told all should come. All have. You choose: all of us enter, or none of us." Riordan felt the Crewe stiffen around him: not in trepidation, but pride.

A long, simian hand reached in from the side, caused the axe-heads to lift merely by touching them: Yidreg.

From behind the hunter, Ulchakh smiled apologetically. "A misunderstanding." He raised his voice so Achgabab's local luminaries could all hear clearly. "Please, Friend Caine who has my *chogruk*, you and *all* your companions are asked to honor us with your presence."

Riordan nodded. "We are honored to be asked to stand before the chief of Achgabab." Smiling, they turned and together paced slowly into the center of the great hall, the Crewe and Bey walking tall and proud behind.

"That was passably said," Ulchakh muttered, "but not quite as I taught you."

"I shall endeavor to be a more apt pupil," Riordan replied from the side of his mouth. He waited as Ulchakh smothered a chuckle. "Why did they block Bey?"

"Because she is not fully human, no matter how much she looks it. No generation alive has seen anyone of her blood in this chamber."

"What was the last generation that did?"

Ulchakh glanced sideways. "None that we know of, Friend Caine." He nodded at Riordan's widened eyes. "Now you feel the importance of this moment. And your place in it."

He led them all to the left side of the raised stone shelf upon which Vaagdjul's chair was already placed. As they came to a halt, Yaargraukh murmured, "It is interesting, who is standing in the other place of honor."

Riordan glanced over—and was too surprised not to stare.

Tirolane nodded at him. Enoran and Orsost were just a step behind to either flank. Slightly off to one side, Ta'rel beamed at the Crewe.

"Hey, Boss," Dora hissed more than whispered, "don't those guys work for *us*?"

Riordan shook his head. "Ta'rel and Tirolane have traveled with us as friends." *Although the* mangle *might have said something!* "The oath we took from the other two was only until we reached Achgabab."

"Still—"

"Don't jump to any conclusions—and don't say anything else." Riordan stood very straight as guards entered from the tunnel that arose from the deeper rock. After them, a much-scarred young h'achgai entered, Chief Vaagdjul's hand on his shoulder. Whether the venerable leader of the Great Tribes did so to steer the youth or use him as support was unclear.

Reaching the chair with slow surety, Vaagdjul waited as he was announced, his audience inclined their heads in respect, and the boy stepped slightly to his right side. He sat with even more care than he had lavished upon each step, drew in a great breath and announced, “Before you stands Djubaran of the family Judhé, second branch of Clan Uksko. He undertook his *cho'urz* to the dunes-that-do-not-move. Determined to learn more, he returned to them before he could be affirmed as a child no more. But now he has returned. Affirm him!”

“Djubaran: a child no more!” shouted all the h'achgai.

“And again, for a second journey and second proving!”

The same chorus rose, even louder.

“Now,” Vaagdjul said through a loud sigh as he leaned back into his chair, “attend Djubaran's words, which bear import to h'achgai and visitors alike.”

Djubaran stepped forward and cried, “I have traveled and seen! Hear the tale I swear is true!” His posture became slightly less rigid, and even though his voice was no longer so loud, it still rang back down from the high, craggy arches of the hall. “You have heard tell of what I found when I reached the end of my cho'urz. The sandy sides of the dunes-that-do-not-move had fallen away to reveal the ancient stone flat-tops that lay beneath them.

“But soon after, I was set upon by a dozen *tadjabbai*—”

“What?” Dora whispered far too loudly.

“Shuddup,” Miles muttered.

“—which chased me for many days before I found rock upon which to walk, scattering sand before me to keep my scent from touching it. The chiefs of old surely watched over me, sending winds to blow the sand away before the tadjabbai arrived. And so I escaped and returned to Achgabab.

“But even as I fled the flat-tops, I saw something that was only reported once before, and so, had been thought a mistake—either in the eye of he who saw it, or the hand that recorded the tale. Some distance away, there were shallow holes among the lower dunes, such as fingers make when plunged down into dry sand. This was why I returned, though all counseled against it: to better see what had not been seen in many generations and perhaps to learn what caused it.”

Djubaran rubbed at one of the healing gashes on his face. “The second journey was harder. The spring hatching filled the air with hungry *kiks*, and that hunger made them bold. But the closer I came to hotside, the fewer there were, until I once again stood before the flat-tops.

"The sands had rehidden all but the largest one, and the strange holes were more shallow. But now I could ascend the flat-top that remained exposed, so I risked a closer approach."

Murmurs rippled through the great hall. Ulchakh leaned toward Caine. "No one has ever dared to touch, let alone stand upon, any of the flat-tops. Djubaran risked much, and has gained much, in this. Not only is his future bright, but many believe it augurs the special favor of our Passed Chiefs."

The young h'achga spoke over the fading whispers. "There I discovered that the top of the ancient stone was as flat as winter ice, but also, that several round doors led down into it, one of which was damaged."

"Hatches?" Duncan whispered from behind. Caine tilted his head slightly, hoped that Solsohn understood that he had heard but also, that a single audible word might be deemed disrespectful.

"I was deciding whether to approach closer," Djubaran continued, "and possibly peer within the flat-top, when 'qo came from the north. They had caught my scent on the wind. So I fled."

Djubaran took a moment to collect himself. "They did not relent. Three full days they pursued me, pushing me ever closer to the great river that flows down to Forkus and beyond. The ground was less even and there were wadis in which I lost the 'qo by going back upon my own tracks. But there were always some more behind me to the east, so I had no safe path to return home.

"So I made the river my destination, bending my steps toward Tajkor. Even though it is on the far side and well back from the high-water bank, I hoped that, if I remained watchful, I could signal to any of our kin who might go there for fresh water or game.

"Once again, our Passed Chiefs watched over me. Less than a day after arriving, hunters appeared along the far bank. They saw me waving my clothes and heard me crying over the rush of the river. They returned with one of their small boats and fetched me to their side of the river when it was at equiflow. The chief of Tajkor welcomed me, saw to my care, and bid me carry news of his people to their cousins here, though some of it was only for the ears of our own chief. He also relayed a strange story that he urged I pass on to the Mangled, but now, Chief Vaagdjul has asked me to share it with you.

"Tajkor is not set beside the river, but its people watch its waters from hidden places. When there is nothing in view, its hunters go forth, as do its merchants. Some days before I arrived, one of the traders they know from Fragkork stopped at the appointed place on the bank. After it was clear his party had not been followed, Tajkor's own traders came forth.

"Not only goods were exchanged, but news as well, including evil tidings from Fragkork. The lieges of that city are indeed selling off their humans to the south, but far more quickly than has been reported. Several mean to send their most valuable breedstock downriver by barge, and so, eliminate most of the risks associated with caravans.

"One name among the first group of humans to be traded in his manner was familiar to the traders: Cruvanor. He is a famed warrior in the stable of Gorzrik, who is the second vassal of Sirvashwekh, sworn to Ormalg. The chief of Tajkor bade me to be sure to bring that name and news to you."

Vaagdjul held up his hand. "Djubaran, you have acquitted yourself as well in the hall as you have upon the wastes. Go, now, with your kin to feast and rest. All others, I thank you for witnessing the completion of his cho'urz. I must now have the hall to discuss matters with our visitors."

The h'achgai other than those who had traveled with the Crewe—and three large guards—exited the cavernous chamber with curious glances and low murmurs. When they were gone, Vaagdjul swung his gaze away from Caine and Ulchakh to the other side of his rude dais. "Ta'rel, though you do not come from the tribes of Ebrekka, is this human, Cruvanor, known to you?"

The mangle's teal eyes half closed in affirmation. "Ne'sar, daughter of the durus'maan of Ebrekka, told me to remain alert for that name. He is indeed a great war leader. Some say the greatest of all the stables of Fragkork, even if he is past his prime. But this is not why the news is important. Well, not directly."

"Explain."

"Ne'sar explained that if Cruvanor was to be sold away from the stable, it would signify two things: that Sirvashwekh is forcing his most ambitious vassal, Gorzrik, to do so in order to weaken him. But secondly, and more importantly, it would be a sign that the lieges of Fragkork are not simply reducing their stables, but eliminating them with almost reckless speed."

"Why would they do that?"

Ta'rel shrugged. "Because the x'qai may have finally found an adequate replacement for humans. And by trading away the greatest of the city's war leaders first, they would also be reducing the possibility that their plans might be foiled. As you are no doubt aware, humans have proven unusually adept at toppling vassals or vavasors through indirect means. Cruvanor would surely be the most proficient—and willing—to silently instigate such trouble and so, disrupt their plans."

Vaagdjul nodded, scanned all the human faces. "I asked you to stay because I foresaw that you would now have matters to discuss and would wish a private place to do so. But also because whatever you do next, it will not be difficult for adversaries to learn that you started out from Achgabab. So in this way, our fates have become intertwined with yours. I mean to hear what you hope to achieve in journeying to the dunes-that-do-not-move, that I may counsel you. In doing so, I intend to protect my people from reprisals that might arise from rash or ill-considered plans."

Riordan nodded. *"Don't screw up my world, humans": a fair enough message.* "I am interested, Chief Vaagdjul, in what you think our objectives might be."

It was Ulchakh who answered. "Such remote ruins often contain artifacts of the world as it was before. You obviously knew that, because you were bedecked with such wonders when we met in Forkus—and your eyes brightened as I told you of the dunes-that-do-not-move." He shrugged. "Those who already possess—and understand—such artifacts always seek more."

Riordan smiled. "True."

Vaagdjul leaned forward. "But now a new concern arises, does it not? You freed two humans from the caravan: those standing by Tirolane. The account sent by the chief of Tajkor suggests that this barge will be carrying more. Possibly *many* more."

Tirolane nodded slowly. "That is almost certain, if Cruvanor is being sent. If Gorzrik failed to include enough humans for a reasonable retinue, he might as well have proclaimed his intention to barter off the war leader. Also, because barges are only used to convey cargos of extraordinary value, it would be plausible that Gorzrik would detail Cruvanor to oversee its protection.

"Still, a renowned war leader such as he might see through the charade, if for no other reason than x'qao vassals are loath to send their most capable and experienced humans into the field. Such a leader's strategic acumen, and ready detection of subtle ploys, is too valuable to the defense of a x'qao stronghold. So if Cruvanor has any suspicions that *he* is the precious cargo, the humans will be watchful for opportunities to escape."

Tirolane's voice tightened as he concluded. "This a *singular* opportunity. We should seize it."

Riordan managed to conceal his surprise. "You mean, to attack the barge?"

Tirolane nodded.

Riordan looked around the Crewe: a few nods, a few shaking heads, mostly shrugs. "As I am sure Arashk or others have told you, we make decisions much as do the h'achgai. I may be the commander for battles—the *dregdo*—but when it comes to steering our course into the future, we are all *dregdir*; all of us have a voice. So we will need to discuss this, first. "

Vaagdjul shook his head. "Caine Riordan, I fear you do not understand the importance of Djubaran's words when he said that these humans were soon to be loaded on the barge. Allowing for the time it took for the traders from Fragkork to carry this news down the river to Tajkor, and then for Djubaran to reach us, a decision must be made swiftly. Very swiftly."

Orsost's neck cords stood out in high relief. "It may already be too late! The current from Fragkork is swift!"

Tirolane gestured for the former stable-warrior to be silent.

Riordan made sure he didn't frown, even as he thought, *Despite their initial oath of fealty to us, you put those two in your pocket, didn't you, Tirolane? I just hope you're the friend we thought you were.* "The only way we can give you an immediate decision is for us to take a vote right now. Study the faces of my friends, Tirolane. They have many questions, perhaps more than I do. Are you willing to answer all of them, standing here?"

Tirolane frowned. "I suspect it would be unwise—for both of us—if I did so."

"Then the alternative is for us to vote without knowing any more than we have heard. But again, look at our faces and consider: do you believe you will get the answer you wish without telling us why you want it so very badly?"

Tirolane's hands became fists. Riordan wondered if the sound he heard was the big swordsman's teeth grinding. "Very well: ask your questions."

Dora stepped out from the Crewe. "Tasvar told us you were looking for your friends. Is one of them with this Cruvanor, maybe?"

"No, but he, of all people, might know where they are. Or how to find them."

Duncan shook his head. "Look, if they're using the river to move Cruvanor, then how many places could they be taking him? To Forkus? Maybe a city further downriver? My point is, why rush to intercept the barge if we can find and grab him later?"

Tirolane shook his head. "You presume you can project Cruvanor's likely journey. You cannot. Besides, the odds of rescuing him grow worse with every passing day."

Solsohn shrugged. "Well, that's just another reason why it would be better if we carry out the rescue *after* our salvage mission to the dunes. With any luck, we'll find a few more useful 'artifacts' to tip the balance in our favor. So as soon as we've taken a quick look—"

"No!" Tirolane snapped. "He may not have that much time."

Ayana inclined her head. "With respect, Djubaran's tale indicates that we, too, could be running out of time. The sands seem to be reclaiming the flat-tops once again."

"Then we can dig!"

"We don't have enough hands to do it."

"But you are likely to, after taking the barge!" Tirolane countered. "As it was after the caravan, any trogs you capture will have no one else to follow. And they will do so gladly because your leadership is wise and gentle. If unconventional."

"And of course, they would *fear* you," added Bey.

Tirolane shrugged. "Tell me: have the trogs not been easier to control, knowing that there is at least one human who has no gentle feelings for them?"

"Yes, it has been a great help," Bey said bitterly, "having them work beneath your death-filled eyes."

Even through his bronzed skin, Tirolane was fair enough that his flush was evident. "I will not deny that my heart was hard when I joined you. But this too, is true: you are not the only one who sees the world differently, now. Still my point stands: after intercepting the barge, we would have more thralls—I misspeak: *followers*—with which to remove the sand."

Bannor shook his head. "Aren't you missing a step in the process, Tirolane? The part where we actually stop a barge, commandeer it, and come away with a lot of prisoners? Because *sinking* it... well, that would pretty much defeat the purpose."

Tirolane folded his large arms. "Barges must stop for the night or when the river's force becomes too great. But there are only so many places they may be beached safely—which is why we must make haste. There is only once such breakwater north of Khorkrag and it would be a hard march to get there before the barge. Once it is downriver, we cannot overtake it." He shrugged. "As for commandeering it, I have seen your artifacts used in battle. I have no doubt they would prove at least as decisive in this one."

Tirolane stepped forward into the lull in their questions, arms slightly raised. "You have told me all the things that you supposed I did not understand. Now, I must list the things of which *you* have little or no knowledge."

"'Catching up' to Cruvanor is a bad idea, and not merely because of the speed with which the barge will carry him to an uncertain fate. You are also assuming that you will be able to inspect the ruin quickly, find useful artifacts, and then discover Cruvanor's whereabouts. Each of those assumptions is flawed."

Solsohn crossed his arms. "And do *you* know how long prospecting will take?"

"No one can say, but I *do* have some knowledge of what other prospectors have encountered. Even if the site's internal structure is mostly intact, and none of its walls or ceilings need to be shored up like a mine shaft, the most time-consuming process will still lay before you."

"Exploration?" Duncan suggested.

Tirolane shook his head. "Cataloging and then removing what you find. Only fools race through these rare ruins, grabbing whatever comes to hand. Often, different objects only make sense when seen in context of each other. Removal must therefore be slow and methodical. Which is further complicated by the dangers of the deep caverns."

Miles screwed up his face. "What deep caverns? Besides, we're not going spelunking—er, cave-crawling beyond the ruins."

Tirolane shrugged. "No, but their denizens are typically inclined to emerge when fresh air sinks in."

"Wait," Craig said, raising both hands, "are you telling me that these ruins are all connected to caves? Filled with, uh, monsters?"

"Not all, but most. Another factor of which you are unaware: creatures of the dark always seek paths to the surface, not only so that they may hunt upon the wastes, but because those are points where rainwater trickles down." Tirolane shook his head. "For these reasons, prospectors must be competent warriors who are prepared for a long campaign fought in the dark. Because once a sealed site is breached, you may not leave until you have removed all the salvage you mean to take away. Whatever you leave behind will be stripped bare."

Newton crossed his arms. "And how long does such removal take?"

Tirolane shrugged. "It depends upon the size of the site and the thoroughness of the prospectors. But even a relatively small find would take weeks if you were near a city such as Forkus. But out in the high desert, a dozen or more days' hard travel to this, the nearest tribal village? You must think in terms of *months*." His hands lowered. "So you see, there will be no speedy 'tracking' of Cruvanor if we do not rescue him. Now."

Eku's voice was quiet but focused, as if he were examining an object very carefully. "I have the impression that you expect to find something other than collapsed ruins at these flat-tops, that it may prove more intact than most. More useful."

Tirolane glanced at the factotum, as if seeing and assessing him for the first time. "'Expect' is too strong a word. But insofar as these structures are rarely exposed, and border on hotside, there is an excellent chance that they have not been accessed before. Also, in such arid lands, rain is rare, so the likelihood of water damage is low."

Caine glanced at the one member of the Crewe who had been conspicuously silent since Vaagdjul entered. "You have no questions, Yaargraukh?"

The Hkh'Rkh's heavy shoulders bunched and shook: dismay, even angry despair. "I am not human, but how may I find fault with any being who wishes to save one of his own kind from the enslavement of a species as inimical as the x'qai?" He ended on a fluting nostril-sigh.

Enoran and Orsost looked hopeful. But Tirolane seemed to understand that the sound Yaargraukh had emitted was not promising.

"Consequently, I have no question," Yaargraukh resumed, "but I do have an observation. One that I take no joy in sharing.

"If we resolved ourselves to finding and freeing all humans, great or humble, who are traded as brute chattel, we would never do anything but that. And because the task is endless, we would help but a fraction of those who deserve it.

"More sobering still is the probability that we would no longer have the time or resources to build our forces and improve our equipment. Instead, all we would have to show for our efforts would be determined pursuit by the most powerful suzerains and too many empty spaces where our friends once sat in our camp circle.

"So I must ask: at what point must our own directives take precedence over local needs? Should we defer such rescues until we can aid all, not just those of especial importance or repute? Or is it best that we *do* rescue this Cruvanor first because his name and reputation precede him and so, best serve the greater cause?" The Hkh'Rkh's neck spasmed. "We can say choosing him is more efficient, but never let us assert that it was 'fair.'"

Tirolane hung his head. "The noble grat'r-that-is-not speaks honorable words. And were Cruvanor here, I imagine he would agree."

Enoran raised an eyebrow. "You speak as if you know him."

Tirolane shook his head. "No, but I know a great deal about him. Which is why it is not chance that I traveled north with Sharat and that I am not stunned to find Cruvanor nearby, in danger of being traded away from Gorzrik's stable."

Orsost shook his head. "But how could you know of Cruvanor? You are from Zrik Whir."

"I grew up in those distant isles, yes, but you can see from my skin I am not *from* there."

"Then how the hell do you know about Cruvanor?" Miles almost shouted.

Tirolane looked up, eyes bright. "Because he is my grandfather."

Chapter Twelve

Vaagdjul rose hastily. "I have heard as much as I need. If I were to remain longer, I would hear more than I should. Or wish.

"The hall shall be sealed. The guards will admit no one. Leave when you will. I am old, and tired, and have presided over too many family squabbles and tragedies. Apprise me of your plans when they are set."

The chief hobbled toward the exit, two of his guards following with his chair. The third walked alongside the venerable h'achga, one hand surreptitiously ready to steady or catch him.

As soon as their footfalls faded, Dora spun toward Tirolane. "*Coño*! Why not start with 'he's my *abuelo*'—eh, grampa?"

Tirolane gritted his teeth "I will not resort to the currency that paid my way as a waif growing to age on Zrik Whir: pity, pity, and more pity." He shook his head sharply. "And yet, that is just what I have done."

Orsost stepped close to him. "Lord Tirolane, we are with you!" He glanced at the Crewe, disappointed frown deepening.

However, Enoran's eyes remained on Tirolane's face. "So, this is why you would not accept our oaths?"

Tirolane nodded, met the technicker's gaze. "I could not, in good conscience, allow you to join your paths to mine. For I could not know, and still do not, what I must hazard to fulfill the oath I took to rescue my only living family."

His attempt at a smile was bleak rue. "And what follows that quest will be no better: rescuing friends who have been taken by the x'qai." He gave up trying to affect jocularity. "The simple truth is that an oath of service made to me is likely to become a suicide pact."

"So," commented Bannor, arms crossed, "it's not chance, you happening to be with Sharat. You must have heard about his mission when you were at the Legate's in Forkus. Although that doesn't seem like the sort of intel Tasvar would share out."

"It was not," Tirolane admitted, "but when one knows what to look for as an assault group is being readied—the type and amount of provisions, the numbers and persons on the team, the region-specific kit—their destination was a near certainty."

Peter nodded. "And your claim that you were setting forth to immediately seek your friends: that was an . . . exaggeration?"

Tirolane started. "I am no liar! Nor have I invited or encouraged anyone to believe anything that is not true! My friends *have* disappeared into the stronghold of some liege here on Brazhgarag. And it is not an 'exaggeration' to assert that, of all the humans on this continent, Cruvanor is more likely to have word of them than any other."

"Why?"

"Because it is known that there are a dozen senior war leaders who have found ways to pass intelligence between them secretly and stay apprised of conditions among not just lieges, but of the suzerains to which they answer."

"Damn," Duncan breathed, "a humint star chamber! Ready-made!"

Miles grinned. "Down boy. Er, sir."

Tirolane walked slowly toward the Crewe, hands out. "I know the magnitude of what I ask, not only in time and risk but compassion for people you do not know. So I swear this upon my ancestors, most especially the only one whom I know to be alive: if you grant me this boon, my fealty is forever yours. A life bound to you for a life set free.

"But know this, as well: I will go alone if I must, and I will take oaths of fealty from all those who, knowing the dangers, still wish to tender them unto me. Including those of any trogans or trogs who wish to follow their former leaders." He gestured to the humans on either side of him.

Miles leaned away. "Damn, I thought you were on our side,

Tirolane. But I guess we see your true colors now, yeah? You'll even take the trogs over us, to get what you want."

Tirolane's jaw became as rigid as his eyes were hard. "That was not my intent. But if that is leverage, and if it helps you make the right decision, then so be it."

"The right decision for you and Cruvanor, maybe, but not us."

"No. It is the right decision for *all* of you." He let his gaze run along the faces of the Crewe. "You more than anyone."

Miles was leaning forward to respond when Caine raised a hand. "Let him finish."

"Yeah"—Bannor nodded shrewdly—"I think the downside—losing Cruvanor—is only half of what Tirolane is talking about. That's the stick . . . but I'm guessing there's a carrot, too. Am I right?"

Tirolane frowned. "I do not know what a carrot is. But if you mean that I have only presented the perils of not saving my grandfather, rather than adding mention of the benefits, then you are correct."

Caine smiled. "Yes, that's what Bannor means. So: tell us."

Tirolane spread his hands in appeal. "Let us dismiss the fact that Enoran and Orsost would then gladly join your efforts—and so, your colors. Let us also leave aside the certainty that Cruvanor and the humans with him will offer you the same, if not greater, gratitude and loyalty. Let us even ignore that, with Cruvanor's name and knowledge, you could build your force not merely through captured trogs but more freed humans."

"That's a lot to ignore," Duncan muttered, rubbing his chin.

"Let us consider only this," Tirolane concluded. "That Cruvanor is one of the great experts of ancient salvage. Certainly the foremost on this continent, and very possibly in the world." He nodded at the group. "None of you have overseen such a project. He has, dozens of times. His eye will discern the value of objects unerringly, and also, assess which artifacts may be refurbished most easily. Very possibly using components of other similar devices that may be found nearby."

"And how do you know this?" Ayana asked mildly.

Tirolane offered the shadow of a courtly bow in her direction. "Because when an artifact is acquired by Zrik Whir, and its black market provenance indicates it was found and assessed by Cruvanor, that is the highest standard of value and reliability."

He surveyed their carefully neutral faces again and his own started to bend into the shape of baffled anger. "Will you not have me? Have I not been honorable at all times, in all ways?"

"None more so," Caine replied.

"Indeed, none so much," Yaargraukh answered, his tone of respect calming the swordsman. "But your honor pulls you in two ways. No one can objectively advocate for themselves in such circumstances."

"Which," Riordan followed, "is why we must ask you to give us the room: so that, as a group, we may decide how to respond."

Tirolane nodded and paced away. Without so much as a glance from him, the two freed humans followed him out of the hall.

Riordan let a full minute pass, then nodded at Bannor.

The Special Forces colonel turned toward Bey. "We need your opinion on what you just heard."

She frowned, uncertain. "Of course, but I did not understand all of it."

Riordan managed not to smile; he was quite sure that whatever parts were unfamiliar, she'd already made some shrewd guesses.

Bannor shook his head. "We're not asking you about prospecting or Cruvanor or any of those matters. Our concern is much narrower. Specifically, if Tirolane was to leave our group, what impact do you think it would have on the trogs?"

Bey nodded, frowned. "This would be a very bad time for any rifts to appear among their highest leaders. There are now three separate groups that have been added to those of us who came north as your prisoners from Forkus. All but one of the twelve newest are kajh, and half of those are trogans. They will soon be competing for places of respect, so strong leadership from familiar figures will be necessary to maintain order. And in this group, that will be more crucial because of your . . . er, unfamiliar means of command."

"Yeah," added Miles with a long sigh, "and if the three humans who leave are the locals who lead them the 'normal' way, that will confirm their suspicion that the rest of us don't know what the hell we're doing." He spat. "Great. Just great."

Caine sought and found Bey's eyes. "Do you feel Tirolane's departure could lead to desertion? Or mutiny?"

Bey shook her head sharply at the suggestion of mutiny. "No. You have won battles and they have seen that you are both fearsome and just." She frowned. "If by desertion you mean slipping off in the night, I do not think any would do that. But they might fade away from the edges of an uncertain battle, and any order to retreat might cause them to flee, instead."

Duncan's voice sounded injured. "Kinda disappointing, given that we've treated them way better than anyone else—including their own kind."

"You have, but their minds are still those of warrior-thralls. They are accustomed to leaders who never give them more than they must. You give them much more, but in their experience, the only leaders who do that are those with a weak hold over their troops."

As if reading Caine's mind, she looked over at him. "But do not change the way you lead. For now, just remember to remain distant from them: that is the behavior of higher leaders who cannot be bothered with the affairs of regular kajh or urldi. And if your lieutenants express authority in familiar ways, they will see your behavior as akin to that of powerful vassals or lieges. Eventually, they will see the true differences in leadership and realize that is what makes this band so successful. But that will require more time and victories."

Bannor nodded. "Thank you, Bey. Now, we will need to speak among ourselves."

She tilted her head, as if she doubted what she had heard. "You are asking me to leave? Even though I am part of your, eh, command staff?"

Bannor nodded.

She turned to look at Caine. "And you agree to this?"

He met her gaze. "I'm the one who made it a rule, in this case," he exaggerated. Because even if there had been enough time, they still could not have explained why it was necessary for her to leave. Discussing Tirolane's ultimatum meant assessing how it affected prospecting, which in turn directly impacted their odds of returning to space. And since Caine had been the one to restrict "Shangri-la" topics to Fireside Chats, *he* was the reason Bey couldn't remain. *Besides: my unit, my responsibility.*

Bey did not make it any easier. "You do not trust me? *You?*" Typically quite professional, her voice had become high and raw.

Caine kept his face unchanged. "Trust has nothing to do with it. The rest of us must now discuss things that would be unsafe for you to know."

Bey's face contorted into tight, intersecting lines of both anger and hurt. "And you think I would share your secrets? Even though I might be tortured?"

Riordan suppressed a sigh of regret. "Bey, none of us know all the, uh, Talents, that x'qai might have to extract secrets. But I do know this: if someone decides to investigate our most powerful artifacts, then anyone with detailed knowledge of them is at great risk. And I refuse to expose anyone to that peril needlessly. That is why I must ask you to leave. This one time." *I hope.*

Without a word, Bey stalked out of the great hall.

The others exchange glances. "Boss," Dora muttered, "I think we may have a problem with her."

"Probably more than one, but that's a conversation for another place and another time." *Or, given how fast things change on this world, maybe never.*

Craig was rubbing his hands—anxiously, Riordan thought. "So we're deciding whether we go after Cruvanor and keep Tirolane, or go straight for the old ruins and lose him, right?" Answered only by nods, Girten continued. "Well, then how's that even a choice? Tirolane is a good guy trying to do a great thing. The ruins—well, it's not like we *know* if we'll find anything useful there. And it sure doesn't seem like anyone else is rushing to find out before we do."

"No, not so far as we know," Peter answered, "although there is probably at least one informer inside Tasvar's fortress. Far more important is what Djubaran reported about the sand rising up against the flat-tops. We cannot know whether it will take days or seasons for the desert to cover them again. But we can be sure of this: the sooner we reach them, the more likely we can get inside."

Riordan nodded. "Those are key variables in the strategic question before us: what is the best way to achieve our primary objective of getting the hell off this planet? Do we rescue Cruvanor before going to the ruins, or after?"

After several seconds of silence, Miles shrugged. "I'll say it if no one else will. The site is a bird in the hand; Cruvanor is one in a very distant bush." He sighed. "So, hold on to the bird. We leave the casino and count our winnings. Going after Cruvanor is tempting Fate. And she'll kick your ass, every time."

"So what're thinkin' then?" Katie Somers asked, eyes widening.

"That we're going to traipse into the wrack and ruin of ages past and find a rocket down there, just waiting for us?"

Newton's counter was testy. "No, but we are likely to learn what kind of technology existed when these 'flat-tops' were built. And that will tell us if it is sensible to keep looking for a means of getting to orbit, and possibly, give hints where to look for them.

"On the other hand, we may learn that their technology was not sufficiently advanced. Either way, we would have an answer to our most urgent question: Can we return to space and regain the ship?"

"Or," O'Garran sighed, "is it just a bridge—well, orbit—too far?"

"Only once we have answered that," Eku mused, "can we be certain that our efforts and energies are focused on achievable ends. It is a very simple choice."

Bannor shook his head. "But it's *not* that simple a choice. You heard Bey. Tirolane could prove key to maintaining control over the forces we need to reach, secure, and explore the ruins. And without Cruvanor, will we even know what to look for? Will we miss warning signs, dangers, that his experienced eyes would spot in time?"

Dora shook her head. "Yeah, yeah, all very logical. Very clever. But you're overlooking something."

Riordan smiled. "Tell us."

"Well, it's like Colonel Green Beanie said about these ruins. We don't know what it's gonna be like. Probably skulking around in the dark, hoping monsters we've never heard of won't kill us before we find something that might not even be there.

"And rescuing Cruvanor? More unknowns. Can we get the barge? Will we win? If we do, will it hurt us so bad that we'll have to go back to Achgabab and lick our wounds—assuming they'll let us?"

Newton crossed his considerable arms. "And your point is?"

"My point, Doctor Ice Water, is one you'd never see." She stared around the faces of the Crewe. "There's only one choice we've got that isn't based on maybes and guesses and calculated risks. And that's rescuing Cruvanor—because it's the *human* thing to do.

"Win or lose, a rescue is a real act; it's *visceral*. Yeah, we might lose more goods, maybe even some lives. But it will bind us all together because we *stood* together. Stood against creatures that make their living by sucking the life out of us all: creatures that everyone—human, crog, trog—hate." She raised her chin, daring anyone to contradict her.

"Assuming we survive as a unit," Peter pointed out.

"No argument," she replied, "but we've got some tricks that they've never seen. And if they've sent a whole army along with this barge, we're sure to spot that way in advance and turn right around."

"Dora's right," Bannor agreed. "There's only one reason to intercept it that transcends debates over optimization: to save the humans on that barge. Everything else—whether Cruvanor can help us, whether the ruins are above or below the sand, and whatever they do or don't contain—is what we worry about *next.*" He glanced over at Riordan.

Who let the silence extend to ensure that the debate had truly wound down. Caine looked around the group. "Every point made was solid." He nodded at Rulaine. "But I agree with your conclusion."

O'Garran cocked an eyebrow. "Not like you seem surprised by any of it, sir. You barely reacted."

"Because, Chief, sometimes the best thing a commander can do is let his staff debate the options and consequences." He nodded his appreciation. "Besides, it wouldn't have been right for me to steer this conversation."

Somers raised an eyebrow. "An' why's that, Commodore?"

"Because, from the moment Tirolane put the choice before us, I knew which option I favored." He saw perplexity in the faces ringing him. "As far as I'm concerned, what we choose now defines who we are. Are odds and percentages going to drive our actions and our objectives? Or will they be determined by what we value most: the people around us?

"We've all seen, and felt, how pragmatism can push human values off the table. In military operations, it's often unavoidable. But if it becomes too frequent, it can become a habit. Then, flesh-and-blood costs are just statistics: wrinkles that spoil the 'bigger picture.'"

He jabbed his finger at the ground. "I won't have that. Ever. We need every one of our people to know we care for our own. But more importantly, we need them to *believe* it—and that means *we* have to act accordingly."

Riordan straightened. "They've seen that we don't make reckless decisions. They've got to see that we won't make heartless ones, either. And if that is the core truth of our unit, then we will stick together *as* a unit. Hell, that's why we're all here now: because we came to know—and feel—that way about each other. And the more we've been the underdogs, the more important that's been."

Caine leaned back. "So: *that's* why we're going after Cruvanor first."

Craig was smiling broadly. "Sir?"

"Yes?"

"Should I go get Tirolane, now?"

Riordan couldn't help smiling back. "Please do, Sergeant Girten."

After hearing the outcome he'd clearly read in Girten's broad smile, Tirolane proved as good as his word: he offered to take an oath of irrevocable fealty then and there.

Riordan shook his head. "Tirolane, you know we don't believe in having vassals. We believe in, and have become, friends who travel together but are free to part if they must and to return as they can. Is that acceptable to you?"

He stood very straight. "It is not merely acceptable; it confirms my conjectures, and highest hopes, about your group from our first meeting. That you were a company so worthy of my fealty that you would forego an oath and make it an agreement of honor instead. So to you I say simply, 'Lead. I shall follow.'"

They shook hands in Bactradgarian fashion and, reflexively, the rest of the Crewe came forward to make a similar welcome to him and then Orsost and Enoran.

Except Girten, who sidled up to Caine. "Sir, you might want to step out into the main corridor for a moment."

Riordan turned. "Why? Is someone waiting for us?"

Craig looked uncomfortable. "Well, they deny it . . . but I think so."

"Spit it out, Sergeant: who's come to see us?"

"Not to see 'us,' sir. Just you. And she didn't come; she *stayed*."

Riordan had to walk around the nearest corner before he discovered Bey sitting on one of the stone benches lining the main approach to the great hall. He sat at the other end. "You're angry."

She didn't look at him, but nodded. "I was. I know I shouldn't be." Bey shut her eyes. "I was furious, was sure you thought I was weak... but I know you do not think so."

"Then what—?"

"So, if you knew I was not weak, then I was certain you sent me out because you thought me a stupid trog who could not keep secrets. But I knew you didn't think that, either. So then I even imagined that you sent me out of the council to prove that you preferred the rest of your trib—eh, Crewe. But that made less sense; had you felt that, you would have shown it long before now."

"So, you are still angry because—?"

"Because even though your precaution and your reasons are prudent, I did not—and do not—*like* them. But that is just stupid and impulsive, which is *exactly* what other races expect of trogs. And that makes me angry at *myself*."

"You have no reason to be angry at yourself."

She almost shouted. "Do you think I don't know that? But then, in the same instant, I am angry at you for having been the cause, the source, of all these doubts and feelings. They are not... not sensible."

Caine shrugged, smiled. "Feelings aren't always sensible."

"They are for me," Bey snapped irritably, but something in her tone suggested that she doubted the words even as she uttered them.

Riordan wondered at her oddly irresolute assertion. "I understand your anger. And also, the frustration of having reactions that, if you were counseling a friend, you would call illogical." He smiled again. "I've certainly done that. Far too often."

Bey looked up. Her eyes bored into his longer than he expected—and apparently, she as well. Bey slapped her thighs and rose. "I must do something."

"What?"

She shook her head fiercely. "Anything that will keep me from thinking or feeling until both become more clear. I presume we march for the river tomorrow?"

Riordan nodded. "At first light."

She returned his nod and walked briskly away.

As she did, Caine had the impression that as much as she was rushing toward her sleeping furs, she was also rushing away from the great hall.

As fast as she could without running.

INTERLUDE ONE

A Surplus in the Colors

May–June 2125
The Scatters, Ktoran Space

Interlude One

Trevor Corcoran leaned back from the Dornaani screen, dismissed yet another prompt asking if he wanted to shift to semi-holographic display, and stared at the block of copy he'd typed. He could have dictated the log entry, of course. Dornaani "AI" was not just astoundingly accurate at rendering speech as text, it was downright unsettling. It also would have taken Trevor, at most, a third the time he'd spent clacking away at the keyboard the Dornaani had excavated from their almost-forgotten collection of "generationally specific human interface resources." Which was tactful code for, "backward technologies usable by equally backward hominids from a wide variety of epochs."

Trevor folded his arms, stared defiantly at the Dornaani complex. *Some tasks* should *take more time. More thought, more reflection.* In that regard, modern human systems actually weren't any better: for more than a century, speed, convenience, and minimal learning curve had been the desiderata driving computer and software design. It had reached the point that, before the turn of the century, every one of the service branches had added remedial courses to help inductees understand how most devices worked at all. Trevor smirked at the untouched Dornaani work interface: a half-HUD with earphones. *No, I will* not *go gently into that good night.*

But even as he celebrated his own, quixotic resolve to resist the rise of machines, Trevor wasn't able to completely escape the nagging knowledge that it was the lesser reason he stuck with the keyboard. The greater part was that he was stubborn. Or at least, an unabashed creature of habit. He smiled: *Got that trait from Mom.*

An unbidden memory of her face and her laugh threatened to burst out of his carefully patrolled emotional vault. He shut them down abruptly, just as he'd soon do to the commplex. She might very well be the last living person from his nuclear family. Reflecting on that made every chore, every duty, every conversation just that much harder. *So stay on task. Edit your damn log entry and move on to the next thing.*

Poising his hands over the keyboard in readiness to enter corrections, he read:

> After leaving the system the Dornaani call Depot (L 1815 5 A, for us), Alnduul kept *Olsloov* moving with minimal turnaround time between shifts. That rapid pace wasn't just because we were almost half a year behind Caine and Company (who, according to Alnduul, dubiously dubbed themselves his "Crewe"). That was the carrot, the thing we were running toward. But at Depot, we also started running away from a big stick: the entirety of the Collective. The system's automated port authority/traffic control computer detected *Olsloov*'s transponder... which should have been five shifts away, back at the edge of CTR space.
>
> Short version: since we were now on damn near everyone's "most wanted" list, we started riding hard for the border.
>
> At least we made good time. *Olsloov* has a whopping sixteen light-year shift limit, whereas the ship we're chasing has just a little over twelve. Both ships have the ability to shift into and out of deep space (i.e. no stellar-size gravity well required for navigation), but Hsontlosh—that's the bastard we're trailing—either hasn't decided to use his, or isn't aware he's got one. And lastly, because we were staying ahead of the Collective's realization that Alnduul was AWOL, we were able to load up on antimatter wherever we stopped. And why not? It's not as if we'll ever be going back that way, not unless the powers-that-be in both governments tell us that all is forgiven and we should come home. In re: to which: I'm not holding my breath.

The cumulative effect of our advantages was that, by the time we arrived at system BD+13 778, we'd cut almost fifty days off Hsontlosh's lead. We were, to use my "Uncle" Richard's British idiom, feeling rather chuffed. Which is, of course, right when the universe-at-large likes to throw curve balls at you. (Richard would probably call it a "googly.")

As soon as we re-expressed in that system, Alnduul knew that the nature of our chase had changed. Up until then, we'd been following signals from a tracking fob that he'd given to Caine before everything went to hell in a hand-basket. After it was activated, the tracker left a data string in every local commo stream like a trail of bread crumbs.

But there was no bread crumb in BD+13 778; there was a buoy. The kind that a Dornaani ship automatically deploys if it is under attack or detects the imminent likelihood that it might mis-shift. And since there was no debris or sign that any other vessel had been present during the eighty-five days since the buoy had been kicked loose from Hsontlosh's ship, the odds tilted toward a mis-shift.

Richard and I thought it was pretty much a death sentence, but Alnduul disagreed, mostly because we were now just one shift away from 13 Orionis: a system at the very limit of the Ktoran Sphere. He suspected (and he was right) that it would have been wild coincidence for Hsontlosh's ship to have a catastrophic failure right as he was about to link up with whatever buyer he'd lined up for Caine and his "Crewe." They'd become extremely valuable political poker chips ever since the Lost Soldiers went missing; too many powers had too much to lose if they ever resurfaced.

Alnduul also pointed to the ship diagnostic that all buoys record when they're jettisoned. There were no developing maintenance problems, no signs of imminent failure, but the navigation system had been damaged—*physically* damaged—at almost the same second the buoy was deployed. And there was only one way to physically damage the navigation system without pulling apart bulkheads or hull sections: you had to do some pretty serious violence to the navigator's console. I suggested that it sounded like everything went sideways during a shootout on the bridge.

Alnduul put on his best professorial demeanor and

corrected my choice of words: it was quite likely that everything went sideways *because* of a shootout on the bridge. Which I had been working up to, but it's his ship so I just nodded. Which was just as well, because he had even more evidence supporting the distinction he'd made.

Turns out that the buoy also contains a log of any commo events just prior to its deployment. In this case, the only such activity hadn't come from the ship itself, but from Caine's tracking fob. Being in the buffer worlds between the Collective and the exile-infested Ktoran Scatters, there was nothing in the system to relay that signal. But, Alnduul added, raising one finger, it also indicated that its beacon function was probably not why Caine triggered it; just shortly before the mis-shift, the fob had been used to override a ship's system.

So yes, it certainly looked as though Caine and Crewe had taken command of the ship. And that certainly appeared to be the cause of the mis-shift. But was there any chance that they had survived?

It took Alnduul and his crew two days of studying whatever quantum-entangled magic they use to detect buoys active in nearby systems. But in the end, that's just what they found: the faintest hint of a signal. But it was so garbled that its fragmentary data strings couldn't be trusted. It also didn't give us a heading any better than "it's somewhere in this half of the universe." But one shift would give us signal differentials that, theoretically, would allow us to come up with a reasonably accurate vector along which to plot the course of our subsequent search.

Of course, all that relatively hopeful news came along with a major problem: how to keep replenishing our antimatter stocks. *Olsloov* has the *means* to do so. The problem is *time*, because converting stellar energy into antimatter is not a speedy solution—as every member-state of the Accord knows all too well. Even the Dornaani have had to invest in large, permanent facilities to make that slow process worth the expense and time.

Happily, Dornaani magic *does* make it faster and easier. After our first shift into the Scatters, I had a ringside seat as they deployed one of their solar collectors. Made of material as thin as spider silk and only a fraction of the mass, it unfolded like the wings of a giant cubist moth. And as it did, Alnduul's crew kept seeking the buoy signal so they could perform their n-space version of triangulation and show the way ahead.

That was a month and three shifts ago. For a portable, frontier antimatter production system, the Dornaani arrays are nothing short of amazing. But generating enough antimatter to power a shift-drive? It's still slow: so slow that we've had to choose our destinations very carefully. You don't set up these arrays and get them producing in a few hours. You're lucky to have them running in a few days. As Richard put it, when you start making antimatter, you're "in for a penny, in for a pound."

So now, it's mostly wait and watch and finish the most depressing task I've ever tackled: deciding which of the Lost Soldiers we're going to thaw out and drop on the first habitable (and receptive) planet we find. Because almost every day, a new warning light shows up on yet another of their coldcells.

The roster of which and how many are failing is too long to include here (see ref# 12b in the mission log), and yeah, it only *feels* as though a new light comes on every day. But even if the list isn't growing quite that fast, the challenge is the same: either we defrost over a hundred of those poor sibs in the next few months, or we're going to start losing them to malfunctions.

Trevor was reading the last sentence before he realized that he hadn't made any corrections. Whatever part of his mind he'd hoped would watch for typos had slipped away to study the same mental worry stone he'd been turning over and over for weeks, even in his dreams. It was increasingly likely that the way forward meant charting a course through the most dense clusters in the Scatters. And if most of the green worlds there had already been settled by Ktoran exiles... then what?

Trevor sighed, called up the transit projections, scrolled to the bottom of the list: the star beyond which they were almost sure to start losing cold sleepers. It was also the last system they could reach without deploying the solar collectors again. In other words, in every possible way, 55 Tauri was the end of the line.

And if things didn't start looking up, they'd have to reanimate and consult a few key cold sleepers whose expertise might prove necessary to facilitate fast provisioning.

At least the system looked promising. The fragmentary data string from a pre-Dornaani robotic survey indicated it had multiple refueling possibilities and at least one green world. But if that world was settled...

Trevor's jaw muscles clenched. *Please, God or whatever is out there, the Lost Soldiers have already been accused of invading Turkh'saar. Don't make them live that all over again at 55 Tauri.*

Richard Downing was not surprised by Melissa Sleeman's reaction to Trevor's invitation to share her "relevant expertise": decidedly guarded. But now that she was in the briefing room with them, he realized he'd underestimated the full measure of her wariness. Her posture was that of a cornered animal, and it intensified as she shifted her gaze from Trevor to Richard.

Her eyes became blank, as if venetian blinds were being shuttered just behind her retinas. "Mr. Downing, did you ask me to meet with you because of the food shortages? Because if you are about to tell me that my husband has to go into—"

"Actually, Melissa," Trevor interrupted, "I was the one who wanted—needed—you here."

"So it's not about the shortages?"

"Not directly," Downing answered. "We need your scientific expertise on a related matter."

"So, this *isn't* about food rationing?"

"No." *Although that could be coming soon enough.* "Right now, we are cautiously optimistic about the next system on our shift plot."

She frowned. "55 Tauri?" Downing nodded. "Hmm. A little birdie told me that 55 Tauri could end up being our *last* stop."

Downing smiled, nodded, and thought, *And was that little birdie named Christopher Robin? Fine soldier, but can't keep a secret from his wife.* Of course, there was more virtue in that than not. "Happily, our present system has no Ktoran exiles, so Alnduul once again has enough time to produce more antimatter. We will almost certainly generate enough to replace what we'll use in the shift to 55 Tauri.

"Why 'almost' certainly? If we are so safe here, isn't it up to us how much antimatter we generate?"

"Yes," Trevor answered, "but every day we spend here, we're risking that a coldcell will fail completely and one of the Lost Soldiers will die. So as soon as we've got enough antimatter to be sure of making at least one shift after 55 Tauri, we've got to go there."

Melissa bit her lip, nodded tightly. "Any more data about it?"

Downing glanced at his compupad. "Alnduul's team has yet to complete the first week of observation, but the preliminary results are promising. Each of the stars has a world solidly in the habitable zone. However, the stars are also nearing periapsis.

"At the closest approach, the weather—both planetary and stellar—will be unusually turbulent. On the surface of the secondary's habitable planet, the change in average temperature could be quite marked. That and the probability that its seasonal norms have already been disrupted by the approach of the primary could make it difficult to locate and gather food."

Trevor tried to add a touch of levity. "So we'll be arriving during a triple-strength El Niño."

Melissa raised an eyebrow. "That would be a very mild variation compared to what Mr. Downing's data suggests." She frowned. "But you certainly didn't ask me here to talk about planetary weather or food supplies."

"You're right," admitted Trevor. "Actually, you're here because of a memo you wrote even before Richard and I joined you at Zeta Tucanae."

Her frown deepened. "I wrote a lot of memos back then. Mostly updates on what we were learning about the Ktoran coldcells. And the symbiopods."

"Yes, and in the course of your research, you flagged one Lost Soldier who might be helpful in that regard. Although he wasn't actually a soldier. He was—"

Sleeman's eyes opened wide. "Yes. His name was Robert Hampson . . . no, that was an alias. He was a brain specialist, mostly developing new treatment and surgical techniques instead of performing them. His actual name was . . . give me a moment."

Downing gave her two, then pushed the compupad toward her. "Dr. Edouard Tedders. He was with the last group of Lost Soldiers that the Ktor kidnapped. He was in Mogadishu for two days to assess a brain injury: nephew of a congresswoman. He was being flown to a secure airfield when his helicopter was shot down over the Indian Ocean."

Sleeman nodded. "I recommended he be reanimated as soon as it was feasible. As both a doctor and a scientist, he was a crucial asset. But given his specialties, he was the only human with us—awake or asleep—who could help me learn more about the Ktor coldcell technology."

"We agree," Downing said with a smile. "With your approval, we'll begin the reanimation process. And I think you'll find him particularly motivated to unravel the mysteries, and apparent risks, of the symbiopods."

"Why so?"

"Because he's in one right now. He should have recovered and finished acclimation at least a few days before we shift to 55 Tauri."

"And when do we tell him that it's not just humans on this ship?"

Trevor glanced at Downing, who shrugged. "In due time," Trevor replied through a long sigh, "in due time."

Trevor glanced at the reports Sleeman had placed before her on the table. "A little more light reading on the good doctor?"

"There is nothing 'light' about him or his career," she asserted. "Or his life."

Trevor nodded. He'd spent less than an hour with Tedder: specifically, the doctor's first twenty minutes of genuine, memory-forming awareness. "Is he having a hard time adjusting?"

Sleeman shook her head. "Frankly, I'd take some comfort in that. But, comparing his post-revival attitude and interaction scores to those of the Lost Soldiers who were awakened on Turkh'saar, I'd say he's had the least disorientation or emotional trauma of all."

Downing nodded slowly. "Is that because of his technological acumen? Less culture shock?"

Trevor almost scoffed at his "uncle's" understatement. "As the CEO and CTO of a neurosurgical consulting firm called The Cutting Edge, I'd say Dr. Tedders already had one foot in the future."

Sleeman shrugged. "Well, that's certainly part of it, but I think it's also that he's genuinely excited to be living in this time."

Trevor stared. "Granted I wasn't with him long, but he seemed like a pretty genial guy. But what you just said makes him sound, well, a bit like a sociopath. What about family? That's usually what hits Lost Soldiers the hardest."

"He didn't have much." Sleeman's voice acquired a hint of

melancholy. "He was the only child of older parents. One had already died, the other had just been moved into assisted care."

Downing looked up. "Why?"

"His father had Alzheimer's."

Trevor knew the term but wasn't sure of the exact definition. "That's, eh, a form of dementia, isn't it?"

Melissa nodded. "Edouard—Dr. Tedders married late, also. They wanted to start a family but medical intervention was required. Before it produced any results, she was killed in a car crash. Reading between the lines, I'd say he threw himself into his work until, three months later, he received a call from the classified side of his research career and was off to Somalia." She shrugged. "I think waking up into a future where he's already valued may be helping him adjust."

Downing nodded. "Part fascination, part work therapy, then. Why don't you bring him in, Doctor Sleeman?"

She returned within the minute with Tedders in tow: a squarely built and quick-eyed man in his fifties. However, he seemed younger; just walking into the room, he exuded a youthful interest in his new surroundings.

Trevor stood, extended his hand. "Dr. Tedders, you may not remember me, but I'm—"

"You called yourself 'Nephew'; of course I remember." He smiled at Downing without having any particular reason to do so. "And you were 'Nuncle.'"

Richard stood, offered his hand as well. "Recognizing us is not a test, Doctor, but if it was, you'd have passed with flying colors. Please, be seated. I hope you're starting to find your way around our century?"

"Starting," Tedders allowed, "but there's a lot of it to get acquainted with. I've been driving poor Melissa crazy with all my questions!"

She smiled and shook her head. "No trouble at all. And many of your questions are, well, very refreshing. And evidently whenever I am no longer sufficiently interesting—or alert—Edouard has been ploughing through a bit of history. And a *lot* of medical journals."

"Making up for lost time," Tedders agreed, nodding so vigorously that his shoulders jogged a bit, too. "Besides, it sounds as if you've already got some work for me."

Trevor smiled. *Now, that's* real *eagerness. Or grief avoidance. Or both.* "How much do you know about our situation?"

"Only a little," Tedders admitted—and then launched into a ten-minute synopsis of where they were from, who they were, why they'd had to flee to their current location, the difficulties of moving swiftly without being detected, and the logistical ramifications of their renegade status. The only thing missing was any reference to the Dornaani as aliens, which had been carefully firewalled from his voracious forays into the databanks.

At the end of his summary, he added a capstone that demonstrated that he already understood exactly why he'd been reanimated. "And that's why you need to get a better handle on the various coldcell technologies you're relying upon, and how to predict and cope with the impending failures."

Trevor saw Downing trying to hide a smile as his nephew nodded and uttered the understatement of the week: "Well, yes, I guess that about sums it up. So, um, where would you start?"

"Well, first I'd want to coordinate with Dr. Sleeman to see if she has pressing needs in any areas. But if I was a completely free agent, I'd go back over reports to look for any indications of post-revival amnesia or what might appear to be mild brain damage."

Downing was suddenly very interested. "Why?"

"Because if some of those prove to be mistaken diagnoses, they could point to the reason there are so many yellow lights on units that have no evidence of mechanical malfunction."

Trevor frowned. "Dr. Franklin suspected it might be the result of software or control failures. So we'd still be getting a warning even though the machinery checked out."

Tedders nodded. "And that could be one hundred percent correct. But it might also be a warning that the occupant's memory is in danger of being compromised."

Downing sat up very straight. "Explain that please, Doctor."

The doctor spread his hands. "Are you familiar with theta waves?"

Sleeman seemed to be in the act of dredging up old memories. Downing's blank stare was, Trevor guessed, a match for his own.

"Okay," said Tedders energetically, "so here's the short version. Theta waves are, crudely put, how your brain turns experiences into memory. They're particularly important when you sleep because that's when your brain takes all the day's data and, for lack of a better analogy, selectively copies it to your permanent memory."

"And this relates to coldcell failures... how?" Trevor asked.

"Your, uh, Terran coldcells have a separate system for maintaining theta waves. It's very straightforward and throws very clear warning codes if failure is imminent. But the units made by the, uh—Ktor? Yes? Well, they're kind of a puzzle box, but it seems that their theta wave functions are failing at almost three times the rate of our far more basic coldcells."

"Why?"

"Exactly what I want to find out. But I have a working hypothesis. Given what you've told me about the Ktor and why they might have grabbed us Lost Soldiers, I suspect they built in a default kill switch."

Responding to their horrified looks, Tedders hastened to explicate. "I mean kill the part of the system that maintains the occupant's theta waves if the Ktor lose possession of the coldcell." He considered. "When you recovered us, did you have to detach the cells from a power plant?"

Sleeman nodded stiffly. "It was inaccessible without major excavation. For which we had neither the tools nor the time."

The doctor nodded. "Understood. Here's my guess: the moment you detached the cells from their original power supply, you were also cutting an authorization signal hidden inside that feed."

Downing had grown slightly pale. "So we started a countdown clock."

Tedders sighed. "Very possibly so. That would explain why the failure rate is way over the estimated life cycle of the units, which should be *way* better than ours. And before you ask, I have no idea how long the clocks will run, or if they're all the same, or what happens when they run out. But since the malfunctions seem to be related to the theta wave maintenance, I think it will have something to do with memories. Anything from compromise or the inability to create new ones, or, well... everything is wiped. Clean slate. I suppose even complete shutdown of autonomic functions—heart, liver, you name it—is possible. Once a system has that much access to the control architecture of the brain and nervous system, you can't rule out anything."

Tedders looked at the stunned faces surrounding him. "I might be able to learn more about what to expect, and maybe some workarounds, if I could actually look at the units themselves."

Trevor swallowed. "I think you'll want to meet our hosts first."

"You mean this Alnduul fellow I keep hearing about?"

"Yes, that's the fellow. Come with us. He's waiting in a different part of the ship."

Tedders' answering smile was eager. "Great! I can't wait to see it all! And meet Alnduul!"

Trevor drew in a deep breath. "Yes, well, I think it might prove a life-changing experience."

PART TWO

Adversaries and Allies

Bactradgaria
June–July 2125

Chapter Thirteen

Bannor felt as much as saw the light of the sun creep over the horizon. The sharp chill began relenting even before the shadows were full. The steep, higher banks across the river leaned out of the fading darkness, their crests a mauve line against the slopes that fell away to their flanks and rear.

As he slipped around the edge of the hide shelter-half and tucked hard against the western side of the wadi's bed, he stepped wide to avoid a puddle—which was no longer there. He scanned the rest of the shelters huddled against the concealing side of the rocky gulch. The ground was finally drying out, and not a moment too soon.

He passed the trogans' shelters and discovered that Bey had already been there to rouse them. Without breaking stride, he decided to take the long route to the alcove they'd designated as their CP just before night closed in on the fifteenth day since they'd left Achgabab.

A march of twelve or thirteen days was what Vaagdjul and other sage h'achgai had predicted for reaching the rocky point on the eastern bank, just a few days north of Tajkor. However, a late spring gale swept in. With more sand than dust underfoot, the resulting mud hadn't been as bad as in the more southerly wastes, but it still slowed them by half. It also made it impossible to either get clean or eat anything other than dried strips of dustkine. More than once, members of the Crewe—including Bannor—had gazed wistfully toward their tightly packed Dornaani camp gear. But the decision to save it for emergencies was reinforced by the need to show their forces that they had the skill and toughness to live under the same conditions. Whether the trogs and related beings were receiving that message remained uncertain.

He edged around one of the large rock formations protruding from the wadi walls, tempted to scratch at the hair tunic in which he'd slept. Always an exercise in futility: the more he scratched, the more it itched. So the sound of squabbling a few meters up the wadi was a welcome distraction. Two of the trog porters—one from Forkus, one from the caravan—were arguing over the correct way to repair a large ration sack that had been damaged during the last near-pass of a tornado. Not good: of all mornings, this one required silence, speed, and discipline.

Bannor kept his voice low and without affect. "You."

Mouths still open, the trogs' hushed bickering ceased and their eyes met his. One swallowed nervously.

"No," he told them, and moved on.

He heard their mouths shut with audible snaps, managed to suppress a smile. More than any personnel he'd ever worked with, trogs responded to the "quiet and lethal" demeanor that had its exemplar in Tirolane. It wasn't that Rulaine or O'Garran or the others were lacking in the art of being daunting instructors, but even that required more nuance. On Bactradgaria, it was just as Bey had told them: until the locals became accustomed to the Crewe's leadership style, there was no point in dangling a carrot of possible approval. Only the stick—or the dead-eyed threat of it—guaranteed swift compliance.

And right now, and right here, that was good enough.

"Good morning, Colonel," murmured Riordan's voice from behind.

"Commodore," Bannor replied with a small grin. "Inspecting the troops?"

"You seem to have that well in hand. My concern is if we're ready to move at speed. Looks like that tornado's wind is going to cost us at least one of the travois."

"We'll be lucky if it's just the one, I think. Speaking of luck, did you have any luck getting Tirolane to open up about his past a little more? I saw you chatting with him after dinner."

Caine shook his head. "He begged off until after the attack."

"What's that about, do you think?"

"No idea. But I think we can wait that long."

"If only all things were like that. Such as today's chalk-talk. Ready for it? No last-minute tweaks?"

Riordan shook his head. "Given how limited our intel is, I don't see how there's much to reconsider." He smiled. "On the other hand: a plan without a last-minute change? Is this group even capable of that?"

Bannor made sure his smile didn't falter. "Who can tell?" Technically, it wasn't a lie.

But it sure did feel like one.

It was crowded in the natural alcove even without Yaargraukh, who had to lean in over hunched heads and shoulders to see the sand table of the projected battlefield. Eku, whose arm was finally out of a sling, was proving to be a good CO's adjutant: likely his permanent role. For Bannor, that was a relief: the factotum showed very few of the aptitudes that would make him a reliable soldier. However, he seemed well-suited for a senior staff officer—assuming he kept working on his brevity.

"Last night's final observation of the enemy confirmed their late arrival at the mooring point," the factotum continued. "However, given their proximity, we were limited to three minutes of monoscope surveillance with negligible elevation advantage."

"Yeah, but at least we didn't have to pretend to be acrobats," Duncan groused.

"Dinna bother me!" Katie smirked.

Bannor's grin was tempered by regret that they hadn't been able to build another human pyramid for their final surveillance. Just after noon the prior day, they'd come across a small, rocky hillock: the only terrain feature higher than two meters and not hopelessly slimed by the recent rains. Yaargraukh held the monoscope aloft on a pole, but even that didn't provide enough elevation to get the needed visible distance downriver or upriver. The former was the most important; they had to be certain their target had not already sailed south of them. The latter was to determine if their enemy was visible yet, and if so, their likely ETA at the natural mooring point where the Crewe hoped to intercept them.

It was Ayana who had suggested the expedient of a human pyramid, putting elfin Katie Somers at the top. Tottering as she stood on her toes and held the scoped pole aloft with both hands, they just managed to catch sight of a slowly approaching barge. Happily, the rest of their own march to the point of engagement was across flat terrain. But once they'd hidden themselves in the closest, driest wadi, they couldn't risk more than briefly raising the monoscope above its still-moist rim.

The sky was darkening into late dusk when the target finally arrived. Trogs dragged the barge up the bank to tie it off, snugged among the scattered rocks that offered the only mooring point on this stretch of the river. The only tactically significant observation was that not all the enemy forces were traveling aboard the flat-hulled vessel. Many, if not most, had paralleled its progress on the bank.

Ulchakh observed that this was common practice. Barges moving at speed became quite unstable on Bactradgaria's energetic and unpredictable rivers, and so, risked capsizing if they moved much faster than a trog might run. The h'achga trader was puzzled by one thing, however; for the barge to have already reached this point from Fragkork, anyone matching its progress on land would have had to run almost constantly, every day.

Eku suggested the answer. "As per the commodore's orders, the last watch raised the monoscope long enough to survey the enemy camp's thermal signatures. Detailed imagery was neither expected nor vouchsafed, but, even prone in sleep, the trogs' silhouettes were irregular and the heat levels were mottled rather than even."

"What would cause such an image?" Newton asked, arms crossing and brows lowering.

Bey glanced at Tirolane, who nodded encouragement. "At Tirolane's suggestion, I put this question to the trog shaman, Zhathragz. He is not certain, but he suspects they are *jalks*."

"Jalks?" echoed several of the Crewe.

"The term is built from the words for 'diseased' and 'dead'—or in this case, deadskins. But these no longer require the attention of a shaman to guide their actions; they are bound to him."

"How?" asked Dora as she crossed herself furtively.

It was Tirolane who answered. "The shaman compels a deadskin to swallow a sample of his or her blood or skin, mixed with a mold that works upon the nerves of whatever it infects. In a creature already suffering from s'rillor, the mold swiftly becomes dominant. In its natural state, it compels the host to feed. Continuously."

"And if the mold is infused with a sample of the shaman's blood or tissue?" Newton asked cooly.

"It is akin to the blood-bonding that x'qai have with the creatures that serve them, such as kiksla and kiktzo. In this way, their creator does not have to control them constantly through his arts; they remain mere extensions of his will until they die."

"Daaayumn!" O'Garran exhaled, stretching. "That sounds like what my meemaw's aunts called 'cabas.' That was their nasty way of referring to 'horses': people controlled or 'ridden' by spirits." He yawned. "My people were voudou folk. Didn't have much regard for Santeria. But I never could see that there was much of a difference."

"Sounds more like zombies," Girten grunted. "But I'm wondering why they bothered with a barge at all. Seems like the target hasn't been traveling much faster than if these, uh, jalks were marching and the rest were on dustkine."

Bey shook her head. "Greater safety is their primary intent, not speed. Caravans can be intercepted by any force that is willing to lay in wait. However, the barge beached there"—she gestured toward the river less than two kilometers to the west—"cannot be engaged when it is upon the water. That ensures near complete protection for as many as forty persons or the equivalent in cargo. Anything following along on land is expendable."

Tirolane nodded. "And in this case, such invulnerability will be the prime concern of those in command. If Cruvanor were to be informed, or come to suspect, that he is not there as a commander but as cargo, he would likely have tried to arrange an ambush. As for those on shore, I suspect the master of the barge was willing to accept the slower pace because they needed the bodies."

Duncan raised an eyebrow. "To serve as Judas goats?"

Tirolane shrugged. "Or bait, if they meant to hunt along the way."

"Or," Bey added reluctantly, "as food."

Bannor considered it a reassuring, yet sad, sign that not one of the Crewe evinced revulsion. He was pretty sure they felt it; they'd just ceased to be surprised by it. "Did you learn anything else about their unit composition?"

"Very little," Bey answered, "except that for such a strong force, they had very few fires."

Caine leaned forward. "What does that tell you?"

She shrugged. "That there will be more x'qa than usual and fewer trogs or other servitors. And the more full x'qai there are, the more likely that we will have to contend with blood-bonded kiksla or kiktzo. Also, some x'qai—but particularly the x'qnarz and x'qrukh—may have unique Talents. But inasmuch as we cannot know which or how many might have such powers, there is no way to be forearmed, only forewarned."

"In short, you can't plan for everything," Dora sighed.

Riordan smiled. "Hell, if we could, we wouldn't be on this, um, continent at all." He started to rise. "So, unless anyone has any last observations—?"

"Well," Duncan said, swallowing, "we did come up with one final refinement to the plan, Commodore."

One of Riordan's eyebrows rose. "'We'?"

Ayana nodded respectfully. "It is an item we suspected you might have overlooked. However, mentioning it before now could have been perceived as questioning your authority." She glanced at Bey, who was frowning, gaze moving from face to face among the Crewe.

Riordan scanned the same faces. "Your input doesn't undercut my authority unless I let it—which I assure you, I won't. Given all the professional experience in this circle, I'd be a lousy leader if I didn't invite maximum input, particularly before I put any of those same lives on the line. My only concern is that we always—*always*—have the best possible plan. So show me what you have."

Solsohn nodded. "Without more intel, it's as good a plan as anyone could come up with, sir. Except for the placement of one asset." Duncan picked up the white pebble just behind the center of the line of archers and crossbowmen positioned in the wadi closest to the enemy. He moved it to the other side of the wadi, where a small upright stick marked the command post. "Our suggestion is to move the CO off the line of engagement."

Riordan stared at the pebble and stick, and then, as Bannor had expected, turned to face *him*, not Solsohn. "You knew about this, of course."

"Of course," Bannor admitted. "Sir, with all due respect, the point of having a command post is to position the commander where he has a full view of the battlefield and can effectively control his forces."

Caine jutted his chin at the small imprint where the pebble had started out. "That's why I put myself where I did. As you know." He turned and looked around the faces of the Crewe. "All of you know that. Strategic opsec requires that we activate only a few radios for very limited use. Consequently, physical proximity between commanders and units is more important than ever. That's the only way to make sure orders get through."

Bannor nodded. "And they will: that's exactly why the rest of us, your cadre, are on the line. But with a force this large, and an enemy this unpredictable, there's a new consideration."

"Which is?"

O'Garran almost shouted, "Keeping you alive! Sir." He flinched when Riordan's eyes snapped toward his. "Commodore, please: no one knows better than I do how much officers willing to lead from the front boost unit morale and cohesion. But..." It was one of the first times Bannor had seen the chief look away from a staring match.

"But, sir," Duncan said calmly, "they lead from the front when they *have* to, not all the time."

Riordan crossed his arms. "Since arriving here, there hasn't been a lot of difference between the two. Besides, I can't lead *at all* without being where it matters: on the battlefield."

Duncan didn't look away. "Sir, 'being where it matters' is not the same thing as taking point every damned time."

Bannor saw Riordan's jaw set, knew he was going to dispute Solsohn's overstatement, didn't wait long enough for that to happen. "Commodore, you need to realize that what we can't afford to lose is *you*."

Yaargraukh chimed in from the other flank. "Caine Riordan, none of us dispute that until now we have had to deploy all our resources—and so, put all of them at risk—in every action. But note my qualifier: 'until now.' The time for that is past."

"And what are you suggesting? That I shouldn't take my fair share of the risks?"

"No, sir," Bannor said quietly, "but you shouldn't take as many as you do."

He'd hoped there would be a few silent moments for Caine to absorb that, but Katie barely waited one second. "Ye've been doing it from the start, even before we, eh, arrived from Shangri-la. You stayed out in the 'sunlight'—and very hard, gene-splitting sunlight it was!—far too long. Could've killed you outright. Or made you so sick once we were here that no one could have reached you in time to help. And it's not just the risks, sir! Even at the hovel, you insisted that you be the first to execute a pris—"

Bannor cut her off; invoking bloody details from Forkus would not help. "Sir, long before we got here, you proved . . . well, whatever you had to prove. Again and again, in Indonesia and all the places and lands beyond it." He waited until he was sure Riordan had seen his eyes. "So please: no more."

The muscles in Riordan's jaw bunched—which was apparently the last straw for Miles O'Garran. "Sir, I told you before and I'll tell you again: we're together because of you. Sure, if we were back in, uh, our own country, this would all roll differently. You're no slouch as a leader or a tactician, but rank notwithstanding, it normally wouldn't make sense to keep you in charge there, would it?"

Riordan's eyebrows rose at the SEAL's blunt assessment.

"Except we're *not* back home and our situation is *not* normal. We're in a blood-filled cesspool where, every time we get close to a battlefield, you get it in your head that you're *just* the CO.

"But you're not. You're also our general and strategist and diplomat and first-contact expert. And we can't afford to lose all *that*."

Bannor waited a beat before adding a formal coda. "Commodore, if you see any flaws in our recommendation, we'd be grateful to hear what they are before you decide on it."

Riordan didn't move, but the fists on his hips were white with contraction.

Dora leaned far across the sand table. "Boss, we're your Crewe. We're with you all the way. We all follow your orders, even me—and I never listen to *anybody*. But on this one point, Boss, please: listen to us. *All* of us. And not for your sake. For *ours*."

Riordan stared at the white pebble for several more seconds before he spoke. "I'll need twice the number of runners currently detailed to me. Eku, ready another monoscope and one more coil carbine." He looked around the group. "What's our highest priority?"

"Secure Cruvanor," answered Peter.

"Incorrect. That is our *objective*. Our highest *priority* is to live to fight another day: *all* of us." He glanced at Tirolane. "That way, we can keep after Cruvanor until we free him."

He straightened. "I will see every one of you back here, regardless of the outcome. Do you all agree with *that*?"

Bannor was part of the spontaneous chorus of "Yes, sir!"

"Then the plan is amended as you suggest. Thank you for your input. Get to your commands. We move out in fifteen minutes."

Not ten strides out of the alcove, Caine heard footsteps thumping into the moist wadi-silt behind him. He turned.

Bey caught up to him and matched his pace. "That was"—she sought the right word—"very different."

He raised an eyebrow. "The council? In what way?"

"I know they are all your friends, but still... it is an odd way to interact with one's leader."

He shrugged. "Well, as you said, they're my friends. And I did ask for their input."

"Even so, I have never met a leader like you."

He laughed. "Probably because I never intended to be one."

She stared at him. "How can that be?"

He shrugged. "I was an analyst."

"An analyst," she repeated. "What is that?"

Hell, sometimes I wondered the same thing. "An analyst is a person who gathers information about military situations and equipment. Then they project what an enemy might do, what their own side might do better, and even explore what new tools could be developed to improve its position."

She listened, shook her head as he concluded. "That does not surprise me. It is also not what strikes me as so odd."

"Well, what does, then?"

"Our leaders start as warriors," she explained in a very matter-of-fact tone. "Trog-kind do not have any leaders who do what you describe. I have only seen such positions given to humans and then, only to very old humans. They are considered too important to be allowed into combat."

She frowned. "But you do both. Quite well. I have seen it. But now your friends mean to protect you as if you are a snowhair."

He laughed. "A what?"

She both smiled and frowned at his reaction. "A snowhair. Because when humans grow very, very old, their hair grows white."

Riordan tilted his head. "Isn't it the same with trogs?"

She sighed. "I do not know. Few of any of the trog breeds live long enough to get truly white hair. A little grey, maybe, but that is all." She stared at him. "But your friends seem to consider you a snowhair already. Do they hope to keep you from being a warrior, also?"

He smiled. "That's a very good question. I think the answer is 'sometimes.' Also, not all of them would define 'warrior' the same way." He exhaled to purge annoyance. "There will be more conversations about what they brought up, but this is not the time for them. We have a battle to fight. And if I see the slightest hint that my friends are in danger—"

She held a hand up before him. "Leader Caine—or is this a moment where I may simply call you Caine?"

He nodded. "Of course."

"I do not speak to you as my chief, er, CO, but personally."

He was surprised when she put her hand on his arm, managed not to show it.

"Caine," she said, "remember this, please: they are right that they need you. And they are right in saying that you have nothing to prove." She glanced at her hand, snatched it away, but her eyes returned to his even more severe and intent. "You have nothing to prove. To anyone."

He had no idea of the expression on his face; her exhortation had surprised him so much that his now habitual command demeanor might have slipped.

Before he could think of a suitable response, she nodded and strode away toward the shelters of the trogs, muttering commands as she went.

Chapter Fourteen

Riordan lifted the monoscope just high enough to clear the rocks mottling the lip of the wadi farthest from the target. He jerked back from the eyepiece when the hideous forms of two x'qai of the same breed swam into focus, close enough to be on him in three of their leaping strides...

Idiot: you left it set for 10X magnification!

Riordan zoomed out to 4X. Now at the equivalent of a hundred meters' distance instead of forty, the wider view of the enemy's camp was both more useful and less startling. It was also relatively reassuring. The target's numbers and positions were close enough to the prior night's estimates that there was no reason to revise the plan. It also gave him the key piece of information asset he'd been lacking: a direct, daylight picture of the terrain in which his forces would engage the enemy.

The wadi that ran just beneath his CP meandered west toward the river, ending with a slight southerly slant. Weathered clusters of stone punctuated most of its sharper twists and turns. Fifty meters from the high-water bank, those protuberances became smaller, rounded, and scattered, ultimately straggling down to the water. Still, they formed a natural water-break, behind which the barge was beached. Sitting on a narrow fan of sand-and-scree, the rocks not only kept it from being washed back into the downriver current but from floating out during contraflow.

Opposite Riordan's CP, the skirt left by the wadi's overflows ran down gently, leveling off a dozen meters beyond its slightly raised lip. From its foot, the land ran south, widening out into the utterly flat wastes. However, from the southwest to northwest, the ground gradually mounted toward the modest plateau which had cut the wadi with untold springsworth of runoffs. From Riordan's vantage point, the anticipated battlefield resembled a low-rimmed amphitheater, a southern opening spreading away from the barge and camp, which marked the limit of the proscenium.

As suggested by the prior night's surveillance, those who'd slept ashore were still quite close to the barge. No tents had been pitched and their few fires had been small and allowed to burn out during the night. But rather than sleeping in fur piles, they were clumped in three immense heaps, each covered by patchwork hide tarps. Four killspawn were kicking at the edges of those covered lumps indifferently, atypically bored at the prospect of inflicting pain.

Time to get a look at the real *opposition.* Riordan tilted the monoscope upward and zoomed in to 8X.

The deck of the barge was alive with x'qai of different types, but two were noticeably larger than the rest, one of which had two pairs of arms and a somewhat feminine head atop a decidedly masculine torso. Caine command-blinked at the image-capture icon at the edge of the Dornaani helmet's HUD and panned slowly, trying to identify other creatures and get tallies of each kind.

After a minute, Riordan accepted that any further survey would be pointless. There was so much activity on the deck, so many bodies abruptly blocking his view and then gone again, that he didn't trust his head count. No reason to add more layers to already questionable data, so he tasked the suit to analyze the images and compare, assess, and separate by approximate types of beings. It returned numbers slightly different from his own, but the ones that mattered the most were identical: the total of each kind of x'qao.

He toggled the command channel open. "Heads up. Visuals incoming. Stand by for local assessment." Riordan popped the visor, nodded to Eku. "Mr. Eku, please set the images for a slow feed, then hold it at an angle that Ulchakh can see."

The factotum nodded, and Ulchakh, hunching to stay beneath the overhang of the rock shielding the CP from aerial eyes, leaned over to inspect the pictures. He grunted disagreeably several times before summarizing. "The leader will be one of the three greater x'qai. You know the one with many arms is an arurkré, yes?" He continued as soon as Riordan nodded. "It is never possible to know all the transformations they may have wrought upon themselves, including new Talents. But I do not think he is very far along that path."

"Why?"

"See his arms. They are as yours or mine. If that transformation happened many years ago, they would be heavy and powerful, almost with the appearance of stone.

"The smaller of the other two—the one that bears no resemblance to other creatures—is almost certainly a M'qrugth. The size and smoothness of his body suggest he is still quite young; likely less than a century. But he could still be very dangerous. In purebloods such as he, Talents arise early and are often those which are rare in other x'qa.

"The large, heavy one covered with bristles could be either a typical x'qao who has grown immense through centuries of conquest, or an arurkré who chose that form."

Riordan felt one of his eyebrows rise. "You sound far less confident of your second guess."

"You are correct. Look at its hands: too large and thick-fingered to handle tools or weapons well. As arurkrés grow older, they also grow wiser: enough to realize, and admit, the benefits of artifacts sized for hands like ours. So I cannot explain why, if his size is due to his age, he would have disregarded that advantage as he shaped his transformation."

"Give us your best guess: which one is the leader?"

Ulchakh sighed, leaned his head away from the helmet. "It could be any of those three. It depends on what our eyes cannot show us: their Talents and temperaments. Their age and patrons might also be factors, particularly in the case of the M'qrugth; they tend to be the elect—or the reviled—of those who shape their fates. They are too powerful for lieges not to use, but also too likely to become a rival."

Ulchakh squinted. "Notice also the trog giving orders to his own kind, the one with less armor and smaller weapons. If there are any jalks beneath those tarps, I suspect he is the shaman to whom they are bound. He is also likely to be tasked with the direction of whatever pawns and deadskins might be among them."

Over Newton's connection, Caine heard Craig's faint but distinctive plea: "Can't we just call 'em all zombies?"

Ulchakh probably hadn't heard, but if he had, probably would not have cared. "The shaman is not a leader above the killspawn, but do not underestimate his importance. The three greater x'qai understand that since beings like us are more vulnerable to injury, we possess greater caution and so, foresight. So a shaman may not give orders, but he may be tasked to advise his superiors on how to respond to an ambush."

"Bannor here, Ulchakh," Rulaine said loudly. "What kind of command struct—eh, leadership tiers are likely among the other x'qai?"

"Probably none. They will follow the greater ones' orders. If any among the same breed of x'qao are given more authority, the others would be more likely to argue than obey their commands. Particularly the five x'qiigh, those whose forms resemble what Newton calls entelodonts. Unless they fear their leaders, they rarely accept orders without some quarreling first. And they often get away with it. More so than other kinds."

"Why?" asked Baruch. "They seem no more dangerous than the others that we have seen. Less so, in fact."

"Yes, but they are far more likely to allow kiktzos to dwell upon them."

"So," Yaargraukh's voice rumbled, "they are the most likely to be aerial reconnaissance assets."

"Er, yes," Ulchakh confirmed after parsing the still unfamiliar terms. "You have counted ten other x'qai, yes?" He acknowledged Caine's nod. "The leaders will not want to risk the x'qiigh in a battle. Keeping them from rushing into it is a different matter."

"Bannor again, Ulchakh. Shouldn't there be more of the smaller x'qa, like we faced at the caravan?"

Ulchakh shook his head. "They would be too numerous and restless to carry on the barge. Keeping them ashore would be pointless: without several x'qai present to both remind and threaten them, they would chase after every bit of prey they saw."

Solsohn was almost whispering. "Commodore, did your suit ever get a final count on the tinkers running around on the deck?"

"Negative, Duncan. The top of their heads hardly show above the gunwales. Besides, they never stop moving." *Probably because the x'qai would have enjoyed stomping them "by mistake."* "But why the heck are you whispering?"

The IRIS sniper chuckled. "Because I forget that the kiktzo can't hear me."

"Are they still out over the river?"

"The HUD's motion and thermal sensors say so. But the movement pattern is damn odd, sir. Like they're circling each other and spiraling higher, rather than maintaining overwatch."

Ta'rel leaned over Ulchakh's shoulder. "I do not think they are lookouts, Duncan. At least, not anymore."

Riordan hated the additional seconds it would take, but asked anyway: "Give us your best guess at what Major Solsohn is seeing, Ta'rel. Quickly." *Because sooner rather than later, one of those damn bugs is going to see something—a shift in a shadow, a brief glint of metal—and we'll have lost the element of surprise.*

Ta'rel thought for a moment, then spoke very rapidly. "They are probably trying to chase off other kiktzo which have followed the barge from Fragkork. Lieges watch each other, particularly unusual activities such as sending cargo by barge rather than caravan. They will dispatch host x'qai to trail the barge at a distance. Their kiktzo keep watch. If the master of the barge detects them, he will send his own to kill or chase them off, helped by more expendable kiksla. I believe this is what Duncan is seeing."

Great: so whatever we do is going to show up on some other liege's scanner. "Well, the master of the barge *must* have kept some watching the area near the mooring."

Ta'rel's smile was rueful. "Never overestimate the x'qa capacity for concentration. Or their ability to keep more than one purpose in mind. Or for closely controlling minions whose brains are truly those of insects."

Riordan sensed that Ta'rel was on the verge of yet another pithy observation; he cut a hand in the air. "Point taken. Melee One and Melee Two?"

"Here," Yaargraukh answered. Riordan could see him, along with Tirolane, at the head of the two melee sections, huddled tight within the shadows of the corner where the wadi ran out from around the far side of the eastern plateau.

"Move to waypoint one. Firing Lines One and Two, you'll move as soon as the observation posts engage. Call out reactions to any of our movement."

"The ground is still moist enough that none of us are raising dust," Ayana murmured. Her voice was uneven. Panning over with the monoscope, Riordan saw her trotting at the head of her Support section, following in column behind Melee One and Two. "We have been very lucky to come so far without being observed,"

"I'll take every second of it," Riordan answered, "because that luck sure won't last forever."

"Indeed," Yaargraukh muttered. "It has just run out."

Chapter Fifteen

Riordan raised his monoscope higher to see whatever Yaargraukh had spotted.

The activity on the barge had become manic. Two of the three greater x'qai were issuing rapid orders with sharp landward gestures, roaring so loudly that they were easily audible along the wadi. Like ripples propagating from an impact point, their wild vitality radiated out, transferring to the other x'qai and the trogans. The third greater x'qai, the arurkré, leaped off the barge as if carrying the bow wave of that mad energy with him. Even as he did, the four x'qai already ashore tore the tarps away and started kicking savagely at the figures that lay beneath.

Jalks—at least forty of them—began rising. Slowly at first, but with fits and starts akin to malfunctioning machines, they jerked upright. Staggering after the x'qai that had roused them, many of them appeared misshapen, particularly around the head and neck. Perhaps a dozen trogs suffering from varying stages of s'rillor—impaired, as Ayana had named them collectively—followed behind, slower and gaunt.

Riordan considered rising to get a better look but in that same moment, had to wave Ulchakh back from trying the same thing.

Which decided Caine against doing so himself: *If it's not a good idea for Ulchakh to stand, it's no better for me.* Close upon the leeward side of a rocky outcropping and hidden beneath its north-leaning overhang, the CP was the only fixed element on the northern side of the wadi. Far enough from the others that it was unlikely to be discovered except by chance, Riordan had nevertheless taken a coil carbine—just in case. The single greatest risk to their plans was that a kiktzo would locate the CP and alert a x'qao capable of disabling a human at range. At the caravan ambush, some such Talent had taken Duncan out of action. But if the same thing happened here and broke both the primary and backup command links—

Riordan frowned as the enemy began to sort themselves out, their frantic action becoming more purposeful. Caine had hoped to get eyes-on Cruvanor and any other humans before opening fire, but in another few seconds, waiting for that would become a luxury they couldn't afford. He took a deep breath as he prepared to order Bannor and Duncan to begin the maneuver they'd nicknamed their "backfield crisscross"—

But instead of leading a general charge toward Yaargraukh's groups, the arurkré emerged from the milling mass of disease-ravaged trogs at a walk, all four arms waving for attention, two of the lesser x'qai from the barge following behind. He was flanked by the shaman and one of the trogans, who raised a bone pole.

A tattered white streamer ran fitfully out from it, riding the ebbs and flows of the morning breeze.

Girten's voice was audible over Newton's connection. "Are they—surrendering?"

Ulchakh heard it as well; he shook his head. "No. That banner signals they mean to parley. They have seen Yaargraukh's force."

As the small enemy delegation moved toward Melee One, the two greater x'qai on the barge continued their torrent of furious orders. In response, the tinkers began scurrying after several of the lesser x'qai. The trogans vaulted the gunwale, heading toward the jalks.

"Do I maintain my advance?" Yaargraukh asked.

"At a slow walk," Riordan muttered. "Duncan: sky sweep?"

"One of the bugs dogfighting over the river just started back this way. Can't see anything smaller."

The parley group continued to close, the arurkré gesturing for the jalks to stay in place like a stern owner commanding a pack of dogs.

"Bannor?"

"In position. Hand cannon ready. Standing by."

"Primary target is the young M'qrugth. Secondary target is the big x'qao with him."

"Acknowledged. Acquiring lock."

The parley group stopped. The arurkré raised his upper arms toward Yaargraukh and the section of warriors following him, palms high to halt them. His lower two arms now held curved swords. They did not merely shine but flashed: probably steel.

"Commodore?" asked the Hkh'Rkh.

"When he waves you to advance, meet him. Maximum gain on the audio pickups in your duty suit."

Even before the Hkh'Rkh could reply, the monster was gesturing for him to approach. "Audio is at maximum sensitivity. Do you wish me to go alone?"

Tirolane's voice added something in the background, too low and swift for Riordan to understand. "Couldn't make that out, Yaargraukh."

"Tirolane strongly urges that I go alone. He clearly wishes to accompany me, but indicates it would not be wise."

No time to get the reasoning behind either recommendation, so... do I trust Tirolane or not? "Follow his advice, Yaargraukh. Duncan?"

"Shifting my aimpoint to their parley group, sir."

Bannor added, "My HUD and hand cannon are now locked on the primary target. Monoscope is angled to observe the parley group. Prepared to retarget."

Sometimes, professionals executing a tight plan are faster than mindspeak. "Stand by."

Riordan craned his neck to get a better look at Yaargraukh: an imposing but solitary figure striding slowly toward five very lethal adversaries.

For a moment, the Hkh'Rkh's stolid advance was the only movement in the entirety of the surreal tableau.

Yaargraukh maintained his pace as he approached. Keeping his enemies waiting sent a strong message, but it also gave him enough time to study them in detail.

If the arurkré was young, it did not act so, and other than its lower arms, its body was made of hard, mature muscle shaped and scarred by equally hard use. The x'qai flanking it were of two different types. One reminded Yaargraukh of the terrestrial rodents that had become nuisances during the occupation of Indonesia. Neither he nor any of the Crewe had encountered this variety of killspawn—a x'qnarz—before, and he was not pleased that it was happening here: they were said to be craftiest of common x'qai.

The other, a x'qrukh, was one of the more common breeds; a broad creature, its body and head hinted at those of terrestrial muskolids, canids, and ursoids without exactly resembling any of them. Tasvar had counseled that they were the most dangerous x'qai simply because when others fled, this breed remained tenacious, sometimes dying where it stood—and so, inflicted just that many more casualties.

The trogan to the arurkré's left had an eye-shaped tattoo on its forehead: a truthteller like Bey. Not typically found among caravan guards, but perhaps the same factors that had compelled the liege to send this cargo by boat had shaped this choice as well.

The other trog's wild array of symbols, tattoos, and shriveled enemy trophy-parts confirmed he was a shaman. He was also a caver, whose sharp features, filed teeth, and red-cornea eyes did not radiate savagery nearly so much as his expression: eager, grinning bloodlust.

The arurkré held up a hand when Yaargraukh had closed to ten meters. He stopped.

The arurkré's black, and decidedly feminine, lips curled in revulsion, then confusion, and finally annoyance. "What are you?"

Intriguing. Pedigree before business. Rather like home. "Why do you ask? Do you believe your eyes deceive you?"

"No. I *know* they do not. But you are—you *cannot* be a grat'r."

"Can I not?"

"You are not like the ones at the front of your own formation." The arurkré jutted its pointed chin over the Hkh'Rkh's shoulder. "You are not like any I have seen. But nor are you a x'qao."

Careful: even if they cannot confirm their own kind by smell, they might have a Talent that does. "I suppose I do not *seem* to be a x'qao."

Its black lips parted to reveal sharklike teeth. "Do not lie to me."

"I did not. I spoke merely of the uncertainty of appearances." *Technically, all in the realm of truth—which is where I must remain, on the chance that they have a Talent to detect falsehoods.*

The arurkré shook the heavy tulwars it held in its smaller

hands. "What is your purpose here, creature? To enrage me with twisted words or to parley?"

"You requested the parley, not I."

The arurkré's eyes narrowed. "So I am speaking with the leader of the forces arrayed against us?"

Yaargraukh let his long, black tongue wriggle out. "Again, it might appear that way."

The x'qao leaned forward as if it might charge—but stopped suddenly, almost as if hitting an invisible barrier. With a thundering hiss like a venting steam pipe, it waved the shaman and trogan truthteller forward.

The shaman bowed slightly. "We would have speech, strange lord."

"I have come to hear it. And in doing so, I give you more time to prepare." Yaargraukh's shrug was a quake of his shoulders. "It shall avail you nothing. But speak quickly. My patience is considerable, but the same cannot be said for my warriors."

The caver made a show of peering around him. "With respect, strange lord, they are not so mighty a horde as your words suggest."

"How they fight, and other powers I possess—and you are unable to detect—are secrets you shall learn only by trying my patience again, and so, failing in whatever you hope to accomplish by this parley. About which: start by telling me why you need to parley at all."

"It is not a need, strange lord. Rather, it is a wish, that we might spare you and—"

"You would far sooner kill me than spare me anything. So I bid you answer my question quickly, or go back to your master and report how you ruined whatever he sent you to achieve."

The caver looked like a snarl was trying to burst out from his eyes. "My master has need of swift travel without impediments. I am sure that under other circumstances, he would have been delighted to indulge your thirst for battle."

The arurkré sneered from behind the shaman. "You are fortunate he is unwilling to spend the hour that it would take to slaughter all of you." The four-armed killspawn pantomimed peering behind Yaargraukh. "My mistake: *half* an hour. At most."

Yaargraukh rested his hand on one of the short broadswords that Achgabab's finest craftsmen had made to fit his hands. "Whoever speaks the next word, either it will explain your terms or will send me back to my forces so that we may then settle our affairs as I intended from the start."

The trogan truthteller stepped forward, hand out in an appeal for patience. "Strange lord, our arurkré master is as spirited for battle as yourself. However, please allow our shaman to put forward the inducements our master offers. Will you hear those terms?"

Yaargraukh ground his teeth in apparent frustration—but in so doing, closed a mandibular circuit that sent a single coded question to Riordan: accept or decline?

Riordan's voice came through the audio induction leads that lay along the resonance cavities near where his nominal head met his neck. "Two minutes. Then get out of there."

Yaargraukh raised his head. "Assuming your offer does not constitute an insult to my intelligence—or tactical advantage—then yes, I will hear your terms. You have half the grains of a small glass to present them. "

The caver offered another gallingly insincere semi-bow. "As the strange lord wishes. The terms are these—"

As the caver began his recitation of what his masters were offering in exchange for uncontested passage, Riordan glanced away from the Hkh'Rkh helmet's scratchy camera feed and surveyed the field. The only significant development was that the rest of the enemy trogans had positioned themselves to the flanks and rear of the jalks. Hardly surprising: even if under complete control, that mindless mass would certainly require drovers if it were to be delivered where and when it was needed on the battlefield.

Caine toggled the open channel and turned so that the others with radios could hear the exchange in the CP. "Ulchakh, about that trogan truthteller: does his presence mean they're dealing in good faith?"

Ulchakh frowned. "In cities and towns, most x'qai hold to commitments made before truthtellers and oathkeepers. But a chance encounter in the wastes, where there are no witnesses they deem important? They are unlikely to honor their pledges unless the other party is a liege or a known vassal."

"And is there any chance they'd believe we are?"

"I doubt it, Caine Riordan. If we were, why have we not shown our master's colors? But they may yet keep their word in order to avoid a battle they could otherwise avoid."

"So," Newton grumbled, "you are saying that sometimes, there *is* honor among thieves?"

"Among monsters, in this case. But yes"—Ulchakh's smile was grim—"when it suits them."

Duncan sighed. "Now *there's* the Bactradgaria I know and loathe."

"The clock is running out," Riordan interrupted. "Odds that this isn't a ruse?"

When no one offered an immediate answer, Ta'rel shrugged. "Probably not a ruse. Cruvanor is a cargo which they dare not lose."

"Tagawa here. Cruvanor remains unseen?"

Duncan answered. "Correct, although there's still a lot of activity on the barge. Looks like a dispute of some kind."

"Explain," Riordan ordered, watching the final seconds of Yaargraukh's allotted time tick away.

"The tinkers were apparently ordered to launch the boat. But they don't have enough muscle, and the x'qai aren't playing. The M'qrugth just got involved. Wait." A brief pause. "Are we *certain* that nothing lives in the river?"

"Yes," Riordan snapped. "Why?"

"Ripples, toward the back of the barge."

Damn. Had someone been rolled over the stern, or—?

"That could be x'qwogh," Ulchakh muttered, "the only x'qai that are at home in water."

Riordan clenched his teeth. *And with more kiktzo overhead or soon to be...* "Yaargraukh, tell the caver you have to bring the terms to your commander. Get back to your troops!"

As confused cross-talking marked the Hkh'Rkh's withdrawal from the parley group, Bannor calmly reported, "Two x'qai just jumped across the deck. They're holding someone down. I see legs thrashing. Either a trog or a human."

Riordan saw Yaargraukh accelerate his return, gesturing for his forces to meet him halfway. Even as he did, the arurkré and shaman turned and started back toward the various trogs waiting behind them. "Bannor, do you still have lock on primary target?"

"Affirmative, but we'll never get Cruvanor if they launch that boat."

"They won't if we take out their leadership."

The parley group was now running full speed back toward the jalks; the mass of them started forward with a collective jerk.

"Commodore," Yaargraukh muttered, "any new orders?"

"No. Follow the plan."

"And then?" Eku gulped, watching the field take on a shape that had not been anticipated in any of their planning sessions.

"And then we improvise. Bannor—"

"Movement in the water!" Duncan shouted. "And humans on the deck! They're up and moving toward—"

Riordan spoke loudly, but calmly, over Solsohn's report. "Bannor: execute crisscross."

Chapter Sixteen

"The ball is in play," Bannor Rulaine confirmed at the same moment he squeezed the trigger on the Dornaani hand cannon.

Set to deliver eleven thousand joules to the target, it quaked in his grip. A wisping tail of fire marked where the hypersonic tengram projectile not only split the air, but plasmated its own coating.

It hit the M'qrugth in the center of the sniper's triangle. Its upper torso vaporized, head and arms spinning away in different directions.

Rulaine barely saw it; he had already turned to run down the wadi's southern slope.

Duncan emerged from a shadowed crevice just east of him. Bannor unlimbered the hand cannon as he reached the floor of the gully and ran directly toward Solsohn.

Just like high school football, Rulaine reflected. Which was how their opening gambit got its name: "backfield crisscross." Although there were variations, the tactic was always the same: the running back who started with the ball cut across the backfield and handed it off to a back heading the opposite direction. The objective: trick the opposing team into chasing the wrong runner.

But here, it was the hand cannon being handed off, and the other running back was Duncan, who would remain in the shadows as he sprinted further west to a new firing position. Bannor, however, would keep running down the middle of the wadi's course. In broad daylight.

So get a good look, you damned kiktzos, he thought as he slowed. He held out the hand cannon, long enough to make sure that the weapon was snug in Solsohn's grip, and then sprinted even harder. *And now, come and get me.*

Rulaine headed toward the entry of a narrow crevice that branched off from the right side of the wadi. Every few steps, he glanced at the motion sensors in the Dornaani HUD. There wasn't even enough time to look over his shoulder, so that would have to do.

Even before Riordan heard the sharp thundercrack of the Dornaani weapon, he'd started down the list of orders it triggered. "Line Two, assume downslope positions. Yaargraukh, advance Melee One and Two. Do not charge the enemy until they are within twenty meters."

The Hkh'Rkh's reply was immediate. "Acknowledged."

Riordan made sure the archers of Line Two were tucking down behind the rocks and into the dips on the slope toward the battlefield before issuing more orders. "Line One, this is a change to your target list. Chief O'Garran is to switch to his carbine. He and Bannor will target the x'qiighs on the barge."

"Sir?" asked Newton.

Just do it! "Killing or even distracting x'qiighs means cutting links to the kiktzo, Line One. The rest of your group is to target the shaman in the retreating parley group. Signal the same to Bey in Line Two."

"But sir, the shaman is moving—sprinting."

Riordan kept his voice steady. "Line One, I repeat: full volley at the shaman, all bows and crossbows. If the target is immobilized, crossbows sustain fire until mission kill is confirmed. Bows will shift to original targeting of enemy field force after their second volley. Execute."

"Commodore," Baruch pressed, "most of our crossbowmen are not skilled enough to—"

"Doctor, do not question my orders. Full volley on the shaman." Riordan gave Baruch one second to reply. "Lieutenant, acknowledge your orders or turn your command over to Lieutenant Wu. Acknowledge."

"Acknowledge all, sir." Newton's voice was cold and irritated but chastened.

Which is good enough... for now. "Execute."

Before Riordan had finished the sentence, six crossbows sent a rattle of dull slaps along the southern lip of the wadi. A moment later, Bey and her eight archers released a rough, whispering volley in the same direction. The arurkré and two other killspawn with the parley group were hit, even though they weren't targets—yet. The truthteller's back sprouted a quarrel and a long shaft; he fell and did not move. But, miraculously—which, Riordan realized, might literally be the case—the shaman ran on, unscathed. Almost two thirds of the missiles cut the air above or between the fleeing parley group.

"Sir," Eku said softly, "these target changes are—"

"Are essential," Riordan snapped. "With the enemy's force split, we have an opportunity to eliminate key command-and-control elements *and* degrade their ability to use the kiktzos as observation platforms." On the slope behind Line One, their own tinkers were handing primed crossbows up to the marksmen along the lip as they received discharged ones in return, claw-foot reloaders at the ready.

Eku's frown threatened to become a request for tactical explication, but Ulchakh interrupted him with a nod. "Killspawn who cannot see all their enemies and are without strong leaders do not fare well in battle."

Riordan didn't have time to thank the old h'achga for deflecting the factotum; he was busy swinging the monoscope to scan along the trench line—*no, wadi*—running west from the CP. The same instant he began checking on the units there, Bannor ran out of the lower half of his field of view, heading toward the crevice. Riordan elevated the scope steadily, tracking over Line One, Line Two, and ending on Duncan, who was already clambering up the northern side of the wadi to his firing position. If any kiktzo or their ilk had seen him, they hadn't acted on it.

Suppressing a sigh of relief, Riordan turned the monoscope ninety degrees to face the battlefield. X'qai had begun to rally the jalks just as Yaargraukh rejoined Melees One and Two, with Support coming up behind.

Yaargraukh turned back toward the enemy as Melee One formed up on him. Its complement—his two grat'r vassals and the prakhbrai that O'Garran had dubbed trogres—leaned inward. "Orders," he bellowed.

Tirolane was already there. Orsost came running from the front of the twenty warriors of Melee Two, glanced at the forward-straining posture of Yaargraukh's grat'r bodyguard. "Do we charge?"

Yaargraukh's tongue snaked out. "My guards no doubt wish it. But we shall advance at the walk until I call for the trot. We shall not charge until they are very close. Tirolane, you are ready?"

The big, broad human nodded. "I am ready."

Yaargraukh's neck quivered. "I do not see how you can do what you propose."

Tirolane smiled. "You will have that answer soon enough."

Orsost pointed out into the field. "The bows and crossbows are at work... but not on the jalks!"

"Commodore Riordan sees new risks, but with them, new opportunities. The two x'qai that accompanied the arurkré are faltering." He drew his second broadsword. "Our part of the plan remains the same. Melee One," he shouted at the large creatures flanking him, "remain close. Do not fight as individuals. We are a wedge. If any of us lag, the wedge breaks. Hit and move on."

He turned toward Orsost. "Melee Two, capitalize on the shock of our attack. Dispatch or hobble any enemies left in our wake. Again, remain behind us as much as possible. But do not lag; without you, our rear is exposed to those we have left for you."

Yaargraukh leaned his mouth toward his helmet's audio pickup. "Ms. Tagawa."

"Ready."

"It is no longer advisable that you remain directly behind Melee Two. I regret having to ask this, but—"

"You need not ask," she replied. "You need Support to swing out to the south, so we may put oblique fire into the jalks as they close."

Orsost had overheard. "But if they swing toward your force, you have only eight scouts! And all but two are newly trained to their bows!"

Ayana's answer was what humans called "wry." "Tell Orsost I also have a grapple gun and Zhathragz. We are far from helpless."

"Excellent," Yaargraukh confirmed as he raised both swords in the direction of the arurkré-led jalks. Two more recently released x'qrukh were bounding from the barge to join them. "But you *must* remain screened until I call for you to swing out to the left."

"*Hai*," she replied.

"We begin," Yaargraukh ordered. Lowering his swords into positions of readiness, he began striding toward the enemy.

Bannor glanced up at the motion sensor; several *somethings* were behind him, closing from above. Rapidly.

He put out his free hand and slowed himself as he turned the corner into the crevice. Ignoring a closet-sized gash in the near wall, he started sprinting again.

From behind, a faint buzzing grew louder—then peaked; the motion contacts in his HUD had swerved into the passage behind him. They'd had to bank sharply to navigate its narrow entry.

Ten meters in, Rulaine stopped and spun.

Three insects—large and with heavy mandibles—abruptly transitioned from a forward rush into a hover. Their antennae flicked, flexed, measuring the suddenly turned prey for unexpected threat. They discovered none.

Bannor smiled. *None that they can recognize.* He toggled his HUD for visual sync mode . . . and tossed the Dornaani stun grenade in his left hand.

The insects, an instant away from driving home their attack, shied back again—just as the grenade's wild, asynchronous, ultrasonic bedlam struck them along with a shuddering, strobing blast of light in the most eye-gouging contrasts the spectrum offered.

Wings humming angrily, they backed up.

Just far enough.

"Now," Bannor said, his external speakers making it loud enough to be heard over the chainsaws-shredding-crystals cacophony.

The lightshow winked off. Enoran stepped out of the closet-sized notch in the side of the passage, holding a smoking canvas cylinder. With a curse that Bannor did not recognize, he underhanded it toward the insects and ducked back as it landed beneath them.

Just as Bannor reactivated the grenade's audio assault, the cylinder came apart with a crash of glass and a brittle shattering of dried bone. A cloud of roaring orange flame rushed out of it, flashing upward and along the narrow channel. The buzz of the insects became a desperate, stuttering screech. Two of them fluttered unevenly, one with a wing afire. The third veered madly forward to escape the flames, dropping when its wings scraped along the wall.

"Again," Bannor ordered.

Enoran leaned out and threw another object: a bag of charcoal dust. The same dust that had lined the canvas cylinder before its framed-fixed oil lamp shattered.

The insect with a burning wing lit like a torch and began bouncing wildly from wall to wall. The other that had been caught in the first flash of flame managed to avoid the second one, wings whining as it reoriented and sped upward out of the crevice, trailing smoke. And the third, just about to regain the air, skittered unevenly away from the blast and fell again. Right in front of Bannor.

Who leaned forward, a Dornaani molecular machete in his right hand as he blinked at the icon that deactivated the stun grenade. "Draw play complete," he muttered into his helmet's pickup as he put the blade through the chitin of the insect's head. He switched to a private channel. "And Caine?"

"Yes?"

"Just checking you're going to stay right where we need you."

Riordan's voice was flat. "I have no plans to move, XO. Now get your carbine in play and put some rounds on the x'qiigh back at the barge."

"On it, sir," Bannor answered, noticing that Caine hadn't actually agreed to stay put. Shaking his head, he picked up the inert grenade and motioned for Enoran to follow him.

Duncan Solsohn finished scaling the hand- and foothold rocks protruding from the northern slope of the wadi and crawled into the sniper's perch designated OP Two. First job: roll on his back so his HUD could scan the immediate overhead, motion sensors at maximum sensitivity.

Nothing. So maybe Bannor's "draw play" had attracted the attention of all the kiktzos that had angled toward the sound and flame-flutter of his first shot.

Cradling the hand cannon, Duncan hastily hooked in the first battery's power cable, rolled back onto his belly, and lifted his head enough to sweep a broader circle of sky.

The HUD's sensors revealed bogies in two rough groupings. One was still over the river, but it had shrunk considerably. The second was back near the barge, hovering rather than moving: almost certainly the majority of the kiktzos. There were a few other individual signals roving around the area, mostly standing off near the crossbowmen and archers of Lines One and Two. Probably kikslas that hadn't yet been vectored in on any specific targets. Which was odd, since the missile fire from the south lip of the wadi was pretty heavy. In addition to the eight archers, there were two weapons per crossbowman and a dedicated loader for each: effectively, every one of them was sending a quarrel downrange every twelve to fifteen seconds. *So why in hell aren't the x'qai using all the kikslas to interdict that base of fire?*

The moment Solsohn raised his monoscope over the rocky lip of OP Two, he had his answer.

Instead of being the nerve center of a focused response to the attack, the barge was a mass of bodies whirling in frenzied chaos. The remaining greater x'qao was bent over, either trying to pick something up or hold it down. The tinkers were rising away from the same point, several holding lengths of rope as the rest pointed angrily at that part of the deck. The other seven x'qai—two x'qrukh and all five x'qiigh—were alternatively roaring at each other and the creatures ashore, flexing their claws and fists violently as they leaned over the gunwale in eagerness to join the impending battle ashore. Occasionally their ire and attention was caught by whatever the last greater x'qao and the tinkers were focused upon: probably the humans, bound and prone, concealed behind the gunwale.

One of the x'qiigh flinched, then another as small wounds sprouted on both of them. Bannor and Miles had brought their carbines into play. The x'qai that hadn't been hit had the same reaction as those that had: shrieking fury as they were forced to duck and dodge rather than flinging themselves in the direction of the nearest enemy. Duncan wondered how long the presence of the greater x'qao could hold them in place while taking fire.

The answer wasn't long in coming. Abruptly, the first one that had been wounded—the largest x'qiigh—began spasming, as if its body were struggling to break free of its skin. With a squealing howl of rage and relief, it vaulted the gunwale and sped toward the point where the masses of its allies and enemies were poised to collide.

The greater x'qao snapped erect, sending a sharp, high screech in the wake of the x'qiigh, then stared, and finally, with gesture of both command and resignation, sent the barge's two remaining x'qrukh after it. Almost as an afterthought, it waved at something beyond the upriver gunwale.

Two x'qwogh leaped out of the river, long sheets of water arcing behind them as they cleared the barge's side. Solsohn barely noticed their strange amalgamation of reptilian and batrachian features, or a pair of indolent, irregular ripples still troubling the water. He finally had a clear shot on the last leader aboard the barge.

He rose just enough to swing the hand cannon toward it and blinked on the greater x'qai to fix it as the primary target. The aimpoint guidons flashed into existence, urging him to adjust aim slightly to the right...

Riordan's voice almost startled him. "OP Two?"

"Acquiring primary target now—shit!"

"Report."

"The big one just disappeared!" But no, that wasn't quite right. Solsohn could still see a fuzzy shape where the greater x'qao had been. "I think—I think it's got some kind of chameleon skin."

"With that fur?" Riordan's voice was calmly incredulous.

"Yeah: I think that's why I can see the outline at all. Bad design feature." But still enough to screw up target lock. *However, assuming the camouflaging effect is strictly visual...* "Shifting primary targeting to thermal sensors. HUD is recalibrating."

As it did, Duncan peripherally noted that the disturbance in the water was now on either side of the barge, but even closer to shore than the two x'qwogh which had leapt over the gunwale. *That way, they can join their two cousins or run up the bank to defend either flank.*

The guidons reappeared in his HUD. He swung the weapon as they directed—and swore. "God *damn* it!"

Riordan's voice was flat. "Report."

"That bastard x'qao boss just picked up a human. Using him as a shield."

"Description."

Solsohn sighed. "He's a ringer for Orsost's description of Cruvanor: silver hair, weathered face, creased skin." *Making him the oldest human I've seen on this damned planet.*

"Concur it's Cruvanor," Riordan replied. Then, after a pause: "Is the primary target tall enough to be taken with a high shot, above Cruvanor?"

"Negative. Might be if target was standing at full height, but he's not being sloppy. Sorry, Commodore: no shot."

A longer pause, during which the x'qao leader snarled orders at the tinkers. To a one, they dropped the gaff poles they'd just picked up and set about readying short bows and javelins. No, Duncan realized, not javelins but darts for the atlatls several were pulling from their belts.

Riordan's voice returned, crisp with determination. "How many x'qiigh are still on the barge?"

"Four, sir," Solsohn replied—just as it was roiled by more furious activity. A human warrior jumped up from the deck toward the x'qao holding Cruvanor. One of the x'qwogh leaped to intercept him, jaws distended into a display of large, curved teeth.

The leader howled at it. The x'qwogh landed with an annoyed snarl; rearing back, it spared the human certain death in its jaws, but not the force of a backhand. Flung almost three meters, the warrior crashed into the gunwale and slid to the deck, limp. Cruvanor clawed to break out of his captor's grip, but at a blink from the greater x'qao, his silver head lolled.

During the two seconds of shipside chaos, Riordan either had a partial view of it or was given a report. "Duncan, status: was Cruvanor hit? Was it friendly fire?"

"Negative to both, sir. Looks like the leader used a Talent that put the old guy's lights out. Still no shot on primary target, sir. But I could take out the damn frogator who smacked Cruvanor's rescuer into next week."

"Negative. You will shift targeting to the x'qiigh."

"Sir, say again? I am to shift target *away* from the leader?"

"Confirmed, Major. Reduce charge to mission-kill against x'qiighs. And they're clustered, maybe enough for column ambush protocol two."

Duncan had to drag his eyes off the greater x'qao before he could see that Riordan might be right about the engagement strategy: the three x'qiigh were, roughly speaking, arrayed in ranged sequence: front, middle, rear.

Solsohn worked quickly, but without rushing. A few extra seconds at the start often reaped large benefits afterward. With the HUD showing the target at one hundred eighty meters, he selected forty-three hundred joules of exit energy, and drifted the cross hairs across all three x'qiigh, blinking on each. He designated the rearmost as primary, the lead as secondary, and then let the weapon's guidons bring him back to his first target. The cross hairs flashed rapidly as he neared it, then stayed lit as the guidon glowed bright aqua: the weapon had acquired and locked on the target's center of mass. Duncan squeezed the trigger.

The hand cannon quaked; the hypersonic projectile split the air like a crisp, close thunderclap. But he barely saw the round punch a hole ten centimeters beneath the base of its neck: Solsohn was already following the guidons to the first in line.

That x'qiigh had twisted to see what had happened to the one in the rear, and had already spun back. It turned slowly as its eyes swept the land to the north and west: the general direction from which its cousin's death had arrived. And just in time to present a full frontal target when Duncan squeezed the trigger again.

Solsohn cursed; for some reason, the round dropped beneath the HUD's aimpoint and hit the monster in its protuberant belly. The entry point cratered slightly, but the exit generated a jet of ichor and fragments: of what, Duncan had no time or need to know. He jogged the gun to the left.

Perhaps the last of the three x'qiighs wasn't stupider than the other two—the interval between the shots was less than four seconds—but he was only starting to emerge from a state of utter bewilderment when Solsohn snugged his cheek close to the Dornaani weapon. As the cross hairs glowed solid, he murmured, "Poor little monkey"—*well, piggy*—"in the middle" and squeezed the trigger.

The creature was turning to flee when the round impacted its flank, hitting ribs and possibly penetrating to the spine. Bone fragments erupted outward along with the green-mauve mass of its species' peculiar lung tissue. The x'qiigh collapsed. Its death cries were an arresting combination of ursine roars and porcine squeals.

"Commodore," Solsohn muttered, checking the weapon's diagnostic panel, "that is three for three. Target the x'qwogh?" Bannor and Miles had already trained their carbines toward the amphibian monstrosities, the low-power plinking inflicting more agitation than damage.

"Good shooting, but negative on the x'qwogh. Stand by." Duncan listened as Riordan ordered Newton to pass new orders to Bey's Line Two: target the mixed mass of jalks and x'qai heading toward Yaargraukh's forces. "OP Two," Caine resumed, "leader is primary target, again."

"Sir, just to confirm: I still have no shot on that target. He might as well be wearing Cruvanor like an apron."

"Understood. Engage at your discretion."

Well, with that order, what else can I do? "Roger that, sir. Looking for the shot, awaiting further orders."

He did however, steal a moment to glance toward the two masses that were almost in contact on the flatland below. The enemy had left a thin scattering of bodies in its wake. "Good luck, Yaargraukh," Solsohn thought. With a sigh, he kept the HUD's cross hairs near the newly furious—and desperate—greater x'qao on the barge.

Chapter Seventeen

The two grat'r flanking Yaargraukh kept leaning forward, as if straining at invisible leashes that kept them from launching into a headlong charge. Still, with frequent side glances, they kept pace with their lord's steady tread, their self-restraint buttressed by the quiet patience of the two unusually astute and alert trogres who rounded out Melee One. Being brothers clearly reinforced their own discipline; when one became a little too eager, the other maintained a steadying example. But their origins—sons of the most revered warrior in their race's living memory—could have played a role as well; their sire's famed composure in the face of adversity may have been inherited as much as emulated.

They also had their father's curiosity, apparently. The one to the left speculated, "Surely, they will charge soon, Leader Yaargraukh. What are your orders?"

The Hkh'Rkh reassessed the distance to the enemy. "We continue to advance at the walk. And wait."

One of the grat'r raised its head. "Wait why, Lord?"

"For the bowmen to do their work." Yaargraukh gestured with one of his swords.

The arrows arcing into the mass of the oncoming jalks were wounding many, dropping a few, but some also struck the arurkré and the two, already feathered x'qao that had accompanied it to the parley. One, the much smaller x'qnarz, fell and did not move. The larger x'qrukh was limping but kept up with its leader. The four that had kicked the jalks awake were mixed in among them. Just behind, the last two that had been released from the barge glanced north as if they might rush the archers. Between the uncertain odds of surviving that charge into massed fire and the tantalizing proximity of Yaargraukh's smaller force, they pressed forward.

"Fight soon?" the senior grat'r muttered querulously.

"Very soon," Yaargraukh answered with a pony-nod. Despite the slight uphill grade as the land rose toward the plateau, neither the jalks nor the x'qai were slowing. Still, any energy they spent running was energy they would not have for fighting. Indeed, the impaired were slowly but steadily falling to the rear of the formation.

"We are not formed to receive a charge," observed the second trogre in a respectful tone.

"Because we shall not do so," Yaargraukh replied. "We shall countercharge. Widen your strides." He glanced back at Tirolane. The human increased his gait to draw alongside the Hkh'Rkh, who spoke loudly enough to be heard by both Melee One and Two. "Stay close to your comrades. Tight formation. Now, at the trot: follow me."

In the background, distant cries of triumph came in over Newton's open channel. Craning his long neck, he spotted what had stirred the marksmen of Lines One and Two. Not only had the last of the arurkré's original parley guards toppled, but so had the shaman, despite having veered south to avoid their volleys. He'd just gone down, one quarrel in his leg and another in his torso. However, the jalks showed no sign of wavering; perhaps even his death would fail to unravel the power of his last command to them.

Tirolane spoke loud enough to be heard over the growing war cries of the kajhs behind them. "With your permission, I shall lead the charge."

Yaargraukh did not have time to express his surprise. "You are already at the front."

"I mean beyond you, just a few strides." The human's eyes were fixed on the arurkré; impatient to kill its foes, the greater x'qao's charge had taken it slightly beyond the wavefront of the jalks and leading x'qrukh.

"That does not sound wise."

"I know—but it is. Please: trust me."

Had Yaargraukh ever detected the faintest hint of recklessness or arrogance in Tirolane, he would have denied the request. But, since the human had invariably demonstrated quite the opposite, he answered, "Then you had best begin now."

Tirolane grinned—it was neither joy nor mirth—and began stretching his strides into a run.

Two running steps onward and Yaargraukh saw a potentially fatal problem. "Tirolane! Your armor!"

The human only broke stride enough to call back, "What of it?"

"It is gapping at the back." Yaargraukh had never before noticed how peculiar the chainmail's fastenings were. "It might come undone!"

Tirolane flashed a smile: friendly, but also a bit—impish? "No, it is just a unique design." Brandishing his bastard sword in one hand, the human turned and charged straight at the arurkré. Roaring savage delight at the challenge, the x'qao ran to meet it, two arms waving its tulwars, the other two now brandishing long daggers, held back in readiness.

Suicide, Yaargraukh thought as the distance between the human and the much larger monstrosity closed—until the human stopped abruptly. Perhaps sanity had prevailed over whatever propelled Tirolane into his mad, headlong charge.

But the human had not stopped to flee; instead he stood ready and lifted his left hand.

The instant Tirolane's palm was fully presented to it, the arurkré spasmed and its eyes dulled, senseless.

Before the muscular contractions had propagated the length of its body, Tirolane closed the last few meters in a single twisting leap: a fluid motion that owed as much to dance as swordsmanship. As he slipped past the aimless flapping of all four of the x'qao's weapons, he dipped his sword just enough to get his left hand on the grip before thrusting upward.

Back muscles bulging with the effort, Tirolane drove the point upward into the flesh just under the arurkré's chin.

Yaargraukh was already too surprised to be freshly amazed when the weapon's tip jetted up through the monster's heavy skull at its hairline. X'qao flesh was hard to pierce, their bone even harder; Tirolane's feat was not within the bounds of sense or reason.

Yet neither kept the monster from collapsing in a heap.

Tirolane turned outside the arc of its nerveless topple, facing Yaargraukh, who had managed to keep his advance to a trot, despite his misgivings and astonishment. Behind the swordsman, the jalks kept coming, but the closest x'qrukhs slowed, unable or unwilling to believe what they had just witnessed.

"You shall lead your followers to great victory!" the human shouted at the Hkh'Rkh, adjusting his armor.

"*We* shall do so!" the Hkh'Rkh objected, breaking stride.

"Not this day, friend. The rest is yours!" Tirolane pulled an object from his belt: surely, his flintlock pistol, Yaargraukh surmised. But what he held as he drew in the flapping folds of his cloak was a small, plain bag.

The jalks were almost upon him.

"Beware!" Yaargraukh shouted, sprinting to defend the remarkable, but foolish, human.

Who, with an apologetic smile, dashed the bag to his feet.

Smoke erupted upward and outward.

Yaargraukh was tempted to run headlong into the billowing cloud, but urgent events pulled his eyes and attention elsewhere. Newton was reporting that the shaman had been hit several more times and was apparently KIA. As if to confirm that assessment, the solid mass of charging jalks abruptly became a rapidly diffusing mob, some of which were now stopping to eat their own dead. Those that kept running forward did so without any consideration of the actions of the rest. The trogan drovers, who had been about to swing wide and take Yaargraukh's own troops under fire with their short bows, abandoned that plan in an attempt to ensure that the jalks completed the charge.

Beyond them, the last two x'qrukhs to jump from the barge were staggering under a withering barrage from the crossbows of Line One. Yaargraukh doubted they would live long enough to trade any blows. The bow fire into the enemy's van was beginning to take a toll, not only upon the jalks, but the four x'qrukhs around which they had formed. None of the latter had fallen yet, but most of them were limping or bleeding—and were ready fodder for the tightly packed wedges of Melee One and Two.

The smoke produced by Tirolane's mysterious bag dissipated just as Yaargraukh reached it. On the ground was the human's armor, its peculiarity revealed; it was fastened by cable-linked clasps that ran down its back. One tug on that cable and a properly trained person would likely be able to shrug out of it in a second or two.

Or maybe less, Yaargraukh conceded. He raised both swords toward the enemy, and in the hooting roars that were among the most ancient birthrights of all Hkh'Rkh warriors, he shouted, "Tighten ranks! Charge!"

Riordan blinked: a puff of smoke, a brief heat-shimmer distortion just beyond it, and then there was nothing where Tirolane had been an instant before. Except Yaargraukh who, undeterred by the warrior's disappearance, called for the charge at the very moment the enemy was not just losing cohesion but becoming an atomized rabble. That had been the point of making the shaman a priority target, but if it had taken even two seconds longer...

The last of the two x'qai who'd broken away from the barge went down. Two of the ones mixed in with the jalks were beginning to resemble pin cushions. Melee One crashed headlong into the less focused jalks and put a deep dent in that mass as they pushed to reach the two closest x'qrukh. Melee Two stayed close behind them, mostly finishing off the wounded and pushing back those jalks who, attracted simply by combat and the smell of uninfected bodies, drifted in behind Melee One once its bow shock had passed them.

Despite surprises and uncertainties, the plan had still not come apart. But the outcome was still far from certain. If the Support section under Ayana were engaged, its recently trained scout-archers hadn't the numbers or experience to keep from being not merely scattered, but run down and devoured where they fell. And with every passing second, that became the likely outcome if Yaargraukh didn't have them swing southward...

"Commodore, this is CP Two." Solsohn's voice sounded perplexed, even confused. "Did you happen to see a—a distortion near that puff of smoke?"

"No—well, yes, maybe. Anyone else?" Negatives came in on all other channels. *They wouldn't have been looking that way, anyhow. Speaking of which*—"How did *you* see it, Major?"

"Sir, just because I'm eyes-on the primary target doesn't mean I haven't called up a thumbnail screen to show me the main battlefield through my monoscope. Right after Tirolane, well, disappeared, I *did* angle the HUD in that direction for a second."

"And?"

"Nothing to see there, but the motion sensor started throwing out intermittent contacts just after the smoke appeared."

"Contacts? Where?"

"Vectoring toward the river."

For one instant, Riordan considered those contacts just one more troubling mystery—before realizing they might be the key to understanding what had happened. "Duncan, those contacts: were they vectoring toward the river or the *barge*?"

"Can't say, sir," Solsohn replied. "Signals were too choppy for—"

His HUD's motion sensor pinged again—right next to the barge. In fact, the signal was headed straight toward—

The greater x'qao flinched as if startled, glanced around—just as Tirolane's head, and then arm, emerged out of a watery-wavering heat mirage that appeared next to the monster. In his hand was his fully cocked flintlock pistol—aimed directly into the greater x'qao's right ear.

Even Duncan's experience as a sniper did not prepare him for the split-second chaos-cascade that followed. The weapon went off. The creature's head snapped over and it started to fall. Cruvanor dropped out of its nerveless hands. A x'qwogh and the last x'qiigh leaped toward Tirolane, whose naked body appeared as if he were casting off a robe with one hand—which is exactly what he was doing. As its folds fell away, the sword in his other hand flashed to meet the x'qwogh in mid-leap.

Tirolane's bastard sword was already slashing sideways at the x'qwogh's outstretched claws before Duncan could send an emergency thumbnail pop-up to the other Dornaani helmets. "CP, situation on the barge. Primary target is down . . . but Christ, Tirolane is alone against three x'qai. Advise!"

The scant second of silence between the last word of his sitrep and Riordan's reply felt like five minutes. "OP Two, new targets: any x'qao threatening Tirolane. Maintain safety margin. Miles, Bannor, Bey, Yidreg: same orders. Target high; friendlies are on the deck. Over."

Affirmatives—either direct or on behalf of those without comms—flooded in as Riordan instructed Bannor and Miles to expend maximum charge in each shot.

Solsohn had swung his weapon around to the frantic scrum on the deck—and realized: *Shit, they're moving so much that I can't pre-designate. Well, old school, then.*

The ebb and flow of the melee on the barge had a rhythm to it, at least enough to discern that when Tirolane's attackers jumped back, Duncan might have just enough clearance to take a shot. *But damn it: the* waiting*. . .!*

Yaargraukh was not in time to intercede on behalf of the grat'r that had followed him since Forkus: as impetuous as ever, it attacked the only unwounded x'qrukh without waiting for a partner.

The x'qao stood as if waiting for the blow, until, in the blink of an eye, it dodged right. Unable to correct in time, the grat'r overextended—and the killspawn grabbed its unarmored arm, claws piercing it. Before Yaargraukh's guard could hoot-moan in pain, the x'qrukh leaned over and, with one wrenching gnash of its serrated jaws, ripped and then severed the arm at the shoulder. Only then did the killspawn detect something approaching from its flank. It started to turn—

Yaargraukh cut high. Leering, the x'qrukh sidestepped—and discovered that the Hkh'Rkh's overhand attack had been a feint. Sweeping low, the other blade hit the killspawn just above the ankle. It went over, roaring, struggling to regain its feet—

Which made it that much easier for Yaargraukh to cut sideways into its neck, deep enough to breach its windpipe. The x'qao wheeze-shrieked and fell back, claws scrabbling futilely after the Hkh'Rkh which had killed it. Who, striding past, tossed a single instruction over his shoulder to the trogan kajhs of Melee Two: "Finish it."

Yaargraukh took five steps before encountering a jalk that was already half dead. Finishing it out of mercy as well as duty, he glanced around and realized that the battle was won. It was not over, but the tide had turned beyond reversal, particularly after Ayana's Support section had shifted south and outward from the point of contact, giving them the angle they needed to fire into the jalks.

The scouts-turned-archers had been surprisingly effective, apparently bearing out Bey's assurance that the shaman, Zhathragz, had access to mysteries and miracles that would aid them. And if that was indeed the cause, it required exacting investigation, although Yaargraukh had grim forebodings of what else might be revealed.

The enemy's trogans had been unsuccessful in their attempts to keep the jalks herded into an effective force. But by the time they abandoned their efforts, they had become too dispersed to regroup for a fighting retreat. Most died where they fell, except those whose entreaties for quarter were heard by a fellow trogan or Orsost. Their fate would be decided later, unless the severity of their wounds ended the discussion before it could begin.

At the southern edge of the battlefield, Yaargraukh spied a tall, heavy figure—one of the x'qrukh—moving in an unexpected direction: back toward the flatland leading south along the river. He allowed himself a satisfied grumble and a spare moment to watch as the other surviving x'qai sped—or in one case, limped—after him.

Riordan's voice was loud in his helmet. "You heard Duncan's sitrep?"

"Affirmative."

"Line One is shifting fire to the barge."

"Wise. We have matters in hand, here. Once I have cleared a corridor, I shall send a detachment to help secure the objective."

"Bravo Zulu. Riordan out."

Yaargraukh used the comparatively archaic Hkh'Rkh paging system to contact Newton.

"Baruch, go."

"Dr. Baruch, please alert both Lines to watch for us entering their field of fire, both as we complete our operations here and move toward the barge. Yaargraukh out."

Duncan finally had a clear shot at the last dodging and leaping x'qiigh; he squeezed the trigger.

Unfortunately, a clear shot wasn't always enough if the target was a killspawn operating at that species' combat speeds: the x'qiigh was already jumping forward again when the weapon cracked.

On the other hand, a shot from the Dornaani hand cannon didn't have to be perfect: it just had to hit. Although the x'qiigh's torso was already blocked by one of the x'qwogh attacking Tirolane, part of its flank and leg were still exposed. The projectile impacted the hip joint, blowing a hemi-circular chunk out of the creature. Its leg collapsed, sprawling it against the killspawn that had been screening it.

That x'qwogh and its cousin—the last aboard the barge—were startled, then backed away, ducking as crossbow bolts and survival rifle projectiles began peppering them.

The resulting decrease in violent movement on the deck improved Duncan's situational awareness—which was why he peripherally detected a hint of motion he would certainly have missed earlier.

The greater x'qao, whom he'd presumed dead when it fell, lurched up behind Tirolane, claws raised, head a one-eyed and bloody ruin.

There was no time to think, no time to engage the target designation system. Duncan reflexively increased the weapon's charge as he swung just far enough so that the crosshairs flickered on the only part of the target higher than Tirolane's head: the bulging muscle joining the shoulder to the neck.

Good enough. Solsohn squeezed the trigger.

It was not a solid hit: only a grazing shot along the neck. But sixty-five hundred joules blasted away enough of the tissue so that the leader's head hinged sharply sideways as it roar-gargled through a gout of blood.

Riordan's voice was urgent and far too loud. "All units: fire on primary target and maintain!"

Bolts, quarrels, four gram slugs from the coil carbines, and two more from the hand cannon cut the air over the barge like a sideways hailstorm. The remaining x'qwogh glanced at each other and came to the same conclusion at the same instant: they leaped long and low for the water. And apparently they kept on going down into the depths: despite his fine vantage point, Solsohn never saw a single bubble marking their submerged route of escape. Just two faint, final ripples where the other two had lurked; either they'd never received a summons from their leader or elected to ignore it.

Duncan smiled. "So, CO: *that's* why x'qwogh weren't a priority."

Riordan's reply was wry. "I have a simple philosophy about enemies. Doesn't really matter if they're a mission kill; if they're running like hell, that's good enough."

"Amen," added Bannor.

"Yaargraukh, here. The field is clear. I shall secure the barge."

"I'll be right behind you," Riordan added. "Everyone else: hold positions and maintain overwatch."

Riordan was running to catch up with Yaargraukh's warriors at the barge, but the Hkh'Rkh held one hand out stiffly behind his large body. "Commodore, you agreed to limit your risks." Then he led Melee One over the gunwale.

His head-neck swiveled slowly from side to side before he straightened. "Please join us, Commodore." He waved for several of the trogans from Melee Two to follow.

Riordan scanned the deck as he jumped aboard. Cruvanor and the human who had leapt to his defense were senseless but alive. There were three other bound humans and, beyond them, a mass of tinkers cowering behind the weapons they'd dropped. Several began prostrating themselves.

Tirolane was propped up against the body of the x'qao he'd dropped with his pistol. His torso and one leg were scored with deep red gashes that had painted most of his body bright red. The big swordsman smiled briefly and nodded, but his motions were slower, less assured, than usual.

Riordan spoke into his comm pickup as he popped the visor. "Doctor Baruch, gather security and get here on the double. At least one surgical case, two more for assessment." He hastened toward Tirolane, two sets of rapid footfalls—a pair of Yaargraukh's trogans—keeping pace behind him: *So I've got bodyguards, now.* He knelt down so that the big warrior did not have to look up. "Tirolane, the doctor will be here in a few minutes."

The swordsman smiled again. "These wounds are not the worst I've known."

Riordan's eyes registered the crosshatched cicatrices that covered almost half of the swordsman's torso and parts of every limb. "Even so, I'll just stay here until the doctor arrives." He palmed the Dornaani autoinjector he'd torn out of his kit while sprinting to the river. Tirolane didn't appear to be in immediate danger, but with wounds like those...

"Your company is very welcome," the other answered, his eyes wavering slightly.

"While we wait, I have a question." Which wasn't pressing, but keeping him alert might help buy extra time.

"Yes?"

Riordan jerked his head in the direction of the battlefield. "That was quite a disappearing act you pulled back there. Would you care to explain it?"

Tirolane's lips bent into a small smile. "No. Not yet. But you could ask a *different* question."

Riordan smiled back. "That's actually the only one I have."

Tirolane nodded gingerly. "I am not surprised. Fortunately, I see the doctor coming, so we need not fear an awkward silence."

Chapter Eighteen

Riordan surveyed the battlefield. Yaargraukh was the only figure still standing in it as he reached down toward the wounded grat'r. It struggled to rise, but could not. Given its doglike backward knee, it could barely manage to hold itself up on trembling arms. It lifted one of them, possibly in supplication—

But instead, last supporting arm tremoring, it reached an unsteady hand for the nearest of Yaargraukh's two swords. The Hkh'Rkh straightened, seemed about to step back... but then his pony-neck sank slowly. The grat'r tugged on the sword, bringing it into contact with the top of its own head. It was the same position with which it had appealed for Yaargraukh to accept its oath of servitude back in Forkus.

The Hkh'Rkh did not move, might have been speaking. The grat'r's head wobbled sharply: as emphatic a negation as its wounds allowed. Yaargraukh's neck and spine straightened as the grat'r released the sword so that its lord could hold it high enough to strike a final, merciful blow.

Riordan turned away, not merely to avoid seeing the grim conclusion, but because of a sudden, related image: his own execution of the first of eight traitorous prisoners taken during their rescue of Eku. The memory pulled at him like a black undertow...

Get moving. Do something. Now.

Riordan closed the last few meters to the impromptu gathering of his command staff near the materiel being unloaded from the barge. Riordan returned their nods and glanced upward, scanning the sky. "How soon before the porters get here?"

"The runner should return with them very shortly." Bey frowned and clarified. "Five of your minutes, I think."

"And in your experience, how long until any remaining kiksla start coming closer?"

She shook her head. "I have no such experience. Kiksla are used less in cities than in the wastes, and when they are, it is not to observe the affairs of trogs."

"Sir," Chief O'Garran asked, "does it matter since all the x'qiigh are dead?"

Riordan shook his head. "Ulchakh's best guess was that the aerial jousting over the river was because another liege had his own bugs shadowing the barge. And there may have been others directly connected to the liege—Gorzrik?—who were just hitching a ride."

Peter nodded. "Sensible. That way he keeps direct watch over his investment."

Caine turned toward Solsohn. "Any bogeys on this side of the river?"

Visor closed, Solsohn was already studying the skies above the far bank. "Only a few contacts, sir, and none closer than five klicks. I'll keep an eye out." He reopened his visor. "Observation, sir?" Riordan nodded. "If any of those bogeys are sending data through some blood-bond, I doubt their master understood what they saw. All the x'qai with this barge should have made it unassailable. Instead, they went down in less than ten minutes, and their command and control was gone in half that time."

Riordan folded his arms. "So if any of those bogeys are connected directly to the liege, he's keeping them at a safe distance, presumably to keep tracking the barge. Almost like having transponders attached to it."

"That's my guess, sir."

"It's a good one. Keep watching. If they start approaching, keep me apprised of speed and vector." Over Ayana's narrow shoulder, he spotted Newton standing up from examining one of the human captives. "We need to be ready to move in thirty minutes. That means getting everyone back into formation, adjusting the order of march for losses, and prioritizing the battlefield salvage. No time to assess or count it: just get it loaded for the porters. If anyone needs me, I'll be getting the casualty count from Dr. Baruch."

A muted chorus of "Aye, aye, sir" followed him to where the surgeon was standing, considering one of the two wounded enemy tinkers. "Dr. Baruch, a moment of your time, please." Newton turned slowly, acknowledging the request with a lugubrious nod.

He met Riordan halfway, his tone more distant than cold. "What do you require, sir?"

I require you to get the stick out of your ass. Riordan resisted the urge to issue the order aloud . . . for now. "I'm dropping rank and formalities, for a second. What I want is a frank conversation."

Newton cleared his throat. "With respect"—and it was unclear how much of that sentiment was actual—"rank is never fully 'dropped,' sir."

"Right now, it can be. But if you choose not to avail yourself of the opportunity to speak freely, that's your business. It's also extremely unwise." When Baruch's demeanor remained unaltered, Riordan folded his arms. "Have it your way, then. One question, Lieutenant: why?"

Baruch's face was carefully blank. "Why what, sir?"

"Lieutenant, this can go from bad to worse in a hurry. You may be our only doctor, but I will bust your ass to private if you are insubordinate. As it is, you've shown little understanding of how to behave as part of the chain of command during a battle." *And you* chose *this career, so you should be a damn sight better than me.* "I've given you more latitude that anyone else. Maybe that was a mistake. So I will ask just one more time: why?"

Baruch swallowed, glanced away. His mouth opened, then closed again.

Riordan wasn't gratified; he was relieved that he'd hit a still-active nerve. *C'mon Newton, if I've got to break you to save you, I will—but please don't make me.*

"I am . . . unaccustomed to being ordered about," Baruch answered. "Especially in a peremptory fashion."

Ignoring the doctor's use of "peremptory"—a telltale sign of the root of the problem—Riordan shook his head. "If there's any difference in the way I give you orders, it's that I've erred to the side of extreme patience. That's over. Now, tell me why I should keep you in a command position."

Baruch's eyes met Caine's. "Respectfully, perhaps you shouldn't."

As Caine's eyes narrowed, he added, "Sir, I mean that sincerely. I am not trying to use my medical qualifications as leverage. I see you are in earnest. But you may be right: I may not be suited for a command position."

Riordan pointed at him. "Those are your words, not mine. Tell me why you think they might be true."

Baruch sighed. "You know what they say about doctors, especially surgeons, Commodore. As a clade, we tend to be head-strong, arrogant, disdainful of other opinions. And as with most generalizations, there is probably a core of truth to it. Given our specialty—to repair a human body tilting toward death—there is no room for doubt or hesitation." He shrugged. "I am aware of the studies showing our typical personality profile is one that 'does not work well with others.'"

Riordan nodded. "And I doubt you became a surgeon so that you could be tapped for IRIS."

Baruch's bitter laugh was more of a parched cough. "You have a rare talent for understatement, sir. But when the offer to join was tendered—ever so obliquely—I could not, in good conscience, refuse." He shook his head. "I operated with small teams, never at the tip of the spear." He gestured at the sere wastes and littered bodies. "This was never what I—or my handlers—envisioned."

Riordan allowed himself a smile. "I assure you, I am very, very familiar with that feeling." He uncrossed his arms. "The ruins are our next objective. We should be there in ten to twelve days. We have enough personnel that I can spare you from command assignments until then. Use that time to decide if you want to return to them or not. To be clear, I want—and *we need*—you as part of the cadre. But if you can't be a team player, I can't keep you there."

Newton nodded very slowly, his already long face seeming longer than ever. "That is more than reasonable, sir."

Riordan nodded and walked back toward the others, gesturing Newton to follow. When they were close enough to be heard, he asked, "Your report, doctor?"

"I have not yet tallied those wounded whose injuries are not life-threatening. As far as fatalities, we suffered five trog kajh KIA and one trogan. I am not counting the grat'r, which apparently despaired of its kind's unusual regenerative powers."

"Well, except for the grat'r," O'Garran observed, "it's pretty much a wash, then. Three enemy trogans surrendered after being wounded, and there's another that was still here on the boat with Cruvanor. So six lost, four gained."

Bey nodded. "Miles O'Garran is correct, but there are other considerations."

Dora shook her head. "Yeah, there always are with new trogs, hey? Can we trust them? Will they start trouble? Do they need training and what type?"

Bey nodded. "All this is true, yet there is more. The mixture of our kajhs is changing, and that must be watched. Closely."

Dora raised an eyebrow. "The 'mix' of them?"

Bey sighed. "When we arrived at Achgabab, our kajhs were almost all trogs, with but a few trogans. Now, almost a third of our kajh are trogans or trogres. This diminishes the importance of the trogs. It brings back what they experience in cities: that they are the lowest of all peoples. But there, that has less impact upon their lives, since almost everyone around them is also a trog. But here, if a trog now looks to the left, they see another trog, but on the right, they see a trogan or larger warrior." She shook her head. "They know what that means."

"I don't!" pressed Dora.

Ayana's answer was quiet but clear. "It means they understand that they are becoming more expendable. And so, possess less status." Bey nodded affirmation.

Riordan crossed his arms. "So, what do you recommend we do about that, Bey?"

Given the speed of her reply, Caine was fairly sure it had already been on the tip of her tongue. "Train the scouts to make them more like true kajh. It not only gives us more fighters, but will help the kajh feel less reduced in stature."

Craig's incredulity almost put a crack in his voice. "You mean, because they have someone new to look down on?"

Bey shrugged. "It is how things are. We could also train the tinkers with bows. Most of them already have basic skill in it. Their fingers are nimble and they learn quickly. That would add many more archers."

"Do we have enough bows?" Duncan wondered aloud.

"Half had their own, as did most of the enemy trogans. We have more than enough."

Bannor rubbed his chin. "We'll have to set a limit on how

many tinkers we designate as combat personnel—even as screened archers—for any operation or formation. We're at . . . what, eighty-eight bodies in total? We need to hold at least half the tinkers back so we always have enough support and maintenance."

Caine nodded. "All good ideas, but not for wrangling on a battlefield. The doctor tells me all the humans are fit to travel. Tirolane's wounds are the worst, but he's already recovering slightly."

Newton's grunt was irritated. "More as a result of strange plants and pastes than any of my ministrations."

Craig perked up. "You mean like what the first grat'r gave Yaargraukh after we rescued Eku?"

"Maybe. Or not. Who knows? Many of the lesser wounds already show signs of healing."

Katie cocked her head. "And who provided these eldritch elixirs?"

"Cruvanor," Newton muttered. "It seems the disfigured trogan on the boat was either an agent of his, or was sent to watch after him. She saw where the x'qai stashed the humans' gear when we appeared. This was apparently part of it."

Duncan let his breath hiss out. "I've got to tell you, I thought for sure the one who tried to free Cruvanor was a goner. He got backhanded *hard*."

"Yeah," Miles agreed, "that was damn near suicidal."

Newton shrugged. "I'm sure you would have done no less if it had been *your* father."

"Wait: what? He's the old guy's son?"

"He is named Rogarran. He sustained a concussion and there may be a hairline crack just below his left orbit." Seeing the question in Riordan's eyes, Baruch nodded. "He can travel. But he should not be given any duties for at least ten days. Ideally, I would prescribe double that time, but . . ." Newton sighed and gestured at the planet around them.

"Anything else?" Caine asked.

Bannor smiled. "Yes, sir: 'thank you.'"

Riordan frowned. "Come again?"

"Commodore, we know you don't like hanging back, but today, part of why we won was because you were free to call the ball as and when needed." There were small but firm nods around the circle. "So thank you for agreeing to our one change of today's plan."

Riordan scoffed. "Not like I had much choice, short of inciting a mutiny."

"I can neither confirm nor deny—"

Riordan held up a hand. "Spare me. We don't have a lot of time and we have a tricky task before us."

"Which is?" Eku asked.

"Talking to Cruvanor."

As Caine, Bannor, and Bey approached Cruvanor, the trogan Newton had described as disfigured rose quickly, hands free of weapons but hovering near them.

The war leader—unusually well preserved for his age—raised a calming hand. "No need for caution, Fwhirki. If they meant to harm me, they'd have done so long before now."

But Bey had stopped in mid-step when he called his apparent guardian by name. "'Fwhirki?' You are kajh?"

"Obviously," said Fwhirki with the faintest hint of a smile. "Just like you."

Having heard the kajh's name twice, and seeing the puzzling exchange with Bey, Riordan recognized and recalibrated a number of assumptions. "So, you're a woman?"

"And a crog, not a trogan!" Bey added as the other smiled, and then frowned.

"Crog? Trogan?" muttered Fwhirki. "What are these words?"

"They shall be explained later," Caine assured her. "But before then, it is necessary we converse with your . . . er, leader?"

Cruvanor laughed: the sound was clear, strong, undimmed by years. If Caine had closed his eyes, he would have guessed the man was half his age. "I am not Fwhirki's leader. At least not until you showed up. It seems her inclusion among the guards on this barge was arranged." He smiled. "Another tale to be shared, but for which there is no time, Lord—?"

"My name is Caine, and I am no person's lord. This is Bannor, my executive officer, and Bey, who commands and trains our, er, praakht forces." It had been so long since he'd used the common name for trogs, Riordan stumbled before recalling it.

The storied war leader let his eyes travel over the persons to whom he'd just been introduced. His expression was genial, but Riordan could see the keen—even ruthless—calculations running behind it. "From your tone, I take it that you also have no lord, Caine."

"You are correct. We came at the behest of Tirolane."

Cruvanor nodded. "My grandson, if such a tale is to be believed."

"He would not lie!" Bey said sharply.

The human's neck stiffened slightly. "I perceive that. I simply meant that it is too happy a tale for me to readily believe. But more of that later. What are your plans?" he finished, eyes sliding toward Bannor.

Reading us—and our roles—like a familiar book, aren't you? But Riordan just nodded at his XO.

The Special Forces colonel pointed east. "As soon as the salvage is ready, we will put fifteen kilometers—uh, we march the rest of the day away from the river. We'll maintain a rearguard to watch for enemies who might arrive at this site or attempt to follow us, and use, eh, magic helmets to watch for kiksla. We spend one day recovering, securing the gear for a longer march, and set out the day after."

"Your destination?"

"The dunes-that-do-not-move."

Rulaine may have been about to add an explanation, but the old man's narrowed eyes and small nod signaled that he was quite aware of them. "I see. I agree: we must move with all haste. But call your scroungers away from searching the bodies of the jalks and pawns. They will have nothing of value. Besides, they are urgently needed just as they are."

Caine exchanged looks with Bannor. "In what way?"

Cruvanor got to his feet in one smooth motion. "Follow me."

Partly because he wanted to ensure security, but even more so to disabuse the war leader of any notion that he was in charge, Riordan put up a hand. "No. Tell us where you wish to go. Bey, two guards, on the double."

Cruvanor laughed. "For me... or for you?"

"For us all, if our enemies are nearer than they seem."

Cruvanor looked into Caine's eyes for a long moment, and then something changed in them. As if he'd been measured and found worthy of an extra measure of respect. "And here come our guards. First, where are the tinkers?" Bannor pointed them out, sitting under the watchful eyes of several kajhs. "Excellent. I must speak to one of them. If I am right, the conversation will also serve as an explanation for why we need the bodies."

When the war leader arrived at the group of squatting tinkers, it took a moment for them to recognize him. They quailed—until realizing that his attention was fixed upon only one of their number.

Riordan raised an eyebrow. "I presume it would be most convenient to speak to this one alone?"

Cruvanor smiled. "Quite right." As the other tinkers were relocated, he subtly continued his reappraisal of Riordan. "I do not believe I have thanked you for rescuing us, yet."

Riordan smiled back. "Not yet. But if I were in your shoes, I wouldn't be in a rush to do so—not until being satisfied that I was truly being rescued, rather than 'appropriated.'"

The old war leader chuckled. "'Appropriated.' Oh, I like that. After all these years, you'd think I'd have come up with that euphemism myself. At any rate, thank you. And you're right: when something is too good to believe—rescue, and at the urging of my grandson no less!—I have learned not to believe it." He turned to the sole remaining tinker, who had begun to shake. "Now, little one, tell me your tale."

"T-tale?" the tinker almost whimpered.

"You don't know the tale I mean?" Cruvanor's voice was like his smile: mirthless.

The tinker shook his head.

Cruvanor glanced at Riordan. "With your permission, War Leader?"

Caine shrugged. "Be aware: they were guaranteed fair treatment."

One of the old man's frosty eyebrows arched high up his forehead. "Well," he said, "we *will* have a lot to talk about. I shall act in accord with your terms. Fwhirki, bring our little friend after me."

As Fwhirki hauled the small humanoid to his feet, she muttered, "We are no longer in Fragkork, so my name is no longer Fwhirki."

"No?" Cruvanor asked as they made their way to the blind side of the barge.

"No. I am Qyza."

The war leader's eyebrow rose again. "Ah, so you are a Breaksister. You are related to Darzmorgar, perhaps?"

She smiled as she towed the tinker along beside her. "Perhaps."

"I have always been fortunate in my friends," Cruvanor acknowledged with a small, respectful nod in her direction. Then he turned to the tinker, his voice a parody of soothing reassurance. "Now, I want you to tell us the story about *this*."

He reached into the rough matrix of shaped and lacquered bone that held the barge's cured-hide hull in place. When he withdrew his hand, it held a heavy cord.

The tinker grew very pale. "It is what the arurkré commanded me to remove just before the battle. But I couldn't."

"I know," Cruvanor agreed in a voice like that of a malevolent uncle. "The x'qai kept giving you orders, first to do this, then to do that, and if you displeased any of them—"

"Great War Leader, you saw how they were! They trampled my cousin underfoot! Crushed him like a slug! I couldn't—"

"Calm, now, little tinker. Just tell me: what were you supposed to do with this line?"

"Pull it. Hard." The small being trembled. "I was to make sure the whole length came out."

"Why?"

"To leave a sign. To Great Liege Sirvashwekh. That we were here."

Riordan exchanged glances with Bannor and Bey. *So the tinker was acting on Sirvashwekh's orders, not his vassal Gorzrik's?*

Cruvanor's question introduced yet another level of uncertainty. "Let us assume it was actually Sirvashwekh who hired you to pull this cord, not someone using his name. My only interest is in this: Did you truly believe it would simply leave a *sign*?"

"Y-yes. What else?"

Cruvanor leaned over the tinker. "This cord is connected to a flaw in the gridwork, fashioned so that normal travel does not affect it. It can only be undone by pulling the cord."

"But-but why?"

"To sink the barge, little fool. A day or two further downstream, the loosened joint at the flaw would finally have given way and we would have all been lost in the river."

"But to what end?"

Cruvanor tossed the cord on the sand, gestured that Fwhirki—*no; Qyza, now*—was to return the tinker to the rest of his kind. "I have seen this before," he muttered to his rescuers. "When a liege fears that a cargo or 'package' might not go where he wishes, he takes steps to ensure that if it does not, it won't reach any other destination, either."

Bannor nodded somberly. "So if you had managed to commandeer the boat—or had some friends intercept it—this was the insurance."

"Exactly."

Riordan smiled. "And that's why we need the bodies. Because once we've picked out the most useful items, we're going to reload the barge and start it downstream. So when it finally capsizes, the agents of whoever rigged the boat for destruction will find what they expect: the right amount of flotsam, jetsam, and bodies."

Cruvanor nodded approvingly. "You have done this before?"

"Something like it," Riordan muttered around a small grin.

Bey glanced at Riordan. "Do you wish me to bear orders to the others?"

He nodded, but kept his focus on Cruvanor. "Clearly, you knew this was coming."

The old man shrugged. "We knew things were not as they seemed. I saw it first, sent a signal to my son and the others from our stable."

"What kind of signal?" Bannor asked. "On a boat full of x'qai, you must have been watched constantly."

The war leader smiled. "The best signals are those given in plain sight, my new friend. In this case, it was arranged that, at meals, each of us who felt all was well would take a drink before they ate. But if there was peril, we would take a bite before we drank. Trust me: no x'qao is patient enough to note such subtleties." He laughed. "Of course, it helps that they deem us stupid."

"Despite keeping you for your intelligence and discipline."

Cruvanor's smile widened. "You are not from x'qai lands, this is clear. If you were, you would surely know that the ability to hold such contradictory convictions is not merely quite possible for x'qai; it is one of their most notable, and exploitable, traits."

As they approached the renewed activity to reload the barge, a figure swayed up from a makeshift pallet: Tirolane.

The old man stopped and stared. As the big swordsman approached with a hitch in his gait and supported by Enoran on that side, Cruvanor's Adam's apple worked hard, twice. His eyes grew bright and the first sign of later years—a geriatric quiver of his lower lip—pushed through before he could shut his mouth against it. The sudden clamping of his jaw was so sudden that his cheeks shook—which freed a single glistening drop to run down the deep creases in his face.

"Grandfather! These men—"

"I have met them, Tirolane. I—" The war leader was suddenly a very old man. "Your grandmother... Her face is in yours. I remember—" The iron war leader whose fame was as wide as the continent of Brazhgarag stifled a sob; it sounded like he was swallowing a boulder. "I would embrace you, but for the wounds."

Tirolane shook loose of Enoran and threw himself into Cruvanor's arms. For a long moment they did not speak.

Had it been any place other than a battlefield in which the enemy might still have interest, Riordan would have eased away.

But Tirolane held himself back from that embrace, large rough hands on either leathery arm of the old warrior. "What you do not know, Grandfather, is the character of these, your rescuers. They did this on trust alone. Even though I could not be fully forthcoming, they still did this. It is a mark of their commitment to freeing our people—all of them—wherever they may be."

Despite age-dimmed teeth, Cruvanor's smile was radiant. "I believe you, my boy. Now, rest. We must move, and you should not have risen."

Tirolane appeared to be on the verge of resisting that advice when his more grievously wounded leg gave out. Enoran had to catch him and guide him back to the pallet that was being hastily converted into a litter.

Cruvanor turned toward Riordan. "I am yours," he said, his voice ragged. "Your vassal, your servitor: however you'll have me and mine. I owe you no less. And I have seen what you can do—the like of which I have never seen before."

Riordan extended his hand. "I told you already, none of us are lords—and we will not answer to any. So, welcome, *Friend* Cruvanor."

The old man's eyes threatened to leak again, but something he saw over Caine's shoulder made them harden. "Stop!" he ordered.

They all turned. Two trogans were in the process of removing gear from an arrow-feathered corpse: the caver shaman.

Cruvanor glanced at Riordan. "Take nothing from his body. It could have been touched and bound by a greater x'qao."

"So they might be able to find us wherever we take any item of his," Bannor concluded through a long, hissing inhalation.

"Exactly. But also, if his body, or his baubles, come ashore, that will assure the saboteur that he was on the boat—along with everyone else—when it capsized."

Riordan nodded at the two trogans: they lifted the body and started toward the barge.

As they passed, Cruvanor spat on the corpse. Had human eyes the power to vaporize objects, Riordan was sure there would have been nothing left of the caver. He noticed the Terrans' reactions. "You do not know of them?"

"Very little," Riordan admitted.

"Then know this: they eat our kind. They eat praakht. They eat each other. And they revel in it. All of it."

Riordan drew a deep breath, put a hand on the older man's age-corded arm, and drew him away from the river.

Chapter Nineteen

Riordan held up the edge of the tarp as Duncan and Bey sprinted in out of the torrent of immense raindrops that were hammering infinities of small craters into the dusty highland soil—before obliterating them with a fresh bombardment in the next instant.

"Damn, rain after tornadoes is *cold*, here!" Solsohn exclaimed.

"Tornados?" Bey repeated.

"*Matjvalkar*," Eku supplied for her.

"Ah," she nodded, turning so that, as she ran her hands down her arms, the water sprayed back out into the sheets of rain. "It usually is colder, even in summer." She glanced at Riordan. "Apologies to keep the council waiting, Leader Caine. We just received the last reports."

Caine smiled. "Everything's running behind, today." *And not just because of the weather; the bigger we grow, the longer everything takes.* "Find a seat and we'll get started."

Solsohn had produced three pieces of parchment from a satchel inside the breastplate of his hide armor. He held one up to peer at it in the grey light. "Get comfortable folks; this is a long list."

Riordan cut through the groans. "That won't be necessary, Duncan. Just touch the wavetops, please."

The CIA analyst who'd become an IRIS sniper almost pouted. "But, sir—"

Riordan shook his head. "We're past the point where we can all track the details. As of today, you and all other section heads won't be reporting on your areas, just *running* them. From now on, you only come to me if there is a problem or an opportunity that isn't part of the normal workflow." He smiled. "I hate micromanaging."

"In a pig's eye—sir!" O'Garran blurted.

Riordan chuckled, both at the SEAL's stunned outburst and his immediate attempt to walk back its borderline insolence by tagging on an honorific. "There's a difference between liking something and doing it, Chief. Our force is now essentially a light company. We have to start running it that way." He turned back to Duncan. "So, what's the *synopsis*, Major?"

Solsohn shrugged. "There was a lot of choice cargo on that barge: fifty kilos of salt, select foods, excellent sleeping furs, hundreds of liters of methanol and ethanol." He smiled. "And enough moss to keep us from becoming any more insane than we already are. For now."

Riordan chose not to speak over the relieved sighs. It was unclear if any of their inoculations were effective against the microbe that brought on s'rillor, but now they had more time to reach Ebrekka, both to be tested and to acquire even more moss.

"T.O.E. status?" Caine requested sharply. The Crewe straightened: back to business.

Duncan nodded. "We've pretty much hit all our marks, Commodore. Everyone, down to the handlers and porters, is now wearing cured hide armor or better. Combat troops have bronze axes or better. We've even got more bows than bowmen. Our real problem is arrows."

Newton shook his head. "I still do not understand why they carry so few."

Solsohn shrugged. "Because the locals don't go through a lot in any given battle. They loose a volley or two and then close. Us? The foundation of our playbook is to maintain a base of fire. All our archers have been emptying a quiver, sometimes two, in every engagement." He shook his head. "Add in all the breakage and the shafts we don't find in after-action sweeps, and we'll be rationing them soon. And that will cut deeply into our primary battlefield advantage: high rate of fire from more and better-trained personnel."

Bannor raised an eyebrow. "So does this mean we need to change our plans and divert to a town?"

Before Riordan could rule it out—the ruins had to come

first—Bey shook her head and sought his eyes. "No. That is not necessary. But Leader Caine, if we mean to keep enough arrows in quivers, we *will* need to cease traveling." If she noticed the curious expressions surrounding her, she gave no indication. "We have thirteen tinkers beneath our colors, now. Almost all of them are fletchers. But they cannot do more than repair what has been reclaimed when we are marching hard."

Wu frowned. "But do they have enough raw materials?"

"Between the caravan and the barge, we possess a great deal of obsidian and workable flint. Bone for shafts is plentiful. However, the hair used for fletching cannot be cooked and shaped except on days in which there is no movement at all."

Yaargraukh was nodding slowly. "Are they at their labors today?"

"To the extent they can be, Leader Yaargraukh, but the fletching requires the heat of the sun, at least."

Most of the command group stared ruefully at the rain pouring off the tarp like a waterfall.

Craig Girten was the first to turn his gaze back to the Crewe. "So, sir, if most folks here are now section heads, who's in charge of all the local *humans* we've added?"

Caine nodded. "That, Sergeant, is a very good question. We could give Cruvanor that role."

Dora raised a long, dark eyebrow. "You mean to bring another person into the group? We're gonna need a bigger tent!" There were laughs, but she pressed forward with the same tone. "Kind of early to give him a seat at this table, don' you think, Boss?"

Riordan nodded. "I do. That's why the real question is what Tirolane wants to do."

"How do you mean?"

"Well, he's a local. If Cruvanor is in charge of all local humans, that would include Tirolane."

Ayana nodded. "So Cruvanor would take Tirolane's place." She glanced at Riordan. "Unless Tirolane could remain with us as an official liaison to Cruvanor, who is given direct oversight of local humans."

Eku frowned. "That is an, er, somewhat inelegant command structure, do you not agree, Commodore?"

"I most certainly do, Mr. Eku, but consistency is less important than fit." The factotum's blank stare invited edification. "The humans who've joined us are used to being servitors. But as they spend more time with us, they seem to be thinking beyond vassal-servitor structure. It's not the way they operated among themselves, anyhow. So I tend to agree with Ms. Tagawa; we let Cruvanor have direct oversight of them for now, and keep Tirolane as a go-between."

"You think that will last, sir?" Duncan asked doubtfully.

"Absolutely not. I don't think *any* of our current organization is going to last. Right now, we have low numbers of humans without spouses, children, or a fixed base of operations. So all organization has to be not only mission-practical, but readily adaptable to altered circumstances. Ms. Tagawa's suggestion balances all those needs. Besides, I want to keep Tirolane a free agent, for now."

Dora smirked. "You mean to keep him out of *abuelo*'s way when it comes to dealing with the other locals?"

"Partly," Riordan answered in a serious tone, "but also because we still don't understand his abilities. But once we do, I can foresee needing his insight on that. That special expertise warrants a separate seat on this council, just as we brought in Bey for her knowledge of trogs." He smiled at her, and she smiled back—but almost guardedly. *Was it something I said or do I have lichen stuck in my teeth?* "Besides, I think Cruvanor will want the same arrangement."

"Why?" Newton asked.

Yaargraukh's rumble was slow and sly. "Because then he still has a family member in our unit's leadership circle." The Hkh'Rkh shifted to ease the weight on the minor leg wound he'd sustained in the battle. "In time, should our paths continue to be the same, I suspect Cruvanor will sit among us here. But for now, he has much to plan and do."

Wu frowned. "He has only seven people under him, not counting Tirolane."

"That is not his source of power nor his primary concern. He is a figure of renown who commands great respect among local humans, particularly those enslaved in other stables. His next actions will be to further aims and objectives appropriate to that position."

Miles' sigh was histrionically "patient." "And how will he do that, stuck out here?"

"Mark my words, Chief O'Garran, he will not wish to remain in the wastes any longer than he must. And I suspect his desired directions will prove worthy of close consideration. He may not know who or what we are, but of all the people we have met—perhaps including Tasvar—he understands the roles we might play."

Ayana's tone was intensely interested. "And how do you know this?"

"I have no knowledge of his intents, if that is what you mean, Ms. Tagawa. But know this: the feudal and warlord mentality of Bactradgaria is far more similar to contemporary Rkh'yaa than you might guess—or be comfortable with. Indeed, it very closely parallels those of our ancient states."

Riordan noticed Solsohn leaning forward eagerly. "Something else, Major?"

"Yes, sir. You asked me to report what kind of weapons Cruvanor and company had in storage on the barge." Riordan nodded as most of the group leaned forward: more firearms meant greater odds of survival.

Solsohn didn't need to check any notes. "Of the three humans beside Cruvanor and Rogarran, one—Polsolun—is young and there because of his sword. No firearm experience, apparently. The other two are in their late thirties, I'd say. The soldier—Marcanas—has an over-under break-breech rifle with short barrels. Un-necked brass cartridges."

O'Garran jumped in before Duncan could breathe. "Artifact or recent manufacture?"

Solsohn shook his head. "Could be either. But what their technical wizard Irisir is toting came out of a factory: a pump shotgun. The tolerances, stampings: it wasn't made in any postapocalyptic wonderland. The ammo: all reloads, but an insane amount of care in the craft."

Riordan discovered his chest was tight. "Any markings?"

Solsohn shook his head. "Nothing legible. It's old, sir: *really* old. Worn smooth but treated like a newborn baby. If there are replacement parts, I can't tell them apart.

"Rogarran's own weapon was never aboard, it turns out. When they undid the wrappings, they found a few well-oiled copper rods in its place."

"What *should* have been there?" Wu asked.

"Bolt action rifle. Necked cartridge. Rogarran says it didn't have markings, but everything he describes makes it another factory piece. Which is probably why Gorzrik swapped it out. I converted the local measurements; it sounds similar to an old .30-06." He shrugged. "Even with black powder reloads, I'm guessing the x'qai didn't want that anywhere within a kilometer of them."

Bannor raised an eyebrow. "And Cruvanor himself?"

Duncan shook his head. "Talk about convergent technological evolution. Semiautomatic pistol. Twelve-round box. Close as dammit to that nine-millimeter museum piece Dora has."

"It is called a Ruger," Eku furnished with a twist of injured pride in his voice. He was its actual owner, but he hadn't touched it since Dora had carried it ever since they seized the crippled ship orbiting above.

Riordan nodded, but felt a frown growing on his face.

"Hey, Boss," Dora quipped, "what were you expecting? A cannon?"

Ayana was also frowning. "I suspect the Commodore is concerned for the same reason I am: not because the firearms are small, but because they are so basic."

Caine nodded. "Compared to the very advanced buildings Miles saw in the trough at the bottom of the river, these weapons are far more consistent with the larger, industrial-era city that was perched above it. And if that's the only technology that survived, or was rebuilt, then our odds of finding a way back to, eh, 'Shangri-la' become a lot worse." He turned toward Newton. "So did you manage to get Rogarran to drop hints about how the local humans *do* manage to trace lineage among the stables?"

"I learned nothing because he had nothing to reveal. However, I strongly suspect his father must know, in part because a stable's senior war leader is the only human who can reliably keep secrets. They are indispensable to their lieges and so, are only rarely investigated, let alone interrogated. However, in my time with him, I noted a most peculiar development, entirely unrelated to the matter of tracking lineage." Riordan nodded. "He and Cruvanor—and apparently all the local humans—are already calling praakht 'trogs.' And adopting the rest of Chief O'Garran's slang for other species, as well."

"Well, sure!" the little SEAL almost shouted. "They know quality word-slinging when they hear it!"

Wu shrugged. "Perhaps, or perhaps they are adding their

authority to Bey's attempt to foster new identity for the trogs through a new name. Could it be an act of, well, solidarity?"

"Solidarity?" Newton's laugh was more of a snort. Then he reconsidered. "Well, perhaps it is, in a way."

"*What* way?" Dora's tone was decidedly impatient.

"They may be attempting to purge every vestige of x'qao authority from trog minds, but the purpose may not be to liberate them. It may be to make them more malleable."

"Why?" Duncan asked sharply. "Or, more importantly, for whom?"

"That is the issue, isn't it?" Newton agreed with a dour nod. "Cruvanor is expert at manipulating the forces within a liege's power structure. Most especially, the ones over which he is not supposed to have any influence. Which is to say, rank and file trogs."

Solsohn frowned. "So he could be trying to sway them away from us."

Dora shrugged. "He's a native. He's got every advantage in that area, and he's too smart not to have already smelled that. Every day, his advantage in managing them is going to grow."

Craig shook his head. "Sounds like we'd better talk to him."

Bannor nodded. "Yes, but I don't think he's trying to undermine us. I think he's trying to help us. We'll know better once we speak with him today. And with Tirolane."

"Speaking of Tirolane," Duncan muttered, "do you think maybe he can give us a better idea about how that x'qao got control of Cruvanor?"

Dora shrugged. "Looked as though he just passed out. Kind of like what Tirolane did to the leader of the caravan."

Duncan's voice was dark. "Kind of *exactly* like that."

"What are you saying?"

"Just this: we have someone with us who does what x'qai do." Solsohn moved restlessly. "Or maybe vice versa. And after the x'qao leader at the caravan blinded me for five critical minutes, I've got a personal interest in how it's done."

"'Done'? Do you mean by the x'qai or Tirolane?"

Duncan looked up from under lowered brows. "How can you be sure there's a difference?"

Craig rocked back. "You think Tirolane's—what? A x'qao in disguise?"

"A half-breed?" Dora muttered.

Riordan stood up. "Hold on. Let's break this down. There are two issues there: defining what are Talents, and learning about Tirolane's origins.

"Let's start with the latter, since we've got more information. We know he's from Zrik Whir. We know Zrik Whir is powerful enough to remain independent. We know he's been there since he was a child. Not one of our reliable and well-informed sources—Ulchakh, Tasvar, Yasla, and now Cruvanor—have ever mentioned or seemed to entertain the possibility that he might be anything other than human. Nor, I'll point out, have any x'qai we've met. So I consider that a pretty strong body of evidence that Tirolane is exactly what he appears to be: *not* a x'qao.

"As for his 'Talents,' all we know is that what he did at the caravan *looks* like what the x'qai leader did to Cruvanor. But that doesn't mean it is the same, either in terms of its source or its specific effects. It's entirely possible—and I suspect this—that what we're calling Talents may be specific to species, even those that might 'look' the same. But no one seems eager to answer those questions, least of all Tirolane himself."

Ayana glanced at Riordan. "Has anyone put such questions to the shaman Zhathragz?"

Riordan frowned. "No, and I'm not sure we can risk that yet. Just asking him to explain his powers would let him know he has a huge information advantage over us." He glanced at Bey—who was already looking at him. She started. "What's your opinion? Would it be safe to ask Zhathragz? Perhaps if the questions came from you?"

She shook her head. "If I tried, he would seek to leave our colors. Shamans are sworn to secrecy by those who initiate them. It is said that if they violate that oath, the source of their power will be aware and withhold their mystic gifts."

Wu looked sideways at Bey. "Is 'gifts' just another word for 'talents'?"

"No, Leader Wu, they are not the same. Shamans' powers are called Gifts because that is literally what they are. There is a connection between them and whatever source or being bestows those powers. A Talent comes from within the being that possesses it. Or so we are told."

Riordan nodded. "And that may be as much clarity as we have for a while."

Duncan shook his head. "Makes optimal planning really difficult, sir."

"Agreed, but let's consider this similar to investing in a new, and very crucial, intelligence asset. For now, I intend to trust both Tirolane's motives and his judgment on how best to use his powers to help our plans without disrupting them. Which is what he's done so far."

Solsohn rubbed his nose. "Any objection to asking him to share a bit more?"

Riordan exchanged a shrug with Bannor. "No. But don't press too hard. I suspect Tirolane has very good reasons for his reticence."

O'Garran looked out into the deluge; a tall grey shape was limping closer. "And speak of the devil..."

"I sincerely hope that label *is* figurative," Newton muttered.

Chapter Twenty

Caine found the speed of Tirolane's recovery not just impressive, but implausible. They'd seen much the same phenomenon after Yaargraukh had been wounded during Eku's rescue, but Hkh'Rkh durability and rapid healing were well-known properties of the species. And the "physick" provided by the recently slain grat'r had presumably amplified that process to unprecedented levels.

However, Tirolane was human, or if not, was such close kin that none of the wise or powerful of Bactradgaria had deemed or treated him otherwise. Yet as the swordsman eased himself down to the only threadbare sitting fur still unoccupied, he evinced only modest discomfort: more stiffness than pain, judging from his controlled reactions.

He was current on most of the day's new information; Baruch had passed it on in conversation while tending the swordsman's rapidly closing wounds. However, the concerns regarding how the humans should be organized—and under whose command—was a new topic. Bannor introduced it without reference to the group's recent discussion.

Tirolane shrugged. "The humans should have my grandfather at their head. His name is known. They consider serving under him a stroke of great good fortune."

"And you?" Ayana asked. "Do you not wish to serve alongside Cruvanor?"

Tirolane smiled. "Your words are more precisely true than

you may intend, Ms. Tagawa. I do wish to serve alongside him, but not *under* him." When several eyes widened in surprise, he shrugged. "My roots are on Zrik Whir. His are not. He is an expert in the way of the x'qai and their stables. I am not. His has been the life of a thrall in durance vile and almost entirely in one city. Mine has been the path of a wanderer, not only searching for what slender thread connects me to my blood relatives, but to become as self-sufficient as I may.

"That path has made me a natural liaison between those I've met all along my way: those I grew up with in Zrik Whir, the Legate, and now you and my grandfather. I am happy to serve in that role. I will oversee some component of our forces, if that proves advisable. But I assure you, I have no hunger for the dull routines of doing so. I would as soon that responsibility remains with someone else."

Riordan had not expected that any of the Crewe would actually sigh in relief at the swordsman's words, but was nonetheless grateful that none did.

"I do have one suggestion, though." Tirolane turned to face Bey directly. "Please understand that my observation is in no way a judgment on the fine work you have done as the commander and trainer of our various trog-kind. But I believe that it might be useful if my grandfather was allowed to walk among them at his leisure. Not an inspection. Nothing formal. Perhaps a meal in your camp circles."

Dora rallied to the defense of her crog friend. "You think that his eye and nose for trogs is better than *hers*?"

Tirolane's very blue eyes were very calm. "Not at all. But Cruvanor's eye is different. His time in a x'qao's stable has made him particularly sensitive to the same subtleties of association and contention that have concerned this council. His insights might help build a cohesive unit with minimal points of friction among its members."

Katie Somers blew a stray bang out of her eyes. "An' why do we need that, if we're set on building an entirely different unit, an entirely different outlook?"

Tirolane opened his large, scarred hands in appeal. "Even as thralls, humans gather power to themselves. That is what ensures their survival. They accrue and conceal resources with which to groom and support undeclared allies, both within a stronghold and outside its walls. To do that, they must be expert at detecting x'qao attempts to insinuate traitorous—or desperate—trogs into their good graces. They must manage the forces they build beyond the confines of the stable, settle their differences, reward or threaten as those groups and circumstances require. Because humans who cannot do all these things either become abject slaves or are short-lived in their attempts to circumvent their liege's constraints. And at the core of all these skills is one thing."

"To understand trogs better than we—they—understand themselves?" Bey anticipated with a hint of asperity.

"No," Tirolane replied patiently. "To foresee how any given group of trogs will interact with any other group: trog, human, or other."

"You make your grandfather sound like a soothsayer," Bannor said amiably.

Tirolane replied in kind. "It does seem that way, I suppose." He shrugged. "Other species deem the mangle ability to find water in the wastes a matter of magic. This may be something like that: a skill so essential that only those who attain it survive to pass it on, and in doing so, refine it."

Bey's frown had not relented, but she nodded. "We shall see that his visit to our camp circles occurs. And in a natural manner."

Tirolane looked around the group, felt the pregnant pause. One eyebrow lifted. "I see I am not done, yet." He glanced at Solsohn with a smile. "You wish to ask me about my *anagogoi*."

Solsohn blinked. "Your what?"

Tirolane nodded, more to himself than at the puzzled response. "I shall rephrase: Why do you wish to know about the effects I can manifest?"

Duncan shrugged. "It's not so much a wish as a need. If we knew what you can do, and how, and when, we could make much more effective plans."

Tirolane's smile had faded. "We are allies and friends. I perceive that you trust me, more than is your wont. I ask you to trust me a while longer."

Miles leaned forward. "I trust you just fine, big guy, but here's the catch: not knowing more about your tricks keeps us from knowing how better to keep us all alive. Including you. You've seen what our weapons and sensors—eh, artifacts—can do. But that's just the surface. If we knew all your potentials, we could—"

Tirolane lowered his eyes and held up his hand. He waited until O'Garran's impatient entreaties sputtered into surly silence. "I have my anagogoi through oaths and inheritances. They are not like your artifacts, are not 'possessions.' I own my sword. I own this pistol. But each anagog is a part of me. And I will not discuss them so quickly or casually as if they were mere objects."

Riordan was peripherally monitoring the faces of the Crewe. Along with Miles, Dora and Katie appeared the most irritated. Duncan appeared more frustrated than upset. Ayana and Bey seemed the most ready to accept Tirolane's explanations and attitudes.

The swordsman was also reading the group carefully, so much so that as Dora's frown deepened and her mouth began to open, he added, "You are clearly unfamiliar with anagogy or the greater spheres of eunogony to which they are related. Understand: asking questions about either, but particularly anagogoi, is not at all like exchanging what you call 'specs' on your different artifacts and weapons. It is an intensely personal question, one which is considered terribly rude."

"How rude?" Katie snapped. "Rude enough to be riskin' lives over?"

Tirolane smiled at her. "I think the best comparison I can make is this: imagine that, within five minutes of meeting you, I casually asked about your sexual preferences and proclivities."

Katie's eyes grew round. "Oh. Aye, aye..." she muttered before looking away.

Newton became thoughtful, Dora became annoyed—at herself or Tirolane or the whole frustrating situation was not clear. Duncan nodded in resignation. Miles crossed his arms. Bannor and Ayana both smiled, which, for just a moment they shared.

Okay: crisis averted. Riordan turned to Tirolane. "Thank you for being patient with our questions. I think we all understand something we did not before: that this is not just a matter of secrecy, but privacy and oath-keeping." The swordsman replied with a slow, grateful nod that was more like a sitting bow.

"However," Caine continued, "until we understand more deeply how and what these phenomena are, we cannot determine if possessing these anagogoi is not just a power, but a peril as well." The mere fact that Tirolane expressed no surprise was almost a confirmation of the conjecture with which Riordan concluded. "It's a paradigm of nature that there are equal and opposite reactions for every force, and that most one-way doors actually aren't. So in having these powers, we have to wonder if you are not marked by, or even made more susceptible to, some of them. For that reason, we may on occasion ask you to absent yourself from the council when we are making final, or highly sensitive, deliberations."

Tirolane nodded somberly. "In your place, I would do no different." He looked up; the hoarse thundering of the rain had relented. The swordsman rose stiffly, raising a palm to stay Yaar-graukh's movement to help him. "Let us go to my grandfather while the skies are more friendly. Even before you asked, he thought you might wish to talk to him. I sense he was correct."

Chapter Twenty-One

Two trogans from the barge rose and stood behind the sitting Cruvanor as Riordan approached with a few others. The crog who had helped save the war leader—Qyza—exchanged nods and small smiles with Bey.

Without bothering to look at his new bodyguards, Cruvanor raised a hand of summons. They were immediately in a position of readiness to either side. "Trogans, you are released from your duty here. When I call you back, bring my meal." His raised hand flipped into a wave of dismissal.

The gesture and implicit presumptions surprised Caine—but not so much that he failed to sense and block Bannor's sudden, aggressive step toward the war leader. "So are those your favorite sharecroppers? Maybe ones with your blood in them?"

Christ, where is this *coming from?* Riordan made sure his shoulder was in front of Bannor's.

Cruvanor was unusually calm but clearly baffled. "I do not know what a sharecropper is."

Bannor might have taken another step forward, but bounced into Caine's shoulder. "I don't care what you call your hand-and-foot servants, here: trogs, praakht, slaves, thralls. Call them free, but it doesn't make them so, you da—!"

Miles put a hand on Bannor's opposite arm. The Special Forces colonel shook it off violently, but it had landed at just the right moment to keep him from adding whatever insult he'd been about to toss at Cruvanor. Instead, he glared at Little Guy. "You're stopping me? *You?*"

"Yes, sir. Customs are different here, so—"

"Not so different at all, maybe." His eyes bored hard into Miles. "I've got my own homespun yarns, Chief. My grandma's mother was killed by the Klan in Alabama because she had the nerve to vote. And *her* mother was a sharecropper who didn't dare say no to the son of the man who still owned them after decades of so-called 'emancipation.'"

Riordan maneuvered so he was more completely in front of Bannor. Tirolane had limped out from behind the others, taking up a position midway between Rulaine and the old war leader.

Whose frown was now more one of concern than puzzlement. "What does he say? There are many words I do not understand."

Riordan spoke before anyone else—especially Bannor—could. "He believes that you treat these trogans as if they are your slaves, that they are beholden to you."

"Or may be your own children," Bey added. She was now directly behind Bannor.

Cruvanor shook his head. "You come from a different place, indeed. As far as siring any you see here, the few assignations I had with trogans or crogs were all in my youth." He stared intently at Bannor, as if he might discern some secret reason behind his rage. "More to the point, if anyone is owned it is us humans. We are the livestock of ruthless masters who forbid us to have families. The trogs and trogans are but their servitors and serfs." He shrugged. "Besides, we do not seek out trog-kind. It is they who approach us."

Bannor's aggressive forward lean diminished. "What?"

Bey explained from behind him. "It was thus with my mother, Leader Bannor. She bore me of a crog from a wandering human tribe. She chose that, even though it increased her, and my, risk among trogs of the Free Tribes."

Rulaine turned to look at her. "Why?"

"Because if my human blood became too obvious, I might be shunned."

"Then why did your mother, er, mate with a human at all?"

She shrugged. "For the reason you have now seen. Crogs and trogans are highly valued beyond the society of trogs."

Bannor jabbed a finger toward Cruvanor. "You mean valued by men like him?"

She shook her head sharply. "No: by ambitious chiefs and gang leaders, but even more, by x'qai. Many take us into direct service, thereby freeing us from an uncertain fate among trogs. The x'qai deem us good partners to the humans."

Cruvanor nodded. "And so they—you—are. But it goes well beyond that. Because lieges know that we work particularly well with crogs and trogans, they hope to suborn as many as they can, to keep eyes and ears on the actions they know we hide from them."

"And that," Qyza muttered, "is how Cruvanor and his men came to be here: because x'qai fear that above all else."

Bey moved so that she stood beside Bannor. "You have seen and heard no different since you arrived in Forkus. Lieges find it safer and easier to recruit the highest kajh to arrange the betrayal of humans who become too powerful, too influential, in their holdings."

"But," Cruvanor said with a small, grim smile, "it usually works otherwise." He smiled up at Qyza. "As it did in this case."

Bannor's voice was so tight that it pained Riordan to hear it. "So you're telling me that trogans are loyal because you care *so* much for them, because you are *such* good masters?"

Cruvanor stood, hands at his sides. "My friend, I fear you are so rage-blind at the injustices that prevail in your lands that you cannot fully perceive the different realities in this one. Bannor Rulaine, most trogans and crogs seek us out because we are so *similar* to each other. Are some more intemperate? They are made to be so. Do most live brutish lives? They are given no chance for anything better.

"Not so the trogs of the Free Tribes"—he nodded toward Bey; she returned it—"and that is why they often rise high among those of the cities. Not only are they unbroken by x'qao masters, but because they have families, they trace lineage. That is how those tribes manage to endure. And if they lack the same crafts and skills and learnings that make humans valuable to the x'qai, it is not because they are without ability. It is because the price of their freedom is to remain beyond the reach of the lieges, out in the savage wastes where there are barely enough resources to survive."

Riordan and the others started when Dora added her thoughts from behind; she and Duncan had evidently rushed over when Bannor started shouting. "It's no different on Ear—in our lands," she explained. "You see it everyplace where life gets bad enough for long enough. African slums, South American shanties, burned-out edges of Western cities: the language is different, but otherwise, they're all the same."

Cruvanor edged closer to Bannor. "I do not speak my next words to suggest I act out of altruism; I do not. But in the struggle to exist beneath the taloned heels of the x'qai, we—humans and trog-kind—benefit from each other. We both survive. More than if we were wholly estranged or, worse yet, in competition with each other."

Bannor had taken a step back, his face flushed: whether with residual anger or embarrassment, Riordan couldn't tell. "The cavers don't seem to fit into that equation."

The face of every native Bactradgarian hardened. "They do not," Cruvanor breathed. "The lieges do not employ them in numbers because they are even less governable than 'qo. When those least of all x'qa finally cower beneath the threats of their master, stubborn cavers simply slip away to find better places in which to indulge their savagery."

Bey nodded. "They are the worst of us—of *all* trog-kind. It is as what has often been said of scythes, Leader Caine: they are the worst of all humans."

He smiled at her. "The more we learn of each other, the more parallels we discover."

Bannor stood straight. "Cruvanor, I formally apologize for my outburst. It was unprofessional and jeopardized an alliance that is important to both of us. It shall not happen again." He turned stiffly toward Caine. "Commodore, I shall withdraw from this conver—"

"Unnecessary, Colonel. As you were." Riordan turned to the old war leader. His expression was—what? Sympathetic? Or maybe empathetic, possibly remembering similar moments from a long and bloody career littered with broken hopes and the faces of dead friends.

"Let us all sit together," Cruvanor said. "Since Bey is here, I assume Tirolane has persuaded you to allow me to walk among the trogs." He shook his head, glanced at her. "I told him that it was too soon, too likely to be understood." He reached wiry fingers to clasp the swordsman's nearest shoulder. "I am learning that my grandson is a very persuasive fellow."

"We've noticed the same thing," Riordan agreed. He turned to look back at Dora and Duncan. "Unexpected, but glad to see you here."

"Yeah, well, it sounded like a lively conversation, Boss." Dora's drollery was so extreme that it was a parody of itself.

"Actually," Riordan continued, angling himself to open a clear path between Cruvanor and Duncan, "Major Solsohn has a great many questions about the dunes-that-do-not-move and what we might find there."

Cruvanor raised an eyebrow. "Only him?"

"No, but he's in charge of that information and certainly has a mind for the relevant details."

"Such as?"

Duncan pushed forward. "Such as, how the *hell* can anything be left in useable condition? What little information we've got tells us that the last war—because it looks like there was more than one—took place well over two millennia ago."

Cruvanor glanced at Tirolane. "It is unusual that anyone has even that much knowledge. You are to be congratulated on gathering it." He settled into a comfortable position, the way many old men did when preparing to embark upon a long tale. "There is much to suggest the wheels and gears of that world did not all stop at once, at least not after the most recent war. Also, since hidden sites from earlier epochs are still found, logically even more were being uncovered in earlier times.

"So, in addition to caches buried toward the end of the last war, there were ongoing discoveries of older, advanced artifacture. Between the two, the knowledge to build and repair sophisticated devices seems to have persisted long after the guns fell silent. I suspect city-states arose around those who possessed such expertise and preserved what they could." He shrugged one narrow shoulder. "The historical record is uncertain, at best."

Duncan grunted. "You're telling me . . . er, War Leader Cruvanor. Most of the records seem to be from several millennia ago, some of which apparently refer to other sources that have since disappeared."

Cruvanor nodded. "I have noticed the same. The reason is probably twofold. Firstly, x'qai—particularly the suzerains—do not want these tales of our kind's earlier greatness to become known. They project that it would only embolden us."

"They're right," Bannor almost snarled.

Cruvanor smiled. "Indeed they are. The other cause is that there is much churn among lieges. They come and they go. Sometimes they endure for centuries, even millennia: sometimes for a score of years or less.

"But there is one constant among that turbulence: when they fall, it is in tides of blood and fire. Preserving documents of no particular use does not enter into the considerations of the attackers. Certainly much of that is because of disinterest, but futility might also be a factor." He added a wintry smile. "Asking rampaging x'qai to exercise mindful restraint when they encounter ancient documents is akin to instructing them to bypass a heap of raw meat."

Duncan was nodding. "That certainly explains why there are so few documents and the historical timeline is so disorganized. But to circle back to my question: If there is a site at the-dunes-that-do-not-move, how will anything inside still be useful? If the last of these human enclaves fell over seven centuries ago, what would resist the rot, rust, and decay?"

Cruvanor shrugged. "Sometimes, it is just as you say: it is like opening a great mausoleum in which only rubbish was interred." A slow, sly smile edged onto his face. "But sometimes, it has been sealed by the elements. And the greatest power of these lands—the sickness which destroys everything that grows to maturity—also annihilates many animalcules which cause decay. If water cannot enter the site, so much the better. And if it has collapsed in such a way that it is sealed from air itself, objects can last a very, very long time indeed."

Solsohn stared at him. "No. There's something else."

The war leader glanced up at Riordan. "You have a very fine team."

Caine smiled. "I know. I believe you have a question to answer." *One you tried to dodge.*

The other nodded. "There is another situation in which there is no decay: no change *at all*. I have only encountered such a ruin three times."

"Which is two times more than anyone else," Tirolane put in. Qyza nodded vigorously.

Cruvanor smiled and waved for them to desist. "There is a compound we call 'ancient amber.' It must either be dissolved or chipped slowly away from what it encases. The means whereby it effects this preservation is unclear, but whatever was captured in it is unaltered by time, more so than a *kik* in amber. Hence, its name." He frowned. "There is one other thing."

Riordan couldn't tell if the old man was overcoming an innate reluctance to share a secret, or having to push through a terrible memory to access it.

Cruvanor sat very straight. "I have been in a place very much like the one the young h'achga described. It contained elements that were—most implausible. And wonders you would scarcely believe."

Riordan smiled. "Try us."

"It was a large complex and very heavily built. Like a great pyramid fortress, sheared away at the top. It had equally fortified tunnels connecting it to other, smaller sites that radiated out from it. The equipment in it was pristine, and some of it reminds me of what you carried into battle at the river, the artifacts I am told that you employed to see and slay the greatest x'qai. And rads—strange, complicated, some with weapons. But this was not the strangest thing of all."

Riordan almost shouted at the old man not to stop talking.

"There was a great chamber. I wish I remembered it better; I was young and it was my first such site. But this much I recall. My war leader in those days walked to an intricately painted wall that made no sense to me... until he placed his finger on one particular spot and said, 'This is where we are right now.' Then he pointed to all the images surrounding it.

"And there were all the mountains and rivers and bays I knew. And the other continents. It was a map of the world." He shook his head. "To think that I ever saw such a thing. It changed me. I knew we—our long forgotten and dust-rendered forebears—had not only built this strange fort that was now half underground, but had ruled the world and the skies above."

"How," Duncan asked quietly, "did you know they ruled the skies, as well?"

"There were curved lines that ran along the surface of the world, lines which matched no physical features. We knew this, for we knew several of the regions through which they ran and they contained nothing where the lines passed. Collectively, they were like a wave made of many lines, always constant, rising to and fro across the middle of the map."

"The moon," Miles whispered—apparently before he could think the better of it.

None of them had ever seen Cruvanor startled before. "How do you know? Have you seen the same map?"

"It is how we navigate," Riordan said quickly. "Those are the tracks where the moon passes over the surface of the world. They change, higher or lower, with the seasons."

Cruvanor leaned back. "So you know. That it is not the sun that moves with the seasons. It is our world that is tilting."

God damn. "Yes," Riordan answered. "We know."

Cruvanor stood. "Then I say to you all, here in the last years of a long life, that you are very well met, indeed. I thought such things, such discoveries and wonders, were all behind me. Perhaps they are not." He reached out toward Tirolane. "You have fallen in with fine friends, Grandson. But now, I must strike a note of discord at the very moment I should be harmonizing gratefully."

Riordan kept his voice calm, level. "How so?"

"I shall help you at this ruin. But immediately after that, you must take me to Zrik Whir, by whatever means may already be, or come, within your compass. I must go there to seek help, or remain behind to find it here.

"Help for what?"

"To free my brothers and sisters that remain in Gorzrik's stable."

Riordan shook his head. "But Zrik Whir is very distant. How can you be so sure that anyone there will help you, or that they could do so in time?"

He sighed. "Because unless I am greatly mistaken, my freedom—and the news I bear—will galvanize them to taking action here on Brazhgarag." He leaned forward. "They do not see what is changing on this continent and beyond. There have always been massacres, cullings, atrocities levied against our kind. But now, something far more sweeping, more deliberate, is coming. It is planned and many lieges have agreed to it. The Grand Council at Paideion must understand that the dissolution of Gorzrik's stable is but a fore-echo of the first volley in a much greater war."

"A war to achieve what?"

Cruvanor met Caine's eyes. "Extermination. To sweep our kind from the face of this planet."

Chapter Twenty-Two

After the blinding midday glare on the streets of Forkus, the great hall of Hwe'tsara's court still seemed dim, a collage of shadows that differed only in shape and darkness. Heavy footfalls—punctuated by the *click-click* of talons—announced the approach of the increasingly irritated liege. Mindful of Fezhmorbal's counsel, Qudzorpla bowed low, much lower than she ever had to any being before as the large x'qao finally appeared and flung himself into his stony throne. "You have news?"

"I do, Your Horror."

"Well, spit it out—no: wait. Before you do, I have news for your master."

Fezhmorbal is my leader, not my master, *you beast.* "I attend your words, Dread Liege." She also rued what he might convey: news about the so-called star splinter. Truth be told, she found it easier to tolerate his contemptuous disregard than the nonsense that had filled gullible mouths when it first appeared. It was an omen! A god! A world-ending meteor! But now? It was just a slightly brighter object, repeating its daily sprint across the night sky, all but forgotten.

Hwe'tsara's distempered snarl brought her awareness back into the dark hall. "Tell Fezhmorbal that the great W'sazz-Ozura has determined that the new star over which he obsesses shall not be above us forever. Close observation, and unthinkably dull measurements, satisfy her that it will ultimately fall from the heavens."

She was so surprised that the information was pertinent that she forgot to add an honorific. "How soon?"

Hwe'tsara was too annoyed to notice her informal query. "Seasons, years, more: how should I know? And why should I believe the scribes who think that they do, and have convinced W'sazz-Ozura? They are the same bloodbags that insist that their own kind—think it; *humans*!—once traveled the night skies with ease!" He shifted on his throne, scanning the room hungrily. "Clearly, the scribes ate the wrong fungi that day. Would they had eaten deadly ones." He fixed his eyes on Qudzorpla. "Now, what is your news? I will be displeased if Fezhmorbal's lieutenant Gasdashrag has discovered nothing of interest since finding and following the thieves' trail from the site of the caravan ambush."

She began her answer with the slightest bow she could risk. "There is news, but the trail itself was old and much ruined by weather. But it did lead to Achgabab, Your Horror, just as you anticipated." *Because* we *told you so.*

The x'qao shifted his thick mass forward. "I know those lands enough to know that if that is all he has to report, he has dawdled, waiting in a safely distant camp for several weeks now." He smiled mirthlessly. "Which will displease me even more."

"Then you shall be pleased, Your Horror. Gasdashrag left behind but a small contingent to monitor the western approaches the thieves followed from the river. However, he moved the balance of his force to a position just under a day's march northwest of the small pass that exits Achgabab's canyon-lands, well to the north."

Hwe'tsara frowned in surprise. "Toward hotside?"

"Your Horror's knowledge of that region is remarkably precise. Yes, that is the pass, and Gasdashrag positioned himself so that he could observe any forces which emerged from there, or from the wider passes into the east."

"Which would be how the thieves would leave Achgabab if they meant to go to Ebrekka."

"Or, Uhrashgrukh, Dread Hwe'tsara. But instead of appearing there, the thieves' formation exited to the north. Although it becomes increasingly difficult to think of them as thieves."

Hwe'tsara's eyes narrowed. "They stole. They are thieves. They shall die for it. And you should remember that. Or do you prize neither your welcome in this court nor your life?"

Qudzorpla managed not to swallow in terror. "I apologize that I did not make my meaning more clear, Dread Liege. Thieves they are, but now, they travel in numbers and in formations that are far more akin to that of a war party. A very well-led war party that marches as do campaign units marshalled by human war leaders. Senior ones, at that."

"So they exited Achgabab to the north. For what purpose? Those lands are among the most barren, and the farther north one goes, the more lethal they are to humans."

"Yes, it puzzled Gasdashrag as well, Your Horror. It was even more puzzling when the thieves angled back toward the river, albeit much higher upstream than where they crossed."

Hwe'tsara's head lifted sharply. "Are they mad?"

"We asked the same question. But the answer is, 'apparently not.' Just today, Gasdashrag arrived at the site of a battle fought near the natural mooring some days north of Tajkor. There were scattered bodies, mostly x'qai and jalks, but our trackers say that there had been far more corpses there, initially. They found only one set of tracks leading to the site: those of the thieves. So evidently, the other force arrived by barge."

"Well, who won?"

"The battlefield itself surrendered few clues. However, only the thieves' tracks left the field. And I must emphasize: they did not flee or withdraw. They left the field at their leisure, and none of the bodies left behind answer to those suspected to be in their formation."

Hwe'tsara's teeth ground audibly. "And has Gasdashrag followed and visited my vengeance upon them?" It sounded like he already knew, or at least feared, the answer.

"That, Your Horror, is why Fezhmorbal is now traveling north to join his lieutenant. Gasdashrag's scouts have since determined that the thieves' force is now more numerous than his own, and yet are increasingly more orderly during both their marches and bivouacs. Given that they are known to have multiple firearms, Gasdashrag consulted with Fezhmorbal, who agrees that their contingents should be combined before engaging the enemy. The latter also asked me to send word that his time in Khorkrag was brief, but useful."

Hwe'tsara extended a single long claw in her direction. "You are smiling. So his time in Khorkrag achieved more than merely the arranged resupply. He discovered something to advance my interests there."

"Your Horror reads me so readily." She was gratified and revolted at the x'qao's evident delight in such petty, and baseless, flattery. "By sheer serendipity, an opportunity presented itself to ruin relations among the h'achgai of the region. Specifically, I refer to the ties that bind the smaller tribal collectives to Achgabab."

Hwe'tsara's hard-rimmed lips were grinning, now. "Tell me more."

"Upon arriving in Khorkrag, Fezhmorbal learned that a scion of a smaller h'achgai community was in the town to conduct trade and seek support for his father's ambitions."

"I know the family of which you speak. And?"

"Fezhmorbal extended the courtesy of his camp to this fellow... after feeding his companions to grateful 'qo."

"So he has the scion hostage?"

Qudzorpla bowed her head. "It is as you say, Your Horror. Fezhmorbal has left behind several trusted agents to exploit this hostage when the time is right."

Hwe'tsara studied her silently for several seconds. He never had before. She tried to remain calm as she reviewed the exits from his stronghold...

"You are welcome here, female stooop," he announced finally. "You are frank, efficient, and spend less time wondering after things that are of no concern to me. When you have more news, return. If you have need of more support, you will be expected to make a firm case for it. Now, begone: I grow irritable when I am hungry."

She bowed and backed out of the chamber. Not out of respect, but out of uncertainty. Despite his words, the monstrous predator might be unable to resist the impulse to devour a receding prey animal such as her.

Fezhmorbal sent a pulse of approval through the mental link Qudzorpla had established. "You handled that monstrosity quite well. Does he suspect that you have skills beyond that of a liaison and warrior?"

"If he does, he gives no sign of it. And he has little skill at dissembling."

"If any. Very well. You shall remain in Forkus with Sorsherreg, gathering forces and building our web of contacts. We may have need of them sooner rather than later."

Her thought paused. "Have your plans or circumstances changed, Commander?"

"The latter has impelled the former. The change is what Gasdashrag reports regarding the activities and tracks of the war party that Hwe'tsara insists on calling 'thieves.' It is too early to be certain, but in addition to many more tinkers, it appears that the proportion of humans has increased. This is not merely reflected in a greater number of their better and narrower sandal and boot prints, but the efficiency of their march."

"It is very like what you always strive to achieve, then, Commander."

"It is, but the more x'qa and praakht I add to our forces here in the north, the more widely spread our own people become. With only sixteen deciqadi to oversee six dozen assorted, intemperate servitors, we are at the point where to increase the numbers of our force means decreasing its speed and flexibility."

"So what is your solution, War Leader? I would learn from you, if you would teach me."

"When I have an answer, I shall share it with you. But this is my misgiving: that the longer it takes us to shape conditions conducive to mounting an attack upon the humans with our greater numbers, the less those greater numbers will matter. Our enemy becomes more nimble; we become less so. This is why you and Sorsherreg must recruit more praakht and, particularly, prakhwa."

A longer pause followed. "Do you mean to send others back to help us in that task?"

"It shall be just you two."

"Is that..." He could feel her thought grow diaphanous as she conceived of various ways to solve the obvious problem before her: finding a tactful way to challenge his judgment.

"You wish to ask... what, Qudzorpla? Is my choice 'wise'? 'Prudent'? 'Safe'? Come, complete the thought that I may know which insult you intend."

"I mean no insult, War Leader Fezhmorbal. But it would be very easy for us to be overcome in the places where Sorsherreg and I must go to secure such new troops. Particularly the prakhwa."

"You have many advantages, and you may use those you have already signed to our cause to support you in gathering more.

Besides, it may be wisest to build the less useful forces first. Many minds are weak, deadskins are plentiful, and your purses grow steadily heavier." He sighed. "I admit having our force now split into three groups is not what I envisioned or what I would choose. But for now, we must prove our capabilities and competence to Hwe'tsara so that not even he will fail to realize that, excluding humans, he could not possibly achieve what he is achieving through us."

"Your words are my wisdom, War Leader."

Let us hope they are. "We shall touch minds again at the appointed day and time." He broke the link.

Fezhmorbal sighed and rubbed his eyes before surveying the camp around him.

"Difficulties in Forkus, camp-brother?"

The commander turned toward his comrade of many campaigns and plots: Meznagruss, whose skill with a sword was almost as great as his mastery of eunogogic patternings. Not a friend, exactly—deciqadi were not plagued by sentimentality like praakht or humans—but the fellow was a near-peer that he would regret losing. Very much.

"Affairs in Forkus are not so much difficult as strained," Fezhmorbal explained. "The thirty of our group were an ample number to change Hwe'tsara's fortunes and make him dependent. But with the onset of these strange humans, we are stretched too thin and too far."

"It was a bold decision to make them so high a priority."

Fezhmorbal allowed a smile to curl one side of his mouth. "If you believe I have erred, say so frankly." It was a shared irony, but also a warning that if Meznagruss presumed too much, he would have a challenge on his hands.

The warrior-magister raised both those hands in mock dismay. "I said you were bold, not a buffoon. But you know that if it does not produce results, and we do not succeed with Hwe'tsara, questions will be asked."

Yes, Fezhmorbal agreed with a nod, *but it is you who will be asked first. The Oligate will wish to know if you supported me. And if you answer in the affirmative, then they will consider unseating you, as well.* "We have seen many things over the years we two have served the race, camp-brother, so tell me this: have you ever seen, or even heard, of something so singular as these humans?"

Meznagruss shook his head without delay or the faintest hint that it was feigned. "You know I have not. I said as much when you divided our focus between the mission at hand and the one that fell from the sky."

Fezhmorbal nodded. "The longer we follow them, and the more we hear of them—their extraordinary knowledge combined with their extraordinary ignorance—the more I believe that they shall lead us to something that dwarfs Hwe'tsara and all of Forkus by comparison."

"You may well be right. And I certainly hope you are." Meznagruss crossed his arms tightly in front of him, either hand resting upon the bony hip opposite: a far more stable posture for deciqadi than humans. He stared out at the force the two of them had built.

It was an excellent vantage point—the very place where the humans had apparently made camp before ambushing the caravan. Just beyond the stony teeth around the small rise, two score praakht and prakhwa kept at weapon drills beneath the unsympathetic eyes of the deciqadi. His one useful x'qa—well, an illithrakz, actually—barked orders in a voice that was far deeper than he would have expected from its female form. But no amount of commands or threats could govern the dozens of x'qa that roved back and forth, sowing disorder the same way that the swaying tails of dustkine spread their dung.

But Fezhmorbal's gaze did not remain on his forces. Once again, he felt it pulled beyond them, to rest upon the flat expanse where the caravan had been attacked. The humans had chosen the ground well, and unlike many deciqadi, he was able to separate his loathing of a foe from the ability to see and appreciate its competence. And this one had been quite competent indeed.

There was little left to assess, but judging from where broken shafts remained and dustkine trampling had marred the ground beyond the power of rain to wash away, there had been three attack elements. The first had appeared directly in the path of the caravan, slowing it. The second had been hidden in a trench-like wadi to the east. It had volleyed into the side of the halted dustkine and no doubt the clumped 'qo and praakht. And then a third element had attacked from a small dry rill from the rear and to the west.

The caravan had been hit from three directions sequentially.

Every time it had turned to address a new threat, yet another group attacked from a different direction, ultimately surrounding it. The attackers had possessed a startling number of bows and crossbows—probably more than Fezhmorbal had even now—and who knew what carnage their harrowlike weapons had wrought. But even so...

"You keep staring at that battlefield," Meznagruss muttered. "Are the ghosts talking to you?"

"Maybe they are. The more I look at it, the more I come to suspect that the caravan was not merely attacked by bows and artifacts."

"What are you saying?"

"I am saying, the sheer mass of the caravan should have inflicted far more harm on the ambushers, unless they had further means to destroy its morale, its commanders, or both. The formation came apart too easily."

"I know that tone, you old war-kine. What are you thinking?"

"That the humans may have either an anagogete or eunogogete among them. Maybe more than one."

Meznagruss crouched down beside him, surveyed the field. "It would explain much. Each time such a power was unleashed could have staggered the caravan yet again."

Fezhmorbal nodded. "Enough to break the much larger force and send the dustkine into frenzied flight."

"Has Gasdashrag seen any indication that they have either kind of practitioner among them?"

"No, but humans with such powers are more circumspect in their use of them than we are. It makes them harder to assess—and so, predict."

Meznagruss frowned and nodded. "You mindspeak with Gasdashrag tomorrow, do you not?"

Fezhmorbal nodded.

"What do you mean to tell him?"

"To be more careful than we planned and to keep the majority of his force further from any point of engagement than he might have otherwise. We shall hasten our march to close with him. What I instructed Qudzorpla to report to Hwe'tsara was completely true: Gasdashrag must be far more cautious until we have joined him." Fezhmorbal watched his deciqadi try to train the prakhwa in the use of crossbows and bit his lip: *Even they are too impatient. And the smaller praakhan species are fearful, so even though they are complying, they are not learning.*

Meznagruss' voice almost startled him. "You told me you would share your theory about why the humans are heading straight toward hotside. I think we may have reached the point where that is necessary."

Fezhmorbal nodded. "Although it was more common in earlier centuries, humans still risk journeys into hotside if they hear of or have learned the location of a site where they may go prospecting for ancient artifacts. And this group of humans seems lavishly equipped with them."

"So you do not believe they are carrying high-value goods to Fragkork or to a desolate rendezvous where none will follow?"

Fezhmorbal shook his head. "Gasdashrag's x'qiigh have ample kiktzos. Even watching from over the horizon, they have plainly shown that this group not only moves as a military formation, but has far too few porters. They have barely enough to carry supplies for their march."

"And you think that they may have learned of a buried ruin from maps they found in the same place as their artifacts?"

"Possibly," Fezhmorbal murmured. But as he did, he looked up into the first shades of dusk and wondered when the new star would appear.

As if it might whisper what lay behind the strange coincidence of its arrival and the appearance of these even stranger—not to say disturbing—humans.

Chapter Twenty-Three

Yidreg shielded his eyes with a long-fingered hand and nodded. "The sands have not taken them back, yet."

Riordan ascended to join him at the spine of the final dune. Its eastern, leeward side stretched longer and leveled off more gradually than the others they'd been crossing for the past week. That gentle slope ended at the periphery of a flatter expanse which disrupted the predictable progression of north-south transverse dunes. Several uneven mounds of sand jutted up from the roughly oval depression, two of them apparently anchored by outcroppings of stone. But those dark surfaces were too smooth and uniform to be any kind of natural rock at all.

Cruvanor's son Rogarran drew up alongside Caine, nodded agreeably. "The dunes-that-do-not-move. Just as they've been described."

"Count yourself lucky to see them," Yidreg muttered. "I made the same cho'urz as Djubaran, hoping to behold a legend." A stuttering grunt escaped his throat: the h'achgan equivalent of an ironic laugh. "They were so covered then that I passed them without noticing." He folded his arms. "I'd never thought to see them in my lifetime. I am glad to do so."

Others were gathering along the subtly serpentine crest of the dune. Eku, wearing Peter's Dornaani vacc suit, glanced toward Yidreg. "Commodore Riordan has asked me to take—eh, gather images of the ruins, but instructed me to ask if that would violate any customs or laws pertaining to them."

It was Ulchakh who wheezed out a reply as he labored through the last few steps of his ascent. "This is not a holy place. There are no taboos."

Riordan nodded his thanks as Eku began building a visual database of the two dark masses protruding from the irregular heaps of sand around them. The larger one appeared to be the top of a trapezoid. The smaller one was no more than a small corner of the same dark material, protruding from the leeward slope of a reconquering dune. "Too late to approach them, I suppose," Caine asked in Rogarran's direction.

It was Cruvanor's voice which answered. "We'll want more light. Besides, that stone is still hot from the day's sun." He edged closer to Riordan. "We'll want to be atop the large one before dawn. Operating this close to hotside, we don't want to be standing out here in the heat—particularly not on a slab of dark rock."

Bannor's voice came up the slope behind them. "Sounds like you might have done this before. So, what has your experience taught you about approaching these sites?"

"That no two are the same." Cruvanor's grin was audible in his reply.

Bannor and several others rising to the lip of the dune laughed.

Rogarran was smiling as well. "The next question of first-time prospectors is usually, 'If it was you entering that ruin, what would you do first?'"

Riordan shook his head. "I won't ask for advice that way."

"Of course not," Rogarran replied with a nod. "You are an experienced leader. You know that if you ask any subordinate to give advice as if they were the commander, it undermines your authority. In the minds of some, it becomes unclear who the real leader is."

Riordan shrugged. "That's not my reason, although if our chain of command could be weakened by a few casual words, I'd get that settled first. In no uncertain terms."

Cruvanor was smiling. "And even if you did ask me what I would do in this situation, you would not follow those steps slavishly. Because you would know they were lacking."

Rogarran sounded upset. "Lacking? In what way?"

"In that my way would not include all the unknown artifacts and powers at our allies' disposal."

Riordan returned the old war leader's smile. "And although it's my intent to reserve the use of those assets for extraordinary circumstances, they still impact our planning. There are some risks I'm more willing to take because those resources are insurance against unexpected outcomes. But I will only include a few of them in our basic plan."

Cruvanor nodded, studied the site. It rose up like a low, dark mesa on the very brink of being drowned under endless waves of sand. "Although I am no stranger to entering ruins, this will be a novel experience for me."

Eku looked up from refining the images he'd gathered. "Why?"

The senior warrior who'd been traveling with Cruvanor—Marcanas—answered with a sardonic snort. "It's the first time he doesn't have a crowd of x'qai watching over his shoulder."

Duncan's voice rose from behind. "Were they worried you'd take a wrong step?"

Cruvanor smiled into the darkening eastern sky. "They were worried I'd pocket something they didn't notice. Which was quite ironic, since their perception of what's valuable in a ruin is laughable." His smile faded. "However, I must admit that prospecting ruins for a x'qao liege was easier in at least one way."

Bannor glanced over at him. "And what was that?"

"Well... we always had deadskins with us."

Eku evidently hadn't heard the rueful drawl at the end of the war leader's reply. "Were they easier to manage as porters?"

The eyes Cruvanor turned upon the factotum were kind but slightly pitying. "They also served as emergency rations for the x'qai. And, during the initial entry, as bait."

"Bait?" In the course of uttering that one word, Eku's tone changed from perplexity to horror.

Chief O'Garran joined him at the crest of the dune. "Better to have one of them on point than one of us." He tried to make it sound jocular, but Riordan heard the grim undertone as well as a hint of disgust.

"What of the tunnels below?" Bey's voice asked from several meters behind. "Can we expect to restore our water from seepage?"

"Yes, but it is likely to be contaminated. Besides"—Cruvanor pointed at the low, irregular dunes surrounding the two ruins—"I suspect this ruin is like the other I entered long ago: near the center of a zone of great destruction. Do you see those faint glints down near the flatter parts of the depression?"

"I noted them while capturing the images," Eku replied as others nodded.

"If your images are very precise, I think you will find them to be small clumps and spherules of glass, mostly green and black."

Riordan swallowed. "And you found similar, er, residues, at the other site like this one?"

Cruvanor nodded. "Many prospectors find them near badly damaged ruins or those that were partially or wholly sealed off from the surface." He glanced at Riordan. "Does this mean something to you?"

Riordan was fairly sure he kept his expression from changing. "It means just what you said: this was once a place of great destruction."

Rogarran was eyeing the sun behind them. "Where shall we make camp, this night? Here, or closer to the ruins?"

Riordan answered quickly. "While you discuss the merits of both, I will confer with Eku to see what, if anything, his images reveal about the site." Putting a hand on Eku's elbow, he steered the factotum back down the side of the dune they'd just ascended.

"Commodore, I did not see anything of relevance in the images of—"

"Eku, reconfigure your HUD for spaceside sensors."

"Sir? I don't—"

"Just do it, and follow me."

Bannor was trailing behind the pair. "Something wrong, Commodore?"

"Not sure. I'll tell you in a moment." He led Eku back up to the spine of the dune.

"What am I looking for, sir?"

Bannor started to draw in a sharp breath, controlled the reflex. "Shit."

Riordan nodded at him. "Eku, what is your REM counter showing?"

Eku started. "Approximately seven times background. No health risk unless we were to live here. Sir, how did you know?"

"Those smooth glass bits twinkling in the sands? They're trinitite."

When Eku frowned at the unfamiliar word, Bannor explained.

"Sand melted into glass by a nuclear blast. It was observed at the first test, which was called Trinity. You only find the term trinitite in history books, now."

Eku stared at the bowl-like depression in which the ruins were located. "So, that's a crater?"

Riordan nodded. "Probably. Assuming we get inside the ruin, you'll have a task in addition to recording everything we see and building a real-time floorplan. I want you to keep the REM sensor running. Especially if we come across any water; that's more likely to retain a higher level of contamination."

Eku swallowed. "Anything else, sir?"

"Yes. I'm pretty sure Cruvanor is going to want to make camp down in the bowl. It's good cover from the wind, gives us distance and good sightlines to all the dune-tops, and allows us the earliest possible start getting up the first ruin. So when we go down to take a closer look, you're coming with me. And if that REM meter begins spiking, you let me know. Right away. No delays. I don't care who's talking or about what. Understood?"

Eku's eyes were wide as he nodded. "Very much so, sir."

Bey heard footsteps approaching, looked up; Qyza was sauntering in her direction, smiling. Bey put aside the shortsword she was sharpening. "And why are you so cheerful?"

"Why shouldn't I be?" the other replied with a sigh and a loose-limbed flop onto the hide beside Bey's. "I am much sought after, here. Even in spite of this," she emphasized, tugging on her misshapen turnip of a nose and surrounding scars.

Bey shrugged. "Still, as a crog, I would have expected you are *always* considered a prestigious mate. Particularly in a city such as Fragkork."

Qyza scoffed. "Unlike you, I had no beauty to be ruined by the breaking of my nose. And as a whakt—crog—I was not truly part of any gang or tribe of trogs. My group was mostly trogans, and never more than a dozen or so."

Bey nodded. Like herself, Qyza had not been in direct service to a x'qao liege. But rather than part of a gang, she had been brought into a group whose axes could be hired by the highest bidder. Or at least, that is how they had made it appear. In fact, through rather tortuous connections, their small band received modest but regular funding from the humans of several different stables. That unrevealed retainer maintained them as unrevealed allies, which was how she had heard of Cruvanor's pending "journey." That in turn brought her enough information to be in the right place, and to offer the right price, to be included in the barge's guard contingent.

Bey glanced back along her path of approach: she'd come from Cruvanor's camp circle. "You rut with the trogs, yet you still stay with the humans."

Qyza shrugged. "Why not?" She smiled at the numerous camp circles that radiated out from Bey's solitary sleeping fur. "No one made *me* the leader of all trogs!"

Bey smiled, raised an eyebrow. "No... but would you *like* to be?"

"Gods, no!"

They laughed, Qyza's eyes wide with horror that was only partly histrionic. "What a curse that must be."

"And an honor, as well," Bey added seriously.

Qyza nodded. "No doubt, but I would not want those worries for my body's weight in moss, my sister! And you certainly don't seem to be any happier for it. Look at you: you should have your choice of trogans and trogs aspiring to join you in your furs. And yet there you lie, night after night, all alone."

Bey shrugged. "I cannot take a fur-mate, or any mate at all, without creating many problems. Both for the group and myself."

Qyza nodded. "Well, yes, that is certainly one reason you remain alone."

Bey heard the hanging tone. "What do you mean, *one* reason?"

Qyza rolled her eyes and leaned closer, voice low. "Please, Bey. I am not a half-blind human. I see what they do not. Yes, you are careful with your glances and your voice, but you are rarely further than a dozen steps away from Leader Caine. Even when you are not looking at him, you always—*always*—know exactly where he is."

Bey's first instinct was to do what she had when Zaatkhur, and occasionally Sho, had made similarly accurate observations: scoff and deny them. But now, without any friends, it would be a great relief to have someone to talk to, someone with whom she could share what she dared not reveal to anyone else. Doing so was also a risk, of course: she and Qyza had become friendly, but not so close that she could be sure the other would keep a secret. On the other hand, that risk was also an opportunity, because if Qyza *did* keep her confidence, that bond of trust would put them on a much faster path to a true friendship. "Do you think our own kind see it?" Bey murmured carefully.

"Our own kind? If you mean trogs, no, but that is because they probably *presume* you wish to mate with a human. And if so, why not their leader? Some may think it is your only choice, if they reflect on how impossible it is for you to be with trogs, given all the different groups in the unit. You cannot choose one without turning all others against you.

"But that is complicated, and any who think of that will also forget it. They simply see what is before their eyes: that you walk among the humans as one of them and have their full trust. And given your looks, it is natural to conclude that you aspire to be one of their mates."

"And do they also forget that as a female kajh, that is quite impossible for me to *be* one of their mates?"

Qyza threw up an exasperated hand. "Who knows what they forget? Before becoming part of this strange band, their masters made sure they had little time—or reason—to think, so their world is one of feelings and first impressions. But are the *humans* aware of our limits as female kajhs?"

Bey frowned. "I do not know. But certainly their females must have noticed, and among the Crewe they share all of what they learn about us. So they must know."

Qyza shook her head. "Whether they do or don't, they are the strangest humans I have ever encountered—and I have met some very strange ones." She rubbed her twisted nose. "Are they from Beyond, do you think?"

"I do not know. They do not speak of it. But they know almost nothing of this land or its ways."

Qyza shrugged. "Then they are from Beyond."

Bey shook her head. "How could that be? They do not know Uhrashgrukh or any of the other places where it is said those from Beyond emerge or reside."

Qyza gestured impatiently in the direction of the Crewe's camp circle. "Their ways are too bizarre to be anything but Beyonders—and especially strange ones at that, sister! They share in the most menial tasks, conceal their feelings, and nurse wounded trogs like their own offspring—assuming they can have any. Gods, do they even have the urge to mate? Ever?"

Bey frowned. "They are circumspect, but yes, Bannor and Ayana are most certainly mated."

"Then why do they not share their furs?"

"I do not know. This group of humans are all very private and very careful. I am not sure why. Some of my band wondered if they were one of the storied groups which foreswore rutting to make themselves greater warriors. But they denied it."

"Given the way they act—or rather, *don't* act—I'm not sure I'd believe them."

Bey shrugged. "I suspect they feel the same urges, perhaps just as strongly. And with just as much variation. From what I have observed, Leader Pandora views males and females with equal interest."

"Hmmm . . . interesting." Qyza's tone suggested more than casual curiosity. "So you are certain it is not simply that they are burntskins, that they have no passions?"

Bey frowned. "I have never put great faith in *that* rumor, either."

Qyza raised an eyebrow. "Oh? And how many burntskins have you encountered before these?"

"None." Bey smiled. "And you?"

"Only a few, but they were all harrows and scythes. They certainly had passions, but mostly for violence, which they gratified by either forcing themselves upon, or killing, others." She sighed. "If these humans of yours were from Beyond, like reapers, I'd expect them to behave similarly. But they could not be more different. They have even more self-control than war leaders like Cruvanor. Of course, that just proves the truth of the old trog saying."

Bey allowed herself a half-grin. "And which of the hundreds of trog sayings do you mean?"

"That with humans, appearances can be deceiving."

Bey almost chuckled. "With humans, appearances are *always* deceiving. That is what makes them so dangerous."

Qyza smiled wickedly. "And yet so interesting, too?"

Bey rolled her eyes but smiled as she waved away Qyza's leer. "Your teasing does not help me."

"Then what would?"

Bey smiled at her fellow kajh's earnest offer. "I need you to stand guard once we are bivouacked in a place where privacy is possible."

Qyza frowned. "Stand guard? Where? Why?"

"So that I will not be interrupted when I speak with the one person who can answer my questions. Are you willing to do that for me?"

"Of course!" Qyza leaned closer, even though there wasn't another being within twenty arm-lengths. "Who do you mean to pull aside?"

Bey looked into her new comrade's eyes, saw only interest and resolve. Her caution melted away and, matching Qyza's inward lean, she discovered that her sudden rush of emotion was not at the promise of understanding Caine and his companions better, but at the relief of gaining what she had been missing for so long: a friend and confidant.

INTERLUDE TWO

Allies or Adversaries

June–July 2125
Bactradgaria

Interlude Two

Richard Downing arrived on *Olsloov*'s bridge with two days' growth of beard and reeking of stale sweat. Thlunroolt appeared at his elbow, handed him a visual relay visor already patched into the ship's active drones, and may have muttered something sympathetic as he glide-floated away.

Everyone, even Trevor, looked worse for wear. His nephew turned in his human-shaped acceleration couch. "Here for the final act?"

Richard nodded, reached out for a handhold. "Yes. Maybe then we'll know if this has been a tragedy or a comedy."

Trevor shrugged. "Maybe both." He turned back to watch the main screen's apparently motionless vista, even though *Olsloov* was heading in-system at very high speed. The many hours at high-gee acceleration had added to everyone's weariness.

Richard connected his duty suit's lanyard to the handhold. *And everyone had been in such high spirits when we arrived.* Now, the only thing anyone really wanted was to see the back of the bloody mess they'd made and, maybe, sleep long enough to forget it had ever happened.

To use a colorful profanity quite popular among the Lost Soldiers of Major Rodger Y. Murphy's era, from the moment *Olsloov* shifted into the 55 Tauri B system, it had been a complete "shit show." Those aboard just hadn't known it at first.

Emerging slightly above the ecliptic of the smaller K3 star that was the secondary of the binary pair, Alnduul had ordered his sensor operator to watch for the typical signs of a spacefaring civilization: pinpoint radiant energy sources, broadcast or microwave activity, small objects on unusual vectors or maintaining usefully close and regular orbits. She found nothing.

Nothing nearby, that is. The primary system—an F7 main sequence star with three planets—was a riot of just such activity and emissions. Most of it was centered on the third planet, but there were also noticeable signatures clustered near planet two. There were also plentiful thermal blooms along trajectories consistent with either high-energy transits or Hohmann transfers between the various planets, their satellites and, by conjecture, space stations. However, as they had encountered since entering the Scatters, there were no high-power broadcast or radar emissions. To use those, or supraluminal drives, was a violation of the terms of their exile and certain to bring swift retribution from the Ktoran Sphere.

The readings emanating from the high-energy transit vehicles were consistent with nuclear thermal rockets. The plenitude of artificial objects in space indicated a highly industrialized population, probably in the billions. However, that made the silence of the secondary system all the more puzzling. *Olsloov* approached the third, and clearly green, planet of the secondary for a better look.

Within the hour, a handful of small objects were detected maneuvering in its vicinity. However, the planet itself showed no radiant energy sources or radio signals. Surprisingly, the only source of those signatures in the system came from asteroids 0.7 AU from the green world, most of them clustered just beyond the gas giant in the fourth orbit. The signatures were unusual in their type and degree of spectral diffusion, and if it had not been for *Olsloov*'s advanced sensors, they would have probably been overlooked.

Their source was narrowed to a volume of space in which there were three objects that shared unusual characteristics: all were long asteroids rolling slowly around their long axis. Their surfaces were also extremely dark, as if any reflective points had been dulled to a matte finish. Trevor's frown had signaled doubt even as he asked if the coloration could be a result of natural phenomena.

Alnduul answered that while nothing was impossible, the selective abrasion needed to create such a nonreflective surface had never been observed in nature. An oblique course was laid in to swing close and get better samples of the faint, brief radio bursts emanating from or near them.

As they approached, revelations mounted quickly. The awkwardly encrypted, and very possibly analog, comm bursts were easily decoded by the Dornaani computers, which identified the underlying language as a devolved form of Ktoran as it had been spoken fourteen hundred years ago. Hardly surprising: since entering the Scatters, every inhabited system evinced Ktoran linguistic roots. Still, the system remained promising. Not only was it distant from the bustling activity around the primary, but the very low technological sophistication of the green world made it likely they could avoid contact while taking on a hold-full of what Alnduul insisted on calling "comestibles." And if peaceful contact could be established with whoever was using radios beyond the fourth orbit, then *Olsloov* might also be able to top off her antimatter bunkers.

The only uncertainty was whether the locals had also inherited their Ktoran ancestors' predilections for aggression and domination. The green world's lack of development was a tentatively hopeful sign they had not: it was unlikely that such a prize would have gone unconquered, otherwise. Instead, other than a few small craft loitering nearby, *Olsloov* detected no signs of local activity other than the very faint and infrequent radio signals beyond the fourth orbit. The only logical conjecture was that the Ktoran instincts toward dominion had either diminished or had been actively rejected in favor of a less ferocious social framework.

Consequently, Downing and Alnduul agreed that, due to their rapidly dwindling supplies, it was worth the risk of making contact. But since they had no facts about the civilization, only conjecture, they agreed it was safest to do so at the furthest inhabited edge of the secondary system. So, continuing their steady approach to the slowly rolling asteroids, they tasked the computer to translate words of greeting into the local Ktoran patois and sent it using the only medium they'd seen used by the locals: medium-power broadcast.

That not only initiated the "shit show" that followed, but triggered its explosion into instantaneous, full-blown chaos.

All radio emanations from the asteroids ended immediately. Previously undetected small craft activated drives, heading outward from the green world's Trojan Point asteroids. The slightly larger ships that had been idling around the planet reacted promptly, crowding gees to intercept the ones that had appeared so abruptly. The perplexing activity finally became clear when one of the ships breaking orbit did not join the chase but rose toward the ecliptic, high enough to send a quick, high-energy broadcast burst back toward the primary system.

Olsloov's computer promptly decoded and translated it: "Investigating local anomaly; stand by for details. Confirm lascom coordinates for subsequent comms."

Downing prided himself on being hard to confuse, disorient, or surprise: a quality that had served him well before medicaling out of the SAS. But on this occasion, he experienced all three mental states simultaneously until he realized that the "local anomaly" was not *Olsloov* or its radio message; it was the small craft which were fleeing the inner system.

It was as if a familiar, expected image had been turned upside down and its actual content finally became clear. The rolling asteroids themselves were the sources of the whisper-faint signals and were almost certainly not facilities belonging to people from the primary system. Rather, they and the small craft that had appeared so suddenly had been hiding from the indolent ships of interlopers from the primary system. All revealed because, in *all* the locals' minds, the *Olsloov*'s strong and straightforward broadcast signal could only be sent by a craft from the primary system. Alarmed, the small craft that had been hiding among the third planet's Trojan asteroids had broken cover: whether to flee or swiftly return to defend their homes in the outer system was known only to them.

Realizations tumbled into place quickly after that. The rolling asteroids were large habitats, and more exacting scans began registering very small energy signatures throughout the outer system. These space dwellers had obviously led a secret existence for a very long time. But how?

It was Trevor who saw the reason: the median distance between the primary and secondary system, twenty-six AU, was a lengthy and costly haul, even for nuclear thermal rockets. So, presuming the culture around the primary had retained the Ktoran impulses toward aggression and conquest, they had probably chosen not to establish a colony on a world that was usually too far to defend against insurgencies or even a complete overthrow. It was far more logical to undertake a wealth-gathering journey of eleven AU once every eighty-eight years: when the systems were at periapsis.

Which was now only six years away.

All of which meant that *Olsloov*'s one message had put the entire population of the second system at imminent risk of subjugation or extermination.

After that, there wasn't enough time to examine any one of the cascading decisions too deeply. Swift action was necessary if the damage was to be contained and controlled. Identification and offers of help were sent to the asteroid habitats. *Olsloov*'s comms and electronic countermeasures suite initiated full-bandwidth jamming of the ships from the primary system. Dornaani drones were launched toward the green world, crowding gees that Downing and Trevor at first suspected of being erroneous; their extraordinary acceleration and duration outstripped what human technical intelligence analysts considered theoretical maximums.

Pushing the drones to their limits proved pivotal. Shortly after the vessels from the primary's system were jammed, several began altering course to rise above the shadow of the combined mass and interference of the planet and the system's star. The only logical reason: to establish line-of-sight communications to the main system. Not knowing their performance characteristics, there was no certainty that the Dornaani drones, despite their blistering speed, would arrive in time to thwart them.

No one slept for forty-eight hours. The locals—who, according to the Dornaani translator, called themselves "SpinDogs"—agreed to a hastily arranged and incompletely defined alliance. Their Matriarch asked for a liaison, so the most senior woman officer among the Lost Soldiers, USAF Captain Mara Lee, was pulled out of suspended animation, briefed in a rush, and sent straight into twelve hours of virtual language training. With a ten-to-one time compression, she was hustled out to join the SpinDogs with the equivalent of one hundred twenty hours of "old Ktoran" language instruction and an overview of the kind of culture she might encounter. Downing was deeply impressed by her resilience and mission focus, and experienced more than one pang of regret that she was one of the Lost Soldiers that would have to be left behind. But like so many others now, her cryocell's yellow warning light had begun to flash; full failure was imminent.

As she was being readied, the ships from the primary's main world—Kulsis—had split into two groups. One continued pursuing the SpinDogs' small craft, which were not, it turned out, fleeing toward the large habitats but their own out-system hiding spots.

However, the other enemy formation crowded gees and headed toward the source of the first, mysterious transmission: *Olsloov*. Unfortunately, that course would also bring them to the SpinDogs' still undiscovered asteroid habitats within twenty-four hours.

Subsequent events and decisions were something of a blur for Downing. The Dornaani drones narrowly intercepted and eliminated the Kulsian ships attempting to establish line-of-sight communication to their home system. The SpinDogs' small craft began slowing, altering course; their pursuers kept after them. *Olsloov* pushed five-gee constant to intercept the Kulsian formation already heading in its general direction, disabling every ship without slowing or taking damage. A swarm of local craft emerging from the asteroid habitats followed in its wake to finish that hurried job. Alnduul released more drones and, his crew in their acceleration couches, maintained speed to hasten in-system.

The drones caught up with the Kulsian ships pursing the small craft, bracketed and pushed them toward an intercept point for Alnduul's second sortie of drones and the SpinDogs' own craft. The most difficult part of the operation was to ensure that the enemy was sufficiently contained before initiating the chaos of battle.

Twelve hours later, the fastest of the SpinDog ships from the asteroid habitats—Mara aboard one as a liaison—were finally in range to begin the last act of the drama: to ensure that no word of the SpinDogs' existence ever reached the primary system.

As if from a great distance, Downing heard a voice calling his name: "Richard?" It was Trevor Corcoran.

Downing awoke to the bridge of *Olsloov*, visor in his hand.

Trevor nodded at him. "Might want to put that on, Uncle Richard. We're coming to the finish line."

Downing nodded, fumbled with the visor, knew he should find out how long he'd been in a sleep-deprivation daydream, but discovered he only cared—really *cared*—about one thing at the moment:

The lad called me Uncle *Richard. Could just be a slip. Happens when you're stupid with lack of food and kip. But still—*

Trevor called me Uncle Richard.

And then *Olsloov*'s screen and Downing's visor were filled with drones and missiles and flaring hulls that trailed glowing fragments.

One of the Kulsians' last remaining rotational habitats—four pods cycling around a central docking hub—was hit by three SpinDog missiles. The structure came apart in a ruin of components that recalled a pair of bolos tearing free from a splintering discus, the rotational tethers hurling away transport pods like bullets from a sling.

Richard was unable to suppress a sharp flinch, whereas, alongside him, Trevor didn't even react. He had seen far worse, and far more, during the invasion of Earth.

The view in the holographic visor changed. The dying station was now a tiny, discorporating smudge of debris, black against the surface of the third planet. The remaining Kulsian hulls were attempting to flee but being unerringly slaughtered before they could make any significant progress. The largest of them was a long trusswork keel with engines at one end, a hab-ring at the other, and cargo and docking frames in between. Shining motes swarmed around it. Had the feed in Richard's visor not come from one of those drones, they and the rest of their small metallic cousins would have been invisible.

Gleaming bursts of ellipses marked where the enemy ship's point defense fire batteries released streams of projectiles at the small Dornaani attack platforms. Futile: the swarming drones' ability to crowd gees rapidly and along very different vectors made nonsense of the Kulsians' rudimentary maneuver projections and intercept algorithms. In reply, the teardrop-shaped harriers swung in wide arcs, their microsecond megawatt-level UV laser bursts carving and shearing away the struts and modules of the fleeing ship. Occasional explosions and tongues of flame marked where they touched oxygenated fuel or missile racks.

Trevor grunted. "Got to hand it to the Dornaani; they sure can put on a show. Considerate, making sure that the visors are synced with their lasers' wavelength." He shared the calm observation as one of the crew modules on the stricken ship's ring habitat sparked as it was rent, and then sent out a weak rush of flame and a litter of writhing stick figures.

"I am glad you appreciate the proximal viewpoint," added Alnduul from behind.

Downing turned and removed his visor. "How much longer now, do you think?"

The Dornaani's two large, pupilless eyes nictated twice, rapidly. "Not more than three minutes. We have interdicted Kulsian craft on vectors that would have brought them into positions with line-of-sight to their home system. The remainder are collected at the center of the lee of the combined masses of this system's sun and the planet below."

"And scratch one more," added Trevor. "That transport, or whatever it is, just vaporized. A hit on its drives. Damn, those drones are fast. And how do you Dornaani pack so much punch in those short focal-length lasers?"

"You know I will not answer that question, Captain."

"Never hurts to try. And here comes the local cavalry to clean up what's left."

Downing put his visor back on.

The new perspective was much closer to the planet: a hazy mix of greens, blues, and a wide equatorial belt of dusty ochre. In the foreground, the spindly craft of the SpinDogs were bearing down upon the last enemy ships. The outsystem workhorses had no need for fuselages: their fuel tanks and modules were held together by spiderweb frames that were part gridwork, part geodesic cradles. Not sturdy, but fast and spare—and loaded with missiles. Which they released in coveys toward the comparatively sluggish enemy hulls.

The comms crackled slightly on the sender's side, then Mara Lee's voice was in their earbuds. "Lee to *Olsloov*."

Alnduul nodded to Downing, who replied, "*Olsloov* Actual. Go, Captain."

"Please switch to secure five."

"Done, Captain. What's troubling you, that you don't want our allies—well, co-combatants—on the channel?"

"Sirs, this is—this is wrong. We're not breaking off to assess, as per the OpOrd you and the locals agreed upon."

Downing ran a tooth over his lip. As long as Lee had to keep communicating through the radio of a SpinDog ship, their allies couldn't be prevented from eavesdropping. "Details please, Captain."

"Sir, I have asked when the flight leader intends to demand that the enemy ships cut thrust, stand down, and prepare to be boarded."

"And?"

"And he has not replied."

Trevor glanced over. "Don't like the sound of that."

Lee sounded like she was speaking through clenched teeth. "Neither do I, sir. This is... wait, what the—?"

The comm channel terminated with a sharp snap, replaced by a hiss of static. Downing glanced quickly at Alnduul.

The Dornaani's mouth flattened. "Transmission terminated at the source."

Downing glanced quickly at the tactical holotank; all the aqua-colored motes—friendly forces—were still there.

Alnduul murmured, "Changing visual feed."

Eyes refocusing on his visor, Downing saw their allies' ships angling in toward the enemy craft. Even though the SpinDog lasers were far weaker, they were still picked out by the spectrum-scanning Dornaani visor as they played over the fleeing ships. The beams tore rents in fuel tanks and caused small, dense, wildly spinning clouds of debris to jet out from the sides of cargo and crew modules.

Silent, the two humans and the Dornaani watched the ruthless and efficient slaughter unfold until the last of the orange motes denoting enemy craft had vanished.

Downing wet dry lips before commenting, "Well, I suspect that whoever cut off Captain Lee's comm channel no longer has anything to hide. Can we raise her?"

Alnduul waved a hand of falling fingers at one of his bridge crew; her hands danced over the almost featureless control surfaces. She stared at them a moment, her gills closing slowly. "No reply."

Trevor cleared his throat. "Richard, I think I know why."

As Downing recentered his attention on the scene in the visor, Mara Lee's voice emerged from the bridge's sound system as an amplified whisper. "*Olsloov*, send pulse to confirm you receive me."

Alnduul nodded at his crewperson, exchanged glances with Downing. "The captain was not to use our secure comm bud except in case of emergency."

"I think Trevor is watching that emergency unfold," Downing answered, swallowing.

In the visor, the SpinDogs' spidery craft had begun to counter-boost, slowing their approach to the debris field. In it, a number of escape pods were flashing their location. Space-suited individuals were waving glove-mounted lights.

Mara Lee's voice, back as an even fainter, huskier whisper, reported. "This ship is still weapons-hot, sir. So are the others, from what I hear. And now—oh, shit!" Her voice became a muffled, pressure-hose hiss. "Shit! *Shit!*"

The SpinDog ships' more modest point defense fire systems began sending short bursts of two or three rounds at the blinking lights of the survivors. One by one, they went out.

All of them.

Fifteen minutes later, the SpinDog commanders restored normal comm channels. Mara Lee was breathing heavily as she reported.

"They killed every one of them. Every. Single. Fucking. One of them. They straight-up lied to us, sirs."

"Yes," Downing answered, "they obviously did. And it will make our upcoming conversation with them quite difficult."

"You think so?" Mara Lee caught herself, then added, "Sir."

"Yes, I do 'think so,' Captain, and you will watch your tone." Downing waved at *Olsloov*'s comms operator, who signaled that they were now connected on their secret link. "Captain, are you now also receiving through the Dornaani comm bud?"

"I hear you, sir. Loud and clear." Lee had to keep her replies consistent with the communication on the SpinDogs' open channel, or their "allies" would realize she was receiving additional transmissions they could not hear.

"Good, Captain. Now: put a stopper in that rage so you can see the bigger picture. Vengeance may be part of the SpinDogs' motive, but that doesn't explain what they just did."

"Waiting on your next send, sir," Mara muttered bitterly.

"They just sacrificed the opportunity to interrogate Kulsian survivors, as well as collect salvage they could have used from the ships they gutted." He switched to the normal comm channel. "Have our allies offered any explanation for their departure from the OpOrd?"

"Haven't received any yet, sir."

Downing went back to the Dornaani channel. "Here is what I suspect. The SpinDogs killed the survivors so that *we* couldn't talk to them. Our new 'allies' have been hiding in this system for centuries, so they are genuinely in fear for their existence. But if they are interested in keeping parts of their own past hidden, particularly what they might have done *before* they went into hiding, allowing survivors to talk is a risk they might not be willing to take. At this moment, they still have absolute control over the narrative of who, what, and why they are here." He went back to the normal channel. "We'll see what explanations they offer when we meet them in an hour."

"Roger that, sir. Although it's hard to imagine any need, any level of caution, that would explain what I just saw. Sir."

"I agree. Downing out."

Alnduul's eyelids cycled slowly, somberly. "It is indeed difficult to understand why they would need such absolute measures. They could have simply restricted your access to the survivors."

Trevor pulled off his visor. "Yeah, but you're forgetting something, Alnduul."

"And what is that, Captain Corcoran?"

"In this system, everyone is a descendant of the Ktor."

Alnduul's mouth tucked in. "Yes. There is that." His eyes half-closed in thought. "Shall I provide a drone escort as you travel to meet the Matriarch?"

Even as Downing returned through *Olsloov*'s starboard airlock, he was still reviewing the conversations and planning sessions that had preceded their joint action against the Kulsians. What worried him the most was that he couldn't find anything that foreshadowed the SpinDogs' sudden, completely autocratic decision that it wasn't enough that the battle end with a decisive slaughter, but a mass execution.

Vacc suits over their arms for return to the locker, Trevor glanced over at Downing. "You've been frowning deeper and deeper since we cut loose from their diplomatic barge. What's eating at you?"

On their way to the bridge, Downing recounted his orderly critique of what he'd said as well as the often terse utterances of the Matriarch and her military advisors. "For three decades, my job was to attend meetings just like that one. So when things go pear-shaped, it's part of my job to discover why they did. That's how we learn more about both enemies and allies. And while I may not be a dab hand at much else, I'm good at my job. So what did I miss?"

Trevor shrugged as they approached the bridge. "Not sure there was anything to miss, Richard. The SpinDogs may be dozens of generations removed from the Ktor, but they are still just as cutthroat."

Downing nodded. *Cutthroat, indeed.* Perhaps the view from the austere room where they'd met the Matriarch and her advisors had been part of their message: looking out across the recent battlespace, glass-shard glints marking the debris field where the Kulsian ships had died en masse. "'Dead men tell no tales,'" Richard muttered.

Trevor nodded back. "Yup. Now, there's just one last question we need to get answered."

Downing sighed as the hatchway to the bridge's briefing room dilated. "Whether the Lost Soldiers we leave behind will fall into the same category."

Alnduul was waiting for them. "Was your meeting with the Matriarch successful?"

"It wasn't a failure. But I'll let you decide if those are the same thing."

Trevor's chair had finished adjusting its shape to conform to the SEAL's tigerish build. "In my opinion, yeah, they pretty much *are* the same thing. As for the meeting itself? They were happy with the outcome, and unpleasantly surprised that we'd even bring up the matter of their tossing out the OpOrd when it no longer suited them."

"Because they presume that they have exclusive authority here?"

"Not exactly. They just assumed that since it's their system, and since the Kulsians have been raiding—well, raping—the third planet for centuries, it's their prerogative to treat them however they please." He scratched the back of his neck. "Given that Kulsis is almost certainly going to send a force to find out what happened to the raiders that just disappeared, I'd say the Matriarch had her hands full making sure that we weren't the next on their gibbet."

"That," Alnduul observed drily, gazing around at *Olsloov*'s bulkheads, "would have resulted in a most disappointing outcome for them."

"Yes," Downing agreed, "which was why I believe most of that was stuff and bluster. They saw what your drones were capable of. They had no desire to be on the receiving end. The only problem is, what if that attitude changes once we're safely gone?"

Alnduul laid his fingers against each other. "You fear that they will prove faithless with Major Murphy and his contingent of Lost Soldiers?"

Downing wished he had a drink—any drink. "Faithless? Perhaps. My greatest worry is that we'll be leaving our lot right in the middle of this predatory scrum without a scorecard."

"I beg your pardon?"

Downing smiled; it was rare, now, but every once in a while, Alnduul still stumbled over an unfamiliar idiom. "Let's leave aside the possibility that the SpinDogs might try to forcibly co-opt, or cut up, the Lost Soldiers once we've shifted on our merry way. As I said, that's a possibility. But it's a bloody surety that Murphy and his cadre will have no understanding of the inner workings and insider politics of the SpinDogs. I consider that a profound handicap."

"Where profound is just a nice way of saying, 'potentially lethal.'" Trevor's grim tone contrasted sharply with the jocularity of his words.

Alnduul rolled a set of long fingers toward Richard. "However, in the main, our allies are satisfied with the outcome of our cooperation?"

"Yes... and by God, they ought to be! All spaceside Kulsian assets have been eliminated, including a bunch of recently deployed satellites. Your drones destroyed the two planetside comm arrays capable of reaching the primary system. Which they call Jrar, I'm told. We have also established handshake and security protocols for data-sharing with the SpinDogs. Their eagerness to receive the technology transfers bordered on the manic."

Trevor shook his head. "I'm still not sure about giving them so many schematics, Richard. If the Ktor ever come here and see old Terran weapons and vehicles in our new friends' hands, that could cause the post-war pot to boil over and scald Earth. Far worse, this time."

Alnduul joined his hands, fingers steepled each to their opposite. "Among your own people, only a very small minority would remember military equipment made in your 1960s. It was all but forgotten by the time either of you gentlemen were born. As for the Ktor, we do not possess many details about their culture, but I am fairly sure that they do not make a habit of memorizing such data. Particularly none of those who would venture among the exiles they've sent out here into the Scatters. Such knowledge would be solely the domain of scholars. If them."

"And you're sure you've sanitized the schematics? Not just the language, but the units of measurement?"

Alnduul attempted a human nod: after almost half a dozen years, Downing still found it painful to watch him try. "As we speak, every part of every device that the SpinDogs will be replicating is being converted to other measures, down to the last detail. Should anyone ever see the actual devices or the schematics from which they were produced, there will be nothing that suggests Terran origin."

For a moment, Trevor looked sheepish. "Yeah, and I'm a fine one to be asking opsec questions."

"Why?"

"Because I let it slip that we have cryocell technology." He shook his head. "It never occurred to me the Dogs wouldn't have it."

Downing nodded. "Completely understandable, lad. The Ktor who came here certainly must have used cryogenic suspension. Since their exiles—er, Exodates—are restricted to slower-than-light drives, they couldn't have survived the multigenerational trip without it."

Trevor squinted at the tabletop. "Gotta wonder how they lost the technology."

"That is an unusual, even suspicious discovery," Alnduul agreed with slightly pinched eyelids. "However, any inquiry would alert the SpinDogs to your knowledge of their origins."

Trevor screwed up his face. "Do you really think they'd be upset that our archenemies are the same people who kicked them off their home worlds? We have an axiom for that scenario: 'the enemy of my enemy is my friend.'"

Alnduul's eyelids tightened further. "That may obtain on Earth, but it might not here."

Trevor appeared at pains to remain deferential. "It's pretty much a human constant, Alnduul."

"So it would seem. Yet, as you say, we do not know the events that led to their exile here. Nor can we be certain that factions—both here and in the main system of Jrar—do not aspire to rejoin the Ktoran Sphere, or at least, elect to continue following its teachings and tactics.

"Which is why we must carefully consider the circumstances in which we leave Major Murphy and his detachment. As you say, Richard Downing, if the SpinDogs have reason to be suspicious or dismissive of us as allies—or as effective protectors of our friends—then the moment we depart, they may attempt to put Major Murphy in a subordinate, or at least difficult, position."

"Or out an airlock." Trevor's face was as glum as his tone.

Alnduul's inner eyelids nictated . . . slowly. "Yes," he admitted, "there is that possibility."

PART THREE

Reclaimed from the Past

Bactradgaria
August 2125

Chapter Twenty-Four

Once the rest of the formation had established outposts and a perimeter around the part of the dune that led to the top of the trapezoidal ruin, Riordan joined the entry team. "So, is it sealed or not?"

By way of answer, Rogarran produced a clay bowl of urine and moved to the edge of the only apparent access point: a hatch designed to close flush with the top. However, the metal disk was slightly askew; the hinge securing it had gapped.

Rogarran brushed away the sand that had already collected around the hatch and slowly poured the urine into the gap. Initially, it pooled, but within a few seconds, the level stabilized and then dropped. A few seconds after the last of the urine was poured out, the remainder disappeared around the rusted hinge.

Cruvanor nodded at Caine. "The tinkers are ready to drive wedges into that gap to unseat the hinge. Normally, I would use iron pry bars. But even if we had any, I am not sure they would be the match of ancient steel, even when it is rusted."

Miles stepped out from under the small pavilion providing shade for the work and assault teams. "But you've used wedges before?" he asked.

Cruvanor nodded.

"Isn't that a bit like knocking on the door to see if someone's at home?"

The war leader smiled. "It certainly is. Which is why you

and the others shall be standing ready with guns and crossbows. Besides, it is our only option. Let us set the tinkers to work. We'd best be inside before the sun climbs much higher."

It took four tinkers to wrestle the hatch out of its housing. Cruvanor's most senior warrior, Marcanas, toed his way carefully toward the meter-and-a-half hole into darkness. He held a large hunk of dried meat: Cruvanor's alternative to using deadskins as bait.

Riordan raised a hand, motioned Eku forward. They waited as the factotum collected sensor data from the underside of the hatch and the void beyond. "REMs are ten percent less than surface, Commodore," the factotum reported, stepping back.

Riordan nodded to Miles, who walked over and lowered a Dornaani stun grenade into the darkness.

"That is the weapon that blinds and deafens x'qai?" Rogarran asked.

"And pretty much everything else," muttered Miles. "But it can be selectively activated."

Rogarran frowned. "I do not understand."

"Today, we may only want it to shed regular light," Caine explained as Miles sealed the visor on his helmet and took a step back. "Anyone with a command link to the grenade can choose how and when it activates." He nodded to Marcanas. "You can position the bait, now."

Marcanas grinned at the word "position." He simply tossed the meat into the hole and unslung his over-under carbine. Cruvanor's youngest follower, Polsolun, positioned himself at the rim. The other elements of the entry team—kajhs, tinkers, and Yaargraukh—edged closer.

"How long?" Eku asked.

Cruvanor shrugged. "Without knowing what lives in the ruins and, if anything does, how far off they are, one cannot even guess. However," he added with a grim smile, "you may be certain that as soon as the scent reaches x'qa, they will not keep us waiting."

Barely fifteen minutes later, the tinkers' slightly pointed ears literally perked up. Rogarran began making a hushed inquiry, but the sound they'd heard was suddenly audible to all: a scraping, scrambling approach of multiple creatures.

"Company coming," O'Garran hissed over his shoulder at

Craig Girten, who detached his Dornaani survival carbine from the solar recharge unit just beyond the shade of the canopy.

The noise grew suddenly louder; the creatures were in the space directly beneath them. Harsh, grating whispers took the place of hurried movement.

"That's Deviltongue," Cruvanor whispered in Riordan's ear. "One x'qao—a x'qrukh, I think—and two or three q'akh. They've been in the chamber before. They want the food but the new opening worries them."

It was very close to what Cruvanor had predicted, if the first response was from x'qa. "What now?"

"We wait."

"For what?"

Cruvanor was distracted, listening, then answered, "For that." Without any warning he stepped forward, nodding toward Polsolun. Riordan followed, a full step behind, and looked down in the hole.

Spotlit in a shaft of sunlight, a x'qrukh was pushing a q'akh aside, grabbing the dried meat out of its claws. Whether it was the sound of Cruvanor's movement, his scent, or his shadow bisecting the pool of brightness, the two killspawn glanced up—and the larger one immediately leaped high, hands grabbing for the human intruder.

Its claws scratched at the edge of the hatchway before it dropped back. As it scream-roared in frustration, Polsolun replaced Cruvanor at the edge of the opening, iron longsword held at the ready, kite shield high. Marcanas tucked in low behind it on the right, Cruvanor was a step back to left, drawing his pistol. As the smaller q'akh jumped upward, Polsolun muttered, "Now," over his shoulder.

Marcanas leaned out around the warrior's shield and discharged one barrel of his carbine down at the x'qa's rising maw. Riordan didn't see exactly where the round hit; there was a splash of mauve ichor and then the q'akh was falling backward, screeching.

No sooner was its body out of the way than the x'qrukh, legs bunched in readiness, launched itself toward the opening. Before it could clear the hatchway, Cruvanor leaned forward and, almost casually, squeezed off three fast rounds.

The creature's left eye burst and the muscle lining its right jaw sheared off. The third bullet apparently went down its gullet, judging from the jet of reddish-purple blood that gouted up. As the x'qao bounced off the rim of the hatch, Marcanas finally got his own line of sight. He fired the second chamber of his carbine, punching a hole in the left side of the nerveless monster's neck. It fell back, landing square atop the wounded q'akh that was just struggling to its feet.

Miles was staring at the old war leader. "First time handling that pistol, huh?"

For a moment, Cruvanor seemed to have missed the ironic tone of the chief's query. Then he laughed. "Every time is like the first time." He turned his attention back to the hatchway. "There is still a q'akh down there. He is startled, but not moving. Yet."

"Craig, on the line!" Miles snapped, resealing his visor. "And here's some light for you."

Just as Sergeant Girten arrived at the edge of the hole, the Dornaani grenade sent out a blinding glare of white light.

The remaining q'akh, a twin to the other, was revealed just beyond the circle of sunlight, throwing its hands up against the brilliance.

Riordan couldn't tell if Craig used the iron sights or the top-mounted monoscope, but he rained a rapid patter of semiautomatic fire down at the unsuspecting creature. The first round missed, the second clipped it at an angle: a flesh wound more startling than grievous. The next several shots scored one hit on its chest and another on its lower abdomen.

The q'akh staggered back, but did not fall; the carbine's setting was very low. Craig repositioned himself and crouched, maintaining fire until it fell over.

"Are we clear?" Riordan called.

"All targets down, sir," the paratrooper replied. "The first one they hit is just getting untangled from the bigger guy."

At a nod from Caine, O'Garran shouted, "First team in!"

The four tinkers ran to the edge of the hole, tossed three secured lines—all Dornaani cable—over the rim and held them steady. Three kajh grabbed hold and slid down. The wounded q'akh swiped blindly at one; the trog swung away from its claws, lost hold of his line, and tumbled off to the side. The other two kajh landed solidly, got their axes in their hands. One circled around to the flank of the crippled monster, the other faced into the darkness, guarding the rear.

"On me!" Yaargraukh bellowed and jumped down, his grat'r follower right behind him, weapons already in their hands.

Riordan watched the brief flashing of blades before Yaargraukh announced, "All clear." As the tinkers began their descent, he nodded to Craig. "Take entry team two down. Set up to guard the lines, then call in the other teams."

Girten nodded. Waving team two over, he turned toward Cruvanor. "I don't get it, si—er, Cruvanor. How can x'qa be so stupid?"

The war leader shook his head. "They are not stupid so much as impulsive. If, at the start, they had seen any of us holding a gun, they would have proceeded differently. That is why Polsolun only held a sword and a shield and why Marcanas and I remained behind him."

Irisir, Cruvanor's technicker, came forward as Girten was about to start down the line and put a pausing hand on his arm. "X'qai become more dangerous as they become more patient. That, more than their Talents, is why M'qrugth or older arurkré are particularly fearsome. And why they must be fought with different tactics."

Girten stared, then nodded and slid down, shouting orders to the three kajh of his team as he did.

Riordan nodded to Irisir. "That's good advice. Feel free to repeat it to us. Frequently."

The technicker nodded. "I will." He took hold of a line. "But for now, my mind is upon what the centuries have kept concealed. Tell Cruvanor I await him below." He led another team down.

When Riordan finally descended into the now torchlit chamber, Irisir was the one holding his line, admiring it. "Truly a marvel," he murmured. "How is it made?"

"I am not really sure," Caine answered truthfully as he peered into the darkness. "What have you discovered?"

Irisir answered with a gesture that invited Riordan to survey the room.

It extended away from the shaft of sunlight in three directions—west, north, and east—but the south wall was almost at their backs. Across from them, a ceiling-high ramp of sand sloped into the room, almost completely obscuring the presumably breached wall behind it. The dune's further intrusion had been blocked by what resembled a narrow altar or platform running along the chamber's longer, east-west axis. Like the walls and everything else in the chamber, its sides and surfaces were not merely smooth; they were geometrically regular, with precise right-angled corners. Smaller, irregular objects were clustered near it.

"Have you ever seen anything like this?" Riordan asked quietly.

"No," Irisir admitted. "Only Cruvanor has. And he'd like your opinion on what it might be."

"Where is he?"

"With the team that went one level down, through there." Irisir nodded at an open hatch in the floor, the glint of a ladder descending into whatever lay below. "I'll get him."

Riordan nodded as Irisir left and Duncan—leader of the Crewe's prospecting team—emerged out of the darkness from the west. "Major," Caine asked, keeping his voice low, "what are we looking at here?"

Solsohn's eyes were unusually wide. "I can show you a picture that's worth a thousand words, sir. And given my tendency to explain things in detail, you *know* that's a bargain."

Retracing his steps to the west, Duncan led Riordan to a wide, utterly flat expanse of wall. He activated his Dornaani hand light and murmured, "Eureka."

That one word proved to be the warning Riordan needed to control his surprise. It wasn't just a wall; it was a map of Bactradgaria. *Probably a match for the one Cruvanor described encountering during an early prospecting mission.*

Riordan turned back toward the center of the room. What had been mysterious objects were now startlingly obvious. The dark object at the center was a long command console with crew stations. And from this angle, he could make out three low-backed chairs facing the north wall, the tops of their seat backs just barely pushing above the sand.

But now, even the intrusion of the dune appeared to be a logical part of the scene. Riordan jutted his chin at the notional north wall. "What do you think? That sand came in through observation slits after they corroded and gave way?"

Duncan drew in a long breath. "Observation slits, yes. Corroded, no." He gestured at several dark sticks or lumps extending out from the fine-grained slope. "Bones, sir. And a boot. North side of the chairs are ruined. My guess? Blast shields didn't cover the observation slits in time." Riordan swallowed, turned as Duncan played his light across the floor of what had clearly been a control room. "We've found—and marked—ten bodies. Except for one, they all fell along lines radiating away from the observation slits. Blown down wherever they were standing or sitting."

"And the other one?"

Solsohn shrugged. "He or she was down before the nuke hit. Their clothes—what's left of them—are different. All clues to figure out what went on here, assuming we get the chance."

Riordan pushed back a haze of surprise and burgeoning questions. "Getting that chance is our number one objective, right now. Any material salvage worth mentioning?"

Duncan chuckled at the question. "Guess you didn't see what was behind you while shinnying down the line, sir." He shined his light up at the space between the overhead hatchway and the south wall.

For a moment, the shadows made Riordan unsure of what he was seeing, but then ... "Is that a rotary weapon of some kind?"

"Yep. Six barrel. Automated mount. Covers the access through the floor as well. Too early to say if it's just a housing with rusted guts or not. Of course the biggest value would be what should be attached to it: a hopper of ammo." Solsohn swept the light across the floor. "See those shapes in the sand? Personal weapons. Size is consistent with pistols, maybe submachine guns."

Riordan ran a hand through his hair as he looked back up to the hatchway. "Are any other parts of the ruin open to the wastes?"

"There are vents in small access alcoves at the southeastern and southwestern corners of this room. There's sand clogging the latter, so the vent cover may have rusted out. Or it could have been a point of, er, kinetic ingress."

Riordan's eyes returned to the mix of bone and cloth that marked the one body that hadn't been flung back by a concussive wave roaring through the observation slits. "You think there was an infiltration team inside when the hammer came down?"

Duncan shrugged. "It's no surprise that there are a lot of guns here, sir. But a surprising number were not in their holsters when the world ended."

"What have you told Cruvanor?"

"Nothing yet, Commodore. I was still doing my first pass

when he went down to Level Two. But it sounds like he's heading back up."

Marcanas emerged through the hatchway in the floor. He nodded to Riordan and stepped aside as Cruvanor came up almost as quickly behind him. He nodded, silver hair bobbing, as he stepped close to Riordan and Duncan. "An interesting find, wouldn't you say?"

Riordan found a smile that was more congenial than stunned. "I'd say you have a talent for understatement, my friend."

Cruvanor grinned. "This site is very like the one I remember from my youth, but far more intact. That one had been crushed as if hit by an immense hammer: floors askew, deep crevices cutting through it from top to bottom."

He glanced at the walls. "But this is . . . is uniquely pristine. Although I remain unsure what its purpose might have been." He finished on a hanging tone, smiled when he had to ask explicitly, "Do you have any thoughts on that topic, Leader Caine?"

"Firstly, I am just 'Caine,' my friend. As to what this was . . ." *It's just a guess, but damned if it doesn't check all the boxes* . . . "I am relatively sure that this is what was called a launch control bunker."

Cruvanor's smile was patient and also a bit sheepish. "I know the meaning of all the words you just used—but I have no idea what a 'launch control bunker' might be."

Riordan nodded. *So his knowledge doesn't extend that far. Apparently.* "In the times when humans made machines of steel that moved on the land, the seas, and even in the air, certain of those vehicles were turned into weapons. Specifically, some were shaped much like heavy darts or javelins, propelled by compounds far more powerful than the fuel in your rads or the powder in your guns. I believe this room is where the controllers of those weapons ensured that they flew into the air at the right time and angle."

Irisir had overheard, leaned in. "And how do you know—?"

Cruvanor held up a hand. "We are here to learn about this ruin, Irisir, not about the origins of our friends' singular knowledge." He smiled at Riordan. "You were saying?"

"Some of these weapons carried explosives of such force that they could destroy entire cities. Others, usually smaller and faster, were built to intercept them before they could reach their targets. I suspect those latter, protective weapons were controlled from this place."

Duncan raised a surprised eyebrow but said nothing.

If Cruvanor noticed, it did not color his tone. "Why do you think it was not the city-killing weapons?"

Riordan shook his head. "It could be. But if so, there are several features which are puzzling."

"Such as?"

Riordan gestured at the walls. "As sturdy as this bunker's sides may seem, it would still have been far too vulnerable to the enemy's city-killing weapons. In the records I have seen, they were more likely to be launched and controlled from subterranean facilities. It is unlikely that they could have been entered so easily as it seems this one may have been. Intruders would have to contend with many checkpoints, each a small fort or bunker unto itself."

Riordan gestured toward the sand-clogged alcove. "However, Major Solsohn found what may have been a breached vent whereby a strike team entered this complex. That would be more consistent with sites where defensive missiles were kept; they were usually on the surface, less armored, and more numerous."

"Why?" Irisir wondered, returning Cruvanor's surprised gaze with a hint of defiance.

Riordan shrugged. "Once the offensive missiles were launched, it was likely that the war would be decided by them, one way or the other. However, commanders made them very hard to reach and destroy; that way, some would remain if a second launch was required to achieve victory.

"However, the defensive missiles were deemed expendable. They were usually more broadly distributed and in smaller numbers. Those struck by the enemy's missiles were not expected to survive."

"Your words paint a picture of a world constantly balanced on a razor's edge of terror."

Riordan nodded somberly. "I suspect that the city-killing weapons were unleashed and that one struck very near this site." He pointed at the north wall. "When we clear that sand, I believe we will find observation slits for controllers who had to confirm the launch of defensive missiles. Whether they had yet to do so or had completed that task is something we may never know."

Cruvanor's eyes became sharp, almost eager. "How close might those defensive missiles have been? And if they did not launch, would they have sustained the same damage as this bunker? More? Less?"

"Those," Riordan answered with a small, slow nod, "may be the most interesting questions of all." *And the answers are likely to determine whether or not we can ever leave Bactradgaria.*

Cruvanor's smile was thoughtful. "Then it seems we should catalog this site with all reasonable haste. Because, the sooner we have completed that, the sooner we are likely to have those answers."

Caine returned his smile. "I could not agree more. Let's assign our prospectors."

Chapter Twenty-Five

Miles O'Garran folded his arms as the clearing team gathered around him. Duncan Solsohn was the officer in charge, but, as tactical commander, the nuts and bolts were the chief's concern. The big-brain types—Duncan, Cruvanor, Irisir, Eku—were only along to assess the structure, tag items for salvage, and set objectives. And hopefully, they'd stick to that, although when it came to combat ops, the old war leader could probably give him a run for his money. "So do we have any intel on the rest of the complex? What did you see down on Level Two?"

Marcanas rolled his eyes in Cruvanor's direction. "*Someone* wanted to go on a mapping expedition, but we kept it to a quick look around the nearest corners. Our best guess is that Level Two's floor plan is at least two times this room's dimensions."

So about fifteen by thirty meters. Miles nodded. "What about inter-floor spaces and conduits?"

Cruvanor's smile was initially surprised but became one of satisfaction. "In all the years I have explored such ruins, you are the only other person who has asked that question."

Yeah, because I'm the only one who's ever been in a modern building. But hey, if that scores me some easy points—"How are they accessed? What are we looking for?"

The war leader shrugged. "Usually they are in small closets that must be opened with special tools or great force. If at all. We did not see any during our 'quick look,' but the inter-floor space is well over a meter thick. So there will be crossways and pipes. And, I predict, conduits for very thick electrical wires. What you call 'cables,' I believe."

Duncan frowned. "Was there another opening beneath this one?" He nodded at the hole around which they were standing.

Irisir nodded. "But it is slightly offset." He anticipated Miles' next question. "There was no evidence that it is regularly used. Of course, if there is as much ancient amber in the rest of Level Two as the small part we saw, it may be impossible to tell if creatures travel there."

"Huh? Whaddya mean?" Girten asked from the clearing group waiting to the side of the command huddle.

Cruvanor frowned. "The floor of Level Two is mostly covered in a kind of ancient amber which the ancients used to smother fires. It is very resilient and not readily scratched by passing boots or claws. It is knee-high in some places," he finished, glancing at Duncan. Who nodded thoughtfully.

But the color had bled out of Girten's already pale face. "Amber? You mean"—he stared at Duncan and Miles—"the same color as the super-cosmolene the Ktor used to preserve our equipment on Turkh'saar?"

Duncan became as pale as the paratrooper. "We'll see when we get down there. Sergeant, tell me if it's *not* the same substance you saw."

"You are familiar with the ancient amber?" Irisir asked, eyes intent upon their faces.

"I think we might be," Duncan answered carefully. He glanced at Cruvanor. "So, just to be clear: both these substances preserve whatever is caught in them?"

Cruvanor narrowly assessed the three strange humans. "Yes, as if no time had passed at all."

"Well," Miles shrugged, jerking a thumb back at the tinkers, "looks like they've got some pick- and spadework ahead of them."

The local humans stared at him, horrified. "You mean to... to break it?"

"Uh, yeah." *Well, so much for those easy points I scored with the old guy.* "What did *you* have in mind?"

"The solvent?" Irisir asked tentatively.

Girten cleared his throat. "Sirs—"

"*I'm* not a 'sir,' dammit," Miles growled.

"Er, sirs, Chief: what Irisir said about a solvent. That could be how the Nazis and Ni—Japanese removed the super-cosmolene. Because there sure weren't any chunks of it laying around."

"Then how do you know it was amber-colored?"

"Just a guess, Chief, but, uh, back in 'Shangri-la,' amber is also the color of the symbiopods."

Sweet Jesus! It is! Miles swallowed, glanced at Duncan, whose eyes had hardened.

Solsohn drew a deep breath. "Okay, there's a solvent. But what's wrong with chipping at it?"

Cruvanor shook his head sharply. "It is not to be trusted until it has been liquefied. And even then, anything it encased, or even touched, must be washed in a thin gruel."

The Crewe members frowned at the word "gruel." "I do not believe we have learned that word." Yaargraukh rumbled.

"Yeah," Miles added. "Gruel is something you eat. Sounds like you're talking about—what? Some kind of cleanser?"

"No," Irisir said slowly. "We mean gruel. Thin porridge."

Girten goggled. "And that kills whatever's left of the, uh, ancient amber?"

"No. It shows if there was any residue left behind. Any remaining amber will infest the gruel, begin to absorb it."

"Is it lethal?" Duncan asked.

Cruvanor looked at the major oddly. "Not that we have ever observed. But death would be preferable. Once within you, it can sap your will at times you do not expect and cannot predict." He shuddered. "It is said to be a tool of the x'qai, but I have seen that they fear it, too."

Miles looked down the ladder. "Is it safe to walk on this damn, er, symbiolene?"

Irisir raised an eyebrow at the latest of Mile's sardonic nicknames. "It is not advisable. And if you must, do not touch the bottoms of your shoes. Best you burn them."

Duncan blew out a long sigh. "Well, I guess we use the solvent. But that will require a lot of water, won't it?"

Irisir nodded. "Yes, but fortunately, the solvent was stored along with water sufficient to both spray and rinse it. Although that machinery no longer has power, one can release the solvent and water at the same time and, with care, mix them upon the surface of the ancient amber. It dissolves just as thoroughly."

When O'Garran had been informed that they would not

sweep the complex swiftly, but stop to scribble floorplans, notes, and tags, he'd groaned aloud. Now, he was happy to take it one, careful step at a time. "Well, the sooner we get about it, the sooner we can bring in all those poor bastards frying outside."

"We can't, Chief: not all at once," Duncan muttered. "We'll limit exposure by keeping surface watches short, but we still need the sun. And the rain."

"The sun is the greatest danger," Polsolun said confidently.

"It may be, but without it, our guns, lights, and sensors will eventually stop working."

Polsolun frowned. "So, your artifacts depend upon sun magic?"

Duncan paused, and Miles knew why: the last thing any of the Crewe wanted to do was pass off technology as "magic." On the other hand, trying to actually *explain* it…

Irisir put a hand on Polsolun's considerable shoulder. "I have wondered if it is sun magic, or some phenomenon akin to what we observe in plants. They gather the sun's rays to gather the power they need to grow. The Crewe's devices gather the sun's rays to gather the power they need to function." Looking at Cruvanor's face while Irisir presented his analogy, Miles would have wagered the old guy already had a pretty good idea of the basics.

Still, getting adequate power was a minor problem compared to getting adequate water. "About the rain, Major: do you actually think there will *be* any this close to hotside? Haven't felt a drop for a week, now."

Irisir gestured toward the walls. "Cruvanor has the knowing of where water may still reside in the walls or beneath the floors."

The august prospector-warrior shook his head. "That is true, but as I have said, this ruin is very like the one I entered in my youth. There, the water almost killed some of us."

Irisir's eyes widened; he'd clearly not heard *that* part of the story.

"You have seen Eku using his artifacts to assess our surroundings. That is because our friends understand that the cataclysm which destroyed this place may have permanently blighted both the land and the water. There is almost certainly some water left in the tanks of the ruin, but I doubt it can be made potable, even by the ministrations of our shaman." He nodded toward Zhathragz, who nodded in return.

What? Mr. Mumbo Jumbo can purify water? Now, if he could turn it into wine, that *would be a trick worth having.* But Miles only said, "Then what do we do when it runs out? Which can't be more than a week or so from now."

"What we find today and tomorrow will determine our alternatives," Cruvanor replied quietly.

Sensing that the preliminaries were finally winding down, Miles tugged at his cured armor in annoyance. "Guess it's time to clean house, then. Nothing you saw down there gave you *any* clues about what we might run into?"

Marcanas smiled. "Down there? No. But up here is a different story." He motioned for the commanders to follow him. He arrived at three trog corpses piled in the far northeast corner. One had been stripped very nearly to the bones. The other two had only been sampled and it was clear why.

"Jalks," O'Garran muttered.

"Zombies." Girten's correction was both deferential and stubborn.

The chief ignored him, turned to face Zhathragz instead. "So this means one of your kind is down there, huh?"

The shaman nodded. "And since the bodies are still fresh, I doubt he is far."

"What was he doing up here, do you think? Looking for a way out?"

Zhathragz was frowning. "I have been wondering that since I was shown these corpses. I do not believe the shaman himself was here. I believe these were scouts, sent ahead to look for metal, possibly water."

"And made enough noise to draw the x'qa?"

The shaman was still frowning. "Perhaps. We will know better if we discover where the killspawn made their lair."

Girten glanced around. "Not here?"

Marcanas shook his head. "No spoor. No trophies. Only one exit."

Miles nodded. "Do you think they used this as a kill zone, then?" When met with puzzled stares, he expanded. "Like you said, until we popped the top on this room, there was only one way in and out. So maybe they laired someplace where they'd hear or smell something heading up into this room, and then come in behind them."

Marcanas smiled. "There is only one flaw in that theory: x'qa aren't tidy. Look around: nothing else has been killed in this room for hundreds, maybe thousands, of years. No sign anything was dragged off, either. To my mind, the surprise is there are bodies here at all—particularly these three."

"What's so strange about them?"

Zhathragz shrugged. "None of them are cavers."

"And again: that is strange . . . why?"

Cruvanor crossed his arms. "Trogs do not venture this close to hotside or into the high desert except in dire need. They are unlikely to survive here: they depend upon access to the surface where game roams. So they dwell in shallow caves or upper tunnels.

"But cavers dwell deep, where neither the deadly heat nor deadly cold ever reaches." The war leader gestured to the corpses, glanced at the shaman. "These trogs are, from the look of them, from Wild Tribes, yes?"

"They are, lord. I recognize two of their tattoos. As you say, it is strange to find them here. Unless they had dire need." Zhathragz frowned. "If they encountered an enemy—a rival tribe, cavers, a creature of the deep rock—and were compelled to flee in this direction, they may have been trying to escape by finding a way to the surface."

"But wouldn't that be almost certain death?" Solsohn asked.

"It would be a great risk, yes, but if the tunnels behind them were held by deadly foes, it might have been their only chance."

To Miles, it sounded like their "clearing operations" would be more like cornering a twitchy, starving animal. "If they're still around, it sounds like they could be pretty desperate with no place to run." He crossed his arms. "That's a recipe for high casualties—on *both* sides."

"Yes, Leader Miles. But properly managed, that could work to our advantage. Which is why I was sent down, when word of these corpses reached the surface."

Girten asked the question Miles had decided to keep to himself. "But where's Bey? Shouldn't she be along for this, too?"

Zhathragz may have concealed a flash of annoyance. "She is busy with the balance of her forces, ensuring they are adequately alert as they guard the approaches to this ruin."

Really? I've gotta deal with Mister Mumbo Jumbo directly? Well, then: "I'm setting some ground rules for how you'll work with us, Zhathragz."

The shaman nodded, but was also frowning. "I will comply—as soon as I know what 'ground rules' are."

O'Garran managed not to roll his eyes or sigh. "Your ground rules are really simple: you ask *me* before you do anything."

"Of course. May I suggest something now?"

Miles wanted to groan but just nodded.

"I can strengthen the eyes of several of our warriors. For an hour or more, their vision will be better in the dark. Do you wish me to call for this boon?"

Miles shrugged "Don't see why you would. We shouldn't be in the dark at all, given that we have torches." *And Dornaani hand lights, but I'm not about to advertise plan B.*

Cruvanor glanced at Duncan and Miles. "If it is acceptable to you, I would like to hear more of what Zhathragz has in mind."

Miles was trying to decide between agreeing and possibly looking like a pushover, or ending the discussion and looking like an arrogant dick, when Yaargraukh's voice rumbled from behind. "I, too, would like to hear the shaman's reasoning."

Duncan shrugged acquiescence. Miles copied the gesture. Reluctantly.

Zhathragz folded his thick-fingered hands. "If those at the front of our group light the way with torches, we will be announcing ourselves to our enemies. If, however, several of our kajh have their vision enhanced, they will be able to start an attack before they are seen. This will work best if they are preceded by two tinkers, as they have the best glowsight of any trog-kind, even cavers."

Miles glanced at Duncan, who was already looking at him. "Glowsight?" they chorused.

Cruvanor raised his chin as puzzled looks passed between his own men and the trogs in the clearing force. "Glowsight," he said calmly, "is what trogs call their ability to perceive heat as faint light when it is very dark."

Solsohn looked at the various trogs in the group. "And none of you thought to tell us about this?"

Their answers were diffident shrugs, surprise, and avoidant eyes.

Cruvanor raised his hand. "The humans of this, eh, continent are all familiar with trog glowsight. Also, unless you traveled in lightless tunnels, it would not have been mentioned."

Miles nodded amiably. *And once again, we're the village idiots.* "But if what they're seeing is heat"—*damn; they've got* natural *thermal vision?*—"then why didn't they tell us when we were marching up from Forkus? Knowing we had sentries who could see the body heat of approaching critters on cold nights would have been *really* useful."

To everyone's surprise, it was Eku who answered, nodding to himself. "If the sensitivity of glowsight is very weak, it might not register heat that is being wicked away by strong winds, no matter how cold."

Zhathragz's head bobbed in agreement. "That is why trogs' glowsight is only useful in tunnels, particularly cold ones."

Duncan gestured toward the tinkers. "And them?"

Cruvanor's smile was wintry. "Oh, their glowsight is quite good." He turned toward the two who'd been tapped to scout ahead for any snares or trip-wired alarms. "Which makes me wonder why none of them bothered to mention it since taking their oaths with you." The tinkers squirmed, looked like they would rather be anywhere else at that particular moment.

Miles was about to join in when Duncan took a different tack. "Maybe they were just forgetful," the major began. "So the best way for them to prove their loyalty is by how boldly they probe ahead of the clearing team. But if they don't, well, we'll have to wonder why they didn't mention this glowsight sooner." His concluding smile was mirthless.

Had the moment not been so serious, Miles might have cheered; Baby Officer Duncan was really outgrowing his rear-echelon cradle! "Orders, sir?"

Solsohn nodded. "Set your formation and point rotation, Chief. This could be a long day."

"Aye, aye, sir."

"And Chief?"

"Sir?"

"You are *not* allowed to take point yourself."

O'Garran bit back a rebuttal, then a curse. Did Major Desk Trooper know that he'd actually trained for tunnel ops? And yes, Peter may have piled up more practical experience in Indonesia, but he hadn't been tapped for the clearing mission and besides, he wasn't a SEAL, dammit! Once Miles was sure he wouldn't sound angry—or petulant—he leaned closer to Solsohn. "Major, I really should be on point, sometimes. Show the noobs how it's done, y'know."

Duncan smiled and whispered back, "Nice try, Chief. The commodore thought you might try to soft-soap me with that 'improving the troops' line." He leaned away, still smiling. "I understand your desire to lead from the front. But just as the commodore had to accept recently—and now me, too—you're too irreplaceable to be on the pointy end."

O'Garran's disappointment became deflation. If Riordan had seen it coming and coordinated with Solsohn, then no argument was going to change the cards he'd just been dealt.

"However," Duncan added, "given what's at stake in getting this site under control quickly and completely, the commodore also acknowledges that this extraordinary situation calls for extraordinary measures."

Miles looked up eagerly. "So we're not going 'old school' on this one?"

"There's no 'we' in this case, Chief. You will be the only one in Dornaani armor besides Eku. We need you coordinating just behind the point of contact, with full comms and sensors. We also need you ready to screen out a shock grenade and put some hurt on blinded enemies if things go sideways. Girten will be corner-checking using his monoscope, and Eku will be linked to your helmet, creating a floorplan from your feed. You've got two minutes to suit up."

About damn time! But Miles O'Garran's only response was a crisp, "Aye, aye, sir!"

Chapter Twenty-Six

Duncan did not just stop, but froze in place, when O'Garran raised his fist into the "hold position" attitude. Cruvanor and his warriors lagged a moment behind, never having seen it before.

From the circle of darkness that marked the hatchway leading down into the third level, there was scrabbling and hissed exchanges.

Duncan heard Girten mutter something to the chief, who took two steps back to pass the word to the support group. "One of the tinkers on point got their arm hooked into a tripwire just as they got off the descent line. Need a little more light so we can see the snag." He nodded toward the trogan carrying the group's only lit torch. "A few steps toward me should do it."

Solsohn nodded the trogan forward. "I thought the tinkers have the best glowsight," he whispered sideways to Cruvanor.

Irisir murmured a reply over his shoulder. "They do, but unless the line was much hotter or colder than the air around it, it would not show up."

O'Garran must have heard; his snicker was well-muffled but he might as well have shouted, "Hey, genius; it's *thermal* vision, remember?" Before planetfall, Duncan would have flinched at the mistake, and of all the Crewe, the chief was still the one whose ribbing he found hardest to abide. But whatever reservation the others—and he himself—harbored over his background as a desk jockey had faded: enough so that the present slipup elicited a smile rather than sweat.

Eku glanced up as the torch shifted forward. "Major, even scanning the hatchway from back here, the REM rate is dropping. So is the temperature of the open area below." He studied the floor as if he suspected it of conspiring to conceal a secret. "It is possible that the level beneath us is partially or wholly subterranean."

As Duncan nodded to acknowledge Eku's report, Girten hissed something back at O'Garran, who shook his head. "What's up, Chief?"

"Damn tinker is now completely tangled in the tripwire. One move and we ring the doorbell of whoever's waiting down there. My recommendation is we get ready to launch a full-on assault. That means doing it with light, since surprise is out of the question."

Duncan felt more than saw Cruvanor's and Marcanas' eyes turning toward him . . . just as Zhathragz's voice came over his shoulder. "Leader Duncan, there is another way."

Solsohn managed not to frown; after his personal experience with "Gifts" and "Talents," he'd be happiest never having to hear about them again, much less deal with them as a CO. But "happy" and "CO" were contradictory concepts, anyhow, so . . . "Tell me. Quickly."

"I can prevent the alarm from working."

Duncan raised an eyebrow. "You seem very sure of that."

Cruvanor leaned in. "I believe he has reason to be. Assuming that whoever set the tripwire has not warded it. "

Zhathragz's reply fit smoothly into the war leader's carefully telegraphed pause. "It is not warded, Lord Cruvanor. I am certain of it."

Cruvanor glanced at Duncan and shrugged. "I believe he could solve the problem."

"Hsssst!" O'Garran sent back toward them. "Time to fish or cut bait!"

"Different plan," Duncan decided and replied in the same moment. "Zhathragz is going to solve our problem."

"How the—?"

"Make way for him. If he needs something, comply."

Zhathragz slipped past both Miles and the kajh watching the human's flank and stopped when he reached Girten and the two scout-archers peering down at the snared tinker. "Can you describe the alarm?"

Girten shrugged. "Looks like hollow bones and some rusted strips of steel."

Zhathragz nodded and leaned forward to peer down at the

tinker. "Can you cut the tripwire?" he whispered into the near-dark. An oath-ridden affirmative rose up in answer. "Then have your knife on it and cut when I nod."

The chief turned to face Duncan directly. "What the hell is Zhathragz going to do—sir?" His mutter was worried and entirely too loud.

"We'll find out together. Be ready to pull up the tinker if things go sideways."

Zhathragz had crouched at the edge of the hatchway, head slightly inclined as he stretched out his palm. He began a crooning whisper—and nodded.

Duncan hadn't the angle to see down into the hole, but from the sudden tensing of O'Garran's shoulders, he knew the tripwire had been cut.

Instead of a loud clunking and clatter, the only sound was a muted thump.

Miles shook his head. "Well, I'll be—"

"Chief, report."

"Uh, yessir." He leaned back. "Damnedest thing, Major. All the junk rigged against the ceiling hit the ground hard; hell, one of the bones broke. But listening to it, I'd have sworn it was just soft rubber wrapped in blankets."

Duncan nodded as Zhathragz backed away from the hole. "Thank you," he said.

Zhathragz looked away, shook his head. "The power is not mine, so no thanks to me." He turned to Miles. "Be careful as you send the warriors down. The Gift of quieting has run its course."

O'Garran glanced at Duncan with a sharp nod; he and the first team were ready.

Duncan nodded back. "Send 'em down, Chief. We'll hang back with the light until you give the all clear."

It took the better part of ten minutes for the entirety of the clearing team to slide down to Level Three. Which was just as well: the last of Bannor's security group was still descending the ladder to Level Two and occupying all the tactical control points, even though there weren't any reports of enemies or other new avenues of ingress.

As Bannor's forces were still hopscotching over stretches of symbiolene to reach their positions, the last of Duncan's command came down the line: Yaargraukh and his grat'r vassal. The Hkh'Rkh pressed close to the wall as he let the two rearguard kajh slip past him to form the last rank of the formation.

Duncan felt a nudge on his left arm; Miles had sidled up and leaned into him. "Waiting on your word, sir,"

Solsohn nodded. "Any report from the corners?" He gestured toward the two passages that led out of the small chamber into which they'd descended.

"Lead scouts tell me there are longer, wider corridors down here," the chief reported. "Sightlines via the monoscope indicate its footprint is at least half again as large as Level Two. There's some rockfall down the western corridor. The tinkers see signs of recent passage by sandaled feet leading into the northern one. They're betting that's the direction in which we'll find whoever left their two pals and the jalk on the top level."

Duncan slipped the crossbow off his back, used the front stirrup to cock it. "Rear guard to hold this chamber. Chief O'Garran, get your team moving."

Level Three had far less symbiolene in general and, although one path was recently trafficked, the first areas they crept through had never been entered. Instead, Solsohn found himself trying not to get distracted by all the desiccated corpses and personal weapons strewn about. Many of the firearms were made of plastics or composites that had succumbed to the centuries, either crumbling or riven by cracks. But others were surprisingly intact, most of which Cruvanor instructed to be left for him and Irisir to handle first. They recognized several of the models from prior salvage missions and were hopeful that at least some could be refurbished.

Far more plentiful were shell casings, most of which were coated in the distinctive dim green-beige patina of ancient brass. They were scattered liberally in areas that had evidently been points of contact between the bunker's personnel and whatever special ops team had been sent to eliminate them.

Evidently the sharpest of these firefights had taken place in two corridors that converged on a slightly larger and heavier door, ajar and hanging on its hinges. After the tinkers confirmed it had not been entered, Girten put his monoscope into the gap between the wall and the door and studied what lay beyond.

When he leaned away, both his eyebrows had climbed into acute arches. "Chief, you might wanna take a look at this."

O'Garran obliged. He leaned back almost immediately and turned to the command group. "Major, Cruvanor, while I am fully aware of the protocol not to manipulate any of the doors or objects during this sweep, I think you may want to make an exception for the chamber on the other side of that door."

Duncan motioned Cruvanor toward Girten, who was holding the monoscope in place, then turned to face Eku. "Best guess; have we seen half of this level?"

The factotum was studying the images on his HUD. "Slightly more than half, sir, assuming the building's shape—a trapezoidal solid—remains consistent."

Miles had drifted closer. "Whaddya thinking, Major?"

Duncan crossed his arms. "That it's probably time to see if Zhathragz can 'Gift' some of our lead ranks with glowsight."

The chief shrugged. "No reason why not."

"You choose which of your point personnel should, eh, get the treatment. Work out the specifics with Zhathragz. But stay handy, in case—"

"Duncan," Cruvanor called from the damaged door as Irisir leaned away from Girten's monoscope. "I agree with Chief O'Garran. We should enter this room now. With your permission?" Marcanas and Polsolun were standing nearby, the latter holding his shield as if he meant to use it as a lever in the gap between the door and the jamb—which, come to think of it, looked more like a hatch coaming. He nodded.

With Cruvanor coaching him, Polsolun inserted his shield as Solsohn had anticipated. But instead of using it as a pry bar, he rocked it back and forth gently. Eventually, the door and hinges started to grind faintly. Rusted bits of metal fell as the movement of the shield widened the margin. Several minutes later, with Marcanas taking some of the weight of the hinges, the door swung slowly open. Eku shined his Dornaani hand light over their collective shoulders.

At first glance, it appeared to be nothing more than a very large chamber with a very high ceiling: so high that it had to rise beyond the footprint of Level Two. But as Duncan's eyes grew accustomed to the light and the odd shapes within, he realized the southern wall of the room was actually a mass of sand which sloped outward to cover half the floor: the utterly smooth concrete floor.

In addition to its pristine condition, unusual geometric markings were still plainly visible on the concrete. Behind Duncan, the trogans peering around the coaming whispered that the bold lines and curves might be mystically incised holy symbols for shamanistic rites, or whatever the ancients had in place of them.

Ironically, that was precisely the moment Duncan realized what they were. He looked up, discovered the other three Crewe members doing what he was: glancing away from the floor to check each other's reactions. The three humans smiled; Yaargraukh's black tongue writhed out of his central nostril and wagged before disappearing again.

Cruvanor had noticed their collective responses, gestured to the markings just beneath his feet. "I take it the trogans are mistaken as to the origin of these lines and curves?"

"You might say that," Miles drawled. Girten didn't manage to completely stifle his guffaw.

"They're movement guidelines. Markings for vehicles—rads and maybe bigger machines—to show the drivers where to move or park them."

Duncan looked up at the ceiling: regularly spaced industrial-sized lights, probably fluorescent. Half were still fully attached; the rest had either shaken loose or were hanging by a few wires.

"We call it a garage," Girten chuckled at the local humans. "What's your word for it?"

Polsolun frowned. "A vehicle park."

"That works, too," Craig said agreeably before glancing toward O'Garran and pointing to an irregular berm in the midst of the sand. "Hey, whaddya bet we find some old, rust-eaten jalopy under that humped-up pile of dirt?"

"Watch your tone," the chief muttered in mock threat. "You could just as easily be describing my meemaw's back yard." Girten chuckled again.

However, Cruvanor was shaking his head. "I do not know what a 'jalopy' is, but I would not presume it is ruined." He pointed just beyond the leading edge of the sand. "Look there."

Duncan did and noticed that at some places, a thin yellowish plaque edged out from beneath the sand. His breath caught, but he was careful to let it out slowly. "Symbiolene."

The war leader nodded. "I suspect that, if this was a vehicle park, the doors were breached by the cataclysm just as was Level

One. If so, the ancient amber would have automatically triggered and coated most of this chamber. I suspect the sand stuck to it much as if it had landed upon glue."

Duncan swallowed. "So any vehicles might still be... functional? As well as whatever else was underneath?"

Cruvanor's nod would normally have been the response in which Solsohn placed the highest confidence. But in this case, it was Craig Girten's casual shrug. "Worked for the Ktor on Turkh'saar, sir. As you might recall."

Duncan nodded at the paratrooper. "I recall, Sergeant. Very, very well. Eku, coordinate with Irisir for however you want to mark and tag this, uh, garage. Everyone else: we can't finish clearing this level if we stay here." He led the way out.

Because if I don't, I might start digging with my bare hands.

The darkness was so near absolute that the only radiance in the formation—one small running light on Eku's vacc suit—seemed dangerously bright.

Its approach was the only warning Solsohn had that the factotum was leaning closer to give him an update. "Chief O'Garran reports that the glowsighted kajh and scouts have spotted the enemy indirectly."

"You mean they see body-glow around corners?"

"The phrasing was his, Major."

Okay, then yes: that's what he means! "Disposition of enemy and their awareness?"

"Sir?"

Jesus: really *Eku?* "How many, how situated, and have they been alerted to our approach?"

"Ah. I will ask, sir."

"You do that." Solsohn regretted his snappish tone, but Eku's inability to pick up military parlance, let alone instincts or habits of thought, was so absolute that it sometimes felt willful.

A large mass moved close to him, which he could only tell by subtle changes in sound coming from that direction. "Yaargraukh?"

"It is I, Major. The trogans are with me."

"No reason to come forward."

"Not yet," the Hkh'Rkh sighed hoarsely, his species' equivalent of a whisper. "And if a reason arises, it is best to be positioned so that I may pass without bumping you."

Duncan was about to whisper that he wholeheartedly agreed when the light on Eku's suit edged toward him again. "Sir, the chief reports an estimate of eight to twelve opponents. They are in what was a communal shower. He believes it is their camp. It is unclear if they are aware of—"

Sudden shouting from the darkness ahead made the enemy's level of awareness unmistakably clear. Sandaled feet thumped forward, were greeted by the whisper of four short bows: two held by scouts, two by tinkers. An enemy trog screamed and fell, even as torchlight flared, bouncing dim reflections off walls and corners as it worked its way around the showers' dividing walls. The fluttering glow picked out the doorway, the jostling silhouettes of heads, and the abrupt motions of shoulders and arms.

A ragged patter of sandals—the enemy, therefore—receded. Quiet reasserted.

Eku's voice was more tense. "Chief O'Garran is shifting to assault protocol three. He will advise—"

Duncan was not surprised that Eku never finished his update. As Miles had pointed out, the enemy were rats in a corner. Time wasn't on their side, so they were coming out fighting again, just as soon as they'd regrouped. More shouting—no, a battle cry—more bow discharges, shadow-axes being brandished—

Abruptly, the attackers were bathed in light; Miles was holding his hand light aloft, angled toward the enemy. The front rank were all jalks, hands raised against the brightness but undeterred.

Axes cut toward them before they could recover from the vulnerability of that reflex. One of the scouts cried out at the same moment that the buzzing snaps of Girten's survival rifle kicked into life like a metronome trying to catch up with itself.

The enemy's reaction was as uniform as it was instantaneous. Cries of dismay rose up behind the already staggered jalks. The trogs in the second rank twitched, ducked—and then ran back into the safety of the showers.

"It seems the 'gravel rounds' had the desired effect," Yaargraukh observed.

Duncan nodded, still a pointless gesture in the marginal light. "Don't know our weapons, can't see what's hitting them, no time to find out. I just hope—"

"Grenade!" yowled O'Garran's voice.

"Cover!" Duncan shouted, shielding his eyes. As he did, he

saw the locals were following the drill—except Polsolun, whose disdain of the Crewe's instructions and expertise had been subtly but steadily increasing. *Guess you'll learn the hard way, sport.*

The eye- and ear-gouging chaos of the Dornaani shock grenade exploded over both friend and foe in an almost tangible wave. A rival bedlam of desperate shouts and pointless orders echoed out of the showers, along with bodies crashing headlong into walls and falling to the floor: blind enemies trying to scramble away from their attackers.

Although the light show continued, the grenade's caterwauling ended and was replaced by the much-amplified voice of Master Chief Miles O'Garran repeating the universal Low Praakht phrase for "lay down your arms": "*Ir-nek! Gruz'k jorgna!*" Transliterated, the words were "Be still or be meat," but the effect was identical.

After a second iteration, a brief scuffling put an extra pause into Little Guy's repetition of the order. A moment later, Eku leaned toward Duncan—

Who already knew the report: "The chief confirms the enemy shaman has been identified and rendered harmless."

As soon as O'Garran discontinued the visual effects of the grenade, the scouts and first two ranks of well-armed and -armored kajhs charged into the showers. Miles had already disarmed the most imposing of the near-blind survivors. And if the first image they saw was that of half a dozen trogs with bronze battle-axes at the ready, it probably made the offer of surrender not merely appealing but compelling.

"Sitrep, Chief?" Duncan shouted.

"Enemy position secured, sir! New orders?"

"Secure the prisoners. Designate guards and see to our casualties, then the enemy's. See if they'll volunteer information on the rest of this level."

"You're willing to trust them, sir?"

"No, but I want to hear what they have to say. After that, restructure our formation to finish the sweep."

"'Finish' is my favorite word in that sentence, sir. Looking forward to being done down here."

Duncan just nodded. *Yeah, your primary job will be over—which means that mine will just be starting.*

Chapter Twenty-Seven

"Hey, Major: CO wants a sitrep!" O'Garran called as he came around the corner of the now well-lit main corridor of Level Three.

"Already?" Duncan grumbled irritably.

"Uh . . . I think maybe you've lost track of time, sir."

Duncan glanced at his chrono. *Damn!* It had been three hours since he'd ordered the chief to secure the prisoners and started a detailed analysis of the complex. "Tell the commodore I'm just finishing up." Which was true. Sort of.

He glared at the one discovery which was confounding not just him, but the whole salvage assessment team, Crewe and local members alike: an immense encysted hatch, located at the end of a switchback tunnel that pushed out beyond the otherwise rectangular footprint of Level Three.

Miles cut his eyes at the symbiolene-encased object. "Tough nut to crack, huh, Major?"

Duncan nodded. "At least. Anything to report, Chief?"

"Zhathragz is babysitting the enemy shaman, and Bey is watching over the two of them with some of her biggest, baddest kajhs."

"She doesn't trust Zhathragz?"

Miles shrugged. "Pretty much, but she's extra-cautious when it comes to these trog witch doctors. It's like she's watching for them to exchange some secret handshake."

Solsohn nodded absently. The reticence of trog shamans went beyond how they worked their so-called miracles; it extended to their interactions with others of their ilk. How they were initiated, trained, rose to full stature, and conferred on matters impacting all of them—if they did—remained carefully guarded mysteries. "And the rest of the prisoners?"

"Got their lead warrior in a room by himself, too. Again, with babysitters. The others are in the showers. All are bound. But I gotta say, they seem pretty relieved."

"How do you mean?"

"Well, I still can't understand their jabber when they're going really fast, but near as I can tell, they didn't come here to hunt or raid. I think they were running from something."

Duncan glanced at him. "Does Cruvanor know about this?"

"Just told him before I came to you. He says it means we'd best mount a heavy guard on the ingress point at the end of the western corridor. I've got some tinkers clearing away the rockfall."

Solsohn frowned. "Does Cruvanor think whatever drove the prisoners here might come calling?"

"Not sure, sir. But looks like you can ask him yourself."

Cruvanor was approaching with Polsolun just behind. "I take it Leader Miles has informed you about my assessment regarding the breach in the west tunnel's wall?"

Solsohn nodded. "But no details."

"It is old, caused by the expansion of a natural fissure. The break starts slightly above the ceiling and runs considerably further down. Only one may pass at a time without risking falling into the crevasse."

"So, easy to defend."

Cruvanor smiled ruefully. "That would depend on what is attacking, but yes, it is certainly better than if the point of entry was wide."

"Yet you feel it necessary to increase the force we'd earmarked to hold it."

Cruvanor evidently inferred what "earmarked" meant from context. "The nature of cavern walls beyond and the depth of the crevasse are typical of deep, extensive tunnels. There are probably sizable caverns beneath us. This complex is certainly connected to the greater subterranean arteries that run the length and breadth of this continent." He shrugged. "There is no predicting what might arrive to challenge us from the deeps, or when. That is also why I suggest investing extra resources for a layered defense. In particular, we should keep a sizable reserve back from the entry itself."

Duncan nodded. "Prudent. Let me guess: you're thinking Yaargraukh and his team are the best for that job."

Cruvanor smiled. "I hate becoming so predictable so quickly, but yes. He is particularly well-suited for these tunnels, and his appearance—as an arurkré arising from a grat'r—should have much the same effect as you've exploited before. X'qai will proceed cautiously because they are unsure whether such a unique being is affiliated with a suzerain and if so, which one."

Solsohn kept nodding. "Which would buy us time, just as it did when we freed you." He frowned. "But if you're that worried about x'qao intruders, then why keep the prisoners on this level?"

Polsolun looked like he was going to offer an exasperated response, but Cruvanor held up a hand, stilling him. "Because," the war leader answered, "if any of our captives are bonded to a x'qao, or are extremely susceptible to their influence, we do not want to give a potential adversary eyes—or allies—on the other levels."

Duncan almost smiled: *Damn, whether its microdrones or mind powers, tactical security follows pretty much the same lines.* "It's pretty clear you've done this a few times before."

Cruvanor chuckled. "I should hope it is."

O'Garran nodded. "You're the reason we had such light casualties: one KIA and two minor WIA. An easy day... but maybe a little too easy."

Duncan glanced at Little Guy. "You're starting to sound as dour as Yaargraukh, chief."

Miles shrugged. "Maybe, but not for the same reason. I'm just a superstitious grunt, Major. When something seems too good to be true, it always is."

Cruvanor gestured at the walls around them. "Often, the sites that have the fewest points of ingress are also the easiest to secure because there has been little or no prior entry." He smiled crookedly. "But with such a breach as we've found on this level, you may consider your superstition justified, Leader Miles." He nodded toward the amber-crusted hatch that Duncan had been contemplating. "And this also complicates matters."

Solsohn studied it anew, realizing that "hatch" wasn't the right term; it was more like the door of an old-style bank vault. "Because of the symbiolene that's in the way?"

"And the fact that, if you look very carefully, you will see that the door is not fully closed. The ancient amber was released when it was very slightly ajar."

Solsohn looked more carefully. *Oh, great.* "Are you worried something might be on the other side of it?"

Cruvanor shrugged. "I am worried that we have no way of knowing *anything* about what is on the other side of it."

Duncan rubbed his nose, pointed to a label beside it, partially covered by a thin plaque of symbiolene. "Were you able to read this?"

Cruvanor shook his head. "We only know fragments of the ancient languages. But you can read it?" He glanced at the Dornaani helmet Duncan was carrying. "Ah. Your artifact can magically decode it?"

Solsohn despaired of finding a short explanation for how all the samples they'd fed it created a web of contexts and linguistic roots that produced an eighty percent read rate. "The translation is not perfect, but it indicates that only authorized personnel are allowed beyond this point. The closest translation is 'restricted access.'"

Cruvanor stared at the vault door. "So, if I understand the emphasis you place on that phrase, the builders considered the contents dangerous, secret, or both." He frowned. "Could the defense missiles be on the other side?"

Well, that conversation sure made an impression on him! "Normally they'd be kept much further from their launch controls. But it's possible."

Cruvanor frowned deeply. "As the world is today, would such missiles have value beyond the materials in them?"

More than you can possibly guess. "Yes. Very much so."

"It could prove very difficult to reach what lies beyond," Cruvanor said, almost more to himself than Solsohn. "This level has far fewer of the narrow closets you call access panels. That could signify that there are fewer reservoirs of the solvent and water. Or that they are difficult to tap. Or that they were reached through the surface."

He folded his arms, considering. "We must hold back a measure of what we find in the reservoirs on Level Two. If we use the solvent sparingly, we might have enough to free the door."

Duncan cocked an eyebrow at the war leader's hanging tone. "Something tells me that won't be the end of the difficulties."

"Mighty portals like this one often portend equally sturdy construction in whatever lays beyond. Even if there are reservoirs within, the access panels might be too thick to breach. Those require special windlass tools to open." He sighed. "I faced such a challenge once. It was a long, arduous process."

"*How* long?"

Cruvanor shook his head. "Until we free the door, there is no way to estimate the total time required. It will depend upon the presence or absence of both the ancient amber and the solvent. But just opening heavy, secured access panels? That could take many days, possibly a third of a season."

Solsohn shook his head. "So, that would create another problem: limited rations and water."

Cruvanor nodded. "Which would have to be fetched from Achgabab. Along with workers to remove the greatest wealth of this place: its many tonnes of fine metal.

"But that will require many bodies for many days. Who might also have to dig us out, should a sandstorm pass over, or a tornado come too near." His concluding laugh was dry and mirthless. "Prospecting and salvage is not only dangerous; it can be very, very aggravating."

Duncan smiled. "Well, it might be a little less so, this time."

"Why so?"

"It just so happens we have an agreement with Tasvar, the Legate's station chief in Forkus. They get half of whatever *they* can carry away. So they're the ones who'll handle the logistical challenges. Which still made them very, very happy."

Cruvanor nodded vigorously. "As well it should."

"There's only one problem," O'Garran sighed. "First, Tasvar has to be *told* we hit the mother lode." He shook his head. "It'll be a hell of a walk, getting a message to Forkus."

"That," Cruvanor said with a sly smile, "might not take as long as you think, my friend."

Duncan sympathized as Caine Riordan shook his head. "Wait a minute. We have *two* ways of reaching Tasvar by mindspeak?"

Tirolane nodded. "My consciousness is known to the mindspeaker traveling with Sharat. And Sharat's is known to Tasvar's mindspeaker."

Riordan took a moment to compose himself. "And there's a second way that involves Ta'rel?"

Who, standing next to the commodore, shrugged. And, of course, smiled.

"How?" asked Riordan.

"Ne'sar gave me her cloak. I am not familiar with such powers, but it is tied to her, much as if it were a living thing with a blood-bond. And she also is known to Sharat's mindspeaker."

Riordan put a hand to his head, as if that were the only way he could get it to stop shaking. "I can't believe it," he muttered after several long moments.

"Do not blame yourself," Ta'rel almost soothed. "If the way of such powers is not known among your people, you would not envision such possibilities."

Miles grinned. "Yeah, and it's not like you've had much else to think about, Commodore."

Cruvanor's laugh was light, pleasant. "Your Master Chief's irony is apt, Caine Riordan."

"And instructive," Riordan added. "I've been thinking of these 'powers' and 'miracles' as sui generis—uh, unique to the individuals who have them." He shook his head again. "Seems like they're not. Or, not exactly."

"About which we may speak later," Cruvanor agreed. "So, shall we send the message to Tasvar?"

Riordan nodded, scanned the deployment roster Duncan had handed him earlier. "I understand why we're so reaction-heavy down on Level Three, but it still worries me. If we put the majority of our reserves on Level Two, we'd have maximum flexibility against threats from underground *and* the surface."

Cruvanor nodded. "It is a calculated risk," he allowed. "But there is no evidence that you were followed from Achgabab, nor any sign that we were trailed from the river. Any other foes would be small bands or creatures who happen upon us as they traverse the dunes. They will not be disposed to press an attack in the teeth of such firepower as we have at our disposal.

"Also, there is still a reasonable reserve on Level Two, and all who are off duty must collect there, with armor and weapons at the ready. One of your own Crewe will be there as per Major Solsohn's requirements, in one of your artifact suits. It will be connected to sensors and shock grenades, also placed as per his instructions."

Riordan nodded. "Very well. He stared around at the defensive preparations for Level One, eyes stopping when they reached the open elevator. "That's secured, correct?"

"Immobile," Solsohn confirmed. "Even if we had power."

Caine walked over to it, looked up, exited smiling. "Well, I have some crap duty for a few folks, but that can wait. What's our setup for surface observation?"

"Two kajhs or scouts, with two fixed monoscopes relaying their feed to—"

Riordan shook his head. "No 'scopes on the surface without someone from the Crewe up there. Let's increase the watch to three and keep the monoscopes in this room."

Uncomfortable looks ping-ponged between the others in the huddle. "Sir," Duncan began, "if the 'scopes are in here, we're not as likely to get as much advance warning about the surface. And if we don't know who or what we're fighting until they hop down to visit—"

"I'm aware of the risks, Major, but the one thing we can't do is leave our, uh, artifacts unattended. They're too vulnerable to enemies and weather, so this is one time where we'll rely on bodies instead of our 'special tools.'"

Riordan looked around the faces of the impromptu council. "Anything else? No? Then it's time to start moving our people inside. Duncan, let's keep the solar systems out as long as we can—with an anchor watch. Ta'rel, find Eku and test all the seeps or other water sources; even with the Legate provisioning us, water rations are still going to be tight. And Bey?"

"Yes, Leader Caine?"

"I want your teams to make a full sweep before we settle in. They have the most experience living underground, so if we've missed anything, I want them to have a clear field in which to spot it. I want everyone inside before we start losing light."

As Riordan left with Cruvanor to inspect the suspected locations of water tanks and solvent, O'Garran sidled over to Duncan. He stared around at the walls. "Gotta say that this sure takes me back, Major."

"To what?"

"My early days as a SEAL. I spent more than a few weeks in a sub, back then."

"Good times?"

The chief stared as if Solsohn had lost his mind. "Worst damn days of my life." He stared at the walls again. "Me? I'll take a room with a view. Every time."

Chapter Twenty-Eight

Bey slipped into the room she shared with Qyza. It was a strange sensation, waking up in the night in a small chamber. Most of the trogs had similar reactions, and its layout—a warren of small rooms—was decidedly unfriendly to forming camp circles. But at least they did not also have to become accustomed to sleeping without a fur-mate.

"Has she settled in?" Bey whispered into the dark.

Qyza's slightly drowsy response might have been feigned; she was still not enthusiastic about Bey's plan. There was a thread of tension in her answering mutter. "Yes."

"And is she alone?"

"Also, yes." Then: "Are you truly determined to do this?"

"I'll tell you what I am determined *not* to do," Bey replied, finding her friend's shoulder in the dark and pulling her up. "I am determined not to spend another day ignorant of how it is that the women of Leader Caine's Crewe are allowed to be warriors. And if so, how it is they think *we* hold those roles."

"What you're really saying is that you are tired of not knowing why Leader Caine seems to like you, but not in the way you want him to."

"No! Well . . . yes. But not as you mean. It is simply that I desire clarity."

"Hmmph. Sounds like you desire something else, as well."

"Stop being foul—well, more foul than usual. Now come along and watch that I am not interrupted!"

✧ ✧ ✧

Bey discovered her teeth were on edge as the two of them waited for the footsteps of the watchman to diminish. The maddening part of evading detection was that if either one of them was seen in a posture suited for stealthy movement, they would be tasked to explain such strange behavior. At worst, they would be mistaken for intruders and attacked.

As if reading and judging her thoughts, Qyza mumbled, "This is madness."

Bey leaned around the near corner. The watchman—one of her own kajh—was just disappearing around the far corner. "Come," she muttered. Qyza emitted a subvocal expression of disapproval and resignation; her sandaled footsteps were close behind Bey's own.

They slipped past the room that had been set aside for the off-duty watch—empty for the moment—and drew close to the next door along the corridor. "Straighten up," Bey muttered.

"And what do I say if I am approached?"

"That you are waiting for me to come back out of this room."

"And if they ask why I'm not in there with you?"

Bey exhaled slowly. "You tell them the truth: that I am here for a private conversation. They need not know about what, and our own kind would never guess the topic. Now: can you do that?"

"Oh, all right," Qyza grumbled, leaning back against the wall. "Anything to get this over with."

Bey nodded her thanks and took the two remaining steps to the door. It was slightly ajar.

She raised her hand to knock on it—and almost jumped at the unexpected invitation from within: "You are welcome to enter, Bey."

Reflecting that she had yet to see any evidence supporting the popular trog assertion that human hearing was inferior, Bey laid her palm against the door and pushed against it gently.

Ayana Tagawa looked up from the sitting posture she often adopted at the end of the day: cross-legged, straight-backed, and strangely serene. Her eyes opened as slowly as the door. "Please be seated. It is the custom of my forebears that I should offer you tea, but all I have is water."

Bey held a hand up to halt the fine-boned human female's reach for the small clay pitcher beside her spartan sleeping arrangement: a thin blanket atop a modest fur. "I am grateful, but am not thirsty... unless it would be graceless to refuse your offer?"

Ayana smiled as her hand returned to her lap. “When one so openly expresses their desire not to give insult, they offer the highest courtesy.” She nodded faintly. “So tell me, Bey, what is it you wish to ask me about? And be assured: unless your words reveal a danger to our group, I shall not share them. I presume they are of a personal nature.”

Bey flinched. “Wh-why do you presume so?”

Ayana’s smile was so small that Bey thought she might have imagined it. “The hour is late for professional discussions.”

I am a fool! Bey was glad the light was very dim; the heat rushing to her face was probably darkening it. “Leader Ayana, I woul—”

The diminutive human held up one slender hand. “I am Ayana. You sit in our council as an equal. There is no need to use terms of rank when our conversation is both personal and private.”

“But some of you do. Even outside the council. They call Leader Caine—the commod—” Her face grew hot again. “Even those of you who are clearly his personal friends call him by his title. As they should.”

Ayana smiled, may have sighed. “I understand your frustration, Bey. My society, and particularly my own family’s reculturated traditions, are far more precise regarding what titles must be used when, and between whom.”

Despite puzzlement over what the word “reculturated” meant, Bey nodded. “There seem to be gestures—or sometimes the kind of glances exchanged—that signal that personal permissions have been granted. But I have not been able to understand or predict them very well.”

Tagawa nodded. “You have no reason to concern yourself with these irregularities. They reflect complexities of which you would not be aware. Dora and Eku have never held rank, so they lack titles which fit into the military customs that prevail in the group. Consequently, they are given great latitude when addressing those who do. My own situation is a mix of the two; I held rank, but as an officer aboard a merchant vessel. So I do not neatly fit into the patterns of rank and formal address, either.”

She put her hand on Bey’s well-developed bicep. “Your case is more difficult still. In the space of one season, you have passed from being our enemy to our prisoner, then to a warrior, and now the commander of all the trog-kind in our formation. So here is what I advise: if others are not using titles, nor should you. In the fullness of time, the maddening inconsistencies of casual Western interactions will become familiar."

"Western?" Bey echoed. "I would have thought most of you were from the east, presumably from lands beyond the islands of Zrik Whir."

Ayana's smile only increased Bey's puzzlement; it was rueful, but wry as well. "I suppose you could get to our lands either by going far enough east *or* far enough west. But it would be a long, long journey indeed." Her lips straightened as she nodded past Bey's shoulder. "Does your companion Qyza not wish to join our conversation?"

Bey had to concentrate not to break eye contact with the human. "She is there to make sure that we are not interrupted."

"Ah." Ayana's gaze was gentle, but also measuring. After a long moment, she leaned forward. "Your face is rigid with the pressure of the questions behind it. Please: ask freely."

This was what Bey had hoped for: an open invitation, given without caveats or precursors. But now that she had it, she was so nervous she had to review how she'd decided to proceed. *First, the roles of females in their society. And of how they choose mates.*

And... if it is true that Leader Caine no longer has a mate. She slammed a mental door against that thought. *No! That is* not *what you are here to ask. Just follow your plan.* "I have come to you because you are the leader of the Crewe's females."

Another small smile worked its way across Ayana's lips. "I believe Pandora would debate that."

Bey shook her head. "She would not. If someone asserted so in the presence of others, I suppose she might; that is her way. But I have watched Leader Dora. She defers to you in all things. And it is only right, given your position."

"My position?"

"Of course." When it became clear that Ayana truly did not understand what Bey was implying, she added, "You and Leader Bannor are mated."

Bey had never seen Ayana's eyes grow so wide. "Tell no one!"

Bey smiled, almost laughed, and then realized: *She is serious! Is it possible?* "But surely, the others in the Crewe know." *The trogs certainly do!*

Ayana sat back on her heels with a very long, very slow sigh.

"Yes, you are probably right. We have attempted to be discreet, but since departing the Legate's fortress, privacy is all but unobtainable." She straightened. "However, be assured that my relationship with Colonel Rulaine does *not* determine my position among my companions or in the force we have gathered to us."

Bey paused to be certain that Ayana was in earnest and discovered that she certainly was. "But... how could it *not* determine your position?"

For a moment, Bey did not understand why Ayana did not answer or why she was looking down with her eyes half closed. Then she realized: *She's composing herself. The question bothers, or possibly insults, her.*

When Ayana looked up again, her gaze and face were serene—almost chillingly so. "Among our people, 'mates' have no bearing upon our personal rank, either professionally or personally. So my standing is not dependent upon Colonel Rulaine any more than his is dependent upon me." While Bey was searching for a tactful way to steer the conversation toward her further, more pressing questions, Ayana added, "You must have noticed that, among my companions, there is little if any difference between the males and females. It seems to be a source of confusion among the trogs, so I presume they brought their questions to you."

"I have noticed. And they have brought their questions. Which is"—*partly*—"why I approach you: to understand what I have seen."

"Understand? In what way?"

Bey shrugged. "How can there be no differences?" Now it was Ayana whose face revealed she was uncertain how to respond. "You are equal to the males, yet you—and all the other females—have moon sign."

Ayana stared at Bey as if she had begun speaking an unknown language—until her eyes opened even wider than they had earlier. "By moon sign, you mean...?"

Bey could not tell if Ayana's sudden halt was because she was striving for words to confirm her understanding of "moon sign" or because she was stunned to silence. Bey offered an alternative. "Moon sign is our word for the fertility stain. You must know, for we have seen that the females of the Crewe all have it."

Perhaps it was the subtle emphasis that Bey put on the word *all*, but Ayana leaned forward, eyes full of sudden, startled comprehension. "And you—*you* do not?"

Bey shrugged. "Of course not."

Ayana's reaction was all the explanation Bey needed for why the Crewe did not understand: in their land, they obviously didn't require—or even *have*—the rite whereby female trogs became kajh. "One cannot be kajh if one can still bear young," she explained.

Ayana sat back hard upon her heels. "I... we never noticed."

Bey provided Ayana with the explanation in the same moment she perceived it. "You wouldn't have. Sho and I were the only two female kajh, and Sho perished early in the journey north."

Ayana leaned forward, stretched out a sympathetic hand, noticed Bey's curious glance, interrupted the gesture. "No, of course," she said, addressing herself as much as her visitor. "It is a choice—a strong choice—and does not seem uncommon enough, here."

Bey shrugged against the overstatement. "I would say it is simply not so unusual that it occasions surprise."

Ayana regarded Bey as if she had never met her before. "I would learn whatever you wish to tell me of this choice that female warriors must make."

Bey exhaled gratefully and started the tale of how she and those like her became a kajh. Finally, the gulf of mutual ignorance was being bridged. And once it was, Ayana would appreciate the significance of the other questions Bey yearned to ask—or more accurately, why it was imperative that she did.

She had once overheard Ulchakh telling Hresh that the greatest truths are actually fairly simple to explain. The rite of female kajh bore out the axiom. It was, after all, a product of necessity. If a female warrior had young, their fates would be sealed the moment she perished, or she was too wounded to fight for them. So it was that females had the same right as males: to choose to be kajh or not. To choose the way of weapons and freedom, or servitude and bondage.

Ayana seemed both fascinated and horrified. "And when must one make that choice?"

"As early as possible," Bey said with a sad smile. "Until one chooses, one is not trained. The later one begins training, the less likely they are to survive."

"How old were you?"

"Not quite four years. Of course, we come to maturity more rapidly than you humans."

"But you are a crog."

Bey smiled. "Yes, I made the decision very early in my growth, long before I showed my first moon sign."

"And how is it done, doing away with your moon sign?"

Bey shrugged. "It is a mixture of roots and fungi, added to one's food shortly after first moon sign. It is not pleasant. It kills some, but that is rare. And it is worth the changes, if you survive."

"Do you mean changes to your body?"

Bey managed to smile rather than laugh. "No: in how we are treated! Until then, you are trained but do not receive any extra food or other privileges. But once the moon sign stops and the scarring ritual is completed, you eat as well as any other young warrior. You are taught more, you sleep deeper in the piles, receive shares of every hunt and raid, and you sit in the warriors' circle when the chief or gang leader speaks."

"And you share all the risks of those warriors?"

Bey shrugged. "How could it be otherwise? Like any other young warrior, you are given the worst jobs and may be tormented by the ones just above you. But you are also protected by the laws that keep warriors from killing—or violating—each other outright." She drew a deep breath. "It is not a fine life, but is better than the fate of a slave, an urld."

"And why did you choose it so early, Bey?"

She sighed: now, she had to touch the only memories that she regretted—partly because they were painful, but also because there were so few. "The day my mother died. Or was left to die. I could never learn which it was, and the warriors had neither reason nor desire to tell me if they'd abandoned her."

Ayana frowned. "Abandoned her? To attackers?"

Bey shook her head. "No. My mother was kajh, but from the Free Tribes. And that was why the gang leader in Forkus never liked her, even though he desired her."

Ayana nodded. "I take it that a woman may be a kajh in the Free Tribes without giving up her fertility."

Bey nodded back. "Yes. And because we—well, *they*—have families, the harsh division between kajh and urld does not exist. I was born into that world but remember so little of it. Almost all my memories are of Forkus, of city-trogs, and the x'qai who enrich those who pursue supremacy and destroy any beings that keep love or laws for anything else."

Ayana studied her, long enough that Bey felt its significance: all the human leader's questions were answered. "And what would you ask of me?"

Bey responded with a half-truth. "Many have already been answered." *Just not the ones that keep me turning and tossing before sleep allows me to escape them.* "There was not such equality between males and females in the Free Tribes, but my mother was a kajh, and it is said she might have become chief. So however that is possible among them, I suspect it is simply more so among your own people, about whom I know almost nothing."

Ayana's nod was slow, almost formal. "I suspect that those observations are all accurate. And I regret that I may not tell you more of our lands. But if you have specific questions about us as individuals, I may be able to answer some of them."

Bey mirrored her host's slow nod, buying time to order her thoughts. *You could ask about Caine's mate. No: too direct. It would be better to learn if their males are like ours: that they will not consider females who cannot maintain their line. No, you fool! She would see the* real *intent of that question in an instant.*

Bey exhaled, felt her realities—female kajh, leader of trogs, member of the command circle—rise up around her like walls. There was no way to ask the questions she wanted. Something like quiet despair began settling in her belly, given weight by self-recriminations. *How could you not foresee that this conversation would*—had to—*end here? Or did you not* want *to see that? Were those dreams so pleasant that you blinded yourself to the cost you must now pay: having them all dashed at the moment you thought you might come closer? You are indeed a fool.*

But at least she had realized her foolishness before destroying all that she had built. *Be thankful that the wiser part of you awakened in time to put a stop to such strange hopes and stranger fantasies.*

Bey cleared her throat. "Any questions I might ask about individuals would surely touch upon the lands that gave rise to them. Or might be so personal and frank that they would offend." She smiled. "The trog-ways with which I grew up are usually blunt where yours are careful. Perhaps when I have a better instinct for those differences, I may return with questions." *Every word of which is true. And also an impossible fungus-dream.*

Ayana nodded, again formally. "Perhaps at a later time, then."

She sat up so her spine was very straight. "All of what you shared is new information for us. This places me in an awkward position."

Bey nodded. "I came to you privately, but what I shared about female kajh is important to understanding the land in which you find yourselves. It must be shared with the others." Before Ayana could respond, Bey shook her head. "No," she told herself as much as Ayana, "it is best that you do exactly that. After all, it is no secret. You or another of the Crewe would have learned it eventually. That it happened tonight, and that it was I who brought it to your attention, does not matter."

Ayana's eyes had become bright, unblinking, and filled with... wondering? Understanding? Pity?

Bey was glad that she did not redden as did burntskins. She stood quickly. "I appreciate your speaking to me at such a late hour and without any prior notice, Leader Ayana. I believe I have a much better understanding of how your ways differ from ours. That is a great help. I thank you."

The human rose, put out a pausing hand. "Bey, I realize you are unable to confide in those who follow you. This is a burden of all leaders." Her voice was almost sorrowful. "I hope you shall come to see me and speak again, if you wish."

A dozen answers—some grateful, some bitter, some sardonic, some agonized—passed through Bey's mind in the space of a second...

But instead of replying, she nodded sharply, turned, and left, tugging the door closed. She marched past Qyza who was so startled that she lagged behind a few steps. "Well, did you learn what you wanted?"

"I learned what I could," Bey mumbled, trying to sound indifferent instead of anguished. "Now, let's get our sleep. By daybreak, the humans will want the sun-catchers outside and my kajh watching over them."

Chapter Twenty-Nine

Gasdashrag was only peripherally aware when the last sliver of the moon sank beneath the horizon. He scanned his formation: well-concealed on the western slope of the dune and ready for movement. He was about to return his focus to the x'qao nearby when a figure rose and approached, apparently sent by Suzbegrog, his second-in-command. Gasdashrag held up his hand and paused the young deciqad: he had to keep his focus directed inward, seeing through the eyes of the x'qiigh's kiktzo.

The enemy had all but disappeared from the slab-capped dune a league south of where he'd positioned the insect. More accurately, it was the x'qiigh which had guided it there. But inasmuch as Gasdashrag was in the killspawn's mind, he was not only able to see through the insect's compound eyes but monitor the accuracy of the orders the x'qao gave it.

He pushed the x'qiigh to send the kiktzo a half mile closer to the ruin. The sudden motion was profoundly disorienting; the multiple lensing effect of insect ommatidia was particularly difficult to adjust to when kiktzo flew at speed. The world became a jumble of wildly changing scenes, in which every feature was not singular, but replicated as visual echoes of the incompletely seen original.

When the insect stopped, Gasdashrag still could not make out many details. There were a handful of figures moving slowly around the hole into which almost a hundred humans, praakht, and assorted others had disappeared over the course of the day. They had just finished collecting the bright, shiny objects they laid out after dawn and which were now being handed down into the bowels of the ruin. When the figures finished, they conferred briefly, received instructions from those in the ruin, and dispersed to sand-covered watch posts arrayed around the hole.

Gasdashrag accepted he'd seen all that he was going to, but it had been enough. The war party that Hwe'tsara still insisted on calling—and considering—"thieves" had repeated the pattern they'd established when they'd entered the site the day before. And when an enemy has begun to demonstrate patterns, a clever attacker can begin formulating plans that capitalize on them.

He sent a mental bump at the consciousness of the x'qiigh: a distasteful whorl of impulses and wildly divergent thoughts that were nonetheless monomaniacally self-focused. Gasdashrag warned the x'qiigh that the mental contact was about to end, and ordered that the kiktzo was to remain near the ground as it flew back: it must not silhouette itself against the sky, even at night.

He looked up at the deciqad who'd waited patiently for him: Zusnesmar. The young warrior was one of the two in Gasdashrag's group who shared the rare distinction of being an ambigogete: an individual capable of exercising both anagogic and eunogogic powers. "Yes, warrior?"

"Suzbegrog bids me tell you that Fezhmorbal has touched his mind and is impatient to have concourse with yours."

Imagine that: Fezhmorbal impatient. Almost as surprising as 'qo being hungry. "Does he wish to initiate the contact?"

"He was waiting on you to complete your observation of the enemy. He says the contact will be brief."

That was comparatively easy to believe; the day Fezhmorbal was not in a hurry was the day they would be carrying him on his bier. And even then... "Return to Suzbegrog. Tell him to approach and wait upon me. I should not be long. And Zusnesmar?"

"War leader?"

"Be well rested. Your varied talents will be required. Very soon."

"I shall be ready, War Leader Gasdashrag!"

Yes, but I wonder if Suzbegrog will allow you to prove it. Gasdashrag waited until Zusnesmar's soft, sand-sibilant footsteps grew distant, faded beneath the sound of the wind. He closed his eyes and concentrated upon conforming his mind to the conceptual shape of his primary anagog. That accomplished, he adjusted it so that it naturally gravitated toward the equally unique shape of Fezhmorbal's own consciousness. He felt the two fit together suddenly.

"What do you observe, Gasdashrag?"

"The enemy has completed moving into the site. Today there was no evidence of combat, but there were signs that prospecting may have begun. They had workers manning a bucket rope that removed a considerable amount of sand."

Fezhmorbal's thoughts were muted for a moment. "If they are excavating sand, the ruin is not fully sealed. Have you observed any other irregularities in the surrounding dunes, such as odd dips or declivities?"

"Nothing that suggests a spot where sand may be draining down into the site."

"Is there any chance that your force has been seen?"

Gasdashrag realized that he had, quite uselessly, shaken his head in negation. "There is no sign they have detected us, War Leader. Indeed, I do not see any way they could have. We are on the far side of a dune almost a day's walk from the site, and the kiktzo only approached close enough to count their numbers."

"What do you mean to do now?"

"We shall approach tonight, stopping behind the last line of dunes northwest of the ruin. If the enemy's surface force continues to be minimal, we will attack tomorrow night."

Fezhmorbal's response was not immediate. "Your forces will not be well slept."

The warning struck Gasdashrag more like a test of his competency, not a true concern. "The x'qa will rest when they become bored, though they hardly need it. The praakht will get enough sleep. And it does not matter if the pawns and deadskins do; they will still follow their orders. Regardless, as soon as the moon is down tomorrow, we shall attack."

"You are confident your force is sufficient?"

"No more or less than yesterday. About which: how far away are you?"

Fezhmorbal's long pause came with an aural whiff of frustration. "Too far. At least fifteen days." His thoughts became restless. "And there is still no sign that they are preparing to send away part of their force to replenish supplies?"

"None, War Leader. What do you make of that?"

"Nothing. We lack sufficient information for conjecture, and there are entirely too many *possible* explanations."

Fezhmorbal's conclusion struck Gasdashrag as the best segue he was likely to get for asking the question it had been wisest to avoid. Until now. "I cannot help but wonder if the explanation might be unique to this region." No reaction through the link. "I have heard the dotard-tales which claim that lands along hotside were not all deserts in the Before-World, and that many works of the ancients were buried in their entirety. While they were still fully functional."

"I have heard such tales, too," came the enigmatic reply. "All my life. And so have our fathers back across generations uncounted."

Gasdashrag did not want to appear gullible, but was just as determined not to ignore any opportunity to gain insight into his commander's true intents. "Do you think there might be a small shred of truth to such tales, War Leader?"

Fezhmorbal did not respond immediately. When he did, it was as though he had not sensed Gasdashrag's query. "These 'thieves' will be watchful. Make sure they are vulnerable before you attack. Destroying their force in battle would be a great achievement, but it will still be a victory if you can control merely the upper reaches of the site. If they are driven to a depth where it would be suicidal for them to counterattack upward, that will be sufficient.

"Signal me immediately if that is achieved. I may have means of furnishing you with some additional x'qa even before I arrive. Either way, inform me of the outcome. Which is to say, your success."

Gasdashrag altered their link to signify a respectful pause. "It shall be as you say, War Leader Fezhmorbal." And immediately after the link dissolved, he added, *If only the outcome was as assured as my blithe assertion of it.*

Chapter Thirty

Peter Wu waited as the last kajh from the prior watch climbed down the ladder from the control room. Almost no one called it Level One anymore, probably because it was just one big room, other than the defunct elevator in the northeast corner.

Peter grabbed hold of a rung just as Bannor's voice called down, "One more on the way."

Peter stood aside, looking up. "I figured you'd have been the first down."

"I would have been, if you'd been awake early," Rulaine chuckled.

Peter yawned. "Maybe next time... sir." One of the unwritten laws of military life—that no one woke up to stand a watch any earlier than they had to—was also the most frequent cause of arguments, good-natured or otherwise. He'd seen fistfights break out over a few minutes more or less of sack-time.

"Lieutenant Wu was still getting his beauty sleep," Duncan's voice added through a yawn.

Rulaine slid down the remainder of the ladder, stared at Peter, shook his head sadly. "Well, it's not working."

Wu grinned. "The colonel is the epitome of wit."

"Yeah," Duncan drawled, "I hear he's pretty funny, too."

"Yes, he is," Peter agreed, "and if you work very hard, Major, I'm sure that, one day, you will be as well."

Bannor snorted out a laugh. "Point goes to Lieutenant Wu.

Tell Miles I'm doubling my bet that he doesn't get a wink of sleep during the next watch. I'm heading for my furs and shrugging out of this armor." He nodded to Tirolane as they passed each other at the corner of the wide, doorless ready room just a few steps along the western corridor.

Duncan was still buckling into his own armor as he glanced up the ladder. "I suspect they're waiting for you up there."

Peter sighed and nodded, "Yes, I suspect they are." He went up two rungs at a time.

His energetic arrival surprised the rest of Level One's third watch: Enoran, one of Arashk's h'achgai, three tinkers, and ten trogs. Peter nodded, went over the standard operating procedures, including the codes for interaction with the three scouts hidden in the sand drifts atop the ruin. They quickly settled into their rotations between performing simple maintenance and remaining on alert—to the extent that anyone could, staring at the walls of one room. Fortunately, Bannor and Miles had come up with a scheme to keep the "active watch" element awake and ready. Unfortunately, it was the part of being watch commander that Peter hated the most.

After positioning the bone ladder beneath the mostly sealed hatch above, and angling a small mirror toward one of the fixed monoscopes, Peter Wu turned to the trogs and tinkers who weren't already repointing shafts for their own self-bows. While not introverted, he enjoyed his own company and felt no need to fill time with needless chatter. But part of his job was to keep the watch alert—and now, that duty called.

Settling his gear near to hand, Wu leaned toward the trog-kind and resumed their conversation from where it had ended the prior night. "So, other than dustkine, what have you hunted?"

As if swept away by the cooling winds, Zusnesmar felt Gasdashrag's consciousness withdraw from his own. The deciqad once again became aware of what his eyes had ceased to register during his contact with the war leader: dark sands, a dozen of his own kind lying in a line just beneath the crest of the last dune that was higher than the ruin. Further down the shielded slope, twice as many praakht waited in similar postures, the pawns among them made obvious by their absolute lack of movement. And down at the bottom—

Eager, hungry eyes and open maws, flecked by glints of the fangs lining them. A dozen 'qo, slightly fewer q'akh, and three x'qnarz waited in the dip between dunes. They stirred and shifted restlessly, their attention switching between the anticipated kills just one dune away and the more immediate temptation of the living, breathing bodies just a few leaps higher up the slope. Allies or food: with killspawn it could change in the blink of an eye, sometimes at the most problematic moments.

"Are you done appreciating the night air?" a voice grated behind Zusnesmar, even though it had been hardly more than a second since the contact with Gasdashrag had faded.

He rolled over to make his report. "Apologies, Suzbegrog. I was considering how to pass on the war leader's message most succinctly."

"Seconds wasted pursuing succinctness have now slowed your relay of critical orders. Speak them!"

He is threatened by my intelligence; he was from the first. "Yes, Second War Leader Suzbegrog. Another far-seeing was attempted by Shavragtur, once War Leader Gasdashrag finished repositioning the balance of our force two dunes back. It was no clearer than his prior two. We only know that the opening in the top of the ruin connects to a large chamber below. It is not a narrow shaft that leads directly into the depths."

Suzbegrog's eyes seemed to bore through the small lip of sand between them and the target. "Does Gasdashrag believe that if I were to try a far-seeing from here, that I would perceive more?" He glanced sideways. "Or did you not think to ask that?"

So sorry to disappoint. "Gasdashrag believes further skrying will be profitless. He has heard that this is frequently the case with the oldest ruins. It is speculated that those with specially layered construction distort what is conveyed from their interiors."

"'Distort,' or 'interfere'? Choose your cosmology with care, pup."

And this was why Suzbegrog had never risen higher, despite his abilities at both anagogy and eunogogy. *Here, less than two hundred paces from our target and with restive x'qa soon to lose their weak hold over ravenous impulses, you stop to argue how and why our powers function. It is not your pettiness that has crippled you; it is your inability to think as a warrior must. That speed is of the essence.* "I submit to whichever term you prefer, Second War Leader." *As if I didn't know which.* "The effect is the same; we have no more than an outline of the volume beneath the opening. However, Shavragtur's last far-seeing conclusively showed that the chamber, as well as the opening into it, are not natural, but crafted. The opening is a perfect tube, and the room beneath, while irregular, is a composition of geometrically precise voids."

Suzbegrog muttered vaguely at the report. *Probably because he cannot find fault with it.* "Well, then, it sounds as if this ruin is indeed worth the time and resources that Fezhmorbal has expended upon it. Such precise construction in undamaged form is characteristic of the oldest sites—and richest finds. His gamble has paid off."

For you as well, you bone-dry rock-turd. Fezhmorbal's proposal was deemed so unlikely to bring us water and wares that the Oligate only sanctioned it because of his reputation. And still, they were not generous in their support. Why else would you *be along as the senior magister of this enterprise?* "Orders, lord?"

Despite his impatience, Suzbegrog did not reply. He did not move, except for a long swallow which sent his prominent Adam's apple on a long, slow journey that ended where it had begun.

Ancestors, please no. Is it true? Has he been unable to act when he must lead? Were those rumors actually—?

Suzbegrog blinked, then nodded. "How long can you sustain mindspeak?"

"Minutes if I must project it. Nearly an hour if it is cooperative, as with Gasdashrag."

"How long will it take you to invoke?"

You'd know if you ever permitted me to give you a complete review of my abilities. "It is an anagog, so instantaneous."

"Then contact him. Tell Gasdashrag we mean to attack now." Suzbegrog raised his head enough to be heard by the other deciqadi down the line. "Wait for us to signal you from the ruin. Tell those below that we shall not be long." He gestured for the nearest four deciqadi to join him, along with three of the senior kajhs.

"Come closer," Suzbegrog muttered once they were together. "And do not move." He closed his eyes, raised his hand into the center of the group, and flexed his fingers. Then he recentered himself and, after a longer period, performed a slightly different crafting gesture.

He opened his eyes. "You see each other?"

"Yes, but oddly," said Hazmalsin, the youngest warrior among them. "It is akin to glowsight."

"It is a powerful version of it. If you were unable to see heat so well, you would no longer see us at all. We will now appear as the sands around us."

"B-but I thought that one must be without clothes or gear for that eunogog to work."

"Those are the limitations of a lesser eunogogete," Suzbegrog said, with the faintest hint of a turn in Zusnesmar's direction. "But this will not last long. Now, we shall walk quickly to our target. But do *not* run; the effect does not conceal abrupt motions reliably."

They crept over the crest and began approaching the ruin on a line that put its one exposed corner between them and the three "hidden" watch posts the humans had sunk into the sand that remained upon the upper surface. The route of advance exposed them to detection slightly longer, but once they were under the rim of the structure's roof, none of the watch posts would have a line of sight to them. But even then, the most troublesome part of their approach would be making their way up the sandy slopes to the top.

Hazmalsin, who had never attacked prepared foes, let alone humans, began walking even faster than Suzbegrog. "Warrior," Zusnesmar muttered. "Follow your leaders. Do as they do." Hazmalsin glanced over, eyes wide, nodded, and reduced the frequency of his strides, lengthening them instead. Zusnesmar nodded approval as they continued.

With the moon down so low that there was not even a faint horizon-glow, they closed their formation once they were in the blind-space beneath the ruin's rim. They spread out, testing the sand along the base of the dune through which the ruin protruded. An area aligned with the most wind-exposed corner of the structure seemed more stable, probably because looser sand blew away from that which time had packed hard against the ruin's strangely perfect sides.

The force's most experienced dune-runner, Islikbraya, led the way up, her fingers silently pointing to places least likely to collapse and gesturing for more space between those ascending when they risked putting too much weight on any one part of the slope.

As she approached the top, she crouched low, moving slowly so that Suzbegrog's effect had ample time to change from the colors and textures of the sand to those of the ruin itself. She peered briefly over the edge before waving the others to follow.

When they reached her, she indicated precisely where the three lookouts were hidden. Suzbegrog let his own image blend with that of the new surroundings, worked some other effect that Zusnesmar did not recognize—some further layer of unnoticeability, probably—and then set about preparing an effect that required much more time: clearly, an ambitious construct. When it was readied, he rose up over the lip of the structure just enough to extend his hand toward the lookouts.

The only indication that anything had occurred was an almost inaudible thump, possibly of armor falling upon stone or a satchel being dropped. Suzbegrog signaled to Islikbraya. Together they crept over the rim and toward the three hidden watch posts where they conferred briefly. They waved the rest over, but without pithing the guards.

Suzbegrog saw Zusnesmar's questioning look as he approached. "If they are bonded, or warded, their death will be an alarm to those who crafted it."

Very well, at least you are as clever as they say. "Shall I signal to our forces?"

Islikbraya interrupted with a hiss. "Not yet. Come see this, er, door." As Hazmalsin positioned their three kajh to stand guard over the comatose praakht watchmen, Zusnesmar joined the other two at the hole.

It was blocked by a round metal plate. Or rather, a door, judging from its perfect fit and rust-eaten hinges. It had been left slightly tilted over the rim, and its thickness promised that it would be very heavy. But worst of all, there was no line of sight into the chamber below. They considered the round metal door again, looked at each other, then at the kajhs. Hazmalsin was clearly the largest and most muscled of the group, but...

Zusnesmar stepped back from the obstacle. "I think we need to bring up the q'akh and x'qai. Quickly."

"Well, of course we do, fool," Suzbegrog muttered. "Did no one notice that there was a heavy door in place here?"

Islikbraya looked away, leaving Zusnesmar with the grim job of pointing out the obvious. "I can contact Gasdashrag to inquire what the kiktzo saw, if you wish."

The magister's eyes widened. "You dare—!"

Islikbraya did not look at him as she interrupted. "He dares nothing. He points to the obvious; that this obstacle was not detected. He also points toward our only means of attacking by surprise: to give the task of removing this great iron disk to the creatures most likely to do so swiftly."

"Summon them," Suzbegrog spat, turning away from the entry. "And bid them hurry."

Islikbraya glanced at Zusnesmar, nodded, and moved to Hazmalsin. Together, they unpacked, unfurled, and raised the signal pennant: bright white cloth shot through with silver threads. They waved it toward the others waiting with the killspawn.

"You," Suzbegrog muttered toward Zusnesmar without bothering to look at him. "I will call for your mindsense when we have cleared the way down. How long will it last?"

"Once I have constructed it, two minutes at most."

He turned, surprise and fury growing on his face. "Once you have *constructed* it? Do you mean to say that you do not have the effect as an anagog but a eunogog?" Zusnesmar nodded, Suzbegrog turned away again, cursing fiercely into the night.

Because you cannot *curse me about this.* Zusnesmar had repeatedly attempted to report his specific abilities to the magister. Who, if he had ever relented in his haughty dismissals, would have realized that his adjutant would require time to produce the effect he now desired.

Which raised a troubling matter. "Why do you need mindsense so swiftly, Magister?"

"Idiot! It is now impossible for us to fully surprise our enemies. No matter how swiftly the x'qai might remove the obstacle, we have no way to incapacitate any of our enemies before sending down the first wave." He glared at Zusnesmar. "Unless you expect them to be so stupid that they will stand directly beneath us, looking up?"

Zusnesmar once again had to admit the magister knew his craft, if nothing else. Unable to see his targets, Suzbegrog's contingency was to have Zusnesmar's mindsense locate the minds below the instant that the obstacle was removed. "I can have it held in readiness," he offered.

The magister shook his head irritably. "The rush to get our first attackers down among them will make it impossible to coordinate activity close to the hole itself." His eyes looked through Zusnesmar, narrowed. "But there may be another way." He returned to his eyes. "I warned you I might require you to mindwatch a pawn or a deadskin. Do you remember?"

"I do."

"How long will that last and how far can you remain in contact?"

"At most, it will last a few minutes. As to range, I cannot say; I have never used the construct in a manner where it was an issue. And I cannot say whether or not the ruin's construction will block it."

"But if there is a clear path to the chamber below, you could manage that, at least?"

Zusnesmar couldn't see any reason why he wouldn't. "Yes, Magister."

"Then we have another way to locate those in the chamber below—and better still, a means of assessing if they are worth another construct such as the one I used on the guards up here." In response to Zusnesmar's questioning look, he added, "It is a very taxing effect. If those in the chamber below are just more of the same"—he jerked his head at the three senseless watchers—"I shall save my strength."

He stood, waving to the first of the x'qa who were already swarming over the lip of the roof. "Now, gather the others and stay close to me." He smiled savagely at Zusnesmar. "Having the eyes of a pawn for a minute will be more than enough."

Zusnesmar sincerely hoped it would be and passed a simple, patterned pulse back to Gasdashrag: a code indicating the attack was about to begin.

Chapter Thirty-One

Peter checked his chrono, and pushed up from the ancient and now hide-cushioned seat. He held up a hand just as the most talkative kajh prepared to share yet another hunting story. "I was not aware so many creatures existed in the wastes. Now, it's your turn to—"

Something scraped at the lid—only once. Not three fast taps, which was how the lookouts were supposed to start a coded message.

All sound and motion in the room stopped—except for Peter leaning over to lay a hand on the ladder.

A second scrape, this time followed by a metallic groan and a clank.

Wu toggled his helmet's comm link for a general alarm, pushed the ladder over—and in so doing, knocked aside the mirror angled so a monoscope could watch the top hatchway.

Enoran reacted just as rapidly, one hand pulling the one h'achgai back against the wall with him, the other drawing his wheellock pistol. The scout-archers copied their retreat to the edges of the room a moment later. The porters and handlers managed to stand their ground, frantically glancing from the probable threat above and back to their leaders.

All except for one of the trogs—who, having somehow forgotten the oft-repeated instruction to never, *ever* stand under the hatchway, stepped forward to look up in startled, open-mouthed curiosity.

✧ ✧ ✧

The Dornaani alarm—a strident groan—filled Duncan's helmet.

"Shit!" was not only Solsohn's first thought, but his first word. However, before it had finished coming out of his mouth, he was already reacting, as much by reflex as thought.

He tipped over the alarm gong, glanced at the thumbnail monoscope feeds—both still functioning, but the hatch-monitoring mirror was gone—and paged Yaargraukh to confirm that there was no simultaneous attack being mounted against the subterranean breach.

In those two seconds—during which Solsohn had reflexively unlimbered his carbine—the rest of Level Two's ready reaction team started to respond. Craig had his survival rifle out and was moving toward the opposite side of the ladder to Level One. Tirolane was already poised a step back from the overhead hatchway, sword in his right hand and newly lanyarded pistol in the other. Marcanas turned toward the corner of the ready room, kicked Rogarran out of his restless doze, and was already reversing back toward the ladder.

Thank you, God-or-Whoever, that it's the start *of the watch*, Duncan thought as he scanned down the stacked status lights of the remote-operated security assets. The shock grenades positioned on Level Three—at the breach, the bottom of the ladder, and vault door—were all green. The grenade just two meters to his right: green. The grenade up in Level One: also green.

As he double-checked the links between the three active Dornaani suits, Yaargraukh's pre-coded sitrep blinked to life: again, green. No assault or probe on Level Three.

Not ten seconds in and all assets were on-line and ready; Solsohn registered a microsecond of pride. *Not a bad plan, even if Caine and Bannor* did *tweak a few—*

The thumbnail screens for Level One suddenly became blurs of confused movement. The damned porter who'd been standing under the hatchway began stumbling out of a sudden shower of sand—

He was knocked sideways, the other trogs' rising cries suddenly silenced by a single, loud thump. Duncan glanced up; something had hit the hide-covered shield they'd secured over the hatchway. Glancing back toward the monoscope thumbnails, he saw the cascade of sand diminish to reveal a form rising from its knees: a trog.

Duncan squinted.

The trog was in rags, limbs wasted, eyes blank. But those blank eyes were nonetheless staring intently, the unkempt head turning in a surprisingly slow, even fashion.

Peter started cursing at the very same instant that Duncan shouted, "Kill it! Kill it *now*!"

Miles O'Garran gasped as his helmet was abruptly filled by hysterically panicked whale-song—which was to say, the Dornaani equivalent of a red alert.

There were shouts, too—one of which was his own as he jerked upright and slammed his head against the top of the elevator shaft. Even through the helmet, the blow put him on his back again—*shit, talk about a low ceiling!*

The desperate cries coming over his comms weren't part of some dream or drill or flashback. Rolling to his side this time, O'Garran checked his gear, glanced at the HUD's data feeds, and began edging closer to the elevator's ceiling access panel. But there was only one thought in his mind as he did so:

Snapping up that absurdly soft watch duty Riordan had offered—sleeping all night long in the access space above the elevator—hadn't proven to be such a great choice, after all.

After playing out his survival rifle's battery cable so it wouldn't catch on the fixtures around him, he kicked the access panel aside. Legs working in short pushes, he squirmed closer to the opening from which sounds of savage combat arose.

Zusnesmar felt the moment that Suzbegrog's brief mindwatch touched the pawn's senses, and most particularly, its eyes. The magister completed and released his eunogog at the surprised enemies in the dim chamber beneath them.

Zusnesmar waited long enough to ensure that the construct had taken hold then waved the waiting 'qos toward the opening.

As the first of the ravenous beasts leaped down, Zusnesmar noted that the defenders were only surprised, not shocked. Several—possibly humans?—had already moved back against the walls of the large room. The rest already had weapons in their hands; they weren't moving decisively, but they *were* standing their ground. But that was only for the first instant.

Before the first 'qo's feet slapped down hard on the ancient floor, almost half of those who'd not yet reacted began moving oddly. Some shrank away from not only the opening above but from everyone else in the chamber, as if they no longer recognized them. Others blinked, groggy and disoriented as if they'd been shaken awake from a deep sleep. A few even swung about themselves desperately, attempting to fight off imagined attackers or even their nearest comrades. But whatever their reactions to Suzbegrog's construct, there was one common thread: within the first few seconds, all were either fending off or fleeing from the first four 'qo which had flung themselves down into the room.

After waving several more into the hole, Zusnesmar ordered Islikbraya to block the remaining 'qo long enough to make room for the first of the two x'qai that had lifted the round metal door out of its frame. He paused the second one long enough to order two q'akh down. As Zusnesmar gestured for the second x'qao to follow, the eyes of the mindwatched pawn showed him just how ferocious hungry 'qo could be.

They unerringly detected which of the guards Suzbegrog's construct had distracted and leapt on them with utter abandon, bearing them down to the ground. Raking claws spattered blood in all directions. The second group landed and rushed any defenders who showed less resolve than the others. They were largely undeterred by the sweeps of bronze hatchets and obsidian axes, accepting deep cuts as the price for closing with the recoiling praakht and sinking their fangs into lagging limbs. The screams of their victims excited them even further; they flung chunks of armor and bone aside to get at the best meat.

Zusnesmar shouted orders, tried to prevent them from clumping up two and even three to a single defender. But even if they heard his commands, it was unlikely they would have obeyed; the 'qo were mindless with hunger-amplified bloodlust.

As Suzbegrog neared the completion of his next construct and Islikbraya held back the wave of killspawn waiting to follow Hazmalsin into the ruin, Zusnesmar compelled the pawn to scan the room once again. Halfway through the slow turning of its head, he spotted a still shape amidst the chaos of thrashing limbs and waving weapons: a figure wearing a strange suit that matched the descriptions of those worn by the thieves. He shouted after the second x'qao as it jumped through the hole, ordering it to attack the presumed human.

But as he did, the figure raised some kind of weapon, reminiscent of a crossbow without bowstaves—and suddenly, the image was gone, along with Zusnesmar's link to the pawn.

Peter paused to make sure the enemy pawn was truly down before resuming his crouched movement along the wall. Enoran, who had also ducked down far enough to be screened by the room's long control console, was moving in the same direction: toward the elevator. The 'qo were rushing after whatever targets they could reach first: mostly trogs who had become either unresponsive, or, to all appearances, delusional.

But when the first q'akh finished literally tearing apart the tinker that had not crawled under a chair in time, it reared up—and paused. Peter motioned for Enoran and the h'achga following him to freeze—

Too late. One moment, the q'akh's head had been half turned away; the next, it was facing them, eyes widening. It lowered its head at Wu and screeched. Abruptly, it was bounding across the room. It dodged the second x'qao, which landed barely a meter away, and extended its final stride into a high arc that would carry it over the control panel.

But Peter had not wasted the thin moment between the q'akh's shriek and charge. In that half second, he'd brought his weapon up near enough to the killspawn that his HUD's targeting guidons snapped into existence. The creature's own movement turned them bright aqua: target locked.

Wu squeezed the trigger, knowing it was a risk not to double-tap the monster, but the battery drained quickly and he had fewer shots than there were enemies.

The round hit the q'akh at the base of the neck. The pebble-skinned humanoid tumbled over the console and landed just short of Peter, kicking as the human moved beyond the reach of its frantic death throes.

Duncan Solsohn gritted his teeth as the sounds of slaughter kept increasing overhead.

"Jesus Christ, Major!" Girten almost wailed. "We've gotta go up there! If we don't—"

"Keep covering the hatch, Sergeant."

"But Lieutenant Wu won't—"

"He has four shots, at a minimum," Solsohn interrupted, watching as Peter edged around the q'akh he'd just taken down with one shot. "And he has one of the grapple guns. Hold steady."

Tirolane's face was unchanged, but the hand on the hilt of his bastard sword was almost white despite being sun-bronzed. "Very well," he muttered. "Then step aside, Major."

Duncan popped his visor to look the swordsman in the eyes. There was no insolence or even impatience; just cold resolve as he uncocked his flintlock pistol and let it swing on its lanyard. He lifted his palm so that it was aimed at the still covered hatchway above.

Resealing his helmet, Duncan stepped aside with a gulp, wishing he could get further away, even though the swordsman was a proven ally.

"Major—" Girten pleaded again.

"Sergeant, get out a flare," Solsohn muttered, watching the monoscope. The x'qao in the room above had turned toward the hole to the surface, just as one of the q'akh had done before attacking Peter. *They're receiving—and probably disobeying—orders from up top.* "Girten, override the flare's minimum arming distance. Ten meters."

"But . . . a flare?" Craig almost wailed. But he continued digging one out of his belt pouch.

Duncan kept forcing himself to ignore the flashing—and sometimes flying—limbs in the monoscope screens so that he could track the two x'qrukhs' movements and positions.

Peter kept Enoran and the h'achga moving along the wall toward the elevator as the other q'akh kicked and pummeled those 'qo that had stopped to gorge on their kills. As they did, the second x'qrukh turned, searching for the other q'akh that he'd almost crushed—and discovered the three crouching defenders. With a roar rising up in its throat, the x'qao started toward them—but then, snarling, turned back toward the hatch down to Level Two.

Wu was about to warn Solsohn when that comm channel opened. "They're looking up for orders," Duncan snapped. "Neutralize." The channel closed. And for good reason: the first x'qrukh was bending over to grasp the hide-covered shield blocking the hatchway down to Level Two—and Duncan's reaction force. *And if Solsohn's right—*

Peter was moving before he had a plan—because there was no time for one. Only a few moments in which to follow instincts honed by almost two decades of experience and training.

He jumped toward the console, quite sure that it was the stupidest thing he'd ever done. *But also, maybe the thing they least expect.* Checking and finding his flanks clear for that one second, he leaned over the console and glanced up at the open hatchway, eyes triangulating the relevant angles faster than his brain could.

Anyone looking down would position themselves for direct line of sight to the hatchway down to Level Two. They'd use the vantage point with least exposure to defenders beneath them. Combine the two. The attackers would be looking down from the side of the top hatchway that faced the south wall.

The part of the hatchway which was now directly over Peter's head.

Absurd, he scolded himself as he shoved forward until his hip was against the center console. He leaned out, twisted around, and swept his carbine toward the hatchway overhead.

He had a brief impression of a black, star-filled hole before the HUD targeting system reimaged it using thermal and light intensification. The hatchway brightened and, peeking over its edge, were the thermal outlines of two heads. They were trog, maybe human.

The targeting guidons offered either for lock.

Peter grimaced: *Damn, which one is in charge? Or more dangerous?*

The one on the left extended a hand—

Okay: you. He blinked to lock the target and fired—

Just as another figured leaped down from the other side of the hatchway.

Wu scrambled back from the console and discovered himself staring at a much bigger human—or was it?—rising up from his landing crouch, a long dagger in one armored hand.

Behind him, the first x'qrukh grabbed the shield covering Level Two. He slung it away, and with a kill-lusting howl, jumped down, the other one moving to follow.

Zusnesmar started at a sound—a sharp buzzing snap—that spiked upward from directly below. He flinched away.

An instant later, Suzbegrog slumped sideways against his arm and Zusnesmar felt wetness on that cheek.

Leaning back from the rim of the hole as more 'qo jumped into it, he touched his face. The hand he brought away was covered with dark deciqadi blood. Careful not to expose himself, he leaned back to peer at the magister.

Some projectile—a bullet?—had punched a hole beneath his left eye and exited near the top of his spine.

Zusnesmar was halfway through reestablishing a full link with Gasdashrag before he realized that he had not been paralyzed by terror. One trial behind him, at least. As the commander's consciousness firmed into his own, he reported, "The magister is dead."

Gasdashrag had probably guessed the news from the emotional surge of the young deciqad's contact. "Yes," he agreed. "Report. Quickly."

"I have only seen two humans. Only one was in artifact armor. At least a dozen enemy are dead, but few or none are warriors. We have sent down half the force. Hazmalsin just joined them to ensure they engage useful targets. The first x'qao just opened the shaft to Level Two. No results yet."

"The speed of their response is troubling," Gasdashrag replied. "As is the lack of humans. You must take complete control of that chamber before more of them appear. Press the attack. Speed is key." The link dwindled.

Zusnesmar turned toward all the remaining killspawn and kajhs. "Go!" he yelled, jabbing his finger toward the hole.

Abruptly, the shield above Duncan was gone and the x'qrukh he had watched grasp it was hurtling down the hole, claws out, maw wide.

Tirolane tensed the palm that was already aimed toward it.

The creature went limp in midair, head lolling, limbs nerveless. It crashed to the floor.

Tirolane had turned his body as he completed the gesture, which gave Marcanas the space to leap forward. His whole weight behind the thrust of his longsword, it sank deep into the killspawn's perversely broad chest. Even so, the warrior had it out in an instant, flipping it over into a two-handed grasp. He drove it down through the x'qrukh's right eye.

Peter's shout over the comms startled Duncan. "Roger enemy cadre overhead. More targets." It clicked off.

Solsohn glanced at Craig Girten. "Stand ready here at the ladder, Sergeant."

"To do what, sir?"

Duncan did not reply; he was too busy double-checking his survival rifle and the HUD's targeting system.

Goddamn Dornaani gear, Miles fumed, *getting hooked on every nut and bolt.* Which was an exaggeration, of course, but it made O'Garran feel less like a failure as he prepared to—finally—drop down from the top of the elevator.

And it's not as if there wasn't some truth to the complaint. The generous loops suited for spaceside gear and big gloves were just snags waiting to happen. As they'd proven repeatedly. Several times, he would have just torn himself free, but two things stopped him: the knowledge that he might ruin the space suit, and that he, like the overwhelming majority of humans, was just not strong enough to actually tear the Dornaani materials.

The chief swung his boots through the hole. *At friggin' last.* He used one hand to hold the survival rifle—no, carbine!—close to his chest. The best use of his other paw had been a real Hobson's choice: either clutch the battery and cable—an unwieldy seven-kilo millstone—or leave the battery on top of the elevator as he used his hand to pay out the cable to keep it from tangling as it uncoiled. Both choices were shit, but hey: welcome to combat in the real world.

O'Garran checked that the battery was well back from the opening, aimed his feet at the hides two meters below, and butt-pushed himself off his perch.

As he started to drop, he felt the cable playing out smoothly. *Perfect!*

Until, that is, it snagged on *his* end.

The loop of slack he'd kept for a little extra control, just in case the cable snagged overhead, caught under a belt pouch. It pulled free almost instantly, but in that same instant, it tugged the mostly extended line with a force equivalent to the still accelerating mass of exactly one Chief Miles O'Garran. With no slack left, the downward pull was exerted against the mass on the higher end—which was to say, the battery.

O'Garran felt the sharp tug, followed by an instant release, and followed his instinct: to lean away as he landed. So instead of conking him straight on his head, the battery glanced off his shoulder—and tore the power jack loose as it did.

Miles managed the worst three-point landing of his life—professional or personal—and recovered into a lopsided kneeling position. He wished he had a moment to lay some truly fine invective on the battery, but his fall had been loud enough that two nearby enemies—*little 'qo bastards, of course*—turned their heads. Their eyes narrowed and jaws opened.

Well, ain't that just my shit life: half my ready shots detached. Here's hoping I've still got enough.

He shot the closest 'qo in the center of mass without waiting for the HUD's targeting system: not enough time and besides, it was like shooting really ugly fish in a bathtub. The other one had been bumped aside by its more agile pal and was still scrambling to its feet as the HUD's targeting guidons tightened around it—just as a bronze axe came down square on its head from behind.

Like most of its kind, the 'qo was absurdly resistant to damage. The axe sheared off its flesh and cracked the skull, but didn't split it. The wielder of the axe—one of Arashk's h'achgai—took another step forward and finished the job. Miles nodded his thanks, scanned for bad guys.

No shortage of them, but even if Duncan hadn't started yammering in his ear, he'd have known which one to hit. Boosting the charge, he swung the weapon smoothly onto target: a big x'qrukh about to jump down to Level Two, just like his pal had moments before.

The guidons flashed and locked green in the same instant. He squeezed the trigger twice.

One round cratered the side of the big killspawn's neck, the next hit near the spine. Its yowl was one-half angry bear and one-half dying trash compactor. It fell over with a limp thud.

The HUD threw up an orange warning light: one full power charge remaining. As it did, Enoran came up alongside the h'achga, which was being driven back by another q'akh. The human moved to help—but had just enough time to bat away the grasping claws of a 'qo charging right through Miles' line of fire.

One shot. Two friendlies. Miles felt the quandary, knew both might die if he grappled with it—and targeted the 'qo. Even though the h'achga had helped him just seconds before.

O'Garran squeezed the trigger, pushing away a regret that was also a question: Was choosing to save Enoran's life kinship—or bigotry? And how the hell could you tell?

I'll worry about it later. If I live. Miles grabbed for the loose end of the cable, hoped that jury-rigged Dornaani equipment was rugged enough to forgive rough handling. As he manhandled the battery to reach the output port, he blinked on the comm link to Duncan and yelled what the watch CO needed to hear:

"Clear skies, Major!"

Duncan winced at the volume of the chief's addition: "And hurry up! Peter's down to shortswords."

Solsohn nodded at Girten. "Straight up the chimney."

Girten leaned into the space beside the ladder and fired his flare upward through both hatchways. Duncan leaned out as soon as it launched, gun aimed after it.

The Dornaani flare was so swift that no one—neither friend nor enemy—even had the time to react. So when it burst an instant later—a small sun suddenly shining down upon the ruin—it backlit the bodies surrounding the star-littered hole that opened to the surface.

A figure's head and shoulders were framed in that light, just visible over the rim: a live silhouette laboring to pull an inert comrade out of the line of fire.

"Gotcha." Duncan squeezed the trigger, hardly needing the target lock.

The moving figure, now struggling to lift the other, actually rose into the shot; what should have been a headshot impacted between the neck and clavicle. The dark outline tottered, fell across the rim and wobbled there for a moment before momentum tipped it over the edge to thump on the floor above.

"Peter, Miles," Solsohn paged in case their visors happened to be up, "here comes the light show." He activated the stun grenade on Level One.

Killspawn yowls vied with the electronic cacophony. Wild sprays of light strobed and spattered down through the hatchway and sparkled off the metal ladder. "Status, Level One."

"Alive," Miles grunted.

"Barely," Peter added. He might have been wheezing.

Solsohn muted the channel. "Doctor Baruch, follow the response team to Level One."

"Acknowledged."

Tirolane stared at the pattern of lights on the floor. "How long do we wait?"

Duncan checked his timer. "You ready to go up?"

Tirolane, Marcanas, and now Rogarran simply stared, their swords held for a swift ascent.

"The 'qo should be blind for about a minute. Can't make any guesses about any others still up there." The constant stream of killspawn leaping down had made a head count impossible.

Another h'achga and a kajh still fastening his armor rushed up as Duncan counted off the last seconds "Three, two, one… go." He switched off the grenade as the three humans began leaping up the ladder two rungs at a time, followed by the other two warriors. For a moment, the only sound was the furious sputtering of blind killspawn.

Then, the death-yowls began.

Chapter Thirty-Two

"Looks like your defense plan was a success, Major."

Solsohn turned toward the source of the praise: Bannor Rulaine, who was rounding the corner from the space reserved for the off-duty watches. "Could have been better."

"That's true of every plan that's ever been executed. The universe makes a mess of the best of them." He arrived at the ladder, a hand on the nearest rung. "Sitrep."

"Level One has been cleared of the enemy and is secure. Dr. Baruch just went up to assess and treat casualties. The reaction force just went topside, led by Chief O'Garran. Yidreg and a few others joined them."

Ayana Tagawa appeared behind Bannor. "Any reports from the surface?"

"Enemy was already retreating. Anyone with bows and crossbows are engaging. As per protocol, no modern resources were authorized once the site was deemed secure."

Rulaine shifted his own crossbow so he could better climb the ladder one-handed. "Tell them we're coming up."

Duncan started forward. "Colonel, I'd like to join—"

"No, Duncan. This was your show; you see it through down here. You've done the first part of the job; now you get to be the constant commo hub for the follow-on." He nodded at both Solsohn and Girten and started up the ladder. Tagawa shot Duncan a quick smile—almost a grin—as she followed.

A comm channel illuminated in his helmet: Yaargraukh. "Solsohn. Go."

"Do you require reinforcements, Major Solsohn?"

"No, we're secure. Wrapping up topside."

"I am glad to hear it." He paused. "Were your forces sufficient?"

"I won't lie, Yaargraukh; having forty percent of our personnel down on Level Three brought us to the edge of our ready resources."

The Hkh'Rkh's voice was somber, quiet. "As we foresaw."

Solsohn grunted, not willing to trust his first reaction on open comms. A bottom-heavy force deployment had been strongly advised by both Cruvanor and Bey, who—rightly—pointed out that the wall breach connecting Level Three to the tunnels was a potential source of innumerable attackers. But still...

Duncan finally found a sufficiently neutral reply. "I think some force rebalancing might be in order."

"Indeed. Yaargraukh out."

Solsohn sighed: *Well, more grist for the next meeting of the command group. Speaking of which*—"Sergeant Girten, I think the commodore will want to be briefed. If he's still asleep, please rouse him."

In response, Girten let loose an explosive guffaw.

Startled, Solsohn turned, worried that some strange mind-talent from an unseen enemy had affected the paratrooper.

But Craig was pointing past Duncan back toward the corner screening the off-duty and sleeping personnel. He tried to speak but couldn't, just pointed more vigorously.

Solsohn followed his finger.

It took him a moment to recognize the disheveled, bleary-eyed apparition that was staggering around the bend: Caine Riordan. Half in his armor, carrying a still sheathed longsword, a crude local helmet tilted rakishly on his head.

He straightened—mostly—and demanded: "Sitrep."

Duncan managed not to smile. Girten had no such self-control: the commodore's "command presence" produced another roar of laughter that was closer to mule-braying.

Riordan, trying to stifle a yawn, goggled at them. "What?" he said.

Uncertain how to answer either of his commander's requests, Solsohn was relieved when Girten saved him. "Gawdamn, sir," the GI chortled, "you look like every green looey that ever woke up *after* an attack was over."

Riordan stared, blinked, and then—as if slowly waking up to the sleep-drunk mess that he was—began to chuckle.

Girten wiped laughter-tears out of his eyes. "Well, now you've gone and ruined it."

"What? Why?" Riordan asked, hand raised to cover another yawn.

"Well, you just did what none of them butter-bars in France and the Lowlands ever did: laughed at yourself. They all got pissy about it." He smiled sadly. "Still, makes me a little homesick."

Riordan began to straighten out his gear and his smile. "Sorry to end the comedy magic," he said, rubbing sleep sand out of his eyes. When he looked up, they were as clear as his tone. "Still, I'll have a full sitrep, now, Major."

Listening to the moment-by-moment breakdown of Solsohn's response to the attack, Riordan forced himself not to sigh. After all, he'd brought it on with his very, very serious request for a full sitrep.

Like they say, "be careful what you ask for; you just might get it." It certainly was good that Duncan had not only put his planning talents on full display, but was now having them fully recognized by the CO. Albeit in painstaking—or would that be painful?—detail.

So it was a relief when Miles came sliding down the ladder, landing with a bounce that turned his jaunty smile into a momentary wince. He allowed his right shoulder to sink a little. Riordan frowned. "Have you had that looked at, Chief?"

"Doc is busy treating folks with real wounds," the SEAL replied, sucking a painful breath in through his teeth. "But I did turn topside ops over to Colonel Green Beanie. Who had the nerve to call me 'Littl*est* Guy'!" He glanced up at Caine. "But I guess tonight everyone is glad I'm little enough to fit on top of the elevator."

Riordan nodded. "The major was telling me that you turned the tide."

Miles glanced at Duncan. "He did, huh? Well, that's just half the story, you know."

"Oh?"

"Yeah . . . because he was the other half. Capping that guy who's leaking all over the floor up there"—he rolled his eyes up toward Level One—"that's what sent them scurrying." He rolled his shoulder carefully. "Although just like always, the SEAL paid the greater price."

Riordan smiled. "Guess you're rethinking sleeping on top of the elevator as—what did you call it?—your 'soft duty'?"

Miles looked like he was about to shrug, but thought the better of it. "Sir, it's a well-known fact that the universe hates me. Me in *particular.* So I'm not really surprised that I only got one night of uninterrupted shut-eye before all hell broke loose.

"But the way I look at it, I'm guessing it gets better from here on. Something tells me we won't be hosting any more late-night visitors for a while. If ever. Secondly—and don't tell anyone I ever said this—I think my present misery was worth the experience."

Girten glanced up. "Worth it? Why?"

"Because I've spent a career having bastards coming out of the walls and floors and ceilings at me. For once, it was *me* coming out at *them*! Felt good switching roles. Kind of like getting revenge on all those bastards—and the universe that put them there."

"Because it hates you?" Solsohn said, one eyebrow raised.

"See? Now you're getting it, Major."

Riordan crossed his arms. "What's the situation up top, Chief?"

"The colonel sent me to report that 'the OpFor is retreating.'"

"And you'd say . . . ?"

"That they're running like hell, sir. Even the 'qo. Those that are left. We also dropped a bunch of their trogs as they 'retreated.' But I'm guessing that—"

A sudden scrambling of boots and sandals came down through the hatchway, followed by muffled questions and orders.

Riordan moved toward the ladder. "News, Major?"

Solsohn shook his head. "No new contacts."

Riordan started up the ladder. "Duncan, you stay here."

"Sir—"

"That's an order," he snapped as his eyes cleared the hatchway to Level One.

Blood. Limbs. Bodies. Everywhere.

"My God," Riordan breathed as he climbed the last few rungs up into the bowels of the slaughterhouse.

Newton was laboring intently on a figure obscured by his broad back, but it was clearly not one of theirs: its boots were knee-high strapped hide, and the armor fringe just above them was light chain mail. Across the room, Peter was propping up the h'achga that had been on duty with him, a blood-sodden wrapping where its belt should be. Enoran was not far away, back against the wall, an arm and a leg swathed in slightly less inundated bandages.

But almost all the noise was coming from the hatchway overhead, where Ayana was guiding a scout and a kajh as they lowered another trog down, a crossbow bolt protruding from the center of his chest. Her rapid speech and glances behind made it pretty clear that there were other casualties awaiting transfer down to what had become Newton's combination operating theater and triage station.

Riordan looked across the room to Peter, whose suit had more than a few gashes in it. "Can you report?"

Wu nodded. "Enoran is stable." He glanced at the h'achga and shrugged. "Those two fellows over there"—he jutted his chin at two scouts behind Riordan—"might regain consciousness. The rest?" Wu shook his head, then glanced up at the sound of Ayana's voice.

"Two friendly-fire casualties," she announced. The two carrying the trog deposited him near Newton and headed back for the ladder.

Peter watched them ascend. "According to the comchatter, the other enemy WIA is a mangle."

Riordan crossed the room to Peter. "A mangle? Working with this bunch?"

Peter shook his head. "I do not know."

Caine kneeled next to Wu. "And how are *you*?"

"I shall be fine, sir."

"Is that what Dr. Baruch said?"

"Dr. Baruch," Newton called over without looking up, "has said nothing. Too busy."

Riordan nodded. "Duncan sent a runner back to get Katie awake and up here."

The surgeon nodded curtly. "That is welcome, but there is very little she can do other than hand me what I need. These wounds are too severe."

Miles' eyes roved across their own dead and wounded trogs. "Do we really give a damn about one of the bastards who tried to kill us?"

"We might. I believe this one is an officer of some kind, and his wound is localized. The others..." Newton shook his head. "I cannot believe I am saying this, but I recommend bringing Zhathragz up. He might be able to stabilize some of our own wounded. By which I mean, the ones I've treated."

That was when Riordan realized that there were at least three others from the Level One watch that only appeared dead; the shallow rise and fall of their cured breastplates was too faint to see without focusing on them carefully. Riordan leaned his mouth toward the comm pickup. "Duncan—?"

"I heard, sir. Already have a runner going for Zhathragz."

Riordan approached Newton at an angle that allowed him to see around the doctor's torso.

The body of the enemy officer was not merely thin, but gaunt. Wherever his skin was not covered by armor—scale, mostly—it was not merely wizened, but dehydrated. A memory jumped up: those physical features were the same they'd noticed upon meeting the monster-riding female warrior who had been both herald and enforcer at the entrance to Forkus.

Miles had come to stand next to Caine. "Damn ugly bastard."

"His features are not without interest, however," Newton observed. "I must begin suturing the primary wound. Pay attention as I do."

Although sedated by one of the local fungi compounds, the being stirred as Newton began working with the needle driver. When he pushed the thread up through the other side of the laceration, the patient flinched, lids flickering long enough to reveal his eyes.

Amber eyes. Just as amber as the guards in Tasvar's fortress. Or, often, the Ktor.

Riordan glanced at Miles, who was already looking up at him.

"Well," the master chief muttered, "that can't be good."

Newton was the last to join the council circle, whose members were sitting in the fixed chairs of the site's briefing room.

Or, more accurately, what was left of them. The cushions had disintegrated at the lightest touch, but with multiple hides layered atop each, they were reasonably comfortable. More so than the floor, at any rate.

Riordan waited until the surgeon had dropped into his waiting chair. The front of his local tunic—they had all started saving their off-world clothes, as well—was almost as bloodstained as his hands. "I regret that we have to start with your report, Doctor."

Newton waved away the concern. "I am happy to dispense with it at the outset.

"We suffered ten dead. Two were tinkers, the rest were trogs: scouts and urldi, no kajh."

Eku looked up from his notes. "I thought there were only eight KIA, Doctor."

"There were, but we lost two within the last half hour, including the friendly-fire incident."

Riordan nodded. "When did that happen?"

Tirolane cleared his throat. "Right as we regained the surface. The flare was already spent. Some of the fleeing enemy were still within bow range. Orders were being shouted, changed, countermanded. I suspect that is what roused one of the lookouts from whatever trance they were in.

"He jumped up suddenly. Rogarran saw the motion on his flank. His crossbow was at the ready." Tirolane sighed. "Rogarran carried the trog to the hatchway but the wound was deep and would not stop bleeding."

Newton nodded. "I black-tagged him."

"Black-tagged?" Bey repeated, frowning.

Ayana leaned forward. "It is a term used by healers. The person so designated is deemed to have a mortal wound."

Bey folded her arms, nodded, stared straight ahead.

Newton continued. "We have four wounded, one of whom is so stubborn that he insisted on being at this gathering." He cut his eyes at Peter.

"If I were a compliant patient," Wu countered, "you would not recognize me."

Newton's grunt combined agreement with reluctant amiability.

"The other friendly fire casualty?" Riordan asked.

Duncan leaned forward. "Technically, only realized as friendly fire afterwards. There were two mangles with the enemy. They were both fleeing. One was hit. He was one of the ones who just died."

Dora put her fists on the table. "And why the hell are mangles helping these bastards?

Duncan shook his head. "They weren't helping, not voluntarily."

"Well, how then?"

Bey raised her chin. "They were under the influence of one of the deciqadi."

"The what?" several voices asked.

"The beings directing the attack—one of whom is still alive, yes, Doctor?"

Newton nodded slowly. "He is hanging on by the thinnest of threads, but yes."

Riordan leaned forward. "What can you tell us about them, Bey?"

She shook her head. "Almost nothing. Their affairs rarely overlap with those of trogs. They are allies of the x'qao lieges."

Bannor folded his hands. "Allies, not servitors?"

"They are not vassals. They answer to their own kind."

"Do they live in cities?"

"Their own, if any. They are apart from the affairs and activities you have seen in your time here. It is said they dwell in ancient caverns, most of which are hotside. Although many of them have taken service with lieges and even suzerains, I have never heard anyone speak of what their purposes might be."

Tirolane looked as if he were about to add something but rubbed his chin instead.

Riordan made note of the swordsman's reticence on the topic of the deciqadi and turned back toward Duncan. "So we're counting the dead mangle as a friendly-fire incident."

"Yes, sir. The other one is no longer under the influence of the deciqadi, to use Bey's term. According to Tirolane, it is the result of, eh, either an anagogic or eunogogic ability."

Tirolane nodded. "That is the most likely explanation. But others are possible. When we converse with the prisoner, we should have a better idea of the agency that compelled the trog's compliance."

Duncan shifted in his seat. "Returning to the topic of enemy casualties, we count eight 'qo, three q'akh, and two x'qrukh killed. Two deciqadi as well. And five trog kajhs: two who jumped down toward the end of the engagement, three who were hit while running toward the nearest dune."

Bannor rested his index finger on the table. "I believe there are POWs, as well?"

"Yes, sir. Three trogs, all of whom were wounded by arrows. Doc Baruch expects them to recover fairly rapidly."

"Also," Newton added, "none of them seem highly motivated to return to their masters."

"Even so," Bey interjected, "they must be carefully watched before they may be trusted."

Bannor frowned. "More so than the ones we found here in the ruin?"

She nodded. "Much more."

Duncan resumed. "There are also seven s'rillor cases who

didn't bother to run when their bosses did. And of course, there's our prisoner, about whom we know next to nothing. Except that he and the older of the two dead ones are clearly literate. They had small books and codices." He scratched the back of his head. "Damned if any of the scribbling matches anything we've seen."

Bey's eyes rested on Tirolane a moment before he raised his chin slightly and offered, "I may have greater luck deciphering them." He glanced at Riordan. "With your permission."

Riordan nodded slowly. "Pending a discussion about what you expect to find in them, yes."

Tirolane returned the nod. "I feel certain of this much: the contents will require considerable study before I have a command of them."

"So you do not think they are journals, or the like?" Wu asked.

"No," Tirolane answered, "I think they will answer how this group possessed the powers that they demonstrated."

Riordan frowned. "Could that include clues regarding whom they are working for, and why?"

Tirolane met his eyes. "It might. Indeed, I very much hope it does."

After leaving a rearguard within a league of the ruin to ensure they were not being followed, Gasdashrag pushed past two more dune lines before calling for a halt.

He and the rest of his force—even the x'qa—were exhausted and drawing great wracking breaths. The killspawn were tired enough that for now, their primary desire was to rest. But as soon as they recovered, hunger and frustrated kill-lust would emerge twice as powerful as it had been when they attacked the ruin.

But as much as he dreaded having to contend with unruly x'qa, that was whelp's play compared to the duty he faced now: contacting Fezhmorbal.

As soon as he touched the counselor's consciousness, he felt foreknowledge radiating out at him. "You failed."

"We did." He realized how the seasoned war leader knew. "Otherwise, we would not have been able to report so swiftly." *And perhaps you have someone working as an informer in my force. Or did. I could see Suzbegrog gladly accepting such a role.*

"Yes, the timing of this contact suggests much, but also the odds of the fight itself. Tell me how the battle unfolded."

"Our approach was routine enough, given the forces we faced. Their surface patrol was quite minimal."

"It was a mere tripwire," Fezhmorbal emended. "No warriors at all, I'll wager."

"I believe that was the case. We did not take the time to either interrogate or dispatch them."

"Prudent. Then?"

"The interior of the ruin remained only vaguely perceived despite multiple far-seeings. Detection of minds within it was entirely unreliable, as you warned might be the case."

"Which is part of why I felt your odds diminished, the more you told me of its nature."

Then why did you bid me attack, you bloodless husk? "I do not have a full account after that. Events unfolded quite rapidly. Suzbegrog and Zusnesmar wasted no time sending down 'qo after they used a mindwatched pawn to scan the first chamber."

"That was well conceived. Zusnesmar's idea?"

"Possibly." *You know more about those in your command than you reveal.* "The spirits of our fathers were very much with us in that first half minute or so. But there were only two humans on that level, and only one wore artifact armor."

Gasdashrag sensed a pulse of grudging respect in his superior. "Again, a tripwire: one who could survive and observe while they held their true force elsewhere."

"It is as you say. There was a similar opening in the floor of the first chamber, almost directly beneath that through which our forces entered. However, the moment we opened it, the battle went against us. Not only did strange weapons hit our race-brothers with almost magical accuracy, but yet another human emerged from a hidden location opposite the opening to the second level. Possibly garbed in artifact armor."

"And thereby, they had you in the flank. What were your losses?" As he relayed them, Gasdashrag could sense Fezhmorbal's growing emotion—and was surprised to discover it was resignation, rather than anger. "No, you did not fail," the war leader added as if he had—*had he?*—read Gasdashrag's private thoughts. "You did well to get as far as you did with as few losses. We know much more about them than we did."

"But this outcome will enrage Hwe'tsara!"

Fezhmorbal's indifferent reaction was the mental equivalent

of a shrug. "Would it have been better to settle the issue of these so-called 'thieves' once and for all? Certainly. Was it likely that we could? Dubious, and more so as time went on and they continued to accumulate resources. And if, as seems likely, they have Cruvanor of Gorzrik's stable with them—yes, I have confirmed those rumors—then their own aptitudes and his experience gave them mastery of the ruins, and possibly its artifacts, far more swiftly than any of us could have anticipated."

"Then what have I achieved, losing so many of my force?"

"A demonstration to Hwe'tsara that we made an honest effort, but will require more resources to achieve his desired goal."

"Which is not possible."

"Ah. But he does not know that, nor will he until it is too late. But for the nonce, his crusade to be avenged upon these 'thieves' will provide all the cover we require to advance the race's objectives. And equally important, you have confirmed that these humans are as singularly dangerous—and unusual—as I suspected. Which, when Hwe'tsara's suzerain becomes acquainted with the fact that I warned him of this from the outset, will make us his only source for understanding and dealing with what has transpired. Well, Hwe'tsara or whoever might be Ormalg's suppliant liege in Forkus, by then.

"Now, one last matter. You lost three of our brethren, did you not?"

"I did."

"And you are sure that they are all, regrettably, dead?" Fezhmorbal's transmission of the concept "regrettably" lacked the emotional undercurrent which a genuine expression of it would have contained.

"Two of them, yes."

"I did not ask about two, Gasdashrag. I asked about all three." Fezhmorbal's link became suffused with dark currents, precursors to black rage.

"I cannot confirm Zusnesmar's demise. His mind detached from mine as abruptly as death, but as the rest fled immediately after he fell, I cannot be certain that death was the cause."

"And have you tried to touch his mind?"

"Yes, but the ruin blocks that just as completely, War Leader Fezhmorbal."

"Now, that *does* upset me," Fezhmorbal responded as slowly as a viper uncoiling to strike from ambush. "That upsets me a great deal."

Chapter Thirty-Three

Trailing Pandora Veriden, Riordan spied the end of the corridor over her shoulder. There were two guards at the vault door and no sign of the symbiolene that had encrusted it just two days earlier.

Caine increased his pace; Dora widened her strides to keep up. "When did Cruvanor clear it?"

"Finished just an hour ago, Boss."

He glanced sideways at her tone: tense, uncertain. "What's the problem?"

"No problem, sir." They'd arrived at the door. "But . . . well, see for yourself."

The two kajh guards stepped aside with the trog equivalent of a salute—an abbreviated nod-bow that reminded him of his time spent in dojos—and Dora reached past him to pull the door open.

Cruvanor was waiting for him inside, smiling.

Riordan glanced at the walls and the floor: no sign of symbiolene. "So the space behind the door was clear?"

Cruvanor chuckled, gestured to small drains in the floor. Yellowish water was pooled around them, distant gurgling audible from well below their louvers. "No. This space was coated in ancient amber. Follow me." He began walking down a long, straight corridor that was more reminiscent of a reinforced shaft. Small pitch-reeking braziers gave it the appearance of an entrance to hell.

Riordan noted that the floor was completely dry. "How long ago did you release the solvent?"

"About an hour, now."

"And it's this dry already?"

Cruvanor's glance was one to which Riordan had become accustomed: mild surprise at the gaps in the Crewe's knowledge. "When deliquescing, the ancient amber mostly turns to vapor. Whatever was encased in it is rarely wet for more than a few seconds."

"And what did it reveal?"

Cruvanor came to the end of the tunnel, pointed through the narrow opening between what looked like a ship's bulkhead doors. "After a few tests, we saw no reason not to dissolve all the remaining ancient amber. The process is just about finished. Have a look."

Riordan stepped through the doors into a T-intersection at the center of an immense chamber. It ran at least sixty meters to both right and left, both arms split by yet more bulkhead-grade steel. And in a line along each of them, were fuming yellow columns: the sign of dissolving symbiolene. A small amount of water ran away from the base of each, disappearing almost as rapidly as it pooled there.

The process concluded abruptly. The vapor dissipated within two, maybe three seconds.

As it faded, it revealed rows of rockets, each snugged in its own bay, a launch sleeve poised above each one.

"My God," Caine exhaled finally. For a moment he couldn't be sure if the surprise had driven all thoughts out of his head or whether it was so filled with ideas and questions that it produced the cognitive equivalent of deafening white noise. "You mentioned a test?" he eventually croaked.

"Yes. We first applied the solvent to those two, down at the end of the left-hand row."

"Condition?"

Cruvanor shrugged. "We found no flaws, but our knowledge does not go beyond gross physical defects. I am sure you and your companions are the best judges of whether any internal damage has occurred. But, as I have said before, I have never heard of anything sealed in ancient amber that is less than perfectly preserved."

Dora came to stand beside Riordan, put her hands on her hips. She leaned toward him. "I heard what you said when you saw them. So: *now* do you believe in God, Boss?"

Riordan swallowed. "I honestly can't say one way or the other, Dora, but if anything was going to make a believer out of me, this might be it." He craned his neck to look up along the matte-grey fuselage of the nearest rocket. "Yes, this just might be it."

The rest of the day was so busy that Riordan still hadn't had dinner when he arrived at the conference room.

Everyone present—the entire council circle, Tirolane, and Cruvanor—were already staring at him as he walked through the doorway. He had never seen a room with so many faces wearing expressions that truly warranted the adjective "expectant."

He smiled. "Okay, yes: the rockets." He turned to Eku and Ayana. "I know there could still be plenty of disappointing surprises, but based on your inspection, how would you rate their condition?"

Eku glanced at Ayana, who had far more experience with the relevant hardware. "They appear as they might have for an inspection. However"—now she glanced sideways—"I defer to Yaargraukh in this matter."

Riordan nodded at the Hkh'Rkh. "So, they are similar to your own systems, after all?"

Yaargraukh's shoulders rolled. "Enough for the purposes of basic assessment, yes. Insofar as my people once made frequent use of such vehicles, I can say that there are no signs of wear, other than what might have been generated during a test-firing. A further, if implausible, indication of the preservative qualities of the symbiolene is that it has maintained their fuel, as well."

"Is that so surprising?" Peter wondered, shifting to better accommodate his bandaged arm. "If these are indeed defense missiles, don't they employ solid-rockets?"

"Not all of them," the Hkh'Rkh corrected. "Although the dimensions and basic frame of the vehicles are all similar, almost a third are liquid-fuel variants." Surprised stares met that revelation. Yaargraukh did not pause to acknowledge them. "They were fueled for launch. With liquid hydrogen and oxygen."

Initial stares of surprise transformed into suppressed horror.

"Do not be alarmed. Their fueling hoses were attached. Although there is no electricity to drive the primary systems, Eku identified and activated an emergency detanking system that had several possible power sources—one of which was an exothermic reactant. The fuel will be in safe storage within the hour. How we refuel—well, that is a problem for another day."

"So is everything having to do with power," Duncan groused.

Cruvanor inspected the faces of the Crewe. "And by power, you mean electricity?"

Riordan nodded. "Given how much of this complex was encased by symbiolene, I suppose it's possible that some of its electrical systems might still function."

"In the meantime," Ayana added, "we discovered a variety of truly 'manual' overrides and access systems in the launch bay, as well as tools and a shop beyond. All of that is still coated in symbiolene, however."

Cruvanor shook his head. "The sheer amount of intact systems, tools, documents, and fixtures makes this the most challenging site I have ever prospected. Also, we usually have at least five or six technickers such as Irisir present to supervise cataloging and assessment, which are carried out by junior members of their specialty."

Tirolane leaned toward his grandfather. "Within two weeks, there should be some aid with that. Tasvar's convoy includes many of his own technickers."

Duncan was slowly turning a graphite stylus that was Bactradgaria's substitute for a pencil. "And still, there's something missing here."

Riordan nodded. "Auxiliary control. A command backup."

Bannor shrugged. "There's no sign of any access to a blank space inside the footprint, according to the map put together by Eku," whom he acknowledged with a grateful nod.

Duncan shook his head. "Old-fashioned bunkers like this sometimes put them in strange places." He turned to Cruvanor. "In your earlier salvage ops, have you ever found schematics—er, floorplans?"

"No. But in a site so intact, and with ancient amber encasing so many spaces, we do discover preserved documents. But they are among the most delicate salvage to retrieve. In this case, we have few hands and no surety of being able to read what they say."

Solsohn nodded, but was already thinking ahead. "Maintenance areas would have to have schematics. At least references to all the facilities for which they're responsible. So if there is an auxiliary control, we may find hints there."

Riordan nodded toward him. "Make it a priority as you coordinate with the cataloguers."

Duncan tapped his temple. "Already at the top of that list, sir."

"I know what I'd like to see at the top of a list," O'Garran exclaimed. "Those vehicles in the garage. And whatever is in them, if they're security rigs. Same with the weapons that are coming out of the amber. Be nice to have a few of those restored."

Cruvanor appeared to take a moment to reinforce his patience. "As I have said before, restoring the contents of the garage will be a significant undertaking. Much of the solvent and water in the chamber was lost through leakage, and we are unable to assess how much remains embedded in the walls which are still blocked by sand. The greatest volume of which is presently choking the exit, which, in turn, is at least three meters under the dunes. So recovering the contents of the garage is likely to involve relocating considerable volumes of water and solvent from Level Two to the garage. After that, a major excavation project would be required to free any vehicles we might find there, assuming their condition warrants the effort."

Miles seemed to be struggling with his own patience. "Okay, but what about the personal weapons, at least? A few of the pistols and submachine guns that you've found would have been pretty helpful a couple of nights ago."

"I completely concur, but what you suggest is not a hasty process. There is much to be done after freeing the weapons." He frowned. "The ones we've uncovered on Level Three were so covered in the symbiolene that they will probably be the easiest to restore. We will prioritize those, as well as the ammunition found with them."

"Besides," Tirolane added, smiling down the conference table at the decidedly grumpy O'Garran, "Sharat will soon be here, so his firearms will be added to ours. Tasvar's task force will bring considerably more."

"We also need more bodies-as-armor, now," Dora added, arms folded tight across her chest. "There aren't enough hands for all the jobs or eyes for all the places that need watching."

Bey nodded. "I agree, but the answer to that problem is ready at hand. The trogs who survived the battle on Level Three are eager to join our force, more than any other group to date."

Bannor rubbed his chin. "Any idea why?"

"If they are to be believed—and I have no reason not to on such a matter—their home tunnels are becoming more dangerous. As they put it, something is 'boiling up' from the deep reaches."

"Did they say what?" Katie Somers asked.

Bey shook her head. "I do not think they know. They were pushed out of their regions by those fleeing the trouble. My guess? Raiding cavers."

"Or cavers being riled up by something worse?" Miles wondered.

"That too, is known to happen."

Bannor nodded. "Either way, until we know that those trogs really want to join rather than just hide behind us, let's keep them away from Level Three. They're familiar with it and know where it connects to the tunnels, so that's where they could become an opsec worry."

Miles nodded. "So we keep them topside?"

Bannor nodded back. "Rotating into Level One to limit exposure, at least until we know they're reliable."

Riordan glanced at Bey. "Have the POWs we took two nights ago revealed anything about their masters?"

She shook her head. "Only that they believe that you and their masters are distant kin."

When that met with stares and frowns, Newton leaned forward. "Actually, they are correct that the deciqadi are a human offshoot of some kind. However, there are a number of marked physiological changes. The most noticeable is the mass of tissue that overlays the scapula and causes a rounding of their shoulders."

Cruvanor tapped the table sharply. "The forward-leaning posture caused by that hump is why many call them stoops," he explained. "However, you will more commonly hear them referred to as 'calluskins.' But whatever you call them, they are quite dangerous: arguably more so than x'qai."

O'Garran shrugged. "They didn't seem so tough."

Cruvanor stared down the table at him. "I do not mean their individual prowess and resilience, Chief O'Garran. I am referring to their organization, aptitudes, and capacity for learning many skills—including the mental powers which make you so uncomfortable." Riordan was glad that no one glanced at Tirolane as the war leader concluded.

Duncan was nodding. "Yeah, those guys had a decent plan,

and if the x'qa were any more disciplined, they'd have hurt us a lot more than they did." He tossed his stylus down. "I can't see any reason to doubt that they're the ones who followed us all the way from Forkus. They weren't just some random group of raiders wandering around hotside hoping to find worthwhile prey. Low-grade morons would be smarter than that, and this bunch were *not* being led by morons."

Tirolane set his hands flat on the table. "I agree. As you say, Duncan, there is no other plausible explanation. And that is also why I doubt we have seen the last of them."

Riordan leaned forward. "Not if they're hired guns for whoever we angered in Forkus." He glanced toward Cruvanor. "Does that sound about right to you?"

The war leader nodded. "Very much so. Deciqadi sell their services to x'qai, but are never their vassals. And they are the only adversaries who could have marshalled so many lesser x'qa to follow you for almost an entire season, rather than attack as soon as they could."

"Why do you think they *didn't* attack?" Peter asked.

"Because following your path meant they also came across all your battlefields. That is how they learned about you." He nodded to the perplexed faces around him. "For instance, the lack of trog corpses indicated that combat was not eroding your force; it is how you were increasing it."

Riordan nodded. "If so, I think their attack on us here was probably more opportunistic than committed. That's why they were able to withdraw so quickly, even with such undisciplined troops. They had contingencies if they were unable to drive home their assault."

Cruvanor shrugged. "That is the deciqadi approach to war as we have seen it waged many times in Fragkork. Which brings me to a topic that today's discoveries may have made more... complicated."

Riordan sighed. "Your need to travel to Zrik Whir."

Cruvanor echoed his sigh. "Yes. It is not as I would have wished. I promised I would help you with the prospecting of this site and I have barely begun. So I understand if you feel I am leaving too early."

Bannor raised an eyebrow. "I mean no disrespect, Cruvanor, but how would you get there if we did not leave, also?"

Tirolane shrugged. "Sharat mentioned that, after concluding his visit here, his next destination was Shrakhupsekh."

Duncan squinted. "That's a coastal city. Down the river from Uhrashgrukh, right?"

Cruvanor smiled. "It is, and it is one of the most common ports of call for the Rocks that sail between the continents."

Solsohn blinked. "The *what* that sails between continents?"

"The Rocks. They are very old, some say ancient, ships with sails that turn in the wind like those of a windrad. They do not resemble a boat so much as a tube with a groove open to the sky. Within that opening, down to the very bottom of the hull, there are shops and shacks stacked high against the inner sides of the tube, built upon and served by various wondrous devices. They are like floating towns that follow both winds and currents to make their way around the world. Or so it is said."

Riordan managed to suppress both his amazement and frustration that here was yet another piece of commonplace knowledge—intercontinental transports, no less—that none of them had heard of. *And why would we, if we don't know to ask?* "How many of these Rocks are there?"

Cruvanor smiled again. "I do not know. I have never been upon the ocean, although I have seen it twice." He shook his head. "I thought all my great adventures were behind me, but since meeting you and your companions, it feels like they are just beginning. So be assured," he stressed, looking up, "I do not wish to leave. But I must. If I do not, it may be the death of my other grandson." In response to more stares, Cruvanor shook his head. "No, I refer to one that is soon to be born. Or may already have been. It is Rogarran's child, carried by his beloved, Dalisa. That is why he is not traveling to Zrik Whir with me. If I am lost, then he still may hope to rescue her and the child."

"From what?"

"From the same fate as my stable's liege Gorzrik meant for me and my son: sold away to lieges in a far city, so that all our lines are scattered to the winds like dust. So that we are no longer a danger to them. Indeed, I suspect our fate was to be even worse, but that is speculation only. Our best hope of rescuing Dalisa and her child—and, if we are the recipients of some miracle, our entire stable—is to bear news to Zrik Whir of the coming war of extermination. We must hope that, between gratitude and practicality, they will contribute resources to that rescue." He shrugged, suddenly looked his age. "It is a desperate hope, but when you have but one, you seize it."

Bannor's voice was quiet, almost gentle. "Which is another reason why you and Rogarran cannot travel together for now." When Cruvanor turned curious eyes on him, Rulaine explained, "We have a saying: 'don't put all your eggs in one basket.'"

The old war leader nodded. "A wise saying, indeed. With your permission, Rogarran will remain here, to continue to gather what allies he might and what news comes out of Fragkork while I am gone."

Riordan looked around the room, saw only three faces that seemed to be mulling over another course of action: Bannor, Ayana, and Duncan. Possibly Yaargraukh as well, but Caine had no confidence in his ability to read subtle Hkh'Rkh expressions. *Well, I guess this is as good a time as ever to throw out an idea that will probably grind a lot of gears.*

Riordan stood. "Cruvanor, we understand you must leave sooner than you foresaw, but it doesn't necessarily follow that you must do so alone. However, the alternative I have in mind could also impact our ability to return to our homeland. So it's a topic we'll take up at our nightly gathering: our 'Fireside Chat.'" He smiled. "Which, given how long that discussion could be, we'll need to start right now." He nodded deeply. "Thank you for bearing with us, and giving us the room."

Grandfather and grandson exchanged long looks, the former clearly far more surprised than the latter. Bey raised an eyebrow, rose, and headed for the door. The two humans nodded and followed her out.

Chapter Thirty-Four

The moment the half-intact door closed, Duncan turned toward Riordan. "Sir, whatever else you may have in mind, we can't leave here, can't just walk away from a functional launch facility and hope it will be here when we get back. Just the danger from the tunnels alone—"

"I'm glad you feel so passionate about it, Major Solsohn—because you will be one of the ones staying behind."

"I—what?" The rest of the room was just as stunned and just as abruptly silent as he was.

Riordan nodded. "You're absolutely right, Duncan. We can't leave this facility. It is the pearl of great price and for all we know, the only one that still exists anywhere on this damned planet."

Miles was half out of his seat at the other end of the table. "Wait a minute, sir, are you saying—?"

"You'll learn what I'm saying by waiting *and* watching your tone, mister."

Miles swallowed, sat.

"There will be time for discussion, but that comes *after* the basic idea is laid out. Actually, it's closely related to the strategy you just heard coming out of Cruvanor's mouth. The one which possesses merits that Colonel Rulaine instantly appreciated."

"I did?" squawked Bannor.

"Absolutely. And we're lucky you did, because I think we've been so laser-focused on surviving, then getting here, and then consolidating our gains, that we missed the same answer that Cruvanor arrived at because he had *no other choice*."

Riordan looked around the table. "We have to split into two teams." He raised his voice over the nascent sputters of surprise or protest. "Cruvanor's got no other choice, not if he wants to maximize the odds of saving his grandson—hell, the whole stable. Crisis drives people to desperate solutions.

"Our situation isn't as desperate as his, but Colonel Rulaine's observation applies just as well to us: 'don't put all your eggs in one basket.' And I'm not suggesting we split into two teams because I feel for Cruvanor and his people—I do—but because it's the smart move.

"Let's say we all stayed here with the pearl of great price. Wonderful—*unless* we discover tomorrow or next month that all those rockets waiting one floor beneath our feet *can't* get us to orbit.

"Now turn it around; we all go with Cruvanor to Zrik Whir, bringing word of how their camphor could give them and the Legate smokeless powder. It would certainly cause some serious, even decisive, damage to the x'qai overlords—*unless* Zrik Whir can't or won't help us. Or because on the way there, we're all lost when one of these Rocks capsizes. Because, damn it: who ever heard of a floating rock?

"But there's a third, even thornier possibility: that we're not in a simple either-or situation, but we don't know it yet. Example: what if it turns out that the only way we can launch the birds downstairs is with help from Tasvar or Zrik Whir? Or maybe other connections *they* have, but that we haven't even heard about yet? Kind of like the way we just this minute learned about the Rocks.

"Bottom line: firstly, we can't tell which of the options—the rockets in this complex or a partnership with Zrik Whir—is the bird in the hand versus the one in the bush. Secondly, what if we need *both* birds to get to orbit? And it all comes back to the same problem: that we just don't know enough. Which is exactly why it's too early to put all our eggs in one basket."

For a moment the whole group stared at him. Then Miles rubbed his nose and asked, "Commodore, all those analogies—you been thinking about birds a lot?"

Riordan laughed. "If you're asking me whether or not I'm birdbrained—"

"Hey, your words, not mine, sir." He grew serious. "But birds or no, something tells me you didn't just think of this right here and now."

Ayana shook her head, a small smile on her face. "Most certainly not."

Riordan shrugged. "The moment I saw those missiles, I knew we had a choice to make. But it took me an hour before I realized it couldn't be one or the other; it had to be both."

"A whole hour?" Dora muttered with a grin.

"Should have been immediate, but our experience here made that thought counterintuitive."

Katie frowned. "How d'yeh mean that, sir?"

Bannor was smiling at Caine and nodding slowly. "I believe the commodore means that our survival on this planet has depended upon one thing above all else: that we stick together. That we had to become more than a team. Instead, like several of you have said before, we've become a family. But being a family on this world goes way beyond caring for each other personally; it means one hundred percent interdependence." He shook his head. "In most families, that would probably be diagnosed as unhealthy, suffocating. But here, it was our recipe for survival... and there really wasn't any alternative."

Riordan nodded, looked around the table, saw the reluctance in almost every face. "That's why it doesn't just feel wrong; it feels dangerous. And before now, I'm not sure we *could* have done so safely. But with growing forces and proven allies, our course of action is no longer driven by immediate, obvious necessity. Now, at long last, we can not only *think* strategically; we can *act* that way."

Newton crossed his arms. "One of the oldest strategic axioms dictates that one should never divide one's forces in the face of the enemy."

Riordan nodded. "And I agree, but in this case, the enemy ran away. Are they still watching us? Probably, at least to the extent they can. But if there was ever a moment to take the steps necessary to undertake two strategic initiatives, this is it."

He leaned forward. "History has shown that at the right moment, a force must divide *to* conquer. I am convinced this is that moment. No matter how wrong or dangerous it might feel after having hung together so tightly for so long." Riordan pushed back from the table. "Comments?"

Craig Girten licked his lips anxiously. "I know I'm the guy always bringing this up, but I've still got to wonder if getting back to the ship isn't... well, a pipe dream. Yes, there are a whole lot of rockets downstairs, but like you said, Commodore, they might not work. Or you might not be able to control them. And to hear you all talk about it, there are about a thousand things that can go wrong and it's still too early to know about *any* of them. Heck, let's say you do get up there to the ship. It's got no fuel left. So how do you get it moving?"

Ayana nodded at his question. "We get it moving by bringing the fuel with us."

"Beg your pardon, ma'am, but how? Looks like there's barely enough room at the top of those rockets to fit a pilot—uh, astronaut?—into 'em."

"There are multiple rockets of the necessary type, Sergeant."

"To do what?"

"To send a payload of fuel to the ship."

"Wait: you mean to tell me that the Dornaani magic engines use the same stuff as these super-fancy V-2s?"

Tagawa smiled. "Strangely, yes. In addition to liquid oxygen, the rockets use liquid hydrogen, a great deal of which we have just emptied from them. And it will be far easier to send up a payload—such as fuel—than it will be to send up a pilot.

"As for the very real concerns of achieving launch, flight control, and rendezvous? We have only had access to the rockets for twelve hours. If we stop now, we have no chance for success. So if we are to act upon this extraordinary discovery, we must start planning with the expectation that we can succeed, though we may ultimately learn otherwise." She studied Craig's growing frown. "Do you have a further concern, Sergeant?"

"Yes, ma'am, I do. Let's say you do get a bunch of these rockets to orbit, and right to where you need them. And let's say you can get the ship to work, even though you've all said half of its wiring and engines are burned out. How do we know we can get home? You've all been looking for familiar stars in the sky and haven't seen any. So how do you know we're not billions of light-years away from Earth? Eku here has said that, uh, mis-shifts can exceed the shift-drive's maximum rated range. So maybe we're in a galaxy on the other side of the universe, yeah?"

Eku shook his head. "All evidence and theory suggests that a fully coherent re-expression—which is to say, the ship comes out *as* a ship rather than a spray of subatomic particles—is impossible at galactic ranges. It is extremely unlikely even over comparatively short ranges; let us say, several dozen light-years. Certainly no more than a hundred or so; that would be the logical limit even if the energy put into the shifts was used with full efficiency and each achieved maximum theoretical range. That is probably what happened with the first shift. Subsequent shifts were attempts by the ship's automatic systems to return to recognized star systems. Unfortunately, it was not possible to determine how many of those corrective shifts were executed or if they were based on data corrupted by the damage done to the navigation console."

Girten had gamely attempted to parse the factotum's explanation. "So... we're still in the same galaxy?"

"Barring a violation of physics as we understand it, yes."

Riordan shrugged. "But even if we couldn't return to Earth, getting the ship back is still our top-priority mission. Once we have the high ground, we have the possibility to effect real change. Quickly."

"Well," Katie muttered, "if we're gon'ta split up, can't we at least have radio communications?"

Eku shrugged. "The ranges of the suit radios do not permit it. Besides, there is the danger of enemy detection."

"Aye, but all the times we've used 'em, and still nary a peep from the bogeymen—?"

"Yes, but it would involve using maximum power."

Bannor rubbed his chin. "We could do it at seemingly random intervals—say, a fractal progression with a preset variable—once a week. Ten minutes per transmission and nothing but squelch breaks."

Eku seemed to be trying to understand why, having been told it was beyond the power limits of the radios, others were still discussing it. "But as I have said, the limitations of the equipment make it quite impossible."

Duncan didn't seem to hear the factotum, either. "You know, we might get around the power problem by setting up a series of skywave tests. We might be able to pull some of the atmospheric data we generated for the drop to get some initial parameters. And we code each send's test settings as part of the message so the Zrik Whir team can send and confirm if they receive.

Assuming, of course, that the commodore will agree to a weekly signal test?" His eyes drifted toward Riordan.

Whether the chance of establishing communication over thousands of kilometers was realistic or not, the Crewe's faces left little doubt of their eagerness to try—maybe because it held out a thin thread of hope that the separation would be less than absolute. Even despite the notional bogeymen, who might not be there at all . . . or might simply have not stumbled across their signals, yet. *On the other hand, at some point, in order to pursue new opportunities, you've got to take new chances . . .*

Riordan nodded. "Sure, we'll see how it works. You'll come up with the details, Major?"

"Already have, sir."

Miles lifted his chin. "One other item, sir."

"What's that?"

"If some of us are heading out, then we ought to have a going-away party!"

Riordan saw his own responding smile on every other face. Even Newton's. "Seems unanimous. Make it so, Master Chief."

Chapter Thirty-Five

Duncan raised a cup. "Long live the dunces! Who have *at least* half the special blessings that God is supposed to give."

"Meaning?" Peter asked.

Duncan stopped in the middle of a generous sip. "Old saying: 'The good lord protects drunkards and fools.' Well, sailing across the sea in a *rock* is certainly not something sensible people would do. So there's half your blessing right there. And if you drink up, you'll be well on your way to the other half! Now: stand and be recognized, dunces!"

Caine smiled, made sure he was the first to rise. The other "dunces"—Dora, Peter, Craig, and Miles—stood as well. And surprisingly, so did Bey, which prompted Ta'rel to his feet also. He had to wave his fellow mangle down to keep him from joining in.

"Long life and safe return!" Duncan yelled, and was answered by the rest of the Crewe.

As cups were drained—and over half immediately refilled—Bey slipped up to Caine, who was still nursing his first drink. "I am not sure why we are the dunces?"

"Well, *you're* not!" he replied. "But the rest of us—the reason we're on the team going to Zrik Whir is because we lack any useful knowledge or skills for launching a rocket."

"Ah," she breathed. "So since I am turning back at Shrakhupsekh, I am not a dunce."

Caine chuckled before he sipped his drink. "I am quite sure they *never* meant it to apply to you, Bey."

"Because I am not really one of you? Not part of your Crewe?"

Riordan extended the sip that hid his eyes from hers. *That tone: is she... envious? Upset?* As he lowered the cup, her eyes were waiting for his as they cleared the rim. "I think they're just being careful," he explained.

"Of what?" She sounded genuinely puzzled.

"Of insulting you." Riordan shrugged. "We still have a lot to learn about trog customs."

"Trog-ways," she corrected. "Yes, you do." She sounded more wistful than impatient, glanced toward Ta'rel and the mangle with him. "Why is the one we captured—well, freed—with Ta'rel?"

Riordan smiled. "I assume it's a misunderstanding, since Ta'rel isn't going to Zrik Whir, either. I don't think he's going any further than our first stop at Ebrekka. But when someone invited him to our send-off, I suspect he passed it on to his friend." Riordan shrugged. "On the other hand, Tirolane *should* be here, but isn't. There was going to be a small send-off for him and Cruvanor organized by Marcanas, but when Sharat's team and the Legate's prospecting group showed up yesterday, it grew into quite a party."

She nodded. "I heard the festivities on my way here." She looked sideways at him. "And why is Ta'rel going to Ebrekka? His community is far away, west of Forkus."

"He's not heading home. He intends to return here—just as soon as he returns Ne'sar's cloak."

She grinned at Riordan's mischievous tone. "Oh? Is that all?"

Caine shared a sly smile with her. "I'm sure he has no other reason for going."

They laughed. Although Bey did so somewhat awkwardly, he thought. Or self-consciously. She fell silent, seemed to be studying her cup far more intently than its simple design deserved. The expression was familiar; it was the one she wore if she had to report a sensitive issue among the trogs. *Well, might as well learn what it's about—*

"Commodore!" Eku called, emerging from a group that had gathered around Katie so closely that it appeared conspiratorial. "I have—" He noticed Bey as he swung out far enough to see her sitting beyond Riordan. "Oh! I am sorry, sir. I did not mean to interrupt."

Riordan shrugged, looked over toward Bey—who was already

gone. "Well," he said, turning back toward the factotum. "Apparently you aren't interrupting at all. Are you enjoying yourself, Eku?"

Eku frowned at the question. "I suppose I am, but that is not what I came to say."

No, probably not. Riordan wondered how factotums socialized with each other—assuming they did. "What's on your mind?"

"That is singularly serendipitous phrasing, Commodore." He produced Riordan's Dornaani helmet. "All the most damning evidence from Hsontlosh's computer—and also, the most galling lacks of detail—have been encrypted and uploaded as I promised."

Caine took the helmet. "Thank you, but you didn't need to spend the past few days rushing to complete it. It's not as if we're leaving Bactradgaria any time soon."

"I know, sir. I am merely following your example by ensuring that all our evidentiary eggs do not remain in one basket. Although you are the ones traveling into the unknown, it is still possible that you shall be the ones who survive, rather than us here. We have attracted attention to ourselves and this site. Surely, that is what you perceive to be *our* risk."

"It is. And again, thank you, Eku." He paused. "I know that being on this world has been, well, difficult for you."

"It is certainly not what I was trained for."

Riordan nodded, wondered if he had any reciprocal gift for the factotum, just in case these *were* the hours the last they'd spend together. *Well, it's not really a gift, and it's none of my damn business, but... Oh, what the hell:* "You know, Eku, despite watching humanity on Earth over the centuries, you may never have seen us so clearly as you do here."

He physically recoiled. "You mean on Bactradgaria? This savagery?"

Riordan shrugged. "This is probably pretty similar to the world in which not just our, but your own, progenitors evolved: brutish, unpredictable, without any daily assurance of food or shelter. This is why we organized ourselves as groups and survived to become a dominant species. Not that you'd know it from our conditions here."

Eku was slightly miffed. "I am quite aware of what early human evolution looked like. I saw the end of what you call the Neolithic Era."

"So then you saw how hard-won the first tools were, the

control of fire, the growth of towns. And then the costs that came along with them: widespread famine, disease, and war."

Eku looked sideways at the word "war": a stare that mixed irony with revulsion.

Caine nodded at it. "Yes, I'm sure we are still savage by your standards. But remember this: we—all us Terrans in the Crewe—are direct products of that unshaped development. You, my friend, are not. Everything you know, every aspect of your growth—and of all the generations of factotums before you—are the results of careful study and operant conditioning. You are humans bred to be partners with the Dornaani. We are just humans."

"And what is your point?"

Riordan shrugged. "That we, your friends, are the products of the natural—arguably necessary—evolutionary trajectory of humans. And that those early days are also the origins of whatever you might respect or like in us."

"I would like to think," the factotum replied, "that the influence of the Dornaani did not alter us, but simply accelerated our attainment of civilization."

Caine shrugged. "That could be the case. All we know for sure is that the Dornaani also shaped you to serve their needs, albeit in the service of your own species. But in doing so, they made you fundamentally unlike the species from which you arose."

"So you are suggesting that to better understand myself, I must somehow revert to your own primit—natural state?"

Caine smiled at Eku's slip and sudden flush. "I don't know about reverting to it, but I think *exploring* it is worth thinking about. And maybe worth experimenting with, too."

"I would hardly know where to start," Eku replied.

"Maybe that's because *thinking* about where to start is part of the problem." Caine grinned at the factotum's earnest frown. "Discovery isn't just about what you think, Eku, but what you feel, how you react."

Eku frowned, shook his head. "But this is at odds with what I have observed in the Crewe—and particularly in you, Commodore. You do not act on emotions or immediate reactions. You are logical. You are measured. You do not allow impulses to shape your behavior."

Caine smiled. "Don't I? Do you think it was logical and

measured that I left my son alone—for two years, now—to seek Elena? Or to endanger myself and others in the process? In short, is there any 'logic' to elevating the value of one life to the point where so many others should be risked—or lost—to save it? For all we know, my mission to find Elena may have started a war, or at least primed events to go in that direction."

Eku's mouth was open in surprise, maybe despair. "So you regret all that you have done?"

Caine shook his head. "Not one bit. The truly important risks we humans take are because of what we feel, not what we think. In my case, it was because of love. But not just love for Elena as my partner, but as a person upon whom injustices were heaped *as she slept*—literally. Elena Corcoran was failed by everyone and every institution that was sworn to protect both her body and her rights. And I could not allow that to stand."

Eku nodded slowly. "The Romans had a saying: '*fiat justitia, ruat caelum.*'"

Caine smiled. "'Let justice be done, though the heavens fall.' It's been a long time since I heard that." He stared out across the sands. "It's pretty much back to basics, in these wastes. I imagine it's a lot like the days when it was us against the sabertooth. You don't have a lot of time to find and form a more perfect union, or a more fair society, on this nasty ball of dust. But on the other hand, it's reassuring that we can return to those basics, that we haven't lost all the lessons of our evolution. It gives me hope that humanity will retain them, regardless of our advances—at least as long as we remain in touch with the hard realities of the universe."

Eku raised an eyebrow. "You truly believe that most humans on Earth would be able to adapt to these barbaric conditions?"

Caine cocked his head. "Most? I don't know about that. A lot of them, yes, and frankly, I think we could use a few more than we have now. My greatest worry is those who believe that being *able* to survive in a place like this somehow marks them as *less* evolved. Because when—not if, but *when*—the universe reminds us just how little power and control we have, it's the people who can endure these conditions who'll be best equipped to keep our finest and proudest accomplishments from sliding down into just so much ruin and wreckage."

Eku nodded. "So those of you who have the closest relationship with their Neolithic selves are the ones most able to preserve all that you've achieved since? Don't you find that contradictory?"

Riordan just smiled. "No, but I do find it ironic."

Eku was frowning, but still nodding. "I shall think on what you have said, Caine Riordan: all of it. And now, I must excuse myself. I occasionally find the local libations somewhat, eh, troubling to my stomach."

"They're certainly not top-shelf liquor."

"Not 'top shelf,' sir?"

"Not the best. By a long shot."

"I'm not even sure they are entirely composed of liquor, but I would say that's the least pressing of our many unknowns. Good night, Commodore. I shall be present to see you off, tomorrow."

Bey reappeared as the remaining revelers collected in a corner of the bare storeroom that had housed the now fading festivities. She sat next to Riordan, flashed a quick smile at him, looked at the others sitting in a dispersed, impromptu circle. "I am not accustomed to such happy leave-takings."

"Oh? What kind *are* you accustomed to?"

"Those where crying is more common than laughing." Seeing his perplexity, she shrugged. "Mostly it is to wish a peaceful journey to what lies beyond this life."

Caine sat straighter. "That's certainly part of what motivated this party."

She nodded. "Yes, but there is much hope in it, too. Our farewells are for those about to face dangers from which there is little chance of return." She sighed. "And usually, that is the result. So these are not times of celebration; they are times to say what has been left unsaid. Or to apologize for things that should *not* have been said. I see little of that, here."

Riordan nodded. "If that happens, it is usually done privately, or at least apart from everyone else."

O'Garran's less-than-steady voice came across the circle at them. "What are you two whispering about over there? Schemes of world conquest, I bet!"

"No, just wondering how much of that rotgut you can stomach, Chief."

"Sir! Questioning a SEAL's ability to hold his or her liquor is a serious insult! But seeing as how you're an officer an' all, I'll just let it slide. But what I can't abide is a person who comes to a party and just sits, alone and lonesome with nothing to say. Like you, Yaargraukh. Not a peep—well, rumble—out of you all evening? What's a matta? 'Ca'tor' got your tongue?" Miles' inebriated play on 'Ktor' earned a round of genuine groans.

Yaargraukh did not play along, however. "You should be grateful I am so quiet, Chief O'Garran. Hkh'Rkh celebrations are typically much louder than this. And our interactions are far more, em, kinetic."

Riordan wasn't sure whether "kinetic" was a euphemism for tests of strength, combat, or sexual prowess—or maybe all three. He also had less than no desire to find out. "Yes, but you've been ruminating on something, Yaargraukh."

"I have. Or mostly, I have been ruminating on the strangeness of a thing. No, that is not entirely correct. I have been ruminating upon how strange it is that something I *used to* find strange does not seem so anymore."

Miles shook his head at the tortuous phrasing. "You sure you haven't been dipping a little deep in the punch bowl?"

"If I understand that tangled idiom, no, I have not been over-imbibing. My trust in the local concoctions is very limited." He turned toward Caine. "But to answer your question, Commodore, I have been examining how it is that I came to feel so comfortable among humans. Or at least, among *this* group of humans. I found my thoughts drifting in this direction when several of you remarked how, if Zrik Whir became an ally, it might also prove to be a logical new home."

"A new home?" Bey's tone was surprised, possibly alarmed. She had not been present for that conversation.

Yaargraukh's neck quivered slightly: a faint nod. "This site is weeks away from allies, water, game. If we tie ourselves to a place so landlocked, so isolated, we invite encirclement—from below, as well as above." His neck circled: a shrug. "Is it useful as a base of operations? Certainly... for now. But once the humans of Fragkork have been freed, the rockets have been launched, and all that may be salvaged from it has been removed, what is it but a hole on the edge of hotside? To dwell in it then would be to live in one's grave.

"And so, when many of you wondered if Zrik Whir might be a place where we could find a true home, a place where we may not only consolidate our strength but live without constant worry, I thought about how congenial that might be. How welcome to live in such a home."

He paused. "And then I looked around at your very alien faces and realized that I was envisioning you, rather than my own kind, as my fellows in that home." His torso shook. "It is strange to think—to feel—that about a different species. And yet, that is the place I have come to."

Katie leaned forward. "And d'yeh never miss your homeworld? Yer own kind?"

Yaargraukh's chest rumbled fitfully. "I should, and yet I do not. I have too many misgivings of what I would find there."

Bannor nodded. "You mean the disputes between the Old and the New Families?"

Yaargraukh pony-nodded. "If I could journey there, I would; it is my duty, and I must devote my energies to what is best for my people. But the prospect of kinslaying looms large"—he shuddered—"and only a monster would long to be drenched in the blood of friends and even relatives."

He glanced upward, as if there were not two levels between himself and the surface. "And yet, every so often, a wind comes out of the west that bears the smell of the far river—and though subtle, there is a scent in it that reminds me of Rkh'yaa."

Katie wiped her eyes, turned toward Dora. "When do you miss home?"

Pandora's arms were so tightly crossed that she appeared to be hugging herself. "What do you mean?"

"I mean, what time of day, or activity, puts yeh back there, if only for a moment?"

"Cooking," Pandora said. The single word had started with an edge but was soft by the time she completed it. "And my *abuela*. She cooked for us. She must be dead by now." Dora chuckled weakly, smiling at the far wall. "*Madre* said that she remembers *abuela* being tough, but then she got softer when all us *nietos* came along." She sniffled. "I guess that's why *madre* was so tough, too. But I was her only child—well, the only one that lived long enough to get out of the slums—so she doesn't have any grandchildren to soften her."

Dora jammed the heel of her palm into the traitorous eye that had almost allowed a tear to escape. "Not that I was ever going to be a mother. *Coño*, I don't know who it would be worse for—me or the kids."

Bannor glanced at Ayana. "And what about you?"

Tagawa closed her eyes. "There are times—more precious because they are rare—when, just before dawn, the rain falls softly, here. I do not rise, do not look, for then I would know it is not home. But for that moment, I can imagine I am there."

Katie and Newton seemed to fold into themselves and started to look away—before Miles' loud contribution rescued them from even deeper melancholy.

"Privies," O'Garran declared firmly. "Yeah, the trogs are human, pretty much. But what comes *out* of 'em?" He shuddered. "It's not like *us*, that's for sure. I figure that anyone with our prissy intestines probably died along with most of this hellhole's biosphere. I'm guessing that, back then, part of being tough enough to survive meant having the gut of an old gator. 'Cause sure as shooting, we've been eating the same food as the locals for half a year now, and we still don't smell like *that*."

"Ye're a charmin' man," Katie muttered.

"And predictable," Dora added.

O'Garran doffed an imaginary hat.

The moment he finished, Duncan looked up at nothing in particular. "Kids. For me, it's kids. Particularly the sounds they make. For whatever reason, whether stateside or deployed, I always seemed to be in a place with kids. The crying, the shouting, the singing, the laughing. Drove me nuts. Never wanted any of my own. But the sound of them was like a promise made to the future."

His sudden frown was bitter, almost ferocious. "Here? Almost no kids around. And those that are? They're all quiet as the tomb. Half-starved faces with big eyes staring out of them. Empty eyes, like whatever else they might have shown is long gone. It's as if s'rillor is just waiting to come along and finish the job."

When the silence became uncomfortable, Tagawa leaned around Bannor and asked, "And what about you, Commodore?"

Caine presumed he wouldn't be spared, so he was ready. "The morning, just after dawn. But I don't think of home because of what's around me, but because of what isn't. I miss it all. The smell of the mountains. The sound of the sea. The way the humidity in each place changes what hits your senses and in what order.

"Because here, there's none of that. No smells of anything growing, no sounds unless something is hunting you. Except there's always the wind, whistling over the wastes."

Katie jumped up and short-circuited any possible silence. "Well, my mug is empty, and I'll pour for anyone willing to learn a Scots drinking song that was old when Robert the Bruce was a wee bairn!" Most rose to join her. Others—notably, Bannor and Ayana—stood and wandered toward the door, hands almost touching.

But Bey remained sitting beside Caine. Her eyes on his, she smiled: an unusually slow and gentle curl of her lips. Then she looked away toward Katie, who was trying—without much success—to teach the remaining revelers how to boom out the lyrics with a semi-genuine highland burr.

Still watching the unpromising rehearsal, Bey murmured, "You must long for your home. Very much."

"Hard not to, given all the things I miss."

She shook her head. "What you said just before: that is not how I know."

He felt an eyebrow rise. "How, then?"

She shrugged. "Because the only times you are surprised here, you are not just shocked: you are horrified. Not by fear, but by disgust. I see it in all of you. So it stands to reason that you must all be from a much more pleasant place."

He shrugged. "I suppose we are," he admitted, wondering how long she had seen that revulsion on his face, on the others'. "I don't really think about it. We don't have the time."

She smiled. "Do you not? When you look toward the horizon, the emptiness of your eyes says otherwise." She shrugged. "Maybe you think about it without even realizing it. It is like that with memories we learn to push away, the ones that can only hurt us." Her smile was like a hand laid on his arm, his heart.

She left him sitting, staring after her.

INTERLUDE THREE

Restored to the Present

August 2125
55 Tauri B (The Scatters)

Interlude Three

Downing and Trevor almost bumped into Edouard Tedders who, head down over a report, charged out of the small lab the SpinDogs had furnished for him.

"Whoa, Doc," Trevor said, catching him at arm's length. "Careful you don't kill yourself! Or me!"

Tedders glanced at the SEAL's broad shoulders and large arms. "I don't think you're at any risk," he grinned. He looked between the two men. "How's Murphy coming along?"

Downing shrugged. "About as well as can be expected, I suppose. He's alert already but damn near motionless. Not weak. Just keeps asking who's in charge. Won't respond otherwise."

Tedders nodded. "Actually, that's a good sign. Self-control and focused suspicion are signs of excellent cognitive function. And studies show that revived individuals who deal with the temporal-dislocation trauma directly and proactively usually have very rapid and complete recoveries. And of course it's also promising given the situation."

"'The situation'?" Trevor repeated.

"Well, from what I've heard, the SpinDogs are not likely to give him a lot of time to prepare for all of the decisions he'll have to make. Almost immediately."

"Indeed," Downing sighed. "We're just on our way to welcome him into that brave new world."

Trevor crossed his arms, frowning. "We're going to have to

put him in the picture in less than two days. Question is, Doc, what picture do we paint?"

Tedders' face didn't change, but the mind behind it was clearly in sudden, and possibly perplexed, operation. "Sirs, you've kept me out of the loop on what comes next, which I fully understand. But since I don't have any of that knowledge, well, why ask me?"

Trevor's grin was decidedly crooked. "For the same reason we just came from asking Missy Katano the same question. Because you both have fine brains that haven't been drilling at the problem for three days straight. And because those two brains grew up in the same world that Murphy did."

Downing nodded. "That shared social context makes it likely you will instinctively have a better grasp of how he will react to, and what he might do with, any information we might give him."

"Hmmm. What did Missy say?"

Trevor shrugged. "Just that she felt it best to read him in as soon as possible. Then she spent almost five full minutes complaining that his dossier was incomplete. Particularly the last few days before you all went down in that helicopter."

Tedders frowned. "Did she happen to mention what she felt was missing?"

"Just some medical notes that were redacted the day before you all went missing."

"Oh, medical notes? That's probably because he had undiagnosed MS."

Downing and Trevor stared.

"I diagnosed him. No time to run tests, mind you, but he was a textbook case. I got a look at the preliminary tests the Army had run in-country." Tedders shrugged. "I suppose the symptoms could be caused by some other condition . . . but nothing comes to mind."

And if nothing comes to your *mind . . .* "Well, that will certainly shape our assessment, Doctor Tedders. And if you think of anything else, please let us know. The more complete a profile we have of Murphy, the more accurate our observations and approaches are likely to be. Whatever 'accurate' happens to mean, in this case." Downing grimaced at Trevor. "Well, lad, no use putting it off: time to meet Major Murphy and tell him that everything he knew is gone."

Murphy was dozing again when Downing and Trevor entered the observation room for the medical bay in which he was recovering. Or being held. It all depended upon one's point of view, his post-revival physician had muttered.

That same physician, pararescue jumper Ike Franklin, was already in the observation room. "Here already?" Downing asked.

"Never left," Ike sighed, signing off on yet another battery of the major's vital signs.

"Doc, you need to get some sleep," Trevor urged.

"I get sleep. Every time I go to one of your guys' meetings. So, are you two ready?"

"Ready? No," Trevor sighed, staring at the door to the medical bay. "But resigned to it. Here goes hell."

"Right behind you, Captain," Downing said, wishing that he could be anywhere else.

Downing cleared his throat. "Major Murphy."

The Lost Soldier awoke with a start, took in the gray, utilitarian walls and lighting just long enough to reorient himself. He glared at them.

Well, well: Tedders certainly was right about the likelihood that he'd be alert and *suspicious.* "Take it easy, Major. You are safe and among friends."

Murphy did not look convinced in the slightest, but struggled to rise up on his elbows. He swayed a moment, then studied his two visitors more carefully: a professional scan of uniforms, insignias, other details. He was not comforted by the results. His jaw came out defiantly. "Murphy, Rodger Y. Major, US Army. Serial number 984—"

I wonder if they are all going to do this? Well, at least they're well trained. Downing waved away both the information and truculence. "Yes. We know. In fact, my companion here—let's call him Mr. Nephew—is still a reservist in your military. Different branch, however."

Trevor looked sideways at being labeled "Mr. Nephew," might have been readying a callous retort, but Murphy sat up abruptly. "The Blackhawk. What—?"

Trevor nodded. "Went down in the Indian Ocean. November 17, 1993 . . ."

Downing saw uncertainty in the major's eyes. *Maybe your memory isn't as complete as Tedders predicted.*

"Copilot and crew chief were KIA," Trevor continued, "although the copilot's body was never found. The pilot and passengers survived."

Murphy frowned. "How? And why? Hell, the second missile wasn't an RPG round; it was homing on us and made a contact hit. The front half of the chopper should have been gone—and me with it."

"As best we can tell, the second missile's warhead was defective. Went off late and weak. Damage to the cockpit, and the copilot, was essentially from the impact. That's why the pilot and everyone else close survived."

Murphy did not even nod. Downing watched his eyes, saw his training take over. No routine or casual exchanges. No communication at all, if possible. But this time, his gaze traveled with slow determination over each of them. *Looking for clues as to who we are.*

But when he spoke, it was clear he'd tweaked to the subtle, and intentional, clue that the situation might be far more irregular than it seemed. "You read out the whole date of the attack on us, year and all. Why?"

The major stopped himself on the verge of another question. Downing saw him measuring, calculating. *What was more important: to stop talking or to learn what was actually going on?*

The slight jut of Murphy's chin indicated he'd chosen the latter. "So, are we being recorded? Is this a—a sanitized debrief? Who are you guys with?"

Trevor smiled, shook his head. "We are not being recorded, although come to think of it, that might have been a good idea. And if anyone is providing debrief information, it's not you conveying it to us." He paused. "It's we who have to convey it to you."

"Huh? What the hell do you mean?"

"I'll let my colleague—'Mr. Nuncle'—explain."

"Mr. Nuncle," is it, Trevor? Well, turnabout is only fair, I suppose. "Captain Murphy, we mentioned the precise date of your crash because you've been unconscious for a while."

"Then why am I still in the same fatigues? Wait a minute, you didn't even bother to change my clothes when you fished me out of the ocean?"

Downing raised a hand to pause his indignation. "We most certainly would have. But we were not the ones who recovered you."

Murphy's gaze flicked back and forth between his visitors. "Okay, what aren't you telling me?" His eyes widened very slightly. "This has something to do with the date of the crash."

Downing sighed. *And here's where we destroy your world, you poor sod.* "You are to be congratulated on your conjecture, Major Murphy. Our recounting of the date is indeed central to what you must learn about what has happened to you."

Murphy's jawline straightened with tension. "Then spit it out: why is the date so important?"

Trevor calmly met Murphy's eyes. "Because it's not that date anymore. Not even close."

Murphy's expression did not change, but his voice tightened. "Stop the theatrics. What's the date?"

"August. 2125."

A moment of shock, then a dismissive, contemptuous smile. "Okay, guys. I don't know who you are, or who put you up to this, but this is a really shitty gag. I mean, maybe if we hadn't lost someone on the chopper, it would be okay. But it's lousy to build a practical joke on the copilot's grave, because that's pretty much what you're doing here."

Trevor nodded very slowly. "You're right. That would be a shitty joke. But this isn't a joke."

Murphy had been watching their eyes, looking for rehearsed lines or the subtle glances of one liar checking his performance with another. And it was the absence of those signs of deceit that finally cracked his armor of denial.

"No," the major rebutted, surging forward, "this is all *bullshit.* Weirdest damn strategy for producing POW disorientation I've ever heard of, but it isn't going to work. It's too freaking ridiculous."

Downing tried to keep his shoulders from slumping. "We presumed you would have that reaction. We'd probably have the same one, put in your place. That is why we're going to let you spend as long as you need with someone from your time. He even served in your theater of operations—Somalia—albeit a few years later."

The door opened, the major's temporal compatriot arriving right on cue. He raised a salute as he halted. "I'm Ike Franklin, Major Murphy," he said almost sadly, lowering his hand. Nice to meet you, sir. Wish it was under better—well, sane—circumstances."

Murphy frowned. "Nice try. Uniform is a complete match. Accent is perfect. You guys have done your homework well. Or are you working for some rogue cell? Is that it?"

Franklin sighed. "I get it, Major, I really do. Those of us who had higher clearances wondered the same thing when we were awakened: was this some elaborate mind game to disorient us, get us to drop classified information? And you know what we figured out?"

Murphy shook his head, swallowed. "No. What did you figure out?"

"That none of us knew anything important enough to warrant all of this."

Downing couldn't tell if it was Franklin's obvious regret, or that Murphy's lizard-hindbrain sniffed out that that this bloke had been where he was now, but the major was clearly shaken.

"Tell me, Major," Franklin continued. "Just what do you know that would make an enemy willing to put on this kind of crazy show? I'm familiar with the info that is dished out at your rank, probably heard a lot of the same material since I served roughly during those years. I heard it because we might have to make snap decisions about badly wounded personnel with sensitive intel. So I know most of the same data points about nukes, particularly small ones. I'm also guessing we both know a bit about comm protocols that probably never made it online, at least not where Netscape could find it."

Murphy blinked at the word "Netscape." It was apparently one of those casual, common references that had not survived the march of time: that only someone from his historical moment would understand. The major's eyes almost seemed to physically recede, as if they and his entire consciousness were begging to fold inward.

Franklin did not stop. "But at the end of the day, you know how it goes: the services are full of folks, mostly between O3 and O5, who have a gambling habit, a drug habit, a sex habit, or alimony payments to beat the band. *Those* are the folks who are spilling the semi-secrets, not us—and for pennies on the dollar, compared to what it would cost to set up something like this."

Murphy struggled to find a reply, but failed.

Downing nodded at Murphy, turned toward the door.

But Trevor lagged behind. "Sorry, Major. I really am. I've

known several people who've had to grapple with this kind of one-way trip into the future. It's never easy, and the longer the time they've been gone, the harder it is. And you—well, you've been gone a very long time." Downing nodded somber agreement and closed the door behind them.

They returned to the observation room. In the main screen, Murphy rallied. His face became red as Franklin became the new center of his angry—and desperate—focus.

From there, the progression followed the same pattern reported by the Lost Soldiers who'd been animated on Turkh'saar. Once Murphy's disbelief wore off, anger took its place. That was the dangerous phase of acclimation: attribution of blame. In general, the ability to ensure that one's rage remained fixed upon its true, proximate causes was not always a well-evolved trait among humans. And, for those who'd been in combat, the need to suppress that very same restraint—in order to kill enemies who'd not done anything to them personally—often led to its erosion in other parts of their lives.

But as Murphy's psych profile had suggested, once he'd heard the details of his abduction, including who had carried it out, for what purpose, and Earth's ongoing war with that species, he'd settled down. He'd also become quite pale.

Trevor leaned back in his chair. "Here we go."

"He might not," Downing countered.

"Yeah? Well, don't forget: I took odds that Murphy *would*."

Franklin had just segued into a casual recounting of his own abduction in the Somali outback. The tale was so matter-of-fact, so filled with the needless details that mark stories as genuine, that there was simply no plausible reason to doubt it was genuine.

That was the realization that drained the rest of the color from Murphy's face and grayed his lips—right before they released a rush of vomit.

"Told you," Trevor sighed. He paused, considering. "I wonder if they're all going to do that."

Downing felt a bit unwell himself. "I wouldn't be surprised. But at least Murphy managed to turn his head at the last moment."

Trevor looked over; for a fleeting instant, he was the spitting image of his assassinated father. "We take the little victories where we can get them, eh, 'Nuncle'?"

"Right you are, 'Nephew.' Well, it's on to the next reanimation."

"And Murphy?"

"We'll see him as soon as he's gone through the brief. Assuming he's still sane on the back end of it."

"Ready for that briefing, sirs," Murphy announced as he entered the meeting room on the restricted section of *Olsloov*: the part where Dornaani were not allowed.

Richard Downing waved Murphy toward a seat: a regular chair, not one of the transmogrifying structures that still unsettled quite a few of the humans aboard. Who knew how a refugee from the late twentieth century would react? *Mental note: if Tedders ever wants to run that as an experiment, the subject must surrender any weapons, first.*

Downing folded his hands. "We are aware that this has been a terrible shock, Major, and that we've thrown a great deal of information at you. And on top of it all, you had a close call during training just an hour ago. So if, all things considered, you'd like to put off this briefing another day or two—"

"I'm good, sir." Seeing Downing's dubiety, Murphy leaned forward. "Let me see if I can boil the situation down to the basics."

Trevor smiled. "Go ahead."

Murphy leaned back. "So, by the numbers. One: we're stuck here.

"Two: if the enemy sends a signal back to Kulsis, we're dead.

"Three: to stop them from signaling, we have to initiate ground ops to keep them from building a makeshift transmitter.

"Four: we can't get to the ground without the SpinDogs' help, so we need to establish a workable *modus vivendi*."

Trevor grinned, surprised at the Latin phrase.

Murphy raised a frowning eyebrow. "Look, I was gonna be a lawyer, once, yeah?"

Trevor nodded. "Please: go on."

Murphy simply picked up where he had left off. "Five: you're not leaving enough of us 'Lost Soldiers' behind to do the job on our own, and you aren't leaving enough of the right kind of equipment.

"Six: even if we did have the gear, we know squat about what's down there. And the SpinDogs don't have much info about the area where the OpFor is building a new transmitter.

"Seven: that means we need the cooperation of the locals to mount the operation and get the necessary gear.

"Eight: we do that by recruiting the indigs, and with their help, grab an equipment cache the last bunch of bad guys left behind about eighty years ago. And in the bargain, we show the indigs that together, we can win.

"Nine: we parlay that alliance, and infusion of modern gear, into strikes to seize other caches. That enables us to equip a large enough force to attack and destroy the transmitter.

"Ten: and if we actually get that far, *then* we think about other plans." Murphy leaned back. "Does that about sum it up?"

Downing managed not to smile in admiration. "More or less," he muttered.

Murphy nodded. "Good. Where do we start?"

PART FOUR

Toward Uncertain Horizons

Bactradgaria
August 2125

Chapter Thirty-Six

Bannor Rulaine half-turned at the sound of someone else exiting the hatch from the Silo: the name the Crewe had given to the ruins. As they had every day at sunup, Newton emerged first, followed by Qyza. Bannor exchanged nods with them as they waved away the sentries' salutes. As Rulaine resumed his pointless vigil, he heard them come to stand alongside him.

"They should have arrived at Ebrekka two days ago," Newton muttered.

Bannor nodded.

Qyza's tone was artificially casual as she jutted her chin southward. "With everyone on rads, they might have reached it sooner."

"They might have," Rulaine agreed.

"So then why are we standing here at dawn yet again?" Newton's rhetorical question sounded more like a snarl than speech.

"Because," Bannor sighed, "it's hard not to *know* that they're there, that they're safe."

"I feel like a schoolchild," the doctor resumed in the same tone. "After all the operations we've been on, you would think we'd grow accustomed to the uncertainty."

Rulaine smiled. "In the days of sail, officers' families erected tall houses in the port from which their husbands, fathers, and sons set to sea. And built out from or atop the roofs of those houses was a place where they could watch them leave, but mostly, to watch for their return."

Newton nodded darkly. "Those overlooks were aptly called 'widows' walks,' I believe."

Qyza frowned. "Because so many of those watching became widows? Or because that was what all of them feared as they waited?"

Rulaine shook his head. "I don't know. Both, I suspect."

"So this is our widow's walk?" Newton grumbled. "Even though it could be months, even a year, before they return from Zrik?"

Bannor shrugged. "I guess so. At least until we get used to them being gone. Or until we have some luck with the radios and the ionosphere." Rulaine crossed his arms. *Best way to stop moping is to start working.* "Have the new Legate personnel provided any new insights on our prisoner?"

Newton sighed. "None, in regard to medical treatment. Very little on anything else. They agree with Rogarran that he was not the commander of the unit we repulsed; the deciqadi do not risk their leaders at the point of contact."

Rulaine smiled. "Guess they don't have the problems we did with the Commodore, then."

"Indeed, they do not. They describe the deciqadi as being almost as ruthless in their treatment of each other as they are in dealing with other beings. They also explained that our prisoner's limited consciousness is not necessarily a direct consequence of his injuries."

Qyza nodded. "Calluskins often enter a mystic trance when they are badly wounded." She made a warding sign. "That healing sleep is one of their many dark arts."

Newton's tone was carefully patient. "Whatever causes it, her description matches what the Legate's personnel describe."

Bannor glanced at the surgeon. "Could it also be used to avoid questioning? Or conceal mindsensing contact with others of his kind?"

Before Newton could reply with the archly clinical lexicon he applied to all parapsychological phenomena, Qyza shook her head. "They cannot use other mystic arts while in the healing sleep."

Rulaine raised an eyebrow. "Then why did Zhathragz and Rogarran both insist that the prisoner be kept in the armory to block those powers? They specifically mentioned the thick, multi-layered walls as being crucial to ensure that."

"I think you may not have understood their concern exactly, Leader Bannor. That is not to stop the prisoner from using his powers, but to prevent his discovery by the mindsensing power of others."

Newton stared at her. "I get the impression that you know quite a lot about the deciqadi. More than any of the other trog-kind."

She nodded. "That is because I did not serve any liege, either in their fortress or beyond. I was—am—a member of a group that forged its own way in the world."

"And in the black market, as well?" Bannor asked.

Qyza's smile was sly. "Especially in the black market. That is why I have this badge of honor." She touched her squashed nose. "I am less likely to be recognized as a crog. And because of that, I have been in places and heard conversations that might not even come to the ears of the greatest war leader. That is how I know of the calluskins."

Bannor smiled back at her. "Then I think we are overdue for a conversation."

Her tone was almost haughty. "You are. But it has not been urgent out here in the wastes. I am a creature of the city. And of Fragkork in particular."

Newton frowned. "Is it so different from other cities?"

She nodded. "Hotside cities grow no food. Trogs must shelter in the heat of the day. Trade is meager and lives are short. I will tell you of these things when there is need. For now, you may be certain that if the calluskin is asleep, he may not exercise his other powers. But whatever magic keeps them alive at all is a mystery."

Newton shrugged. "I may offer some insight on that. Although the deciqadi are human in origin, they have either adapted, or been altered, to operate in very arid environments. While treating our prisoner, I have not only had to learn their anatomical differences, but also how their bodies process and store water."

Qyza was frowning at the uncommon words. "You are saying they live without the aid of magic? Then how can they be so thin, and yet so strong?"

Baruch's diction slid toward the didactic. "Their dermal layers, and epidermis in particular, have changed, being both less hydrated and less sensate. They are more of a structural sheathe. That is why their muscles stand out in very high relief. Also, their joints have evolved to be more load-bearing, reducing the amount of active strength required to remain upright.

"This trend toward leathery toughness is observable in their organs as well, one of which is unique to them: the raised area on their back. As Cruvanor's initial description suggested, it is roughly analogous to a camel's hump. Its tissue is comprised of cells which function much like sacs to hold a great deal of water which is released at need into the body. This was particularly pronounced during the days before I found a way to hydrate the prisoner via infusion; his body released the water extremely slowly. I presume this is not only optimal for storing water during long dry periods, but for facilitating the near-hibernatory state we observe currently."

Bannor crossed his arms again. "My medical knowledge is limited to battlefield intervention, but if a deciqadi's hump hoards water, how do the rest of its metabolic processes keep ticking?"

Newton raised an eyebrow. "An astute question, Colonel. I have wondered the same thing. I note that the fluids and cellular matter of the body is more viscous. I suspect a connection, but I have had neither the time nor equipment to test my theories."

"Speaking of theories," Duncan Solsohn's voice shouted from the hatchway, "wanna come test one of mine?"

Bannor turned, tamping down a surge of unwarranted hope. "Which theory? You have so many."

Solsohn, chin level with the sand, chuckled. "Guilty as charged. But . . . are you coming, or what?"

Bannor nodded to the other two, who showed no inclination to witness the proving or disproving of one of the IRIS major's innumerable speculations. "Well, make way, so I can climb down the ladder."

Duncan grinned. "About 'climbing down the ladder,' sir . . ."

"Yes?"

"Hold that thought."

Irisir and a small guard detachment were waiting for them at the end of Level Three's only dead-end corridor. He held out a key to Duncan. "It fits, as you predicted. The lubricant has unfrozen the lock." The expression on the senior technicker's face mirrored the suppressed excitement on Solsohn's.

Bannor stood before the access panel at the dead-end, which backed on one of the three rotary-gun defense blisters they'd found in the complex. "So, are we expecting to find a lot of unexpended ammo?" Whether or not the automated defense weapons could ever be restored to operating condition was almost a moot point. Their ammunition was too valuable to be blasted away in a few seconds; it was a match for several assault rifles liberated from various patches of symbiolene.

Duncan turned toward Rulaine with a smile. "Let's find out." He inserted the uniquely shaped key and turned it slowly, gently. This area had also been coated—anomalously—in symbiolene, but Cruvanor's lessons had finally caught hold: treat everything as if it were ready to break.

The key turned. The panel gapped. At a nod from Irisir, one of the guards inserted the equivalent of a putty knife and pried it open.

On the far wall of the closet-sized space was an access panel that was a match for the majority found throughout the complex. Its lock was as well; no chance the key would fit it.

But in the center of the floor, there was a hole. The ladder in it disappeared down into lightless black.

"What the hell—?" Bannor began.

Duncan was too excited to let him finish. "It's all due to Cruvanor. If we weren't tagging and cataloging everything—and I mean *everything*—we'd never have put this key together with this lock."

Irisir shook his head. "The major failed to mention that it is *he* who saw an anomaly on one of the floorplans and brought us here."

Rulaine stared down the dark shaft. "Yes, but brought us to *what*?"

Duncan's grin broadened. "Let's go see."

"You weren't joking about remembering my 'climb down the ladder' remark," Bannor muttered, glancing between his feet at the leading guard's light. "I count one hundred rungs, already."

The light below stopped. "Bottom!" the guard called up. "Only room for four people, maybe five."

Irisir, who was just one place above Bannor, called up to the tail-end guard. "Five more rungs, then hold position." A bobbing light—he was wearing a miner's cap—conveyed the warrior's nod.

At the bottom, Bannor hopped off the last rung. Irisir followed and moved to the one door in the small space around the base of the ladder. He found its lock, tried yet another uniquely shaped key. It slipped in the lock, which he duly doused with lubricant.

After inspecting their utterly blank-walled surroundings, Bannor glanced at Duncan, who was still catching his breath. Although he had better wind than when they'd dropped dirtside, he was regaining the stamina he'd lost during too many years as a desk jockey. "Major, is this what I think it is?"

Before Solsohn could answer, Irisir moved the key in the lock; yellow fluid leaked out. "There is symbiolene in the mechanism itself. Probably some in whatever lies beyond."

"I'm betting on it," Solsohn said. "Let's take a look."

A turn of the key and the door swung open easily. Just one foot beyond the threshold, a solid wall of symbiolene stared back at them.

Irisir reached inside, up behind the top of the door frame. "Every room has the same manual release for the solvent. Be prepared to close the door when I pull the lever. We should be able to enter in half a minute." He nodded to the guard holding the door, released the solvent and stepped back hastily. A moment after the guard sealed the room, a faint hissing arose from the other side of the door.

Solsohn turned to Bannor. "Remember what we said when we found the rockets, Colonel? A couple of us had the nagging suspicion that the floor plan of the site didn't seem complete. And I'm not just talking about all the open spaces behind access panels and the maintenance crawlways."

Bannor nodded. "You're talking about operating systems."

Duncan nodded back, just as the hissing faded.

Irisir opened the door. Wisps of yellowish vapor were still rising from the machinery and consoles that filled a room barely three by four meters.

Duncan waved a hand at it. "Colonel, allow me to present auxiliary control."

Fearful that the major's enthusiasm might also lead him to speak too freely in front of the locals, Bannor remarked, "This is truly a Shangri-la moment, Major Solsohn."

"Indeed it is," Duncan responded with a knowing smile; he'd obviously reminded himself, very pointedly, not to mention anything about what they hoped to achieve with the rockets.

Irisir was frowning into the small control room. "I do not understand. Why hide it so far underground? And if it was to be concealed, surely the master architects of this place could have crafted an entry that was almost totally unnoticeable, rather than through an access panel in a conspicuously odd location."

Solsohn nodded. "You are correct. But they weren't trying to *hide* this room; they were trying to *protect* it."

Irisir's frown deepened. "But if attackers can detect it, that makes it much harder to protect."

Bannor pointed upward repeatedly. "The danger was not from attackers in the site, but from the skies above. The terrible energies that ruined it could have been even greater, enough to reduce it to dust.

"The attacking missiles may have been designed to explode overhead—airburst—which creates the widest possible area of damage beneath. But it is also possible that they were designed to explode upon contact with the bunker, or even penetrate into it, or the land nearby. The damage from such a hit is not so wide, but much more focused."

"But they failed," concluded a guard whose eyes were round with awe and horror.

"Or were intercepted," Duncan emended. "Many of the rockets in the bays above us were probably designed for that purpose. We will know when we've finished examining them."

"Which could require a long time," Bannor qualified.

"Or," Solsohn muttered as he stepped into the room, squinting as he reached behind the tallest console, "maybe not so long after all." His hand reappeared holding the ancient equivalent of a folio-sealed ring binder. "This exceeds even my most hopeful theories."

Bannor nodded, smiled, but felt himself tempted to turn southward, toward Ebrekka. If all the luck at the Silo was good, the universe's law of equal and opposite reaction might mean bad—very bad—luck for the others. Or maybe it meant they were already—

No. That's just grunt superstition. Snap out of it, you idiot!

But even though Rulaine knew it was just the habitual cynicism of a life lived as a soldier, nothing would have pleased him more to learn that Tirolane or some other local mindspeaker had broken protocol and sent a quick pulse.

To let Bannor know that they were still alive.

Chapter Thirty-Seven

As the Legate convoy neared the approximate location of Ebrekka, Ta'rel's mangle friend stood up in the lead rad and pointed ahead. Riordan smiled and loaned Sharat the monoscope. "Is it the lookout?"

"It is," the Legate's captain replied as he peered through the instrument. He signaled to the other windrads to follow the one carrying the mangle. Although not from Ebrekka or one of its larger outlying communities, he had known where to seek the watcher who would show them the best approach.

Sharat returned the monoscope to Caine, his eyes following the device as it left his hand. "It would take some bartering, but I believe I could get you a real rad in trade for that artifact."

Caine's smile was genuinely one of regret. *Sharat, I wish I could* give *one to every independent human force we meet.* But he forced himself to say, "I am sorry, but I can't do so. It is not my personal possession."

Sharat nodded knowingly. He hung on to the real rad's pitted rail of shaped bone as it angled toward a narrow defile between two loaf-shaped rises. "We shall not be here long, not if you are to get to Shrakhupsekh in time to sail upon the Rock to Zrik Whir."

"They are so infrequent?" asked Bey from the bed of the vehicle, currently configured for passengers rather than cargo.

"It is more a matter of seasons," Sharat answered. "Travel in winter is particularly treacherous. But even during the rest of the year, the currents and winds often change."

"I shall regret not seeing that great port city," Ulchakh said, somehow sounding wistful even as he shouted over the brief revving of the rad's engine.

"You are welcome to travel on with us," Sharat shouted over his shoulder while tapping the driver's arm to guide him toward a waypoint.

Ulchakh shook his head. "I may not, Friend Sharat. My place is with the rest of my people, at Achgabab."

"Surely they can spare you a little longer."

"Surely they already shall, since I foresee that I will often be at the Silo. What has been found there shall impact us h'achgai for all times to come."

"You mean the increased access to metals and other treasures?"

"That, too, but more what comes along with it: unwanted attention." Ulchakh's voice suddenly seemed loud over the diminished muttering of the engine; the rad had begun cruising over flatter ground. "Achgabab is no longer safely beyond the margin of great events and the attention of lieges. That, I fear, may have put my trading days behind me, that I may be an intermediary to regional powers. So as soon as I finish my business here, I must turn my back on any journey to Shrakhupsekh. And even more so, to Zrik Whir—assuming they would allow me to set foot on their island at all."

"What *is* your business in Ebrekka, anyway?" Sharat asked, glancing behind briefly. "And I can't believe it was sheer chance that we came across the three h'achgai warriors who joined us as we neared the Orokrosir."

Ulchakh smiled. "It is not chance. Indeed, it is a matter that is long overdue. And I would probably have put it off a bit longer, if I was not traveling with my friend Caine and his Crewe."

Riordan glanced at him. "And when were you going to tell me about this?"

Ulchakh's smile broadened. "Now seemed like the perfect time."

"And what is this business of yours?"

"You will see as soon as we arrive." He leaned over. "Patience, Friend Caine. This shall benefit you as well. I have named you chogruk; I would not involve you in anything that would compromise you."

Caine smiled. "I'm not worried; I'm curious."

Ulchakh laughed. "It is one of your best traits. And you shall have your answer soon enough."

Ulchakh was surprised when his estimate of their remaining travel—"soon enough"—extended into another two hours. "I have never been to Ebrekka itself, only rendezvous points surrounding it, but I had no idea it was this close to the heart of the Orokrosir."

After the balance of the formation had dismounted, the drivers followed three mangles—children, from the look of them—toward a safe place where it was said not even the most determined kiktzo would espy them. As the vehicles moved off, a pair of mangle scouts emerged from the shadows at the mouth of a wadi. With deep bows, they gestured toward a winding path that appeared to meander through gullies and along the western sides of low ridges. Having reasonable command of their language, Peter asked them how far they had to go on foot. He translated their answer from the native units of measure: just over two kilometers.

Ulchakh remained close to Riordan, close enough to indicate to others that they were having a private conversation. "There is another reason I am traveling no further than Ebrekka. Doing so would require traveling with the forces of the Legate."

Riordan lifted an eyebrow. "I was under the impression that the h'achgai and the Legate are friends."

Ulchakh made a dyspeptic noise. "Let us say instead that Achgabab is friendly with Tasvar and leave it at that. As far as the Legate in general . . ." He sighed, scratched his arms in a decidedly simian fashion. "Sometimes, the Legate's many groups travel as traders, sometimes as war bands. It is becoming the latter, more and more."

"Do you know why?"

"Do I know? Certainly not. But I suspect that the elimination of stables like Cruvanor's is not unique to Fragkork. Rather, I believe such events are becoming both more frequent and widespread."

Riordan shrugged. "He has said as much."

"Yes, but those incidents send out ripples. It is not chance that Tasvar sends you as an intermediary to Zrik Whir. And with so rich a salvage site located so close to Fragkork—" He shuddered. "Many fortunes and fates are being blown about by these winds. I fear they may amplify each other into a whirlwind." He emitted another dyspeptic grunt. "The Legate's group travels toward such tornados, and Achgabab has no desire to be pulled along with them. If it becomes necessary, we will know, and act, in due course." He straightened, rubbed his large, round shoulder against Caine's high, narrower human one. "But now, let me educate you in the ways of the mangles, who you may hear referring to themselves as *yekhwhir*."

"Is that their own tongue?"

"No, but those who do not speak Low Praakht may not understand 'mangle.' Yekhwhir is Deviltongue for 'disfigured' or 'malformed' men."

"And the, eh, yekhwhir prefer to be known by a name given to them by x'qai?"

"No, but they do not care, either. Mangles rarely share their native language with others. I myself know but a few words in it."

"So Peter's knowledge of *yekhwhir* is—"

"Is very rare," interrupted Ulchakh in a hushed tone. "I suspect Ebrekka's durus'maan—Raam'tu—will already be aware; his daughter, Ne'sar, will not have failed to mention it. But it will not be widely known, so Leader Wu may hear much of interest spoken by those unaware he can understand their words."

"Thank you, Friend Ulchakh. And since you are so kind as to instruct me in the ways of the yekhwhir, what other knowledge do I lack?"

"Most everything. That applies to me, as well. For so amiable a people, mangles are quite accomplished at conversing broadly about themselves and the world at large while, somehow, revealing little of their race or its secrets. However, it is well known that their skill with the growing of plants and concocting philters is unsurpassed. I suspect that is connected to their ability to measure the level of s'rillor in any species. No doubt Ta'rel will once again insist on taking samples from you and your companions."

"He has already done so."

"It is a wise precaution. Lastly, as you may have already conjectured, mangles cannot breed with any other species, although their kind often grow to express their physical traits. Except those of cavers: that never occurs."

"And why is that?"

"No one knows. Maybe they themselves do not. What little

more I can tell you about mangle breeding is that they never have twins, and the expression of certain traits is fatal."

Riordan frowned. "Intrinsically fatal, or . . . socially?"

"To my knowledge, they do not kill their young for any reason. Indeed, they do not kill each other at all." He shook his head when Caine's face apparently revealed his disbelief. "That is how most react upon learning this. But time goes on and still there is no kinslaying among them." He shrugged. "It is said to be a magic particular to mangles. Perhaps it is the universe showing pity; perhaps because everything preys upon them, they have been spared the strife that leads races to prey upon themselves."

Riordan nodded. "And now, have we come far enough that you will share your true business here?"

Ulchakh elbowed him lightly. "Unless I miss my guess, you'll see for yourself soon enough." Up ahead, one of their guides had tapped on a rock. A moment later, further on in the wadi, a much larger rock on the opposite side swung outward. "I believe we have arrived."

After a long series of rammed-earth chambers and short tunnels lit by faintly glowing fungi, Riordan and the other visitors were escorted into a much larger room: a veritable cathedral that had been cored out from within the first rock formation they'd encountered since entering. Scouts—apparently the closest thing mangles had to "guards"—were posted along the walls. Several glanced curiously at Bey, then at each other. One or two shrugs were exchanged.

But neither their reactions, the soaring ceiling with dagger-shaped stalactites, or even the mysterious platform at the other end of the chamber commanded Caine's attention. It was the wild disparity among the mangles themselves.

He had become accustomed to the mismatched physiognomies and features of Ta'rel and Ne'sar, but seeing dozens of such beings in one place imparted the feeling of a surreal dream. All the variform eyes, ears, noses, faces reminded him of books from his earliest childhood, where creatures of all sorts acted and spoke as humans. But even in those fantasies, the species of each character was complete and separate: there were badgers or weasels or bears or rabbits, but never mixes of them. He could perceive only one genetic constant among the mangles; no matter the mix of characteristics, they were all recognizably terrestrial in origin. Some had been dramatically altered, or perhaps, like the entelodont Baruch had identified, were of lost species. But Riordan saw nothing in any of them that recalled the xenobiologies he'd seen elsewhere.

One stood apart from the rest, waiting near a platform at the other end of the chamber, and gestured them to approach. "I am Raam'tu, durus'maan of Ebrekka," he announced as they neared. "I bid you welcome. It is a privilege to have you as our guests."

"And we thank you for allowing us to visit you here," Riordan added when the others had finished making replies to their host, who was mostly human—except for the white and silver fur that covered his face. "We know few are permitted to enter Ebrekka."

Ta'rel glanced between him and Raam'tu, mouth open to speak—but the durus'maan addressed his visitors first. "It is a special place," he affirmed, gesturing to the chamber around them, "and it is fitting that we should meet you here, in particular." He stood aside. "Even fewer have seen what I show you now." He gestured them to approach the wall behind him.

Except it wasn't exactly a wall; what Riordan had taken to be a slightly outthrust portion of the rock was a slab that had partially separated from the surface behind. It was quite thick and the wall around it showed the marks of profitless mining or chipping. There were several bone wedges in the gap, splintered from the work of hammers.

Raam'tu waved them toward the slab. "Look more closely. In the largest gap, here."

Riordan and the others nearest did so.

A bright metallic gleam stared back at him, not quite even with the rest of the wall. It wasn't a vein of ore; few were so pure. As he followed the shining seam where it ran up behind the slab, he saw another reason the metal could not be a natural feature: it was as perfectly flat and smooth as if it had been manufactured.

Riordan straightened. "This is part of some object from ancient times."

Raam'tu nodded.

Dora looked around the other side of the slab. "I can see it here, too."

Miles' voice rose behind her. "Looks like the bottom of some container. A big one. The kind used for shipping freight."

Whereas Riordan had stepped away, Peter crouched low, almost seemed intent on wriggling his way into the aperture, though it was hardly wider than a pocketknife. "How long has it been exposed?"

"We found it as you see it," Raam'tu explained. "And in the years since then, we have made almost no progress freeing the metal from the rock. As you see. So it would indeed be a great occasion—and an auspicious omen—if the task were to be completed while you are our guests here."

Riordan glanced at the durus'maan: his face had become just as serious, even somber, as his tone. "Why would it be so beneficial to complete this task now?"

"It would signal great favor for the other reason we are gathered here."

"Which is?"

Raam'tu glanced at Ulchakh, who almost completely hid his surprise. "The salving of an old wound between Vaagdjul of Achgabab and Boghram of Atorsír. The latter is bringing one of his daughters to be life-mated to one of Vaagdjul's grandsons."

"Here?"

The durus'maan worked hard, but unsuccessfully, to keep a frown of perplexity from bending his brow. "No, she will accompany Ulchakh back to Achgabab." He glanced at the old trader.

So did Riordan—who discovered that his h'achga friend had evidently chosen this moment to study an interesting feature among the stalactites. "So," Riordan answered Raam'tu, without taking his eyes off Ulchakh, "when does the party from Atorsír arrive?"

"Soon, but this was arranged so hastily that Boghram's group is still traveling here, albeit as swiftly as prudence allows."

Riordan tried not to frown. "And why is it that Boghram was only invited recently?"

The durus'maan shrugged, obviously resigned to the fact that he could no longer leave Ulchakh out of the conversation as he clearly desired. The mangle nodded toward the h'achga. "You must ask him."

But of course. Riordan turned fully toward his friend, raising an inquisitive eyebrow.

Ulchakh's reply had a faint undercurrent of pleading. "There are many reasons for the suddenness of this gathering. First and foremost is that Sharat's return north to the dunes could not have been foreseen as few as thirty days ago. And your own errand that brings him back south so quickly was not known until fifteen days ago." Ulchakh shrugged. "Journeying with a well-armed Legate group is swift and safe and a rare opportunity. Particularly for my kind. So Vaagdjul thought it prudent to act quickly on Boghram's unexpected acceptance of his offer."

"By offer, you mean the wedding?"

Ulchakh blinked uncertainly at the word "wedding," but nodded. "For almost two years, Boghram's only response has been sullen silence. When Sharat left Achgabab to trade in Atorsír, he was also carrying a message from Vaagdjul: that his grandson could wait no longer to take a mate. It was becoming . . . let us say 'unseemly.' Families who had reason—and daughters—to make such a life-mating were being rebuffed for no apparent reason."

"And that explanation convinced Boghram to agree?"

"Evidently. Shortly after the message was delivered, he sent word back through Sharat's group."

Which means either Boghram has a mindspeaker of his own, or relied on the one with Sharat. "So this is why you are actually here."

Ulchakh raised a pausing finger. "I told you there are *many* reasons. One of the others you see before you. It has been at least a score of years that Raam'tu's people have come here, driving in wedges of stone or bone. You see what progress there has been."

"We have little skill with rockwork," the durus'maan explained. "Similarly, we do not work metal so often or so skillfully as our h'achga neighbors, and it is not our way to invite outsiders into our hidden places. It takes only one loose tongue to cause disaster."

Riordan shook his head. "But why did you invite the h'achgai at this time? And why become the exchange point for Boghram's daughter?"

Raam'tu shrugged. "Boghram required neutral ground and neutral parties present. And since Ulchakh's visit promised to finally bring resolution to the quandary of reaching the metal that time entombed in the rock, we felt that it was worth the risk of allowing visitors." He smiled at Riordan, then glanced at Peter. "We also know how you saved Ta'rel upon the wastes west of Forkus. If anyone deserves our trust, it is you. Who are also, we believe, the answer to this problem." He gestured toward the wall.

Now we come to it. "And how do you believe we could help you with that?"

"Our tools, Commodore," Peter said from behind. "Not our unusual, er, artifacts. Just the tools from our kits."

Ulchakh nodded. "Your hammers, your pitons: I remarked upon all your tools' wondrousness, even as we crossed the great river above Khorkrag. They are harder than our best steel."

Peter nodded at the wedges jammed into the gap behind the stone surface facing them. "They've got the right idea, but I suspect that none of the wedges they try to drive in have the right combination of hardness and tensile strength to stand up to the resistance while being hammered."

Raam'tu nodded. "It is as your friend says. So we decided to set aside our prohibition of bringing outsiders into this special place to both help our neighbors rediscover their lost friendship through joining mates and free a heart of metal that shall profit, and protect, all of us."

'All of us'? Well, that's a novel twist. Riordan crossed his arms. "So, is it your intent to share the metal with the h'achgai?"

Raam'tu shrugged. "And with you, if you wish it. And even with peaceable praakht, one of whom is said to travel with you." He nodded a personal welcome to Bey. "And yes, I know you are whakt—none could miss it—but I am told that you are a lord in your own right, and that your forces are governed by laws very like those of the h'achgai and humans. We of Ebrekka would have all share in this metal."

Bey sounded skeptical. "That is very generous of you."

Raam'tu smiled. "It is also very wise of us. Those who have ownership of a thing almost never seek to destroy it."

"No," she said with a frown, "but they often come to covet it for themselves alone."

"That is very true. But ask yourself: who would wish to do so, beyond the heart of the Orokrosir, so far from a trading place or river?" He indicated the walls around them. "Who but those who already live here? Savage bands and gangs have this in common: they only value that which they can sell or use without effort. But this metal, even once freed, will require long, difficult work to draw forth." The durus'maan smiled. "I have never seen or heard of a raider that would be attracted by such a proposition."

He returned his steady gaze to Riordan. "However, these two reasons give rise to the third that determined us to free the metal now, if possible." He folded his hands. "Humans rarely give credence to fate. I am told it is even more rare among you and your friends.

"But we mangles see, and heed, omens when they arise. There have been many in just this year alone, several attached to yourselves. Perhaps that is why you are so unable to see them; how can a being truly see its own face?"

Dora frowned. "In a mirror."

"Which is my further meaning: that we can *only* see ourselves reflected in that which is outside us." He smiled. "Perhaps, at this time and place, we may prove to be your mirror. Suffice it to say that if your people are not only present, but instrumental, in freeing the metal that has resisted us for so long, that would be a powerful portent. And all things done within the scope of that event would be favored."

"Such as mending wounds between kin," Ulchakh put in from the side. "I am reluctant to speak of omens and signs with you, Friend Caine, let alone ask for your help based upon them. You and the Crewe make plain the profound doubt you have regarding even the most forthright display of arcane powers.

"But such powers and portents are as real to us as your artifacts are to you. So in the name of our beliefs, and our reality, I make bold to add my voice to Raam'tu's. I ask you: will you help us bring peace not only to my people, but to make this place a hallowed ground? A place where all our races came together in peace to forge peace? Not only through the bonds we make with each other, but the metal weapons with which our peoples can resist the terrors of the x'qai?"

Well, when you put it like that... "Yes, we will help." Riordan stared at the rock. "To the extent that we are able."

The durus'maan inclined his head. "One can ask no more, particularly of honored guests. We are your humble hosts. Please: come walk among us."

As Raam'tu led the way out of the chamber, Riordan trailed well behind and managed to draw Ulchakh aside as they walked. "And when were you going to tell me about the other reasons you are here?"

"Once again, I had hoped to do so a little bit later than events allowed."

"I don't know that I think much of your sense of timing, Ulchakh."

"I know, Friend Caine. Right now, I have a poorer opinion of it than you do. My apologies."

Riordan put a hand on the old trader's shoulder. "I understand you were probably waiting for a quiet, private place. But in the future . . . don't wait. Be sure to tell me things like this ahead of time. *Way* ahead of time."

"Commodore?" Peter had fallen well behind the throng following Raam'tu. He was staring back at the slab they'd inspected.

Riordan smiled. "You want to stay behind, get a better look?"

Wu nodded. "My grandfather cut stone the traditional way. This is . . . a little bit like being with him again, like being at home. And with some subtle use of an artifact, I think I can get this done before—"

"Lieutenant Wu?"

"Commodore?"

"Permission granted. Stay as long as you wish. Presume you have access to any of our gear to get it done. Give me a report when you've settled on a plan."

"Yes, sir."

As Riordan turned to catch up to the others, Dora lagged for a moment, smiling. "You know we're not going to see him for hours, right, Boss?"

"And maybe not even then," Caine answered. "Lead on, Ms. Veriden."

Chapter Thirty-Eight

Fezhmorbal stared at the sky, striving for patience as he sent a disapproving pulse back through the link to Qudzorpla. She had no reason to become so excitable. "Yes, I am certain it is the thieves. Or at least, some of them."

Qudzorpla did not reply immediately. "So, they have divided their force?"

"I would not say divided. Rather, they have sent out a detachment on some errand to Ebrekka. As I thought."

He felt her become distracted; probably managing subordinates. The base in Forkus was growing once again. "I do not understand how you foresaw this," she sent with renewed focus. "Please: instruct me."

Whether those words are flattery or genuine is of no consequence so long as she continues to serve adequately. "Firstly, the prey had a mangle with them from the time they fled Forkus. So, although they chose to go to Achgabab first, it did not mean they would not also travel to Ebrekka at some later point. Even if that is not their mangle's home, it is his species' most powerful community; surely he would seek its advantages.

"Secondly, after withdrawing from his attack on the ancient site, Gasdashrag detected Sharat's group heading there, but doubled in size. He probably achieved this by absorbing another Legate group that hunters sighted moving north into the Orokrosir. Already in Atorsír, Sharat would have been able to effect a swift rendezvous before traveling north to the ruin.

"Yet after only a few days there, all six of the Legate's rads headed back south, this time making for the eastern edge of the Orokrosir. Given that course, their only logical destination was Ebrekka."

Qudzorpla sent a pulse of comprehension and appreciation. "How much of this convoy is comprised of Sharat's forces, and how much the thieves'?"

"We cannot be certain. Gasdashrag remains at a distance that prevents detection by the prey. Unfortunately, that means it provides little detailed information. However, crewing six rads and their dedicated security force would take up at least a third of the seats. Adding supplies and minimal cargo, that would only leave room for a dozen passengers. The thieves would keep a bodyguard at least equal to their own numbers, so we may conjecture that leaves room for but five or six of them. So it is not the thieves' whole force, but a detachment."

Qudzorpla pulsed gladness. "A small fraction of the force of almost ninety that arrived at the site. So, truly, it is just as you say: a detachment. But to what end?"

"That, Qudzorpla, is the most important question. With any luck, our coming operation should provide us with some answers. Or at least, indications."

"And when shall that operation commence?"

"As soon as our agents arrive."

"How are you tracking their progress?"

"Kiktzo, of course. Our agents are close. Gasdashrag shall remain at a greater distance until our first gambit opens a path for a more general attack."

Qudzorpla could not mute her surprise in time. "What do you mean by 'a more general' attack? Surely you do not mean to take Ebrekka?"

"Surely, if you ask such foolish questions, your career will be shortened. Dramatically."

"Apologies, War Leader: my query was rhetorical. I rephrase: what is your intent?"

Fezhmorbal felt an urge toward pedantry, mentally swatted it aside. "This attack has several aims. It would be enough to sow fear, discord, and distrust among these groups at any time, but given the ceremonies that they will ruin, I suspect the effect will be even greater. Any movements toward a productive alliance should be either prevented or slowed. The Mangled are particularly sensitive to casualties, and an attack into their own community is likely to send them scurrying into the shadows like so many cowardly roaches."

Qudzorpla broke in before he could continue. "Do you expect that, like the mangles, the prey will become less aggressive, more likely to remain in a single, safe place?"

"Quite the contrary. Their decision to send off a detachment so soon after repulsing Gasdashrag's attack further indicates that they think like warriors, not thieves. They are expanding by both retaining the site as a base of operations while initiating another mission in league with the Legate.

"But regardless of how many casualties we inflict, we will accrue greater knowledge of them by assessing how they respond to our new attack. If all goes well, I have detailed a forward assault group to secure any gains until Gasdashrag and I can converge upon that position. If it is possible to control the area, we shall. If not, we will take what we wish and bring the 'thieves' back to Hwe'tsara." He reconsidered the ramifications of bringing live prisoners in front of the liege. "It is a pity that they will be dead by the time we bring them to Forkus."

"As a result of the combat?"

"Yes, that is likely. But even if we do capture any of the thieves or their associates, it will likely prove unwise to turn them over to Hwe'tsara. I suspect that once we have tortured their origins and intents out of them, we will possess information too beneficial to our own purposes to be shared with x'qai. But in the case of Hwe'tsara, that will hardly matter. He will revel simply in the act of despoiling the bodies, of that you may be sure."

Fezhmorbal felt Qudzorpla forming her response to his plans. "You are bold and risk much, War Leader."

"And you are foolish to think so, since I do not risk near so much as you presume. But now, what news of Hwe'tsara?"

"Little other than his continued impatience. However, I suspect he has voiced that impatience to other war leaders."

"*Our* war leaders?"

"Yes, Fezhmorbal. I suspect he has contacted other deciqadi captains in an attempt to ascertain whether the time and expense being 'lavished' on his vengeance seems excessive."

"And?"

"And he received no answers, I suppose because they are unsure what best to say, given that you are known to have the support of the Oligate. However, several of these captains have learned that you not only have forces closing on Ebrekka, but that you may have a means of getting inside. As such, they have begun to urge that your mission be broadened to include them, as well. That if you have a way into Ebrekka, your duty to the race is to throw wide those entrances, rather than pursue your own limited objectives." Qudzorpla waited. When Fezhmorbal did not reply, she asked, "War Leader, what would you have me do?"

"Nothing. Let them wait for an answer that will never need to be sent—because within days, the deeds will be done and they can only suggest what might have been. But without any knowledge of the particulars, it will be random speculation and soon forgotten."

"And Hwe'tsara? What should I tell him?"

"Even less. You shall tell him of the attack after it has occurred, and only those details which are strategically wise to share with him. If he presses you before then, simply avoid him for the few remaining days."

Qudzorpla signaled agreement, then speculated, "If the plan is to be concluded within days, your agents must be very near to the target, indeed."

"They are. The necessary parties know that the son of Boghram of Atorsír remains in our possession and lives in a state of peril worse than death itself. As that son is the full brother of the female being sent as a peace offering to Achgabab, our agents fear the displeasure of their own tribal leaders as much as they do us."

"And has the entourage arrived at Ebrekka yet?"

"You only need know this: they will be in place very soon."

"And those with rank and status remain unaware of the attack or how it will occur?"

"Not even the one carrying it out knows the plan. The only use of our leverage was to ensure that he was included in the entourage."

"War Leader Fezhmorbal, there is just one thing I do not understand."

"Just one?"

Qudzorpla may have been slightly amused or slightly insulted; neither mattered. "What I cannot fathom is this: How shall you attack if none of our own forces are actually present?"

Fezhmorbal tried very hard not to preen, at least not in a way that Qudzorpla could detect. "You may recall that, after I helped increase the bounties on humans in Khorkrag, Hwe'tsara urged Suzerain Ormalg's 'liege' there to be of assistance to us. Suffice it to say that through his offices, I came to 'interview' the town's oldest and most successful raiders. They confirmed that a force that had once been near the target was, in fact, not only there, but very close. Almost inside."

"But that cannot be the total of your attack force, War Leader."

Interesting. Qudzorpla *was* insightful at times. "And why do you say that?"

"Because I cannot believe that a force that is so small that it can hide close to Ebrekka could be sufficient to achieve your ends. And also, because your efforts have been mostly focused upon getting an agent inside, I suspect that the great balance of the attack will be carried out by a larger force that depends upon the actions of that agent."

"You are correct," Fezhmorbal answered, giving no hint of the unwitting ironies of her deductions. He sent a pulse that warned Qudzorpla against pressing for more details, and then dissolved the link. As his mentor had told him long ago, by definition, a secret plan will not remain secret if it is shared. No matter with whom.

Not until it is put into motion.

Chapter Thirty-Nine

Riordan heard the distinctive rustle and faint metallic clicks and clacks of a person wearing a Dornaani vacc suit. He turned.

Peter Wu leaned his helmeted head around the corner of the doorway. "Another update for you, sir."

Caine smiled, waved him in. "What's the good word today?"

Wu pulled up a seat—a bone framework shaped like an ottoman—and put his hands on his knees. "We're ready to go, sir."

Riordan leaned away from the mission log he'd finally had a chance to update. "Already?"

"I'm as surprised as you are, sir. And I wish I could take the credit, but I can't." He sighed despite his smile. "Chalk up another victory for Dornaani technology."

"The pitons?"

Wu nodded. "The smart metal in them is a lot more effective than the manual indicated. Or maybe the pitons in our packs are a later model."

Riordan nodded. Of all the Crewe, Peter had made the most thorough study of their survival pack's documentation and technical specifications. However, except for their stays at Achgabab and the Silo, it had been a catch-as-catch-can project. Long weeks of marching all day, every day, left little time or energy for reading translated, jargon-laden references to materials or phenomena that required explanations from Eku. "So can I tell our hosts we won't need to put out the solar rechargers anymore?"

Peter frowned. "Just one more day, sir. I want to make sure

there's enough energy for the kind of sustained molecular expansion that will give us a satisfying grand finale." He grinned. "Anything to build our legend."

Caine raised an eyebrow. "It makes me a little uneasy, all the local talk about our 'legend.' We seem to be the only ones who consider it either dubious or amusing. But I'll pass along the word to Raam'tu that after today, we won't have to put our equipment out in the sun." While not subterranean by preference, the mangles spent most of each day in concealment, and exposing even the smallest solar array alarmed them. Riordan had persuaded them to allow it for an hour after dawn and again just before dusk.

"That will be a help, sir. What comes next?"

"The hardest part of all," Riordan sighed. "Talking to the powers that be."

"It is necessary that we wait until the day *after* tomorrow," Raam'tu explained to the "leaders of peoples" he had asked to witness the freeing of the metal.

Riordan glanced back at Peter. They both concentrated on responding with slow, somber nods of understanding. For Caine, it was as good a way as any to conceal his discomfort with the steadily increasing formality, almost severity, surrounding the impending event. Every successive announcement sounded a bit more like a proclamation, and the tone was steadily shifting from serious to sonorous.

Ulchakh crossed his arms. "What is the cause of the delay?"

Ne'sar, who'd become her father's assistant in seeing to the preparations, gestured in the direction that Riordan gathered was west. "Boghram's journey from Atorsír has been slower than hoped. Only now have our farthest watchers caught sight of the entourage. They will not arrive until dusk tomorrow, and we shall not bring them within until evening."

Bey frowned. "You fear they are being observed?"

"No more than anyone else who approaches this place," Raam'tu answered with a rueful smile. "We have many hidden ways that pass underground before they emerge near one of our secure entrances."

Cruvanor leaned toward Caine as the durus'maan shared sad anecdotes of why they had adopted such layered precautions. "All places should be so well protected: rings of walls are far easier to penetrate than multiple, separate tunnels."

Caine nodded. "An all-axis tiered defense. Textbook."

Cruvanor stared at him. "I must read this book. Also, thank you for insisting that I be included as one of the witnesses at the coming ceremony."

Riordan shook his head. "No thanks necessary, and they didn't resist."

"But why is Sharat not here?"

Caine shook his head. "He claimed he was not a high enough officer to represent the Legate."

The war leader's answering frown was skeptical.

Riordan's reaction to Sharat's demurral had been similar. "He didn't offer any further explanation. But in your case, I felt it was right—and necessary—that every human in a stable has a senior representative here." And one day, Caine hoped he'd be able to share his additional reason: that, not being native to Bactradgaria, he could not legally or ethically speak for *any* of its peoples.

Bey nodded as Raam'tu finished his cautionary tale of the tragedies that had led the mangles of Ebrekka to evolve such sophisticated defenses. "I am privileged to be the guest of such a wise and clever people," she said with a deep nod. "And I am honored to stand as witness to an event that promises to gather all our species around a shared resource. And cause."

But rather than returning her bow-nod, Raam'tu folded his hands loosely over his belly. Although superficially avuncular, the gesture also suggested a step back from the conversational intimacy of the moment before. "I am glad you mention your status as a leader of your people. In speaking with your prakhwa—er, trogan—guards, I have come to learn that they have never witnessed your affirmation as chief."

Riordan heard the hanging tone. *What the—?*

Bey straightened, was suddenly stiff. "But I have been given command over all the trog-kind that serve beneath Caine Riordan's banner."

He confirmed her claim with a vigorous nod.

"And a worthy position that is—but still, it is not that of a chief or a band leader."

"But nor is she a vassal," Riordan pointed out.

Now it was Bey who nodded—and looked both grateful and slightly panicked. "Lead—Caine Riordan specifically wished me to remain independent, that I might be a fully free voice for my people." She pointed to the circle tattooed on her forehead. "I am a truthteller. If I lie, I die."

Raam'tu waved away her protestations. "Your veracity is evident both in that sign and, more importantly, in your actions and demeanor. But your veracity is not at issue. You have not been confirmed as a chief or band leader—and you must be such, to represent your people at this ceremony. Which, if omens align, may have expanding and enduring influence upon many subsequent events—and alliances."

"Alliances?" I've never heard any *mangle use that term, let alone the durus'maan of Ebrekka.* Riordan moved his eyes slightly, peripherally measuring the reactions of the other gathered leaders.

If anything, his own response was the most muted. Cruvanor seemed to have narrowly suppressed a surprised blink. Ulchakh was already straightening out his surprised smile. Ne'sar herself had not foreseen that her father might make such a statement: she hastily closed her open mouth.

Bey, however, was staring at Caine, her look of anxiety replaced by determination and a question he could not fathom. *But if she has a way out of this...* He allowed his eyelids to droop in assent. *Do whatever you need to.*

She turned her eyes back toward Raam'tu. "Then I shall become a chief. The trogans who are our guards have long been made legal witnesses to the desire of my forces to have me declared so."

Wait: what—? Riordan hoped his face hadn't given away his surprise the way his peers' had just a moment earlier.

Raam'tu leaned forward, not just interested but unabashedly hopeful. "I would not ask this given your tattoo, except that it concerns your own affairs: Can another attest to this?"

She nodded. "Hresh, h'achga oathkeeper, was called to witness the vote among my people." She glanced at Ulchakh. "I requested he report it to Ulchakh. Confidentially."

The h'achga nodded, glanced at Riordan. "She did not seek the vote, Friend Caine. She did not want you to worry that it might signify disapproval of your leadership, or that of the Crewe in general."

Riordan's only reply was a raised eyebrow. *But later, I'm going to have a conversation with all concerned.*

However, Raam'tu was not only mulling Bey's claims, but sidebarring with his daughter, who had tugged on his sleeve and was now whispering urgently in his white-furred ear. Caine almost smiled as he watched an exchange he'd been sure he'd never see on Bactradgaria: a neolithic equivalent of legal formalities and bureaucratic wrangling. *Guess it's as universal as death and taxes.*

Raam'tu nodded at Ne'sar and straightened to face Bey again. "My daughter, who has already forgotten far more about trog-ways than I ever learned, bids me ask if you have shared trust, yet?"

Bey may have grown pale, and she pointedly did not look at Riordan. "I have not. There was no reason to share trust, since I was not chief." As she replied, Cruvanor stole a glance at Caine, whereas Ulchakh looked away. Sharply.

Riordan almost asked, "And what the hell is 'shared trust'?" but reminded himself: *No, this is Bey's gambit. Questions could derail it. Let her play it out.*

"Then, if I understand your own traditions and codes correctly, you cannot yet be called Caine Riordan's ally."

"No," she answered, "but our laws were not at issue when Caine Riordan and I mutually determined how I, and my forces, would serve beneath his standard."

"I understand, and that arrangement remains entirely between you and him. But it does not change the fact that it is incumbent upon you, as a chief, to confirm any and all allies by jointly participating in the rite of shared trust. So, if you become chief, you must share trust with him before the ceremony, or part from his command until you do."

Bey glanced at Caine. "He is not aware of the rite."

Raam'tu seemed utterly unsurprised. "Then perhaps it is time to acquaint him with it."

Okay, now she's definitely *gone pale.* "Tell me about this rite, Bey. I will do whatever is required so that you may become a chief of your people. I would have insisted upon it long before now, if I had been aware that your followers wished it."

She looked away—which told him just how uncomfortable this topic made her. "The rite of shared trust is performed by all chiefs with any other leaders—trog-kind or not—that acknowledge each other as equals. This is true even if one agrees to obey the orders of the other."

Riordan nodded. "What does the rite involve?" *Probably swapping blood or something like it.*

"The two leaders drink together, then dance together, then

sleep in the same space. Assuming one is not dead in the morning, they are deemed allies."

Riordan almost laughed at an unbidden mental image: two wildly tattooed, scarred, bone-and-trophy-bedecked trog chieftains cutting a dainty gavotte in the middle of a bloodstained cave. On the other hand, spending a night in the same room with Bey... Caine felt his face grow warm at the images *that* notion conjured. *And if that's how you're reacting, then you* can't *agree to it.*

No: you must *agree to the rite. Damn it, get a hold of yourself. Too much is at stake, both for the unit and for Bey.* Mentally and physically, he stood straighter: random sexual thoughts were part of everyday life, so there was no reason to get spooked by one. *Frankly, it's strange you haven't had any about her before now.* Not sure if that was reassuring or troubling, Caine lifted his chin: "I will be proud to participate in the rite of sharing trust."

Bey stared at him, eyes wide—with horror or surprise, he couldn't tell.

"Then it is settled," Raam'tu declared, clearly expecting the nods he received from the homely group of luminaries he'd gathered.

"Excellent," Ne'sar exclaimed. "We shall begin our preparations. We shall have the rite of sharing tomorrow, just in time for the ceremony the day after. Is that agreeable to everyone?"

Riordan nodded, almost chortled: her voice had become as eager and intent as every other event coordinator he'd ever encountered.

Raam'tu nodded happily. "I have kept you all long enough." Ne'sar on his arm, he turned to go, then turned back. "And it shall be all the more auspicious that the freeing of the metal shall be carried out by one of the star people!"

The what? *How in hell did they learn—?*

Peter leaned over, whispering to Caine as the others began wandering away. "Nothing to worry about, Commodore."

"Nothing to worry about? How did they find out—?" That was when he realized that he was the only person who'd reacted to the term "star people."

"They are still completely unaware of our origins," Peter continued. "It's just a coincidence that—" Peter leaned away abruptly, glanced meaningfully past Riordan's cheek. Caine turned.

Bey was right in front of him. "Why did you start so, Leader Caine?"

Why is she standing so close? "Being called star people: I'd never heard that before." *Damn:* is *she closer or does she just* seem *closer?* "I'm . . . I'm not sure why Raam'tu called us that."

She shrugged. "All the mangles here call you 'star people.'"

Great. "Uh, why?"

She stared at him. "Because ever since the moving star arrived last winter, their fortunes have reversed most wonderfully. Starting with your own rescue of Ta'rel, whom they feared dead." She smiled tentatively. "The mangles spend more time outside at night than during the day, so they watch stars. They believe the future can be read in the shapes they make, that they reveal omens. Like the star that arrived shortly before you arrived." She frowned. "Why *else* would they call you star people?"

"I don't—" *No: do* not *tell her you "don't know." That's a bald-faced lie.* "I . . . I'll explain later. It's a silly story. About something that happens all the time, back home."

She was still frowning. "I doubt the story is 'silly,' not judging from the look on your face."

"What look?"

Her frown relented, a small smile replacing it. "The look which tells me that, after all the battles and trials and labors, now more than ever, you should celebrate. This is a good time and a good place to let loose the burdens of both the past and the present and to welcome the possibilities before us. And maybe, if you find that too boring, you will explain why this story from your homeland makes you so worried that the mangles call all of you star people."

"Agreed." *But I will never find anything boring enough to tell you* that *tale.*

Not unless and until I can tell you all *of it.*

Chapter Forty

Ulchakh nudged Riordan and nodded toward the far end of the large, high chamber. Two tables had been placed on the low platform of rock that jutted out from beneath the slab now ringed by Dornaani pitons. "It is traditional that the more powerful leader sits at the table on the right. But that can be changed, according to his preference."

"Or her preference," Caine emended.

"True," the h'achga sighed. "There has never been a reason to say it thusly until now." He shook his head. "Even when you do not mean to, you and your companions spawn changes wherever you go."

Just you wait, Caine thought as he nodded agreeably.

"However," Ulchakh continued, "whereas you would normally be the first to ascend the platform, you must wait until Bey has been confirmed as chieftain."

"How will I know?"

"Oh, you cannot miss it, my friend! She will finish by fire-spinning!"

Riordan frowned, noticed that the mangles wandering in were wearing slightly different garments. Their breeches were longer and less threadbare, and many wore adornments of various kinds in their hair. Also, it was either common practice with both sexes or all the women had been allowed in first. But no, he spied Ta'rel talking with Dora and Miles, and next to them Cruvanor and Tirolane were standing near Craig Girten.

Caine leaned toward Ulchakh, aimed his eyes at their mangle friend. "Now, I confess: I expected to see him with Ne'sar, not my friends."

"You may yet, but until the festivities begin, he is to stay with the visitors."

"Even though he is known here?"

Ulchakh glanced sideways. "It is more important he remains apart *because* he is known here. If he was among the mangles, it would signify that he *belonged* among them. And that would signify—"

"—that Raam'tu would have an announcement to make about the betrothal of his daughter." Caine smiled. Although the mangles were physically the most alien of Bactradgaria's peoples, their lives were the most familiar. Riordan smiled, momentarily homesick as he let the congenial buzz of the crowd wash through him: here were all the nuances of doting parents and hopeful couples, relatives reunited, old jokes rehashed as the younger generation groaned, busy gossip and furtive glances. Not really so different from gatherings back home, except for the perverse lack of snobbery, dispute, and rancor. Riordan smiled ruefully at the many-featured throng and allowed that, yes, it was just like home—except better.

A modest hush swept over the room as faces turned toward the entry. Riordan expected to see Raam'tu and his family before remembering that, as in all other ways, the durus'maan—the senior worrier—had no greater wealth or status than anyone else. Caine leaned forward, peering around Ulchakh's girth to see what the room was reacting to.

At first, Riordan did not even realize it was Bey striding in, framed at the center of a square formed by her four trogan guards, one on each corner. Indeed, their presence was the first reason Caine knew it was she, because instead of tightly wound braids, her hair was free. It was charcoal black, flowing in waves and curls that lifted slightly as she made her way to the other end of the room.

Only then did he notice that he'd almost never seen her wearing anything other than armor or a convenient, simple hair shift for sleeping. It was not that her new garment was striking—it was little more than a worn hide tunic, cinched at the waist—but that her physique was visible. Her body was muscled, broad, well-shaped—and almost entirely without the soft curves he'd become accustomed to growing up amidst human women. By comparison, even Dora's lithe athletic build seemed delicate. Riordan took care not to look at Bey's face—at least until he could be sure he didn't stare or, just as bad, look quickly away. *You are an officer. She is your subordinate and ally, and you have less than no business—*

Ulchakh poked him in the ribs. "They have given her the *zhadgi*."

"The what?" Riordan glanced at Bey. She had been handed what looked like small cages hung from long straps.

"Zhadgi. Ah, of course: you have never seen fire-spinning."

"Well, we have something like it back on—back home." He studied the zhadgi. "I think those are what we call poi. It's a word from one of the places that Newton lived. Except I don't think I've ever seen one like that. Does the flame burn very hot?"

Ulchakh shook his head. "No, the worry is that it will go out. You have seen how difficult it is to make fires, that we haven't the fuels you say are common in your lands. For fire-spinning, it is often scented tar, but it must be kept moving very rapidly lest the flame dies or becomes too faint to see." He leaned back, arms crossed. "It is strange to think you have never seen fire-spinning, particularly from Bey."

"You have seen her?"

"No, but she was known for it in Forkus. I am told that there were many who came to, eh, admire her as a result of her performances." He frowned at Riordan. "I told you this, not long after we fled—er, left—Forkus."

Had he? Riordan couldn't recall—or maybe, had decided not to remember. "Those were busy times," he offered.

"Busy? I was glad for every day that I didn't wake up inside some beast's belly!" He straightened. "You have a visitor."

Riordan looked up. Bey was approaching. Her gait had changed slightly: still the smooth movements of a swordswoman, but the rhythm had changed slightly and each step was more on the balls of her feet. More like a dancer.

She nodded at Ulchakh, then smiled at Caine. "He has told you of fire-spinning?"

"A bit." *Hell, what do I even say?* "Yes."

She raised an eyebrow as Ulchakh moved off; she slipped into his spot beside Caine. "This will help all the trog-kind, you know."

"In what way?"

"The alliance is something they will understand. It is all they have known."

Riordan laughed. "I thought you were talking about the dance—er, fire-spinning."

She shrugged. "But that is a part of it. The rite is a symbol of joining. That, as do the leaders of two groups, so may their followers drink together, dance together, share furs together." She regarded him with mild surprise. "You are very silent. Particularly for you."

He chuckled. "Thank you for finding a nice way of saying I talk too much."

Her laugh was light, brief. "I am told the same thing by my kind. But trust me, though it may seem strange to you, the trog-kind will see this as allowing them to take mates among your companions or other humans. I know there has been no remedy until now and, fortunately, little need: there are so few females among them. But in time that will change, and knowing that we have performed the rite of sharing trust, they will be less uncertain in expressing their interests in mates who are not trogs. Now I must go. I must speak to my guards before I begin." With a businesslike nod, she adopted her warrior-stride and headed toward the platform.

Riordan was startled out of watching her go by Ulchakh's voice back beside him. "Fire-spinning is a form my kind does not do well; our limbs and body are not shaped for it. But among trogs, particularly the Free Tribes, it has had many significances beyond the honoring of leaders before the rite of sharing trust."

"Wait: so she is honoring herself?"

"By tradition, yes, and you as well. But this is what I mean by all the change you bring. I suspect that in all the history of this world, there has never been a chieftain who spun fire to honor herself!" He shook his head. "No part of that last sentence would have made sense to me a year ago, and yet here I am, uttering it! Still, I am sure she will find a way to shift the focus away from herself: she is a kind person, in spite of her hardness."

Riordan nodded. "How do you think she might shift it? To one of the other significances you mentioned?"

"I hope not!" the h'achga laughed. "The other times fire is spun it is because a tribe member has died or that a female of age is signaling that she is willing to consider the approach of prospective mates. Sometimes it is used for both of those at the same time."

Riordan noticed a new scent in the room, as if musk had been mixed with nutmeg. He raised his head, spotted the source the moment Ulchakh pointed it out: burning tapers inside the cage-poi.

"*Ikli* shell," he explained.

"Shell?"

"Ikli are burrowing insects. Very small. When dried and aged, their carapaces release that scent. Pleasant, is it not?"

Surprisingly, it was—although given the other odors that predominated on Bactradgaria, the threshold for pleasing scents was very low indeed.

Riordan watched as Bey played out the straps—well, tethers—that connected the cage-poi to her wrists. He gauged their length, the wild profusion of her hair—and felt a hint of panic. "Shouldn't she bind her hair, to keep it from—?"

With the conversation in the room fading to a low buzz, Ulchakh made a quiet *tsking* noise to interrupt him. "Friend Caine, that is part of what makes her fire-spinning famous: she takes such challenges in stride." He glanced up. "Welcome, friends!"

Riordan looked away from Bey, discovered Peter standing next to him, a bemused smile on his face. He put one of the mangle ottoman-seats next to Caine. "Distracted, Commodore?"

"Worried that Bey might turn herself into a torch!"

Wu glanced at her. "Something tells me she has done this before. The seat is for you, by the way."

"What?"

Ulchakh muttered from the other side. "Since she is spinning the fire, you are the only leader free to be seated. You are the only one who may. It honors you."

He stepped back. "Look: she begins."

Chapter Forty-One

Bey walked down from the platform, two of the trogans flanking it on either side. Riordan stared: her gait had changed again. It resembled the kind of stately but solid progress he associated with vid portrayals of warrior-queens he'd seen as a kid. Had Bey never walked in these different ways all the time he'd known her, or had he just never noticed?

She stopped, feet planted widely, solidly. The entire chamber grew quiet.

"It is customary," she began, "that fire is spun when a new leader is made." She nodded to the trogans. "They bear the responsibility to carry that out, on behalf of those who have expressed that wish in the presence of an oathkeeper. Let anyone who doubts this, now ask."

After waiting through five silent seconds, she lowered her head slightly. "In better circumstances, someone other than me would spin the fire, thus signaling that all gathered recognize Caine Riordan as the leader of his people, and me the leader of mine. Alas, that there is no one here to spin but me. It is an act of necessity, and I am not prideful in the doing of it.

"That is why I spin not just for approaching events, but to remember one whose death could not be remembered with any flames before those I spin today."

Her voice caught; she paused long enough to control it. "I spin for he who was my friend, my fur-mate, and my father-of-the-heart.

His name was Zaatkhur. He gave his life to save others he barely knew. In these flames, and through my sweat, may you glimpse a faint shadow of his great spirit."

She let a moment pass before she started the weighted poi moving in slow, rolling circles. As their tempo increased, so did the brightness of the flames and the sound of their whirring. It was surprisingly peaceful, or at least serene, and Riordan found himself relaxing into the steady, comforting pattern.

Just in time to be startled by an explosive change in Bey's movements and the increasingly violent arcs of fire that struck gleams from her bared teeth. There were moments it seemed that the tethers had to become tangled, that they would set her flying hair ablaze, that the whining cages would snap free and slay those who hemmed her in. Instead, at every point when the frenzied orbits of fire seemed about to finally stabilize, they raised gasps of surprise as their speed and force increased yet again.

Until, with a suddenness that seemed to defy whatever notions of gravity were coded into Riordan's brain, the rings of fire decelerated into twin stars that began to follow and even parallel each other, fading along with the diminished rush of air moving through the cages and over the flame. What had been mad, furious patterns bordering on asynchrony and disaster had eased into a dance of the spheres.

From this emerged new patterns—daring, soaring, impossible—that moved toward hints of supernal freedom, as if tracing the flickering wings of angels in a place as far removed from Bactradgaria as heaven was from mortals. The fiery arcs and her movements became increasingly fluid, sensual, as if both poi and dancer existed only to express their existence through each other and needed no justification other than that: simply to be.

Caine was not sure how much time had passed—it could have been minutes or hours—but as the tempo changed again, he felt a foreshadow of the finale. But it was an end that gestured toward a beginning, toward an existence that was far beyond binary values such as life and death, joy and grief. The easy flow of the cycles of fire became a pair of glowing waves pursuing each other through midair, Bey following behind.

Then, in a feat that owed as much to extraordinary athleticism as it did to inspiration, Bey appeared to not just chase the fire but catch up with it. In a penultimate burst of power and high leaps, she seemed to run alongside it, racing the flames to the ends of the earth and beyond. Far, far beyond.

With a single mighty twist, the cages swirled down in a complex pattern, smoking as they did. The tethers whined and twined around each other so swiftly that the flames went out and the motion was stilled—all in the time it took to utter two gasps.

Bey turned—chest and back heaving, limbs glistening—and waited as the trogans came slowly forward, ready to confirm her as chief. As they did, a thunder of stamping began to swell. Riordan glanced around, understood: because not all mangles had hands, they applauded with their feet.

Riordan started when Peter's voice prompted, "Sir, you should start thinking about going up to the platform."

Caine was about to comply, suddenly realized he couldn't. "Not right now." *At least, not without causing a scene. And maybe some very awkward laughter.*

Miles looked around Peter's shoulder, concerned. "Why the delay, sir?"

Riordan turned to look at them, hoped that his stare was sufficiently stern, yet pleading. "I really shouldn't stand up just yet."

"Sir, is something wrong?"

"In a manner of speaking." When they continued to stare at him, he rolled his eyes. "I found Bey's performance a little too . . . compelling."

Miles, the first to catch on, had the good grace not to glance downward to confirm his hypothesis. "You should have worn a space suit; conceals all *sorts* of embarrassments. Sir." He chortled. "We'll be back in a bit. And Commodore?"

"Yes?"

"Good to know you're human."

Hoping no one noticed as he inched one leg strategically higher, Riordan sighed. "Right now, I'm all *too* human, Chief. Carry on."

Bey bowed deeply as she took Raam'tu's gift into her own hands: a scabbarded shortsword that he claimed had been bestowed with shamanic charms. It was a little early to be congratulating her on becoming chief, but she appreciated the confidence of the gesture. As she returned to the platform, she saw that Riordan had finally seated himself at his table. His smile dispelled any suspicions that he had become less eager to embrace a future as allies.

Bey gestured toward the youngest of the trogans to bring forward the clay pitcher in which the mangles had readied the ritual drink. Before taking her own seat, she stole a glance toward Riordan.

He had not even tried to speak to her since the trogans had finished the rather tiresome process of repeating the same proclamation four times. If anything, he seemed uncomfortable even being seated on the same platform.

Which made less than no sense to her. Although she had been careful—very careful—not to look at him as she spun the fire, she had peripherally seen that his eyes had been upon her the entire time. She was fairly sure he had not even blinked. That is not the behavior of a male who is disinterested.

She looked away from him quickly, lest he notice she was staring. *You are not here to find a mate. You are here to become chief and lead your people. You are here to work with the humans to free as many of us as possible from the x'qai. That is* all *that matters.*

And yet...

Males didn't watch females that way unless they were interested in them. Nor was it the first time she'd felt Riordan watching her in that fashion. *And why should he not? I am strong, I am healthy, I am very nearly as tall as he is! He should be so lucky to have me return his interest!*

But then why in the name of death itself am I so concerned with what he thinks of me? That is of no consequence compared to our duties as—

"Chief Bey!"

The voice of her senior trogan, Kogwhé, startled her—partly because she had fallen into the bottomless pool of her own thoughts, and partly because it was the first time anyone had addressed her as "Chief." She awoke out of her distraction, smiled at Kogwhé... and discovered his jaw was rigid and his eyes hard. "Chief Bey, I regret that my first report to my chief should disappoint her."

She waved away his concern. "What troubles you, Kogwhé?" Then she realized that the pitcher of the ritual drink for the leaders had not arrived yet.

"The humans, my chief. They have taken the drink."

"What?" Had it been anyone but Riordan's Crewe, she might have suspected a subtle attempt to undermine the solemnity of the proceedings. After all, she was not only a female chief, but had been placed in the awkward position of having to perform her own fire-spinning.

But no, although the Crewe had intercepted the pitcher, they weren't drinking from it. As she'd suspected, they were examining it. She rose. It was a very different kind of insult, but it was an insult, nonetheless. "Come with me," she tossed over her shoulder at Kog-whé. "Do not do anything without express instructions from me."

By the time she'd finished uttering the orders, they'd closed half the distance. Peter Wu and Miles O'Garran looked up as she approached—and were smiling, completely unaware of their offense. *Typical.*

"My fellow Leaders," she said, stopping in front of them, "I regret to intervene, but we require that pitcher. It is part of the ritual."

Their smiles dropped away at her tone. "That's what the trogan who fetched it told us," Miles answered with a steady nod. "And we'll get it to you right away."

"Leader O'Garran, I require it now. Why do you object?" *If you dare accuse me of—*

She didn't get a chance to finish the thought. Peter Wu leaned in gently. "Chief Bey, firstly congratulations from all of us. In answer to your question, we have sent Sergeant Girten to bring one of our, er, artifacts. The chemical analyzer."

"We need to test it," O'Garran explained with the bluntness she expected from him.

"It has nothing to do with you, Bey," Dora added. "But what's in that pitcher didn't come from our stash, er, supplies. So there's no knowing what might be in it."

Bey straightened to her full height, which left her looking far down at the two shortest men in the Crewe and gave her a full half-head over Dora. "You do not need to know what is in it, because *I* know."

Miles rubbed the back of his close-shorn head. "No offense, ma'am, but I don't think you have a reliable way to test if something's been poisoned. Well, not without drinking it."

"Which is exactly what I did, first thing this morning. No one but my guard has touched that vessel since."

Peter's eyes widened. "Why did you do that? You could have been kil—at grave risk!"

You and your obsessions with risk! she wanted to shout in their faces. But instead she chose to give them a lesson in manners that most trog children learned before they could walk. "To test the ritual drink in front of the mangles who prepared it for us would have been a terrible insult. It demonstrates that we believe there may be assassins among them and further, that they lack the competence to detect and remove such traitors." She watched their reactions to both points; they clearly understood, even looked embarrassed—but she saw no change in their resolve.

"Or is it that you don't trust *me*?" She knew she was daring them to cross a disastrous line, but didn't care one drop of caver piss what the outcome would be.

It was Dora who stepped forward to face—confront?—her directly. Her tone told Bey which: it was as calm and patient and diplomatic as anything that had ever come out of Veriden's mouth. "Bey, please, we have a duty to our commander. You have to understand that. You've seen us doing it—whether he knew it or not—countless times."

Which was true, but it did not help. However, the fact that it was Pandora who'd stepped forward, and was seeking cooperation rather than confrontation, was a singular opportunity.

"Pandora," she said, gentling her own tone and nodding slightly, "I ask you, please: trust me. And if not by the dangers and battles and camp circles we have shared, then by this." Bey tapped the tattoo on her forehead. "If I am false in this, it is not merely a lie, but a mortal betrayal. I am as good as dead—and before I could leave this chamber." She saw Veriden's eyes start to relent—but not enough.

"And I would welcome that same death if I were ever, in *any* way, responsible for Cai—Leader Caine's death." As she said it, she stared—hard, but also pleading—at the human. *See my eyes, Dora. Do not just look into, but* see *them!*

For the slightest moment, Pandora Veriden's brow bent toward a confused frown—then her eyes widened as if something had appeared out of thin air, right in front of her. She leaned away, eyes still wide, and nodded slowly. "She's okay," Dora muttered sideways to O'Garran. "Bey wouldn't lie to begin with. But sure as hell, not about *this*."

"What? But—"

Dora's voice acquired an edge: not hot, but cold. "Trust me; she's okay. Call it a woman's intuition, if you like." Then she hastened away, casting one glance behind at Bey, a hint of a smile fighting up through the surprise lingering on her face.

As Miles extended the pitcher outward, Polsolun stepped in from the adjoining group around Cruvanor and Tirolane. With a glance at the two stunned Crewe members, he asked, "Chief Bey, with respect, can you tell me which of the mangles prepared the ritual drink?" Seeing her frown, he held up a pausing hand. "I have no doubt of their loyalty, but, well, we are familiar with the different ways such drinks are made. It would be of interest to learn what they use in Ebrekka."

Bey did not like doing so, but in the interest of conceding on so minor a point, and given the crisis that had been averted, she nodded even as she gestured her junior guard over to reclaim the pitcher. As Miles prepared to surrender it, she discovered that she was once again able to see past his bluff pugnacity to what lay below: intense loyalty and concern.

As the pitcher left his unwilling hands, she leaned in. "Leader Miles," she murmured, "please be at ease. A cup of this is not only harmless, but often helpful. I would not allow Leader Caine to come to harm. That is why I tested it once it was out of the sight of our hosts."

His expression was grateful, but also, slightly curious at her words. "If you say so, Bey—I mean, Chief."

She smiled at him and followed the pitcher bearer back to the platform.

Riordan stared at the ritual drink of sharing trust as it was poured into a clay cup. The cup was a treat regardless of what it held. He'd never become entirely comfortable drinking out of bone-worked mugs that were often too reminiscent of skulls—probably because most of them had started out that way. But as for the drink itself...

He glanced over at Bey, who smiled and raised her own cup. "To sharing trust," she said with a cadence that suggested it, too, was part of the ritual.

"To sharing trust," he answered.

She watched him for movement, leaned over and whispered,

"You are the much greater leader. It is you who has the honor of drinking first."

He smiled. "I say to hell with tradition."

She smiled. "I like that idea. How do we send tradition to hell?"

He chuckled at her reworking of the colloquial oath. "We drink together on the count of three. And we count together, too."

She positively beamed. "One..."

They finished counting down together and on three, put the cups to their mouths and drank.

Riordan was the first to finish his share and just barely resisted the impulse to slam it down on the table. Firstly, it might be considered disrespectful. Secondly, it might shatter the clay cup. He was also too distracted by the taste of the liquor: it was even worse than most of what he'd sampled on Bactradgaria. It recalled the nastiest shot of mezcal he'd ever had—largely because he discovered the worm too late.

He put the cup down carefully and turned to smile at Bey.

She was looking at him in a mix of shock and horror. Her cup was still near her lips. She had, at most, sipped from it.

Okay, so this is not *like drinking with Russians.* "Sorry. Did I just break a ritual taboo?"

She shook her head. "N-no, not at all. But perhaps we should dance now."

"Yes, best get that over with," he agreed, realizing that was also not the most diplomatic reply that had ever come out of his mouth.

As they rose, he saw that she meant to meet him at the center of the platform before stepping down. Well, that certainly made sense. As they prepared to descend, he murmured sideways, "I presume this dance is fairly simple? That if it was complicated, you would have shown me the steps?"

Her chuckle ended as a giggle. "Yes, you are correct. You worry about a great many things."

"Well, maybe," he replied as they stepped forward to the same space in which she had spun fire. "But in this case, my only worry is not to insult your traditions."

She glanced over at him. "Yes. I know. I am sorry I teased you."

He grinned. "Don't mind it at all. Shall we dance?"

Riordan realized why she had found his concern so amusing. To say the ritual dance was simple would be a bit like describing water as being "slightly wet." It was not only slow, but it involved no touching or coordinated action at all. It was just two people following the same, very predictable steps. Which, Caine reflected, was probably the only kind of dance two glowering trog gang leaders were willing to do with each other: one that did not require any learning or physical contact.

And yet, he once again became intensely aware of Bey's movement. It was not just that she was graceful, but every step and movement was sure and strong. No, powerful. If he had to liken her to an animal, he decided it would be a tigress. Her eyes were a bit similar to those of a great cat, also—which, he realized were widening and glancing at the place where they had started the dance. *Ah, so we end as we began.* As he'd expected, the final steps were a simple reversal of their first, except that when they stopped, she turned toward him. He did the same.

And she smiled. Good grief, how she smiled! *Have her teeth always been so bright and strong?* As she nodded faintly toward their chairs, Caine couldn't remember if he'd had the presence of mind to smile back at her. He hoped he had.

As he sat, he picked up his cup, remembered it was empty, smiled beatifically—he hoped—at the trogan with the pitcher, who dutifully poured half a measure into it. He turned to Bey, raised his cup, noticed her do the same—albeit with a slight frown and apparent reluctance. He sipped before asking her, "Is it something I said?"

Her frown became bewilderment. "But we have not spoken since before the dance."

Well, whatever else might be universal, that tired old chestnut certainly isn't. Just as well, probably. Hell, the last time I heard that—

His mental attempt to locate "the last time" went sideways, stuttered like a broken video, spewed images:

Annapolis. Indonesia. Opal bleeding out in Jakarta. Elena backstabbed by a Ktor. Knowing he'd been killed the same way. His fault. Awakening from cold sleep—again, and again, and again. Gasping what should have been his last breaths on Disparity. Lost Soldiers dying by the dozens. His fault. Elena. Connor on their sloop. A smile as big as Bey's. As big as Elena's. As big as every sun-bleached skull he'd seen in Virtua. On Bactradgaria. His fault. Elena. His fault. All his—

"Fault!" Riordan said aloud as the room full of strange, mixed, and malformed faces returned, abruptly wiping away the disjointed rush of memories. Most of the mangles weren't even looking in his direction. Everything was going on just as it had before he'd tumbled backwards, fallen into pictures of his past life—

He reached after the images. They and the feelings attached to them slipped through his mental grasp, bled away like watercolors in rain. They'd been so vivid a moment ago, but now...

He glanced over at Bey.

She was staring at him, face stiff with worry and uncertainty. "Woo," he murmured across the gap between them. "This drink has a strange kick." On the other hand, it didn't taste so bad any more.

"Leader Caine," she said as he took another very small sip. It was as if he were hearing her words a full second after she uttered them. Her voice was—had been?—tense. "Yes?"

"If by saying the drink 'has a kick' you mean that it is strong, then, yes, it is. Very much so."

"Well, I've always had a pretty fair tolerance for alcohol. And it doesn't taste that strong. Or that bad. Anymore."

"Even so, it *is* very strong. This part of the rite is now finished," she added as the four trogans reappeared, bearing what appeared to be rawhide wristlets.

Bey stood. He did the same. A trogan approached each of them with a wristlet. The one who'd been charged with overseeing the pitcher now stood between the first two, his hand on the hilt of his weapon. The last and senior nodded at Caine and then Bey, apparently seeking any sign of reservation or rejection.

He nodded, turned and faced the room. "So long as neither strikes the wristlet from their arms, these two leaders are allies. And so, our peoples are joined even as they are." Under other circumstances, Caine would have asked the trogan to repeat the last sentence; it contained a usage or idiom that either he had never heard or he had forgotten. But the wristlet was placed on his wrist, there was a somber thumping of feet and Bey was signaling that the time had come for them to depart in the midst of the same moving square of trogans which had escorted her in.

Following her lead, he joined her at the center of the platform, stepped down, and made sure that this time, he did remember to smile at her as they made their way to the entrance.

✧ ✧ ✧

Peter turned toward Tirolane, who had joined him and Miles near the door, waiting to see the new allies off as they were led to their shared chamber. "Did the trogan just say what I think he said?"

"It depends. What do you believe you heard?"

Wu stared. "That 'our peoples will be joined once the allies have been joined.' In the conjugal sense of that word."

Tirolane waved a hand at the phrase. "That is an old usage, usually reserved for new mates among the Free or Wild Tribes, and only those in which exclusively paired mates are predominant." He shrugged. "Here, and in the context of the rest of the diction, it is merely symbolic."

"Still, could it be taken, well, the other way?"

Tirolane's first answer was a dubious pout. "I do not think so. At least no one in this setting would hear it as you mean. But 'could' it?" His new shrug only required one shoulder. "We are speaking of trog-ways, Friend Peter. They have no laws beyond those traditions that each tribe decides to follow according to their own fashion. From that perspective, far be it from me to declare anything *im*possible."

Miles shook his head. "And you didn't think to say anything about that ahead of time?"

Tirolane smiled. "You gentlemen believe me far more expert in the ways of trogs than I am. Unless you believe Bey has intentionally misled you, there is no cause for concern. If such a strange thing were to be the case, it would not stand. The only true bond forged in this ceremony was one of allies, and that can be severed as easily as those wristlets."

"Well, I guess that's sort of reassuring," O'Garran muttered as Bey and Caine approached, surrounded by the trogans.

"It should be. And if it is not, would that be such a bad thing after all?" He stepped out of the chamber before the procession reached them. "I bid you both a good night."

As the new allies passed them, Caine was set to exit on the opposite side of the entry and, to Peter's eyes, looked very distracted. He was attempting to discern the finer details of the commodore's behavior when he felt a hand on his arm.

It was Bey, who glanced at the senior trog who was next to pass. She nodded at Wu before exiting the chamber.

The trogan stopped long enough to pass a small vial into

Peter's hand as he muttered, "If Leader Caine experiences ill-effects tomorrow, this draught will help." And then he, too, was gone.

Peter looked at the vial, then at Miles—and nearly jumped when Polsolun came up behind him. "Cruvanor was right," the warrior panted. "The mangles made the ritual drink from this." He opened his palm just long enough to reveal what looked like a squashed polyp.

"Is that poison?" Miles muttered through his teeth.

"No, no! It is the source of the extract used in the ritual drink."

"What? The drink isn't alcohol?"

"Mostly, yes, but this is added to it."

"And what is it, exactly?"

"It is a fungus, despite its appearance. You have had experience with it, but not in drink."

"Then in what?"

Peter nodded, understanding. "In the local painkillers. This is probably what they had on hand in the hovel when Eku was so badly wounded."

"It was also used to treat Tirolane after the battle at the barge. And most recently, you yourself, Peter Wu. But there are two differences."

Miles cross his arms. "Which are?"

"Concentration," Peter guessed. "And possibly different varieties that are more likely to induce sleep and pain relief."

"Yes," Polsolun agreed, "but also, the strength of this particular form of the fungus. Mangles are masters of cultivating them, living underground as they do. Their fungi are said to be the most powerful, but for most, that is mere rumor and hearsay. However, Cruvanor encountered some as black market products, long ago. He became concerned." Polsolun stared after the receding procession. "He says he would be very surprised if Bey was aware of the difference."

Peter looked at the vial in his hand. "So this is . . . what? An antidote?"

"I do not know, although it was almost certainly provided by the mangles as well."

Miles shook his head. "It's hair of the dog, whatever else you might call it."

Peter shook his head, started toward the entry. "We've got to tell Caine, warn him—"

Miles' hand was on his arm. "What good would it do to warn him, Lieutenant? And do you really want to crash their downtime in the 'shared chamber' and ruin the rite? Because if you do, then Bey won't be a chief for the ceremony tomorrow. So maybe this time we take a page from the commodore's book: focus on the bigger mission, which means making sure the alliance is secured."

"But if the effects of the fungus"—Peter had almost said "mushrooms"—"are particularly severe—"

"Then they'll let us know. But I'm betting the trogan passed you that vial not because there's anything to worry about, but because Riordan is going to have a hell of a high-concept hangover. And he's got to be bright-eyed and bushy tailed if he's going to be one of the formal witnesses of your splitting-rock trick tomorrow night."

Miles put his hand on Wu's shoulder. "Lieutenant, there's no use shutting the barn door after the cows have left. They know where to find us. And as for the commodore?" O'Garran smiled ruefully. "To borrow a phrase from some of the later-century Lost Soldiers, he's now on his very own magic carpet ride. Might as well let him enjoy the trip."

Peter glared as the SEAL smiled around the word "trip." "That was a lousy pun, Chief. Even for you."

O'Garran just grinned wider. "I live for those moments, Lieutenant. C'mon, let's not be the last ones in the joint when they start stacking the chairs."

Chapter Forty-Two

Bey shook her head when the trogan proffered the pitcher, but, seeing her cup in his other hand, she took it back for a moment and drank. She nodded thanks for his help and patience before releasing the hide curtain behind her.

There were two more such hangings along the taper-lit dog-legs that led to the ritual sleeping chamber. When she reached the final and thickest hanging, she pushed it aside along with a sudden reluctance and planted herself just over the threshold, surveying the room.

It was lit by two larger tapers, each one on a low table alongside the separate piles of their own sleeping furs, one on either side of the chamber. As she'd requested of Ne'sar, Caine's furs were heaped atop a large, bagged mass of hair and old hide strips. Humans called it a mattress, and were said to prefer sleeping on them. She wasn't sure if that was because it was more comfortable or because it had become a traditional fixture and sign of prestige among them. Regardless, it had occurred to her that Caine might have slept on one in Tasvar's fortress and come to prefer it. If not, he could always toss the furs on the floor to sleep in the normal fashion.

Riordan was sitting on the heavy hide rug that lined the expanse of wall between the two piles of furs, holding one of the room's true extravagances in his hands: a cushion. It took a long moment for him to notice her. Clearly, the ritual drink had slowed his usually swift reflexes.

He smiled, held up the cushion. "Do they think we're royalty?"

She smiled back. "This night we are," she proclaimed as she joined him on the rug and scooped up a cushion of her own. She glanced toward his sleeping furs. "Is that arrangement to your liking?"

He followed her eyes. "Well, I *think* so." His quick backward glance was uncertain. "Is that a mattress?"

Is that, too, so different from what you have in your homeland? "It is our version of it. Or so I am told."

"It looks very comfortable," he hurried to assure her.

She rolled her eyes but smiled as she did. "Leader Caine, you are a very poor liar."

"I try not to be a liar at all," he answered with sudden, and maddening, earnestness. But what he said next was both a relief and unexpectedly exciting. "Bey, you must start calling me Caine, now. Just Caine. On a battlefield . . . well, that's different. But we were just joined as allies." He chuckled. "I think that puts us on a first-name basis, don't you?"

"I do," Bey replied, surprised to find that she could feel her pulse in her temples and neck. "But I am never certain of what is proper when I am with you and those of the Crewe."

"Well, let's talk about that. Because when we wake up tomorrow, people should be able to see that our interactions are different: more casual, more familiar."

She only nodded; the conversation was moving in the best possible direction. *Or maybe the worst!* She decided not to risk diverting it.

"So," Riordan concluded, "what is it about us that confuses you the most?"

"Everything!" she replied through a laugh. He joined her, smiled encouragingly. "I think it is your kajh—well, soldier-females—that I have the hardest time understanding. Leader Tagawa—eh, Ayana—explained some of it, but I still do not perceive how your people manage to reproduce."

Riordan blinked. "Uh . . . reproduce? What does that have to do with female—women—soldiers?"

"How can it not? Your fema—women fight as close to the enemy as the most daring male warriors. Yet they still show moon sign. How is it that they may bear young and fight? I do not understand how your people manage this."

Riordan looked even more lost, and also, a bit more influenced by the drink. "Moon sign?" he repeated.

Truly, you have had too much of the drink! "The time of their greatest fertility."

"Ah," he responded. He'd clearly never heard the term before.

But if he doesn't know what it means—"Did Ayana not tell you about the restrictions that are placed upon female kajhs?"

He nodded uncertainly. "She told me that female kajhs are not allowed to have children."

Stars and moons! "And is that *all* she said?"

Riordan nodded again, his eyes unsteady. "She spoke to me just an hour before the deciqadi attacked. We were both coming off duty and needed sleep. We were supposed to speak again, but with all that went on afterward..." He shrugged.

Bey clenched her hands into fists, willed her growing fury to flow into them and nowhere else. *Will nothing with the strange humans ever work correctly or be simple?* Worst of all, there wasn't really anyone to blame, since details about the lives of female kajhs had hardly been an urgent matter in the wake of the attack. But now, Riordan *had* to know; becoming the ally of female kajh had ramifications of which neither he nor any of the other Crewe seemed to be aware.

Her hands still balled into tight, pale fists, she muttered, "It is not that female kajhs are not allowed to have children. It is that we *cannot* have children."

His mouth sagged open. At any other time, she would probably have chuckled. "What?"

She had to close her eyes as she explicated, "We are *physically unable* to have children."

He shook his head: not in negation, but as if a fly had become trapped in his ear. "I think you'd better explain how that happens." He looked up, almost sorrowful. "And why. And how that relates to mating and fur-mates and, well, everything."

Just one minute ago, I was looking forward to a personal conversation with him. Now I am dreading it. She squared her shoulders, took a deep breath, and began.

As with Ayana, it turned out to be easier than she thought, probably because she had rehearsed the basic explanation dozens of times. Once she realized that the attitudes toward female warriors was different with the new humans, she knew that at some point, she would have to address it. And as her leaders, it was their right to insist that she was the one to educate them, not the other way around.

Happily, Riordan not only followed the logic of this aspect of trog-ways, but asked intelligent questions and was not at all offended when he misunderstood or made incorrect conjectures. Better still, he clearly understood that she was uncomfortable having to be the source of the information; his tone and expression was always one of encouragement, even compassion.

Still, as she completed her explanation, she realized that she had not focused so much on her words, or his, but on Caine's eyes. She watched them for any sign of attitudes that would indicate his opinion of her had changed: pity, scorn, aloofness, dismay, sadness, disinterest. No leader, no matter how minor or foolish, weakened their future fortunes by taking a mate who could not bear kajhs and inheritors, who would fate his line to extinction. Males *did* seek them for rutting, yes: often eagerly. But among trog chiefs vying for power, and eager for the support of young warriors who had the same blood in their veins, a female had no place except that which she could carve out for herself.

But she detected none of the reactions she dreaded to see in Caine's eyes. He simply listened carefully, which seemed to sober him, and at the end, asked, "I am very glad to know this, but I still do not understand why you felt it necessary—urgent, even—to tell me this right now."

It took a moment before she realized, *Now* I *am the one who is speechless.* "We are allies. If you agreed to that in the hope that I might mate advantageously and bring greater strength to our alliance, or"—*say it, quickly!*—"or if you had such an interest in me for your own line, then I am duty bound to inform you that I can bear no young." He nodded calmly. "This is a very important political consideration among trog-kind. And among free humans as well."

"I understand," he said, still nodding. "But it's not a concern to me. I am pretty certain it's not a concern to any of my companions, either."

She frowned. "But... why? How can that be?"

He smiled. "Now, that would be a very long conversation. The short answer is that very few of us are warriors for a living, and most of us do not remain so to the end of our lives."

"But one cannot cease to be a warrior! Once one chooses the path of the kajh, one is on it unto death!"

His smile widened. "Not among us. Hell, I never thought I'd be a soldier at all."

She shook her head. "This is not possible. You are a leader. I would know it even if I had never seen you wield a weapon or command warriors." She snorted. "I have been a mate with kajhs—many—who were not so clearly a leader as you."

Caine shrugged, but as he did, interest—or maybe curiosity—kindled in his eyes. "I would like to understand more about how kajhs—both male and female—find mates, and what it means to them. If that is too personal a question, I will not—"

She felt her eyebrows rise. "Personal? No, it is so obvious to us that no one would even think to pose it *as* a question." She frowned. "How different can it be? Our bodies are the same. Although if you mean when and whether we mate to rut or to be attached to another...?"

"Yes," he said, "that."

Bey settled back and began explaining. In the process, she found useful examples from her own life. She didn't know exactly where it became less a survey of trog-ways and mating and more a recounting of the many times she'd been in the furs, but by the end, she and Caine were laughing over her many amorous misadventures. She asked finally, "And what of you? It seems that you have experienced much of what I have."

He nodded. "As you said, 'how different can mating be?'" He chuckled again. "How true that is!"

"So," she said, "did most of your matings occur after you became a leader?" She leaned back into the cushions as she let the end of the question roll off her tongue. She ran her fingers over the softness of the hide and had the sudden, heady realization that in the morning, she would awaken to a reality that few female kajh even dared to dream about: she would be a chief. It sent a thrill through her body, which was already warm with many pleasant sensations.

Her ears told her that Caine had begun answering her, but along with the familiar eagernesses that arose with the rutting urge, there were new ones. Being treated effortlessly as an equal while sharing stories with a male human that was so different and strange and attractive were proving to be a new aphrodisiac, almost as powerful as—

Bey felt her body resist the stiffening she imposed upon it. *No: remember why you are here. If there is to be more with Caine, do not rush that union. Do not pay attention to what your body is saying.* Which, she discovered, was far easier to resolve than accomplish.

"Bey, are you well?"

She sat upright quickly. "I believe I am also more affected by the drink than I knew. Please forgive me: I did not hear all of what you said." Where "not all" actually meant "almost nothing."

He smiled. "You didn't miss much. We can talk about it some other—"

"No!" she interrupted. "Please, continue. I am just easily... distracted right now. You were about to tell me how many mates you had in your furs after you became the youngest snowhair I ever met!"

He laughed. "I forgot that term. Well, I seem like a snowhair because of my profession—er, what I did before my country called me to war."

"You mean, being an analyst?"

"Well, yes, I was an analyst. But most analysts don't like speaking in front of other people. Or aren't very good at it. I was comfortable with it. Over time, I spoke before a great many people, and was asked to answer a great many questions."

"Ha!" she said, pointing. "So that *is* how you became a young snowhair! I knew it. Just as I know you had more mates, after that."

Riordan shook his head. "Sorry, but you're wrong, there. In fact, you have it backward."

She sat up, surprised. "What do you mean, I have it backward?"

"I mean that, when I was in college—er, in a special place of learning—I had more 'mates' than later."

At first, Bey suspected he might be joking, but then saw his steady gaze and knew he wasn't. "Yours *is* a strange country," she muttered. *Not to say foolish!* "But those later mates—surely they were superior in every regard."

Riordan's laugh was too sudden to be anything than genuine. "Wrong again! In fact, one of my last mates was the worst! By far!"

"Worst? In what way?"

His smile was suddenly less ready, more rueful. "She wasn't trustworthy. If she was my mate here, I wouldn't feel safe."

"She would kill you in your sleep?" Bey was glad she did not have her dagger handy and that the woman was far away.

"Well, not literally—but, figuratively, yes." He chuckled. "Toward the end, she might actually have been willing to slip a knife in between my ribs because I had the nerve not to chase her whenever she became distant."

Bey frowned, not understanding. "Chase her? Oh! So you were supposed to ravish her!"

Riordan's expression turned to horror. "Good God, no! We were partners—well, mated, you'd say—but I learned that she had manipulated earlier mates the same way. I put up with it for a while, thought she might feel differently about our relationship. But either she didn't or she couldn't trust me. Or maybe herself." He shrugged. "It wasn't until later that I discovered how many lies she'd told about herself, her past, her feelings. Hell, she'd even changed her name."

"And what was wrong with her original name?"

"Well," Riordan said with a bit of sympathy creeping into his voice, "her parents didn't do her any favor in that department. I doubt any baby girl had been named 'Ethel' in half a century. Maybe more." He sighed, leaned back. "Either way, she was a walking disaster. Almost got me killed. Didn't mean to, but she wouldn't listen to sense."

"What became of her?"

"She got herself into a dangerous situation. I warned her, tried to help her. She didn't—or couldn't let herself—believe me." Riordan shrugged.

Bey nodded solemnly. It seemed that Caine's strange homeland had its own share of dangers. "So, after Ethel, who was your next mate?"

Riordan's face softened and saddened. "Her name was Elena."

Bey nodded, saw Caine's eyes empty as if every bit of awareness had drained into a vast pool of memory within. Although she desperately wanted to hear the tale, she said, "I do not wish you to dwell upon sad things, Caine."

He shrugged; she couldn't tell if the nonchalance was genuine or feigned. "It's not so much sad as it's a long story. A very long story. And pretty convoluted."

"Well," Bey observed, "we do have all night."

He smiled weakly. "Yes, but you think I talk too much as it is. Besides, we should also get some sleep."

Bey relaxed back into the cushions with a shrug of her own. "We shall see." Far bolder answers clamored to get past her lips. She tried to ignore the images those unspoken replies conjured, failed, pressed for him to return to the topic most likely to douse them, to wash away any chance that they would return.

"Tell me about Elena," Bey said.

Chapter Forty-Three

Riordan pushed back the fear that rose in response to Bey's simple request. *Tell you about Elena? So after almost half a year of trying to leave those thoughts behind, I get to reopen the scars all over again?*

He couldn't tell if Bey's incipient frown was in response to whatever look was on his face or a growing concern that he was shutting her out: that she was "just a crog."

Caine licked his suddenly dry lips. "There's so much to tell. Maybe it's better if you just ask me questions." *And maybe that way I can keep those old scars from gapping so wide that I bleed out all over this nice hide rug.*

Bey remained well back upon the cushions. "Where is Elena?"

"She's dead, but we could not recover her body."

Bey's expression became very somber, respectful. "If you do not know the location of her body, how can you know that she is dead?"

Riordan nodded. "Because there is no way she could be alive. It is rather like someone who goes on the ship that travels to the middle of an empty ocean. Then you find wreckage of the ship, but no bodies. It was like that with her; the way she died would have left no trace of her body. She was in an artifact that kept her alive despite very serious wounds. But a sickness grew out of those wounds and became so dire that she never awoke. She either slept away or her body was allowed to fail. The records we found do not say which. But they make it quite clear that she did not survive. I only hope that when she passed, it was painless."

Bey had straightened, leaned forward. "Your voice—did you learn this just recently?"

Damn, how do I explain that? "In a manner of speaking, yes. After a long search. We actually met a long time before she was injured, but we spent very little of that time together. Shortly after we mated, I was put into a very long sleep."

Bey recoiled. "You mean, like a calluskin?"

"No, no!" *Well, now that you mention it...* "The sleep I am talking about is not a trance. It is the work of an artifact like the one she was in. It slows the processes of one's body and makes it so cold that it does not decay even though years may pass."

"And how much time passed between meeting Elena and seeing her again?"

"Thirteen years."

Bey shuddered. "I would not submit myself to such an artifact."

"I didn't want to, either. But the first two times I was placed in it, I wasn't given a choice."

Bey's eyes widened. "The *first two* times? How many times have you been imprisoned in this terrible object?"

She grew increasingly horrified as Caine had to think back and count—which wasn't helped by whatever had been in the ritual drink. Every time he touched on a memory, his mind pulled the rest of him down like a sudden ocean undertow, determined to drag him out of the present. "Five times," he answered finally. "And about as many times again—but those were just a few weeks each—while the Crewe and I tried to find her.

"In the middle of all that, I realized that I had to become a soldier. When our country was invaded, so much happened so fast that first I became a kind of diplomat. Then I was given a military rank that I never deserved. It took almost two years before I was awake—and alone—long enough to learn enough about the many artifacts and wars, strategy and tactics of both the past and the present. It didn't make me a true soldier, but it was a start."

Bey looked like she might be at the edge of vertigo. "And so when you finished that, you finally took Elena as your mate?"

"No. Elena was wounded shortly after I was made an officer and was put into the cold-sleep artifact. We were pledged to each other in our hearts, but never had the chance to marry." Bey's frown at that unfamiliar word prompted Caine to add, "To marry is to become lifemates."

Bey frowned, nodded. "So your leaders used the sleep artifact to stop her wounds along with her body. They hoped she could still be healed."

Damn, she's a quick study! But Riordan only nodded. "And she was taken to another, um, country that has better healers than our own."

"So you and the Crewe journeyed there?"

He shook his head. "Not until much later. We were still at war." *Sort of.* "By the time it ended, I had no way to follow her trail. I had been stripped of my rank and lost my ship."

Bey leaned forward, chin on her fist. "'Stripped of your rank': what does that mean?"

Riordan shrugged. "It means I was accused of a crime and forbidden from serving beneath the banners of my nation."

Bey's dark, straight eyebrows rose sharply at this news. "And what did you do to warrant this punishment?"

"A band of my country's warriors were marooned in another country where they had to fight for their very survival. My leaders sent me to retrieve them. After a bloody battle, I brought them back to our borders where many war leaders had gathered. Most insisted that I turn those warriors over to them, yet would not guarantee fair treatment or a fair trial. I told them I would not turn over the warriors unless those assurances were given. When my leaders refused, I arranged for the ship of a friendly country to take the warriors—and my Crewe—to safety."

"And you remained behind?"

Riordan nodded. "I hoped to convince my leaders to change their minds. They did not." He shrugged. "Still, it was my duty to try."

"And for this they called you a criminal?" Bey had reared back, eyes bright, wide, and very angry. "Your leaders were the criminals, not you!"

Caine managed a smile. "You're not the first to say so."

"And they found you guilty?"

"No, but those who felt I was had enough influence to force the others to take away my rank. Worse, my Crewe and the warriors we rescued could not return to our country."

She shook her head. "So what did you do then?"

"I went home. I spent two happy years with my son."

"A son!" She spoke through a long, relieved exhale. "So, you finally took a mate, at least for a while."

"Actually, Elena gave birth to our son during my first, longest sleep, so he was almost a young man when we met. We had to live incognito, for it was thought that many of the leaders who deemed me guilty might try to send assassins. Which they did, when they finally found me."

"What did you do?"

He shrugged. "After making sure that my son would be safe, my friends among the leaders helped me journey to the country where Elena had been taken in the artifact. But it was a strange land, with almost no humans in it at all, and the other species did not help me. But my Crewe followed me there, and together we followed Elena's trail to the very end. At which point the captain of the ship we were on betrayed us. As we were fighting back, the ship was crippled and we landed on these shores."

Bey nodded, still digesting the mad flurry of events. "Then why have you not taken another mate? You are no longer beneath the banners of your country. Surely you are free to do as you wish. I mean no disrespect, but all the trog-kind are aware that Leaders Bannor and Ayana are mated."

Riordan nodded. "The lower one's rank, the fewer the rules there are about mating. But the higher the rank, the more rules there are. The highest rank must usually refrain."

Bey shook her head. "This sounds very, well, unhealthy."

Riordan grinned. "Again, you are not the first one to say it. But it is how all of us were trained, and there is reason to follow those rules when one is in a place where battles are frequent."

"And you feel these rules are wise?"

Riordan shrugged. "They were set by snowhairs who were deemed quite wise." He smiled. "That is not to say that all, or any, of their decisions were enduring examples of great wisdom."

Her smile mirrored his. "So, Caine, you are a leader of renegades." She looked at him with newfound approval—and interest. "It is strange to hear."

"Why?"

"Because all your actions here are so shaped by rules, yet you are here because you broke those of your own country." She shook her head. "And you would have me believe that, in all the years since you were last with Elena, you have not had a mate?"

Riordan smiled, worried that he might have blushed. "Well, yes, that's true."

She leaned forward, almost shouted. "Gods! Did you never feel the needs of your body?"

He forced himself to laugh. "Oh, I felt them." He cast about for a quip—anything to forget all the years that had passed, and to distract him from Bey's bright teeth and eyes. "Of course," he finally muttered, "I *did* spend a lot of the time asleep." Her eyes were utterly disbelieving and yet utterly accepting of him. The combination made him look away for fear of—what?

Bey's voice was as gentle as it had been loud. "Caine, I have seen you are troubled. I have seen it many times before tonight. Many times before you spoke of how you hate the dawn in these lands."

Caine shook his head—for whose benefit, he was unsure. "I wouldn't say I'm troubled. Not exactly."

"Then what would you call this feeling that gnaws at you?"

"It's the feeling that, although I'm working hard to become accustomed to this life, I can't be sure I ever will."

"You mean, you will never become accustomed from being exiled from your homeland?"

"No. I'm not sure that I can become used to what this journey has taught me: that the very notion of closure is an illusion."

Bey frowned. "Explain what these words mean to you."

Riordan shrugged, but had to look away from her again. "Things happen. People are lost without a trace. You look for them and wind up so far away from home that you don't know if you can ever return.

"But none of those answers are final. Any of them might change if you only persevere one more day. And then another and another. But you can't live in hope of the next day forever. Because if you do, you never move on."

She stared at him with a small, doubtful smile. "And you are just learning this now?

He smiled. "No, I already know it. But *reconciling* myself to it? That's very different. There's a whole life we left behind but I have no way of knowing whether we can get back to it: whether the next day will get us there, or will be just another one we've wasted. But I can't show that uncertainty to the Crewe."

"Why?"

"Because if we don't keep believing we can return home, we *never* will. So as the leader, I can't share my own doubts."

"And yet...?"

How did you know there was an "And yet..." at the end of that sentence, Bey? "And yet, as time goes on, common sense says you have to start spending more energy on the world you're in than getting back to the one you left behind. But still, I have to exhort us to do *both* every day... and I'll never know if I've struck the right balance."

Bey was looking at him over steepled fingers. "Everything that lives does so by moving its focus and energy from what was to what is. That is what you are struggling to reconcile: which deserves your new focus most? The life you live here, or the life you lived back there?"

Riordan nodded at her summation. "Particularly since the energy we spend trying to return could not only improve our life here, but save countless others."

She nodded. "In these lands, we reconcile ourselves to such quandaries so young and so fully that they rarely arise in later life. Anything but the present is a luxury we cannot afford. This is particularly true among trog-kind. We learn that if the things of your past no longer exist in your present, they are akin to stones that will drag you down to the bottom of the sea. Because to survive, you must be free to swim to safety in whatever waters you find yourself, at any given moment."

She glanced at him. "Resisting this wisdom is a trait particular to you—by which I mean all humans, not just those of your Crewe. Even those like Cruvanor, who wear the yoke of stable-keeping x'qai, are not so very different. The worlds you humans make for yourselves weigh heavy upon you."

She nodded as she introduced her own caveat. "Those worlds also give much focus and purpose to your actions of the moment. But when you lose what you have built, or gained, or dreamed of, I have seen many of your kind die because they held on to what was already gone. Rather than live to move forward and build anew."

Caine discovered that a tension had left his chest, a tension that had become so constant that he could no longer remember when he'd first felt it. "Thank you, Bey, both for listening to my words and sharing yours." He smiled. "I can't tell you what it means to discuss these things out loud, to feel that I'm not alone with them."

She inclined her head. "I am glad." She smiled. "Just sitting here this night, we have already spoken more than I did with any of my mates, even those with whom I shared furs for many months."

Caine became acutely aware of her aroma and her breath. "But to talk so little over such a long time... didn't you miss it?"

"Yes, but many of them had little to say. Besides, that is the past." Her eyes were very fixed upon his. "It is strange to think that it is *words* that make you feel less alone, rather than the touch of another."

Riordan smiled. "Oh, I never said *that*." He'd meant to put a humorous spin on his reply, but either failed or forgot to do so.

"That is true," she murmured. "You never did say that." She smiled, settled back on the cushions, but nearer than before. "And now that we are allies—that we have been joined—there will be more opportunities to talk."

Caine felt his body reacting to her closeness, tried to reply, couldn't, and didn't care.

"But what has *not* been possible before this night," Bey continued, "was an opportunity to join." This time, her emphasis on the word "join" was unmistakable.

She searched his eyes. "So do you not also miss the touch of another?" As if reaching out toward a skittish animal, Bey put a hand on his arm.

He looked at it, then up at her. "Oh, no. I've missed that very much. More than I can say."

"Then do not try. There have been enough words." Her wide-set eyes scanned his face, then his body. She leaned into him, found his lips and opened her own.

As they fell sideways, some final fragment of Caine's mind was struggling to be heard, to be heeded:

Is this the right thing to do?

Hell, no.

Is this the smart *thing to do?*

Probably not.

But after doing the right thing, the careful thing, the conscientious thing—time after time, year after year—the other voice he'd kept silent broke through and asked:

But right now—right this instant—do you care about any *of that?*

No.

Hell, no.

Chapter Forty-Four

Wishing there was any alternative, Bey adjusted her shift, steeled herself, and leaned close to the curtain door of the room shared by Peter Wu and Miles O'Garran. "Is anyone awake? It is I, Bey."

The hide curtain was yanked aside almost immediately: Wu was already fully dressed, eyes worried. "I was informed that the commodore was not in his chamber to take a morning meal. Is he well?"

"I . . . I am not sure," Bey admitted. "He is not moving. I would be grateful if—"

As Peter slipped into the short hallway, he turned and kicked some object deeper into the room. It clattered loudly. Chief O'Garran groaned in irritation as Peter released the hanging and insisted, "Show me."

Bey held aside the final curtain to the ritual chamber, motioned for Peter to enter. Nodding, he passed her—and stopped. Even the sight of his commander, insensate and sprawled across the mattress, was not sufficient to jar him out of a prolonged survey of the space.

It was, Bey had to admit, a complete shambles. There were furs in various clumps, but none of them resembled a pile anymore. Some of the cushions were mixed in with them, some flung against walls or into corners. One of the low tables was overturned. The thick rug was no longer just up against the far wall; it appeared to have attempted to scale it.

Feeling heat rise into her face, Bey clarified, "There have been no injuries. No blows were struck."

The words jarred Wu back into motion. "Thank you," he murmured as he walked briskly to Riordan, across whom Bey had thrown the lightest fur: the Crewe were all strangely averse to nudity.

As the short human felt for Riordan's pulse and then delicately opened one eyelid, Bey added, "I feared that the drink's effects worsened during the night. That he might have slipped into an unwaking sleep." When Wu didn't answer, she stepped toward them. "You have the training to help him, do you not?"

Peter straightened as Caine's hand came up, sweeping at the eyelid that his friend had touched.

Suppressing a sigh of relief, Bey struggled to focus on Peter's answer.

"I only have basic medical training for combat injuries. However, if by 'unwaking sleep' you mean a coma, you have no reason to be concerned. His pulse is within normal range, his pupils are normal, and he is responsive, now."

As if to dispute Wu's last assertion, Riordan rolled over heavily. After one groaning sigh, his breathing became deep and slow: asleep again.

Footsteps approached; the gait was O'Garran's. The small warrior rounded the corner rapidly, an unfamiliar pistol held low in one hand. Continuing his brisk approach, he nodded at Bey and asked in a carefully neutral voice, "Is the commodore well?"

"Yes," she answered, moving into the room so as not to obstruct the entrance. "The commodore is just very deeply sedated."

Miles nodded, rounded the doorway—and stopped as if struck in the forehead. His jaw sagged slightly as he took in the condition of the room. "Gawd-daaammnn," he breathed, a smile starting at the corners of his mouth, "it sure doesn't look like *anyone* was sedated in here! Did you crazy kids order another round of drinks?"

Bey straightened, somehow found a haughty tone. "Nothing that happened in this room is *any* of your business, Chief O'Garran."

Bey presumed his response—a startled stare—was the prelude to an argument. But instead, Miles' face stretched into a broad smile: the one that the Crewe called his "shit-eating" grin. "You could not be more right! It's none of *anyone's* gawdamm business, ma'am! Wait: I mean, *Chief*!" He glanced around the room. "Because it must be *really* official now!"

She couldn't resist smiling, but was also frowning as she explained, "I do not understand what happened to Caine. I know that all of you have sampled and toasted with many of our drinks, including those that have much the same mixture as the one used for the rite of shared trust."

Wu looked over. "By the same mixture, do you mean the inclusion of the fungus?"

"Yes. That extract is fairly common. It is almost always present in several of the drinks that your group said were offered to you in Tasvar's fortress."

Wu exchanged knowing looks with Miles before explaining. "That is no doubt true, but you probably did not notice that, during the march north, Doctor Baruch ran assays on every alcoholic beverage we were offered. He did the same during our time at Tasvar's."

When Bey frowned at the word "assay," Miles added, "He nixed any drink that had anything in it besides alcohol and water. So I'm betting that his, er, drink-checking artifact tweaked to even a small amount of the fungus."

Bey stared. "So none of you have ever had any drink with the fungus extract?"

Wu shook his head. "Not except what you gave to Eku as a painkiller. Or what the healers gave to those of us whose wounds were deep and required many sutures."

O'Garran frowned. "Yeah, but even then, that fungus wasn't *this* fungus."

"What do you mean?"

Miles shrugged. "Cruvanor told us—and Ne'sar confirmed it—that the polyp-fungi here are really strong. *Really* strong. By which I mean drop-a-dustkine-in-its-tracks strong."

Bey folded her arms, shook her head. "I should not have assumed you had any experience of it. I put Caine in danger. He could have consumed even more, in which case—"

Miles waved her to silence. "Usually it's us who make mistakes by assuming we understand things about which we know squat-all." He smiled. "I'm sure the commodore will be relieved that, just for once, one of *you* guys got it wrong. I know *I'm* relieved." He glanced back at Wu, who was never so jocular as O'Garran and seemed even less so now.

Bey nodded at Miles. "You are very kind, even if you are not telling the truth." She smiled. "Thank you for coming so quickly. And without waking others. Although"—she glanced toward the gun he held low—"I see you came prepared for any eventuality." She looked more carefully at the pistol. "That is one of the weapons reclaimed from the Silo, is it not?"

The SEAL raised it, his trigger finger lying against the part that contained the barrel. "Yes, ma'am, it is." He regarded it skeptically. "It's a little bit different from our own, though."

"You mean Pandora's pistol?"

"Well, that's actually Eku's antique—but yes, ma'am. I'd better get used to this damn thing."

"Why so?"

O'Garran shrugged. "Turns out the bigwigs from Atorsír will be here before sundown, so the metal-freeing ceremony is on for tonight. Ne'sar said we should be in our martial finery."

Peter rolled his eyes. "She simply said that the other leaders would be in *their* finery. Which includes their best weapons."

"Probably just some gaudy, ceremonial pigstickers," the chief sneered.

Peter stared at him. "Tell me, Chief: do you think the concept of a 'ceremonial weapon' even exists here?"

O'Garran sighed. "Damn, I do hate it when you're right, Lieutenant." He winked at Bey when Wu rolled his eyes. "Well, ma'am, we'll be going now."

She lifted a hand to pause him. "One last matter: if I am chief, then we are both leaders. So as I understand your customs, we may call each other by our given names when we are having a personal conversation . . . Miles." She ended on a smile.

He returned it. "Right you are, ma'a—I mean, Bey." Without any hint of hurrying, he was back around the first dogleg before Peter could produce a vial from one of the small pouches on his belt.

He held it out to Bey. "We appreciate that you had your guard pass this remedy to us, in the event that the commodore reacted poorly to the ritual drink." He glanced behind him; Riordan was stirring slightly. "But it looks like it will be needed here, rather than back in his quarters."

She took it from Wu and smiled at the small, calm man. He appeared to be the sort of human that would manage sums on an abacus, but in actuality, had repeatedly proven almost as dangerous as she when he had shortswords in both hands. "Thank you, Peter. You are very thoughtful."

"And you are very welcome, Bey." His bow was rather like those of trogs. "We shall be attired as appropriately as we may, since we never anticipated a need to dress for anything other than travel and combat."

She laughed. "Dress for combat is always best. That is what impresses the most."

He smiled and headed after Miles.

She watched him turn the corner. *They care for each other so deeply. Perhaps...* She pushed away imagination of what it would be like to be held so closely, so gently, in another's heart. *That is not my life; that is not this land. Their soft emotions are the products of their land. Here, they are just another vulnerability.*

She let the door curtain swing closed behind her, turned—and saw that Caine had rolled over. His eyes were barely open, his hair was tousled—and for an instant she could see what he must have looked like when he was a boy, just waking up. Alarmed at the image, she pushed it away even harder.

She crawled up on the mattress—so cumbersome and uneven!—and urged the remedy into his hand. "Here. Drink this." She regretted the flat tone she put in her voice, but she had to be careful not to become too attached, to begin to dream of things that could not be. She reminded herself of the danger of that, recalling the words she'd used to explain it to Riordan just last night: "Anything but the present is a luxury we cannot afford." And the gentle feelings and deep attachments had never been a part of her world's present—and never would be.

Bey watched as Riordan fumbled at the vial. *Really? Must I open it for him?* She did. He mumbled thanks, tilted the contents into his mouth, but was so groggy that a few drops dribbled out. Bey had to exert a great surge of will to keep from laughing—or from letting that amusingly vulnerable image of him touch her heart and become a memory.

Whatever was in the remedy worked very quickly. A minute later, his eyes were fully open. Shortly after, they were quick, aware, and scanning the room. They opened wider still as they tracked across the wreckage of the prior night's lovemaking—and then ended on her face.

His tone was surprised, possibly abashed. "I did not expect this."

"Nor did I," she answered. It was very hard not to smile as he once again stared at the irrefutable evidence that he—a human known for self-control—had lost every vestige of it as repeatedly and vigorously as she had.

But this was a dangerous moment for smiles. "To be frank," Bey added, "I am not sure it could have occurred any other way."

His eyes returned to her face. "What do you mean?"

At the moment she least wished to, she forced herself to shrug. "The ritual, the drink, the privacy: all of that helped us consummate an act of profound political prudence. For both of us."

"Political prudence?" he echoed. He looked behind him, as if disbelieving they could be talking about the same act or the room in which it had taken place. "This is the result of 'political prudence'?"

Careful now, careful. "I assure you, Caine Riordan, if joining had not been wise, I would not have taken you as I did. Both of us have duties to our peoples, and first among those is to make wise alliances with powerful partners. That is, after all, what we both intended when we entered the hall last night." *But please, please do not ask me what was in my mind when we entered* this *room.*

Fearful that he might ask exactly that, she filled the air with her own words first, fully aware that she had chided him for doing exactly that not so many fateful hours ago. "Our people will now be at ease with each other. Trog-kind will be far less likely to doubt the way you and your companions lead, despite how unfamiliar—even contrary—they seem."

He seemed to be growing as disoriented by her words as he had been by the fungus extract. "And you think this one night will lead to all that?"

She crafted another shrug to go along with her oblique reply. "One can only do what one can do."

He nodded. "I suppose so." His voice sounded very empty. He made to leave the bed.

Before she was even aware of doing it, she grabbed his arm: hard. He looked at it, then her, surprised at first but with questions multiplying behind his eyes. But this time, it was he who eschewed words: he simply remained where he was, waiting.

She, too, had to remain silent, had to let go of his arm: *had to.* But instead, words came out of her mouth. "What do you remember of last night?"

He frowned, his eyes wandered away from hers, the way one does when trying to recall a vague memory.

"Do you remember *nothing*?" *Gods, I sound desperate!*

He shook his head. "A lot of what I recall is just brief flashes." His voice became hollow. "I can't even be sure which of them are real."

"But . . . were they unpleasant?" *No: don't answer! I should not have asked.*

He frowned, eyes still focused inward.

Truly? You cannot remember? How could you forget, how could you even doubt—?

He looked up, was surprised by whatever he saw in her face. He moved the arm she held so that his hand slid down into hers. "Yes," he said, "I remember, but it's like fitting a puzzle back together." He brought his other hand over to hers, holding it firmly but gently. He grinned. "And no, it wasn't unpleasant." He laughed. "Anything but! I'm just—well, I'm just getting used to waking up to all this."

She managed not to exhale in relief—not merely at his reassuring answer, but what it signified: that as foolish as her secret dreams might be, they were stronger than the dour wisdom of suppressing them.

But shouting for joy would make her appear quite insane, so she shifted her emotion sideways into an ironic taunt. "Well, of course you are not used to waking up from a night of passion! Your people seem so averse to mating, I suspect you have forgotten what it is like. Indeed, I still wonder if you secretly *are* a member of one of the warrior cults that swears abstinence. Why else would you try to erase memories of such lovemaking from your mind?"

One of Caine's eyebrows arched. "I thought you said that this was just politics."

She rolled her eyes, but discovered she was leaning toward him. "I never said this was *just* politics."

"No," he replied, mirroring the smile she felt starting on her own face, "you didn't say that, did you?"

Peter Wu glanced toward the open doorway. "The commodore has not returned yet."

Miles smiled knowingly. "You actually expected him?" He chuckled. "Lieutenant, you need to get out more."

Wu was silent, for he could not share his thoughts. *I do not need to "get out more," you inane jester. I need to get back home, back to where I can look into the eyes of the one I left behind.*

O'Garran seemed to read his mind—or maybe, just his facial expression. "Damn, Lieutenant, I forgot—sir, forgive me: I'm just a knuckle-dragging asshole. I know you and Susan Phillips are serious. Damn serious. Which is probably the only kind of serious a man can have with a prim Brit intel officer from the old, old days." He rolled his eyes at his own japery. "Jesus, I just keep putting my foot in it, don't I?"

Wu smiled. "I will interrupt when I disagree, Chief."

O'Garran chuckled. "You're a good sport, sir. But why are you pulling on that Dornaani suit? They said dress to impress, not shock the locals speechless."

"It hasn't had that effect yet, Chief. Besides, I need to be wearing it when the time comes to give the last expansion command to the smart pitons."

"Yeah, well, don't forget to pack your new pistol as well. That's instant status around here." Miles checked his wrist comp. "Y'know, if the commodore doesn't get back soon, *someone* is going to have to remind him we have another ritual, tonight."

"This is a ceremony, Chief."

"Ceremony, ritual, shindig: all the same to me. They've all got the same cardinal rule: Don't be too early, but don't be late. According to Ne'sar, the bunch from Atorsír is just going to make it under the wire, too. Right about now, they should be cutting loose their bearers and entering another of the mangles' mazes."

"Any idea how far away that puts them?"

"I think about ten klicks or so. Far enough so that if some damned kiktzo sees the bearers, it's too far away to be of any help finding this joint."

"Sounds like the bearers are in considerable danger, though."

Miles's answering look was baleful. "Sounds like they're bait, sir."

Chapter Forty-Five

Fezhmorbal huddled tighter into the shadows of one of the few stony ravines that cut through the Orokrosir. Despite his proximity to the x'qiigh whose mind he was watching, he had to tap its repulsive hide to bring its attention back to the work at hand.

The deciqadi war leader had long ago grown accustomed to the necessity of such regrettable contact. But simply being linked to the mind of x'qai did not always guarantee that their focus would remain on a mission. Between their innate inattention and their reluctance at the intensity of his connection, they were often more focused on getting the deciqadi war leader out of their minds than on accomplishing the tasks he set them. So, sometimes they needed physical reminders. When that didn't work, there was always the costly but effective alternative of not bothering to connect, but to directly control them.

He hoped that would not prove necessary in this case. It promised to be a very taxing plan and he had no associates who could be of much assistance. It not only required the war leader's deep reserves of power and precise control, but his unique knowledge of the target.

The lesser x'qiigh's kiktzo had detected Boghram's party easily enough, following them at a distance of several leagues since midday. But the column had slowed when small figures emerged out of the ground itself: mangle outlooks, waiting to guide the chief of Atorsír's entourage toward the ceremony where he was to surrender his daughter to Vaagdjul's intermediary.

Not that the event was of particular importance; the affairs of the h'achgai had become increasingly dull in the course of Fezhmorbal's career. Whereas in his youth the bestial humanoids had frequent tribal wars and succession assassinations, Vaagdjul's tenure had been long, successful, and unusually peaceful. In short, the h'achgai had become regrettably dull, so much so that the little bit of betrothal drama that would soon unfold was not even occurring naturally, but had been encouraged—nay, almost scripted—by none other than Fezhmorbal himself.

With the x'qiigh attentive again, the deciqadi commander used it to guide the kiktzo until it was among the score of bearers and young guards who had not been included with the actual entourage when it was shepherded into a chamber, blindfolded, and led the rest of the way to their final destination.

Most of the bearers were poverty-stricken h'achgai, but several praakht had been hired by the chief's functionaries in Khorkrag. From his broken gait, one was deep enough into the ravages of s'rillor that he qualified as a pawn. Fezhmorbal pushed the x'qiigh to guide the kiktzo to that figure, slumped at some distance from the rest of the porters: even though the disease did not spread by contact among beings, they nonetheless shunned those who displayed its symptoms.

"There," Fezhmorbal prompted, "pester that one."

Although the x'qiigh's control was overhasty and clumsy, the insect alit on top of the afflicted praakh's head, biting, moving, biting again.

Before long, the praakh lurched upright, swatting in vain at its tiny tormentor.

One of the young guards noticed and strode over. Fezhmorbal smiled. A distant cousin of the chief's son: the same one he held captive. So far, so good.

As the guard approached the praakh, he began speaking but was difficult to understand. The simpler the mind that heard speech, the more garbled it became, as if not having the concept of words changed what the creature heard.

But between what he could understand, and that fact that he had scripted the exchange taking place, Fezhmorbal was once again gratified to see that his plan was still unfolding adequately.

The guard shooed away the insect—which the x'qiigh effected too swiftly, but none of the other porters noticed or would have likely detected anything unusual in what they saw. The afflicted porter responded to some simple queries, was confused as to what had become of the satchel in which he carried his rations. The guard rolled his eyes, scolded the porter, then produced the missing satchel, warning him that his punishment was the empty stomach on which he'd been marching since sunup.

The porter nodded numbly, started opening the satchel, but the guard intervened, noting that the other had also not relieved himself yet and should take care of that as well. He pointed off to a blind corner just a few dozen steps down a shallow ravine, telling the porter to return when he was done. None of the other porters, who'd already distanced themselves from the afflicted praakh, had paid any attention to the exchange: certainly not enough to notice anything peculiar about it.

The x'qiigh extended a question into the link. "Kill the guard now?" It was the first sign that the x'qao had any interest in the activities.

Typical. No attention to a mission until it sees an opportunity to indulge its one persistent impulse: brutal blood lust. "Kill it with what?" Fezhmorbal thought at it. "The guard will be removed later. And no, probably not by you." Fezhmorbal considered, added, "Such a slaying is beneath you." The x'qiigh's mood swelled slightly: a brief preening.

And just enough to improve its reliability somewhat. No matter that it was a laughably transparent lie: the x'qao didn't know or didn't care that it was not heartfelt and Fezhmorbal would find the beast marginally easier to control.

The kiktzo followed the praakh, buzzing and shepherding it around the blind corner into a small crevice, the back of which opened out into a smaller, round gap in the surrounding rock. Fezhmorbal smiled: *a very* familiar *gap.*

"Send the kiktzo into the wound," he instructed the x'qiigh.

"Where is the wound, again?"

"There, there: just beneath the rip in the pawn's shift! Quickly!"

The x'qao wasted no time and certainly devoted no particular attention as it complied. The kiktzo slipped through the rent in the porter's garment, found the ready wound that Fezhmorbal's agent had cut there several days before, and burrowed into it. Without waiting for the command from the deciqadi, the x'qiigh ordered it to begin tearing and rending at the open flesh.

"Idiot!" Fezhmorbal hammered at its consciousness, which quailed from that assault in a most satisfying fashion. "Wait! Slowly, lest the pawn cry out!"

But by chance, the unintended suddenness of both the agony and terror of being attacked from inside its body caused the afflicted praakh to rear back sharply, scratching madly at the wound. In so doing, the ration sack flew off its shoulder.

Well, that wasn't the way it was supposed to occur, but success is success. "Now," Fezhmorbal commanded the x'qiigh, "send the first kiktzo off to hide in that shadowed crevice." Once it had, he ordered, "Awaken the smaller kiktzo and the kiksla that are waiting in the meat."

As the praakh collapsed weeping against the wall of the chimneylike gap, the flap of the satchel moved slightly, and two more insects emerged. Fezhmorbal instructed the x'qiigh to make the first one—the smallest species that could function as a kiktzo—fly a slow circuit around the interior of the chimney. Watching through its eyes, Fezhmorbal momentarily feared that decades had dimmed his recollection, that he might not recognize the small aperture he sought.

His fears were wholly ungrounded. Within the first orbit of the gap, he spied the shape he sought: the aftermath of a rockfall that left two great, flat slabs of basalt leaning almost flush against each other. "Stop. There. Send the kiktzo to the top of the gap between the rocks."

The x'qiigh complied, and there, just where Fezhmorbal remembered it, was a slit-like opening, just wide enough for the kiktzo to slip through. "Send it in."

The insect's vision was not optimal for darkness, but its ability to detect air currents and its own stunted sense of smell revealed the chamber as he'd remembered it: before it had been sealed by several of his mentor's most powerful anagogoi. The ceiling rose as it moved further away from the slit and the ground was piled high with sand.

"Bones!" the x'qiigh sent in surprise and typically morbid excitement.

"Yes," Fezhmorbal answered, inspecting the remains: many half-buried praakh skeletons, almost as many polyglot mangle remains, and at the far end of the room, a mummified forearm wearing a vantbrass. The crest of a familiar helmet poked up through the sand where the sand-covered body's head would be.

"That is calluskin armor," the x'qiigh sent as a subdued observation, finally realizing that the actions of the preceding weeks—ensuring that the young guard was bribed through sources unconnected to the deciqadi; locating the special insects; carefully scouting the region from great distances and heights—were anything but random.

"Yes," Fezhmorbal replied, "it is the armor of my people. Now, bring in the kiksla."

The other insect, even smaller, entered. Seen through the kiktzo's eyes, it was almost invisible in the dark. "Let it sing," Fezhmorbal instructed. He restricted his growing satisfaction to a physical smile, thereby leaving the x'qiigh unaware of his state of mind.

"You mean, in this chamber—there are those in the sleep of the sands?"

"I said, let the kiksla sing. Do not task me for answers again."

It was several long minutes—made longer by the x'qiigh's cognitive fidgeting—before several of the sand drifts began trembling.

"Excellent." Fezhmorbal envisioned the slightly larger kiktzo. "Bring it through the gap."

"It may not fit."

"If it loses some legs, I do not care. It will live to the end of the day. That is all I require."

The larger kiktzo did, in fact, lose a leg. It was unlikely to prove fatal, but it was beneath a war leader to attain expertise in the physiology of bugs. He bid the x'qiigh send it to the furthest part of the chamber. "Examine the rear wall, near the arm with the vantbrass." Again, little had changed: the fallen rocks were still piled high, but air was certainly moving through gaps between them.

The sands began to heave, as if they rested upon turbulent waves. At last, the kiksla's song was having the desired effect.

"The sleepers!" the x'qiigh said aloud.

"Yes," Fezhmorbal sent as several explosions of sand, gravel, and dirt jetted upward. From the rapidly refilling craters, figures dragged themselves erect, looming like emaciated specters in the dimness. They began moving listlessly.

"Four—no, six x'qai!" the x'qiigh squealed aloud.

"Be silent." Fezhmorbal inspected them as others began

pushing up. They were almost cadaverous, but he'd seen worse. Badly wounded or starving x'qai had been known to survive for centuries in the strange state they called the sleep of the sands. But typically, they were awakened by the passing of prey, which not only roused them but sent final reserves of strength coursing through their veins: one last chance to hunt, kill, and live again.

But these, having been awakened by the song of the right kind of kiksla, were somnambulistic rather than frenzied. At least it would be some time before they began to prey upon each other.

"Now what?" the x'qiigh pushed, finally eager to witness what plans of mayhem were sure to unfold before the eyes of its kiktzo.

Fezhmorbal smiled. "Lead them to the far wall." The kiksla moved in that direction; the lumbering monsters followed slowly. "Now, let it sing as loudly as it may."

The almost inaudible drone that had awakened the x'qai suddenly ascended into a multi-tonal blend of crossing screeches and buzzing. The x'qai straightened, some of their heads snapping erect and turning, as if seeking the source of an elusive scent.

Without warning, one of the smaller ones—a x'qnarz—launched itself at the amalgam of rock and dust at the back of the chamber, clawing vigorously. Others joined it. The rush of air from a chamber beyond touched the senses of all the insects.

"Now," Fezhmorbal ordered, "send the injured kiktzo through the gap, and prepare to follow my instructions closely."

"To do what?"

Fezhmorbal could not help but gloat slightly. "To pick along a path I once knew. The x'qai and other insects shall wait. Do not tarry, damn you! Send it on its way!"

Chapter Forty-Six

Riordan glanced at Raam'tu, who was standing just beyond the ritual platform, watching the last of Boghram's entourage file into the cathedral-like chamber.

"That's what I call cutting it close," Miles muttered sideways at Caine, glancing at the newly arrived h'achgai from Atorsír.

Caine nodded, the motion almost dislodging the open visor of his Dornaani helmet. Although he'd originally pondered having everyone but Peter wearing their best local armor, all who heard weighed in against the idea—including several whose opinions had not been solicited.

Indeed, it was the locals who'd been most emphatic for the Crewe to wear their "magic armor," in part because it was in keeping with their identity as the collective manifestation of the omens that had preceded their arrival. Beyond that, the suits' identical, precise manufacture radiated a promise of power among the homely garb and gear of the locals.

Besides, Riordan had admitted, it wasn't as if it put any wear or tear on the suits just to walk around in them for an hour or so. And there was no question that they left a profound impression upon locals who had never seen them before. Every mangle had stared after them, wide-eyed.

And now, Boghram's h'achgai were doing no less, albeit on the sly. Their brief, haughty stares were almost comic attempts to mask what clearly lay beneath: surprise, awe, and the oblique fear of warriors who discover themselves to be profoundly outclassed by new rivals.

Judging from the muttering among them, it seemed that the warriors from Atorsír had decided that tangling with the "star people" would fall someplace between "idiotic" and "suicidal" on the risk spectrum.

Their chief hushed them to silence and nodded at Raam'tu. He bowed to Boghram, turned to the other leaders, reached out his hands, then brought them back toward his chest in a gathering gesture. Caine stepped forward. Off to the right, Cruvanor and Bey advanced out beyond their small entourages; to the left, Ulchakh did the same. Well beyond him, Boghram stood forth from his restless warriors.

"We come to see an omen fulfilled!" Raam'tu shouted in a surprisingly strong voice. "This moment was whelped half a lifetime ago. Now, we give birth to it and a new era by freeing the metal of ages long past." He nodded toward Peter, who, visor down, moved to stand alongside Caine, raising one palm toward the piton-outlined slab on the wall. The gesture was the same one Tirolane used as he prepared to call forth one of his effects, or anagogoi.

"Nice bit of theater," O'Garran muttered.

"Shhh," Riordan whispered.

Peter flexed his palm; not necessary, but the subtle *krak!* that emerged from the slab hushed the room.

Riordan would have smiled, but knew he was probably being watched. *And now that he's got their attention...*

Another flex. Another *krak!*

And... one, two, three.

Peter pushed his palm at the slab.

The resulting *KRRRAAK!* caused the entire gathering to start back... and again when the slab literally sprang off the wall. It crashed forward, splitting the platform with a sound, and smell, like lightning. The sharp tang of ozone hung in the air...

Until a roar of triumph, joy, and even relief seemed to displace the odor, as if the nuance of smell was annihilated by the wave of sound that rushed out from the gathering and then echoed down again from the stalactites high overhead.

As a thunder of stamped feet—and other appendages—added to the din, Little Guy stared up at Riordan. "Why, you sly dog... sir. And after all that pushback on 'spectacle.'"

Caine shrugged, couldn't quite smother a smile. "I conceded to the strategic value of theater, Chief. And once I did—well, in for a penny, in for a pound."

✧ ✧ ✧

After Fezhmorbal had compelled the kiksla to follow the injured kiktzo through the winding tunnels, he sent them both up a long shaft he remembered all too well. They emerged into a warren of small, long-deserted chambers; there was no sign of habitation. As he'd expected, the mangles had abandoned that part of the complex. They'd probably hoped that if they no longer saw it, they would no longer recall the terrible losses they had suffered there. He doubted that it had erased those memories.

The x'qiigh was as good as a puppet, now, sensing that savage violence was imminent. Regrettably, it was also beginning to form ideas of its own. "The awakened x'qai: they lag far behind. If you sent the kiksla back, it could hasten them."

"No. Just keep the smaller kiktzo buzzing and following the path of the other two insects. When the time comes and they are closer, we will make its sound loud and irritating enough to quicken them in the direction I wish."

Having no reasonable counter to the near surety that its kin would do just as the deciqadi predicted, the x'qiigh resentfully returned its full attention to the other two insects. In the space of three breaths, it had forgotten its disappointment; it was once again fixed on the promise of slaughter.

Fezhmorbal had it steer the lead kiktzo through a small cluster of larger chambers filled with mementos: remembrances of the mangles who had fallen here and further below. Some of the memorials were relatively new. Excellent: since it still had visitors, it was still open to the upper levels.

He pushed the insects harder now, through broader passages and wider chambers, some of which showed signs of occasional habitation. Then, as the air freshened, they began flying past kits and sleeping furs; temporary workers or visitors. And, if he listened very carefully, there was a murmur of activity someplace above.

Fezhmorbal smiled. So: they had brought Boghram and his h'achgai to their holy of holies. No doubt they had their other visitors there as well. Showing off their pathetic little fragment of the ancient past. As if they'd ever find a way to make use of it.

But it did mean that with almost all the mangles attending whatever rude celebration was in process, the path to it—and all of them—would be largely or completely clear.

"Now," he urged the x'qiigh with a cruelly abrupt mental prod, "send them toward that sound. As quickly as they can fly!"

Riordan and the other leaders hung back as Raam'tu not only allowed but encouraged the entire gathering to come and behold the fulfillment of the omen. As they filed past, he invited them to touch not only the stone but the metal, some of which had been pulled out of the wall by the slab's weight. Riordan watched as Ta'rel picked up a twisted spike of gleaming steel—if that's what it was—and wonder at it, turning it over as if inspecting a blade.

Raam'tu smiled at the young mangle. The durus'maan caught the wrist of the hand with which Ta'rel held the bright shard and raised it over their heads. "Once freed, the shape of the metal foretells its own future! To repel x'qai so we may live in safety, in peace! Come with me, all who wish to show the fruits of the omen to the source that sent it down to us!" He gestured toward the exit, glancing briefly at Bey and Peter as he did.

Wu shut his visor. In the same instant, the icon of Peter's comm channel glowed just in front of Riordan's cheek. Caine closed his own visor and blinked at the light. "Go ahead, Lieutenant."

"Raam'tu is on the move. But he's bringing Ta'rel with him. Cordon as planned?"

"Affirmative," Riordan answered. "We'll be right behind you."

Miles snickered as Bey led her trogans forward and formed them up in a square around Raam'tu and Ta'rel. "Gotta hand it to you, Commodore. You sure can put on a show when you've a mind to."

Caine nodded. It was theater, yes, but it was also prudent: a constant reminder to anyone with dubious intentions that acting upon them meant contending with the star people.

Peter swung in behind the trogans, softly muttering a cadence. To the crowd's surprise, and Peter's obvious delight, they actually fell into march step. Who could have foreseen that the military discipline they'd resisted at Achgabab had become ingrained enough to be useful now?

Fezhmorbal physically reared back as the lead kiktzo turned a corner and came face-to-face with an approaching mass of mangles. A square of prakhwai was in the lead, a human—or was she a whakt?—walking to the side. At the center of those guards was an ancient mangle, clinging to the hand of a younger, somewhat large one.

Who was holding a bright metal shard.

Well, well, how in the name of death and blood did you manage to extract that?

And then the answer marched into view: one of the thieves, sealed in his—her?—artifact armor.

If Fezhmorbal had the time to gloat, he might have. But instead he thrust orders into the x'qiigh's mind as quickly and savagely as an assassin's dagger. "Bring the insects back around the corner and keep them in the shadows! Yes, that's it! Send both ahead of the mangles—and, yes, *of course* they should follow the scent of the fresh air, you imbecile!

"Now, make the kiktzo with the x'qai screech as loud as it might. Excellent! Keep it just ahead of the killspawn so that they will run after it as quickly as possible. For how *long*? Until they arrive at the top of the tunnels and charge into the rear of the crowd, idiot!"

As Raam'tu made to lead the impromptu procession through the wide, hidden exit, Bey quickened her step and got out in front of her trogans. She nodded at Peter, who'd expected the cue.

Continuing his steady advance, he joined her in a brisk exit of the passage, one peeling off to each side. The only things there were a few small insects that flew up at their intrusion and the very bright stars that filled the narrow slice of sky that shone down into the wadi. It was a different opening than the one through which they'd entered upon arriving at Ebrekka. Bey and Peter had confidentially shared their worry about trusting so completely to concealment without a watch, but it was hard to argue with the mangles' assertion that even a few regular guards would give away a point of entry as surely as a constant bonfire.

But, on this night at least, the mangles' experience proved the wisdom of their ways. Peter and Bey exchanged resigned shrugs, and leaned into the passage, waving that it was safe to exit.

As Raam'tu and Ta'rel emerged, Peter popped his visor, took in a deep lungful of air and relished the dull unison of marching sounds as the trogans went past. The rhythmic thud and clatter of scabbards bouncing against cured hide cuisses was a strong sound, a safe sound, one which promised that, with time, the locals could become more than warriors: they could become soldiers.

Raam'tu led Ta'rel into a wider part of the wadi, encouraged him to hold the shard of metal even higher, but the mangle winced; the wicked edges of the twisted fragment had cut his palm. He pulled a spare face-wrapping from a handy pouch, wrapped it around his hand, and held the glittering object aloft. He aimed it as Raam'tu instructed, pointing to the place where, it was said, the moving star had first appeared.

Fezhmorbal, guiding the injured kiktzo through the now eager x'qiigh, made sure the kiksla had followed it out into the night. He sent them up higher, out of the line of sight of the rapidly growing crowd in the wadi. He looked in all directions, trying to find landmarks from long ago...

The three buttes to the south were unmistakable. He adjusted his mental map, looked at the pattern the nearby wadi etched through the land, saw the familiar point where it met and blended into a nearby ravine. The one the mangles were using was a new entry, yes, but not very far away from one of those he had kept under observation as a young warrior. He scanned the ground slightly above the rim of the wadi.

"There!" he pulsed and cried aloud at the x'qiigh. "There! I know that spot. Send the kiksla down to it, singing the song of the sands as loud and fierce as it can."

The x'qiigh complied but wondered, "How can you know that it holds any who are caught in the sleep of the sands?"

"Because I was *there*, you fool. Send it down, faster! Now!"

"Commodore," Peter asked before finishing his update on the crowd and dignitaries, "you might want to skip the stargazing part of the ceremony." He adjusted the visor so that it blocked a little more of the constant rush of mutters and murmurs that was now starting to bounce back from the walls of the wadi.

"So you're saying the outdoor part of the ceremony is dull?"

"Well, I can't honestly call it 'compelling.' Every few minutes, Raam'tu offers a pretty repetitious litany of thanks to the heavens for the omen and the metal. But the real trouble is how crowded the wadi is becoming."

"Yeah, we're at the back of the line and it's barely moving, now. How many are outside, do you think?"

"Well over half of the original audience, sir. The ones still trying to get out are backed up against the others. Seems like everyone wants to be able to say they were here the night a new age began." Wu frowned. "But now that we're outside—"

"Yes?"

"The highlands to the east look further than I expected. In fact, I'm not sure—"

Sudden movement—inbound—in the upper periphery of Wu's vision.

He ducked.

The mangle to Peter's left howled as a flailing mass of limbs and claws crashed into it.

A 'qo. It was already tearing great, bloody chunks out of the writhing body beneath it.

Peter drew his pistol before he thought to do so. He thumbed the safety off—

And discovered it was gone.

No, damn it! It's not *your service weapon!*

By the time Wu had primed the resurrected weapon from the Silo, the mangle had gone limp and the 'qo was hungrily scanning the panicked bystanders as they struggled to push away from it.

Its eyes fell upon Peter the same instant he leveled the gun at the space between them.

Wu two-tapped the creature; he'd only fired the weapon twice and never in combat. He instantly regretted expending the second round; the first punched a hole through the 'qo's skull. It snapped its fangs at him, blinked in surprise, then collapsed.

Wu pushed himself back against the side of the wadi, raised his eyes and the weapon.

Half a dozen 'qo—every silhouette a different size and shape—were plummeting from the top of the gorge into the crowd. He slapped down his visor, scanned for similar signatures above him: no targets but several thermal blooms cresting the lip. And fainter ones further back.

"Wu, report!" Riordan's voice hammered in his ear.

"Under attack," he replied. 'Qo jumping down from the lip of the wadi. Numbers unknown." He saw another shadow rise, ready to fling itself down into the milling, wailing crowd. "The ceremony is no longer dull, sir. Please attend."

Chapter Forty-Seven

Riordan shouted at Cruvanor. "Killspawn jumping into the wadi. No organized defense." Dora and Miles had already drawn their weapons and were scanning the crowd ahead for openings.

"No way through, sir," Dora reported. The sounds of the carnage weren't audible this far back in the passageway, so the direction of movement hadn't reversed—yet. "Where's Craig?" she snapped as she surveyed who was with them.

"Left to catch up to his favorite, Uncle Peter," Miles spat irritably.

Tirolane began pushing through the packed bodies. Before Riordan could speak, Miles grabbed the swordsman's arm. "Not the way to handle this situation, big guy." He turned toward Caine. "With your permis—?"

"Go, Chief."

Miles got Tirolane to relent as Riordan tugged Cruvanor closer to listen. Once those two were focused on the SEAL, the growing huddle drew in the rest: Polsolun, two of Sharat's trogans and his largest trogre.

"Listen up," O'Garran said, checking their twelve and their six hastily, "you can't get through the crowd or get 'em to duck down. But soon they'll see what's happening outside and come screaming back *this* way.

"So, we stay on this side of the passage and let 'em go past. Push them off hard if they bump into you. It's gonna feel wrong, but it's the fastest way to reach the enemy as a team. Understood?"

Riordan made his voice sharp enough to cut through the chorus of varied affirmatives. "One addition. Dora—"

She started, nodded.

"You're going to watch our six; it could become a hell of a hot spot."

She frowned. "Why?"

"We're about to reflex-charge our enemy, stop and ask. But what if that's what he *wants*?"

Cruvanor nodded as he went to join Veriden at the rear of their small assault column. "Now her keen senses and skills have the benefit of my experience and dirty tricks."

"They are coming back our way!" Tirolane shouted from the front. "Wukhzak," he called to Sharat's hulking trogre, "stand with me. None will dare to push us back."

As the large humanoid lumbered to join the swordsman, Riordan realized he hadn't armed himself yet. He reached behind to unlimber his survival rifle—

It wasn't there.

Shit. The mangles had asserted that anything bigger than a pistol would *not* be seen as a symbolic weapon. The result: Caine and Craig had strapped on their swords.

Riordan cross-drew his long- and shortswords, and regretted—deeply—that the Dornaani molecular machete was useless for parrying.

Peter kept hoping for a free second—just one second—to rattle off an update, but there wasn't even that thin sliver of time to spare.

'Qo were still leaping down from the lip of the wadi but nowhere near as frequently and not from the same places. Despite being a good shot with a pistol and the HUD's night vision, he'd put only two out of four shots on target before deciding to ignore the ones overhead. They were rarely visible for more than a half-second at a time and still too far.

But aiming at ground-level targets wasn't going much better. Yes, he wasted fewer rounds, but the constant rush of fleeing mangles and h'achgai left him checking fire at the last moment almost half the time. A clear line of sight didn't stay that way very long.

Finally, a lane opened across the entire width of the civilian-clogged wadi and a 'qo scuttled into it. Despite its low, squat build and broad body, it was surprisingly gaunt; folds of flesh hung down its front like bunched drapes. All of which he noticed in the instant it took him to draw a bead on it and—

Almost shoot the figure that gunned it down from behind: Sharat.

Peter jerked his trigger finger out of the guard as the Legate captain unfroze and, checking his flanks, charged across the wadi. He turned at the last second, his back whumping into the packed sand and dirt right alongside Wu's.

"Can you cover us?"

"Yes." Peter drifted his aimpoint to wherever desperate shrieks rose up from the crowd. "How long?"

"Another three seconds. Maybe four."

Wu glanced sideways. Sharat had already removed the spent cylinder of his percussion cap revolver, torn the wax covers off both ends of a preloaded one, and seated it. His current focus: fitting a pair of three-cap speed-loaders—well, speed-seaters—onto the nipples of the new cylinder.

He swung the barrel back down, locking the cylinder in place just as another killspawn loped out of the scattering crowd, stopping when it caught sight of the two humans.

"'Q'akh," Sharat muttered, raising his weapon as he thumbed back the hammer.

"Save your rounds," Peter muttered as the creature crossed half the distance in a single leap, claws extended like daggers. "I've got enough."

As its foot hit the ground and pushed it up into another bound, Wu let its torso rise into his sights and squeezed the trigger.

The round hit low in the abdomen. Ichor streamed, droplets flying as the 'q'akh wobbled, its foot-claws just leaving the ground. It fell hard, rolled, struggled to get up . . .

Sharat took two steps toward it, a short, bright blade in his left hand. As the killspawn tried to rise up to bite him, he plunged the point directly into its face. The weapon went in with surprising ease.

Glancing back at Peter's approving stare, Sharat smiled. "You should get some of these. Let's help Raam'tu."

Following the Legate officer at a run, Peter asked, "Where is he?"

"Down the wadi the other way. Yidreg and Ulchakh are

protecting him, along with my h'achgai and some of Boghram's. One of my drivers, too—but I think they were swarming him."

"Why didn't you stay?"

"Heard that gun of yours. We need it." They wrestled free of a knot of mangles now rushing back into the safety of the entry. "How many shots do you have left?"

"Twenty-one. Well, twenty, now."

Sharat smiled despite the carnage. "That should do. C'mon, short-legs: keep up!"

Even the solid, muscular masses of Tirolane and the trogre Wukhzak were staggered by the crush of mangles now fleeing the wadi. They managed to push the flow to the other side of the passage, but the buffeting was still transferred behind them to Riordan and Miles.

Little Guy glanced at Riordan's swords. "Sir, you shouldn't be here."

"*None* of us should be here," Caine shot back.

Miles barked out a laugh.

Tirolane spoke over his shoulder. "The crowd is thinning! We should be able to move!"

Riordan nodded at O'Garran, who in turn nodded for Sharat's trogan to be prepared to swing out and lead the way into the wadi.

"Boss," Dora shouted from the rear of their small column, either forgetting or not bothering with her helmet comms, "I think we've got—"

"Killspawn!" Cruvanor shouted—at the very same instant that the passage back to the great hall became a bedlam of death screams, terrified shrieks, and the stone-grating howls of not just killspawn, but x'qai.

Without warning, Tirolane pivoted into a leaping bound to the rear. Wukhzak, seeing no threat ahead, turned with him. Following that momentum, Sharat's two trogans, eyes wide with terrified resolve, spun in place and gulped down the contents of readied vials. They joined Polsolun as he struggled back toward Cruvanor through suddenly motionless mangles. The sounds of slaughter up ahead had ended their flight toward the great hall, but they were still terrified by the massacre in the wadi behind them.

In two chaotic seconds, Caine and Miles had gone from being in the column's second rank to its rear. They exchanged glances.

"Well, fuck," Miles said.

"You said it," Riordan muttered and started forward.

Heading to the new point of contact, they began bouncing off mangles running in both directions, the nearest wall, and occasionally each other.

Peter charged toward a wildly fleeing mass of mangles as they scattered to avoid a wounded 'qo. It was startled at the sight of the two humans, hobbled around to confront them.

Peter stopped, drew down, missed, put the second round in its belly. The squat killspawn squalled, fell, started rising again. A third round: it collapsed.

Sharat had pressed on and was nearing a mob heading for a nearby ravine just as two 'qo leaped down among them. Swerving to avoid the new threat, the crowd broke apart like a wave around a headland—in this case, a protective knot of bloodied figures. A pair of Sharat's h'achgai and two of Ebrekka's scouts were standing close by Ta'rel and Raam'tu, two obscured figures covering their rear.

As the two killspawn raced to engage the defenders, three more 'qo appeared at roughly the same place on the lip. They screeched at the ones below.

The attacking pair broke off their charge at spear-length, just as one of the obscured defenders swung out from the rear: Yidreg, his two-handed sword coated in ichor. The 'qo above spread out, one backing up slightly.

"They wake!" wailed Raam'tu, gesturing toward the ledge above.

"Wake from what?" Peter wondered aloud.

"From the sleep of the sands, of course!" Sharat snapped, moving to flank the two killspawn that were, in turn, trying to flank the defenders.

Bey appeared from behind Ta'rel, newly gifted sword in her right hand; it caught what little light there was and sent it back as painfully bright glints. Not entirely unlike the shard in Ta'rel's own hand—which, Peter was surprised to see, was also coated in ichor.

Wu measured the widening space between the two 'qo circling the weary defenders. He glanced toward the three on the lip, discovered that only two remained in view. That decided him; waiting would cost more lives than acting. Even rashly.

Peter holstered his pistol, drew his molecular machete, and muttered, "Be ready, Sharat. And don't shoot me!"

"What—?"

But Wu was already sprinting toward the gap between the two 'qo threatening the defenders. He hadn't completed his first running step before they spun toward him, screeched, and broke off their flanking movement.

A second running step—

Yowls sounded from the lip of the wadi. The two on the edge jumped down awkwardly, evidently earlier than they had wished. Their third, longer-legged cousin charged over the edge, launching into a broad jump that carried it far beyond the other two.

Third running step—

The 'qo's leap carried it almost all the way to Ta'rel, who saw the movement and dodged back—just as a confused scout jumped in to take his place. The young mangle took the full weight of the plummeting 'qo on his back.

Fourth running step—

Before the scout could even gasp, the 'qo was raking and slashing, blood-misted claws exposing his spine. Ta'rel leapt forward with an agonized cry. Bey took a step in Peter's direction, eyes puzzled.

Fifth running step—

Yidreg angled himself to intercept the two that had just jumped down. Sharat's h'achgai formed up on him. Raam'tu was either chanting or praying, eyes half-closed. Bey stepped to the edge of the defensive circle, eyes now sharp with understanding. Ta'rel swept the omened metal at the back of the 'qo still savaging the scout.

A last running step—

Which Peter turned into a leap. Anything to close with the defenders before the two circling 'qos reached him. He saw the gleaming point of Ta'rel's shard slice through the distracted killspawn's hide as if it was soft leather—just as Wu's helmet squawked a proximity warning.

He rolled with the impact as the charging 'qo crashed into him from the left. Its claws dug at his guts, but scraped off the Dornaani suit. Which reacted by activating its defensive hardening grid. Peter struggled up to one knee, caught a glimpse of Bey charging toward him—

The other 'qo hit him from the right, bearing him down. It was surprisingly heavy, given its small size and withered condition.

Unable to cut through the maddening human's armored back, it screeched, determined to roll the prey over. Peter did not resist.

Quivering with anticipation, the monster lunged at the waiting neck—and then blinked. Its dive forward had brought it into sharp contact with a small, odd blade that the human was holding edge-outward across his own chest. Abruptly awash in its own spurting ichor, the 'qo kept attacking, but each new lunge against the molecular machete just opened more gaping seams in its body.

The other 'qo had regained its feet and dove in, evidently expecting a different outcome. But it never got the chance to find out; Bey had angled around to strike from behind. She plunged her bright blade into its back. When it reared up, and was safely clear of Peter, she drove the point into the back of its squat skull.

As Bey helped Wu to his feet, Ta'rel rose from the body of the killspawn he had slashed to pieces. Without the faintest hint of his characteristic smile, he stalked in the direction of the two 'qo facing Yidreg and the h'achga guards.

With nothing to show for their efforts except wounds, and the sudden realization that they were also the last of their kind in sight, the two 'qos' eyes roved for a route of escape.

They never found one.

Chapter Forty-Eight

Not since his first days fighting Hkh'Rkh and their Indonesian collaborators in Jakarta had Caine Riordan felt so utterly, embarrassingly useless in a fight.

No gun. No idea where anyone was except for Miles and the trogans, who were in arm's reach. Lousy visibility around or over heads and shoulders, some higher than his own. No ability to hear or speak over the passage-compressed screams of terror, death, and killspawn battle-lust. No real comms: even with his visor down, they were barely audible. And, sealed up, even moving was uncertain; no direct sensory cues meant no physical awareness.

Riordan accepted the sad tactical calculus. He wasn't good enough with blades to hold his own against x'qai. He had reasonable parrying weapons and was sealed in a Dornaani vacc suit, so he *might* be able to protect someone who was armed with a decisive weapon. Which was to say, the pistol in Miles O'Garran's hand. But giving orders? Even if they were needed, it was unlikely he'd have the time, comms, or situational awareness.

He muttered into his helmet's pick up. "Chief, I'm your shield."

"Uh, sir, do you—?"

"Might be my last order. Follow it. And shoot straight."

"Uh . . . roger tha—"

"Here they come," Veriden muttered. "Falling back with Cruvanor."

But it was impossible to see exactly when and where she and

the war leader repositioned themselves. The tide that had carried fleeing mangles past them was ebbing, even as the flow of those streaming back toward the wadi was increasing. Rapidly. Some of the noise went with them. What remained was an eerie soundscape of whimpers, occasional shrieks, and fang-grinding growls.

Miles nodded into the darkness ahead. "Can't be any worse than what was outside, right?"

As if answering the chief's rhetorical question, heavy-headed silhouettes with large shoulders and withered bodies began to emerge from the blackness ahead of them. Their movement was erratic: a slow, lumbering advance that intermittently erupted into savage attacks upon unseen mangles or h'achgai. The shadow figures tore into their shrieking prey with great, gulping bites, then tossed them aside like rag dolls.

Riordan decided against tapping a direct relay from Veriden's HUD; any more light in his helmet and he'd be half-blind. "Dora, threat count."

"Six. No, eight, or maybe... *Coño*, there's *lots*, Boss. They're—"

Roars preceded the monsters that rushed out of the darkness and into wild combat. Shoulder to the left side of the passage, Polsolun was hacking at a x'qrukh. Cruvanor fired over his shoulder, the muzzle flashes strobing against bestial eyes, snouts, and fangs. In the center, Tirolane's sword whirred; yowls replied. A single flash of Dora's Ruger on the right illuminated Wukhzak and a x'qiigh struggling over the trogre's halberd. One of Sharat's trogans rushed forward to help.

Polsolun and Tirolane both discharged their guns; heavy bodies fell. The trogan came flying back out of the front rank, cured armor and the belly beneath ripped wide. Riordan's comms deafened him as Dora shouted at Wukhzak to stand back, swore as her gun jammed on a bad ejection, then shrieked when the x'qiigh snapped the trogre's halberd and leaped in, slashing and biting. Veriden's gun spoke as Wukhzak fell. It spoke again; the x'qiigh collapsed over him. Miles started forward, stumbled over the gutted trogan's corpse, tilting into Riordan's left arm as he steadied himself, all the while shouting, "No shot, damn it! No shot!"

With Wukhzak down, the ragged line of contact began collapsing closer to Dora. Tirolane, Polsolun and the last trogan kajh exchanged fast glances and came to the same grim choice: yield ground rather than being overwhelmed by the press of larger, more powerful foes. Miles squeezed off a few shots. Cruvanor and Dora did the same. X'qai fell. The three warriors edged toward the rear. It bought a few seconds, but the fight kept moving backward.

Riordan saw the trogan was tiring, stepped forward, uncertain how to replace him in the line: there wasn't even enough space—

Miles' voice: "Down!" Riordan ducked. A deafening fusillade went over his head. A x'qao toppled. Dora's Ruger spoke a moment later; because the trogan screening her was smaller, it was now easier to line up targets.

But more x'qai came forward. Tirolane had taken down another but was already fending off two more. Polsolun managed to lame his own adversary and turned to help the big swordsman, lunging at the nearer x'qao's flank. As his swordpoint plunged into the monster, the darkness in front of him deepened. A pair of long talons swept out of the shadow and ripped a bloody X across his chest. With a strangled cry, Polsolun collapsed. Dripping gore, the claws preceded a grotesquely emaciated x'qiigh out into the light of the movement-excited glow-fungi.

The killspawn strode over the warrior, neared the person he'd been protecting: Cruvanor. The war leader was only halfway through inserting a fresh magazine into his pistol.

Tirolane saw the threat, leaped forward, but the last of his two opponents—a massive x'qrukh—swept a paw at him, knocking the sword out of his hand.

But no, Riordan realized, Tirolane had released its hilt even before the x'qao struck—leaving that palm free to bring up in front of his opponent's vaguely canine face.

As if hit in the forehead by a piledriver, the x'qrukh pitched backward. It fell against another, smaller of its kind, sprawling it sideways.

The x'qiigh was almost upon Cruvanor. Tirolane prepared to leap into the narrowing gap, unable to even pull up his lanyarded sword in time to interpose it.

But instead, the porcine killspawn sprang past the old war leader—and straight at Miles.

The speed of the beast and its unexpected action left Riordan no time to think. He jumped in from the side, landed an awkward slice that drew some ichor, but barely slowed the x'qiigh.

Still, the blow put a slight hitch in its last step. Miles jumped back. He fired once, twice, and then—cursing at having to spend so many rounds—squeezed off another two. "Out!" he shouted as the creature fell and he grabbed for a new magazine.

The breech on Cruvanor's pistol clacked home as he raised it toward a x'qnarz emerging from the diminishing dark beyond Polsolun's body. As calm as if he'd been at a firing range, the silver-haired war leader fired three fast rounds. The x'qao snarled, stumbled back into the shadows. Across the passage, Dora was reloading, cursing as yet another x'qao charged through the gap in the center of their line. It also headed toward Miles but was intercepted by Tirolane, sword back in hand. The two traded blows in the space directly between her and Cruvanor.

As the last trogan moved to assist the swordsman, a smaller x'qnarz leaped out of the darkness, its bronze broadsword already descending through an overhand cut.

The blow staggered the trogan kajh; the x'qnarz slipped around him, past Tirolane, and ran at Miles.

Who was in the last second of getting the fresh magazine into his unfamiliar pistol.

Partially screened by the recovering trogan, Riordan waited, hoping the x'qnarz wouldn't see him until it was passing, flank exposed. But its pupilless black eyes snapped over at him; it swerved to close, broadsword raised for another overhand cut.

Rather than parry, Riordan retreated out of the blade's downward arc and angled back into the open space between the killspawn and Miles. The SEAL shouted for Riordan to duck. But there wasn't enough time; the x'qao's reflexes were too quick.

As if to prove it, the x'qnarz detected that the trogan had recovered and was threatening its rear flank. It danced away from Riordan and twisted to stab at the kajh. As it did, Caine stepped closer, longsword level, shortsword in a low guard.

The x'qnarz was fast, but not skilled: its broadsword's point skittered off the trogan's cured armor. Still, it was enough to sprawl the kajh toward Dora's legs.

Riordan jumped in with a fast thrust before the killspawn could recover. The steel longsword's point went into its side but dragged, as if being driven through a heavy tire tread. Riordan leaned back quickly. Ichor leaked out as the skeletal x'qao started to spin back around.

Caine knew that the smart move, the prudent move, was to complete his retreat and recover his guard. But this x'qao was almost as quick as thought. So the only way to win was to act before it did. Which meant doing what it would least expect.

Instead of completing his retreat, Riordan jumped forward, leading with the point.

The x'qnarz was twisting back toward him, somehow leaning away while also sweeping its broadsword around to intercept the human's lunge.

But Caine completed his jump by dropping into a near-kneel and rolling his wrist until his primary blade was aimed at the floor. As the x'qnarz's weapon cut the air over his head, Caine drove his longsword through the killspawn's foot.

The x'qnarz emitted a screeching howl: part bat, part hyena. It staggered, trying to recover its balance and its guard at the same time: a fleeting moment of vulnerability.

Riordan drove himself up out of his kneel, angling both swords' points toward the monster as he closed with it.

As the x'qao finished its turn, it started—its snout grazed Caine's visor—and then jerked; the killspawn's own motion had driven it hard against the two swords. Their points dragged, but Riordan's forward push overcame the tough outer hide; the blades ran deep into its body.

The x'qnarz's initial shriek became a wheezing gargle. Riordan stepped back, pulling his weapons free—but was suddenly airborne, head snapped over by the force of an unseen blow.

Caine didn't feel the pain of it until his body slammed into the wall. He fell. Yellow lights glared at him from the helmet's status strip. But he couldn't focus on them. He couldn't focus on anything. Except for the unceasing explosion of agony inside his head.

Or was that sound partly from another rush of point-blank pistol fire?

Caine discovered that he was pushing himself back along the wall. A purely primal reflex. Anything to put distance between himself and whatever had sent him flying with one blow.

Riordan got his left palm against the floor. *Where's my short-sword?* Tried to lift himself, collapsed. Saw a massive silhouette looming over him. An immense x'qrukh.

A scream came from behind Caine, soared over him. But whereas killspawns' roars were stony and terrifying, this shrill howl almost set the air trembling with its intensity. And its resolve. And its passion.

The source of the scream—a vaguely humanoid shadow—crashed headlong into the specter of the x'qrukh. The giant killspawn staggered back, almost recovered its balance, but the smaller shadow kept slashing and stabbing in a precise, murderous frenzy. Two more faltering rearward steps, and the monstrous shadow toppled backward with a guttering groan.

Riordan tried to squint through his blurred vision. Flashes from multiple pistols. Craig Girten running toward the x'qai, a bright metal shard in his hand. Two mangles helping each other toward the exit, trailing blood. Miles stalking past, reloading and cursing as he went.

Time to get up and take charge. Caine almost laughed at the absurdity of the thought; he was struggling just to get his back against the wall. He gathered his legs under him—

Then there was a face, right in front of his. A riot of hair around it. Bright, wide-set eyes. A mouth that said his name.

He smiled: Bey.

It was Bey.

Now everything is going to—

Darkness crushed in from every side. The world became a black void. Into which he sent a final thought:

Bey.

Qudzorpla returned the touch of Fezhmorbal's mind with strange, intense suddenness. "War Leader, are you at risk?"

"Why do you ask?"

"I just had word from your adjutant that our forces were defea—that they failed you, War Leader. I was concerned that our enemies might have located and attacked your position."

"I sense you have not yet studied the details of my adjutant's report." When she pulsed a confirmation, he instructed her, "Examine it again." He waited. "Now: how much of *my* force did I lose?"

She either missed or allowed the small tendril of relief to slip through with her reply. "None. All the attackers were Sleepers in the Sand. So you were not proximal to the battlefield."

"Correct."

"But—"

"Yes?"

"The attack was profitless."

"You are smarter than that."

Her reassessment was tentative. "You gathered useful knowledge. You learned that the leader of the thieves was not the one indicated by the caver who escaped the force they sent into the Orokrosir this spring. You also confirmed that they are no longer operating in one group. They have divided their forces."

"Yes. I suspect their commander will take the precaution of maintaining patrols at greater distance now, seeking to detect our scouts. It is an old game: hide and seek with daggers."

"And what of the large caravan the kiktzo have detected approaching from the east? Are they also bound for Ebrekka?"

"They mean to trade with the mangles but will surely be directed to one of the temporary communities Ebrekka maintains for such purposes."

"Are they all as large as the one you attacked, War Leader?"

"No one knows the answer to that question but the mangles themselves. But I suspect not." He felt Qudzorpla's mind wrestling with contending intents: curiosity and reluctance. "Ask your question."

"The community you just struck: how did you come to know it in such detail, War Leader Fezhmorbal?"

"Many years ago, my mentor lost a team there. He believed he could rally more forces to him at a key moment. He was mistaken."

"Were you there?"

"I was one of the few who returned."

"And your mentor? Did he return?"

"He did."

"And what became of him?"

Fezhmorbal sent the mental equivalent of a shrug. "I killed him as he crossed the threshold of our station house." Qudzorpla's horror was palpable. "His failure was not because of fate's caprice, but his own carelessness. It is the way of our race to eliminate all weakness, or have you failed to notice that?"

"No, War Leader."

"Then refresh your knowledge of those teachings. Your memory of them seems to have dimmed."

"And... what if it had been *your* fault, that day?"

Fezhmorbal admired the boldness of her query. "One day, it *will* be me. In time, all of us fall victim to arrogance, ambition, error, or age. Considering the alternative—withering away on a death-pallet—would you have it any other way?"

She did not answer, but returned to the practical matters at hand. "How do you mean to keep the enemy under observation, War Leader?"

"That task will be given to one of Gasdashrag's lieutenants. I am returning to Khorkrag, there to commission a barge back to Forkus."

She became very attentive. "Do you intend to raise more forces for the Orokrosir?"

"No. I am returning to expedite a transition to more effective leadership."

"Do you mean to confront the other war leaders who contended that you should include them in your strike upon the mangles?"

"I was not speaking of *deciqadi* leadership."

"So . . . x'qai leadership?"

"A word of advice, young Qudzorpla. Stating the obvious never impresses one's superiors. Indeed, it has the opposite effect. Now see to your duties in Hwe'tsara's fortress. I will have business there when I arrive; of this you may be certain."

Chapter Forty-Nine

Riordan liked to think he was a fairly patient person, but he was rapidly becoming annoyed at his present status: that of an invalid.

Every damn one of the Crewe acted as if he'd just broken all his limbs. And his spine, as well.

The individuals gathered in Raam'tu's austere meeting room hadn't proven to be much better. While walking to the meeting of the leaders, Tirolane and—*God help me!*—even Cruvanor were always near his elbow, ready to steady him. Sharat hadn't been much better and Ta'rel insisted on treating Riordan as if he was far more infirm than the durus'maan. Of all of them, only Ulchakh had an apt instinct for how to remain moderately concerned while proceeding as if nothing unusual had happened. Probably a skill learned over decades of striking business deals with beings that might try to kill you after breakfast. Or eat you for dinner.

Bey had started out even more unsure than the others. On the other hand, she had been at her most endearing when she was at her most flustered. In the hours immediately after Riordan had been struck in the head, she alternated between the extremes of how trogs treated injured friends—gruff, infrequent encouragement—and her imagination of the human equivalent: quarter-hour check-ins of great solicitude, but conducted from the other side of the room.

However, she'd become more comfortable after Riordan sat up from their combined sleeping furs and declared that something was definitely wrong with their chamber.

She'd frowned. "What do you mean?"

"Well, we did just spend the night here, didn't we?"

"Yes. But . . . ?"

"But all the cushions and rugs are still in their original places." He frowned. "That just doesn't seem like us. Did you leave, during the night?"

To her credit, she rolled her eyes at his sorry excuse for a pillow-talk quip—a form of conversation that was unknown to her. To her further credit, she did not let that prevent her from forcibly initiating a mutual attempt to render the room an even greater mess than it had been the night before. But as soon as they'd arrived at the meeting—separately, of course—she resumed her furtive monitoring of him.

Raam'tu and Ta'rel laid cups, pulverized spices, and a pitcher of sun-heated water on the low, long table before settling themselves at the central rug. Just as mangles did not allow any significant imbalances in prestige or possessions, they did not abide servitude: to assist another was a personal choice and privilege, never a commodity. So it was that the revered leader of the greatest known mangle community on Bactradgaria personally served his guests the equivalent of midday tea. Riordan would have liked the leaders of the Accord to have been present: they could afford to take notes.

"Your eyes are distant, Caine Riordan," Raam'tu murmured. "Are you certain that you would not benefit from more rest before we address the matters which have arisen as a result of last night's attack?"

"I am quite well rested, thank you, durus'maan," he said, while thinking, *The next person who suggests I retire to my fainting couch for a spell . . .* "I would like to get started, though."

Raam'tu nodded. "The number of those injured and slain has not changed since the last report. There is much sorrow, but for those who have asked if there is a way to salve or share in the mourning of our people, do not be offended if they demur. We do not bring our grief to others until we are ready. So they will not interpret your silence or restraint as callousness, but consideration."

Riordan nodded. It had probably been his and the Crewe's inquiries which had prompted Raam'tu's general advice; it seemed unlikely that the others would have been unaware of mangle death rituals. Of which there would be many in the days to come: over a hundred had been killed, as many again lamed, and twice as many wounded. Had it not been for Ebrekka's renowned healers, the casualties would have been far greater.

The durus'maan nodded toward Cruvanor. "I understand that Polsolun has not succumbed to his wounds."

The war leader inclined his head. "We are very grateful for the care and Gifts your healers have lavished on him. He shall not only live, but will almost certainly resume his life as a warrior with both eyes and all limbs." He sighed. "However—"

"However, he cannot be moved," Raam'tu finished with a knowing nod. "Nor is it likely that he can until the vernal equinox. My eldest daughter tells me his wounds were as severe as a human may have and live."

Cruvanor's mouth was a crumpled, lipless line as he nodded. "I apologize for such an imposition. I know your people are sworn not to allow outsiders to tarry long in Ebrekka. If there is a service or resource I may gift you to lessen our unavoidable violation of that law, please, tell me."

"You are kind to offer such gifts, but we do not need them. More to the point, Polsolun's recuperation here does not violate our law." Cruvanor's facial reaction was a match for Riordan's inner bafflement: *How can that be*?

But Raam'tu raised a finger as he moved to the next topic. "Caine Riordan, I believe Ta'rel has good news for you and your companions."

Riordan glanced at the mangle, wondered if the x'qao's blow had knocked a few marbles loose despite the Dornaani helmet. Ta'rel never had anything to report because he had no such responsibilities.

The young mangle laid his bandaged hand atop the other. "The samples you gave us upon arrival show only a slow progression of the animalcule that causes s'rillor. There are some among you in whom the signs of progression are so small that they defy detection."

Ta'rel had looked away from Riordan as he finished. *Because he doesn't want anyone to get the idea that mine is the sample that "defies detection." And it almost certainly* is, *thanks to the Slaasriithi theriac.* "I shall pass that glad news on to my friends. Is it still advisable that we consume the preventive moss?"

"At the very least, it is *extremely* advisable. It could be crucial. On the other hand, it may be that your bodies are learning what is beneficial in the moss and are growing that inside you." He shrugged. "It is said that such things happen, but I have no knowledge of it."

Riordan nodded gratefully. *If any of the Dornaani inoculations work like long-duration immune boosters, we may all be walking vaccine labs. But, one step at a time. Particularly after yesterday.*

Raam'tu put his hands on his knees. "I understand you have a report for us, as well."

Riordan frowned, then remembered, smiling. "Yes! Sergeant Girten's whereabouts during the ambush outside. Several 'qo charged him all at once, chasing him into a narrow notch in the rocks, just alongside the entry. They couldn't get in, but there was no other way out. He baited several in far enough to take off a few fingers."

"He was in a 'notch'?" Ta'rel asked.

Raam'tu waved away the question. "I know of what he speaks. Before centuries of runoff widened the wadi, much of what is now open to the sky was sheltered. In those days, the notch Sergeant Girten sheltered in was a watch post that was not open to the sky—and so, hidden from the eyes of kiktzo." The old mangle shrugged. "But the land is always changing, and it is no longer safe for that purpose."

Bey frowned. "So, your enemies *have* known the location of Ebrekka? They just did not know the secret entrances into it?"

Raam'tu smiled, gestured at the walls. "This is not Ebrekka, my friends." He turned to Cruvanor. "That is why keeping Polsolun—as long as he remains at this location—violates no prohibitions against outsiders."

Neither Sharat nor Ulchakh seemed surprised; the latter was actually nodding and smiling to himself.

"But you spoke of this place as Ebrekka," Bey insisted.

"Chief Bey, you are a truthteller. You cannot wear that tattoo without an excellent memory to recall what you have seen and heard. Think back on the words my people have used in referring to this place. Especially my own."

Bey was already nodding as Riordan smiled and shook his head. "It was *we* who spoke of this place as Ebrekka. But you and Ne'sar—what did you call it, durus'maan? A special place, I think?"

"You are correct. We refer to it with many labels, but not once did we point, or refer, to *this exact place* as Ebrekka."

Bey was nodding, her eyes closed as she reviewed her memories. "No, you did not." Her eyes opened into slits, one brow raised. "But as a truthteller, I must say you did not make your meaning clear."

"True, but nor were we taking an oath. Had you asked us directly, we would not have lied."

"No, but it is a most profound subterfuge."

"I agree, but there are profound reasons for maintaining it. Do you think it is possible we would have survived here for centuries—longer—if we did not maintain other places that we might meet with outsiders? And which we would allow them to believe were Ebrekka? Shall I tell you how many of those other places have been destroyed or abandoned over the years? Or how many we are always building, bit by bit, because we know that in the fullness of time, the others will all be raided, or betrayed, or discovered?"

Ulchakh was shaking his head. "I knew you had many safe places. I presumed you had more than I imagined. But so many? And so big as this? How do you manage to do this and survive?"

"Because it is necessary for us to be able to both trade and evade all those who would destroy us. Losing such safe places is like any other investment."

Riordan looked at Ta'rel's hand, thought of all the bodies brought past him in the passage just after he'd regained consciousness, Bey at his side. "I am unsure how you can be so philosophical after this investment has proven so terribly... expensive."

Raam'tu nodded. "I do not understand all the ways that your life is shaped by your peoples' natural means of surviving. Conversely, you do not understand all of mine. I may only assure you of this: our investment in this place has proven to be anything but futile; and the expense, while terribly high, is also the cost of securing a better, safer future for increasing numbers of us."

"What I truly do not understand," Riordan replied, "is where all the x'qa came from, all at once." All the leaders' eyes turned toward him. He almost shrugged. *Yes, I'm impossibly ignorant about this world. But right now, I can't afford to care about that—because we sure as hell can't afford a repeat of last night. If a few exchanges had gone the other way...*

Raam'tu glanced at Ulchakh, who asked, "You have heard of 'the sleep of the sands,' have you not?"

"I have now." *As in, about an hour ago.* "But why haven't we run into it before? My God, we marched all the way north from Forkus, and it didn't happen once. Not *once*."

Ulchakh frowned. "I am not sure that is entirely accurate. You may recall, when Yidreg joined the column, we were set upon by x'qa?"

"Yes."

Bey nodded, eyes fixed on Ulchakh.

"Do you remember how your magic helmets did not detect all of their heat before they appeared above rises in the land?"

Bey nodded again. "It is because they weren't there to be seen... not until they were awakened from the sleep."

Ulchakh shrugged. "So I suspected, but we did not follow their tracks to their origins, and I do not have the mastery of your artifacts.

"And as for the rest of our march? Certainly we were lucky, in part, but killspawn trapped in the sleep of the sands are most frequently found in places where they have lost battles, either against one of our species or each other. Those who are rendered senseless but not slain may be covered over by the sand and dust and so, fall into a deep sleep. Such a x'qao's body gathers a cocoon, after which it almost ceases to live."

"Sounds a bit like symbiolene," Riordan muttered, glancing at Cruvanor. The war leader nodded grimly.

"So there was a great battle here?" Caine asked Raam'tu.

The old mangle nodded. "There have been several, or so it is said."

"Was it over the metal?"

Raam'tu frowned. "Not over the metal freed yesterday, but there may have been other metal—or even artifacts—here before. We knew of this place but had abandoned it and ultimately forgot its exact location. It was when we rediscovered it generations ago that we found the new metal. That activity evidently attracted those who may have hoped they had found Ebrekka, or who just wished to take our lives and our goods."

"And yet you came back *again*?"

"Obviously."

"For the metal?

Raam'tu shrugged. "Partly."

"You mean, you would have come back anyway?"

The durus'maan's smile made him look both very young and very old. "Leader Caine, shall I tell you the real reason we survive here in the wastes, among such terrible creatures?"

"Yes, please do."

"It is because we are stubborn. Not obstinate, not prideful: just stubborn. In the same fashion as the seasons and the tides. They come, they go; they wax, they wane—but they always return, and they are never wholly gone."

Shod bone tapped on the packed earth floor, a few meters beyond the opening.

Raam'tu looked at the others. "The reason we meet has arrived. You are ready to hear him?"

Riordan's nod was just as somber as the rest of the leaders'.

Raam'tu stood—and Ulchakh grunted. "You would stand for this murderer, this betrayer of every people known—including his own?"

Raam'tu nodded. "I do so because these are my rooms and he is here at my bidding. I neither ask, nor expect, that you should stand as well." He raised his voice. "Enter."

A h'achga—wounded and in the colors of Atorsír—appeared on one side of the doorway, a mangle scout at the other. They scanned the occupants, nodded to each other and stepped back.

Chief Boghram entered, face expressionless. Raam'tu pointed to a place just beyond the limit of the rug. The grim h'achga went to that spot and waited.

"We have all heard what you claim, Boghram: that after years of refusing the rapprochement offered by Chief Vaagdjul of Achgabab, you recently agreed to accept his proposal that his eldest grandson and your daughter be joined as lifemates. You were displeased to learn that you would not meet the chief personally. You were further displeased when Vaagdjul bade you bring your daughter to this place to be gently conveyed to Ulchakh, his deputy, who would then decide if it was advisable to bring all, part, or none of your entourage to Achgabab for the ceremony. Are my words correct and true?"

"They are," Boghram said tonelessly.

"Yet, throughout these negotiations, you meant to deceive Chief Vaagdjul and avenge yourself on him for slights and dishonors that you have attested to over many years?"

"Also true."

From what Riordan understood, lying would have been pointless: Boghram had been extremely vocal about his opinion of Vaagdjul.

"How did you mean to exact this vengeance?"

"It had been my intent to recruit malcontents in Achgabab as well as lesser leaders of ambition and take the town for my own."

"But you abandoned those plans before you even spoke to Ulchakh. Indeed, you didn't even bother to kill your enemy's deputy. You also didn't recruit your own guards to help exact your revenge, but, curiously, entrusted the bloody deed to the claws of ravenous x'qai. Stranger still, it seems they did not even know they were serving you at all, inasmuch as they killed several of your personal guard, your mate, and tried quite hard to bring the same fate to you." Raam'tu waited. "Please, tell me where I speak incorrectly."

The only change in Boghram was that his face and posture had become rigid.

Raam'tu sighed. "In this room, there is a h'achga whose deputization includes the right to slay you for betraying and plotting to kill the high chief of the Greater Tribe of which you are a part. If you refuse to reply, I no longer have any right to hold you in this place, whereas Ulchakh has every right to demand that you be placed in his custody."

Finally, a significant change flitted across Boghram's features: not just relaxation, but relief.

Judging from their subtle increase in attentiveness, Bey and Ulchakh had seen the same thing.

Raam'tu's detection of it was there in his slow smile. "It is interesting that you find ease in the guarantee of death. So before you commit to such a strange step with your silence, you should know one more thing.

"A few leagues from here, our scouts came upon a body: a junior member of your guard. Cowering nearby was a single trog porter, far along the path of s'rillor. Little more than a pawn, he was grateful for food, and upon the promise of more, revealed where he had sheltered the night."

Boghram's look of relief had fallen away. He was rigid again, his jaw shifting from side to side.

"The place to which he led them was a cave entrance we collapsed almost two decades ago. What is even more interesting is that when we sent other scouts to find from whence the x'qai had risen to attack us, their tracks led to a chamber in which they had spent many years as Sleepers in the Sands." Raam'tu paused. "That chamber was the sealed cave outside which the first scouts stood, but an arm's reach away."

Boghram was no longer able to keep his eyes open, but when he shut them tight, tears streamed out the corners.

"What is this?" Ulchakh muttered, almost as alarmed as he was surprised.

"They have him," the traitor wept. "My son."

"Who has him?"

"I do not know. But if I did not do as they asked, his fate was sealed."

Ulchakh's voice was hard, harsh. "You could have died trying to rescue him."

"Yes, and that would have been an honorable death, but even if I knew who held him, and where, the outcome would have been no different. To even start toward him was to seal his fate."

Cruvanor's sharp intake of breath was like the hiss of a snake in reverse.

"What?" Riordan asked.

"They threatened to infest him."

"Or they already have!" wailed Boghram. "I could expect him to die—he is a warrior; he is ready—but this? To be eaten from the inside until the loathsome killspawn erupt from his body?"

Ulchakh leaned in. "Why did they care about Achgabab?"

"Did you not hear? I was a tool, nothing more. One day the young guard came to me, explained he'd been contacted by my son's captors. They promised to restore him to me so long as I gave the young guard freedom to give orders to the pawn and see to his provisioning. So of course I agreed!"

He looked up in horror at the faces around him. "And then, all . . . this. My own mate slain! My daughter injured! And all the dead . . ." He stared at them, eyes hard. "I will not pretend I have generous feelings for your races. In my years, I have hated many and killed a few. But this—this!"

He almost dove across the rug toward Ulchakh. "Please, kill me. Execute me as a traitor. Let it be known wide, that they will see my son is worth nothing to them."

"And do you think," Riordan asked sadly, "that they would release him?"

"Why not?"

"Because," Caine sighed, "whoever is behind this did not even bother to tell you that you were likely to be one of the victims. They might have preferred that. But they certainly didn't want the young guard to live long enough to reveal anything. And I wouldn't be surprised if the go-between they used to contact him has already met the same fate.

"So, tell me: given the assassins' determination to leave no trace of themselves on this crime, do you really think they would allow your son to live—the only one who's ever seen them?" Riordan shook his head. "Other than their objective—whatever it is—they only care about one thing: no loose ends."

Boghram gaped at Riordan as if he'd become a x'qao in front of his eyes. "Who are you?"

Cruvanor was nodding slowly. "A person who might—*might*—be able to get your son back alive."

Caine's stomach grew cold. Bactradgaria had been populated with enough terrors. But now? There were enemies out there, leveraging local "Talents" and "Gifts" with all the finesse of operators he'd seen achieve the same ends with technology. *Damn: all is for the worst in this worst of all possible worlds.*

He found a smile to show to Cruvanor. *Did you just involve me because it's a genuine opportunity to trick these operators into revealing themselves, or because you wanted to see how I'd respond? Or both?*

But still, as long as the father was known to have survived, and had worthwhile contacts—"Raam'tu, could you keep Boghram here?"

Raam'tu, who seemed largely impervious to surprise, blinked. "Perhaps. But why?"

"Because he may be our backdoor into finding out whoever caused this massacre." Caine pointed at Boghram. "And if we can get the answer to that, we might be able to find, maybe even rescue, your son. But your fate is in Ulchakh's hands." He turned toward the stunned h'achga trader. "Assuming Vaagdjul will permit Raam'tu to hold on to Boghram for a while."

"I do not know if Vaagdjul would agree to that with a dagger held over his heart."

"I wonder if he'd think differently if the life-mating went ahead as planned."

Ulchakh's eyes widened then narrowed appraisingly. "Yes, he

just might—with Boghram under his thumb and his daughter the most prominent person remaining in Atorsír, that might be a very agreeable arrangement." He clapped Caine on the shoulder. "I shall try. That is all any of us can do."

Raam'tu called for the escorts to take Boghram away, who glanced at Riordan right before he disappeared around the doorway.

Riordan was ready—very ready—to leave when the durus'maan announced that Sharat had a final announcement, now that the hearing had concluded.

Without a moment's delay, the Legate commander turned to Riordan. "You ready to leave?"

"What? You mean for Shrakhupsekh? Already?"

"Change of plans, my friend. The irony? It's you and your Crewe who changed them."

Caine slumped back, noticed that Bey was sitting slightly more erect. He knew her well enough to see that although nothing in her expression had changed, she had become very, very watchful. "What is this all about, Sharat?"

"It's about the Silo. And now, what's happened here. You know that Uhrashgrukh sends out large caravans several times a year, yes?"

Riordan wasn't entirely sure, but he nodded because everyone else did.

"Well, the biggest was about to turn south and follow the river to Shrakhupsekh when Tasvar relayed what had been found at the Silo, and in what condition. Within a day, it was decided to bring that big caravan westward to join us here. Three of my rads will go back north to the Silo with almost all that convoy's technickers and salvage specialists. I'll attach to the balance of the convoy which will head overland toward Shrakhupsekh. That also means that the camphor mission to Zrik Whir remains with me alone, so don't talk about it with any of the Legate force from Uhrashgrukh."

"Compartmentalization," Riordan said with a nod. "Got it."

Sharat paused at the strange word, then continued. "It's going to be a lot of value in one formation with a lot of rads and troops. But that just makes us a big target, so we will be traveling as fast as we can."

"All real rads?" Cruvanor inquired over steepled fingers.

"Enough to tow the few windrads if we have to for a day or two." He turned toward Bey, which surprised Riordan almost as much as it surprised her. "Sorry, but you are also needed elsewhere."

"Yes, I know. Shrakhupsekh, with Leader Caine."

Sharat shook his head in what looked like genuine regret. "Chief Bey, the group heading north has almost no one who's been to the Silo. And none of them have even been near Achgabab."

"Yes, and . . . ?"

Ulchakh looked crestfallen. "Bey, my friend. I must be escorted back to Achgabab, but we anticipated that would be carried out later and with at least some of Sharat's men. Now, none of them will be with us. You know the ways for these rads; I do not. And once you have delivered me to Achgabab—with Boghram's daughter, I suspect—you will then need to guide the rest of the Legate's technickers to the Silo."

"Where," Sharat sighed, shifting in his seat, "there is a situation that the Legate only trusts you to handle."

"And what would that be?"

"Trogs trying to push through on Level Three. I'm told there's a breach there."

She nodded. "And trogs are attacking? They must be mad."

"They're not attacking, and they're not mad. They're desperate."

"For food, for water?"

"No: to escape the cavers." He held up a hand to forestall her questions. "I'm told the reason they need you there so badly is that you are the one person that all the peoples speak to—and trust." He pointed to the truthteller tattoo on her forehead.

Riordan frowned. "And did any of the mindspeakers bother to ask the Crewe what they think of the idea?"

Sharat stared at his hands. "They were the ones who reported the situation—and asked for Bey."

Caine looked at Bey. She looked at him. They shared a shrug.

Raam'tu stood again. "I thank you all for sharing your thoughts in my rooms. I am sorry to have kept you so long, but Ta'rel, I do hope you can remain behind for a while longer. It concerns Zrik Whir."

Curiosity held all the others in place.

"What about Zrik Whir?" the mangle asked, genuinely baffled.

"You must go there. With our friends Caine and Cruvanor."

"But, that means I must sail upon the sea."

Raam'tu's smile was impish. "Well unless you grow wings or gills, I suspect that you must, yes."

"But the Rock is—is—"

"Is one of the great wonders of the world I am told. You shall have to tell me all about it when you return."

"But"—the young hero of the wadi looked toward Caine—"I have not been invited."

"No, but I have spoken with Cruvanor, and he agrees." A conspiratorial look passed between the two old statesmen. The mangle turned toward Caine. "Do you wish to remain, to discuss the matter?"

Riordan made sure not to glance at Bey when he answered, "I figure we'll have a lot of time to talk about it on the road to Shrakhupsekh."

"So you agree to it?" Ta'rel sounded like he might become sick.

"I do, actually," Riordan answered emphatically, because he could already see a host of ways in which it could prove to be a very good idea. "Now, if you'll excuse me, I think I'm ready to get some rest."

As Bey led him out, she glanced back at him. "'Rest'?"

He grinned at her. "Yes. 'Rest.' Lots of it."

"I think we forgot to get lunch." Riordan sighed, enjoying the feel of their legs moving along and past each other.

"Dinner, by now," Bey murmured.

He rolled over. "I know that voice. Deep thoughts are stirring."

But Bey did not rise to the light jibe. "Two nights ago, I spoke of how much time and energy you—all your Crewe—spend striving to return to what is behind and to shape what is to come. That it is a great luxury, to devote so much time on dreams that cannot come true. But now, I feel as though I have seen something I did not before: why you clutch so firmly, so desperately to those dreams. Maybe the impossible ones most of all."

"And what opened your eyes?"

She reached for his hand, held it tightly. "This. Feelings like these." Her eyes were so serious they almost looked hard. "I want more of this. Even if the time we share cannot feel this way in every passing moment—what could?—this is what I want from the moments we do have together. I want to feel your flesh and blood and to know you feel mine. Want to know the taste and smell and touch of us until I know—*know*—that this is not a dream, but a reality."

Riordan pushed a long strand of hair away from her cheek. “I want the same thing.”

“I know you do.” She rose up on her elbow. “But I also know that you want more.” She put her hand on his heart. “You have lived your whole life allowing love to dwell here, even when it was an agony and a constant risk to your life. Still, you will not be happy unless that is how you feel about a lifemate. I know this.”

“Does that disturb you?”

“No.” She took his hand and placed it on her heart. “In me, it still feels unfamiliar, strange. But strange and wonderful. And I want more of that. Right now.”

Epilogue

Bactradgaria and the Hyades Cluster (deep space)
September–October 2125

Two shifts beyond 55 Tauri

Richard Downing stared into the holotank, eyes fixed on the star near which *Olsloov* had emerged. "How much longer will it take to replenish the antimatter?"

Before Alnduul could reply, Thlunroolt padded behind Downing with an answer that sounded more like a snarl than any sound he'd ever heard come out of a Dornaani. "It would take many weeks to do so fully, *ex*-Director Downing. This ship has unusually voluminous magnetic containment baffles. Which you would know if you bothered to peruse the ship's specification . . . which *you* requested."

The old Custodian's final additions—imprecations, likely—faded as he made his way to the other side of the bridge.

Alnduul's mouth everted and twisted slightly. "I see that Thlunroolt has, to use your idiom, taken a shine to you."

"That is 'taking a shine' to me?" Downing shook his head, which instantly reminded him it was inadvisable to do so when a ship was rotating rapidly to produce a fractional gee-equivalent. "How does he treat people he dislikes?"

"He doesn't interact with them at all." Alnduul's mouth twisted slightly further; a full grin, now. "That's how I know he has come to consider you acceptable company."

Wish I could say the same for him, old chap. "So, allow me to rephrase my question—"

"No need," Alnduul assured him with a blithe wave of the smallest of his four fingers. "I understood your intent. We will require another week before we have sufficient stocks to effect at least two more shifts."

"And why did you choose this star?"

"In part, convenience. The innermost planet has proven an excellent location for our solar collection arrays. Also, the rare earth prospecting robots have found an exploitable vein."

Downing crossed his lean arms. "And the other reason?"

Alnduul gestured toward one of the acceleration couches; it began transforming into a shape not unlike an armchair. "I will answer that as soon as—ah: Trevor Corcoran," he finished as the iris valve dilated to admit the tall SEAL. "Please, join us." Another of the seats began a similar transmogrification.

"Sorry I'm late," the captain muttered. "Still trying to sort out how best to utilize all the coldcells that freed up after we dropped those poor sibs off with the SpinDogs."

Alnduul laid his two longest fingers side by side in the air. "That is what I wished to discuss."

Corcoran glanced at Downing. "Some new wrinkle?"

Richard shrugged. "Just got here myself, lad."

"It is not a new wrinkle," Alnduul commented. "It is an old wrinkle that is becoming much, much more troublesome."

Richard sighed. "I know that tone, Alnduul. By 'troublesome,' you mean 'perilous in the extreme.'"

Alnduul let air leak slowly out of his gills. "You are fundamentally correct, Richard Downing. Very soon, we could find ourselves desperately short of comestibles. The phased array we have fashioned from our multipurpose satellites has begun producing useful, albeit very imprecise, data."

"And?" Trevor urged.

"We have determined that many of the closest stars are unlikely to have planets in the habitable zone. Those that do are more likely to be home to Ktoran Exodates."

"Because they are the right spectral classes and sizes?" Trevor guessed.

"Yes, but also because most lie in a cluster, or along chains, where other similarly promising stars are within five light-years of each other."

Downing nodded. "So, not only are those systems more

promising, their proximity means shorter journeys for the Exodates' STL craft. Which correlates with higher success rates."

Trevor sighed, leaned back. "So, we could be heading toward more occupied worlds that could be dangerous to approach. We sure don't want another fiasco like 55 Tauri."

"No," Alnduul agreed, "we do not. This is why we remain here producing fuel: so we will not find ourselves pressed to replenish reserves in a problematic system. However, whereas fuel can be gathered anywhere the local population does not have a pervasive spatial presence, food requires much greater proximity—and time.

"Thlunroolt has led a small team in projecting the likelihood of systems along our probable path that are suitable for gathering food. If observed trends hold, we will start becoming malnourished within twenty days, thirty if we initiate rationing now."

"So the only answer is to feed fewer mouths," Trevor concluded with a grunt. "Damn, just when it looked like our biggest problems were behind us."

Alnduul's inner eyelids nictated. "I would still assert they are behind us, given the attitudes of our respective governments."

Trevor replied with a lopsided smile. "Point taken." He sat straighter in the chair that was clearly shaped for reclining. "Okay, so if you've got that projection, I'm betting you've also got a solution."

"I—we—do, Trevor Corcoran, but I suspect you will not be any more pleased by it than I am."

Downing steepled his fingers. "I already don't like it, Alnduul, and I haven't even heard it yet. But let's get to it—and without any caveats. What must we do?"

Thlunroolt, passing behind them yet again, grunted, "We reduce to one-third crew. Both you and us. If we do not, we will all starve before securing sufficient provisions."

Well, thought Downing, *he may be a crusty old sod, but he's direct.* "I thought that's where you might be heading, particularly since the SpinDogs had so little food to spare right before the Searing." He sighed. "At least we have lots of spare coldcells after 55 Tauri."

"Not so many as you think, 'Nuncle,'" Trevor corrected. "More than half of the ones emptied were at high risk of failure. I've just finished running the numbers on how many we'll have left after we move the folks who are still in similarly risky cells into the good ones now available. Not a lot of margin after that, Richard."

Downing folded his hands. "Right. So we need to sleep in three shifts. That's a lot of cycles. Not advisable, but no choice."

"It can be ameliorated," Alnduul asserted. "Firstly, we have a few of our own coldcells for humans. They dramatically decrease both the short- and long-term effects of reanimation. They also allow those just revived to reattain full functionality in less than a third of the time. We recommend that these be reserved for command staff and a cadre optimized for food-gathering operations. We also recommend that a one-month waking interval is optimal for both safety and maintaining a relatively high level of operational awareness in all watches."

"Agreed," Downing sighed. "That way, no one wakes up more than two months out of date. Still, each watch will need a commander. And a medico."

Trevor nodded. "We've only got three real doctors, so they're all in the rota. Cadre need to be current section heads and a few more from the Cold Guard. Locating edibles and pulling them together is going to require a lot of the same skills as a rapid reaction force."

"Your own Cold Guard soldiers are an excellent choice," Alnduul affirmed. "Not only do they have much higher technical expertise with contemporary equipment, but many of them have qualifications as reanimation assistants for your own systems. In the balance, that should prove more valuable than the greater sophistication of the Ktoran units." He glanced between them. "I presume you two will each be commanding officers of one of the watches, but who shall be the third?"

"Hansen would probably volunteer," Richard mused, "but he's almost the oldest among us and is well behind the technical curve. The doctors have to be excluded; they can't wear more than one hat. The Cold Guard are up to snuff on systems, but—"

"Karam Tsaami," Trevor announced confidently. "He's our guy. He's from our time, a pilot, and a bit of a legend. According to scuttlebutt, he's the only one of Caine's crew who didn't get blacklisted when they thumbed their noses at the politicos after Turkh'saar. Gives us a pilot of our own in that shift, too. Helpful for getting dirtside to grab food. Sound like our guy?" he ended, looking at Downing.

Who beamed at his "nephew." "Very much so," Richard replied

before turning to Alnduul. "But there remains one, last, burning question, doesn't there?"

Alnduul's breath fluted out his gills; resignation but also frustration. "Yes: locating Caine Riordan and those we presume are still with him. There is still one buoy we have yet to reach. Hopefully, that will lead to others or some other useful clue."

Trevor looked askance. "That's a whole lot of hope and not a lot of 'plan,' Alnduul." He grew more serious. "So if this buoy is a dead end, then what? How do we continue? Or do we have to start considering that their mis-shift from BD+13 778 was, well, a catastrophic failure?"

Alnduul let all his fingers on both hands droop. "No, I think that most unlikely. Mis-shifts have been so infrequent in the last five millennia that almost all speculation on them is from older records. But the prevailing wisdom remains that if a mis-shift is catastrophic, it will occur in the first shift, not one of the subsequent attempts to correct and return to a familiar region of space."

Downing nodded. "Logical. If the re-expression data was corrupt when the first mis-shift occurred, the ship would never reform. But if it *did* re-express successfully, than any later shifts would possess that same data."

"That is the thinking. But mis-shift has never actually been observed, so neither outcome can be asserted with absolute confidence."

"So," Trevor extrapolated, frowning, "there might have been more mis-shifts to greater distances. Which could mean there are buoys we haven't detected yet."

"That, too, is possible. But once again, there are no certainties."

Downing sighed. "Bloody fitting, if you ask me."

"No certainties? How so?"

"Just like life itself."

Alnduul stared at Richard. "Do you come to this observation from reading Dornaani philosophy?"

"Naah," Trevor groused with a hint of a smile, "it comes from him being *English*. Now let's figure out who to put on those three watches."

The Silo

Bannor came to stand alongside Newton and Bey, their shadows long in the light of the dawn. For some reason, Qyza had stopped coming to their morning ritual: staring south toward Shrakhupsekh.

"The Legate's mindspeaker tells me that the caravan—well, convoy—is nearing the bay," Bannor reported. "They can see the Rock. It's just started off-loading. Our people will probably be aboard in a few days."

Duncan, who'd been following him up the ladder, clambered out of the hatch. "And once they are, it's going to make finding the right radio settings harder."

Bey turned, eyes worried. "Why?"

Solsohn shrugged as he joined them. "As long as they were headed toward Shrakhupsekh, we had a rough idea of their latitude and longi—eh, where they were located."

"I have become familiar with your terms, Duncan Solsohn. I am even learning some of the language that Eku is teaching."

Solsohn's smile was not just friendly, but appreciative: Bey was proving to be as good a student as she was an instructor. "Sorry; I forget who's got what proficiencies, these days. Anyhow, once they're at sea, there's a lot more possibility for error. There's variation in weather, currents, and the courses followed by the different Rocks. Each one's master apparently has their own secret set of waypoints and heading changes to get to Zrik Whir. Makes finding a good skywave result more dependent on good luck."

Bey's pursed lips seemed to resist her words. "So it is less likely that we shall be able to talk to . . . to our people."

"Yes. Sorry, Bey."

She stared south again. "You are doing all that you can. We all know this. It is just that we all miss them."

The three ex-IRIS operatives were silent, knowing full well which one of "their people" Bey was envisioning as she spoke.

She apparently sensed that it was up to her to change the topic. "Regarding this language that Eku is teaching: it is very, very different."

Newton's lips became a grim slit. "It is very, very annoying. And I am not sure it is necessary. You, at least, are learning it voluntarily. The rest of us have been forced into it." His sideways glance at Bannor was not warm. "Some of us believe, as does Eku, that it is necessary."

Rulaine shrugged. "Doctor, you've made that opinion well known already, so give it a rest. And yes, I do agree with Eku. And no, I don't like learning Dornaani any better than you do. But every technical manual we may need to return to 'Shangri-la' is written in that language. As are the programs to organize and search the damn-near complete archive of our 'country's' writings and science. And I have yet to hear anyone refute his assertion that if he died right now, we'd lose access to over ninety-eight percent of *all* that material." Newton crossed his arms, but made no reply.

Duncan started chuckling. "Ah, don't mind Doc, Colonel. He just has to have a good grump, occasionally."

"He's welcome to do so . . . but not around me."

"Because you're the CO?"

"*Acting* CO. And no, because I've had about as much as I can stand. So, as your *friend*, Newton, I'm telling you: cut it out if you want to *stay* friends."

Baruch sighed and actually nodded before inquiring sardonically, "I trust you will not deem a report on our prisoner to be a needless aggravation?"

Can't resist having the last word or dig, can you, Baruch? "Not if you drop the sarcastic tone, no."

Newton frowned. "Very well. Our prisoner—my patient—does awake from time to time. But very briefly. He eats, defecates, and then collapses again. By 'collapse,' I mean that his whole body shuts down."

"That's been going on for so long that I've got to wonder if it's part of his healing process or a way to evade interrogation."

Baruch shook his head. "I cannot tell. But I am working on getting an answer. The first step is compiling a baseline of his normative vital signs and metabolism. It is nearing completion but, until now, there has been no means of monitoring neurological activity."

Duncan raised an eyebrow. "Until now?"

"I'm currently in the process of adapting the biomonitors from one of our own duty suits to function as a crude EEG sensor. Initial tests with the biomonitors have demonstrated high compatibility with the prisoner's physiology, which further confirms that the deciqadi are indeed some offshoot of humanity. I deem it quite likely that once complete, the EEG sensor will alert us if his brain activity changes."

Rulaine nodded. "So once it's operational, we can safely wake him up and start asking some questions."

"Colonel," Duncan murmured, "I'd like to suggest a different approach."

And Major Solsohn once again leads the charge for the forces of optimalization. "Go ahead."

"Sir, the trogs who were with the deciqadi revealed a few interesting facts. Firstly, several were recruited back in Forkus, so their knowledge stretches over a very long timeline. Secondly, they are all convinced that our prisoner—or more likely, one of his commanders—were *still* getting orders from someone back there."

Bannor frowned. "How? Mindspeak? Blood-bonded to a x'qao?"

Solsohn rubbed his nose. "Sir, the language for different categories of parapsychological phenomena still leave us scratching our heads sometimes." He glanced at Bey. "Chief Bey is the person to ask about that."

Bey nodded sharply. "It is rare for intelligent species to be blood-bonded to x'qai, though they may be controlled through Talents. I believe the calluskins are using a form of mindsensing that is reportedly theirs alone. It is not exactly common among them, but it occurs frequently enough that they may place individuals with that anagog among separated groups and so, coordinate distant actions."

Newton crossed his arms. "That explains much about how they followed us from Forkus. But why did you not tell us about this trait before?"

She stared at him. "Because I did not know of it until I spoke at length with many at Ebrekka who are learned in such things. The trogs who traveled with the deciqadi also had some speculations, but patience was required to separate their superstitions from their observations."

Bannor nodded. "Did they know the names of the ones following us?"

"They never addressed each other by anything other than code names in the presence of the forces they had hired, or compelled, into their service."

Duncan shook his head glumly. "Opsec. Compartmentalization."

Rulaine felt the way the major looked. "Yeah, just like us."

"That's what worries me, sir. That's why I'm advising that we proceed very, very carefully."

Okay, Duncan; this time, your optimalization might be worth wading through all the details. "So what's your plan?"

Solsohn leaned eagerly into his recommendations. "First, we find out if what we now know about this group of deciqadi can get us more intel. My thinking is that if these guys tracked us from Forkus and gathered more forces along the way, they're pretty crafty and powerful players. So if they were, or are still, based out of Forkus, I'll bet Tasvar knows of them."

Bannor nodded. "Yep, because, ultimately, they are his true competition. And their boss is one of his opposite numbers."

Newton glanced from one to the other. "And other than gathering generally useful information, what purpose does this serve?"

Duncan looked surprised at the question, perhaps a little disappointed. "The more we know about the prisoner's group when we question him—not just who he is, but who the other officers are, where they come from, what they were planning—the more likely that he'll tell us even more. If he thinks someone else has already spilled those beans, he's likely to dump the rest in our laps."

Newton nodded tightly. "Particularly if we apply sufficient forms of coercion."

Bey glanced sharply at Baruch, surprised.

Bannor shook his head. "Doctor, I didn't think I needed to say this, but we don't use torture. We're not our enemies."

Newton crossed his arms. "And I didn't think you would misread my euphemism so profoundly. I shall be more specific. If we knew more about their biology—specifically, their blood chemistry and toxicity reactions—I could explore pharmacological approaches tailored to diminish his resistance. I could also investigate if some local compounds might erode his short-term memory."

"To what end?" Bey's expression had changed to intense interest.

"So that we may extract information from him in brief, initial sessions that he will not recall. By confronting him with the information from those, he will be more likely to believe that his group has already been fully compromised, and that there are no secrets left to protect."

Bey nodded appreciatively, but was frowning. "That is a long strategy, Doctor Baruch. Given his powers, whatever they might be, it would require keeping him in isolation for the foreseeable future."

Duncan shrugged, grinned at Bannor. "Well, it's not like we're going to get our ship to Shangri-la built overnight."

Bey's glance was both patient and bored. "I know that means you are speaking of what you have called the 'rockets' when you forget local ears are listening."

Well, good God damn! "I'm sorry we haven't explained them yet. It's a little bit—"

"I am in no rush, Colonel Rulaine. Besides, when it comes to *your* secrets, I have adopted Caine's philosophy regarding Tirolane's abilities. In time, you will come to feel it wise, or safe, to tell me about Shangri-la. Until then?" She shrugged and turned her eyes back southward. "I have enough to think about."

Bannor didn't put a sympathetic hand on her shoulder, fearing she might suspect it signaled he had doubts about her emotional toughness and strength. "We all have far too much to think about," he agreed gently, "but perhaps not as much as you."

After a moment, she nodded. But her gaze did not move away from the southern horizon and the path to Shrakhupsekh.

Shrakhupsekh

Careful to stay in the shade, Riordan looked down at Shrakhupsekh's glittering bay from his vantage point: a small ruin on the low uplands that sheltered the city's lichen fields. Not having smelled a real ocean in—well, a very long time—he put his face into the wind running in from the water. He drew in a deep breath.

It had nothing in common with any terrestrial sea, or any of those he'd encountered on other planets. There were none of the punky odors that actually gave them their character: none of the faintly sulfurous decay of flora and fauna. Because, after all, it didn't really have either: just diatoms and perhaps a few euglena-analogs.

He stared at the distant whitecaps, resisted a rueful smile; no matter how low he set his hopes for finding beauty on Bactradgaria, it almost always seemed to underperform. There either wasn't enough life, or there was just a bit too much, to create the effect of the austere, majestic vistas that he'd seen on totally barren worlds. Still, it was worth one more try; he drew an even deeper breath.

The breeze did carry a hint of brine, but the closest it came to exuding the scent of a living ocean was something closer to rain on very old leaves. It was so faint that Caine wasn't entirely sure whether it was there or just his hopeful imagination that was hard—*very* hard—at work.

However, no imagination was required to detect the powerful, rank odors of two lines of dirtkine carrying, respectively, the goods of two sizeable caravans. They had both drifted toward the Legate's truly imposing convoy as they all converged toward Shrakhupsekh. Neither had made any formal arrangements with the convoy's senior officer: a renowned commander from Uhrash-grukh, according to Cruvanor. However, such agreements were not deemed necessary until and unless one formation came so close to another that its actual intent might be to mount a surprise attack. In general, though, caravans kept a reasonable distance and welcomed others nearby, because the iron law of the waste was that there was always greater safety in numbers.

In the case of paralleling the Legate convoy, it was more akin to traveling in the protective shadow of a full company of motorized infantry, albeit a shabby one. The only attack over the long month of repetitive travel had not been made *against* it, but rather, *by* it. After a loose rabble of q'akh and 'qo had followed it for a week, the convoy master decided it was not hunting behavior but purposeful shadowing by some greater power. Riordan had deemed it no less suspicious; during the journey south, far larger groups of wandering x'qai had avoided engagement with the large force of highly mobile and well-armed humans.

The only significant danger they had encountered came in the form of a towering, twister-spawning storm that, upon reaching the river, slowed slightly. Until then, there had been no point trying to outrun it or its wide, devastating tornados. On the flat wastes of Bactradgaria, tornados were far less likely to change course often or rapidly, except in response to strong changes in weather or wind. While that seemed like a predictive advantage at first, the storms so dominated the horizon and sky that the lack of perspective made it difficult to gauge their true direction—until, because of their equally immense speed, it was too late.

Riordan drew in one last breath of the sea breeze, reluctant to leave the shade of the ruin, perched beside the ancient trade lane down into Shrakhupsekh.

"Call has come to mount up, Commodore," Miles called as he approached from the direction of the convoy's van. "By the way, the bastard you wanted to inspect is *behind* you, sir."

Caine nodded, glanced over his shoulder. A single 'q'akh, riddled by bullets and partially decapitated by the blow of a trogan's battle-ax, lay stretched upon the ground. It had been yet another anomalous encounter. The x'qa was entirely alone—odd enough—but had persisted in watching from the shadows of the ruin even after the convoy sent out a reaction force. It defied belief that it had not understood the range, or lethality of the approaching weapons, but nonetheless, it had not fled in time. Cruvanor, who got informal messages passed down from the convoy's commander, reported that they were all in agreement; while not identical, the strange behavior of this killspawn was reminiscent of the first group that had been following the formation.

Miles did not seem to agree. He stood over the long-limbed, blue-black monster and spat on it. "I'm not convinced it doesn't have friends around here somewhere. Damn x'qa are like rats in my meemaw's woodpile; if you saw one, you knew there were twenty more."

Riordan shrugged. "I think the Legate commander is right. This one was either sent here to watch for us, or we didn't see it tailing us until today."

"Yeah, but what'd it be following out here?"

Riordan scanned the ruin and the otherwise utterly open terrain. "Us. Maybe."

"Us?" Miles snorted. "Sir, I think maybe you're feeling ghost-crosshairs on you after Ebrekka. Well, *not*-Ebrekka, if you know what I mean."

"I know what you mean, Chief. After all, dodging assassins is how we met."

O'Garran glanced at Riordan, then smiled as what was obviously a long-ignored memory arrived with considerable force. "Sheee-it! That's right! They were trying to kill you in that safe-house, outside DC."

"Alexandria. First of many times." He stared at the dead 'q'akh. "This feels a bit like that."

"Well," O'Garran mused, "maybe it does. Hell, I sure felt like I was on someone's hit list when all those x'qai kept coming at me in the passage. Particularly with them ignoring all sorts of perfectly fine targets to charge a guy with a gun!" He frowned. "Makes a guy wonder. Is it just your imagination? Or a random, chance event? Or are you actually someone's target du jour?"

"Welcome to the club, Chief O'Garran." With so much chaos and confusion on both sides, it was hard to remember everything that happened, let alone discern if the x'qai's murderous focus on Miles had been purposeful. There was no evidence to support that conclusion, but still, it was worth keeping in mind.

"Let's get back," Riordan muttered, glancing toward the long shape upon the bay: the Rock, just visible between the tall ruins around which, and even into which, Shrakhupsekh had been built.

The convoy master was waiting for them, and the subsequent journey from the lonely ruin was quite short. Centuries of caravans had flattened the outlying land into a perfect surface for both wind- and realrads. Furthermore, rather than trying to enter the city proper, the convoy angled away from the two caravans and stopped on the outskirts. There, Sharat gathered Riordan and the others, loaded them and their gear into three rads, and sped into one of the homeliest parts of the rude metropolis.

As the vehicles raced up within meters of a close pair of hovels, the Legate's troops bailed out of their rads and took covered positions, weapons trained outward. Riordan had seen—hell, had been delivered to—forces with far less proficiency than that demonstrated by the men and women around him now. With O'Garran chuckling something about "just like home, sweet home," and Cruvanor lagging to admire their escort's professionalism, they were ushered into the larger of the two hovels.

A young human in bronze scale armor emerged from a loose cluster of trogs, trogans, and trogres that had initially blocked him from view. "I'm Erdor. I'll help you on your way to Zrik Whir." After shaking hands sharply with each of his guests, he gestured at their surroundings. "Sorry for the accommodations, but things have been—well, they've been a bit rough."

Sharat came over to the fellow, put a hand on his shoulder. "We heard. We've brought some resources for you. While we're here, you don't have to worry about your neighbors. You've got some time to recover."

"How long?"

Sharat squinted, estimating. "Seven days, maybe eight."

Erdor nodded gratefully. "Is there a healer with you?"

"Yes. No Gifts, but well trained in the basic art. I'll get her."

Caine glanced around at the walls. "There's been a fight in here."

"Several," Peter amended.

Sharat returned with the healer, whom Erdor escorted down a steep staircase with a narrow opening: very like the one in the hovel where the Crewe had rescued Eku. And where Caine had met Bey.

Sharat slipped over to the group. "I know it looks a little shabby, but it's very defensible and we're stationing a team here. Also, when you go to board the Rock, you won't be walking out the front door."

Riordan glanced back at the stairs that rose up through the floor.

Sharat nodded. "The other end emerges in a friendly place. Far enough that anyone who might be watching for you to leave here won't see. No one will follow you to the Rock."

"Why would anyone do that?" Dora asked.

Sharat smiled. "Well, you'll want to be wearing your artifact armor when you board, so that will attract a little attention. At least you won't have to dicker about price, and you won't have to wait in a line for one of the ship-to-shore boats that will take you out." He glanced sideways at Cruvanor. "And there is a reasonable chance that someone will recognize this old fellow."

The war leader chuckled. "I shall miss you, Sharat."

"Well, you're not rid of me yet. I'll be nearby. At all times." He leaned over. "That's on orders from the convoy commander. I'm told he got them from the station-chief at Uhrashgrukh."

That seemed to impress Cruvanor deeply, but before Caine could think of a subtle means of inquiring why, Ta'rel asked, "Sharat, what happened here? And why?"

"Long story made short? The leaders of Zrik Whir finally decided to commit to establishing a regular station here. They have small ships and a few hidden havens here on Brazhgarag. But given how wary the suzerains are about Zrik Whir on their territory, the Families behind the mission were forced to keep it as small and unnoticeable as possible. So they sent a small group with Erdor."

"He doesn't look as dark as Zrik Whirans are said to be."

"He's not, Sergeant Girten, and that was part of the plan. He was able to pass for a newly independent human, even an incognito crog. That's why there are no other humans here: all to make sure that no undue attention was attracted."

Sharat sighed. "But having that small and untrained a force means one is also very vulnerable. In this case, as Erdor started expanding, he did so quickly. That *did* draw some attention." The Legate officer looked at the gouges and divots in the wall. "You'd have to ask him about the fight, but he lost almost half his group—and his life—holding on to this place."

Erdor appeared at the top of the stairs, scanned the group more carefully than the first time, stopped when his eyes came to rest on Tirolane. "You are he, are you not?"

Tirolane raised an eyebrow. "And who do you believe I am?"

"The swordsman from Zrik Whir."

"And how do you know that?"

"Because I've heard your name before, Tirolane. Just recently, too."

Tirolane tensed. "Who spoke my name?"

"Your friends, Axanar and Rylhus. They sailed from here on a hull from home, just forty days ago."

Tirolane grabbed Erdor by both arms. "They live? They are free?" Sharat appeared even more surprised than Tirolane.

Erdor nodded. "Yes, unless the sea has taken them on their way back to Paideion. They claim to have quite a story to tell." Erdor frowned slightly. "But it was not safe for my ears."

Tirolane clutched a very startled Erdor close to his broad chest. "Thank you, Friend Erdor. From the bottom of my heart, I thank you many, many times!"

"Speaking of hearts," Erdor grunted over his shoulder, "I think you're crushing mine."

Forkus

Qudzorpla watched Fezhmorbal stare after the pawn that had staggered into their stronghold after he bade the sentries admit her. She approached, cautious but also curious why he watched the wretch stagger off into the streets of Forkus.

"News, War Leader," she announced over his shoulder.

He did not turn. "Report."

"We have tracked the thieves to Shrakhupsekh. They remained with the large Legate convoy all the way from the Orokrosir."

"Yes, I know."

Wondering if she had not been the first to learn, she asked, "Who reported it to you?"

Fezhmorbal nodded after the pawn as she disappeared into Forkus' summer dust and throngs of praakht. "W'sazz-Ozura."

Qudzorpla was unsure she had heard correctly. "And that... that pawn was she? The advisor to Suzerain Ormalg? She herself in that husk?"

"Yes. She had full control of the pawn. It was her puppet." He sighed in what might have been envy. "It was... very impressive."

Qudzorpla shook her head, unable to fit such disparate information and events together. "But why did she take that form to do so? And why did she have word of the thieves? Surely they are too insignificant for her to follow?"

Fezhmorbal seemed to break out of a trance, began walking back into the marshalling yard of their small stone fortress. "W'sazz-Ozura could not care less about the affairs of the thieves or anything having to do with Hwe'tsara. But she cares very much about affairs pertaining to Zrik Whir. Or rather, what suzerains beside Ormalg have in mind for it and the relevant plots they are bringing to fruition."

"So... ?"

"So, any action taken against the thieves at this time would also call attention to the Rock they mean to board in Shrakhupsekh. And since that Rock is bound for Zrik Whir, such action might also call attention to that destination. Consequently, other suzerains have requested that Ormalg ensure the vessel's operations remain as routine and uninteresting as possible—for the present."

Qudzorpla frowned. "But suzerains cooperating thusly? And an elder arurkré such as the much-Talented and renowned scholar W'sazz-Ozura conveying a message in the form of a pawn? War Leader, instruct me: I do not understand."

"You will. In time. Be patient." Fezhmorbal's smile chilled her. "I am quite sure the outcome shall be worth waiting for."

Aboard the Rock, *Shrakhupsekh*

"No one knows what it is made of, honored lord," replied the Master's Second Agent as he guided Caine and the group to their quarters high above the main deck. "All the Rocks are very, very old. It is known that they are neither metal nor rock. Their sides are said to be harder than steel yet lighter than bones. Many suspect there is ancient magic behind their creation!"

"Personally," Peter muttered near Caine's ear, "I suspect plasticrete. Unless, of course, magic artifacts get pitted in just the same way and also show the same blended laminations as smart composites."

"Noah's ark," Craig Girten pronounced, looking up to the peaks of the four rotary sails and following their masts down into small, nacreous pyramids spaced evenly along the centerline of the weather deck. "But Noah's ark with a crew and cargo that's straight outta hell."

Cruvanor leaned toward Riordan. "The real wonders—the mechanisms that propel this craft—must be beneath the rabble down there," he muttered, jutting his chin at the long deck. Beings of every kind, including several they had not seen before, were busy dragging packs and gear about, answering questions, and submitting themselves to the same examination that the group itself had just endured: a thorough check for disease and parasites. Riordan had wondered which of the two trogans conducting it—one dressed like a technicker, the other bedecked with the fetishes and skulls of a shaman—was the more effective.

Tirolane clearly had an interest in the Rock's engineering, as well. "Agent," he called to their guide, "I would welcome a visit to the great devices that push the Rock through the seas."

The Second Agent slipped back among them until he could speak in a low tone. "It would please me to allow you to do as you ask, but alas, you are not known to the Master and his officers. Besides," he murmured, leaning closer, "there are always eyes watching. Come away, now, that you may become familiar with the special amenities of your private cabin." The swordsman shrugged and followed the Second Agent.

Miles bumped into Riordan; he was craning his neck looking up along the masts of the rotary sails. "Sorry, sir—but damn it, that's got to be more smart materials. Those things are forty meters high if they're a millimeter, and I'm sure they reach far down under the deck, too."

Peter nodded. "They may have telescoping extensions, given the space between them. Eighty meters, I make it, with similar clearance at the bow and the stern."

"So, just over four hundred meters long?" Girten exclaimed. "I don't know what that is in cubits, but I'm sticking with this being the Ark from Hell."

Riordan took in the squalor of the deck, the smell of unwashed bodies, the x'qa brutally pushing aside any who obstructed their movement, the emaciation of the few pawns and deadskins who'd been loaded more like cargo than living creatures. "Sergeant, I don't disagree with you; it does look like hell. I just hope Zrik Whir is worth the journey."

"Worth the journey?" The Second Agent had spun about, eyes wide and disbelieving. "Are you mad?"

"No," Riordan replied cooly, "I am a fully paid passenger of the highest class. But if you require that my sanity be confirmed, I shall happily accede to your test. Just so long as you bring your requirement, and your reason, to the attention of the Rock's Master."

The Second Agent moved closer. "Firstly, Lord, I do not hear that as a threat, for the Master would certainly welcome any pretext to enter into civilized discourse with such an . . . an unusual group as your august selves. As for my sharp words, please forgive them, but as I said, eyes are always watching. And ears are always listening."

Riordan shook his head. "Who must the Master answer to, then, if he cannot speak with whom he chooses on his own ship?"

The Second Agent pressed closer still. "Please, lord, I implore you: keep your voice low and your words careful. Do you think we humans exist here, even on this ship, for any reason other than that it suits the present needs of the lieges? Or the whims of the x'qai in general?"

He leaned close enough to whisper, face ashen despite his very dark Bactradgarian complexion. "No ship, no fortress, no artifact, *nothing* has any value except to the degree it ensures the only thing that matters to the suzerains: dominion over us. And yes, I mean us humans in particular."

Cruvanor nodded. "You speak truth, but it need not be so. Not forever, and not everywhere."

"I hope—I pray—that you are correct, Cruvanor. Yes, I know who you are. But I fear that we shall always teeter at the brink of extinction, a perpetually endangered species."

Riordan nodded. "Yet you upbraid me for wondering if it is worth going to Zrik Whir. If no place is more promising for our kind than any other, why should that particular destination matter?"

He grimaced. "At least there we hold some sway, can stand off the killspawn and hope for some measure of safety."

"You mean, as a breed banished to a preserve, a protected species?"

He looked at Riordan with haunted eyes. "It is better than the alternative, is it not?"

Caine nodded. "It is. If the Master of this Rock finds a reasonable pretext to meet with us, we would welcome it. Very much. If not?" Riordan shrugged. "We shall follow you and prepare for the voyage to Zrik Whir."

Appendix A

Dramatis Personae

HUMANS AND ALLIES

Alnduul: Dornaani renegade; former Senior Mentor of the Custodians of the Accord, Dornaani Collective

Ayana Tagawa: former XO of SS *Arbitrage*; former Japanese Intelligence

Bannor Rulaine: colonel, crew of UCS *Puller*; former US Special Forces/IRIS

Caine Riordan: commodore, USSF (ret.); former IRIS

Craig Girten: Lost Soldier; former US Army

Dora Veriden: security specialist; crew of UCS *Puller*

Duncan Solsohn: major, former CIA/IRIS; crew of UCS *Puller*

Edouard Tedders (alias Robert Hampson): neurosurgeon/researcher, CEO/CTO of The Cutting Edge, DARPA contractor

Eku: factotum in the service of Alnduul

Katie Somers: corporal, UCAS Armed Forces

Mara "Bruce" Lee: captain, USAF

Melissa Sleeman: advanced science and technology expert; crew of UCS *Puller*

Miles O'Garran: master CPO, former SEAL/IRIS; crew of UCS *Puller*

Newton Baruch: lieutenant, Benelux/EUAF; former IRIS; crew of UCS *Puller*

Peter Wu: captain, ROCA/UCAS; former IRIS; crew of UCS *Puller*

Richard Downing: former Director of IRIS

Rodger Y. Murphy: major, United States Army

Thlunroolt: former Custodian of the Accord and Senior Mentor of the Terran Oversight group, Dornaani Collective

Trevor Corcoran: captain, USSF; SEAL/IRIS

Yaargraukh Onvaarkhayn of the moiety of Hsraluur: exile from the Hkh'Rkh Patrijuridicate, former Advocate of the Unhonored

THE HUMANS OF BACTRADGARIA

Cruvanor: senior war leader, stable of Liege Gorzrik of Fragkork

Enoran: technicker, stable of a vassal of Liege Azhdrukh of Fragkork

Irisir: master technicker, stable of Liege Gorzrik of Fragkork

Orsost: warrior, stable of a vassal of Liege Azhdrukh of Fragkork

Marcanas: senior warrior, stable of Liege Gorzrik of Fragkork

Polsolun: warrior, stable of Liege Gorzrik of Fragkork

Rogarran: war leader, stable of Liege Gorzrik of Fragkork

Sharat: captain, forces of the Legate

Tasvar: station head, forces of the Legate

Tirolane: warrior and ambigogete from Zrik Whir

THE BEINGS OF BACTRADGARIA

Arashk: h'achgan band chief

Bey: crog kajh and truthteller

Fezhmorbal: deciqadi senior war leader and anagogete

Gasdashrag: deciqadi war leader and ambigogete

Hresh: h'achgan oathkeeper

Hwe'tsara: x'qao Liege in Forkus, sworn to Suzerain Ormalg

Ne'sar: mangle healer

Qudzorpla: deciqadi warrior and anagogete

Qyza: (formerly Fwhirki) crog kajh

Raam'tu: mangle, durus'maan of Ebrekka

Suzbegrog: deciqadi lieutenant and ambigogete

Ta'rel: mangle merchant

Ulchakh: h'achgan trader

Vaagdjul: h'achgan Great Chief of Achgabab

W'sazz-Ozura: greater M'qrugth, Second Vizier of Suzerain Ormalg

Yidreg: h'achgan hunter-of-clan

Zusnesmar: deciqadi warrior and ambigogete

Appendix B

Glossary

deciqadi: Also known as stoops (they have a water-suffused "hump" on their back) and calluskins (from the leathery/callus texture of their epidermis). A human offshoot evolved/geneered for survival in hot, arid climates.

Deviltongue: Generally, the language of the x'qa. However, it usually refers to a "pidgin" dialect that can be spoken by species with soft palates. The x'qai refer to this as "Slavetongue."

grat'r: Proto-sapient Hkh'Rkh.

gruh: A day's worth of the most basic food (mostly edible lichen). Approximately one kilogram. Higher caloric content commands a much greater price. (A kilogram of meat may cost as much as five gruhs.)

h'achga: A being derived from an uplifted orang gene code.

jalk: A human or related being that has been infested by a fungus/spore and is "blood bound" to the one whose blood was the medium of initial infection. The condition is not contagious. Jalks have minimal mental functions and are under the direct control of the one who infected them.

liege: A usually greater x'qao that is the direct lieutenant of a given suzerain in a city. They have broad discretionary powers in their area of influence. Towns also have "lieges," but they are typically less powerful than most city-based "vassals."

moss: The only known antidote for s'rillor. It reduces the presence of the microbe that causes the disease but does not confer immunity. Reinfection/resurgence is inevitable.

Powers: Apparently "parapsychological" phenomena, most of which effect changes or links upon one's own or others' minds, but which may also extend to the physical environment:

anagogy: An innate (or "conferred") Power that is refined through practice and reflection

eunogogy: The only Power that may be "learned" through study

Gifts: Ostensibly "miracles" conferred by patron beings or "deities"

Talents: Similar to anagogy in that it is innate. But its progression is directly related to the growth of the being (either physically or mentally) and is strictly innate.

reapers: Select guards and shock troops of suzerains, lieges, and some vassals. They are usually human or related species and are only rarely from Bactradgaria's known communities. Most are said to come from Beyond.

s'rillor: A noncontagious disease inflicting neurological deterioration in all biota that has a distinct life-cycle change enabling sexual reproduction. Invariably fatal. When one so afflicted requires guidance by others to survive, they become known as "pawns." When they are effectively mindless, their physical condition deteriorates noticeably and they are referred to as "deadskins."

suzerain: The highest political/social rank among x'qai. They are what Bactradgaria has in place of nations. The greatest have major holdings in every major city (see "liege"). With rare exception, suzerains are always greater x'qai or extraordinarily powerful individuals of other species.

symbiolene: Also known as "ancient amber." An enigmatic substance that preserves anything it encases (living or nonliving material) without noticeable change or decay for centuries or even millennia. It seems to be partly biogenic, hence the "symbio-" prefix.

trog-kind: A variety of species which seem to be primarily drawn from Neanderthal stock, although other (unrecognizable) species seem to have been blended in as well. Almost all trog-kind are interfertile, but the greater the genetic separation between the parents, the more likely a mother cannot carry to term or that offspring will be neuter, have birth defects, or both:

caver: One of the two trog-kinds with a high proportion of an unidentified gene code. Mostly carnivorous and subterranean. Cannibalistic. Their name for themselves is not presently known.

crog: Only considered part of trog-kind because x'qai insist on that classification. Overwhelmingly human/Cro-Magnon genetics with some Neanderthal. In local Low Praakht, or "Slavetongue," they are called *whakt*.

tinker: Apparently a smaller version of cavers, but omnivorous and not cannibalistic. Their name for themselves is not presently known.

trog: Almost completely Neanderthal genetics with trace elements of the same unidentified gene code that is more prevalent in cavers. In local Low Praakht, or "Slavetongue," they are called *whakt*.

trogan: Any roughly equal blending of human and trog. In local Low Praakht, or "Slavetongue," they are called *prakhwa*.

trogre: A larger trog with a heavier build and minor (or no) microcephaly. The cause of this genetic variation is unknown. Interbreeding with other trog-kind is typically unsuccessful or results in neuter offspring. In local Low Praakht, or "Slavetongue," they are called *prakhbra*.

The Mangled: So-called because they appear as a pastiche of (almost invariably Terran) species blended into a foundational hominid genetic matrix. Their origins are unknown, as is the process that produced them and the reason (if any) for their creation. The most peaceful of the species of Bactradgaria. They are expert horticulturists and are extremely skilled in growing moss. Consequently, they rarely suffer from s'rillor. They are not viable hosts for x'qai spores.

Vassal: Any being that answers directly to a liege. They typically have physically large holdings that dominate the key production domains in any city or town (agricultural, hunting, crafts). Consequently, their compounds may be larger than that of their liege, but they have only a fraction of their master's combat forces, which are also far better trained and equipped.

Vavasor: Any being that answers directly to a vassal. The relationship is similar to the liege:vassal dynamic. The vassal has greater combat power; the vavasor has proportionally higher numbers of production-devoted thralls. The one difference is that while there are a great many more vavasors than vassals, their holdings (both in size and numbers) are considerably smaller.

X'qa: Also, killspawn. A tough, vicious species with various sub-varieties that is not a product of sexual reproduction. Rather, it infests a host with a sporipositor, only one spore of which comes to maturity via solitary larval endoparasitoidism. Its separation kills the host. It is not merely carnivorous but carnophagic (i.e. it can *only* eat meat):

M'qrugth: Great or royal/pure. They are either unusual arurkré or completely unique in shape. Their maximum lifespans are not known, although several are known to have lived several millennia. They belong to the category of "greater x'qai." They invariably have Talents, usually more than one.

arurkré: Which roughly means "self-transforming." They have the ability to shape their own evolution, through a mix of research and physical self-mastery. They are known to have multi-century lifespans. They belong to the category of "greater x'qai."

x'qao: Bipedal with hands. They have four broad types but these are not subspecies; they simply reflect the kind of creature which hosted the spore that gave rise to them. They occasionally possess Talents.

q'akh: Mostly bipedal, but within that, there is great variety. They almost all have hands, but not all are optimal for tool use. They belong to the category of "lesser x'qa." They never possess Talents.

’qo: Multipedal and if bipedal, optionally so. The smallest, least intelligent, and most impetuous of all x’qa. Their physiology exhibits profound variety. They belong to the category of “lesser x’qa.” They never possess Talents.

Zrik Whir: An autonomous human archipelago. This is the Deviltongue term for it. Transliterated, it renders as “Fodder Islands.”